THE
YEAR'S BEST
SCIENCE FICTION
Fourth Annual Collection

BOOKS BY GARDNER DOZOIS

Strangers (novel)
The Visible Man (collection)
Nightmare Blue (novel—with George Alec Effinger)
A Day in the Life (anthology)
Another World (anthology)
Beyond the Golden Age (anthology)
*Best Science Fiction Stories of the Year,
Sixth Annual Collection* (anthology)
*Best Science Fiction Stories of the Year,
Seventh Annual Collection* (anthology)
*Best Science Fiction Stories of the Year,
Eighth Annual Collection* (anthology)
*Best Science Fiction Stories of the Year,
Ninth Annual Collection* (anthology)
*Best Science Fiction Stories of the Year,
Tenth Annual Collection* (anthology)
*The Year's Best Science Fiction,
First Annual Collection* (anthology)
Future Power (anthology—with Jack Dann)
Aliens! (anthology—with Jack Dann)
Unicorns! (anthology—with Jack Dann)
Magicats! (anthology—with Jack Dann)
Bestiary! (anthology—with Jack Dann)
Mermaids! (anthology—with Jack Dann)
The Fiction of James Tiptree, Jr. (critical chapbook)
*The Year's Best Science Fiction,
Second Annual Collection* (anthology)
*The Year's Best Science Fiction,
Third Annual Collection* (anthology)
Sorcerers! (anthology—with Jack Dann)
Demons! (anthology—with Jack Dann)

THE YEAR'S BEST SCIENCE FICTION

Fourth Annual Collection

Edited by
Gardner Dozois

ST. MARTIN'S PRESS

New York

FOR
Pat Cadigan and Arnie Fenner
and
Robert Michael Fenner,
otherwise known as
"Bobzilla, Scourge of the Midwest"

THE YEAR'S BEST SCIENCE FICTION: FOURTH ANNUAL COLLECTION.
Copyright © 1987 by Gardner R. Dozois. All rights reserved.
Printed in the United States of America. No part of this book may be used or reproduced in any manner whatsoever without written permission except in the case of brief quotations embodied in critical articles or reviews. For information, address St. Martin's Press, 175 Fifth Avenue, New York, N.Y. 10010.

A Bluejay Book

Library of Congress Cataloging-in-Publication Data

The Year's best science fiction.

1. Science fiction, American.   I. Dozois, Gardner R.
PS648.S3Y38   1987   813'.0876'08   87-4445
ISBN 0-312-00709-4 (pbk.)

First Edition
10 9 8 7 6 5 4 3 2 1

Acknowledgment is made for permission to print the following material:

"R & R," by Lucius Shepard. Copyright © 1986 by Davis Publications, Inc. First published in *Isaac Asimov's Science Fiction Magazine*, April 1986. Reprinted by permission of the author and the author's agent, Patrick Delahunt.

"Hatrack River," by Orson Scott Card. Copyright © 1986 by Davis Publications, Inc. First published in *Isaac Asimov's Science Fiction Magazine*, August 1986. Reprinted by permission of the author.

"Strangers on Paradise," by Damon Knight. Copyright © 1986 by Mercury Press, Inc. First published in *The Magazine of Fantasy and Science Fiction*, April 1986. Reprinted by permission of the author.

"Pretty Boy Crossover," by Pat Cadigan. Copyright © 1986 by Davis Publications, Inc. First published in *Isaac Asimov's Science Fiction Magazine*, January 1986. Reprinted by permission of the author.

"Against Babylon," by Robert Silverberg. Copyright © 1986 by Omni Publication International, Ltd. First published in *Omni*, May 1986. Reprinted by permission of the author.

"Fiddling for Waterbuffaloes," by Somtow Sucharitkul. Copyright © 1986 by Davis Publications, Inc. First published in *Analog*, April 1986. Reprinted by permission of the author.

"Into Gold," by Tanith Lee. Copyright © 1986 by Davis Publications, Inc. First published in *Isaac Asimov's Science Fiction Magazine*, March 1986. Reprinted by permission of the author.

"Sea Change," by Scott Baker. Copyright © 1986 by Mercury Press, Inc. First published in *The Magazine of Fantasy and Science Fiction*, April 1986. Reprinted by permission of the author and the author's agent, Merilee Heifetz.

"Covenant of Souls," by Michael Swanwick. Copyright © 1986 by Omni Publication International, Ltd. First published in *Omni*, December 1986. Reprinted by permission of the author and the author's agent, Virginia Kidd.

"The Pure Product," by John Kessel. Copyright © 1986 by Davis Publications, Inc. First published in *Isaac Asimov's Science Fiction Magazine*, March 1986. Reprinted by permission of the author.

"Grave Angels," by Richard Kearns. Copyright © 1986 by Mercury Press, Inc. First published in *The Magazine of Fantasy and Science Fiction*, April 1986. Reprinted by permission of the author.

"Tangents," by Greg Bear. Copyright © 1986 by Omni Publication International, Ltd. First published in *Omni*, January 1986. Reprinted by permission of the author.

"The Beautiful and the Sublime," by Bruce Sterling. Copyright © 1986 by Davis Publications, Inc. First published in *Isaac Asimov's Science Fiction Magazine*, June 1986. Reprinted by permission of the author.

"Tattoos," by Jack Dann. Copyright © 1986 by Omni Publication International, Ltd. First published in *Omni*, November 1986. Reprinted by permission of the author.

"Night Moves," by Tim Powers. Copyright © 1986 by Tim Powers. First published in *Night Moves* (Axolotl Press). Reprinted by permission of the author and the author's agent, Russell Galen.

"The Prisoner of Chillon," by James Patrick Kelly. Copyright © 1986 by Davis Publications, Inc. First published in *Isaac Asimov's Science Fiction Magazine*, June 1986. Reprinted by permission of the author.

"Chance," by Connie Willis. Copyright © 1986 by Davis Publications, Inc. First published in *Isaac Asimov's Science Fiction Magazine*, May 1986. Reprinted by permission of the author.

"And So to Bed," by Harry Turtledove. Copyright © 1986 by Davis Publications, Inc. First published in *Analog*, January 1986. Reprinted by permission of the author and the author's agent, Russell Galen.

"Fair Game," by Howard Waldrop. Copyright © 1986 by Howard Waldrop. First published in *Afterlives* (Vintage). Reprinted by permission of the author.

"Video Star," by Walter Jon Williams. Copyright © 1986 by Davis Publications, Inc. First published in *Isaac Asimov's Science Fiction Magazine*, July 1986. Reprinted by permission of the author.

"Sallie C.," by Neal Barrett, Jr. Copyright © 1986 by Western Writers of America. First published in *Best of the West* (Doubleday). Reprinted by permission of the author.

"Jeff Beck," by Lewis Shiner. Copyright © 1986 by Davis Publications, Inc. First published in *Isaac Asimov's Science Fiction Magazine*, January 1986. Reprinted by permission of the author.

"Surviving," by Judith Moffett. Copyright © 1986 by Mercury Press, Inc. First published in *The Magazine of Fantasy and Science Fiction*, June 1986. Reprinted by permission of the author and the author's agent, Virginia Kidd.

"Down and Out in the Year 2000," by Kim Stanley Robinson. Copyright © 1986 by Davis Publications, Inc. First published in *Isaac Asimov's Science Fiction Magazine*, April 1986. Reprinted by permission of the author and the author's agent, Patrick Delahunt.

"Snake-Eyes," by Tom Maddox. Copyright © 1986 by Omni Publication International, Ltd. First published in *Omni*, April 1986. Reprinted by permission of the author.

"The Gate of Ghosts," by Karen Joy Fowler. Copyright © 1986 by Karen Joy Fowler. First published in *Artificial Things* (Bantam-Spectra). Reprinted by permission of the author.

"The Winter Market," by William Gibson. Copyright © 1986 by William Gibson. First appeared in *Stardate*, February 1986. Reprinted by permission of the author and the author's agent, Martha Millard.

ACKNOWLEDGMENTS

The editor would like to thank the following people for their help and support: Susan Casper, Virginia Kidd, Ellen Datlow, Sheila Williams, Emy Eterno, Tina Lee, Michael Swanwick, Pat Cadigan, Orson Scott Card, Janet and Ricky Kagan, Shawna McCarthy, Lou Aronica, Edward Ferman, Susan Allison, Ginjer Buchanan, Beth Meacham, Claire Eddy, Pat LoBrutto, Patrick Delahunt, Tim Powers, David Hartwell, Martha Millard, Lewis Shiner, Howard Waldrop, Neal Barrett, Jr., Bob Walters, Tess Kissinger, Jim Frenkel, and special thanks to my own editor, Stuart Moore.

Thanks are also due to Charles N. Brown, whose magazine *Locus* (Locus Publications, Inc., P.O. Box 13305, Oakland, CA 94661, $32.00 for a one-year first-class subscription, 12 issues) was used as a reference source throughout the Summation, and to Andrew Porter, whose magazine *Science Fiction Chronicle* (Algol Press, P.O. Box 4175, New York, NY 10163-4157, $23.40 for 1 year, 12 issues) was also used as a reference source throughout.

CONTENTS

Introduction
SUMMATION: 1986   ix

R & R
Lucius Shepard   1

HATRACK RIVER
Orson Scott Card   67

STRANGERS ON PARADISE
Damon Knight   91

PRETTY BOY CROSSOVER
Pat Cadigan   105

AGAINST BABYLON
Robert Silverberg   115

FIDDLING FOR WATERBUFFALOES
Somtow Sucharitkul   133

INTO GOLD
Tanith Lee   155

SEA CHANGE
Scott Baker   181

COVENANT OF SOULS
Michael Swanwick   198

THE PURE PRODUCT
John Kessel   229

GRAVE ANGELS
Richard Kearns   247

TANGENTS
Greg Bear   274

THE BEAUTIFUL AND THE SUBLIME
Bruce Sterling   289

TATTOOS
Jack Dann   314

NIGHT MOVES
Tim Powers   333

THE PRISONER OF CHILLON
James Patrick Kelly   352

CHANCE
Connie Willis   384

AND SO TO BED
Harry Turtledove   411

FAIR GAME
Howard Waldrop   425

VIDEO STAR
Walter Jon Williams   439

SALLIE C.
Neal Barrett, Jr.   469

JEFF BECK
Lewis Shiner   490

SURVIVING
Judith Moffett   499

DOWN AND OUT IN THE YEAR 2000
Kim Stanley Robinson   529

SNAKE-EYES
Tom Maddox   544

THE GATE OF GHOSTS
Karen Joy Fowler   562

THE WINTER MARKET
William Gibson   581

Honorable Mentions: 1986   599

INTRODUCTION

Summation: 1986

There were a few storm clouds on the horizon in 1986, and many industry insiders began to talk with gloomy certainty of the inevitability of a serious sales slump and another recession in the publishing industry somewhere down the road. On the other hand, more SF books were published in 1986 than ever before, and several new programs were announced.

The biggest negative news of the year was probably the demise of Bluejay Books, the ambitious SF line started in 1981 by Jim Frenkel. Bluejay was forced under late in 1986 by major cash-flow problems, as primary sources of funding dried up. The death of Bluejay is a major blow to SF, but not quite the total disaster it might have been. So far, Bluejay has not declared bankruptcy, which could have been a catastrophe of major proportions—the bankruptcies of Pinnacle and Lancer, for instance, tied some literary properties up for years—and both Bluejay's creditors and Jim Frenkel himself deserve credit for this, the creditors for their patience and forbearance, Frenkel for the integrity to resist the pressure to declare bankruptcy in the face of major debts, something which would certainly have been an easier way out for him. Instead, Frenkel has been working behind the scenes with various other editors in an attempt to place with other publishers those Bluejay books which were under contract, and to date has been successful in placing the majority of them (as testified to by the fact that you're reading these words in the first place—since St. Martin's Press has taken this anthology series over from Bluejay). Frenkel has also worked out a deal with his creditors to repay them on a schedule of monthly proportional payments, although it may take years to settle all the debts involved. Still, the demise of Bluejay has cost us an innovative and ambitious SF line, one that frequently produced books of high literary quality; Bluejay will be missed.

In other news, St. Martin's Press bought Tor books on the last day of 1986. Tor has been the fastest-growing company in SF for a couple of years now, experiencing a 35 percent growth rate in 1986, and apparently expanded too far too fast; the $1.5 million in uncollected accounts receivable from the

Pinnacle bankruptcy, the sudden dramatic increase in inventory caused by the demise of Bluejay (Tor probably picked up the lion's share of the titles that were forced to find new homes), the money tied up in inventory by the constant expansion, and the flight of major financial backers because of the new changes in tax laws on passive investments and capital gains (certainly not the *last* effect the new tax laws will have on the publishing industry), have all been talked about as contributing factors to the sale. Tom Doherty will continue to run Tor independently of St. Martin's, except for the accounting and financial end, and Beth Meacham will remain as senior editor (no major changes in editorial personnel have as yet come about because of this sale).

Elsewhere: Doubleday, NAL, Dell, and Dutton were all sold to other publishers during the year—what effect this will have on the SF lines at Doubleday and NAL is as yet unknown. Ace and Berkley will be merging their SF lines, with the Berkley line being phased out—this will result in fewer overall titles yearly. The giant bookstore chain B. Dalton was sold to Barnes and Noble, part of a long trend of increasing centralism; independent bookstores are on the verge of becoming an endangered species. Ace/Berkley, Daw, Bantam, and Arbor House all cut their lists in 1986 (the cuts at Arbor House were the most dramatic; several editors there have also been let go, although so far the SF editorial staff is untouched), and further cuts are likely in 1987.

On the positive side, however, several new lines were announced, and the new titles created will probably at least balance the cutbacks in old titles. St. Martin's Press has announced two new mass-market paperback lines, one for SF and one for horror; Stuart Moore will run the SF line, Lincoln Child the horror line. Walker & Co., in conjunction with Byron Preiss Visual Publications, will publish a new line of illustrated young adult hardcovers, Millennium Books, to be edited by David Harris. Franklin Watts is starting a new SF line, to be edited by Charles Platt. And Davis Publications, Inc., in conjunction with Contemporary Books, is starting up a new SF line, *Isaac Asimov Presents,* which will be published under Contemporary's Congdon & Weed imprint, and which will concentrate primarily on novels by new young authors; the editor of the series is Gardner Dozois. (It's interesting to note that between Terry Carr's Ace Special line, Ben Bova's Discovery Series for Tor, Charles Platt's series for Franklin Watts, and the new *Isaac Asimov Presents* line from Congdon & Weed, all of which have announced their intention to emphasize the work of new writers, it may well be easier for a young author to sell a first novel these days than it will be for him to sell a second or third novel a bit further down the road. Interesting times indeed . . .) And SF and fantasy books continue to make their presence strongly felt on nationwide bestseller lists, with King, Asimov, Heinlein, Donaldson, Hubbard, and Anthony staying on those lists throughout much of the year.

So, contradictory signals and ambiguous omens. Will the recession inevitably come, as the doomsayers predict? Only time will tell. It's hardly a daring prediction, after all, to forecast a coming recession—SF publishing has followed a periodic boom-and-bust cycle ever since there *was* such a thing as SF as a distinct publishing category. The real question is, how severe will the recession be, and how many authors will it affect . . . and to what degree? During the last recession, a few years back, some authors were frozen out of print altogether, while a number of others were not only adversely affected by the recession, they actually *prospered* throughout it, their books going on to top nationwide bestseller lists at a time when most other authors were selling very poorly indeed. I suspect that there will be authors who will be similarly immune to the coming recession, however severe it may be—the intriguing question is, will these lucky writers be the *same* ones as last time? I suspect that they will *not* be, at least in part.

It was another year of changes for the SF magazine market, some of them good, some bad, some of them very hard to call. Many of the biggest changes, however, were negative. The proposed *L. Ron Hubbard's to the Stars Science Fiction Magazine,* which had been relentlessly hyped throughout 1985, died stillborn in 1986, being "indefinitely postponed" after the death of L. Ron Hubbard at the beginning of the year. Although those connected with the magazine still talk about the possibility of it being started up again at some point in the future, all manuscripts purchased for the abortive first three issues have been returned, and most industry insiders consider the magazine to be dead. *Stardate* also died, after two 1986 issues, leaving a number of angry creditors behind; it's supposed to be resurrected in 1987, but this time purely as a gaming magazine. Two other new magazines were launched in 1986: the resurrected *Worlds of If,* edited by Clifford Hong, which produced one issue in 1986, and *Aboriginal SF,* edited by Charles Ryan, a tabloid-format "magazine" which produced two issues. Most industry observers seem to be doubtful about the chances of either of these two magazines surviving, perhaps a little *more* dubious about *If*'s chances; even those who thought *Aboriginal SF* did have a shot at making it seemed dubious about the tabloid format. Well, we'll see. The fourth incarnation of *Weird Tales* died in 1986, but almost immediately a fifth incarnation was announced, with rights to the title being purchased by George Scithers, Darrell Schweitzer, and John Betancourt. Michael Blaine was abruptly fired as editor of *The Twilight Zone Magazine,* after only a few months on the job, and replaced by Tappan King—since King has as much energy, ability, and ambition as any editor in the business, this could bode interesting changes ahead for the magazine.

Night Cry, TZ's sister publication, and *Interzone,* the British SF magazine, both continue to develop promisingly throughout 1986. *Night Cry,* with its manic energy, cheerful bloodthirstiness, and love of the grotesque, is filling the hardcore horror fiction niche well enough that one wonders if *TZ* will not be forced to find a new editorial direction, away from horror fiction per se, in order not to be superfluous; King could probably find it for them—if they'll let him. *Interzone* continues to attract some very good stuff, much of it from American authors, in spite of the fact that it is almost impossible to find in the United States, except in SF specialty bookstores. At year's end, a big-budget Canadian SF magazine, *SF: New Science Fiction Stories,* edited by John R. Little, was announced for 1987.

As most of you probably know, I, Gardner Dozois, am also editor of *Isaac Asimov's Science Fiction Magazine.* And that, as I mentioned last year, poses a problem for me in compiling this summation, particularly the magazine-by-magazine review that follows. As *IAsfm* editor, I could be said to have a vested interest in the magazine's success, so that anything negative I said about another SF magazine (particularly another digest-sized magazine, my direct competition), could be perceived as an attempt to make my own magazine look good by tearing down the competition. Aware of this constraint, I've decided that nobody can complain if I only say *positive* things about the competition . . . and so, like last year, I've a listing of some of the worthwhile authors published by each.

Omni published first-rate fiction this year by Michael Swanwick, Jack Dann, Greg Bear, Tom Maddox, Robert Silverberg, Howard Waldrop, Suzy McKee Charnas, Roger Zelazny, and others. *Omni*'s fiction editor is Ellen Datlow.

The Magazine of Fantasy and Science Fiction featured excellent fiction by Damon Knight, Scott Baker, James Patrick Kelly, Karen Joy Fowler, Judith Moffett, O. Neimand, Richard Kearns, David S. Garnett, Stephen Gallagher, Pamela Sargent, and others. *F & SF*'s longtime editor is Edward Ferman.

Isaac Asimov's Science Fiction Magazine featured critically acclaimed work by Lucius Shepard, Pat Cadigan, Orson Scott Card, Isaac Asimov, John Kessel, Bruce Sterling, Connie Willis, Kim Stanley Robertson, Robert Silverberg, Nancy Kress, Neal Barrett, Jr., and others.

Analog featured good work by Somtow Sucharitkul, Harry Turtledove, Charles L. Harness, Vernor Vinge, Charles Sheffield, Eric Vinicoff, and others. *Analog*'s longtime editor is Stanley Schmidt.

Amazing featured good work by Avram Davidson, Lisa Goldstein, Alexander Jablokov, Keith Roberts, and others. *Amazing*'s new editor is Patrick L. Price, although I suspect that the majority of the stuff that saw print in 1986 was still former editor George Scither's backlog.

The Twilight Zone Magazine featured good work by Steven Popkes, Andrew Weiner, Robert Silverberg, Kim Antieau, Garry Kilworth, Robert R. McCammon, and others. *TZ*'s new editor is Tappan King.

Night Cry featured good work by Robert Bloch, Steven Popkes, Avram Davidson, Augustine Funnell, A.R. Morlan, and others. *Night Cry*'s editor is Alan Rogers.

Interzone featured good work by Gregory Benford, Rachel Pollack, Michael Blumlein, Simon Ounsley, Ian Watson, and others. *Interzone*'s editors are Simon Ounsley and David Pringle.

Short SF continued to appear in many magazines outside genre boundaries, from *Atlantic* to *Redbook*. Since the departure of former fiction editor Kathy Green, *Penthouse* no longer seems to be running much, if any, short SF, but Alice K. Turner, fiction editor at *Playboy,* is fortunately running as much or more of it as ever—one of the year's major stories, in fact, a Lucius Shepard novelette, appeared in *Playboy*.

(Subscription addresses follow for those magazines hardest to find on the newsstands: *The Magazine of Fantasy and Science Fiction,* Mercury Press, Inc., Box 56, Cornwall, CT, 06753, annual subscription—12 issues—$19.50; *Amazing,* TSR, Inc., P.O. Box 72069, Chicago, IL, 60690, annual subscription $9.00 for 6 issues; *Interzone,* 124 Osborne Road, Brighton BN1 6LU, England, $14.00 for an airmail one-year—4 issues—subscription.)

There were a few sparks of interest in the semiprozine scene this year. There was no *Whispers,* and *Shayol* is still dead, alas, but there was a new and fairly slickly executed semiprozine called *New Pathways,* edited by Michael G. Adkisson, which seems quite promising, and Scott Edelman's *The Last Wave* appeared again after an extended absence. *Fantasy Book* produced three issues this year, and the British *Fantasy Tales* one, but as usual, although they were competent and sincere, I was unable to muster up a great deal of enthusiasm for them. *Locus* and *SF Chronicle* remain your best bets among the semiprozines if you're looking for an overview of the genre. Among the semiprozines that concentrate primarily on literary criticism, *Fantasy Review,* which recently gained a new publisher and a new lease on life, is worthwhile, as is *Thrust*. The most outspoken and audacious criticalzine of them all, *Cheap Truth,* died in 1986, but two new ones that look interesting are starting up, Orson Scott Card's *Short Form* and Steve Brown's *Science Fiction Eye*.

(*Fantasy Review*, Dept. VV, P.O. Box 3000, Denville, NJ 07834, $27.95 for a one-year subscription; *Locus,* Locus Publications, Inc., P.O. Box 13305, Oakland, CA 94661, $32.00 for a one-year first-class subscription, 12 issues; *Science Fiction Chronicle,* Algol Press, P.O. Box 4175, New York, NY 10163-4157, $23.40 for one year, 12 issues; *Thrust,* Thrust Publications, 8217 Langport Terrace, Galthersburg, MD 20877, $8.00 for 4 issues; *The Last Wave,* Box 3022, Saxonville St. N., Framingham, MA 01701, $10.00 for 4 issues; *Science Fiction Eye,* Box 3105, Washington, DC 20010-0105,

$7.00 for one year; *Short Form,* P.O. Box 18184, Greensboro, NC 27419-8184; $10.00 for 4 issues; *New Pathways, MGA* Services, P.O. Box 863994, Plano, TX 75086-3994, $15.00 for a one-year—6 issues—subscription, $25.00 for a two-year subscription.)

Overall, 1986 was not a particularly good year for original anthologies. Terry Carr's *Universe* series usually produces one of the best anthologies of the year, but this year's *Universe 16* (Doubleday) was rather weak—in fact, one of the weakest *Universe* volumes in some time, although it did feature a good story by Lucius Shepard. Most of the work in *L. Ron Hubbard Presents Writers of the Future, Vol. II,* edited by Algis Budrys, is also pretty bland. It seems unfair to criticize the stuff therein for being novice work, since that's the point of the whole anthology . . . nevertheless, although some of the writers here may be Big Name Professionals someday, they're not that good *yet,* and it shows; this is a problem common to all such collections of novice work. The best original anthology of the year was probably *Afterlives* (Vintage), edited by Pamela Sargent and Ian Watson—this is actually a mixed reprint-and-original anthology, but about half the contents are original, and include some good work by Howard Waldrop, Rudy Rucker, Gene Wolfe, Leigh Kennedy, and others (although the best story in the book is James Blish's "A Work of Art," which was published in 1956, and may still be the best science fiction treatment of its subject). Elizabeth Mitchell's *Under the Wheel* (Baen) was also interesting. The new anthology series *Far Frontiers* published a couple of solid, if not highly innovative volumes this year—there were reports at year's end that Jerry Pournelle is stepping down as series editor; James Baen will carry on alone, changing the series name to *New Destinies.*

There were no particularly good high fantasy anthologies this year, unlike last year, which saw the publication of the excellent *Imaginary Lands.* Best of the lot was probably Will Shetterly and Emma Bull's *Liavek: The Players of Luck* (Ace). Janet Morris' *Heroes in Hell* (Baen) had some interesting stuff in it but the contents were wildly uneven. Terry Windling and Mark Arnold's *Borderland* (Ace) was simply a failure: a silly concept—punk elves—and mostly indifferent execution.

The big event in the horror anthology market this year was the publication of Dennis Etchison's enormous original anthology *Cutting Edge* (Doubleday). This much-ballyhooed collection was hyped as the *Dangerous Visions* of horror fiction—and to a certain extent lives up to the name. Some of the stuff here is a little too gruesome for my taste—the anthology certainly contains some of the year's grimmest, most violent, and most despairing stories—but the level of craft is generally pretty high, and the book contains an excellent story by Peter Straub, and good work by Joe Haldeman, Steve Rasnic Tem, Clive Barker, Karl Edward Wagner, Marc Laidlaw, and others;

it's an unrelievedly black and intense anthology, though, so don't try to read it all in one sitting. Although equally well-crafted, the stories in Charles L. Grant's *Shadows 9* (Doubleday) were considerably less grotesque—the schism between the "quiet" school of horror writing (typified by *Shadows*) and the gleefully gore-splattered Grand Guignol school widens daily. (On the whole, I prefer the "quiet" stuff myself—and think it is more likely to actually *scare* people, something both horror writers and splatter-film makers sometimes lose sight of.) *Shadows 9* probably has no award-winners on board this time around, but does feature good work by Stephen Gallagher, Kim Antieau, Nina Kiriki Hoffman, Steve Rasnic Tem, and others. Also interesting were *Night Visions 3* (Dark Harvest), edited by George R. R. Martin, and *Halloween Horrors* (Doubleday), edited by Alan Ryan.

An intriguingly offbeat item is *The Best of the West* (Doubleday), the annual Western Writers of America anthology. This year it was edited by Joe R. Lansdale, who's an SF writer as well as a western writer, and he has included several strange western/SF/fantasy hybrids in this year's volume, including a brilliant piece of work by Neal Barrett, Jr. (The straight western stories are all pretty good, too, and even the most conventional of them are pretty quirky.) An interesting book.

According to *Locus*, there were 294 new SF novels and 263 new fantasy novels released during 1986—and these are only *estimates*; no doubt there were many books released that didn't even show up in the count. I'm not sure I understand how anyone could keep up with all of those new titles, let alone anyone with anything *else* to do. Certainly *I* can't keep up with all the new novel releases—busy as I am with the extensive reading at shorter lengths demanded both by this anthology and the editorship of *Isaac Asimov's Science Fiction Magazine*—and so, reluctantly, I have given up even trying to read them all. So therefore, as usual, I'm going to limit myself here to commenting that of the novels I *did* read this year, I was the most impressed by: *The Journal of Nicholas the American*, Leigh Kennedy (Atlantic Monthly Press); *Soldier in the Mist*, Gene Wolfe (Tor); *Count Zero*, William Gibson (Arbor House); *A Hidden Place*, Robert Charles Wilson (Bantam Spectra); *Talking Man*, Terry Bisson (Arbor House); *The Hercules Text*, Jack McDevitt (Ace); *The Falling Woman*, Pat Murphy (Tor); *Free Live Free*, Gene Wolfe (Tor); *Hardwired*, Walter Jon Williams (Tor); and *Homunculus*, James P. Blaylock (Ace).

Other novels which have gotten a lot of attention this year include: *Speaker for the Dead*, Orson Scott Card (Tor); *Foundation and Earth*, Isaac Asimov (Doubleday); *The Handmaid's Tale*, Margaret Atwood (Houghton Mifflin); *This Is the Way the World Ends*, James Morrow (Holt); *The Coming of the Quantum Cats*, Frederik Pohl (Bantam Spectra); *Godbody*, Theodore Sturgeon (Donald I. Fine); *Wizard of the Pigeons*, Megan Lindholm (Ace); *The*

Cross-Time Engineer, Leo Frankowski (Del Rey); *Blood of Amber*, Roger Zelazny (Arbor House); *Radio Free Albemuth*, Philip K. Dick (Arbor House); *Star of Gypsies*, Robert Silverberg (Donald I. Fine); *The Serpent Mage*, Greg Bear (Berkley); *Huysman's Pets*, Kate Wilhelm (Bluejay); *Human Error*, Paul Preuss (Tor); *Dorothea Dreams*, Suzy McKee Charnas (Arbor House); *A Door into Ocean*, Joan Slonczewski (Arbor House); *Songs of Distant Earth*, Arthur C. Clarke (Del Rey); *Marooned in Real Time*, Vernor Vinge (Bluejay); *Yarrow*, Charles de Lint (Ace); *It*, Stephen King (Viking); *Winter in Eden*, Harry Harrison (Bantam); *Chanur's Homecoming*, C. J. Cherryh (Phantasm Press); and *Heart of the Comet*, Gregory Benford and David Brin (Bantam Spectra).

My subjective impression is that 1986 was not as strong a year for novels overall as last year or the year before, although several excellent individual novels *did* appear—and the reviews seem to bear this out, for the most part. First novels continued to make their presence felt—*Locus* lists twenty-seven of them, and there probably were more—but they didn't seem to have as much impact this year as they've had in the past couple of years (particularly in 1984, when first novels dominated the awards lists, and one of them, William Gibson's *Neuromancer*, won both the Nebula and the Hugo); of the first novels, only the Kennedy, the McDevitt, the Wilson, and the Frankowski seemed to generate much critical excitement.

It's interesting to note that although 1986 saw the publication of a number of heavily advertised novels by some of the biggest names in the genre—Clarke, Asimov, Pohl, Silverberg, Donaldson, Harrison—none of them came even close to making it onto the final Nebula ballot. All were passed over in favor of novels by middle-level writers such as Wolfe and Card, and by new writers such as Gibson, Kennedy, Morrow, and Atwood. The same thing happened to a certain extent in 1985 and 1984. Does this indicate a shift in the demographics of the Nebula electorate? Or just a shift in which portion of the electorate still bothers to vote?

There were few important small-press novels this year. One worthwhile project was announced by Chris Drumm, who intends to publish R. A. Lafferty's tetralogy *In a Green Tree* as a series of mimeographed booklets, starting with Chris Drumm booklet, No. 24: *My Heart Leaps Up, Part 1*. It will take twenty booklets to complete the project, each booklet containing two chapters. Let's hope that they can manage to actually complete this enormous project, because the first part of the first novel, contained in the first booklet, is quirky and interesting, sure to appeal to Lafferty fans, and I can't help but wonder if it's the strong strain of offbeat but powerfully devout Catholicism here that has kept this novel off the trade market for all these years. (Chris Drumm's address: P.O. Box 445, Polk City, Iowa, 50226. Regular edition $2.75, signed edition, $6.)

If 1986 was only a so-so year for novels, it was a terrific one for short story collections. The year saw the publication of several landmark collections, all of which belong on everyone's basic bookshelf. The year's best short story collections were *Howard Who?*, Howard Waldrop (Doubleday); *Burning Chrome*, William Gibson (Arbor House); *The Planet on the Table*, Kim Stanley Robinson (Tor); *Dreams of Dark and Light*, Tanith Lee (Arkham House); *Artificial Things*, Karen Joy Fowler (Bantam Spectra); *Close Encounters with the Deity*, Michael Bishop (Peachtree); and *Tales of the Quintana Roo*, James Tiptree, Jr. (Arkham House). If you absolutely have to choose among these, the Waldrop, the Gibson, the Lee, and the Robinson are probably the most essential, and the Waldrop in particular contains fine material from obscure places that the average reader is unlikely to have already seen.

Also outstanding this year were: *Beyond the Safe Zone*, Robert Silverberg (Donald I. Fine); *In Alien Flesh*, Gregory Benford; *Robot Dreams*, Isaac Asimov (Berkley); *Blue Champagne*, John Varley (Dark Harvest); *Merlin's Booke*, Jane Yolen (Ace); *The Complete Nebula Award-Winning Fiction*, Samuel R. Delany (Bantam Spectra); *The Starry Rift*, James Tiptree, Jr. (Tor); *The Curious Quests of Brigadier Ffellows*, Sterling E. Lanier (Donald M. Grant); and *Tuf Voyaging*, George R. R. Martin (Baen).

Small presses played an important role here, as you can see—Peachtree, Dark Harvest, Donald M. Grant, and especially Arkham House, which is becoming one of the most important sources for quality short story collections. It's good to see small presses taking up some of the slack here, since trade publishers still issue fewer short story collections than they should—although things have improved a bit in this regard over the last few years. Still, even though 1986 was a good year for collections, I'd like to see even *more* collections issued in coming years—there've been too few of them, for too long.

The reprint anthology market was a bit more solid this year than it was last year. As usual, your best bet in the reprint market were the various "Best of the Year" collections—there are three covering science fiction, one for fantasy, one for horror, plus the annual Nebula Award anthology. This year also saw the publication of *The Hugo Winners, Vol. 5* (Doubleday), edited by Isaac Asimov, and *The Science Fiction Hall of Fame, Vol. IV* (Avon), edited by Terry Carr, valuable reference anthologies. The best reprint anthology of the year, though, is *Mirrorshades: The Cyberpunk Anthology* (Arbor House), edited by Bruce Sterling. Sterling muddies the already confusingly roiled critical water on this subject a bit more by including in this supposedly canonical anthology several stories (like Rudy Rucker's excellent "Tales of Houdini") that are clearly *not* cyberpunk by any reasonable definition; I also question the wisdom of using William Gibson's least characteristic story but of not including any of Sterling's own brilliant Shaper/Mechanist stories, definitive hardcore cyberpunk. Nevertheless, in spite of these quibbles, this is not only a historically important anthology, but a very *good* one; all the stories are worthwhile, whether cyberpunk or not, and a few of them—notably the Cadigan and the Kelly—are as good as short SF has gotten in the eighties. Also worthwhile this year were: *Tales from the Spaceport Bar* (Avon), edited by George H. Scithers and Darrell Schweitzer; *Alternative Histories* (Garland), edited by Charles G. Waugh and Martin H. Greenberg; *Strange Maine* (Lance Tapley), edited by Charles G. Waugh, Martin H. Greenberg and Frank D. McSherry, Jr.; *Hitler Victorious* (Garland) edited by Gregory Benford and Martin H. Greenberg; and *Isaac Asimov Presents the Great SF Stories: 15* (DAW), edited by Isaac Asimov and Martin H. Greenberg. Two interesting reprint horror anthologies were *Masters of Darkness* (Tor), edited by Dennis Etchison, and *After Midnight* (Tor) edited by Charles L. Grant. Noted without comment are *Mermaids!* (Ace) and *Sorcerers!* (Ace), edited by Jack Dann and Gardner Dozois.

It was a moderately good year for the SF-oriented nonfiction/SF reference book field. 1986 saw the creation of a valuable new reference—*Science Fiction in Print: 1985* (Locus Publications), compiled by Charles N. Brown and William G. Contento—and an updated reissue of a valuable old reference—*Twentieth-Century Science-Fiction Writers, 2nd Edition* (St. James Press), edited by Curtis C. Smith. Also worthwhile were: *The Penguin Encyclopedia of Horror and the Supernatural* (Viking), edited by Jack Sullivan; and *Science Fiction, Fantasy and Weird Fiction Magazines* (Greenwood), edited by Marshall B. Tymn and Mike Ashley. Discounting straight reference books, the best SF-oriented nonfiction book of the year was the huge, highly readable, and highly controversial history of SF by Brian W. Aldiss and David Wingrove, *Trillion Year Spree: The History of Science Fiction* (Atheneum), an extensive update of Aldiss' earlier *Billion Year Spree*. They'll be arguing over *this* one for years to come, just as they argued about its predecessor. There's plenty to argue *about* here, too—Aldiss pulls no punches! The section on the last fifteen years in SF is still a bit sketchy, and Aldiss sometimes gets his facts a bit wrong, but it's all fascinating reading. Just as fascinating, and perhaps even more opinionated, is Aldiss's second collection of essays, . . . *And the Lurid Glare of the Comet* (Serconia Press). Even quirkier reading— and even more fascinating— is Paul Williams's book-long "interview" with the late Philip K. Dick, *Only Apparently Real* (Arbor House). Also worthwhile are: *The John W. Campbell Letters, Vol. 1* (AC Projects, Inc.), edited by Perry A. Chapdelaine, Sr., Tony Chapdelaine, and George Hay; *Inside Outer Space: Science Fiction Professionals Look at Their Craft* (Ungar), edited by Sharon Jarvis; *Hard Science Fiction* (Southern

Illinois University Press), edited by George E. Slusser and Eric S. Rabkin; and *Galaxy Magazine: The Dark and the Light Years* (Advent), edited by David L. Rosheim.

Reviewing last year's anthology in *Mile High Futures,* Ed Bryant took me to task for obviously not knowing anything about film. Well, another year has gone by, and I *still* don't know much about film—as the old joke goes, I only know what I like. And there was not a hell of a lot I liked in the SF/ fantasy film field in 1986, which, to my eyes at least, seemed like a moderately disappointing year. There were some good films lost among the ruck, though, and let's start with them.

Brazil was the best film I saw last year, and one of the best I've ever seen: funny, sad, brilliant, bizarre, absolutely original—it seems to me that, although it's not based on anything by Dick, *Brazil* catches the strange, gentle, and tragic atmosphere of a Philip K. Dick novel better than any film I've ever seen, even better than *Blade Runner,* which merely *looks* like a Philip K. Dick novel. *Aliens* was a first rate SF adventure film, though it lacked the mythic overtones of its predecessor, *Alien. The Little Shop of Horrors* was funny and enjoyably weird. *Labyrinth* had some interesting touches, as did *Peggy Sue Got Married,* although the latter had big holes in its plot-logic. *Star Trek IV* was pleasant but minor.

Everything *else—The Golden Child, Poltergeist II, Psycho III, Legend, Howard the Duck, Maximum Overdrive, Vamp, Invaders from Mars, Highlanders, Solarbabies,* and *King Kong Lives*—I didn't like much. In fact, with a few of those, that's putting it mildly.

On television, *The Twilight Zone* and *Alfred Hitchcock* were canceled, and *Amazing Stories* isn't looking too good, either. A new version of *Star Trek—Star Trek: The Next Generation*—is going to be on the tube next season, but somehow I can't muster up a great deal of enthusiasm for this news; perhaps I've grown jaded.

The 44th World Science Fiction convention, ConFederation, was held in Atlanta, Georgia, over the Labor Day weekend, and drew an estimated attendance of 5,500. The 1986 Hugo Awards, presented at ConFederation, were: Best Novel, *Ender's Game,* by Orson Scott Card; Best Novella, "24 Views of Mount Fuji, by Hokusai," by Roger Zelazny; Best Novelette, "Paladin of the Lost Hour," by Harlan Ellison; Best Short Story, "Fermi and Frost" by Frederik Pohl; Best Non-Fiction, *Science Made Stupid,* by Tom Weller; Best Professional Editor, Judy-Lynn del Rey (refused); Best Professional Artist, Michael Whelan; Best Dramatic Presentation, *Back to the Future*; Best Semi-Prozine, *Locus*; Best Fanzine, *Lan's Lantern*; Best Fan Writer, Mike Glyer; Best Fan Artist, Joan Hanke-Woods; plus the John W. Campbell Award for Best New Writer to Melissa Scott.

The 1985 Nebula Awards, presented at a banquet at the Claremont Hotel in Berkeley, California, on April 26, 1986, were: Best Novel, *Ender's Game*, by Orson Scott Card; Best Novella, "Sailing to Byzantium," by Robert Silverberg; Best Novelette, "Portraits of His Children," by George R. R. Martin; Best Short Story, "Out of All Them Bright Stars," by Nancy Kress; plus the Grand Master Award to Arthur C. Clarke.

The World Fantasy Awards, presented at the Twelfth Annual World Fantasy Convention in Providence, Rhode Island, on November 2, 1986, were: Best Novel, *Song of Kali*, by Dan Simmons; Best Novella, "Nadelman's God," by T. E. D. Klein; Best Short Story, "Paper Dragons," by James Blaylock; Best Anthology/Collection, *Imaginary Lands*, edited by Robin McKinley; Best Artist (tie), Jeff Jones and Thomas Canty; Special Award (professional), Pat Lo Brutto; Special Award (Non-Professional), Douglas E. Winter; Special Convention Award, Donald A. Wollheim; plus a (long overdue) Life Achievement Award to Avram Davidson.

The 1985 John W. Campbell Memorial Award–winner was *The Postman*, by David Brin.

The fourth Philip K. Dick Memorial Award–winner was *Dinner at Deviant's Palace*, by Tim Powers.

The 1985 Rhysling Awards for the best speculative poetry of 1985 went to Andrew Joron for the long poem, "Shipwrecked on Destiny Five" (*IAsfm*, May 85) and to Susan Palwick for the short poem "The Neighbor's Wife" (*Amazing*, May 85).

This volume will, alas, contain another long, grim list of obituary notices for those lost in 1986 and early 1987. The dead included: **Manly Wade Wellman,** 82, one of the masters of the modern fantasy story, author of the landmark collection *Who Fears the Devil?* as well as a large number of other books and stories (many of them about his best-known character, John), and winner of the World Fantasy Award for Life Achievement; **Robert F. Young,** 71, veteran author whose work was published primarily in *The Magazine of Fantasy and Science Fiction* and collected in *The Worlds of Robert F. Young* and *A Glass of Stars*; **Thoma N. Scortia,** 59, author, scientist, and editor, co-author (with Frank M. Robinson) of the bestselling novel *The Glass Inferno* (on which the film *The Towering Inferno* was based), as well as many other novels, stories, and anthologies; **Russel M. Griffin,** 42, highly promising new writer, author of four novels, of which the best known is the brilliant black comedy *The Blind Men and the Elephant*, a friendly acquaintance of mine if not a close personal friend; **Jorge Luis Borges,** 86, one of the giants of world literature and a dominant figure in South American letters, winner of the 1979 World Fantasy Award for Life Achievement; **John D. MacDonald,** 70, one of the most prolific and successful writers of our times, author of the SF novels *Wine of the Dreamers* and *Ballroom of the Skies*, although he was best known as a mystery writer, particularly for the long-running and best-selling Travis McGee series; **Bernard Malamud,** 71, Pulitzer Prize–winning novelist and winner of the National Book Award, author of the associational novels *The Natural* and *God's Grace*; **V. C. Andrews**, bestselling author of gothic novels, best known for *Flowers in the Attic*; **Chesley Bonestell,** 98, brilliant space and astronomical artist whose paintings, particularly for *Life* and *Colliers* in the 1950s, established the "look" of space art for decades of readers and influenced generations of SF and astronomical artists, and much of whose best work is collected in the recent *Worlds Beyond: The Art of Chesley Bonestell*; **Mike Hodel,** 46, producer and host of *Hour 25* for KPFK-FM in Los Angeles, the longest-running SF radio program in the world; **R. Glenn Wright,** 54, professor of English at Michigan State University and longtime director of the Clarion Writer's Workshop; **Lee Wright,** 82, longtime mystery editor and occasional editor of associational fantasy items; **Clyde S. Kilby,** 84, noted J. R. R. Tolkien and C. S. Lewis scholar; **William Barrett,** 85, veteran author; **Marjorie Brunner,** 65, wife of author John Brunner; **Rhoda Katerinsky,** 55, well-known fan under her maiden name of "Ricky" Slavin, long an editor at *MS*; **Jerry Jacks,** 39, well-known fan, active in gay-rights circles; **Forrest Tucker,** star of numerous SF "B" movies such as *The Crawling Eye*; **Keenan Wynn,** 70, best known to SF fans for his role in Kubrick's *Dr. Strangelove*; and **Paul Frees,** who provided the voice characterizations for dozens of animated fantasy characters such as Boris Badinov and Ludwig Von Drake.

LUCIUS SHEPARD

R & R

Lucius Shepard began publishing in 1983, and in a very short time has become one of the most popular and prolific new writers to enter the science fiction field in many years. In 1985, Shepard won the John W. Campbell Award as the year's best new writer, as well as being on the Nebula Award final ballot an unprecedented three times in three separate categories. Since then, he has turned up several more times on the final Nebula ballot, as well as being a finalist for the Hugo Award, the British Fantasy Award, the John W. Campbell Memorial Award, the Philip K. Dick Award, and the World Fantasy Award. His short fiction has appeared in *Playboy, Isaac Asimov's Science Fiction Magazine, The Magazine of Fantasy and Science Fiction, Universe,* and elsewhere. His acclaimed first novel, *Green Eyes,* was an Ace Special. Upcoming is a major new novel, *Life During Wartime,* from Bantam's New Fiction line, and a collection, *The Jaguar Hunter,* from Arkham House. His stories "Salvador" and "Black Coral" were in our Second Annual Collection, and his stories "The Jaguar Hunter" and "A Spanish Lesson" were in our Third Annual Collection. He is currently at work on two new novels, *Mister Right* and *The End of Life as We Know It,* and is living somewhere in the back country in Alaska, with no fixed address.

Shepard has become known for powerful, hard-hitting, sometimes controversial work, but "R & R" is unusually powerful even for Shepard. It is probably his best story to date . . . and quite likely the single best story to appear in the genre this year.

R & R

Lucius Shepard

1

One of the new Sikorsky gunships, an element of the First Air Cavalry with the words Whispering Death painted on its side, gave Mingolla and Gilbey and Baylor a lift from the Ant Farm to San Francisco de Juticlan, a small town located inside the green zone which on the latest maps was designated Free Occupied Guatemala. To the east of this green zone lay an undesignated band of yellow that crossed the country from the Mexican border to the Caribbean. The Ant Farm was a firebase on the eastern edge of the yellow band, and it was from there that Mingolla—an artillery specialist not yet twenty-one years old—lobbed shells into an area which the maps depicted in black and white terrain markings. And thus it was that he often thought of himself as engaged in a struggle to keep the world safe for primary colors.

Mingolla and his buddies could have taken their r&r in Rió or Caracas, but they had noticed that the men who visited these cities had a tendency to grow careless upon their return; they understood from this that the more exuberant your r&r, the more likely you were to wind up a casualty, and so they always opted for the lesser distractions of the Guatemalan towns. They were not really friends: they had little in common, and under different circumstances they might well have been enemies. But taking their r&r together had come to be a ritual of survival, and once they had reached the town of their choice, they would go their separate ways and perform further rituals. Because they had survived so much already, they believed that if they continued to perform these same rituals they would complete their tours unscathed. They had never acknowledged their belief to one another, speaking of it only obliquely—that, too, was part of the ritual—and had this belief been challenged they would have admitted its irrationality; yet they would also have pointed out that the strange character of the war acted to enforce it.

The gunship set down at an airbase a mile west of town, a cement strip

penned in on three sides by barracks and offices, with the jungle rising behind
them. At the center of the strip another Sikorsky was practicing take-offs
and landings—a drunken, camouflage-colored dragonfly—and two others
were hovering overhead like anxious parents. As Mingolla jumped out a hot
breeze fluttered his shirt. He was wearing civvies for the first time in weeks,
and they felt flimsy compared to his combat gear; he glanced around, nervous,
half-expecting an unseen enemy to take advantage of his exposure. Some
mechanics were lounging in the shade of a chopper whose cockpit had been
destroyed, leaving fanglike shards of plastic curving from the charred metal.
Dusty jeeps trundled back and forth between the buildings; a brace of crisply
starched lieutenants were making a brisk beeline toward a fork-lift stacked
high with aluminum coffins. Afternoon sunlight fired dazzles on the seams
and handles of the coffins, and through the heat haze the distant line of
barracks shifted like waves in a troubled olive-drab sea. The incongruity of
the scene—its What's-Wrong-With-This-Picture mix of the horrid and the
common place—wrenched at Mingolla. His left hand trembled, and the light
seemed to grow brighter, making him weak and vague. He leaned against
the Sikorsky's rocket pod to steady himself. Far above, contrails were fraying
in the deep blue range of the sky: XL-16s off to blow holes in Nicaragua.
He stared after them with something akin to longing, listening for their
engines, but heard only the spacy whisper of the Sikorskys.

Gilbey hopped down from the hatch that led to the computer deck behind
the cockpit; he brushed imaginary dirt from his jeans and sauntered over to
Mingolla and stood with hands on hips: a short muscular kid whose blond
crewcut and petulant mouth gave him the look of a grumpy child. Baylor
stuck his head out of the hatch and worriedly scanned the horizon. Then he,
too, hopped down. He was tall and rawboned, a couple of years older than
Mingolla, with lank black hair and pimply olive skin and features so sharp
that they appeared to have been hatcheted into shape. He rested a hand on
the side of the Sikorsky, but almost instantly, noticing that he was touching
the flaming letter W in Whispering Death, he jerked the hand away as if
he'd been scorched. Three days before there had been an all-out assault on
the Ant Farm, and Baylor had not recovered from it. Neither had Mingolla.
It was hard to tell whether or not Gilbey had been affected.

One of the Sikorsky's pilots cracked the cockpit door. ''Y'all can catch
a ride into 'Frisco at the PX,'' he said, his voice muffled by the black bubble
of his visor. The sun shined a white blaze on the visor, making it seem that
the helmet contained night and a single star.

''Where's the PX?'' asked Gilbey.

The pilot said something too muffled to be understood.

''What?'' said Gilbey.

Again the pilot's response was muffled, and Gilbey became angry. ''Take
that damn thing off!'' he said.

"This?" The pilot pointed to his visor. "What for?"

"So I can hear what the hell you sayin'."

"You can hear now, can'tcha?"

"Okay," said Gilbey, his voice tight. "Where's the goddamn PX?"

The pilot's reply was unintelligible; his faceless mask regarded Gilbey with inscrutable intent.

Gilbey balled up his fists. "Take that son of a bitch off!"

"Can't do it, soldier," said the second pilot, leaning over so that the two black bubbles were nearly side by side. "These here doobies"—he tapped his visor—"they got micro-circuits that beams shit into our eyes. 'Fects the optic nerve. Makes it so we can see the beaners even when they undercover. Longer we wear 'em, the better we see."

Baylor laughed edgily, and Gilbey said, "Bull!" Mingolla naturally assumed that the pilots were putting Gilbey on, or else their reluctance to remove the helmets stemmed from a superstition, perhaps from a deluded belief that the visors actually did bestow special powers. But given a war in which combat drugs were issued and psychics predicted enemy movements, anything was possible, even micro-circuits that enhanced vision.

"You don't wanna see us, nohow," said the first pilot. "The beams mess up our faces. We're deformed-lookin' mothers."

" 'Course you might not notice the changes," said the second pilot. "Lotsa people don't. But if you did, it'd mess you up."

Imagining the pilots' deformities sent a sick chill mounting from Mingolla's stomach. Gilbey, however, wasn't buying it. "You think I'm stupid?" he shouted, his neck reddening.

"Naw," said the first pilot. "We can *see* you ain't stupid. We can see lotsa stuff other people can't, 'cause of the beams."

"All kindsa weird stuff," chipped in the second pilot. "Like souls."

"Ghosts."

"Even the future."

"The future's our best thing," said the first pilot. "You guys wanna know what's ahead, we'll tell you."

They nodded in unison, the blaze of sunlight sliding across both visors: two evil robots responding to the same program.

Gilbey lunged for the cockpit door. The first pilot slammed it shut, and Gilbey pounded on the plastic, screaming curses. The second pilot flipped a switch on the control console, and a moment later his amplified voice boomed out: "Make straight past that fork-lift 'til you hit the barracks. You'll run right into the PX."

It took both Mingolla and Baylor to drag Gilbey away from the Sikorsky, and he didn't stop shouting until they drew near the fork-lift with its load of coffins: a giant's treasure of enormous silver ingots. Then he grew silent and lowered his eyes. They wangled a ride with an MP corporal outside the

PX, and as the jeep hummed across the cement, Mingolla glanced over at the Sikorsky that had transported them. The two pilots had spread a canvas on the ground, had stripped to shorts and were sunning themselves. But they had not removed their helmets. The weird juxtaposition of tanned bodies and shiny black heads disturbed Mingolla, reminding him of an old movie in which a guy had gone through a matter transmitter along with a fly and had ended up with the fly's head on his shoulders. Maybe, he thought, the helmets were like that, impossible to remove. Maybe the war had gotten that strange.

The MP corporal noticed him watching the pilots and let out a barking laugh. "Those guys," he said, with the flat emphatic tone of a man who knew whereof he spoke, "are fuckin' nuts!"

Six years before, San Francisco de Juticlan had been a scatter of thatched huts and concrete block structures deployed among palms and banana leaves on the east bank of the Rió Dulce, at the junction of the river and a gravel road that connected with the Pan American Highway; but it had since grown to occupy substantial sections of both banks, increased by dozens of bars and brothels: stucco cubes painted all the colors of the rainbow, with a fantastic bestiary of neon signs mounted atop their tin roofs. Dragons; unicorns; fiery birds; centaurs. The MP corporal told Mingolla that the signs were not advertisements but coded symbols of pride; for example, from the representation of a winged red tiger crouched amidst green lilies and blue crosses, you could deduce that the owner was wealthy, a member of a Catholic secret society, and ambivalent toward government policies. Old signs were constantly being dismantled, and larger, more ornate ones erected in their stead as testament to improved profits, and this warfare of light and image was appropriate to the time and place, because San Francisco de Juticlan was less a town than a symptom of war. Though by night the sky above it was radiant, at ground level it was mean and squalid. Pariah dogs foraged in piles of garbage, hardbitten whores spat from the windows, and according to the corporal, it was not unusual to stumble across a corpse, probably a victim of the gangs of abandoned children who lived in the fringes of the jungle. Narrow streets of tawny dirt cut between the bars, carpeted with a litter of flattened cans and feces and broken glass; refugees begged at every corner, displaying burns and bullet wounds. Many of the buildings had been thrown up with such haste that their walls were tilted, their roofs canted, and this made the shadows they cast appear exaggerated in their jaggedness, like shadows in the work of a psychotic artist, giving visual expression to a pervasive undercurrent of tension. Yet as Mingolla moved along, he felt at ease, almost happy. His mood was due in part to his hunch that it was going to be one hell of an r&r (he had learned to trust his hunches); but it mainly spoke to the fact that towns like this had become for him a kind of afterlife, a reward for having endured a harsh term of existence.

The corporal dropped them off at a drugstore, where Mingolla bought a box of stationery, and then they stopped for a drink at the Club Demonio: a tiny place whose whitewashed walls were shined to faint phosphorescence by the glare of purple light bulbs dangling from the ceiling like radioactive fruit. The club was packed with soldiers and whores, most sitting at tables around a dance floor not much bigger than a kingsize mattress. Two couples were swaying to a ballad that welled from a jukebox encaged in chicken wire and two-by-fours; veils of cigarette smoke drifted with underwater slowness above their heads. Some of the soldiers were mauling their whores, and one whore was trying to steal the wallet of a soldier who was on the verge of passing out; her hand worked between his legs, encouraging him to thrust his hips forward, and when he did this, with her other hand she pried at the wallet stuck in the back pocket of his tight-fitting jeans. But all the action seemed listless, half-hearted, as if the dimness and syrupy music had thickened the air and were hampering movement. Mingolla took a seat at the bar. The bartender glanced at him inquiringly, his pupils becoming cored with purple reflections, and Mingolla said, "Beer."

"Hey, check that out!" Gilbey slid onto an adjoining stool and jerked his thumb toward a whore at the end of the bar. Her skirt was hiked to mid-thigh, and her breasts, judging by their fullness and lack of sag, were likely the product of elective surgery.

"Nice," said Mingolla, disinterested. The bartender set a bottle of beer in front of him, and he had a swig; it tasted sour, watery, like a distillation of the stale air.

Baylor slumped onto the stool next to Gilbey and buried his face in his hands. Gilbey said something to him that Mingolla didn't catch, and Baylor lifted his head. "I ain't goin' back," he said.

"Aw, Jesus!" said Gilbey. "Don't start that crap."

In the half-dark Baylor's eye sockets were clotted with shadows. His stare locked onto Mingolla. "They'll get us next time," he said. "We should head downriver. They got boats in Livingston that'll take you to Panama."

"Panama!" sneered Gilbey. "Nothin' there 'cept more beaners."

"We'll be okay at the Farm," offered Mingolla. "Things get too heavy, they'll pull us back."

" 'Too heavy?' " A vein throbbed in Baylor's temple. "What the fuck you call 'too heavy?' "

"Screw this!" Gilbey heaved up from his stool. "You deal with him, man," he said to Mingolla; he gestured at the big-breasted whore. "I'm gonna climb Mount Silicon."

"Nine o'clock," said Mingolla. "The PX. Okay?"

Gilbey said, "Yeah," and moved off. Baylor took over his stool and leaned close to Mingolla. "You know I'm right," he said in an urgent whisper. "They almost got us this time."

"Air Cav'll handle 'em," said Mingolla, affecting nonchalance. He opened the box of stationery and unclipped a pen from his shirt pocket.

"You *know* I'm right," Baylor repeated.

Mingolla tapped the pen against his lips, pretending to be distracted.

"Air Cav!" said Baylor with a despairing laugh. "Air Cav ain't gonna do squat!"

"Why don't you put on some decent tunes?" Mingolla suggested. "See if they got any Prowler on the box."

"Dammit!" Baylor grabbed his wrist. "Don't you understand, man? This shit ain't workin' no more!"

Mingolla shook him off. "Maybe you need some change," he said coldly; he dug out a handful of coins and tossed them on the counter. "There! There's some change."

"I'm tellin' you . . . ."

"I don't wanna hear it!" snapped Mingolla.

"You don't wanna hear it?" said Baylor, incredulous. He was on the verge of losing control. His dark face slick with sweat, one eyelid fluttering. He pounded the countertop for emphasis. "Man, you better hear it! 'Cause we don't pull somethin' together soon, *real* soon, we're gonna die! You hear that, don'tcha?"

Mingolla caught him by the shirtfront. "Shut up!"

"I ain't shuttin' up!" Baylor shrilled. "You and Gilbey, man, you think you can save your ass by stickin' your head in the sand. But I'm gonna make you listen." He threw back his head, his voice rose to a shout. "We're gonna die!"

The way he shouted it—almost gleefully, like a kid yelling a dirty word to spite his parents—pissed Mingolla off. He was sick of Baylor's scenes. Without planning it, he punched him, pulling the punch at the last instant. Kept a hold of his shirt and clipped him on the jaw, just enough to rock back his head. Baylor blinked at him, stunned, his mouth open. Blood seeped from his gums. At the opposite end of the counter, the bartender was leaning beside a choirlike arrangement of liquor bottles, watching Mingolla and Baylor, and some of the soldiers were watching, too: they looked pleased, as if they had been hoping for a spot of violence to liven things up. Mingolla felt debased by their attentiveness, ashamed of his bullying. "Hey, I'm sorry, man," he said. "I . . . ."

"I don't give a shit 'bout you're sorry," said Baylor, rubbing his mouth. "Don't give a shit 'bout nothin' 'cept gettin' the hell outta here."

"Leave it alone, all right?"

But Baylor wouldn't leave it alone. He continued to argue, adopting the long-suffering tone of someone carrying on bravely in the face of great injustice. Mingolla tried to ignore him by studying the label on his beer bottle: a red and black graphic portraying a Guatemalan soldier, his rifle upheld in victory. It was an attractive design, putting him in mind of the poster work he had done before being drafted; but considering the unreliability of Guatemalan troops, the heroic pose was a joke. He gouged a trench through the center of the label with his thumbnail.

At last Baylor gave it up and sat staring down at the warped veneer of the counter. Mingolla let him sit a minute; then, without shifting his gaze from the bottle, he said, "Why don't you put on some decent tunes?"

Baylor tucked his chin onto his chest, maintaining a stubborn silence.

"It's your only option, man," Mingolla went on. "What else you gonna do?"

"You're crazy," said Baylor; he flicked his eyes toward Mingolla and hissed it like a curse. "Crazy!"

"You gonna take off for Panama by yourself? Un-unh. You know the three of us got something going. We come this far together, and if you just hang tough, we'll go home together."

"I don't know," said Baylor. "I don't know anymore."

"Look at it this way," said Mingolla. "Maybe we're all three of us right. Maybe Panama *is* the answer, but the time just isn't ripe. If that's true, me and Gilbey will see it sooner or later."

With a heavy sigh, Baylor got to his feet. "You ain't never gonna see it, man," he said dejectedly.

Mingolla had a swallow of beer. "Check if they got any Prowler on the box. I could relate to some Prowler."

Baylor stood for a moment, indecisive. He started for the jukebox, then veered toward the door. Mingolla tensed, preparing to run after him. But Baylor stopped and walked back over to the bar. Lines of strain were etched deep in his forehead. "Okay," he said, a catch in his voice. "Okay. What time tomorrow? Nine o'clock?"

"Right," said Mingolla, turning away. "The PX."

Out of the corner of his eye he saw Baylor cross the room and bend over the jukebox to inspect the selections. He felt relieved. This was the way all their r&rs had begun, with Gilbey chasing a whore and Baylor feeding the jukebox, while he wrote a letter home. On their first r&r he had written his parents about the war and its bizarre forms of attrition; then, realizing that the letter would alarm his mother, he had torn it up and written another, saying merely that he was fine. He would tear this letter up as well, but he wondered how his father would react if he were to read it. Most likely with anger. His father was a firm believer in God and country, and though Mingolla understood the futility of adhering to any moral code in light of the insanity around him, he had found that something of his father's tenets had been ingrained in him: he would never be able to desert as Baylor kept insisting. He knew it wasn't that simple, that other factors; too, were responsible for his devotion to duty; but since his father would have been happy to accept

the responsibility, Mingolla tended to blame it on him. He tried to picture what his parents were doing at that moment—father watching the Mets on TV, mother puttering in the garden—and then, holding those images in mind, he began to write.

Dear Mom and Dad,

In your last letter you asked if I thought we were winning the war. Down here you'd get a lot of blank stares in response to that question, because most people have a perspective on the war to which the overall result isn't relevant. Like there's a guy I know who has this rap about how the war is a magical operation of immense proportions, how the movements of the planes and troops are inscribing a mystical sign on the surface of reality, and to survive you have to figure out your location within the design and move accordingly. I'm sure that sounds crazy to you, but down here everyone's crazy the same way (some shrink's actually done a study on the incidence of superstition among the occupation forces). They're looking for a magic that will ensure their survival. You may find it hard to believe that I subscribe to this sort of thing, but I do. I carve my initials on the shell casings, wear parrot feathers inside my helmet . . . and a lot more.

To get back to your question, I'll try to do better than a blank stare, but I can't give you a simple Yes or No. The matter can't be summed up that neatly. But I can illustrate the situation by telling you a story and let you draw your own conclusions. There are hundreds of stories that would do, but the one that comes to mind now concerns the Lost Patrol . . .

A Prowler tune blasted from the jukebox, and Mingolla broke off writing to listen: it was a furious, jittery music, fueled—it seemed—by the same aggressive paranoia that had generated the war. People shoved back chairs, overturned tables and began dancing in the vacated spaces; they were crammed together, able to do no more than shuffle in rhythm, but their tread set the light bulbs jiggling at the end of their cords, the purple glare slopping over the walls. A slim acne-scarred whore came to dance in front of Mingolla, shaking her breasts, holding out her arms to him. Her face was corpse-pale in the unsteady light, her smile a dead leer. Trickling from one eye, like some exquisite secretion of death, was a black tear of sweat and mascara. Mingolla couldn't be sure he was seeing her right. His left hand started trembling, and for a couple of seconds the entire scene lost its cohesiveness. Everything looked scattered, unrecognizable, embedded in a separate context from everything else: a welter of meaningless objects bobbing up and down on a tide of deranged music. Then somebody opened the door, admitting a wedge of sunlight, and the room settled back to normal. Scowling, the whore danced away. Mingolla breathed easier. The tremors in his hand subsided.

He spotted Baylor near the door talking to a scruffy Guatemalan guy . . . probably a coke connection. Coke was Baylor's panacea, his remedy for fear and desperation. He always returned from r&r bleary-eyed and prone to nosebleeds, boasting about the great dope he'd scored. Pleased that he was following routine, Mingolla went back to his letter.

    . . . Remember me telling you that the Green Berets took drugs to make them better fighters? Most everyone calls the drugs 'Sammy,' which is short for 'samurai.' They come in ampule form, and when you pop them under your nose, for the next thirty minutes or so you feel like a cross between a Medal-of-Honor winner and Superman. The trouble is that a lot of Berets overdo them and flip out. They sell them on the black market, too, and some guys use them for sport. They take the ampules and fight each other in pits . . . like human cockfights.

    Anyway, about two years ago a patrol of Berets went on patrol up in Fire Zone Emerald, not far from my base, and they didn't come back. They were listed MIA. A month or so after they'd disappeared, somebody started ripping off ampules from various dispensaries. At first the crimes were chalked up to guerrillas, but then a doctor caught sight of the robbers and said they were Americans. They were wearing rotted fatigues, acting nuts. An artist did a sketch of their leader according to the doctor's description, and it turned out to be a dead ringer for the sergeant of that missing patrol. After that they were sighted all over the place. Some of the sightings were obviously false, but others sounded like the real thing. They were said to have shot down a couple of our choppers and to have knocked over a supply column near Zacapas.

    I'd never put much stock in the story, to tell you the truth, but about four months ago this infantryman came walking out of the jungle and reported to the firebase. He claimed he'd been captured by the Lost Patrol, and when I heard his story, I believed him. He said they had told him that they weren't Americans anymore but citizens of the jungle. They lived like animals, sleeping under palm fronds, popping the ampules night and day. They were crazy, but they'd become geniuses at survival. They knew everything about the jungle. When the weather was going to change, what animals were near. And they had this weird religion based on the beams of light that would shine down through the canopy. They'd sit under those beams, like saints being blessed by God, and rave about the purity of the light, the joys of killing, and the new world they were going to build.

    So that's what occurs to me when you ask your questions, mom and dad. The Lost Patrol. I'm not attempting to be circumspect in order to make a point about the horrors of war. Not at all. When I think about the Lost Patrol I'm not thinking about how sad and crazy they are. I'm wondering what it is they see in that light, wondering if it might be of help to me. And maybe therein lies your answer . . .

It was coming on sunset by the time Mingolla left the bar to begin the second part of his ritual, to wander innocent as a tourist through the native quarter, partaking of whatever fell to hand, maybe having dinner with a Guatemalan family, or buddying up with a soldier from another outfit and going to church, or hanging out with some young guys who'd ask him about America. He had done each of these things on previous r&rs, and his pretense of innocence always amused him. If he were to follow his inner directives, he would burn out the horrors of the firebase with whores and drugs; but on that first r&r—stunned by the experience of combat and needing solitude— a protracted walk had been his course of action, and he was committed not only to repeating it but also to recapturing his dazed mental set: it would not do to half-ass the ritual. In this instance, given recent events at the Ant Farm, he did not have to work very hard to achieve confusion.

The Rio Dulce was a wide blue river, heaving with a light chop. Thick jungle hedged its banks, and yellowish reed beds grew out from both shores. At the spot where the gravel road ended was a concrete pier, and moored to it a barge that served as a ferry; it was already loaded with its full complement of vehicles—two trucks—and carried about thirty pedestrians. Mingolla boarded and stood in the stern beside three infantrymen who were still wearing their combat suits and helmets, holding double-barreled rifles that were connected by flexible tubing to backpack computers; through their smoked faceplates he could see green reflections from the read-outs on their visor displays. They made him uneasy, reminding him of the two pilots, and he felt better after they had removed their helmets and proved to have normal human faces. Spanning a third of the way across the river was a sweeping curve of white cement supported by slender columns, like a piece fallen out of a Dali landscape: a bridge upon which construction had been halted. Mingolla had noticed it from the air just before landing and hadn't thought much about it; but now the sight took him by storm. It seemed less an unfinished bridge than a monument to some exalted ideal, more beautiful than any finished bridge could be. And as he stood rapt, with the ferry's oily smoke farting out around him, he sensed there was an analogue of that beautiful curving shape inside him, that he, too, was a road ending in mid-air. It gave him confidence to associate himself with such loftiness and purity, and for a moment he let himself believe that he also might have—as the upward-angled terminus of the bridge implied—a point of completion lying far beyond the one anticipated by the architects of his fate.

On the west bank past the town the gravel road was lined with stalls: skeletal frameworks of brushwood poles roofed with palm thatch. Children chased in and out among them, pretending to aim and fire at each other with

stalks of sugar cane. But hardly any soldiers were in evidence. The crowds
that moved along the road were composed mostly of Indians: young couples
too shy to hold hands; old men who looked lost and poked litter with their
canes; dumpy matrons who made outraged faces at the high prices; shoeless
farmers who kept their backs ramrod-straight and wore grave expressions
and carried their money knotted in handkerchiefs. At one of the stalls Mingolla bought a sandwich and a Coca Cola. He sat on a stool and ate con-
tentedly, relishing the hot bread and the spicy fish cooked inside it, watching
the passing parade. Gray clouds were bulking up and moving in from the
south, from the Caribbean; now and then a flight of XL-16s would arrow
northward toward the oil fields beyond Lake Ixtabal, where the fighting was
very bad. Twilight fell. The lights of the town began to be picked out sharply
against the empurpling air. Guitars were plucked, hoarse voices sang, the
crowds thinned. Mingolla ordered another sandwich and Coke. He leaned
back, sipped and chewed, steeping himself in the good magic of the land,
the sweetness of the moment. Beside the sandwich stall, four old women
were squatting by a cooking fire, preparing chicken stew and corn fritters;
scraps of black ash drifted up from the flames, and as twilight deepened, it
seemed these scraps were the pieces of a jigsaw puzzle that were fitting
together overhead into the image of a starless night.

Darkness closed in, the crowds thickened again, and Mingolla continued
his walk, strolling past stalls with necklaces of light bulbs strung along their
frames, wires leading off them to generators whose rattle drowned out the
chirring of frogs and crickets. Stalls selling plastic rosaries, Chinese switch-
blades, tin lanterns; others selling embroidered Indian shirts, flour-sack trousers, wooden masks; others yet where old men in shabby suit coats sat cross-
legged behind pyramids of tomatoes and melons and green peppers, each
with a candle cemented in melted wax atop them, like primitive altars.
Laughter, shrieks, vendors shouting. Mingolla breathed in perfume, charcoal
smoke, the scents of rotting fruit. He began to idle from stall to stall, buying
a few souvenirs for friends back in New York, feeling part of the hustle,
the noise, the shining black air, and eventually he came to a stall around
which forty or fifty people had gathered, blocking all but its thatched roof
from view. A woman's amplified voice cried out, *"LA MARIPOSA!"* Excited
squeals from the crowd. Again the woman cried out, *"EL CUCHILLO!"*
The two words she had called—the butterfly and the knife—intrigued Mingolla, and he peered over heads.

Framed by the thatch and rickety poles, a dusky-skinned young woman
was turning a handle that spun a wire cage: it was filled with white plastic
cubes, bolted to a plank counter. Her black hair was pulled back from her
face, tied behind her neck, and she wore a red sundress that left her shoulders
bare. She stopped cranking, reached into the cage and without looking plucked
one of the cubes; she examined it, picked up a microphone and cried, *"LA*

LUNA!'' A bearded guy pushed forward and handed her a card. She checked the card, comparing it to some cubes that were lined up on the counter; then she gave the bearded guy a few bills in Guatemalan currency.

The composition of the game appealed to Mingolla. The dark woman; her red dress and cryptic words; the runelike shadow of the wire cage; all this seemed magical, an image out of an occult dream. Part of the crowd moved off, accompanying the winner, and Mingolla let himself be forced closer by new arrivals pressing in from behind. He secured a position at the corner of the stall, fought to maintain it against the eddying of the crowd, and on glancing up, he saw the woman smiling at him from a couple of feet away, holding out a card and a pencil stub. "Only ten cents Guatemalan," she said in American-sounding English.

The people flanking Mingolla urged him to play, grinning and clapping him on the back. But he didn't need urging. He knew he was going to win: it was the clearest premonition he had ever had, and it was signaled mostly by the woman herself. He felt a powerful attraction to her. It was as if she were a source of heat . . . not of heat alone but also of vitality, sensuality, and now that he was within range, that heat was washing over him, making him aware of a sexual tension developing between them, bringing with it the knowledge that he would win. The strength of the attraction surprised him, because his first impression had been that she was exotic-looking but not beautiful. Though slim, she was a little wide-hipped, and her breasts, mounded high and served up in separate scoops by her tight bodice, were quite small. Her face, like her coloring, had an East Indian cast, its features too large and voluptuous to suit the delicate bone structure; yet they were so expressive, so finely cut, that their disproportion came to seem a virtue. Except that it was thinner, it might have been the face of one of those handmaidens you see on Hindu religious posters, kneeling beneath Krishna's throne. Very sexy, very serene. That serenity, Mingolla decided, wasn't just a veneer. It ran deep. But at the moment he was more interested in her breasts. They looked nice pushed up like that, gleaming with a sheen of sweat. Two helpings of shaky pudding.

The woman waggled the card, and he took it: a simplified Bingo card with symbols instead of letters and numbers. "Good luck," she said, and laughed, as if in reaction to some private irony. Then she began to spin the cage.

Mingolla didn't recognize many of the words she called, but an old man cozied up to him and pointed to the appropriate square whenever he got a match. Soon several rows were almost complete. *"LA MANZANA!"* cried the woman, and the old man tugged at Mingolla's sleeve, shouting, *"Se gano!''*

As the woman checked his card, Mingolla thought about the mystery she presented. Her calmness, her unaccented English and the upper class background it implied, made her seem out of place here. Maybe she was a student, her education interrupted by the war . . . though she might be a bit too old for that. He figured her to be twenty-two or twenty-three. Graduate school, maybe. But there was an air of worldliness about her that didn't support that theory. He watched her eyes dart back and forth between the card and the plastic cubes. Large, heavy-lidded eyes. The whites stood in such sharp contrast to her dusky skin that they looked fake: milky stones with black centers.

"You see?" she said, handing him his winnings—about three dollars— and another card.

"See what?" Mingolla asked, perplexed.

But she had already begun to spin the cage again.

He won three of the next seven cards. People congratulated him, shaking their heads in amazement; the old man cozied up further, suggesting in sign language that he was the agency responsible for Mingolla's good fortune. Mingolla, however, was nervous. His ritual was founded on a principle of small miracles, and though he was certain the woman was cheating on his behalf (that, he assumed, had been the meaning of her laughter, her "You see?"), though his luck was not really luck, its excessiveness menaced that principle. He lost three cards in a row, but thereafter won two of four and grew even more nervous. He considered leaving. But what if it *were* luck? Leaving might run him afoul of a higher principle, interfere with some cosmic process and draw down misfortune. It was a ridiculous idea, but he couldn't bring himself to risk the faint chance that it might be true.

He continued to win. The people who had congratulated him became disgruntled and drifted off, and when there were only a handful of players left, the woman closed down the game. A grimy street kid materialized from the shadows and began dismantling the equipment. Unbolting the wire cage, unplugging the microphone, boxing up the plastic cubes, stuffing it all into a burlap sack. The woman moved out from behind the stall and leaned against one of the roofpoles. Half-smiling, she cocked her head, appraising Mingolla, and then—just as the silence between them began to get prickly—she said, "My name's Debora."

"David." Mingolla felt as awkward as a fourteen-year-old; he had to resist the urge to jam his hands into his pockets and look away. "Why'd you cheat?" he asked; in trying to cover his nervousness, he said it too loudly and it sounded like an accusation.

"I wanted to get your attention," she said. "I'm . . . interested in you. Didn't you notice?"

"I didn't want to take it for granted."

She laughed. "I approve! It's always best to be cautious."

He liked her laughter; it had an easiness that made him think she would celebrate the least good thing.

Three men passed by arm-in-arm, singing drunkenly. One yelled at Debora, and she responded with an angry burst of Spanish. Mingolla could guess what had been said, that she had been insulted for associating with an American. "Maybe we should go somewhere," he said. "Get off the streets."

"After he's finished." She gestured at the kid, who was now taking down the string of light bulbs. "It's funny," she said. "I have the gift myself, and I'm usually uncomfortable around anyone else who has it. But not with you."

"The gift?" Mingolla thought he knew what she was referring to, but was leery about admitting to it.

"What do you call it? ESP?"

He gave up the idea of denying it. "I never put a name on it," he said.

"It's strong in you. I'm surprised you're not with Psicorp."

He wanted to impress her, to cloak himself in a mystery equal to hers. "How do you know I'm not?"

"I could tell." She pulled a black purse from behind the counter. "After drug therapy there's a change in the gift, in the way it comes across. It doesn't feel as hot, for one thing." She glanced up from the purse. "Or don't you perceive it that way? As heat."

"I've been around people who felt hot to me," he said. "But I didn't know what it meant."

"That's what it means . . . sometimes." She stuffed some bills into the purse. "So, why aren't you with Psicorp?"

Mingolla thought back to his first interview with a Psicorp agent: a pale, balding man with the innocent look around the eyes that some blind people have. While Mingolla had talked, the agent had fondled the ring Mingolla had given him to hold, paying no mind to what was being said, and had gazed off distractedly, as if listening for echoes. "They tried hard to recruit me," Mingolla said. "But I was scared of the drugs. I heard they had bad side-effects."

"You're lucky it was voluntary," she said. "Here they just snap you up."

The kid said something to her; he swung the burlap sack over his shoulder, and after a rapid-fire exchange of Spanish he ran off toward the river. The crowds were still thick, but more than half the stalls had shut down; those that remained open looked—with their thatched roofs and strung lights and beshawled women—like crude nativity scenes ranging the darkness. Beyond the stalls, neon signs winked on and off: a chaotic menagerie of silver eagles and crimson spiders and indigo dragons. Watching them burn and vanish, Mingolla experienced a wave of dizziness. Things were starting to look disconnected as they had at the Club Demonio.

"Don't you feel well?" she asked.

"I'm just tired."

She turned him to face her, put her hands on his shoulders. "No," she said. "It's something else."

The weight of her hands, the smell of her perfume, helped to steady him. "There was an assault on the firebase a few days ago," he said. "It's still with me a little, y'know."

She gave his shoulders a squeeze and stepped back. "Maybe I can do something." She said this with such gravity, he thought she must have something specific in mind. "How's that?" he asked.

"I'll tell you at dinner . . . that is, if you're buying." She took his arm, jollying him. "You owe me that much, don't you think, after all your good luck?"

"Why aren't *you* with Psicorp?" he asked as they walked.

She didn't answer immediately, keeping her head down, nudging a scrap of cellophane with her toe. They were moving along an uncrowded street, bordered on the left by the river—a channel of sluggish black lacquer—and on the right by the windowless rear walls of some bars. Overhead, behind a latticework of supports, a neon lion shed a baleful green nimbus. "I was in school in Miami when they started testing here," she said at last. "And after I came home, my family got on the wrong side of Department Six. You know Department Six?"

"I've heard some stuff."

"Sadists don't make efficient bureaucrats," she said. "They were more interested in torturing us than in determining our value."

Their footsteps crunched in the dirt; husky jukebox voices cried out for love from the next street over. "What happened?" Mingolla asked.

"To my family?" She shrugged. "Dead. No one ever bothered to confirm it, but it wasn't necessary. Confirmation, I mean." She went a few steps in silence. "As for me . . ." A muscle bunched at the corner of her mouth. "I did what I had to."

He was tempted to ask for specifics, but thought better of it. "I'm sorry," he said, and then kicked himself for having made such a banal comment.

They passed a bar lorded over by a grinning red-and-purple neon ape. Mingolla wondered if these glowing figures had meaning for guerrillas with binoculars in the hills: gone-dead tubes signaling times of attack or troop movements. He cocked an eye toward Debora. She didn't look despondent as she had a second before, and that accorded with his impression that her calmness was a product of self-control, that her emotions were strong but held in tight check and only let out for exercise. From out on the river came a solitary splash, some cold fleck of life surfacing briefly, then returning to its long ignorant glide through the dark . . . and his life no different really, though maybe less graceful. How strange it was to be walking beside this woman who gave off heat like a candle flame, with earth and sky blended into a black gas, and neon totems standing guard overhead.

"Shit," said Debora under her breath.

It surprised him to hear her curse. "What is it?"

"Nothing," she said wearily. "Just 'shit.' " She pointed ahead and quickened her pace. "Here we are."

The restaurant was a working-class place that occupied the ground floor of a hotel: a two-story building of yellow concrete block with a buzzing Fanta sign hung above the entrance. Hundreds of moths swarmed about the sign, flickering whitely against the darkness, and in front of the steps stood a group of teenage boys who were throwing knives at an iguana. The iguana was tied by its hind legs to the step railing. It had amber eyes, a hide the color of boiled cabbage, and it strained at the end of its cord, digging its claws into the dirt and arching its neck like a pint-size dragon about to take flight. As Mingolla and Debora walked up, one of the boys scored a hit in the iguana's tail and it flipped high into the air, shaking loose the knife. The boys passed around a bottle of rum to celebrate.

Except for the waiter—a pudgy young guy leaning beside a door that opened onto a smoke-filled kitchen—the place was empty. Glaring overhead lights shined up the grease spots on the plastic tablecloths and made the uneven thicknesses of yellow paint appear to be dripping. The cement floor was freckled with dark stains that Mingolla discovered to be the remains of insects. However, the food turned out to be pretty good, and Mingolla shoveled down a plateful of chicken and rice before Debora had half-finished hers. She ate deliberately, chewing each bite a long time, and he had to carry the conversation. He told her about New York, his painting, how a couple of galleries had showed interest even though he was just a student. He compared his work to Rauschenberg, to Silvestre. Not as good, of course. Not yet. He had the notion that everything he told her—no matter its irrelevance to the moment—was securing the relationship, establishing subtle ties: he pictured the two of them enwebbed in a network of luminous threads that acted as conduits for their attraction. He could feel her heat more strongly than ever, and he wondered what it would be like to make love to her, to be swallowed by that perception of heat. The instant he wondered this, she glanced up and smiled, as if sharing the thought. He wanted to ratify his sense of intimacy, to tell her something he had told no one else, and so— having only one important secret—he told her about the ritual.

She laid down her fork and gave him a penetrating look. "You can't really believe that," she said.

"I know it sounds . . ."

"Ridiculous," she broke in. "That's how it sounds."

"It's the truth," he said defiantly.

She picked up her fork again, pushed around some grains of rice. "How is it for you," she said, "when you have a premonition? I mean, what happens? Do you have dreams, hear voices?"

"Sometimes I just know things," he said, taken aback by her abrupt change of subject. "And sometimes I see pictures. It's like with a TV that's not working right. Fuzziness at first, then a sharp image."

"With me, it's dreams. And hallucinations. I don't know what else to call them." Her lips thinned; she sighed, appearing to have reached some decision. "When I first saw you, just for a second, you were wearing battle gear. There were inputs on the gauntlets, cables attached to the helmet. The faceplate was shattered, and your face . . . it was pale, bloody." She put her hand out to cover his. "What I saw was very clear, David. You can't go back."

He hadn't described artilleryman's gear to her, and no way could she have seen it. Shaken, he said, "Where am I gonna go?"

"Panama," she said. "I can help you get there."

She suddenly snapped into focus. You find her, dozens like her, in any of the r&r towns. Preaching pacifism, encouraging desertion. Do-gooders, most with guerrilla connections. And that, he realized, must be how she had known about his gear. She had probably gathered information on the different types of units in order to lend authenticity to her dire pronouncements. His opinion of her wasn't diminished; on the contrary, it went up a notch. She was risking her life by talking to him. But her mystery had been dimmed.

"I can't do that," he said.

"Why not? Don't you believe me?"

"It wouldn't make any difference if I did."

"I . . ."

"Look," he said. "This friend of mine, he's always trying to convince me to desert, and there've been times I wanted to. But it's just not in me. My feet won't move that way. Maybe you don't understand, but that's how it is."

"This childish thing you do with your two friends," she said after a pause. "That's what's holding you here, isn't it?"

"It isn't childish."

"That's exactly what it is. Like a child walking home in the dark and thinking that if he doesn't look at the shadows, nothing will jump out at him."

"You don't understand," he said.

"No, I suppose I don't." Angry, she threw her napkin down on the table and stared intently at her plate as if reading some oracle from the chicken bones.

"Let's talk about something else," said Mingolla.

"I have to go," she said coldly.

"Because I won't desert?"

"Because of what'll happen if you don't." She leaned toward him, her voice burred with emotion. "Because knowing what I do about your future, I don't want to wind up in bed with you."

Her intensity frightened him. Maybe she *had* been telling the truth. But he dismissed the possibility. "Stay," he said. "We'll talk some more about it."

"You wouldn't listen." She picked up her purse and got to her feet.

The waiter ambled over and laid the check beside Mingolla's plate; he pulled a plastic bag filled with marijuana from his apron pocket and dangled it in front of Mingolla. "Gotta get her in the mood, man," he said. Debora railed at him in Spanish. He shrugged and moved off, his slow-footed walk an advertisement for his goods.

"Meet me tomorrow then," said Mingolla. "We can talk more about it tomorrow."

"No."

"Why don't you gimme a break?" he said. "This is all coming down pretty fast, y'know. I get here this afternoon, meet you, and an hour later you're saying, 'Death is in the cards, and Panama's your only hope.' I need some time to think. Maybe by tomorrow I'll have a different attitude."

Her expression softened but she shook her head, No.

"Don't you think it's worth it?"

She lowered her eyes, fussed with the zipper of her purse a second and let out a rueful hiss. "Where do you want to meet?"

"How 'bout the pier on this side? 'Round noon."

She hesitated. "All right." She came around to his side of the table, bent down and brushed her lips across his cheek. He tried to pull her close and deepen the kiss, but she slipped away. He felt giddy, overheated. "You really gonna be there?" he asked.

She nodded but seemed troubled, and she didn't look back before vanishing down the steps.

Mingolla sat a while, thinking about the kiss, its promise. He might have sat even longer, but three drunken soldiers staggered in and began knocking over chairs, giving the waiter a hard time. Annoyed, Mingolla went to the door and stood taking in hits of the humid air. Moths were loosely constellated on the curved plastic of the Fanta sign, trying to get next to the bright heat inside it, and he had a sense of relation, of sharing their yearning for the impossible. He started down the steps but was brought up short. The teenage boys had gone; however, their captive iguana lay on the bottom step, bloody and unmoving. Bluish-gray strings spilled from a gash in its throat. It was such a clear sign of bad luck, Mingolla went back inside and checked into the hotel upstairs.

*   *   *

The hotel corridors stank of urine and disinfectant. A drunken Indian with his fly unzipped and a bloody mouth was pounding on one of the doors. As Mingolla passed him, the Indian bowed and made a sweeping gesture, a parody of welcome. Then he went back to his pounding. Mingolla's room was a windowless cell five feet wide and coffin-length, furnished with a sink and a cot and a chair. Cobwebs and dust clotted the glass of the transom, reducing the hallway light to a cold bluish-white glow. The walls were filmy with more cobwebs, and the sheets were so dirty that they looked to have a pattern. He lay down and closed his eyes, thinking about Debora. About ripping off that red dress and giving her a vicious screwing. How she'd cry out. That both made him ashamed and gave him a hard-on. He tried to think about making love to her tenderly. But tenderness, it seemed, was beyond him. He went flaccid. Jerking-off wasn't worth the effort, he decided. He started to unbutton his shirt, remembered the sheets and figured he'd be better off with his clothes on. In the blackness behind his lids he began to see explosive flashes, and within those flashes were images of the assault on the Ant Farm. The mist, the tunnels. He blotted them out with the image of Debora's face, but they kept coming back. Finally he opened his eyes. Two . . . no, three fuzzy-looking black stars were silhouetted against the transom. It was only when they began to crawl that he recognized them to be spiders. Big ones. He wasn't usually afraid of spiders, but these particular spiders terrified him. If he hit them with his shoe he'd break the glass and they'd eject him from the hotel. He didn't want to kill them with his hands. After a while he sat up, switched on the overhead and searched under the cot. There weren't any more spiders. He lay back down, feeling shaky and short of breath. Wishing he could talk to someone, hear a familiar voice. "It's okay," he said to the dark air. But that didn't help. And for a long time, until he felt secure enough to sleep, he watched the three black stars crawling across the transom, moving toward the center, touching each other, moving apart, never making any real progress, never straying from their area of bright confinement, their universe of curdled, frozen light.

2

In the morning Mingolla crossed to the west bank and walked toward the airbase. It was already hot, but the air still held a trace of freshness and the sweat that beaded on his forehead felt clean and healthy. White dust was settling along the gravel road, testifying to the recent passage of traffic; past the town and the cut-off that led to the uncompleted bridge, high walls of vegetation crowded close to the road, and from within them he heard monkeys and insects and birds: sharp sounds that enlivened him, making him conscious

of the play of his muscles. About halfway to the base he spotted six Guatemalan soldiers coming out of the jungle, dragging a couple of bodies; they
tossed them onto the hood of their jeep, where two other bodies were lying.
Drawing near, Mingolla saw that the dead were naked children, each with
a neat hole in his back. He had intended to walk on past, but one of the
soldiers—a gnomish, copper-skinned man in dark blue fatigues—blocked
his path and demanded to check his papers. All the soldiers gathered around
to study the papers, whispering, turning them sideways, scratching their
heads. Used to such hassles, Mingolla paid them no attention and looked at
the dead children.

They were scrawny, sun-darkened, lying face down with their ragged hair
hanging in a fringe off the hood; their skins were pocked by infected mosquito
bites, and the flesh around the bullet holes was ridged-up and bruised. Judging
by their size, Mingolla guessed them to be about ten years old; but then he
noticed that one was a girl with a teenage fullness to her buttocks, her breasts
squashed against the metal. That made him indignant. They were only wild
children who survived by robbing and killing, and the Guatemalan soldiers
were only doing their duty: they performed a function comparable to that of
the birds that hunted ticks on the hide of a rhinoceros, keeping their American
beast pest-free and happy. But it wasn't right for the children to be laid out
like game.

The soldier gave back Mingolla's papers. He was now all smiles, and—
perhaps in the interest of solidifying Guatemalan-American relations, perhaps
because he was proud of his work—he went over to the jeep and lifted the
girl's head by the hair so Mingolla could see her face. *"Bandita!"* he said,
arranging his features into a comical frown. The girl's face was not unlike
the soldier's, with the same blade of a nose and prominent cheekbones. Fresh
blood glistened on her lips, and the faded tattoo of a coiled serpent centered
her forehead. Her eyes were open, and staring into them—despite their
cloudiness—Mingolla felt that he had made a connection, that she was
regarding him sadly from somewhere behind those eyes, continuing to die
past the point of clinical death. Then an ant crawled out of her nostril,
perching on the crimson curve of her lip, and the eyes merely looked vacant.
The soldier let her head fall and wrapped his hand in the hair of a second
corpse; but before he could lift it, Mingolla turned away and headed down
the road toward the airbase.

There was a row of helicopters lined up at the edge of the landing strip,
and walking between them, Mingolla saw the two pilots who had given him
a ride from the Ant Farm. They were stripped to shorts and helmets, wearing
baseball gloves, and they were playing catch, lofting high flies to one another.
Behind them, atop their Sikorsky, a mechanic was fussing with the main
rotor housing. The sight of the pilots didn't disturb Mingolla as it had the
previous day; in fact, he found their weirdness somehow comforting. Just

then, the ball eluded one of them and bounced Mingolla's way. He snagged it and flipped it back to the nearer of the pilots, who came loping over and stood pounding the ball into the pocket of his glove. With his black reflecting face and sweaty, muscular torso, he looked like an eager young mutant.

"How's she goin'?" he asked. "seem like you a little tore down this mornin'."

"I feel okay," said Mingolla defensively. " 'Course"—he smiled, making light of his defensiveness—"maybe you see something I don't."

The pilot shrugged; the sprightliness of the gesture seemed to convey good humor.

Mingolla pointed to the mechanic. "You guys broke down, huh?"

"Just overhaul. We're goin' back up early tomorrow. Need a lift?"

"Naw, I'm here for a week."

An eerie current flowed through Mingolla's left hand, setting up a palsied shaking. It was bad this time, and he jammed the hand into his hip pocket. The olive-drab line of barracks appeared to twitch, to suffer a dislocation and shift farther away; the choppers and jeeps and uniformed men on the strip looked toylike: pieces in a really neat GI Joe Airbase kit. Mingolla's hand beat against the fabric of his trousers like a sick heart.

"I gotta get going," he said.

"Hang in there," said the pilot. "You be awright."

The words had a flavor of diagnostic assurance that almost convinced Mingolla of the pilot's ability to know his fate, that things such as fate could be known. "You honestly believe what you were saying yesterday, man?" he asked. " 'Bout your helmets? 'Bout knowing the future?"

The pilot bounced the ball on the cement, snatched it at the peak of its rebound and stared down at it. Mingolla could see the seams and brand name reflected in the visor, but nothing of the face behind it, no evidence either of normalcy or deformity. "I get asked that a lot," said the pilot. "People raggin' me, y'know. But you ain't raggin' me, are you, man?"

"No," said Mingolla. "I'm not."

"Well," said the pilot, "it's this way. We buzz 'round up in the nothin', and we see shit down on the ground, shit nobody else sees. Then we blow that shit away. Been doin' it like that for ten months, and we're still alive. Fuckin' A, I believe it!"

Mingolla was disappointed. "Yeah, okay," he said.

"You hear what I'm sayin'?" asked the pilot. "I mean we're livin' goddamn proof."

"Uh-huh." Mingolla scratched his neck, trying to think of a diplomatic response, but thought of none. "Guess I'll see you." He started toward the PX.

"Hang in there, man!" the pilot called after him. "Take it from me! Things gonna be lookin' up for you real soon!"

The canteen in the PX was a big, barnlike room of unpainted boards; it was of such recent construction that Mingolla could still smell sawdust and resin. Thirty or forty tables; a jukebox; bare walls. Behind the bar at the rear of the room, a sour-faced corporal with a clipboard was doing a liquor inventory, and Gilbey—the only customer—was sitting by one of the east windows, stirring a cup of coffee. His brow was furrowed, and a ray of sunlight shone down around him, making it look that he was being divinely inspired to do some soul-searching.

"Where's Baylor?" asked Mingolla, sitting opposite him.

"Fuck, I dunno," said Gilbey, not taking his eyes from the coffee cup. "He'll be here."

Mingolla kept his left hand in his pocket. The tremors were diminishing, but not quickly enough to suit him; he was worried that the shaking would spread as it had after the assault. He let out a sigh, and in letting it out he could feel all his nervous flutters. The ray of sunlight seemed to be humming a wavery golden note, and that, too, worried him. Hallucinations. Then he noticed a fly buzzing against the windowpane. "How was it last night?" he asked.

Gilbey glanced up sharply. "Oh, you mean Big Tits. She lemme check her for lumps." He forced a grin, then went back to stirring his coffee.

Mingolla was hurt that Gilbey hadn't asked about his night; he wanted to tell him about Debora. But that was typical of Gilbey's self-involvement. His narrow eyes and sulky mouth were the imprints of a mean-spiritedness that permitted few concerns aside from his own well-being. Yet despite his insensitivity, his stupid rages and limited conversation, Mingolla believed that he was smarter than he appeared, that disguising one's intelligence must have been a survival tactic in Detroit, where he had grown up. It was his craftiness that gave him away: his insights into the personalities of adversary lieutenants; his slickness at avoiding unpleasant duty; his ability to manipulate his peers. He wore stupidity like a cloak, and perhaps he had worn it for so long that it could not be removed. Still, Mingolla envied him its virtues, especially the way it had numbed him to the assault.

"He's never been late before," said Mingolla after a while.

"So what he's fuckin' late!" snapped Gilbey, glowering. "He'll be here!"

Behind the bar, the corporal switched on a radio and spun the dial past Latin music, past Top Forty, then past an American voice reporting the baseball scores. "Hey!" called Gilbey. "Let's hear that, man! I wanna see what happened to the Tigers." With a shrug, the corporal complied.

". . . White Sox six, A's three," said the announcer. "That's eight in a row for the Sox . . ."

"White Sox are kickin' some ass," said the corporal, pleased.

"The White Sox!" Gilbey sneered. "What the White Sox got 'cept a buncha beaners hittin' two hunnerd and some coke-sniffin' niggers? Shit!

Every spring the White Sox are flyin', man. But then 'long comes summer and the good drugs hit the street and they fuckin' die!''

"Yeah," said the corporal, "but this year . . ."

"Take that son of a bitch Caldwell," said Gilbey, ignoring him. "I seen him coupla years back when he had a trial with the Tigers. Man, that guy could hit! Now he shuffles up there like he's just feelin' the breeze.''

"They ain't takin' drugs, man," said the corporal testily. "They can't take 'em 'cause there's these tests that show if they's on somethin'."

Gilbey barreled ahead. "White Sox ain't gotta chance, man! Know what the guy on TV calls 'em sometimes? The Pale Hose! The fuckin' Pale Hose! How you gonna win with a name like that? The Tigers, now, they got the right kinda name. The Yankees, the Braves, the . . ."

"Bullshit, man!" The corporal was becoming upset; he set down his clipboard and walked to the end of the bar. "What 'bout the Dodgers? They gotta wimpy name and they're a good team. Your name don't mean shit!"

"The Reds," suggested Mingolla; he was enjoying Gilbey's rap, its stubbornness and irrationality. Yet at the same time he was concerned by its undertone of desperation: appearances to the contrary, Gilbey was not himself this morning.

"Oh, yeah!" Gilbey smacked the table with the flat of his hand. "The Reds! Lookit the Reds, man! Lookit how good they been doin' since the Cubans come into the war. You think that don't mean nothin'? You think their name ain't helpin' 'em? Even if they get in the Series, the Pale Hose don't gotta prayer against the Reds." He laughed—a hoarse grunt. "I'm a Tiger fan, man, but I gotta feelin' this ain't their year, y'know. The Reds are tearin' up the NL East, and the Yankees is comin' on, and when they get together in October, man, then we gonna find out alla 'bout everything. Alla 'bout fuckin' everything!" His voice grew tight and tremulous. "So don't gimme no trouble 'bout the candyass Pale Hose, man! They ain't shit and they never was and they ain't gonna be shit 'til they change their fuckin' name!"

Sensing danger, the corporal backed away from confrontation, and Gilbey lapsed into a moody silence. For a while there were only the sounds of chopper blades and the radio blatting out cocktail jazz. Two mechanics wandered in for an early morning beer, and not long after that three fatherly-looking sergeants with potbellies and thinning hair and quartermaster insignia on their shoulders sat at a nearby table and started up a game of rummy. The corporal brought them a pot of coffee and a bottle of whiskey, which they mixed and drank as they played. Their game had an air of custom, of something done at this time every day, and watching them, taking note of their fat, pampered ease, their old-buddy familiarity, Mingolla felt proud of his palsied hand. It was an honorable affliction, a sign that he had participated in the heart of the war as these men had not. Yet he bore them no resentment.

None whatsoever. Rather it gave him a sense of security to know that three such fatherly men were here to provide him with food and liquor and new boots. He basked in the dull, happy clutter of their talk, in the haze of cigar smoke that seemed the exhaust of their contentment. He believed that he could go to them, tell them his problems and receive folksy advice. They were here to assure him of the rightness of his purpose, to remind him of simple American values, to lend an illusion of fraternal involvement to the war, to make clear that it was merely an exercise in good fellowship and tough-mindedness, an initiation rite that these three men had long ago passed through, and after the war they would all get rings and medals and pal around together and talk about bloodshed and terror with head-shaking wonderment and nostalgia, as if bloodshed and terror were old, lost friends whose natures they had not fully appreciated at the time . . . Mingolla realized then that a smile had stretched his facial muscles taut, and that his train of thought had been leading him into spooky mental territory. The tremors in his hand were worse than ever. He checked his watch. It was almost ten o'clock. *Ten o'clock!* In a panic, he scraped back his chair and stood.

"Let's look for him," he said to Gilbey.

Gilbey started to say something but kept it to himself. He tapped his spoon hard against the edge of the table. Then he, too, scraped back his chair and stood.

Baylor was not be found at the Club Demonio or any of the bars on the west bank. Gilbey and Mingolla described him to everyone they met, but no one remembered him. The longer the search went on, the more insecure Mingolla became. Baylor was necessary, an essential underpinning of the platform of habits and routines that supported him, that let him live beyond the range of war's weapons and the laws of chance, and should that underpinning be destroyed . . . In his mind's eye he saw the platform tipping, him and Gilbey toppling over the edge, cartwheeling down into an abyss filled with black flames. Once Gilbey said, "Panama! The son of a bitch run off to Panama." But Mingolla didn't think this was the case. He was certain that Baylor was close at hand. His certainty had such a valence of clarity that he became even more insecure, knowing that this sort of clarity often heralded a bad conclusion.

The sun climbed higher, its heat an enormous weight pressing down, its light leaching color from the stucco walls, and Mingolla's sweat began to smell rancid. Only a few soldiers were on the streets, mixed in with the usual run of kids and beggars, and the bars were empty except for a smattering of drunks still on a binge from the night before. Gilbey stumped along, grabbing people by the shirt and asking his questions. Mingolla, however, terribly conscious of his trembling hand, nervous to the point of stammering, was forced to work out a stock approach whereby he could get through these brief interviews. He would amble up, keeping his right side forward, and say, "I'm looking for a friend of mine. Maybe you seen him? Tall guy. Olive skin, black hair, thin. Name's Baylor." He came to be able to let this slide off his tongue in a casual unreeling.

Finally Gilbey had had enough. "I'm gonna hang out with Big Tits," he said. "Meet'cha at the PX tomorrow." He started to walk off, but turned and added, "You wanna get in touch 'fore tomorrow, I'll be at the Club Demonio." He had an odd expression on his face. It was as if he were trying to smile reassuringly, but—due to his lack of practice with smiles—it looked forced and foolish and not in the least reassuring.

Around eleven o'clock Mingolla wound up leaning against a pink stucco wall, watching out for Baylor in the thickening crowds. Beside him, the sun-browned fronds of a banana tree were feathering in the wind, making a crispy sound whenever a gust blew them back into the wall. The roof of the bar across the street was being repaired: patches of new tin alternating with narrow strips of rust that looked like enormous strips of bacon laid there to fry. Now and then he would let his gaze drift up to the unfinished bridge, a great sweep of magical whiteness curving into the blue, rising above the town and the jungle and the war. Not even the heat haze rippling from the tin roof could warp its smoothness. It seemed to be orchestrating the stench, the mutter of the crowds, and the jukebox music into a tranquil unity, absorbing those energies and returning them purified, enriched. He thought that if he stared at it long enough, it would speak to him, pronounce a white word that would grant his wishes.

Two flat cracks—pistol shots—sent him stumbling away from the wall, his heart racing. Inside his head the shots had spoken the two syllables of Baylor's name. All the kids and beggars had vanished. All the soldiers had stopped and turned to face the direction from which the shots had come: zombies who had heard their master's voice.

Another shot.

Some soldiers milled out of a side street, talking excitedly."... fuckin' nuts!" one was saying, and his buddy said, "It was Sammy, man! You see his eyes?"

Mingolla pushed his way through them and sprinted down the side street. At the end of the block a cordon of MPs had sealed off access to the right-hand turn, and when Mingolla ran up one of them told him to stay back.

"What is it?" Mingolla asked. "Some guy playing Sammy?"

"Fuck off," the MP said mildly.

"Listen," said Mingolla. "It might be this friend of mine. Tall, skinny guy. Black hair. Maybe I can talk to him."

The MP exchanged glances with his buddies, who shrugged and acted otherwise unconcerned. "Okay," he said. He pulled Mingolla to him and pointed out a bar with turquoise walls on the next corner down. "Go on in there and talk to the captain."

Two more shots, then a third.

"Better hurry," said the MP. "Ol' Captain Haynesworth there, he don't have much faith in negotiations."

It was cool and dark inside the bar; two shadowy figures were flattened against the wall beside a window that opened onto the cross-street. Mingolla could make out the glint of automatic pistols in their hands. Then, through the window, he saw Baylor pop up from behind a retaining wall: a three-foot-high structure of mud bricks running between a herbal drugstore and another bar. Baylor was shirtless, his chest painted with reddish-brown smears of dried blood, and he was standing in a nonchalant pose, with his thumbs hooked in his trouser pockets. One of the men by the window fired at him. The report was deafening, causing Mingolla to flinch and close his eyes. When he looked out the window again, Baylor was nowhere in sight.

"Fucker's just tryin' to draw fire," said the man who had shot at Baylor. "Sammy's fast today."

"Yeah, but he's slowin' some," said a lazy voice from the darkness at the rear of the bar. "I do believe he's outta dope."

"Hey," said Mingolla. "Don't kill him! I know the guy. I can talk to him."

"Talk?" said the lazy voice. "You kin talk 'til yo' ass turns green, boy, and Sammy ain't gon' listen."

Mingolla peered into the shadows. A big, sloppy-looking man was leaning on the counter; brass insignia gleamed on his beret. "You the captain?" he asked. "They told me outside to talk to the captain."

"Yes, indeed," said the man. "And I'd be purely delighted to talk with you, boy. What you wanna talk 'bout?"

The other men laughed.

"Why are you trying to kill him?" asked Mingolla, hearing the pitch of desperation in his voice. "You don't have to kill him. You could use a trank gun."

"Got one comin'," said the captain. "Thing is, though, yo' buddy got hisself a coupla hostages back of that wall, and we get a chance at him 'fore the trank gun 'rives, we bound to take it."

"But . . ." Mingolla began.

"Lemme finish, boy." The captain hitched up his gunbelt, strolled over and draped an arm around Mingolla's shoulder, enveloping him in an aura of body odor and whiskey breath. "See," he went on, "we had everything under control. Sammy there . . ."

"Baylor!" said Mingolla angrily. "His name's Baylor."

The captain lifted his arm from Mingolla's shoulder and looked at him with amusement. Even in the gloom Mingolla could see the network of broken capillaries on his cheeks, the bloated alcoholic features. "Right," said the captain. "Like I's sayin', yo' good buddy Mister Baylor there wasn't doin' no harm. Just sorta ravin' and runnin' round. But then 'long comes a coupla our Marine brothers. Seems like they'd been givin' our beaner friends a demonstration of the latest combat gear, and they was headin' back from said demonstration when they seen our little problem and took it 'pon themselves to play hero. Wellsir, puttin' it in a nutshell, Mister Baylor flat kicked their ass. Stomped all over their *esprit de corps*. Then he drags 'em back of that wall and starts messin' with one of their guns. And . . ."

Two more shots.

"Shit!" said one of the men by the window.

"And there he sits," said the captain. "Fuckin' with us. Now either the gun's outta ammo or else he ain't figgered out how it works. If it's the latter case, and he does figger it out . . ." The captain shook his head dolefully, as if picturing dire consequences. "See my predicament?"

"I could try talking to him," said Mingolla. "What harm would it do?"

"You get yourself killed, it's your life, boy. But it's my ass that's gonna get hauled up on charges." The captain steered Mingolla to the door and gave him a gentle shove toward the cordon of MPs. " 'Preciate you volunteerin', boy."

Later Mingolla was to reflect that what he had done had made no sense, because—whether or not Baylor had survived—he would never have been returned to the Ant Farm. But at the time, desperate to preserve the ritual, none of this occurred to him. He walked around the corner and toward the retaining wall. His mouth was dry, his heart pounded. But the shaking in his hand had stopped, and he had the presence of mind to walk in such a way that he blocked the MPs' line of fire. About twenty feet from the wall he called out, "Hey, Baylor! It's Mingolla, man!" And as if propelled by a spring, Baylor jumped up, staring at him. It was an awful stare. His eyes were like bulls-eyes, white showing all around the irises; trickles of blood ran from his nostrils, and nerves were twitching in his cheeks with the regularity of watchworks. The dried blood on his chest came from three long gouges; they were partially scabbed over but were oozing a clear fluid. For a moment he remained motionless. Then he reached down behind the wall, picked up a double-barreled rifle from whose stock trailed a length of flexible tubing, and brought it to bear on Mingolla.

He squeezed the trigger.

No flame, no explosion. Not even a click. But Mingolla felt that he'd been dipped in ice water. "Christ!" he said. "Baylor! It's me!" Baylor squeezed the trigger again, with the same result. An expression of intense frustration washed over his face, then lapsed into that dead man's stare. He looked directly up into the sun, and after a few seconds he smiled: he might have been receiving terrific news from on high.

Mingolla's senses had become wonderfully acute. Somewhere far away a radio was playing a country and western tune, and with its plaintiveness, its intermittent bursts of static, it seemed to him the whining of a nervous system on the blink. He could hear the MPs talking in the bar, could smell the sour acids of Baylor's madness, and he thought he could feel the pulse of Baylor's rage, an inconstant flow of heat eddying around him, intensifying his fear, rooting him to the spot. Baylor laid the gun down, laid it down with the tenderness he might have shown toward a sick child, and stepped over the retaining wall. The animal fluidity of the movement made Mingolla's skin crawl. He managed to shuffle backward a pace and held up his hands to ward Baylor off. "C'mon, man," he said weakly. Baylor let out a fuming noise—part hiss, part whimper—and a runner of saliva slid between his lips. The sun was a golden bath drenching the street, kindling glints and shimmers from every bright surface, as if it were bringing reality to a boil.

Somebody yelled, "Get down, boy!"

Then Baylor flew at him, and they fell together, rolling on the hard-packed dirt. Fingers dug in behind his Adam's apple. He twisted away, saw Baylor grinning down, all staring eyes and yellowed teeth. Strings of drool flapping from his chin. A Halloween face. Knees pinned Mingolla's shoulders, hands gripped his hair and bashed his head against the ground. Again, and again. A keening sound switched on inside his ears. He wrenched an arm free and tried to gouge Baylor's eyes; but Baylor bit his thumb, gnawing at the joint. Mingolla's vision dimmed, and he couldn't hear anything anymore. The back of his head felt mushy. It seemed to be rebounding very slowly from the dirt, higher and slower after each impact. Framed by blue sky, Baylor's face looked to be receding, spiraling off. And then, just as Mingolla began to fade, Baylor disappeared.

Dust was in Mingolla's mouth, his nostrils. He heard shouts, grunts. Still dazed, he propped himself onto an elbow. A little ways off, khaki arms and legs and butts were thrashing around in a cloud of dust. Like a comic strip fight. You expected asterisks and exclamation points overhead to signify profanity. Somebody grabbed his arm, hauled him upright. The MP captain, his beefy face flushed. He frowned reprovingly as he brushed dirt from Mingolla's clothes. "Real gutsy, boy," he said. "And real, real stupid. He hadn't been at the end of his run, you'd be drawin' flies 'bout now." He turned to a sergeant standing nearby. "How stupid you reckon that was, Phil?"

The sergeant said that it beat him.

"Well," the captain said, "I figger if the boy here was in combat, that'd be 'bout Bronze-Star stupid."

That, allowed the sergeant, was pretty goddamn stupid.

" 'Course here in 'Frisco''—the captain gave Mingolla a final dusting—"it don't get you diddley-shit.''

The MPs were piling off Baylor, who lay on his side, bleeding from his nose and mouth. Blood thick as gravy filmed over his cheeks.

"Panama," said Mingolla dully. Maybe it *was* an option. He saw how it would be . . . a night beach, palm shadows a lacework on the white sand.

"What say?" asked the captain.

"He wanted to go to Panama," said Mingolla.

The captain gave an amused snort. "Don't we all."

One of the MPs rolled Baylor onto his stomach and handcuffed him; another manacled his feet. Then they rolled him back over. Yellow dirt had mired with the blood on his cheeks and forehead, fitting him with a blotchy mask. His eyes snapped open in the middle of that mask, widening when he felt the restraints. He started to hump up and down, trying to bounce his way to freedom. He kept on humping for almost a minute; then he went rigid and—his gone eyes fixed on the molten disc of the sun—he let out a roar. That was the only word for it. It wasn't a scream or a shout, but a devil's exultant roar, so loud and full of fury, it seemed to be generating all the blazing light and heat-dance. Listening to it had a seductive effect, and Mingolla began to get behind it, to feel it in his body like a good rock 'n' roll tune, to sympathize with its life-hating exuberance.

"Whoo-ee!" said the captain, marveling. "They gon' have to build a whole new zoo for that boy."

After giving his statement, letting a Corpsman check his head, Mingolla caught the ferry to meet Debora on the east bank. He sat in the stern, gazing out at the unfinished bridge, this time unable to derive from it any sense of hope or magic. Panama kept cropping up in his thoughts. Now that Baylor was gone, was it really an option? He knew he should try to figure things out, plan what to do, but he couldn't stop seeing Baylor's bloody, demented face. He'd seen worse, Christ yes, a whole lot worse. Guys reduced to spare parts, so little of them left that they didn't need a shiny silver coffin, just a black metal can the size of a cookie jar. Guys scorched and one-eyed and bloody, clawing blindly at the air like creatures out of a monster movie. But the idea of Baylor trapped forever in some raw, red place inside his brain, in the heart of that raw, red noise he'd made, maybe that idea was worse than anything Mingolla had seen. He didn't want to die; he rejected the prospect with the impassioned stubbornness a child displays when confronted with a hard truth. Yet he would rather die than endure madness. Compared to what Baylor had in store, death and Panama seemed to offer the same peaceful sweetness.

Someone sat down beside Mingolla: a kid who couldn't have been older than eighteen. A new kid with a new haircut, new boots, new fatigues. Even his face looked new, freshly broken from the mold. Shiny, pudgy cheeks; clear skin; bright, unused blue eyes. He was eager to talk. He asked Mingolla about his home, his family, and said, Oh, wow, it must be great living in New York, wow. But he appeared to have some other reason for initiating the conversation, something he was leading up to, and finally he spat it out.

"You know the Sammy that went animal back there?" he said. "I seen him pitted last night. Little place in the jungle west of the base. Guy name Chaco owns it. Man, it was incredible!"

Mingolla had only heard of the pits third- and fourth-hand, but what he had heard was bad, and it was hard to believe that this kid with his air of homeboy innocence could be an afficionado of something so vile. And, despite what he had just witnessed, it was even harder to believe that Baylor could have been a participant.

The kid didn't need prompting. "It was pretty early on," he said. "There'd been a coupla bouts, nothin' special, and then this guy walks in lookin' real twitchy. I knew he was Sammy by the way he's starin' at the pit, y'know, like it's somethin' he's been wishin' for. And this guy with me, friend of mine, he gives me a poke and says, 'Holy shit! That's the Black Knight, man! I seen him fight over in Reunion awhile back. Put your money on him,' he says. "The guy's an ace!'"

Their last r&r had been in Reunion. Mingolla tried to frame a question but couldn't think of one whose answer would have any meaning.

"Well," said the kid, "I ain't been down long, but I'd even heard 'bout the Knight. So I went over and kinda hung out near him, thinkin' maybe I can get a line on how he's feelin', y'know, 'cause you don't wanna just bet the guy's rep. Pretty soon Chaco comes over and asks the Knight if he wants some action. The Knight says, 'Yeah, but I wanna fight an animal. Somethin' fierce, man. I wanna fight somethin' fierce.' Chaco says he's got some monkeys and shit, and the Knight says he hears Chaco's got a jaguar. Chaco he hems and haws, says Maybe so, maybe not, but it don't matter 'cause a jaguar's too strong for Sammy. And then the Knight tells Chaco who he is. Lemme tell ya, Chaco's whole attitude changed. He could see how the bettin' was gonna go for somethin' like the Black Knight versus a jaguar. And he says, 'Yes sir, Mister Black Knight sir! Anything you want!' And he makes the announcement. Man, the place goes nuts. People wavin' money, screamin' odds, drinkin' fast so's they can get ripped in time for the main event, and the Knight's just standin' there, smilin', like he's feedin' off the confusion. Then Chaco lets the jaguar in through the tunnel and into the pit. It ain't a full-growed jaguar, half-growed maybe, but that's all you figure even the Knight can handle."

The kid paused for breath; his eyes seemed to have grown brighter. "Anyway, the jaguar's sneakin' 'round and 'round, keepin' close to the pit wall, snarlin' and spittin', and the Knight's watchin' him from up above, checkin' his moves, y'know. And everybody starts chantin', 'Sammee, Sam-mee, Sam-mee,' and after the chant builds up loud the Knight pulls three ampules outta his pocket. I mean, shit, man! Three! I ain't never been 'round Sammy when he's done more'n two. Three gets you clear into the fuckin' sky! So when the Knight holds up these three ampules, the crowd's tuned to burn, howlin' like they's playin' Sammy themselves. But the Knight, man, he keeps his cool. He is *so* cool! He just holds up the ampules and lets 'em take the shine, soakin' up the noise and energy, gettin' strong off the crowd's juice. Chaco waves everybody quiet and gives the speech, y'know, 'bout how in the heart of every man there's a warrior-soul waitin' to be loosed and shit. I tell ya, man, I always thought that speech was crap before, but the Knight's makin' me buy it a hunnerd percent. He is so goddamn cool! He takes off his shirt and shoes, and he ties this piece of black silk 'round his arm. Then he pops the ampules, one after another, real quick, and breathes it all in. I can see it hittin', catchin' fire in his eyes. Pumpin' him up. And soon as he's popped the last one, he jumps into the pit. He don't use the tunnel, man! He jumps! Twenty-five feet down to the sand, and lands in a crouch.''

Three other soldiers were leaning in, listening, and the kid was now addressing all of them, playing to his audience. He was so excited that he could barely keep his speech coherent, and Mingolla realized with disgust that he, too, was excited by the image of Baylor crouched on the sand. Baylor, who had cried after the assault. Baylor, who had been so afraid of snipers that he had once pissed in his pants rather than walk from his gun to the latrine.

Baylor, the Black Knight.

''The jaguar's screechin' and snarlin' and slashin' at the air,'' the kid went on. ''Tryin' to put fear into the Knight. 'Cause the jaguar knows in his mind the Knight's big trouble. This ain't some jerk like Chaco, this is Sammy. The Knight moves to the center of the pit, still in a crouch.'' Here the kid pitched his voice low and dramatic. ''Nothin' happens for a coupla minutes, 'cept it's tense. Nobody's hardly breathin'. The jaguar springs a coupla times, but the Knight dances off to the side and makes him miss, and there ain't no damage either way. Whenever the jaguar springs, the crowd sighs and squeals, not just 'cause they's scared of seein' the Knight tore up, but also 'cause they can see how fast he is. Silky fast, man! Unreal. He looks 'bout as fast as the jaguar. He keeps on dancin' away, and no matter how the jaguar twists and turns, no matter if he comes at him along the sand, he can't get his claws into the Knight. And then, man . . . oh, it was so smooth! Then the jaguar springs again, and this time 'stead of dancin' away, the Knight drops onto his back, does this half roll onto his shoulders, and when the jaguar passes over him, he kicks up with both feet. Kicks up hard! And smashes his heels into the jaguar's side. The jaguar slams into the pit wall and comes down screamin', snappin' at his ribs. They was busted, man. Pokin' out the skin like tentposts.''

The kid wiped his mouth with the back of his hand and flicked his eyes toward Mingolla and the other soldiers to see if they were into the story. ''We was shoutin', man,'' he said. ''Poundin' the top of the pit wall. It was so loud, the guy I'm with is yellin' in my ear and I can't hear nothin'. Now maybe it's the noise, maybe it's his ribs, whatever . . . the jaguar goes berserk. Makin' these scuttlin' lunges at the Knight, tryin' to get close 'fore he springs so the Knight can't pull that same trick. He's snarlin' like a goddamn chainsaw! The Knight keeps leapin' and spinnin' away. But then he slips, man, grabs the air for balance, and the jaguar's on him, clawin' at his chest. For a second they're like waltzin' together. Then the Knight pries loose the paw that's hooked him, pushes the jaguar's head back and smashes his fist into the jaguar's eye. The jaguar flops onto the sand, and the Knight scoots to the other side of the pit. He's checkin' the scratches on his chest, which is bleedin' wicked. Meantime, the jaguar gets to his feet, and he's fucked up worse than ever. His one eye's fulla blood, and his hindquarters is all loosey-goosey. Like if this was boxin', they'd call in the doctor. The jaguar figures he's had enough of this crap, and he starts tryin' to jump outta the pit. This one time he jumps right up to where I'm leanin' over the edge. Comes so close I can smell his breath, I can see myself reflected in his good eye. He's clawin' for a grip, wantin' to haul hisself up into the crowd. People are freakin', thinkin' he might be gonna make it. But 'fore he gets the chance, the Knight catches him by the tail and slings him against the wall. Just like you'd beat a goddamn rug, that's how he's dealin' with the jaguar. And the jaguar's a real mess, now. He's quiverin'. Blood's pourin' outta his mouth, his fangs is all red. The Knight starts makin' these little feints, wavin' his arms, growlin'. He's toyin' with the jaguar. People don't believe what they're seein', man. Sammy's kickin' a jaguar's ass so bad he's got room to toy with it. If the place was nuts before, now it's a fuckin' zoo. Fights in the crowd, guys singin' the Marine Hymn. Some beaner squint's takin' off her clothes. The jaguar tries to scuttle up close to the Knight again, but he's too fucked up. He can't keep it together. And the Knight he's still growlin' and feintin'. A guy behind me is booin', claimin' the Knight's defamin' the purity of the sport by playin' with the jaguar. But hell, man, I can see he's just timin' the jaguar, waitin' for the right moment, the right move.''

Staring off downriver, the kid wore a wistful expression: he might have been thinking about his girlfriend. ''We all knew it was comin',' he said. ''Everybody got real quiet. So quiet you could hear the Knight's feet scrapin' on the sand. You could feel it in the air, and you knew the jaguar was savin' up for one big effort. Then the Knight slips again, 'cept he's fakin'. I could see that, but the jaguar couldn't. When the Knight reels sideways, the jaguar springs. I thought the Knight was gonna drop down like he did the first time, but he springs, too. Feetfirst. And he catches the jaguar under the jaw. You could hear bone splinterin', and the jaguar falls in a heap. He struggles to get up, but no way! He's whinin', and he craps all over the sand. The Knight walks up behind him, takes his head in both hands and gives it a twist. Crack!''

As if identifying with the jaguar's fate, the kid closed his eyes and sighed. ''Everybody'd been quiet 'til they heard that crack, then all hell broke loose. People chantin', 'Sam-mee, Sam-mee,' and people shovin', tryin' to get close to the pit wall so they can watch the Knight take the heart. He reaches into the jaguar's mouth and snaps off one of the fangs and tosses it to somebody. Then Chaco comes in through the tunnel and hands him the knife. Right when he's 'bout to cut, somebody knocks me over and by the time I'm back on my feet, he's already took the heart and tasted it. He's just standin' there with the jaguar's blood on his mouth and his own blood runnin' down his chest. He looks kinda confused, y'know. Like now the fight's over and he don't know what to do. But then he starts roarin'. He sounds the same as the jaguar did 'fore it got hurt. Crazy fierce. Ready to get it on with the whole goddamn world. Man, I lost it! I was right with that roar. Maybe I was roarin' with him, maybe everybody was. That's what it felt like, man. Like bein' in the middle of this roar that's comin' outta every throat in the universe.'' The kid engaged Mingolla with a sober look. ''Lotsa people go 'round sayin' the pits are evil, and maybe they are. I don't know. How you s'posed to tell 'bout what's evil and what's not down here? They say you can go to the pits a thousand times and not see nothin' like the jaguar and the Black Knight. I don't know 'bout that, either. But I'm goin' back just in case I get lucky. 'Cause what I saw last night, if it was evil, man, it was so fuckin' evil it was beautiful, too.''

3

Debora was waiting at the pier, carrying a picnic basket and wearing a blue dress with a high neckline and a full skirt: a schoolgirl dress. Mingolla homed in on her. The way she had her hair, falling about her shoulders in thick, dark curls, made him think of smoke turned solid, and her face seemed the map of a beautiful country with black lakes and dusky plains, a country in which he could hide. They walked along the river past the town and came to a spot where ceiba trees with slick green leaves and whitish bark and roots like alligator tails grew close to the shore, and there they ate and talked and listened to the water gulping against the clay bank, to the birds, to the faint noises from the airbase that at this distance sounded part of nature. Sunlight dazzled the water, and whenever wind riffled the surface, it looked as if it were spreading the dazzles into a crawling crust of diamonds. Mingolla imagined that they had taken a secret path, rounded a corner on the world and reached some eternally peaceful land. The illusion of peace was so profound that he began to see hope in it. Perhaps, he thought, something was being offered here. Some new magic. Maybe there would be a sign. Signs were everywhere if you knew how to read them. He glanced around. Thick white trunks rising into greenery, dark leafy avenues leading off between them . . . nothing there, but what about those weeds growing at the edge of the bank? They cast precise fleur-de-lis shadows on the clay, shadows that didn't have much in common with the ragged configurations of the weeds themselves. Possibly a sign, though not a clear one. He lifted his gaze to the reeds growing in the shallows. Yellow reeds with jointed stalks bent akimbo, some with clumps of insect eggs like seed pearls hanging from loose fibers, and others dappled by patches of algae. That's how they looked one moment. Then Mingolla's vision rippled, as if the whole of reality had shivered, and the reeds were transformed into rudimentary shapes: yellow sticks poking up from flat blue. On the far side of the river, the jungle was a simple smear of Crayola green; a speedboat passing with a red slash unzipping the blue. It seemed that the rippling had jostled every element of the landscape a fraction out of kilter, revealing each one to be as characterless as a building block. Mingolla gave his head a shake. Nothing changed. He rubbed his brow. No effect. Terrified, he squeezed his eyes shut. He felt like the only meaningful piece in a nonsensical puzzle, vulnerable by virtue of his uniqueness. His breath came rapidly, his left hand fluttered.

"David? Don't you want to hear it?" Debora sounded peeved.

"Hear what?" He kept his eyes closed.

"About my dream. Weren't you listening?"

He peeked at her. Everything was back to normal. She was sitting with her knees tucked under her, all her features in sharp focus. "I'm sorry," he said. "I was thinking."

"You looked frightened."

"Frightened?" He put on a bewildered face. "Naw, just had a thought is all."

"It couldn't have been pleasant."

He shrugged off the comment and sat up smartly to prove his attentiveness. "So tell me 'bout the dream."

"All right," she said doubtfully. The breeze drifted fine strands of hair across her face, and she brushed them back. "You were in a room the color of blood, with red chairs and a red table. Even the paintings on the wall were done in shades of red, and . . ." She broke off, peering at him. "Do you want to hear this? You have that look again."

"Sure," he said. But he was afraid. How could she have known about the red room? She must have had a vision of it, and . . . Then he realized that she might not have been talking about the room itself. He'd told her about the assault, hadn't he? And if she had guerrilla contacts, she would know that the emergency lights were switched on during an assault. That had to be it! She was trying to frighten him into deserting again, psyching him the way preachers played upon the fears of sinners with images of fiery rivers and torture. It infuriated him. Who the hell was she to tell him what was right or wise? Whatever he did, it was going to be *his* decision.

"There were three doors in the room," she went on. "You wanted to leave the room, but you couldn't tell which of the doors was safe to use. You tried the first door, and it turned out to be a façade. The knob of the second door turned easily, but the door itself was stuck. Rather than forcing it, you went to the third door. The knob of this door was made of glass and cut your hand. After that you just walked back and forth, unsure what to do." She waited for a reaction, and when he gave none, she said, "Do you understand?"

He kept silent, biting back anger.

"I'll interpret it for you," she said.

"Don't bother."

"The red room is war, and the false door is the way of your childish . . ."

"Stop!" He grabbed her wrist, squeezing it hard.

She glared at him until he released her. "Your childish magic," she finished.

"What is it with you?" he asked. "You have some kinda quota to fill? Five deserters a month, and you get a medal?"

She tucked her skirt down to cover her knees, fiddled with a loose thread. From the way she was acting, you might have thought he had asked an intimate question and she was framing an answer that wouldn't be indelicate. Finally she said, "Is that who you believe I am to you?"

"Isn't that right? Why else would you be handing me this bullshit?"

"What's the matter with you, David?" She leaned forward, cupping his face in her hands. "Why . . ."

He pushed her hands away. "What's the matter with me? This"—his gesture included the sky, the river, the trees—"that's what's the matter. You remind me of my parents. They ask the same sorta ignorant questions." Suddenly he wanted to injure her with answers, to find an answer like acid to throw in her face and watch it eat away her tranquility. "Know what I do for my parents?" he said. "When they ask dumb-ass questions like 'What's the matter?', I tell 'em a story. A war story. You wanna hear a war story? Something happened a few days back that'll do for an answer just fine."

"You don't have to tell me anything," she said, discouraged.

"No problem," he said. "Be my pleasure."

*   *   *

The Ant Farm was a large sugar-loaf hill overlooking dense jungle on the
eastern border of Fire Zone Emerald; jutting out from its summit were rocket
and gun emplacements that at a distance resembled a crown of thorns jammed
down over a green scalp. For several hundred yards around, the land had
been cleared of all vegetation. The big guns had been lowered to maximum
declension and in a mad moment had obliterated huge swaths of jungle,
snapping off regiments of massive tree trunks a couple of feet above the
ground, leaving a moat of blackened stumps and scorched red dirt seamed
with fissures. Tangles of razor wire had replaced the trees and bushes, forming
surreal blue-steel hedges, and buried beneath the wire were a variety of mines
and detection devices. These did little good, however, because the Cubans
possessed technology that would neutralize most of them. On clear nights
there was little likelihood of trouble; but on misty nights trouble could be
expected. Under cover of the mist Cuban and guerrilla troops would come
through the wire and attempt to infiltrate the tunnels that honeycombed the
interior of the hill. Occasionally one of the mines would be triggered, and
you would see a ghostly fireball bloom in the swirling whiteness, tiny black
figures being flung outward from its center. Lately some of these casualties
had been found to be wearing red berets and scorpion-shaped brass pins, and
from this it was known that the Cubans had sent in the Alacran Division,
which had been instrumental in routing the American Forces in Miskitia.

There were nine levels of tunnels inside the hill, most lined with little
round rooms that served as living quarters (the only exception being the
bottom level, which was given over to the computer center and offices); all
the rooms and tunnels were coated with a bubbled white plastic that looked
like hardened seafoam and was proof against anti-personnel explosives. In
Mingolla's room, where he and Baylor and Gilbey bunked, a scarlet paper
lantern had been hung on the overhead light fixture, making it seem that they
were inhabiting a blood cell: Baylor had insisted on the lantern, saying that
the overhead was too bright and hurt his eyes. Three cots were arranged
against the walls, as far apart as space allowed. The floor around Baylor's
cot was littered with cigarette butts and used Kleenex; under his pillow he
kept a tin box containing a stash of pills and marijuana. Whenever he lit a
joint he would always offer Mingolla a hit, and Mingolla always refused,
feeling that the experience of the firebase would not be enhanced by drugs.
Taped to the wall above Gilbey's cot was a collage of beaver shots, and
each day after duty, whether or not Mingolla and Baylor were in the room,
he would lie beneath them and masturbate. His lack of shame caused Mingolla
to be embarrassed by his own secretiveness in the act, and he was also
embarrassed by the pimply-youth quality of the objects taped above his cot:
a Yankee pennant; a photograph of his old girlfriend, and another of his
senior-year high school basketball team; several sketches he had made of the

surrounding jungle. Gilbey teased him constantly about this display, calling him "the boy-next-door," which struck Mingolla as odd, because back home he had been considered something of an eccentric.

It was toward this room that Mingolla was heading when the assault began. Large cargo elevators capable of carrying up to sixty men ran up and down just inside the east and west slopes of the hill; but to provide quick access between adjoining levels, and also as a safeguard in case of power failures, an auxiliary tunnel corkscrewed down through the center of the hill like a huge coil of white intestine. It was slightly more than twice as wide as the electric carts that traveled it, carrying officers and VIPs on tours. Mingolla was in the habit of using the tunnel for his exercise. Each night he would put on sweat clothes and jog up and down the entire nine levels, doing this out of a conviction that exhaustion prevented bad dreams. That night, as he passed Level Four on his final leg up, he heard a rumbling: an explosion, and not far off. Alarms sounded, the big guns atop the hill began to thunder. From directly above came shouts and the stutter of automatic fire. The tunnel lights flickered, went dark, and the emergency lights winked on.

Mingolla flattened against the wall. The dim red lighting caused the bubbled surfaces of the tunnel to appear as smooth as a chamber in a gigantic nautilus, and this resemblance intensified his sense of helplessness, making him feel like a child trapped in an evil undersea palace. He couldn't think clearly, picturing the chaos around him. Muzzle flashes, armies of ant-men seething through the tunnels, screams spraying blood, and the big guns bucking, every shellburst kindling miles of sky. He would have preferred to keep going up, to get out into the open where he might have a chance to hide in the jungle. But down was his only hope. Pushing away from the wall, he ran full-tilt, arms waving, skidding around corners, almost falling, past Level Four, Level Five. Then, halfway between Levels Five and Six, he nearly tripped over a dead man: an American lying curled up around a belly wound, a slick of blood spreading beneath him and a machete by his hand. As Mingolla stooped for the machete, he thought nothing about the man, only about how weird it was for an American to be defending himself against Cubans with such a weapon. There was no use, he decided, in going any farther. Whoever had killed the man would be somewhere below, and the safest course would be to hide out in one of the rooms on Level Five. Holding the machete before him, he moved cautiously back up the tunnel.

Levels Five through Seven were officer country, and though the tunnels were the same as the ones above—gently curving tubes eight feet high and ten feet wide—the rooms were larger and contained only two cots. The rooms Mingolla peered into were empty, and this, despite the sounds of battle, gave him a secure feeling. But as he passed beyond the tunnel curve, he heard shouts in Spanish from his rear. He peeked back around the curve.

A skinny black soldier wearing a red beret and gray fatigues was inching toward the first doorway; then, rifle at the ready, he ducked inside. Two other Cubans—slim bearded men, their skins sallow-looking in the bloody light—were standing by the arched entranceway to the auxiliary tunnel; when they saw the black soldier emerge from the room, they walked off in the opposite direction, probably to check the rooms at the far end of the level.

Mingolla began to operate in a kind of luminous panic. He realized that he would have to kill the black soldier. Kill him without any fuss, take his rifle and hope that he could catch the other two off-guard when they came back for him. He slipped into the nearest room and stationed himself against the wall to the right of the door. The Cuban, he had noticed, had turned left on entering the room; he would have been vulnerable to someone positioned like Mingolla. Vulnerable for a split-second. Less than a count of one. The pulse in Mingolla's temple throbbed, and he gripped the machete tightly in his left hand. He rehearsed mentally what he would have to do. Stab; clamp a hand over the Cuban's mouth; bring his knee up to jar loose the rifle. And he would have to perform these actions simultaneously, execute them perfectly.

Perfect execution.

He almost laughed out loud, remembering his paunchy old basketball coach saying, "Perfect execution, boys. That's what beats a zone. Forget the fancy crap. Just set your screens, run your patterns and get your shots down."

Hoops ain't nothin' but life in short pants, huh, Coach?

Mingolla drew a deep breath and let it sigh out through his nostrils. He couldn't believe he was going to die. He had spent the past nine months worrying about death, but when it got right down to it, when the circumstances arose that made death likely, it was hard to take that likelihood seriously. It didn't seem reasonable that a skinny black guy should be his nemesis. His death should involve massive detonations of light, special Mingolla-killing rays, astronomical portents. Not some scrawny little shit with a rifle. He drew another breath and for the first time registered the contents of the room. Two cots; clothes strewn everywhere; taped-up polaroids and pornography. Officer country or not, it was your basic Ant Farm decor; under the red light it looked squalid, long-abandoned. He was amazed by how calm he felt. Oh, he was afraid all right! But fear was tucked into the dark folds of his personality like a murderer's knife hidden inside an old coat on a closet shelf. Glowing in secret, waiting its chance to shine. Sooner or later it would skewer him, but for now it was an ally, acting to sharpen his senses. He could see every bubbled pucker on the white walls, could hear the scrape of the Cuban's boots as he darted into the room next door, could feel how the Cuban swung the rifle left-to-right, paused, turned . . .

He *could* feel the Cuban! Feel his heat, his heated shape, the exact position of his body. It was as if a thermal imager had been switched on inside his head, one that worked through walls.

The Cuban eased toward Mingolla's door, his progress tangible, like a burning match moving behind a sheet of paper. Mingolla's calm was shattered. The man's heat, his fleshy temperature, was what disturbed him. He had imagined himself killing with a cinematic swiftness and lack of mess; now he thought of hogs being butchered and piledrivers smashing the skulls of cows. And could he trust this freakish form of perception? What if he couldn't? What if he stabbed too late? Too soon? Then the hot, alive thing was almost at the door, and having no choice, Mingolla timed his attack to its movements, stabbing just as the Cuban entered.

He executed perfectly.

The blade slid home beneath the Cuban's ribs, and Mingolla clamped a hand over his mouth, muffling his outcry. His knee nailed the rifle stock, sending it clattering to the floor. The Cuban thrashed wildly. He stank of rotten jungle air and cigarettes. His eyes rolled back, trying to see Mingolla. Crazy animal eyes, with liverish whites and expanded pupils. Sweat beads glittered redly on his brow. Mingolla twisted the machete, and the Cuban's eyelids fluttered down. But a second later they snapped open, and he lunged. They went staggering deeper into the room and teetered beside one of the cots. Mingolla wrangled the Cuban sideways and rammed him against the wall, pinning him there. Writhing, the Cuban nearly broke free. He seemed to be getting stronger, his squeals leaking out from Mingolla's hand. He reached behind him, clawing at Mingolla's face; he grabbed a clump of hair, yanked it. Desperate, Mingolla sawed with the machete. That tuned the Cuban's squeals higher, louder. He squirmed and clawed at the wall. Mingolla's clamped hand was slick with the Cuban's saliva, his nostrils full of the man's rank scent. He felt queasy, weak, and he wasn't sure how much longer he could hang on. The son of a bitch was never going to die, he was deriving strength from the steel in his guts, he was changing into some deathless force. But just then the Cuban stiffened. Then he relaxed, and Mingolla caught a whiff of feces.

He let the Cuban slump to the floor, but before he could turn loose of the machete, a shudder passed through the body, flowed up the hilt and vibrated his left hand. It continued to shudder inside his hand, feeling dirty, sexy, like a post-coital tremor. Something, some animal essence, some oily scrap of bad life, was slithering around in there, squirting toward his wrist. He stared at the hand, horrified. It was gloved in the Cuban's blood, trembling. He smashed it against his hip, and that seemed to stun whatever was inside it. But within seconds it had revived and was wriggling in and out of his fingers with the mad celerity of a tadpole.

"Teo!" someone called. *"Vamos!"*

Electrified by the shout, Mingolla hustled to the door. His foot nudged the Cuban's rifle. He picked it up, and the shaking of his hand lessened— he had the idea it had been soothed by a familiar texture and weight.

"Teo! Donde estas?"

Mingolla had no good choices, but he realized it would be far more dangerous to hang back than to take the initiative. He grunted *"Aqui!"* and walked out into the tunnel, making lots of noise with his heels.

"Dete prisa, hombre!"

Mingolla opened fire as he rounded the curve, The two Cubans were standing by the entrance to the auxiliary tunnel. Their rifles chattered briefly, sending a harmless spray of bullets off the walls; they whirled, flung out their arms and fell. Mingolla was too shocked by how easy it had been to feel relief. He kept watching, expecting them to do something. Moan, or twitch.

After the echoes of the shots had died, though he could hear the big guns jolting and the crackle of firefights, a heavy silence seemed to fill in through the tunnel, as if his bullets had pierced something that had dammed silence up. The silence made him aware of his isolation. No telling where the battle lines were drawn . . . if, indeed, they existed. It was conceivable that small units had infiltrated every level, that the battle for the Ant Farm was in microcosm the battle for Guatemala: a conflict having no patterns, no real borders, no orderly confrontations, but like a plague could pop up anywhere at any time and kill you. That being the case, his best bet would be to head for the computer center, where friendly forces were sure to be concentrated.

He walked to the entrance and stared at the two dead Cubans. They had fallen blocking his way, and he was hesitant about stepping over them, half-believing they were playing possum, that they would reach up and grab him. The awkward attitudes of their limbs made him think they were holding a difficult pose, waiting for him to try. Their blood looked purple in the red glow of the emergencies, thicker and shinier than ordinary blood. He noted their moles and scars and sores, the crude stitching of their fatigues, gold fillings glinting from their open mouths. It was funny, he could have met these guys while they were alive and they might have made only a vague impression; but seeing them dead, he had catalogued their physical worth in a single glance. Maybe, he thought, death revealed your essentials as life could not. He studied the dead men, wanting to read them. Couple of slim, wiry guys. Nice guys, into rum and the ladies and sports. He'd bet they were baseball players, infielders, a double-play combo. Maybe he should have called to them, Hey, I'm a Yankee fan. Be cool! Meet'cha after the war for a game of flies and grounders. Fuck this killing shit. Let's play some ball.

He laughed, and the high, cracking sound of his laughter startled him. Christ! Standing around here was just asking for it. As if to second that opinion, the thing inside his hand exploded into life, eeling and frisking about. Swallowing back his fear, Mingolla stepped over the two dead men, and this time, when nothing clutched at his trouser legs, he felt very, very relieved.

Below Level Six, there was a good deal of mist in the auxiliary tunnel, and from this Mingolla understood that the Cubans had penetrated the hillside, probably with a borer mine. Chances were the hole they had made was somewhere close, and he decided that if he could find it he would use it to get the hell out of the Farm and hide in the jungle. On Level Seven the mist was extremely thick; the emergency lights stained it pale red, giving it the look of surgical cotton packing a huge artery. Scorchmarks from grenade bursts showed on the walls like primitive graphics, and quite a few bodies were visible beside the doorways. Most of them Americans, badly mutilated. Uneasy, Mingolla picked his way among them, and when a man spoke behind him, saying, "Don't move," he let out a hoarse cry and dropped his rifle and spun around, his heart pounding.

A giant of a man—he had to go six-seven, six-eight, with the arms and torso of a weightlifter—was standing in a doorway, training a forty-five at Mingolla's chest. He wore khakis with lieutenant's bars, and his babyish face, though cinched into a frown, gave an impression of gentleness and stolidity: he conjured for Mingolla the image of Ferdinand the Bull weighing a knotty problem. "I told you not to move," he said peevishly.

"It's okay," said Mingolla. "I'm on your side."

The lieutenant ran a hand through his thick shock of brown hair; he seemed to be blinking more than was normal. "I'd better check," he said. "Let's go down to the storeroom."

"What's to check?" said Mingolla, his paranoia increasing.

"Please!" said the lieutenant, a genuine wealth of entreaty in his voice. "There's been too much violence already."

The storeroom was a long, narrow L-shaped room at the end of the level; it was ranged by packing crates, and through the gauzy mist the emergency lights looked like a string of dying red suns. The lieutenant marched Mingolla to the corner of the L, and turning it, Mingolla saw that the rear wall of the room was missing. A tunnel had been blown into the hillside, opening onto blackness. Forked roots with balls of dirt attached hung from its roof, giving it the witchy appearance of a tunnel into some world of dark magic; rubble and clods of earth were piled at its lip. Mingolla could smell the jungle, and he realized that the big guns had stopped firing. Which meant that whoever had won the battle of the summit would soon be sending down mop-up squads. "We can't stay here," he told the lieutenant. "The Cubans'll be back."

"We're perfectly safe," said the lieutenant. "Take my word." He motioned with the gun, indicating that Mingolla should sit on the floor.

Mingolla did as ordered and was frozen by the sight of a corpse, a Cuban corpse, lying between two packing crates opposite him, its head propped against the wall. "Jesus!" he said, coming back up to his knees.

"He won't bite," said the lieutenant. With the lack of self-consciousness of someone squeezing into a subway seat, he settled beside the corpse; the two of them neatly filled the space between the crates, touching elbow to shoulder.

"Hey," said Mingolla, feeling giddy and scattered. "I'm not sitting here with this fucking dead guy, man!"

The lieutenant flourished his gun. "You'll get used to him."

Mingolla eased back to a sitting position, unable to look away from the corpse. Actually, compared to the bodies he had just been stepping over, it was quite presentable. The only signs of damage were blood on its mouth and bushy black beard, and a mire of blood and shredded cloth at the center of its chest. Its beret had slid down at a rakish angle to cover one eyebrow; the brass scorpion pin was scarred and tarnished. Its eyes were open, reflecting glowing red chips of the emergency lights, and this gave it a baleful semblance of life. But the reflections made it appear less real, easier to bear.

"Listen to me," said the lieutenant.

Mingolla rubbed at the blood on his shaking hand, hoping that cleaning it would have some good effect.

"Are you listening?" the lieutenant asked.

Mingolla had a peculiar perception of the lieutenant and the corpse as dummy and ventriloquist. Despite its glowing eyes, the corpse had too much reality for any trick of the light to gloss over for long. Precise crescents showed on its fingernails, and because its head was tipped to the left, blood had settled into that side, darkening its cheek and temple, leaving the rest of the face pallid. It was the lieutenant, with his neat khakis and polished shoes and nice haircut, who now looked less than real.

"Listen!" said the lieutenant vehemently. "I want you to understand that I have to do what's right for me!" The bicep of his gun arm bunched to the size of a cannonball.

"I understand," said Mingolla, thoroughly unnerved.

"Do you? Do you really?" The lieutenant seemed aggravated by Mingolla's claim to understanding. "I doubt it. I doubt you could possibly understand."

"Maybe I can't," said Mingolla. "Whatever you say, man. I'm just trying to get along, y'know."

The lieutenant sat silent, blinking. Then he smiled. "My name's Jay," he said. "And you are . . . ?"

"David." Mingolla tried to bring his concentration to bear on the gun, wondering if he could kick it away, but the silver of life in his hand distracted him.

"Where are your quarters, David?"

"Level Three."

"I live here," said Jay. "But I'm going to move. I couldn't bear to stay in a place where . . ." He broke off and leaned forward, adopting a conspiratorial stance. "Did you know it takes a long time for someone to die, even after their heart has stopped?"

"No, I didn't." The thing in Mingolla's hand squirmed toward his wrist, and he squeezed the wrist, trying to block it.

"It's true," said Jay with vast assurance. "None of these people"—he gave the corpse a gentle nudge with his elbow, a gesture that conveyed to Mingolla a creepy sort of familiarity—"have finished dying. Life doesn't just switch off. It fades. And these people are still alive, though it's only a half-life." He grinned. "The half-life of life, you might say."

Mingolla kept the pressure on his wrist and smiled, as if in appreciation of the play on words. Pale red tendrils of mist curled between them.

"Of course you aren't attuned," said Jay. "So you wouldn't understand. But I'd be lost without Eligio."

"Who's Eligio?"

Jay nodded toward the corpse. "We're attuned, Eligio and I. That's how I know we're safe. Eligio's perceptions aren't limited to the here and now any longer. He's with his men at this very moment, and he tells me they're all dead or dying."

"Uh-huh," said Mingolla, tensing. He had managed to squeeze the thing in his hand back into his fingers, and he thought he might be able to reach the gun. But Jay disrupted his plan by shifting the gun to his other hand. His eyes seemed to be growing more reflective, acquiring a ruby glaze, and Mingolla realized this was because he had opened them wide and angled his stare toward the emergency lights.

"It makes you wonder," said Jay. "It really does."

"What?" said Mingolla, easing sideways, shortening the range for a kick.

"Half-lives," said Jay. "If the mind has a half-life, maybe our separate emotions do, too. The half-life of love, of hate. Maybe they still exist somewhere." He drew up his knees, shielding the gun. "Anyway, I can't stay here. I think I'll go back to Oakland." His tone became whispery. "Where are you from, David?"

"New York."

"Not my cup of tea," said Jay. "But I love the Bay Area. I own an antique shop there. It's beautiful in the mornings. Peaceful. The sun comes through the window, creeping across the floor, y'know, like a tide, inching up over the furniture. It's as if the original varnishes are being reborn, the whole shop shining with ancient lights."

"Sounds nice," said Mingolla, taken aback by Jay's lyricism.

"You seem like a good person." Jay straightened up a bit. "But I'm sorry. Eligio tells me your mind's too cloudy for him to read. He says I can't risk keeping you alive. I'm going to have to shoot.''

Mingolla set himself to kick, but then listlessness washed over him. What the hell did it matter? Even if he knocked the gun away, Jay could probably break him in half. ''Why?'' he said. ''Why do you have to?''

''You might inform on me.'' Jay's soft features sagged into a sorrowful expression. ''Tell them I was hiding.''

''Nobody gives a shit you were hiding,'' said Mingolla. ''That's what I was doing. I bet there's fifty other guys doing the same damn thing.''

''I don't know.'' Jay's brow furrowed. ''I'll ask again. Maybe your mind's less cloudy now.'' He turned his gaze to the dead man.

Mingolla noticed that the Cuban's irises were angled upward and to the left—exactly the same angle to which Jay's eyes had drifted earlier—and reflected an identical ruby glaze.

''Sorry,'' said Jay, leveling the gun. ''I have to.'' He licked his lips. ''Would you please turn your head? I'd rather you weren't looking at me when it happens. That's how Eligio and I became attuned.''

Looking into the aperture of the gun's muzzle was like peering over a cliff, feeling the chill allure of falling and, it was more out of contrariness than a will to survive that Mingolla popped his eyes at Jay and said, ''Go ahead.''

Jay blinked but he held the gun steady. ''Your hand's shaking,'' he said after a pause.

''No shit,'' said Mingolla.

''How come it's shaking?''

''Because I killed someone with it,'' said Mingolla. ''Because I'm as fucking crazy as you are.''

Jay mulled this over. ''I was supposed to be assigned to a gay unit,'' he said finally. ''But all the slots were filled, and when I had to be assigned here they gave me a drug. Now I . . . I . . .'' He blinked rapidly, his lips parted, and Mingolla found that he was straining toward Jay, wanting to apply Body English, to do something to push him over this agonizing hump. ''I can't . . . be with men anymore,'' Jay finished, and once again blinked rapidly; then his words came easier. ''Did they give you a drug, too? I mean I'm not trying to imply you're gay. It's just they have drugs for everything these days, and I thought that might be the problem.''

Mingolla was suddenly, inutterably sad. He felt that his emotions had been twisted into a thin black wire, that the wire was frayed and spraying black sparks of sadness. That was all that energized him, all his life. Those little black sparks.

''I always fought before,'' said Jay. ''And I was fighting this time. But when I shot Eligio . . . I just couldn't keep going.''

''I really don't give a shit,'' said Mingolla. ''I really don't.''

"Maybe I *can* trust you." Jay sighed. "I just wish you were attuned. Eligio's a good soul. You'd appreciate him."

Jay kept on talking, enumerating Eligio's virtues, and Mingolla tuned him out, not wanting to hear about the Cuban's love for his family, his posthumous concerns for them. Staring at his bloody hand, he had a magical overview of the situation. Sitting in the root cellar of this evil mountain, bathed in an eerie red glow, a scrap of a dead man's life trapped in his flesh, listening to a deranged giant who took his orders from a corpse, waiting for scorpion soldiers to pour through a tunnel that appeared to lead into a dimension of mist and blackness. It was insane to look at it that way. But there it was. You couldn't reason it away; it had a brutal glamour that surpassed reason, that made reason unnecessary.

". . . and once you're attuned," Jay was saying, "you can't ever be separated. Not even by death. So Eligio's always going to be alive inside me. Of course I can't let them find out. I mean"—he chuckled, a sound like dice rattling in a cup—"talk about giving aid and comfort to the enemy!"

Mingolla lowered his head, closed his eyes. Maybe Jay would shoot. But he doubted that. Jay only wanted company in his madness.

"You swear you won't tell them?" Jay asked.

"Yeah," said Mingolla. "I swear."

"All right," said Jay. "But remember, my future's in your hands. You have a responsibility to me."

"Don't worry."

Gunfire crackled in the distance.

"I'm glad we could talk," said Jay. "I feel much better."

Mingolla said that he felt better, too.

They sat without speaking. It wasn't the most secure way to pass the night, but Mingolla no longer put any store in the concept of security. He was too weary to be afraid. Jay seemed entranced, staring at a point above Mingolla's head, but Mingolla made no move for the gun. He was content to sit and wait and let fate take its course. His thoughts uncoiled with vegetable sluggishness.

They must have been sitting a couple of hours when Mingolla heard the whisper of helicopters and noticed that the mist had thinned, that the darkness at the end of the tunnel had gone gray. "Hey," he said to Jay. "I think we're okay now." Jay offered no reply, and Mingolla saw that his eyes were angled upward and to the left just like the Cuban's eyes, glazed over with ruby reflection. Tentatively, he reached out and touched the gun. Jay's hand flopped to the floor, but his fingers remained clenched around the butt. Mingolla recoiled, disbelieving. It couldn't be! Again he reached out, feeling for a pulse. Jay's wrist was cool, still, and his lips had a bluish cast. Mingolla had a flutter of hysteria, thinking that Jay had gotten it wrong about being attuned: instead of Eligio becoming part of his life, he had become part of

Eligio's death. There was a tightness in Mingolla's chest, and he thought he
was going to cry. He would have welcomed tears, and when they failed to
materialize he grew both annoyed at himself and defensive. Why should he
cry? The guy had meant nothing to him . . . though the fact that he could
be so devoid of compassion was reason enough for tears. Still, if you were
going to cry over something as commonplace as a single guy dying, you'd
be crying every minute of the day, and what was the future in that? He
glanced at Jay. At the Cuban. Despite the smoothness of Jay's skin, the
Cuban's bushy beard, Mingolla could have sworn they were starting to
resemble each other the way old married couples did. And, yep, all four
eyes were fixed on exactly the same point of forever. It was either a hell of
a coincidence or else Jay's craziness had been of such magnitude that he had
willed himself to die in this fashion just to lend credence to his theory of
half-lives. And maybe he was still alive. Half alive. Maybe he and Mingolla
were now attuned, and if that were true, maybe . . . Revolted by the prospect
of joining Jay and the Cuban in their deathwatch, Mingolla scrambled to his
feet and ran into the tunnel. He might have kept running, but on coming out
into the dawn light he was brought up short by the view from the tunnel
entrance.

At his back, the green dome of the hill swelled high, its sides brocaded
with shrubs and vines, an infinity of pattern as eye-catching as the intricately
carved facade of a Hindu temple; atop it, one of the gun emplacements had
taken a hit: splinters of charred metal curved up like peels of black rind.
Before him lay the moat of red dirt with its hedgerows of razor wire, and
beyond that loomed the blackish-green snarl of the jungle. Caught on the
wire were hundreds of baggy shapes wearing bloodstained fatigues; frays of
smoke twisted up from the fresh craters beside them. Overhead, half-hidden
by the lifting gray mist, three Sikorskys were hovering. Their pilots were
invisible behind layers of mist and reflection, and the choppers themselves
looked like enormous carrion flies with bulging eyes and whirling wings.
Like devils. Like gods. They seemed to be whispering to one another in
anticipation of the feast they were soon to share.

The scene was horrid yet it had the purity of a stanza from a ballad come
to life, a ballad composed about tragic events in some border hell. You could
never paint it, or if you could the canvas would have to be as large as the
scene itself, and you would have to incorporate the slow boil of the mist,
the whirling of the chopper blades, the drifting smoke. No detail could be
omitted. It was the perfect illustration of the war, of its secret magical
splendor, and Mingolla, too, was an element of the design, the figure of the
artist painted in for a joke or to lend scale and perspective to its vastness,
its importance. He knew that he should report to his station, but he couldn't
turn away from this glimpse into the heart of the war. He sat down on the
hillside, cradling his sick hand in his lap, and watched as—with the ponderous

aplomb of idols floating to earth, fighting the cross-draft, the wind of their descent whipping up furies of red dust—the Sikorskys made skillful landings among the dead.

4

Halfway through the telling of his story, Mingolla had realized that he was not really trying to offend or shock Debora, but rather was unburdening himself; and he further realized that by telling it he had to an extent cut loose from the past, weakened its hold on him. For the first time he felt able to give serious consideration to the idea of desertion. He did not rush to it, embrace it, but he did acknowledge its logic and understand the terrible illogic of returning to more assaults, more death, without any magic to protect him. He made a pact with himself: he would pretend to go along as if desertion were his intent and see what signs were offered.

When he had finished, Debora asked whether or not he was over his anger. He was pleased that she hadn't tried to offer sympathy. "I'm sorry," he said. "I wasn't really angry at you . . . at least that was only part of it."

"It's all right." She pushed back the dark mass of her hair so that it fell to one side and looked down at the grass beside her knees. With her head inclined, eyes half-lidded, the graceful line of her neck and chin like a character in some exotic script, she seemed a good sign herself. "I don't know what to talk to you about," she said. "The things I feel I have to tell you make you mad, and I can't muster any small-talk."

"I don't want to be pushed," he said. "But believe me, I'm thinking about what you've told me."

"I won't push. But I still don't know what to talk about." She plucked a grass blade, chewed on the tip. He watched her lips purse, wondered how she'd taste. Mouth sweet in the way of a jar that had once held spices. She tossed the grass blade aside. "I know," she said brightly. "Would you like to see where I live?"

"I'd just as soon not go back to 'Frisco yet." Where you live, he thought; I want to touch where you live.

"It's not in town," she said. "It's a village downriver."

"Sounds good." He came to his feet, took her arm and helped her up. For an instant they were close together, her breasts grazing his shirt. Her heat coursed around him, and he thought if anyone were to see them, they would see two figures wavering as in a mirage. He had an urge to tell her he loved her. Though most of what he felt was for the salvation she might provide, part of his feelings seemed real and that puzzled him, because all she had been to him was a few hours out of the war, dinner in a cheap restaurant and a walk along the river. There was no basis for consequential emotion. Before he could say anything, do anything, she turned and picked up her basket.

"It's not far," she said, walking away. Her blue skirt swayed like a rung bell.

They followed a track of brown clay overgrown by ferns, overspread by saplings with pale translucent leaves, and soon came to a grouping of thatched huts at the mouth of a stream that flowed into the river. Naked children were wading in the stream, laughing and splashing each other. Their skins were the color of amber, and their eyes were as wet-looking and purplish-dark as plums. Palms and acacias loomed above the huts, which were constructed of sapling trunks lashed together by nylon cord; their thatch had been trimmed to resemble bowl-cut hair. Flies crawled over strips of meat hung on a clothesline stretched between two of the huts. Fish heads and chicken droppings littered the ocher ground. But Mingolla scarely noticed these signs of poverty, seeing instead a sign of the peace that might await him in Panama. And another sign was soon forthcoming. Debora bought a bottle of rum at a tiny store, then led him to the hut nearest the mouth of the stream and introduced him to a lean, white-haired old man who was sitting on a bench outside it. Tio Moises. After three drinks Tio Moises began to tell stories.

The first story concerned the personal pilot of an ex-president of Panama. The president had made billions from smuggling cocaine into the States with the help of the CIA, whom he had assisted on numerous occasions, and was himself an addict in the last stages of mental deterioration. It had become his sole pleasure to be flown from city to city in his country, to sit on the landing strips, gaze out the window and do cocaine. At any hour of night or day, he was likely to call the pilot and order him to prepare a flight plan to Colon or Bocas del Toro or Penonome. As the president's condition worsened, the pilot realized that soon the CIA would see he was no longer useful and would kill him. And the most obvious manner of killing him would be by means of an airplane crash. The pilot did not want to die alongside him. He tried to resign, but the president would not permit it. He gave thought to mutilating himself, but being a good Catholic, he could not flout God's law. If he were to flee, his family would suffer. His life became a nightmare. Prior to each flight, he would spend hours searching the plane for evidence of sabotage, and upon each landing, he would remain in the cockpit, shaking from nervous exhaustion. The president's condition grew even worse. He had to be carried aboard the plane and have the cocaine administered by an aide, while a second aide stood by with cotton swabs to attend his nosebleeds. Knowing his life could be measured in weeks, the pilot asked his priest for guidance. "Pray," the priest advised. The pilot had been praying all along, so this was no help. Next he went to the commandant of his military college, and the commandant told him he must do his duty. This, too, was something the pilot had been doing all along. Finally he went to the chief of the San Blas Indians, who were his mother's people. The chief told him he must accept his fate, which—while not something he had been doing all along—was hardly encouraging. Nonetheless, he saw it was the only available path and he did as the chief had counseled. Rather than spending hours in a pre-flight check, he would arrive minutes before take-off and taxi away without even inspecting the fuel gauge. His recklessness came to be the talk of the capital. Obeying the president's every whim, he flew in gales and in fogs, while drunk and drugged, and during those hours in the air, suspended between the laws of gravity and fate, he gained a new appreciation of life. Once back on the ground, he engaged in living with a fierce avidity, making passionate love to his wife, carousing with friends and staying out until dawn. Then one day as he was preparing to leave for the airport, an American man came to his house and told him he had been replaced. "If we let the president fly with so negligent a pilot, we'll be blamed for anything that happens," said the American. The pilot did not have to ask whom he had meant by "we." Six weeks later the president's plane crashed in the Darien Mountains. The pilot was overjoyed. Panama had been ridded of a villain, and his own life had not been forfeited. But a week after the crash, after the new president—another smuggler with CIA connections—had been appointed, the commandant of the air force summoned the pilot, told him that the crash would never have occurred had he been on the job, and assigned him to fly the new president's plane.

All through the afternoon Mingolla listened and drank, and drunkenness fitted a lens to his eyes that let him see how these stories applied to him. They were all fables of irresolution, cautioning him to act, and they detailed the core problems of the Central American people who—as he was now—were trapped between the poles of magic and reason, their lives governed by the politics of the ultra-real, their spirits ruled by myths and legends, with the rectangular computerized bulk of North America above and the conch-shell-shaped continental mystery of South America below. He assumed that Debora had orchestrated the types of stories Tio Moises told, but that did not detract from their potency as signs: they had the ring of truth, not of something tailored to his needs. Nor did it matter that his hand was shaking, his vision playing tricks. Those things would pass when he reached Panama.

Shadows blurred, insects droned like tambouras, and twilight washed down the sky, making the air look grainy, the chop on the river appear slower and heavier. Tio Moises' granddaughter served plates of roast corn and fish, and Mingolla stuffed himself. Afterward, when the old man signaled his weariness, Mingolla and Debora strolled off along the stream. Between two of the huts, mounted on a pole, was a warped backboard with a netless hoop, and some young men were shooting baskets. Mingolla joined them. It was hard dribbling on the bumpy dirt, but he had never played better. The residue of drunkenness fueled his game, and his jump shots followed perfect arcs down through the hoop. Even at improbable angles, his shots fell true. He lost himself in flicking out his hands to make a steal, in feinting and leaping high to snag a rebound, becoming—as dusk faded—the most adroit of ten arm-waving, jitter-stepping shadows.

The game ended and the stars came out, looking like holes punched into fire through a billow of black silk overhanging the palms. Flickering chutes of lamplight illuminated the ground in front of the huts, and as Debora and Mingolla walked among them, he heard a radio tuned to the Armed Forces Network giving a play-by-play of a baseball game. There was a crack of the bat, the crowd roared, the announcer cried, "He got it all!" Mingolla imagined the ball vanishing into the darkness above the stadium, bouncing out into parking-lot America, lodging under a tire where some kid would find it and think it a miracle, or rolling across the street to rest under a used car, shimmering there, secretly white and fuming with home run energies. The score was three-to-one, top of the second. Mingolla didn't know who was playing and didn't care. Home runs were happening for him, mystical jump shots curved along predestined tracks. He was at the center of incalculable forces.

One of the huts was unlit, with two wooden chairs out front, and as they approached, the sight of it blighted Mingolla's mood. Something about it bothered him: its air of preparedness, of being a little stage set. Just paranoia, he thought. The signs had been good so far, hadn't they? When they reached the hut, Debora sat in the chair nearest the door and looked up at him. Starlight pointed her eyes with brilliance. Behind her, through the doorway, he made out the shadowy cocoon of a strung hammock, and beneath it, a sack from which part of a wire cage protruded. "What about your game?" he asked.

"I thought it was more important to be with you," she said.

That, too, bothered him. It was all starting to bother him, and he couldn't understand why. The thing in his hand wiggled. He balled the hand into a fist and sat next to Debora. "What's going on between you and me?" he asked, nervous. "Is anything gonna happen? I keep thinking it will, but . . ." He wiped sweat from his forehead and forgot what he had been driving at.

"I'm not sure what you mean," she said.

A shadow moved across the yellow glare spilling from the hut next door. Rippling, undulating. Mingolla squeezed his eyes shut.

"If you mean . . . romantically," she said, "I'm confused about that myself. Whether you return to your base or go to Panama, we don't seem to have much of a future. And we certainly don't have much of a past."

It boosted his confidence in her, in the situation, that she didn't have an assured answer. But he felt shaky. Very shaky. He gave his head a twitch, fighting off more ripples. "What's it like in Panama?"

"I've never been there. Probably a lot like Guatemala, except without the fighting."

Maybe he should get up, walk around. Maybe that would help. Or maybe he should just sit and talk. Talking seemed to steady him. "I bet," he said, "I bet it's beautiful, y'know. Panama. Green mountains, jungle waterfalls. I bet there's lots of birds. Macaws and parrots. Millions of 'em."

"I suppose so."

"And hummingbirds. This friend of mine was down there once on a hummingbird expedition, said there was a million kinds. I thought he was sort of a creep, y'know, for being into collecting hummingbirds." He opened his eyes and had to close them again. "I guess I thought hummingbird collecting wasn't very relevant to the big issues."

"David?" Concern in her voice.

"I'm okay." The smell of her perfume was more cloying than he remembered. "You get there by boat, right? Must be a pretty big boat. I've never been on a real boat, just this rowboat my uncle had. He used to take me fishing off Coney Island, we'd tie up to a buoy and catch all these poison fish. You shoulda seen some of 'em. Like mutants. Rainbow-colored eyes, weird growths all over. Scared the hell outta me to think about eating fish."

"I had an uncle who . . ."

"I used to think about all the ones that must be down there too deep for us to catch. Giant blowfish, genius sharks, whales with hands. I'd see 'em swallowing the boat, I'd . . ."

"Calm down, David." She kneaded the back of his neck, sending a shiver down his spine.

"I'm okay, I'm okay," He pushed her hand away; he did not need shivers along with everything else. "Lemme hear some more 'bout Panama."

"I told you, I've never been there."

"Oh, yeah. Well, how 'bout Costa Rica? You been to Costa Rica." Sweat was popping out all over his body. Maybe he should go for a swim. He'd heard there were manatees in the Rio Dulce. "Ever seen a manatee?" he asked.

"David!"

She must have leaned close, because he could feel her heat spreading all through him, and he thought maybe that would help, smothering in her heat, heavy motion, get rid of this shakiness: He'd take her into that hammock and see just how hot she got. *How* hot *she got, how* hot *she got.* The words did a train rhythm in his head. Afraid to open his eyes, he reached out blindly and pulled her to him. Bumped faces, searched for her mouth. Kissed her. She kissed back. His hand slipped up to cup a breast. Jesus, she felt good! She felt like salvation, like Panama, like what you fall into when you sleep.

But then it changed, changed slowly, so slowly that he didn't notice until it was almost complete, and her tongue was squirming in his mouth, as thick and stupid as a snail's foot, and her breast, oh shit, her breast was jiggling, trembling with the same wormy juices that were in his left hand. He pushed her off, opened his eyes. Saw crude-stitch eyelashes sewn to her cheeks. Lips parted, mouth full of bones. Blank face of meat. He got to his feet, pawing the air, wanting to rip down the film of ugliness that had settled over him.

"David?" She warped his name, gulping the syllables as if she were trying to swallow and talk at once.

Frog voice, devil voice.

He spun around, caught an eyeful of black sky and spiky trees and a pitted bone-knob moon trapped in a weave of branches. Dark warty shapes of the huts, doors into yellow flame with crooked shadow men inside. He blinked, shook his head. It wasn't going away, it was real. What was this place? Not a village in Guatemala, naw, un-uh. He heard a strangled wildman grunt come from his throat, and he backed away, backed away from everything. She walked after him, croaking his name. Wig of black straw, dabs of shining jelly for eyes. Some of the shadow men were herky-jerking out of their doors, gathering behind her, talking about him in devil language. Long-legged licorice-skinned demons with drumbeat hearts, faceless nothings from the dimension of sickness. He backed another few steps.

"I can see you," he said. "I know what you are."

"It's all right, David," she said, and smiled.

Sure! She thought he was going to buy the smile, but he wasn't fooled. He saw how it broke over her face the way something rotten melts through the bottom of a wet grocery sack after it's been in the garbage for a week. Gloating smile of the Queen Devil Bitch. She had done this to him, had teamed up with the bad life in his hand and done witchy things to his head. Made him see down to the layer of shit-magic she lived in.

"I see you," he said.

He tripped, went backward flailing, stumbling, and came out of it running toward the town.

Ferns whipped his legs, branches cut at his face. Webs of shadow fettered the trail, and the shrilling insects had the sound of a metal edge being honed. Up ahead, he spotted a big moonstruck tree standing by itself on a rise overlooking the water. A grandfather tree, a white magic tree. It summoned to him. He stopped beside it, sucking air. The moonlight cooled him off, drenched him with silver, and he understood the purpose of the tree. Fountain of whiteness in the dark wood, shining for him alone. He made a fist of his left hand. The thing inside the hand eeled frantically as if it knew what was coming. He studied the deeply grooved, mystic patterns of the bark and found the point of confluence. He steeled himself. Then he drove his fist into the trunk. Brilliant pain lanced up his arm, and he cried out. But he hit the tree again, hit it a third time. He held the hand tight against his body, muffling the pain. It was already swelling, becoming a knuckle-less cartoon hand; but nothing moved inside it. The riverbank, with its rustlings and shadows, no longer menaced him; it had been transformed into a place of ordinary lights, ordinary darks, and even the whiteness of the tree looked unmagically bright.

"David!" Debora's voice, and not far off.

Part of him wanted to wait, to see whether or not she had changed for the innocent, for the ordinary. But he couldn't trust her, couldn't trust himself, and he set out running once again.

Mingolla caught the ferry to the west bank, thinking that he would find Gilbey, that a dose of Gilbey's belligerence would ground him in reality. He sat in the bow next to a group of five other soldiers, one of whom was puking over the side, and to avoid a conversation he turned away and looked down into the black water slipping past. Moonlight edged the wavelets with silver, and among those gleams it seemed he could see reflected the broken curve of his life: a kid living for Christmas, drawing pictures, receiving praise, growing up mindless to high school, sex, and drugs, growing beyond that, beginning to draw pictures again, and then, right where you might expect the curve to assume a more meaningful shape, it was sheared off, left hanging, its process demystified and explicable. He realized how foolish the idea of the ritual had been. Like a dying man clutching a vial of holy water, he had clutched at magic when the logic of existence had proved untenable. Now the frail linkages of that magic had been dissolved, and nothing supported him: he was falling through the dark zones of the war, waiting to be snatched by one of its monsters. He lifted his head and gazed at the west bank. The shore toward which he was heading was as black as a bat's wing and inscribed with arcana of violent light. Rooftops and palms were cast in silhouette against a rainbow haze of neon; gassy arcs of blood red and lime green and indigo were visible between them: fragments of glowing beasts. The wind bore screams and wild music. The soldiers beside him laughed and cursed, and the one guy kept on puking. Mingolla rested his forehead on the wooden rail, just to feel something solid.

At the Club Demonio, Gilbey's big-breasted whore was lounging by the bar, staring into her drink. Mingolla pushed through the dancers, through heat and noise and veils of lavender smoke; when he walked up to the whore, she put on a professional smile and made a grab for his crotch. He fended her off. "Where's Gilbey?" he shouted. She gave him a befuddled look; then the light dawned. "Meen-golla?" she said. He nodded. She fumbled in her purse and pulled out a folded paper. "Ees frawm Geel-bee," she said. "Forr me, five dol-larrs."

He handed her the money and took the paper. It proved to be a Christian pamphlet with a pen-and-ink sketch of a rail-thin, aggrieved-looking Jesus on the front, and beneath the sketch, a tract whose first line read, "The last days are in season." He turned it over and found a handwritten note on the back. The note was pure Gilbey. No explanation, no sentiment. Just the basics.

I'm gone to Panama. You want to make that trip, check out a guy named Ruy Barros in Livingston. He'll fix you up. Maybe I'll see you.
G.

Mingolla had believed that his confusion had peaked, but the fact of Gilbey's desertion wouldn't fit inside his head, and when he tried to make it fit he was left more confused than ever. It wasn't that he couldn't understand what had happened. He understood it perfectly; he might have predicted it. Like a crafty rat who had seen his favorite hole blocked by a trap, Gilbey had simply chewed a new hole and vanished through it. The thing that confused Mingolla was his total lack of referents. He and Gilbey and Baylor had seemed to triangulate reality, to locate each other within a coherent map of duties and places and events; and now that they were both gone, Mingolla felt utterly bewildered. Outside the club, he let the crowds push him along and gazed up at the neon animals atop the bars. Giant blue rooster, green bull, golden turtle with fiery red eyes. Great identities regarding him with disfavor. Bleeds of color washed from the signs, staining the air to a garish paleness, giving everyone a mealy complexion. Amazing, Mingolla thought, that you could breathe such grainy discolored stuff, that it didn't start you choking. It was all amazing, all nonsensical. Everything he saw struck him as unique and unfathomable, even the most commonplace of sights. He found himself staring at people—at whores, at street kids, at an MP who was talking to another MP, patting the fender of his jeep as if it were his big olive-drab pet—and trying to figure out what they were really doing, what special significance their actions held for him, what clues they presented that might help him unravel the snarl of his own existence. At last, realizing that he needed peace and quiet, he set out toward the airbase, thinking he would find an empty bunk and sleep off his confusion; but when he came to the cut-off that led to the unfinished bridge, he turned down it, deciding that he wasn't ready to deal with gate sentries and duty officers. Dense thickets buzzing with insects narrowed the cut-off to a path, and at its end stood a line of sawhorses. He climbed over them and soon was mounting a sharply inclined curve that appeared to lead to a point not far below the lumpish silver moon.

Despite a litter of rubble and cardboard sheeting, the concrete looked pure under the moon, blazing bright, like a fragment of snowy light not quite hardened to the material; and as he ascended he thought he could feel the bridge trembling to his footsteps with the sensitivity of a white nerve. He seemed to be walking into darkness and stars, a solitude the size of creation. It felt good and damn lonely, maybe a little too much so, with the wind flapping pieces of cardboard and the sounds of the insects left behind.

After a few minutes he glimpsed the ragged terminus ahead. When he reached it, he sat down carefully, letting his legs dangle. Wind keened through the exposed girders, tugging at his ankles; his hand throbbed and was fever-hot. Below, multicolored brilliance clung to the black margin of the east bank like a colony of bioluminescent algae. He wondered how high he was. Not high enough, he thought. Faint music was fraying on the wind—the inexhaustible delirium of San Francisco de Juticlan—and he imagined that the flickering of the stars was caused by this thin smoke of music drifting across them.

He tried to think what to do. Not much occurred to him. He pictured Gilbey in Panama. Whoring, drinking, fighting. Doing just as he had in Guatemala. That was where the idea of desertion failed Mingolla. In Panama he would be afraid; in Panama, though his hand might not shake, some other malignant twitch would develop; in Panama he would resort to magical cures for his afflictions, because he would be too imperiled by the real to derive strength from it. And eventually the war would come to Panama. Desertion would have gained him nothing. He stared out across the moon-silvered jungle, and it seemed that some essential part of him was pouring from his eyes, entering the flow of the wind and rushing away past the Ant Farm and its smoking craters, past guerrilla territory, past the seamless join of sky and horizon, being irresistibly pulled toward a point into which the world's vitality was emptying. He felt himself emptying as well, growing cold and vacant and slow. His brain became incapable of thought, capable only of recording perceptions. The wind brought green scents that made his nostrils flare. The sky's blackness folded around him, and the stars were golden pinpricks of sensation. He didn't sleep, but something in him slept.

A whisper drew him back from the edge of the world. At first he thought it had been his imagination, and he continued staring at the sky, which had lightened to the vivid blue of pre-dawn. Then he heard it again and glanced behind him. Strung out across the bridge, about twenty feet away, were a dozen or so children. Some standing, some crouched. Most were clad in rags, a few wore coverings of vines and leaves, and others were naked. Watchful; silent. Knives glinted in their hands. They were all emaciated, their hair long and matted, and Mingolla, recalling the dead children he had seen that morning, was for a moment afraid. But only for a moment. Fear flared in him like a coal puffed to life by a breeze and died an instant later, suppressed not by any rational accommodation but by a perception of those ragged figures as an opportunity for surrender. He wasn't eager to die, yet neither did he want to put forth more effort in the cause of survival. Survival, he had learned, was not the soul's ultimate priority. He kept staring at the children. The way they were posed reminded him of a Neanderthal grouping in the Museum of Natural History. The moon was still up, and they cast vaguely defined shadows like smudges of graphite. Finally Mingolla turned away; the horizon was showing a distinct line of green darkness.

He had expected to be stabbed or pushed, to pinwheel down and break against the Rio Dulce, its waters gone a steely color beneath the brightening sky. But instead a voice spoke in his ear: "Hey, macho." Squatting beside him was a boy of fourteen or fifteen, with a swarthy monkeylike face framed by tangles of shoulder-length dark hair. Wearing tattered shorts. Coiled serpent tattooed on his brow. He tipped his head to one side, then the other. Perplexed. He might have been trying to see the true Mingolla through layers of false appearance. He made a growly noise in his throat and held up a knife, twisting it this way and that, letting Mingolla observe its keen edge, how it channeled the moonlight along its blade. An army-issue survival knife with a brass-knuckle grip. Mingolla gave an amused sniff.

The boy seemed alarmed by this reaction; he lowered the knife and shifted away. "What you doing here, man?" he asked.

A number of answers occurred to Mingolla, most demanding too much energy to voice; he chose the simplest. "I like it here. I like the bridge."

The boy squinted at Mingolla. "The bridge is magic," he said. "You know this?"

"There was a time I might have believed you," said Mingolla.

"You got to talk slow, man." The boy frowned. "Too fast, I can't understan'."

Mingolla repeated his comment, and the boy said, "You believe it, gringo. Why else you here?" With a planing motion of his arm he described an imaginary continuance of the bridge's upward course. "That's where the bridge travels now. Don't have not'ing to do wit' crossing the river. It's a piece of white stone. Don't mean the same t'ing a bridge means."

Mingolla was surprised to hear his thoughts echoed by someone who so resembled a hominid.

"I come here," the boy went on. "I listen to the wind, hear it sing in the iron. And I know t'ings from it. I can see the future." He grinned, exposing blackened teeth, and pointed south toward the Caribbean. "Future's that way, man."

Mingolla liked the joke; he felt an affinity for the boy, for anyone who could manage jokes from the boy's perspective, but he couldn't think of a way to express his good feeling. Finally he said, "You speak English well."

"Shit! What you think? 'Cause we live in the jungle, we talk like animals? Shit!" The boy jabbed the point of his knife into the concrete. "I talk English all my life. Gringos they too stupid to learn Spanish."

A girl's voice sounded behind them, harsh and peremptory. The other children had closed to within ten feet, their savage faces intent upon Mingolla, and the girl was standing a bit forward of them. She had sunken cheeks and deep-set eyes; ratty cables of hair hung down over her single-scoop breasts. Her hipbones tented up a rag of a skirt, which the wind pushed back between her legs. The boy let her finish, then gave a prolonged response, punctuating his words by smashing the brass-knuckle grip of his knife against the concrete, striking sparks with every blow.

"Gracela," he said to Mingolla, "she wants to kill you. But I say, some men they got one foot in the worl' of death, and if you kill them, death will take you, too. And you know what?"

"What?" said Mingolla.

"It's true. You and death"—the boy clasped his hands—"like this."

"Maybe," Mingolla said.

"No 'maybe.' The bridge tol' me. Tol' me I be t'ankful if I let you live. So you be t'ankful to the bridge. That magic you don't believe, it save your ass." The boy lowered out of his squat and sat cross-legged. "Gracela, she don' care 'bout you live or die. She jus' go 'gainst me 'cause when I leave here, she going to be chief. She's, you know, impatient."

Mingolla looked at the girl. She met his gaze coldly: a witch-child with slitted eyes, bramble hair, and ribs poking out. "Where are you going?" he asked the boy.

"I have a dream I will live in the south; I dream I own a warehouse full of gold and cocaine."

The girl began to harangue him again, and he shot back a string of angry syllables.

"What did you say?" Mingolla asked.

"I say, 'Gracela, you give me shit, I going to fuck you and t'row you in the river.' " He winked at Mingolla. "Gracela she a virgin, so she worry 'bout that firs' t'ing."

The sky was graying, pink streaks fading in from the east; birds wheeled up from the jungle below, forming into flocks above the river. In the half-light Mingolla saw that the boy's chest was cross-hatched with ridged scars: knife wounds that hadn't received proper treatment. Bits of vegetation were trapped in his hair, like primitive adornments.

"Tell me, gringo," said the boy. "I hear in America there is a machine wit' the soul of a man. This is true?"

"More or less," said Mingolla.

The boy nodded gravely, his suspicions confirmed. "I hear also America has builded a metal worl' in the sky."

"They're building it now."

"In the house of your president, is there a stone that holds the mind of a dead magician?"

Mingolla gave this due consideration. "I doubt it," he said. "But it's possible."

Wind thudded against the bridge, startling him. He felt its freshness on his face and relished the sensation. That—the fact that he could still take simple pleasure from life—startled him more than had the sudden noise.

The pink streaks in the east were deepening to crimson and fanning wider; shafts of light pierced upward to stain the bellies of some low-lying clouds to mauve. Several of the children began to mutter in unison. A chant. They were speaking in Spanish, but the way their voices jumbled the words, it sounded guttural and malevolent, a language for trolls. Listening to them, Mingolla imagined them crouched around fires in bamboo thickets. Bloody knives lifted sunwards over their fallen prey. Making love in the green nights among fleshy Rousseau-like vegetation, while pythons with ember eyes coiled in the branches above their heads.

"Truly, gringo," said the boy, apparently still contemplating Mingolla's answers. "These are evil times." He stared gloomily down at the river; the wind shifted the heavy snarls of his hair.

Watching him, Mingolla grew envious. Despite the bleakness of his existence, this little monkey king was content with his place in the world, assured of its nature. Perhaps he was deluded, but Mingolla envied his delusion, and he especially envied his dream of gold and cocaine. His own dreams had been dispersed by the war. The idea of sitting and daubing colors onto canvas no longer held any real attraction for him. Nor did the thought of returning to New York. Though survival had been his priority all these months, he had never stopped to consider what survival portended, and now he did not believe he could return. He had, he realized, become acclimated to the war, able to breathe its toxins; he would gag on the air of peace and home. The war was his new home, his newly rightful place.

Then the truth of this struck him with the force of an illumination, and he understood what he had to do.

Baylor and Gilbey had acted according to their natures, and he would have to act according to his, which imposed upon him the path of acceptance. He remembered Tio Moises' story about the pilot and laughed inwardly. In a sense his friend—the guy he had mentioned in his unsent letter—had been right about the war, about the world. It was full of designs, patterns, coincidences, and cycles that appeared to indicate the workings of some magical power. But these things were the result of a subtle natural process. The longer you lived, the wider your experience, the more complicated your life became, and eventually you were bound in the midst of so many interactions, a web of circumstance and emotion and event, that nothing was simple anymore and everything was subject to interpretation. Interpretation, however, was a waste of time. Even the most logical of interpretations was merely an attempt to herd mystery into a cage and lock the door on it. It made life no less mysterious. And it was equally pointless to seize upon patterns, to rely on them, to obey the mystical regulations they seemed to imply. Your one effective course had to be entrenchment. You had to admit to mystery, to the incomprehensibility of your situation, and protect yourself against it. Shore up your web, clear it of blind corners, set alarms. You had to plan aggressively. You had to become the monster in your own maze, as brutal and devious as the fate you sought to escape. It was the kind of militant acceptance that Tio Moises' pilot had not had the opportunity to display, that Mingolla himself—though the opportunity had been his—had failed to display. He saw that now. He had merely reacted to danger and had not challenged or used forethought against it. But he thought he would be able to do that now.

He turned to the boy, thinking he might appreciate this insight into "magic," and caught a flicker of movement out of the corner of his eye. Gracela. Coming up behind the boy, her knife held low, ready to stab. In reflex, Mingolla flung out his injured hand to block her. The knife nicked the edge of his hand, deflected upward and sliced the top of the boy's shoulder.

The pain in Mingolla's hand was excruciating, blinding him momentarily; and then as he grabbed Gracela's forearm to prevent her from stabbing again, he felt another sensation, one almost covered by the pain. He had thought the thing inside his hand was dead, but now he could feel it fluttering at the edges of the wound, leaking out in the rich trickle of blood that flowed over his wrist. It was trying to worm back inside, wriggling against the flow, but the pumping of his heart was too strong, and soon it was gone, dripping on the white stone of the bridge.

Before he could feel relief or surprise or any way absorb what had happened, Gracela tried to pull free. Mingolla got to his knees, dragged her down and dashed her knife hand against the bridge. The knife skittered away. Gracela struggled wildly, clawing at his face, and the other children edged forward. Mingolla levered his left arm under Gracela's chin, choking her; with his right hand, he picked up the knife and pressed the point into her breast. The children stopped their advance, and Gracela went limp. He could feel her trembling. Tears streaked the grime on her cheeks. She looked like a scared little girl, not a witch.

"*Puta!*" said the boy. He had come to his feet, holding his shoulder, and was staring daggers at Gracela.

"Is it bad?" Mingolla asked. "The shoulder?"

The boy inspected the bright blood on his fingertips. "It hurts," he said. He stepped over to stand in front of Gracela and smiled down at her; he unbuttoned the top button of his shorts.

Gracela tensed.

"What are you doing?" Mingolla suddenly felt responsible for the girl.

"I going to do what I tol' her, man." The boy undid the rest of the buttons and shimmied out of his shorts; he was already half-erect, as if the violence had aroused him.

"No," said Mingolla, realizing as he spoke that this was not at all wise.

"Take your life," said the boy sternly. "Walk away."

A long powerful gust of wind struck the bridge; it seemed to Mingolla that the vibration of the bridge, the beating of his heart, and Gracela's trembling were driven by the same shimmering pulse. He felt an almost visceral commitment to the moment, one that had nothing to do with his concern for the girl. Maybe, he thought, it was an implementation of his new convictions.

The boy lost patience. He shouted at the other children, herding them away with slashing gestures. Sullenly, they moved off down the curve of the bridge, positioning themselves along the railing, leaving an open avenue. Beyond them, beneath a lavender sky, the jungle stretched to the horizon, broken only by the rectangular hollow made by the airbase. The boy hunkered at Gracela's feet. "Tonight," he said to Mingolla, "the bridge have set us together. Tonight we sit, we talk. Now, that's over. My heart say to kill you. But 'cause you stop Gracela from cutting deep, I give you a chance. She mus' make a judgmen'. If she say she go wit' you, we"—he waved toward the other children—"will kill you. If she wan' to stay, then you mus' go. No more talk, no bullshit. You jus' go. Understan'?"

Mingolla wasn't afraid, and his lack of fear was not born of an indifference to life, but of clarity and confidence. It was time to stop reacting away from challenges, time to meet them. He came up with a plan. There was no doubt that Gracela would choose him, choose a chance at life, no matter how slim. But before she could decide, he would kill the boy. Then he would run straight at the others: without their leader, they might not hang together. It wasn't much of a plan and he didn't like the idea of hurting the boy; but he thought he might be able to pull it off. "I understand," he said.

The boy spoke to Gracela; he told Mingolla to release her. She sat up, rubbing the spot where Mingolla had pricked her with the knife. She glanced coyly at him, then at the boy; she pushed her hair back behind her neck and thrust out her breasts as if preening for two suitors. Mingolla was astonished by her behavior. Maybe, he thought, she was playing for time. He stood and pretended to be shaking out his kinks, edging closer to the boy, who remained crouched beside Gracela. In the east a red fireball had cleared the horizon; its sanguine light inspired Mingolla, fueled his resolve. He yawned and edged closer yet, firming his grip on the knife. He would yank the boy's head back by the hair, cut his throat. Nerves jumped in his chest. A pressure was building inside him, demanding that he act, that he move now. He restrained himself. Another step should do it, another step to be absolutely sure. But as he was about to take that step, Gracela reached out and tapped the boy on the shoulder.

Surprise must have showed on Mingolla's face, because the boy looked at him and grunted laughter. "You t'ink she pick you?" he said. "Shit! You don't know Gracela, man. Gringos burn her village. She lick the devil's ass 'fore she even shake hands wit' you." He grinned, stroked her hair. " 'Sides, she t'ink if she fuck me good, maybe I say, 'Oh, Gracela, I got to have some more of that!' And who knows? Maybe she right."

Gracela lay back and wriggled out of her skirt. Between her legs, she was nearly hairless. A smile touched the corners of her mouth. Mingolla stared at her, dumbfounded.

"I not going to kill you, gringo," said the boy without looking up; he was running his hand across Gracela's stomach. "I tol' you I won' kill a man so close wit' death." Again he laughed. "You look pretty funny trying to sneak up. I like watching that."

Mingolla was stunned. All the while he had been gearing himself up to kill, shunting aside anxiety and revulsion, he had merely been providing an entertainment for the boy. The heft of the knife seemed to be drawing his anger into a compact shape, and he wanted to carry out his attack, to cut down this little animal who had ridiculed him; but humiliation mixed with the anger, neutralizing it. The poisons of rage shook him; he could feel every incidence of pain and fatigue in his body. His hand was throbbing, bloated and discolored like the hand of a corpse. Weakness pervaded him. And relief.

"Go," said the boy. He lay down beside Gracela, propped on an elbow, and began to tease one of her nipples erect.

Mingolla took a few hesitant steps away. Behind him, Gracela made a mewling noise and the boy whispered something. Mingolla's anger was rekindled—they had already forgotten him!—but he kept going. As he passed the other children, one spat at him and another shied a pebble. He fixed his eyes on the white concrete slipping beneath his feet.

When he reached the mid-point of the curve, he turned back. The children had hemmed in Gracela and the boy against the terminus, blocking them from view. The sky had gone bluish-gray behind them, and the wind carried their voices. They were singing: a ragged, chirpy song that sounded celebratory. Mingolla's anger subsided, his humiliation ebbed. He had nothing to be ashamed of; though he had acted unwisely, he had done so from a posture of strength and no amount of ridicule could diminish that. Things were going to work out. Yes they were! He would make them work out.

For a while he watched the children. At this remove, their singing had an appealing savagery and he felt a trace of wistfulness at leaving them behind. He wondered what would happen after the boy had done with Gracela. He was not concerned, only curious. The way you feel when you think you may have to leave a movie before the big finish. Will our heroine survive? Will justice prevail? Will survival and justice bring happiness in their wake? Soon the end of the bridge came to be bathed in the golden rays of the sunburst; the children seemed to be blackening and dissolving in heavenly fire. That was a sufficient resolution for Mingolla. He tossed Gracela's knife into the river and went down from the bridge in whose magic he no longer believed, walking toward the war whose mystery he had accepted as his own.

5

At the airbase, Mingolla took a stand beside the Sikorsky that had brought him to San Francisco de Juticlan; he had recognized it by the painted flaming letters of the words Whispering Death. He rested his head against the letter G and recalled how Baylor had recoiled from the letters, worried that they might transmit some deadly essence. Mingolla didn't mind the contact. The painted flames seemed to be warming the inside of his head, stirring up thoughts as slow and indefinite as smoke. Comforting thoughts that embodied no images or ideas. Just a gentle buzz of mental activity, like the idling of an engine. The base was coming to life around him. Jeeps pulling away from barracks; a couple of officers inspecting the belly of a cargo plane; some guy repairing a fork-lift. Peaceful, homey. Mingolla closed his eyes, lulled into a half-sleep, letting the sun and the painted flames bracket him with heat real and imagined.

Some time later—how much later, he could not be sure—a voice said, "Fucked up your hand pretty good, didn'tcha?"

The two pilots were standing by the cockpit door. In their black flight suits and helmets they looked neither weird nor whimsical, but creatures of functional menace. Masters of the Machine. "Yeah," said Mingolla. "Fucked it up."

"How'd ya do it?" asked the pilot on the left.

"Hit a tree."

"Musta been goddamn crocked to hit a tree," said the pilot on the right. "Tree ain't goin' nowhere if you hit it."

Mingolla made a non-committal noise. "You guys going up to the Farm?"

"You bet! What's the matter, man? Had enough of them wild women?" Pilot on the right.

"Guess so. Wanna gimme a ride?"

"Sure thing," said the pilot on the left. "Whyn't you climb on in front. You can sit back of us."

"Where your buddies?" asked the pilot on the right.

"Gone," said Mingolla as he climbed into the cockpit.

One of the pilots said, "Didn't think we'd be seein' them boys again."

Mingolla strapped into the observer's seat behind the co-pilot's position. He had assumed there would be a lengthy instrument check, but as soon as the engines had been warmed, the Sikorsky lurched up and veered northward. With the exception of the weapons systems, none of the defenses had been activated. The radar, the thermal imager and terrain display, all showed blank screens. A nervous thrill ran across the muscles of Mingolla's stomach as he considered the varieties of danger to which the pilots' reliance upon their miraculous helmets had laid them open; but his nervousness was subsumed by the whispery rhythms of the rotors and his sense of the Sikorsky's power. He recalled having a similar feeling of secure potency while sitting at the controls of his gun. He had never let that feeling grow, never let it rule him, empower him. He had been a fool.

They followed the northeasterly course of the river, which coiled like a length of blue-steel razor wire between jungled hills. The pilots laughed and joked, and the ride came to have the air of a ride with a couple of good ol' boys going nowhere fast and full of free beer. At one point the co-pilot piped his voice through the on-board speakers and launched into a dolorous country song.

> *"Whenever we kiss, dear, our two lips meet,*
> *And whenever you're not with me, we're apart.*
> *When you sawed my dog in half, that was depressin',*
> *But when you shot me in the chest, you broke my heart."*

As the co-pilot sang, the pilot rocked the Sikorsky back and forth in a drunken accompaniment, and after the song ended, he called back to Mingolla, "You believe this here son of a bitch wrote that? He did! Picks a guitar, too! Boy's a genius!"

"It's a great song," said Mingolla, and he meant it. The song had made him happy, and that was no small thing.

They went rocking through the skies, singing the first verse over and over. But then, as they left the river behind, still maintaining a northeasterly course, the co-pilot pointed to a section of jungle ahead and shouted, "Beaners! Quadrant Four! You got 'em?"

"Got 'em!" said the pilot. The Sikorsky swerved down toward the jungle, shuddered, and flame veered from beneath them. An instant later, a huge swath of jungle erupted into a gout of marbled smoke and fire. "Whee-oo!" the co-pilot sang out, jubilant. "Whisperin' Death strikes again!" With guns blazing, they went swooping through blowing veils of dark smoke. Acres of trees were burning, and still they kept up the attack. Mingolla gritted his teeth against the noise, and when at last the firing stopped, dismayed by this insanity, he sat slumped, his head down. He suddenly doubted his ability to cope with the insanity of the Ant Farm and remembered all his reasons for fear.

The co-pilot turned back to him. "You ain't got no call to look so gloomy, man," he said. "You're a lucky son of a bitch, y'know that?"

The pilot began a bank toward the east, toward the Ant Farm. "How you figure that?" Mingolla asked.

"I gotta clear sight of you, man," said the co-pilot. "I can tell you for true you ain't gonna be at the Farm much longer. It ain't clear why or nothin'. But I 'spect you gonna be wounded. Not bad, though. Just a goin'-home wound."

As the pilot completed the bank, a ray of sun slanted into the cockpit, illuminating the co-pilot's visor, and for a split-second Mingolla could make out the vague shadow of the face beneath. It seemed lumpy and malformed. His imagination added details. Bizarre growths, cracked cheeks, an eye webbed shut. Like a face out of a movie about nuclear mutants. He was tempted to believe that he had really seen this; the co-pilot's deformities would validate his prediction of a secure future. But Mingolla rejected the temptation. He was afraid of dying, afraid of the terrors held by life at the Ant Farm, yet he wanted no more to do with magic . . . unless there was magic involved in being a good soldier. In obeying the disciplines, in the practice of fierceness.

"Could be his hand'll get him home," said the pilot. "That hand looks pretty fucked up to me. Looks like a million-dollar wound, that hand."

"Naw, I don't get it's his hand," said the co-pilot. "Somethin' else. Whatever, it's gonna do the trick."

Mingolla could see his own face floating in the black plastic of the co-pilot's visor; he looked warped and pale, so thoroughly unfamiliar that for a moment he thought the face might be a bad dream the co-pilot was having.

"What the hell's with you, man?" the co-pilot asked. "You don't believe me?"

Mingolla wanted to explain that his attitude had nothing to do with belief or disbelief, that it signaled his intent to obtain a safe future by means of securing his present; but he couldn't think how to put it into words the co-pilot would accept. The co-pilot would merely refer again to his visor as testimony to a magical reality or perhaps would point up ahead where— because the cockpit plastic had gone opaque under the impact of direct sunlight—the sun now appeared to hover in a smoky darkness: a distinct fiery sphere with a streaming corona, like one of those cabalistic emblems embossed on ancient seals. It was an evil, fearsome-looking thing, and though Mingolla was unmoved by it, he knew the pilot would see in it a powerful sign.

"You think I'm lyin'?" said the co-pilot angrily. "You think I'd be bullshittin' you 'bout somethin' like this? Man, I ain't lyin'! I'm givin' you the good goddamn word!"

They flew east into the sun, whispering death, into a world disguised as a strange bloody enchantment, over the dark green wild where war had taken root, where men in combat armor fought for no good reason against men wearing brass scorpions on their berets, where crazy, lost men wandered the mystic light of Fire Zone Emerald and mental wizards brooded upon things not yet seen. The co-pilot kept the black bubble of his visor angled back toward Mingolla, waiting for a response. But Mingolla just stared, and before too long the co-pilot turned away.

ORSON SCOTT CARD

Hatrack River

Here's a brilliantly evocative story of life and death and dark forces in the early days of the American frontier, in 1805, when places like Pennsylvania and Ohio were deep, forbidding wildernesses, and dark magic was afoot. . . .

Orson Scott Card began publishing in 1977, and by 1978 had won the John W. Campbell Award as best new writer of the year. His short fiction has appeared in *Omni, Isaac Asimov's Science Fiction Magazine, Analog, The Magazine of Fantasy and Science Fiction,* and elsewhere. His novels include *Hot Sleep, A Planet Called Treason, Songmaster,* and *Hart's Hope.* In 1986, his novel *Ender's Game* won both the Hugo and the Nebula awards. His most recent novel is *Speaker For the Dead.* Upcoming are four novels —*Wyrms,* from Arbor House, and *Seventh Son, Red Prophet,* and *'Prentice Alvin,* from Tor—and two collections, *Cardography,* from Hypatia Press, and *Tales of the Mormon Sea,* from Phantasia Press. The prolific Mr. Card is also editing an anthology, *Eutopia,* upcoming from Tor, and somehow also finds time to edit a reviewzine called *Short Form.* His story "The Fringe" appeared in our Third Annual Collection. Card lives in Greensboro, North Carolina, with his family.

HATRACK RIVER

Orson Scott Card

Little Peggy was very careful with the eggs. She rooted her hand through the straw till her fingers bumped something hard and heavy. She gave no never mind to the chicken drips. After all, Mama never even crinkled her face to open up Cally's most spetackler diapers. Even when the chicken drips were wet and stringy and made her fingers stick together, little Peggy gave no never mind. She just pushed the straw apart, wrapped her hand around the egg, and lifted it out of the brood box. All this while standing tip-toe on a wobbly stool, reaching high above her head. Mama said she was too young for egging, but little Peggy showed her. Every day she felt in every brood box and brought in every egg, every single one, that's what she did.

Every one, she said in her mind, over and over. I got to reach into every one.

Then little Peggy looked back into the northeast corner, the darkest place in the whole coop, and there sat Bloody Mary in her brood box, looking like the devil's own bad dream, hatefulness shining out of her nasty eyes, saying Come here little girl and give me nips. I want nips of finger and nips of thumb and if you come real close and try to take my egg I'll get a nip of eye from you.

Most animals didn't have much heartfire, but Bloody Mary's was strong and made a poison smoke. Nobody else could see it, but little Peggy could. Bloody Mary dreamed of death for all folks, but most specially for a certain little girl five years old, and little Peggy had the marks on her fingers to prove it. At least one mark, anyway, and even if Papa said he couldn't see it, little Peggy remembered how she got it and nobody could blame her none if she sometimes forgot to reach under Bloody Mary who sat there like a bushwhacker waiting to kill the first folks that just tried to come by. Nobody'd get mad if she just sometimes forgot to look there.

I forgot forgot forgot. I looked in every brood box, every one, and if one got missed then I forgot forgot forgot.

Everybody knew Bloody Mary was a lowdown chicken and too mean to give any eggs that wasn't rotten anyway.

I forgot.

She got the egg basket inside before Mama even had the fire het, and Mama was so pleased she let little Peggy put the eggs one by one into the cold water. Then Mama put the pot on the hook and swung it right on over the fire. Boiling eggs you didn't have to wait for the fire to slack, you could do it smoke and all.

"Peg," said Papa.

That was Mama's name, but Papa didn't say it in his Mama voice. He said it in his little-Peggy-you're-in-dutch voice, and little Peggy knew she was completely found out, and so she turned right around and yelled what she'd been planning to say all along.

"I forgot, Papa!"

Mama turned and looked at little Peggy in surprise. Papa wasn't surprised though. He just raised an eyebrow. He was holding his hand behind his back. Little Peggy knew there was an egg in that hand. Bloody Mary's nasty egg.

"What did you forget, little Peggy?" asked Papa, talking soft.

Right that minute little Peggy reckoned she was the stupidest girl ever born on the face of the earth. Here she was denying before anybody accused her of anything.

But she wasn't going to give up, not right off like that. She couldn't stand to have them mad at her and she just wanted them to let her go away and live in England. So she put on her innocent face and said, "I don't know, Papa."

She figgered England was the best place to go live, cause England had a Lord Protector. From the look in Papa's eye, a Lord Protector was pretty much what she needed just now.

"What did you forget?" Papa asked again.

"Just say it and be done, Horace," said Mama. "If she's done wrong then she's done wrong."

"I forgot one time, Papa," said little Peggy. "She a mean old chicken and she hates me."

Papa answered soft and slow. "One time," he said.

Then he took his hand from behind him. Only it wasn't no single egg he held, it was a whole basket. And that basket was filled with a clot of straw—most likely all the straw from Bloody Mary's box—and that straw was mashed together and glued tight with dried-up raw egg and shell bits, mixed up with about three or four chewed-up baby chicken bodies.

"Did you have to bring that in the house before breakfast, Horace?" said Mama.

"I don't know what makes me madder," said Horace. "What she done wrong or her studying up to lie about it."

"I didn't study and I didn't lie!" shouted little Peggy. Or anyways she meant to shout. What came out sounded espiciously like crying even though little Peggy had decided only yesterday that she was done with crying for the rest of her life.

"See?" said Mama. "She already feels bad."

"She feels bad being caught," said Horace. "You're too slack on her, Peg. She's got a lying spirit. I don't want my daughter growing up wicked. I'd rather see her dead like her baby sisters before I see her grow up wicked."

Little Peggy saw Mama's heartfire flare up with memory, and in front of her eyes she could see a baby laid out pretty in a little box, and then another one only not so pretty cause it was the second baby Missy, the one what died of pox so nobody'd touch her but her own Mama, who was still so feeble from the pox herself that she couldn't do much. Little Peggy saw that scene, and she knew Papa had made a mistake to say what he said cause Mama's face went cold even though her heartfire was hot.

"That's the wickedest thing anybody ever said in my presence," said Mama. Then she took up the basket of corruption from the table and took it outside.

"Bloody Mary bites my hand," said little Peggy.

"We'll see what bites," said Papa. "For leaving the eggs I give you one whack, because I reckon that lunatic hen looks fearsome to a frog-size girl like you. But for telling lies I give you ten whacks."

Little Peggy cried in earnest at that news. Papa gave an honest count and full measure in everything, but most especially in whacks.

Papa took the hazel rod off the high shelf. He kept it up there ever since little Peggy put the old one in the fire and burnt it right up.

"I'd rather hear a thousand hard and bitter truths from you, Daughter, than one soft and easy lie," said he, and then he bent over and laid on with the rod across her thighs. Whick whick whick, she counted every one, they stung her to the heart, each one of them, they were so full of anger. Worst of all she knew it was all unfair because his heartfire raged for a different cause altogether, and it always did. Papa's hate for wickedness always came from his most secret memory. Little Peggy didn't understand it all, because it was twisted up and confused and Papa didn't remember it right well himself. All little Peggy ever saw plain was that it was a lady and it wasn't Mama. Papa thought of that lady whenever something went wrong. When baby Missy died of nothing at all, and then the next baby also named Missy died of pox, and then the barn burnt down once, and a cow died, everything that went wrong made him think of that lady and he began to talk about how much he hated wickedness and at those times the hazel rod flew hard and sharp.

I'd rather hear a thousand hard and bitter truths, that's what he said, but little Peggy knew that there was one truth he didn't ever want to hear, and so she kept it to herself. She'd never shout it at him, even if it made him break the hazel rod, cause whenever she thought of saying aught about that lady, she kept picturing her father dead, and that was a thing she never hoped to see for real. Besides, the lady that haunted his heartfire, she didn't have no clothes on, and little Peggy knew that she'd be whipped for sure if she talked about people being naked.

So she took the whacks and cried till she could taste that her nose was running. Papa left the room right away, and Mama came back to fix up breakfast for the blacksmith and the visitors and the hands, but neither one said boo to her, just as if they didn't even notice. She cried even harder and louder for a minute, but it didn't help. Finally she picked up her Bugy from the sewing basket and walked all stiff-legged out to Old pappy's cabin and woke him right up.

He listened to her story like he always did.

"I know about Bloody Mary," he said, "and I told your papa fifty times if I told him once, wring that chicken's neck and be done. She's a crazy bird. Every week or so she gets crazy and breaks all her own eggs, even the ones ready to hatch. Kills her own chicks. It's a lunatic what kills its own."

"Papa like to killed me," said little Peggy.

"I reckon if you can walk somewhat it ain't so bad altogether."

"I can't walk much."

"No, I can see you're nigh crippled forever," said Oldpappy. "But I tell you what, the way I see it your mama and your papa's mostly mad at each other. So why don't you just disappear for a couple of hours?"

"I wish I could turn into a bird and fly."

"Next best thing, though," said Pappy, "is to have a secret place where nobody knows to look for you. Do you have a place like that? No, don't tell me—it wrecks it if you tell even a single other person. You just go to that place for a while. As long as it's a safe place, not out in the woods where a Red might take your pretty hair, and not a high place where you might fall off, and not a tiny place where you might get stuck."

"It's big and it's low and it ain't in the woods," said little Peggy.

"Then you go there, Maggie."

Little Peggy made the face she always made when Oldpappy called her that. And she held up Bugy and in Bugy's squeaky high voice she said, "Her name is Peggy."

"You go there, *Piggy*, if you like that better—"

Little Peggy slapped Bugy right across Oldpappy's knee.

"Someday Bugy'll do that once too often and have a rupture and die," said Oldpappy.

But Bugy just danced right in his face and insisted, "Not piggy, *Peggy!*"

"That's right, Puggy, you go to that secret place and if anybody says, We got to go find that girl, I'll say, I know where she is and she'll come back when she's good and ready."

Little Peggy ran for the cabin door and then stopped and turned. "Old-pappy, you're the nicest grown-up in the whole world."

"Your papa has a different view of me, but that's all tied up with another hazel rod that I laid hand on much too often. Now run along."

She stopped again right before she closed the door. "You're the *only* nice grown-up!" She shouted it real loud, halfway hoping that they could hear it clear inside the house. Then she was gone, right across the garden, out past the cow pasture, up the hill into the woods, and along the path to the spring house.

They had one good wagon, these folks did, and two good horses pulling it. One might even suppose they was prosperous, considering they had six big boys, from mansize on down to twins that had wrestled each other into being a good deal stronger than their dozen years. Not to mention one big daughter and a whole passel of little girls. A big family. Right prosperous if you didn't know that not even a year ago they had owned a mill and lived in a big house on a streambank in west New Hampshire. Come down far in the world, they had, and this wagon was all they had left of everything. But they were hopeful, trekking west along the roads that crossed the Hio, heading for open land that was free for the taking. If you were a family with plenty of strong backs and clever hands, it'd be good land, too, as long as the weather was with them and the Reds didn't raid them and all the lawyers and bankers stayed in New England.

The father was a big man, a little run to fat, which was no surprise since millers mostly stood around all day. That softness in the belly wouldn't last a year on a deepwoods homestead. He didn't care much about that, anyway—he had no fear of hard work. What worried him today was his wife, Faith. It was her time for that baby, he knew it. Not that she'd ever talk about it direct. Women just don't speak about things like that with men. But he knew how big she was and how many months it had been. Besides, at the noon stop she murmured to him, "Alvin Miller, if there's a road house along this way, or even a little broke-down cabin, I reckon I could use a bit of rest." A man didn't have to be a philosopher to understand her. And after six sons and six daughters, he'd have to have the brains of a brick not to get the drift of how things stood with her.

So he sent the oldest boy, Vigor, to run ahead on the road and see the lay of the land.

You could tell they were from New England, 'cause the boy didn't take no gun. If there'd been a bushwhacker the young man never would've made it back, and the fact he came back with all his hair was proof no Red had spotted him—the French up Detroit way were paying for English scalps with liquor and if a Red saw a white man alone in the woods with no rifle he'd own that white man's scalp. So maybe a man could think that luck was with the family at last. But since these Yankees had no notion that the road wasn't safe, Alvin Miller didn't think for a minute of his good luck.

Vigor's word was of a road house three miles on. That was good news, except that between them and that road house was a river. Kind of a scrawny river, and the ford was shallow, but Alvin Miller had learned never to trust water. No matter how peaceful it looks, it'll reach and try to take you. He was halfway minded to tell Faith that they'd spend the night this side of the river, but she gave just the tiniest groan and at that moment he knew that there was no chance of that. Faith had borne him a dozen living children, but it was four years since the last one and a lot of women took it bad, having a baby so late. A lot of women died. A good road house meant women to help with the birthing, so they'd have to chance the river.

And Vigor did say the river wasn't much.

The air in the spring house was cool and heavy, dark and wet. Sometimes when little Peggy caught a nap here, she woke up gasping like as if the whole place was under water. She had dreams of water even when she wasn't here—that was one of the things that made some folks say she was a seeper instead of a torch. But when she dreamed outside, she always knew she was dreaming. Here the water was real.

Real in the drips that formed like sweat on the milkjars setting in the stream. Real in the cold damp clay of the spring house floor. Real in the swallowing sound of the stream as it hurried through the middle of the house.

Keeping it cool all summer long, cold water spilling right out of the hill and into this place, shaded all the way by trees so old the moon made a point of passing through their branches just to hear some good old tales. That was what little Peggy always came here for, even when Papa didn't hate her. Not the wetness of the air, she could do just fine without that. It was the way the fire went right out of her and she didn't have to be a torch. Didn't have to see into all the dark places where folks hid theirselfs.

From her they hid theirselfs as if it would do some good. Whatever they didn't like most about theirself they tried to tuck away in some dark corner but they didn't know how all them dark places burned in little Peggy's eyes. Even when she was so little that she spit out her corn mash 'cause she was still hoping for a suck, she knew all the stories that the folks around her kept all hid. She saw the bits of their past that they most wished they could bury, and she saw the bits of their future that they most feared.

And that was why she took to coming up here to the spring house. Here she didn't have to see those things. Not even the lady in Papa's memory. There was nothing here but the heavy wet dark cool air to quench the fire and dim the light so she could be—just for a few minutes in the day—a little five-year-old girl with a straw puppet named Bugy and not even have to *think* about any of them grown-up secrets.

I'm not wicked, she told herself. Again and again but it didn't work because she knew she was.

All right then, she said to herself, I *am* wicked. But I won't be wicked anymore. I'll tell the truth like Papa says, or I'll say nothing at all.

Even at five years old, little Peggy knew that if she kept that vow, she'd be better off saying nothing.

So she said nothing, not even to herself, just lay there on a mossy damp table with Bugy clenched tight enough to strangle in her fist.

Ching ching ching.

Little Peggy woke up and got mad for just a minute.

Ching ching ching.

Made her mad because nobody said to her, Little Peggy, you don't mind if we talk this young blacksmith feller into settling down here, do you?

Not at all, Papa, she would've said if they'd asked. She knew what it meant to have a smithy. It meant your village would thrive, and folks from other places would come, and when they came there'd be trade, and when there was trade then her father's big house could be a forest inn, and when there was a forest inn all the roads would kind of bend a little just to pass the place, if it wasn't too far out of the way—little Peggy knew all that, as sure as the children of farmers knew the rhythms of the farm. A road house by a smithy was a road house that would prosper. So she would've said, sure enough, let him stay, deed him land, brick his chimney, feed him free, let him have my bed so I have to double up with Cousin Peter who keeps trying to peek under my nightgown, I'll put up with all that—just as long as you don't put him near the spring house so that all the time, even when I want to be alone with the water, there's that whack thump hiss roar, noise all the time, and a fire burning up the sky to turn it black, and the smell of charcoal burning. It was enough to make a body wish to follow the stream right back into the mountain just to get some peace.

Of course the stream was the smart place to put the blacksmith. Except for water, he could've put his smithy anywhere at all. The iron came to him in the shipper's wagon clear from New Netherland, and the charcoal—well, there were plenty of farmers willing to trade charcoal for a good shoe. But water, that's what the smith needed that nobody'd bring him, so of course they put him right down the hill from the spring house where his ching ching ching could wake her up and put the fire back into her in the one place where she had used to be able to let it burn low and go almost to cold wet ash.

A roar of thunder.

She was at the door in a second. Had to see the lightning. Caught just the last shadow of the light but she knew that there'd be more. It wasn't much after noon, surely, or had she slept all day? What with all these blackbelly clouds she couldn't tell—it might as well be the last minutes of dusk. The air was all a-prickle with lightning just waiting to flash. She knew that feeling, knew that it meant the lightning'd hit close.

She looked down to see if the blacksmith's stable was still full of horses. It was. The shoeing wasn't done, the road would turn to muck, and so the farmer with his two sons from out West Fork way was stuck here. Not a chance they'd head home in *this*, with lightning ready to put a fire in the woods, or knock a tree down on them, or maybe just smack them a good one and lay them all out dead in a circle like them five Quakers they still was talking about and here it happened back in '90 when the first white folks came to settle here. People talked still about the Circle of Five and all that, some people wondering if God up and smashed them flat so as to shut the Quakers up, seeing how nothing else ever could, while other people was wondering if God took them up into heaven like the first Lord Protector Oliver Cromwell who was smote by lightning at the age of ninety-seven and just disappeared.

No, that farmer and his big old boys'd stay another night. Little Peggy was an innkeeper's daughter, wasn't she? Papooses learnt to hunt, pickaninnies learnt to tote, farmer children learnt the weather, and an innkeeper's daughter learnt which folks would stay the night, even before they knew it right theirselfs.

Their horses were champing in the stable, snorting and warning each other about the storm. In every group of horses, little Peggy figgered, there must be one that's remarkable dumb, so all the others have to tell him what all's going on. Bad storm, they were saying. We're going to get a soaking, if the lightning don't smack us first. And the dumb one kept nickering and saying, What's the noise, what's that noise.

Then the sky just opened right up and dumped water on the earth. Stripped leaves right off the trees, it came down so hard. Came down so thick, too, that little Peggy couldn't even see the smithy for a minute and she thought maybe it got washed right away into the stream. Oldpappy told her how that stream led right down to the Hatrack River, and the Hatrack poured right into the Hio, and the Hio shoved itself on through the woods to the Mizzipy, which went on down to the sea, and Oldpappy said how the sea drank so much water that it got indigestion and gave off the biggest old belches you ever heard, and what came up was clouds. Belches from the sea, and now the smithy would float all that way, get swallered up and belched out, and someday she'd just be minding her own business and some cloud would break up and plop that smithy down as neat as you please, old Makepeace Smith still ching ching chinging away.

Then the rain slacked off a mite and she looked down to see the smithy still there. But that wasn't what she saw at all. No, what she saw was sparks of fire way off in the forest, downstream toward the Hatrack, down where the ford was, only there wasn't a chance of taking the ford today, with this rain. Sparks, lots of sparks, and she knew every one of them was folks. She didn't hardly think of doing it anymore, she only had to see their heartfires and she was looking close. Maybe future, maybe past, all the visions lived together in the heartfire.

What she saw right now was the same in all their hearts. A wagon in the middle of the Hatrack, with the water rising and everything they owned in all the world in that wagon.

Little Peggy didn't talk much, but everybody knew she was a torch, so they listened whenever she spoke up about trouble. Specially this kind of trouble. Sure the settlements in these parts were pretty old now, a fair bit older than little Peggy herself, but they hadn't forgotten yet that anybody's wagon caught in a flood is everybody's loss.

She fair to flew down that grassy hill, jumping gopher holes and sliding the steep places, so it wasn't twenty seconds from seeing those far-off heartfires till she was speaking right up in the smithy's shop. That farmer from West Fork at first wanted to make her wait till he was done with telling stories about worse storms he'd seen. But Makepeace knew all about little Peggy. He just listened right up and then told those boys to saddle them horses, shoes or no shoes, there was folks caught in the Hatrack ford and there was no time for foolishness. Little Peggy didn't even get a chance to see them go—Makepeace had already sent her off to the big house to fetch her father and all the hands and visitors there. Wasn't a one of them who hadn't once put all they owned in the world into a wagon and dragged it west across the mountain roads and down into the forest. Wasn't a one of them who hadn't felt a river sucking at that wagon, wanting to steal it away. They all got right to it. That's the way it was then, you see. Folks noticed other people's trouble every bit as quick as if it was their own.

Vigor led the boys in trying to push the wagon, while Eleanor hawed the horses. Alvin Miller spent his time carrying the little girls one by one to safety on the far shore. The current was a devil clawing at him, whispering, "I'll have your babies, I'll have them all," but Alvin said no, with every muscle in his body as he strained shoreward he said no to that whisper, till his girls stood all bedraggled on the bank with rain streaming down their faces like the tears from all the grief in the world.

He would have carried Faith, too, baby in her belly and all, but she wouldn't budge. Just sat inside that wagon, bracing herself against the trunks and furniture as the wagon tipped and rocked. Lightning crashed and branches broke; one of them tore the canvas and the water poured into the wagon but Faith held on with white knuckles and her eyes staring out. Alvin knew from her eyes there wasn't a thing he could say to make her let go. There was only one way to get Faith and her unborn baby out of that river, and that was to get the wagon out.

"Horses can't get no purchase, Papa," Vigor shouted. "They're just stumbling and bound to break a leg."

"Well we can't pull out without the horses!"

"The horses are *something*, Papa. We leave 'em in here and we'll lose wagon and horses too!"

"Your mama won't leave that wagon."

And he saw understanding in Vigor's eyes. The *things* in the wagon weren't worth a risk of death to save them. But Mama was.

"Still," he said. "On shore the team could pull strong. Here in the water they can't do a thing."

"Set the boys to unhitching them. But first tie a line to a tree to hold that wagon!"

It wasn't two minutes before the twins Wastenot and Wantnot were on the shore making the rope fast to a stout tree. David and Measure made another line fast to the rig that held the horses, while Calm cut the strands that held them to the wagon. Good boys, doing their work just right, Vigor shouting directions while Alvin could only watch helpless at the back of the wagon, looking now at Faith who was trying not to have the baby, now at the Hatrack River that was trying to push them all down to hell.

Not much of a river, Vigor had said, but then the clouds came up and the rain came down and the Hatrack became something after all. Even so it looked passable when they got to it. The horses strode in strong, and Alvin was just saying to Calm, who had the reins, "Well, we made it not a minute to spare," when the river went insane. It doubled in speed and strength all in a moment, and the horses got panicky and lost direction and started pulling against each other. The boys all hopped into the river and tried to lead them to shore but by then the wagon's momentum had been lost and the wheels were mired up and stuck fast. Almost as if the river knew they were coming and saved up its worst fury till they were already in it and couldn't get away.

"Look out! Look out!" screamed Measure from the shore.

Alvin looked upstream to see what devilment the river had in mind, and there was a whole tree floating down the river, endwise like a battering ram, the root end pointed at the center of the wagon, straight at the place where Faith was sitting, her baby on the verge of birth. Alvin couldn't think of anything to do, couldn't think at all, just screamed his wife's name with all his strength. Maybe in his heart he thought that by holding her name on his lips he could keep her alive, but there was no hope of that, no hope at all.

Except that Vigor didn't know there was no hope. Vigor leapt out when the tree was no more than a rod away, his body falling against it just above the root. The momentum of his leap turned it a little, then rolled it over, rolled it and turned it away from the wagon. Of course Vigor rolled with it, pulled right under the water—but it worked, the root end of the tree missed the wagon entirely, and the shaft of the trunk struck it a sidewise blow.

The tree bounded across the stream and smashed up against a boulder on the bank. Alvin was five rods off, but in his memory from then on, he always saw it like as if he'd been right there. The tree crashing into the boulder, and Vigor between them. Just a split second that lasted a lifetime, Vigor's eyes wide with surprise, blood already leaping out of his mouth, spattering out onto the tree that killed him. Then the Hatrack River swept the tree out into the current. Vigor slipped under the water, all except his arm, all tangled in the roots, which stuck up into the air for all the world like a neighbor waving good-bye after a visit.

Alvin was so intent on watching his dying son that he didn't even notice what was happening to his own self. The blow from the tree was enough to dislodge the mired wheels, and the current picked up the wagon, carried it downstream, Alvin clinging to the tailgate, Faith weeping inside, Eleanor screaming her lungs out from the driver's seat, and the boys on the bank shouting something. Shouting "Hold! Hold! Hold!"

The rope held, one end tied to a strong tree, the other end tied to the wagon, it held. The river couldn't tumble the wagon downstream; instead it swung the wagon in to shore the way a boy swings a rock on a string, and when it came to a shuddering stop it was right against the bank, the front end facing upstream.

"It held!" cried the boys.

"Thank God!" shouted Eleanor.

"The baby's coming," whispered Faith.

But Alvin, all he could hear was the single faint cry that had been the last sound from the throat of his firstborn son, all he could see was the way his boy clung to the tree as it rolled and rolled in the water, and all he could say was a single word, a single command. "Live," he murmured. Vigor had always obeyed him before. Hard worker, willing companion, more a friend or brother than a son. But this time he knew his son would disobey. Still he whispered it. "Live."

"Are we safe?" said Faith, her voice trembling.

Alvin turned to face her, tried to strike the grief from his face. No sense her knowing the price that Vigor paid to save her and the baby. Time enough to learn of that after the baby was born. "Can you climb out of the wagon?"

"What's wrong?" asked Faith, looking at his face.

"I took a fright. Tree could have killed us. Can you climb out, now that we're up against the bank?"

Eleanor leaned in from the front of the wagon. "David and Calm are on the bank, they can help you up. The rope's holding, Mama, but who can say how long?"

"Go on, Mother, just a step," said Alvin. "We'll do better with the wagon if we know you're safe on shore."

"The baby's coming," said Faith.

"Better on shore than here," said Alvin sharply. "Go *now*."

Faith stood up, clambered awkwardly to the front. Alvin climbed through the wagon behind her, to help her if she should stumble. Even he could see how her belly had dropped. The baby must be grabbing for air already.

On the bank it wasn't just David and Calm, now. There were strangers, big men, and several horses. Even one small wagon, and that was a welcome sight. Alvin had no notion who these men were, or how they knew to come and help, but there wasn't a moment to waste on introductions. "You men! Is there a midwife in the road house?"

"Goody Guester does with birthing," said a man. A big man, with arms like oxlegs. A blacksmith, surely.

"Can you take my wife in that wagon? There's not a moment to spare." Alvin knew it was a shameful thing, for men to speak so openly of birthing, right in front of the woman who was set to bear. But Faith was no fool— she knew what mattered most, and getting her to a bed and a competent midwife was more important than pussyfooting around about it.

David and Calm were careful as they helped their mother toward the waiting wagon. Faith was staggering with pain. Women in labor shouldn't have to step from a wagon seat up onto a riverbank, that was sure. Eleanor was right behind her, taking charge as if she wasn't younger than all the boys except the twins. "Measure! Get the girls together. They're riding in the wagon with us. You too, Wastenot and Wantnot! I know you can help the big boys but I need you to watch the girls while I'm with Mother." Eleanor was never one to be trifled with, and the gravity of the situation was such that they didn't even call her Eleanor of Aquitaine as they obeyed. Even the little girls mostly gave over their squabbling and got right in.

Eleanor paused a moment on the bank and looked back to where her father stood on the wagon seat. She glanced downstream, then looked back at him. Alvin understood the question, and he shook his head no. Faith was not to know of Vigor's sacrifice. Tears came unwelcome to Alvin's eyes, but not to Eleanor's. Eleanor was only fourteen, but when she didn't want to cry, she didn't cry.

Wastenot hawed the horse and the little wagon lurched forward, Faith wincing as the girls patted her and the rain poured. Faith's gaze was somber as a cow's, and as mindless, looking back at her husband, back at the river. At times like birthing, Alvin thought, a woman becomes a beast, slack-minded as her body takes over and does its work. How else could she bear the pain? As if the soul of the earth possessed her the way it owns the souls of animals, making her part of the life of the whole world, unhitching her from family, from husband, from all the reins of the human race, leading her into the valley of ripeness and harvest and reaping and bloody death.

"She'll be safe now," the blacksmith said. "And we have horses here to pull your wagon out."

"It's slacking off," said Measure. "The rain is less, and the current's not so strong."

"As soon as your wife stepped ashore, it eased up," said the farmer-looking feller. "The rain's dying, that's sure."

"You took the worst of it in the water," said the blacksmith. "But you're all right now. Get hold of yourself, man, there's work to do."

Only then did Alvin come to himself enough to realize that he was crying. Work to do, that's right, get hold of yourself, Alvin Miller. You're no weakling, to bawl like a baby. Other men have lost a dozen children and still live their lives. You've had twelve, and Vigor lived to be a man, though he never did get to marry and have children of his own. Maybe Alvin had to weep because Vigor died so nobly; maybe he cried because it was so sudden.

David touched the blacksmith's arm. "Leave him be for a minute," he said softly. "Our oldest brother was carried off not ten minutes back. He got tangled in a tree floating down."

"It wasn't no *tangle*," Alvin said sharply. "He jumped that tree and saved our wagon, and your mother inside it! That river paid him back, that's what it did, it punished him."

Calm spoke quietly to the local men. "It run him up against that boulder there." They all looked. There was a smear of blood on the rock.

"The Hatrack has a mean streak in it," said the blacksmith, "but I never seen this river so riled up before. I'm sorry about your boy. There's a slow, flat place downstream where he's bound to fetch up. Everything the river catches ends up there. When the storm lets up, we can go down and bring back the—bring him back."

Alvin wiped his eyes on his sleeve, but since his sleeve was soaking wet it didn't do much good. "Give me a minute more and I can pull my weight," said Alvin.

They hitched two more horses and the four beasts had no trouble pulling the wagon out against the much weakened current. By the time the wagon was set to rights again on the road, the sun was even breaking through.

"Wouldn't you know," said the blacksmith. "If you ever don't like the weather hereabouts, you just set a spell, cause it'll change."

"Not this one," said Alvin. "This storm was laid in wait for us."

The blacksmith put an arm across Alvin's shoulder, and spoke real gentle. "No offense, mister, but that's crazy talk."

Alvin shrugged him off. "That storm and that river wanted us."

"Papa," said David, "you're tired and grieving. Best be still till we get to the road house and see how Mama is."

"My baby is a boy," said Papa. "You'll see. He would have been the seventh son of a seventh son."

That got their attention, right enough, that blacksmith and the other men as well. Everybody knew a seventh son had certain gifts, but the seventh son of a seventh son was about as powerful a birth as you could have.

"That makes a difference," said the blacksmith. "He'd have been a born douser, sure, and water hates that." The others nodded sagely.

"The water had its way," said Alvin. "Had its way, and all done. It would've killed Faith and the baby, if it could. But since it couldn't, why, it killed my boy Vigor. And now when the baby comes, he'll be the sixth son, cause I'll only have five living."

"Some says it makes no difference if the first six be alive or not," said a farmer.

Alvin said nothing, but he knew it made all the difference. He had thought this baby would be a miracle child, but the river had taken care of that. If water don't stop you one way, it stops you another. He shouldn't have hoped for a miracle child. The cost was too high. All his eyes could see, all the way home, was Vigor dangling in the grasp of the roots, tumbling through the current like a leaf caught up in a dust devil, with the blood seeping from his mouth to slake the murderous thirst of the Hatrack.

Little Peggy stood in the window, looking out into the storm. She could see all those heartfires, especially one, one so bright it was like the sun when she looked at it. But there was a blackness all around them. No, not even black—a nothingness, like a part of the universe God hadn't finished making, and it swept around those lights as if to tear them from each other, sweep them away, swallow them up. Little Peggy knew what that nothingness was. Those times when her eyes saw the hot yellow heartfires, there were three other colors, too. The rich dark orange of the earth. The thin gray color of the air. And the deep black emptiness of water. It was the water that tore at them now. The river, only she had never seen it so black, so strong, so terrible. The heartfires were so tiny in the night.

"What do you see, child?" asked Oldpappy.

"The river's going to carry them away," said little Peggy.

"I hope not."

Little Peggy began to cry.

"There, child," said Oldpappy. "It ain't always such a grand thing to see afar off like that, is it."

She shook her head.

"But maybe it won't happen as bad as you think."

Just at that moment, she saw one of the heartfires break away and tumble off into the dark. "Oh!" she cried out, reaching as if her hand could snatch the light and put it back. But of course she couldn't. Her vision was long and clear, but her reach was short.

"Are they lost?" asked Oldpappy.

"One," whispered little Peggy.

"Haven't Makepeace and the others got there yet?"

"Just now," she said. "The rope held. They're safe now."

Oldpappy didn't ask her how she knew, or what she saw. Just patted her shoulder. "Because you told them. Remember that, Margaret. One was lost, but if you hadn't seen and sent help, they might all have died."

She shook her head. "I should've seen them sooner, Oldpappy, but I fell asleep."

"And you blame yourself?" asked Oldpappy.

"I should've let Bloody Mary nip me, and then father wouldn't't've been mad, and then I wouldn't't've been in the spring house, and then I wouldn't't've been asleep, and then I would've sent help in time—"

"We can all make daisy chains of blame like that, Maggie. It don't mean a thing."

But she knew it meant something. You don't blame blind people 'cause they don't warn you you're about to step on a snake—but you sure blame somebody with eyes who doesn't say a word about it. She knew her duty ever since she first realized that other folks couldn't see all that she could see. God gave her special eyes, so she'd better see and give warning, or the devil would take her soul. The devil or the deep black sea.

"Don't mean a thing," Oldpappy murmured. Then, like he just been poked in the behind with a ramrod, he went all straight and said, "Spring house! Spring house, of course." He pulled her close. "Listen to me, little Peggy. It wasn't none of your fault, and that's the truth. The same water that runs in the Hatrack flows in the spring house brook, it's all the same water, all through the world. The same water that wanted them dead, it knew you could give warning and send help. So it sang to you and sent you off to sleep."

It make a kind of sense to her, it sure did. "How can that be, Oldpappy?"

"Oh, that's just in the nature of it. The whole universe is made of only four kinds of stuff, little Peggy, and each one wants to have its own way." Peggy thought of the four colors that she saw when the heartfires glowed, and she knew what all four were even as Oldpappy named them. "Fire makes things hot and bright and uses them up. Air makes things cool and sneaks in everywhere. Earth makes things solid and sturdy, so they'll last. But water, it tears things down, it falls from the sky and carries off everything it can, carries it off and down to the sea. If the water had its way, the whole world would be smooth, just a big ocean with nothing out of the water's reach. All dead and smooth. That's why you slept. The water wants to tear down these strangers, whoever they are, tear them down and kill them. It's a miracle you woke up at all.''

''The blacksmith's hammer woke me,'' said little Peggy.

''That's it, then, you see? The blacksmith was working with iron, the hardest earth, and with a fierce blast of air from the bellows, and with a fire so hot it burns the grass outside the chimney. The water couldn't touch him to keep him still.''

Little Peggy could hardly believe it, but it must be so. The blacksmith had drawn her from a watery sleep. The smith had *helped* her. Why, it was enough to make you laugh, to know the blacksmith was her friend this time.

There was shouting on the porch downstairs, and doors opened and closed. ''Some folks is here already,'' said Oldpappy.

Little Peggy saw the heartfires downstairs, and found the one with the strongest fear and pain. ''It's their Mama,'' said little Peggy. ''She's got a baby coming.''

''Well, if that ain't the luck of it. Lose one, and here already is a baby to replace death with life.'' Oldpappy shambled on out to go downstairs and help.

Little Peggy, though, she just stood there, looking at what she saw in the distance. That lost heartfire wasn't lost at all, and that was sure. She could see it burning away far off, despite how the darkness of the river tried to cover it. He wasn't dead, just carried off, and maybe somebody could help him. She ran out then, passed Oldpappy all in a rush, clattered down the stairs.

Mama caught her by the arm as she was running into the great room. ''There's a birthing,'' Mama said, ''and we need you.''

''But Mama, the one that went downriver, he's still alive!''

''Peggy, we got no time for—''

Two boys with the same face pushed their way into the conversation. ''The one downriver!'' cried one.

''Still alive!'' cried another.

''How do you know!''

''He can't be!''

They spoke so all on top of each other that Mama had to hush them up just to hear them. ''It was Vigor, our big brother, he got swept away—''

''Well he's alive,'' said little Peggy, ''but the river's got him.''

The twins looked to Mama for confirmation. ''She know what she's talking about, Goody Guester?''

Mama nodded, and the boys raced for the door, shouting, ''He's alive! He's still alive!''

''Are you sure?'' asked Mama fiercely. ''It's a cruel thing, to put hope in their hearts like that, if it ain't so.''

Mama's flashing eyes made little Peggy afraid, and she couldn't think what to say.

By then, though, Oldpappy had come up from behind. "Now Peg," he said, "how would she know one was taken by the river, lessun she saw?"

"I know," said Mama. "But this woman's been holding off birth too long, and I got a care for the baby, so come on now, little Peggy, I need you to tell me what you see."

She led little Peggy into the bedroom off the kitchen, the place where Papa and Mama slept whenever there were visitors. The woman lay on the bed, holding tight to the hand of a tall girl with deep and solemn eyes. Little Peggy didn't know their faces, but she recognized their fires, especially the mother's pain and fear.

"Someone was shouting," whispered the mother.

"Hush now," said Mama.

"About him still alive."

The solemn girl raised her eyebrows, looked at Mama. "Is that so, Goody Guester?"

"My daughter is a torch. That's why I brung her here in this room. To see the baby."

"Did she see my boy? Is he alive?"

"I thought you didn't tell her, Eleanor," said Mama.

The solemn girl shook her head.

"Saw from the wagon. Is he alive?"

"Tell her, Margaret," said Mama.

Little Peggy turned and looked for his heartfire. There were no walls when it came to this kind of seeing. His flame was still there, though she knew it was afar off. This time, though, she drew near in the way she had, took a close look. "He's in the water. He's all tangled in the roots."

"Vigor!" cried the mother on the bed.

"The river wants him. The river says, Die, die."

Mama touched the woman's arm. "The twins have gone off to tell the others. There'll be a search party."

"In the dark!" whispered the woman scornfully.

Little Peggy spoke again. "He's saying a prayer. I think. He's saying—seventh son."

"Seventh son," whispered Eleanor.

"What does that mean?" asked Mama.

"If this baby's a boy," said Eleanor, "and he's born while Vigor's still alive, then he's the seventh son of a seventh son, and all of them alive."

Mama gasped. "No wonder the river—" she said. No need to finish the thought. Instead she took little Peggy's hands and led her to the woman on the bed. "Look at this baby, and see what you see."

Little Peggy had done this before, of course. It was the chief use they had for torches, to have them look at an unborn baby just at the birthing time. Partly to see how it lay in the womb, but also because sometimes a torch could see who the baby was, what it would be, could tell stories of times to come. Even before she touched the woman's belly, she could see the baby's heartfire. It was the one that she had seen before, that burned so hot and bright that it was like the sun and the moon, to compare it to the mother's fire. "It's a boy," she said.

"Then let me bear this baby," said the mother. "Let him breathe while Vigor still breathes!"

"How's the baby set?" asked Mama.

"Just right," said little Peggy.

"Head first? Face down?"

Little Peggy nodded.

"Then why won't it come?" demanded Mama.

"She's been telling him not to," said Little Peggy, looking at the mother.

"In the wagon," the mother said. "He was coming; and I did a beseeching."

"Well, you should have told me right off," said Mama sharply. "Speck me to help you and you don't even tell me he's got a beseeching on him. You, girl!"

Several young ones were standing near the wall, wide-eyed, and they didn't know which one she meant.

"Any of you, I need that iron key from the ring on the wall."

The biggest of them took it clumsily from the hook and brought it, ring and all. Mama dangled the large ring and the key over the mother's belly, chanting softly,

> *"Here's the circle, open wide,*
> *Here's the key to get outside,*
> *Earth be iron, flame be fair,*
> *Fall from water into air."*

The mother cried out in sudden agony. Mama tossed away the key, cast back the sheet, lifted the woman's knees, and ordered little Peggy fiercely to *see*.

Little Peggy touched the woman's womb. The boy's mind was empty, except for a feeling of pressure and gathering cold as he emerged into the air. But the very emptiness of his mind let her see things that would never be clearly visible again. The billion billion paths of his life lay open before him, waiting for his first choices, for the first changes in the world around him to eliminate a million futures every second. The future was there in everyone, a flickering shadow that was never visible behind the thoughts of the present moment; but here, for a few precious moments, little Peggy could see them clearly.

And what she saw was death down every path. Drowning, drowning, every path of his future led this child to a watery death.

"Why do you hate him so!" cried little Peggy.

"What?" demanded Eleanor.

"Hush," said Mama. "Let her see what she sees."

Inside the unborn child, the dark blot of water that surrounded his heartfire seemed so terribly strong that little Peggy was afraid he would be swallowed up.

"Get him out to breathe!" shouted little Peggy.

Mama reached in, even though it tore the mother something dreadful, and hooked the baby by the neck with strong fingers, drawing him out.

In that moment, the dark water retreated inside the child's mind, and just before the first breath came, little Peggy saw ten million deaths by water disappear. Now, for the first time, there were some paths open, some paths leading to a dazzling future. And all the paths that did not end in early death had one thing in common. On all those paths, little Peggy saw herself doing one simple thing.

So she did that thing. She took her hands from the slackening belly and ducked under her mother's arm. The baby's head had just emerged, and it was still covered with a bloody caul, a scrap of the sac of soft skin in which he had floated in his mother's womb.

His mouth was open, sucking inward on the caul, but it didn't break, and he couldn't breathe.

Little Peggy did what she had seen herself do in the baby's future. She reached out, took the caul from under the baby's chin, and pulled it away from his face. It came whole, in one moist piece, and in the moment it came away, the baby's mouth cleared, he sucked in a great breath, and then gave that mewling cry that birthing mothers hear as the song of life.

Little Peggy folded the caul, her mind still full of the visions she had seen down the pathways of this baby's life. She did not know yet what the visions meant, but they made such clear pictures in her mind that she knew she would never forget them. They made her afraid, because so much would depend on her, and how she used the birth caul that was still warm in her hands.

"A boy," said Mama.

"Is he," whispered the mother. "Seventh son?"

Mama was tying the cord, so she couldn't spare a glance at little Peggy. "Look," she whispered.

Little Peggy looked for the single heartfire on the distant river. "Yes," she said, for the heartfire was still burning.

Even as she watched, it flickered, died.

"Now he's gone," said little Peggy.

The woman on the bed wept bitterly, her birth-wracked body shuddering.

"Grieving at the baby's birth," said Mama. "It's a dreadful thing."

"Hush," whispered Eleanor to her mother. "Be joyous, or it'll darken the baby all his life!"

"Vigor," murmured the woman.

"Better nothing at all than tears," said Mama. She held out the crying baby, and Eleanor took it in competent arms—she had cradled many a babe before, it was plain. Mama went to the table in the corner and took the scarf that had been blacked in the wool, so it was night-colored clear through. She dragged it slowly across the weeping woman's face, saying, "Sleep, Mother, sleep."

When the cloth came away, the weeping was done, and the woman slept, her strength spent.

"Take the baby from the room," said Mama.

"Don't he need to start his sucking?" asked Eleanor.

"She'll never nurse this babe," said Mama. "Not unless you want him to suck hate."

"She can't hate him," said Eleanor. "It ain't his fault."

"I reckon her milk don't know that," said Mama. "That right, little Peggy? What teat did the baby suck?"

"His mama's," said little Peggy.

Mama looked sharp at her. "You sure of that?"

She nodded.

"Well, then, we'll bring the baby in when she wakes up. He doesn't need to eat anything for the first night, anyway." So Eleanor carried the baby out into the great room, where the fire burned to dry the men, who stopped trading stories about rains and floods worse than this one long enough to look at the baby and admire.

Inside the room, though, Mama took little Peggy by the chin and stared hard into her eyes. "You tell me the truth, Margaret. It's a serious thing, for a baby to suck on its mama and drink up hate."

"She won't hate him, Mama," said little Peggy.

"What did you see?"

Little Peggy would have answered, but she didn't know the words to tell most of the things she saw. So she looked at the floor. She could tell from Mama's quick draw of breath that she was ripe for a tongue-lashing. But Mama waited, and then her hand came soft, stroking across little Peggy's cheek. "Ah, child, what a day you've had. The baby might have died, except you told me to pull it out. You even reached in and opened up its mouth— that's what you did, isn't it?"

Little Peggy nodded.

"Enough for a little girl, enough for one day." Mama turned to the other girls, the ones in wet dresses, leaning against the wall. "And you, too, you've had enough of a day. Come out of here, let your mama sleep, come out and get dry by the fire. I'll start a supper for you, I will."

But Oldpappy was already in the kitchen, fussing around, and refused to hear of Mama doing a thing. Soon enough she was out with the baby, shooing the men away so she could rock it to sleep, letting it suck her finger.

Little Peggy figured after a while that she wouldn't be missed, and so she snuck up the stairs to the attic ladder, and up the ladder into the lightless, musty space. The spiders didn't bother her much, and the cats mostly kept the mice away, so she wasn't afraid. She crawled right to her secret hiding place and took out the carven box that Oldpappy had given her, the one he said his own papa brought from Ulster when he came to the colonies. It was full of the precious scraps of childhood—stones, strings, buttons—but now she knew that these were nothing compared to the work before her all the rest of her life. She dumped them right out, and blew into the box to clear away dust. Then she laid the folded caul inside and closed the lid.

She knew that in the future she would open that box a dozen times. That it would call to her, wake her from her sleep, tear her from her friends, and steal from her all her dreams. All because a baby boy downstairs had no future at all, except a death from the dark water, excepting if she used that caul to keep him safe, the way it once protected him in the womb.

For a moment she was angry, to have her own life so changed. Worse than the blacksmith coming, it was, worse than Papa and the hazel wand he whupped her with, worse than Mama when her eyes were angry. Everything would be different forever and it wasn't fair. Just for a baby she never invited, never asked to come here, what did she care about any old baby?

She reached out and opened the box, planning to take the caul and cast it into a dark corner of the attic. But even in the darkness, she could see a place where it was darker still: near her heartfire, where the emptiness of the deep black river was all set to make a murderer out of her.

Not me, she said to the water. You ain't part of me.

Yes I am, whispered the water. I'm all through you, and you'd dry up and die without me.

You ain't the boss of me, anyway, she retorted.

She closed the lid on the box and skidded her way down the ladder. Papa always said that she'd get splinters in her butt doing that. This time he was right. It stung something fierce, so she walked kind of sideways into the kitchen where Oldpappy was. Sure enough, he stopped his cooking long enough to pry the splinters out.

"My eyes ain't sharp enough for this, Maggie," he complained.

"You got the eyes of an eagle. Papa says so."

Oldpappy chuckled. "Does he now."

"What's for dinner?"

"Oh, you'll like this dinner, Maggie."

Little Peggy wrinkled up her nose. "Smells like chicken."

"That's right."

"I don't like chicken soup."

"Not just soup, Maggie. This one's a-roasting, except the neck and wings."

"I hate *roast* chicken, too."

"Does your Oldpappy ever lie to you?"

"Nope."

"Then you best believe me when I tell you this is one chicken dinner that'll make you *glad*. Can't you think of any way that a partickler chicken dinner could make you glad?"

Little Peggy thought and thought, and then she smiled. "Bloody Mary?"

Oldpappy winked. "I always said that was a hen born to make gravy."

Little Peggy hugged him so tight that he made choking sounds, and then they laughed and laughed.

Later that night, long after little Peggy was in bed, they brought Vigor's body home, and Papa and Makepeace set to making a box for him. Alvin Miller hardly looked alive, even when Eleanor showed him the baby. Until she said, "That torch girl. She says that this baby is the seventh son of a seventh son."

Alvin looked around for someone to tell him if it was true.

"Oh, you can trust her," said Mama.

Tears came fresh to Alvin's eyes. "That boy hung on," he said. "There in the water, he hung on long enough."

"He knowed what store you set by that," said Eleanor.

Then Alvin reached for the baby, held him tight, looked down into his eyes. "Nobody named him yet, did they?" he asked.

"Course not," said Eleanor. "Mama named all the other boys, but you always said the seventh son'd have—"

"My own name. Alvin. Seventh son of a seventh son, with the same name as his father. Alvin Junior." He looked around him, then turned to face toward the river, way off in the nighttime forest. "Hear that, you Hatrack River? His name is Alvin, and you didn't kill him after all."

Soon they brought in the box, and laid out Vigor's body with candles, to stand for the fire of life that had left him. Alvin held up the baby, over the coffin. "Look on your brother," he whispered to the infant.

"That baby can't see nothing yet, Papa," said David.

"That ain't so, David," said Alvin. "He don't *know* what he's seeing, but his eyes can see. And when he gets old enough to hear the story of his birth, I'm going to tell him that his own eyes saw his brother Vigor, who gave his life for this baby's sake."

It was two weeks before Faith was well enough to travel. But Alvin saw to it that he and his boys worked hard for their keep. They cleared a good spot of land, chopped the winter's firewood, set some charcoal heaps for Makepeace Smith, and widened the road. They also felled four big trees and made a strong bridge across the Hatrack River, a covered bridge so that even in a rainstorm people could cross that river without a drop of water touching them.

Vigor's grave was the third one there, beside little Peggy's two dead sisters. The family paid respects and prayed there on the morning that they left. Then they got in their wagon and rode off westward. "But we leave a part of ourselves here always," said Faith, and Alvin nodded.

Little Peggy watched them go, then ran up into the attic, opened the box, and held little Alvin's caul in her hand. No danger, for now at least. Safe for now. She put the caul away and closed the lid. You better be something, baby Alvin, she said, or else you caused a powerful lot of trouble for nothing.

DAMON KNIGHT

Strangers on Paradise

A multitalented professional whose career as writer, editor, critic, and anthologist spans almost fifty years, Damon Knight has long been a major shaping force in the development of modern science fiction. He wrote the first important book of SF criticism, *In Search of Wonder,* and won a Hugo Award for it. He was the founder of the Science Fiction Writers of America, cofounder of the prestigious Milford Writer's Conference, and, with his wife, writer Kate Wilhelm, is still deeply involved in the operation of the Clarion workshop for new young writers. He was the editor of *Orbit,* the longest-running original anthology series in the history of science fiction, and has also produced important works of genre history such as *The Futurians.* His other books include the novels *A for Anything, The Other Foot,* and *Hell's Pavement,* and the collections *Rule Golden and Other Stories* and *The Best of Damon Knight,* as well as dozens of anthologies. His most recent books are the novels *The Man in the Tree* and *CV.* Upcoming is another novel, *The Mirror,* from Tor. Knight lives with his family in Eugene, Oregon.

As a writer, Knight established a reputation as one of the very finest short-story writers ever to work in the genre, and although he has produced relatively few stories in recent years, he has not lost any of his skill—as the incisive story that follows aptly demonstrates.

STRANGERS ON PARADISE

Damon Knight

Paradise was the name of the planet. Once it had been called something else, but nobody knew what.

From this distance, it was a warm blue cloud-speckled globe turning in darkness. Selby viewed it in a holotube, not directly, because there was no porthole in the isolation room, but he thought he knew how the first settlers had felt ninety years ago, seeing it for the first time after their long voyage. He felt much the same way himself; he had been in medical isolation on the entryport satellite for three months, waiting to get to the place he had dreamed of with hopeless longing all his life: a place without disease, without violence, a world that had never known the sin of Cain.

Selby (Howard W., Ph.D.) was a slender, balding man in his forties, an Irishman, a reformed drunkard, an unsuccessful poet, a professor of English literature at the University of Toronto. One of his particular interests was the work of Eleanor Petryk, the expatriate lyric poet who had lived on Paradise for thirty years, the last ten of them silent. After Petryk's death in 2106, he had applied for a grant from the International Endowment to write a definitive critical biography of Petryk, and in two years of negotiation he had succeeded in gaining entry to Paradise. It was, he knew, going to be the peak experience of his life.

The Paradisans had pumped out his blood and replaced it with something that, they assured him, was just as efficient at carrying oxygen but was not an appetizing medium for microbes. They had taken samples of his body fluids and snippets of his flesh from here and there. He had been scanned by a dozen machines, and they had given him injections for twenty diseases and parasites they said he was carrying. Their faces, in the holotubes, had smiled pityingly when he told them he had had a clean bill of health when he was checked out in Houston.

It was like being in a hospital, except that only machines touched him, and he saw human faces only in the holotube. He had spent the time reading and watching canned information films of happy, healthy people working and playing in the golden sunlight. Their faces were smooth, their eyes bright. The burden of the films was always the same: how happy the Paradisans were, how fulfilling their lives, how proud of the world they were building.

The books were a little more informative. The planet had two large continents, one inhabited, the other desert (although from space it looked much like the other), plus a few rocky, uninhabitable island chains. The axial tilt was seven degrees. The seasons were mild. The planet was geologically inactive; there were no volcanoes, and earthquakes were unknown. The low, rounded hills offered no impediment to the global circulation of air. The soil was rich. And there was no disease.

This morning, after his hospital breakfast of orange juice, oatmeal, and toast, they had told him he would be released at noon. And that was like a hospital, too; it was almost two o'clock now, and he was still here.

"Mr. Selby."

He turned, saw the woman's smiling face in the holotube. "Yes?"

"We are ready for you now. Will you walk into the anteroom?"

"With the greatest of pleasure."

The door swung open. Selby entered; the door closed behind him. The clothes he had been wearing when he arrived were on a rack; they were newly cleaned and, doubtless, disinfected. Watched by an eye on the wall, he took off his pajamas and dressed. He felt like an invalid after a long illness; the shoes and belt were unfamiliar objects.

The outer door opened. Beyond stood the nurse in her green cap and bright smile; behind her was a man in a yellow jumpsuit.

"Mr. Selby, I'm John Ledbitter. I'll be taking you groundside as soon as you're thumbed out."

There were three forms to thumbprint, with multiple copies. "Thank you, Mr. Selby," said the nurse. "It's been a pleasure to have you with us. We hope you will enjoy your stay on Paradise."

"Thank you."

"Please." That was what they said instead of "You're welcome"; it was short for "Please don't mention it," but it was hard to get used to.

"This way." He followed Ledbitter down a long corridor in which they met no one. They got into an elevator. "Hang on, please." Selby put his arms through the straps. The elevator fell away; when it stopped, they were floating, weightless.

Ledbitter took his arm to help him out of the elevator. Alarm bells were ringing somewhere. "This way." They pulled themselves along a cord to the jump box, a cubicle as big as Selby's hospital room. "Please lie down here."

They lay side by side on narrow cots. Ledbitter put up the padded rails. "Legs and arms apart, please, head straight. Make sure you are comfortable. Are you ready?"

"Yes."

Ledbitter opened the control box by his side, watching the instruments in the ceiling. "On my three," he said. "One . . . two . . ."

Selby felt a sudden increase in weight as the satellite accelerated to match the speed of the planetary surface. After a long time the control lights blinked; the cot sprang up against him. They were on Paradise.

The jump boxes, more properly Henderson-Rosenberg devices, had made interplanetary and interstellar travel amost instantaneous—not quite, because vectors at sending and receiving stations had to be matched, but near enough. The hitch was that you couldn't get anywhere by jump box unless someone had been there before and brought a receiving station. That meant that interstellar exploration had to proceed by conventional means: the Taylor Drive at first, then impulse engines; round trips, even to nearby stars, took twenty years or more. Paradise, colonized ninety years ago by a Geneite sect from the United States, had been the first Earthlike planet to be discovered; it was still the only one, and it was off-limits to Earthlings except on special occasions. There was not much the governments of Earth could do about that.

A uniformed woman, who said she had been assigned as his guide, took him in tow. Her name was Helga Sonnstein. She was magnificently built, clearskinned and rosy, like all the other Paradisans he had seen so far.

They walked to the hotel on clean streets, under monorails that swooped gracefully overhead. The passersby were beautifully dressed; some of them glanced curiously at Selby. The air was so pure and fresh that simply breathing was a pleasure. The sky over the white buildings was a robin's-egg blue. The disorientation Selby felt was somehow less than he had expected.

In his room, he looked up Karen McMorrow's code. Her face in the holotube was pleasant, but she did not smile. "Welcome to Paradise, Mr. Selby. Are you enjoying your visit?"

"Very much, so far."

"Can you tell me when you would like to come to the Cottage?"

"Whenever it's convenient for you, Miss McMorrow."

"Unfortunately, there is some family business I must take care of. In two or three days?"

"That will be perfectly fine. I have some other people to interview, and I'd like to see something of the city while I'm here."

"Until later, then. I'm sorry for this delay."

"Please," said Selby.

That afternoon Miss Sonnstein took him around the city. And it was all true. The Paradisans were happy, healthy, energetic, and cheerful. He had never seen so many unlined faces, so many clear eyes and bright smiles. Even the patients in the hospital looked healthy. They were accident victims for the most part—broken legs, cuts. He was just beginning to understand what it was like to live on a world where there was no infectious disease and never had been.

He liked the Paradisans—they were immensely friendly, warm, outgoing people. It was impossible not to like them. And at the same time he envied and resented them. He understood why, but he couldn't stop.

On his second day he talked to Petryk's editor at the state publishing house, an amiable man named Truro, who took him to lunch and gave him a handsomely bound copy of Petryk's *Collected Poems*.

During lunch—lake trout, apparently as much a delicacy here as it was in North America—Truro drew him out about his academic background, his publications, his plans for the future. "We would certainly like to publish your book about Eleanor," he said. "In fact, if it were possible, we would be even happier to publish it here first."

Selby explained his arrangements with Macmillan Schuster. Truro said, "But there's no contract yet?"

Selby, intrigued by the direction the conversation was taking, admitted that there was none.

"Well, let's see how things turn out," said Truro. Back in the office, he showed Selby photos of Petryk taken after the famous one, the only one that had appeared on Earth. She was a thin-faced woman, fragile-looking. Her hair was a little grayer, the face more lined—sadder, perhaps.

"Is there any unpublished work?" Selby asked.

"None that she wanted to preserve. She was very selective, and of course her poems sold quite well here—not as much as on Earth, but she made a comfortable living."

"What about the silence—the last ten years?"

"It was her choice. She no longer wanted to write poems. She turned to sculpture instead—wood carvings, mostly. You'll see when you go out to the Cottage."

Afterward Truro arranged for him to see Potter Hargrove, Petryk's divorced husband. Hargrove was in his seventies, white-haired and red-faced. He was the official in charge of what they called the New Lands Program: satellite cities were being built by teams of young volunteers—the ground cleared and sterilized, terrestrial plantings made. Hargrove had a great deal to say about this.

With some difficulty, Selby turned the conversation to Eleanor Petryk.

"How did she happen to get permission to live on Paradise, Mr. Hargrove? I've always been curious."

"It's been our policy to admit occasional immigrants, when we think they

have something we lack. *Very* occasional. We don't publicize it. I'm sure
you understand.''

"Yes, of course.'' Selby collected his thoughts. "What was she like,
those last ten years?''

"I don't know. We were divorced five years before that. I remarried.
Afterward, Eleanor became rather isolated.''

When Selby stood up to leave, Hargrove said, "Have you an hour or so?
I'd like to show you something.''

They got into a comfortable four-seat runabout and drove north, through
the commercial district, then suburban streets. Hargrove parked the runabout, and they walked down a dirt road past a cluster of farm buildings.
The sky was an innocent blue; the sun was warm. An insect buzzed past
Selby's ear; he turned and saw that it was a honeybee. Ahead was a field
of corn.

The waves of green rolled away from them to the horizon, rippling in the
wind. Every stalk, every leaf, was perfect.

"No weeds," said Selby. Hargrove smiled with satisfaction. "That's the
beautiful part," he said. "No weeds, because any Earth plant poisons the
soil for them. Not only that, but no pests, rusts, blights. The native organisms
are incompatible. We can't eat them, and they can't eat us.''

"It seems very antiseptic," Selby said.

"Well, that may seem strange to you, but the word comes from the Greek
sepsis, which means 'putrid'. I don't think we have to apologize for being
against putrefaction. We came here without bringing any Earth diseases or
parasites with us, and that means there is *nothing* that can attack us. It will
take hundreds of thousands of years for the local organisms to adapt to us,
if they ever do.''

"And then?''

Hargrove shrugged. "Maybe we'll find another planet.''

"What if there aren't any other suitable planets within reach? Wasn't it
just luck that you found this one?''

"Not luck. It was God's will, Mr. Selby.''

Hargrove had given him the names of four old friend of Petryk's who were
still alive. After some parleying on the holo, Selby arranged to meet them
together in the home of Mark Andrevon, a novelist well known on Paradise
in the sixties. (The present year, by Paradisan reckoning, was A.L. 91.) The
others were Theodore Bonwait, a painter; Alice Orr, a poet and ceramicist;
and Ruth-Joan Wellman, another poet.

At the beginning of the evening, Andrevon was pugnacious about what
he termed his neglect in the English-Speaking Union; he told Selby in considerable detail about his literary honors and the editions of his works. This

was familiar talk to Selby; he gathered that Andrevon was now little read even here. He managed to soothe the disgruntled author and turn the conversation to Petryk's early years on Paradise.

"Poets don't actually like each other much, I'm sure you know that, Mr. Selby," said Ruth-Joan Wellman. "We got along fairly well, though—we were all young and unheard of then, and we used to get together and cook spaghetti, that sort of thing. Then Ellie got married, and . . ."

"Mr. Hargrove didn't care for her friends?"

"Something like that," said Theodore Bonwait. "Well, there were more demands on her time, too. It was a rather strong attachment at first. We saw them occasionally, at parties and openings, that sort of thing."

"What was she like then, can you tell me? What was your impression?"

They thought about it. Talented, they agreed, a little vague about practical matters ("which was why it seemed so lucky for her to marry Potter," said Alice Orr, "but it didn't work out"), very charming sometimes, but a sharp-tongued critic. Selby took notes. He got them to tell him where they had all lived, where they had met, in what years. Three of them admitted that they had some of Petryk's letters, and promised to send him copies.

After another day or so, Truro called him and asked him to come to the office. Selby felt that something was in the wind.

"Mr. Selby," Truro said, "you know visitors like yourself are so rare that we feel we have to take as much advantage of them as we can. This is a young world, we haven't paid as much attention as we might to literary and artistic matters. I wonder if you have ever thought of staying with us?"

Selby's heart gave a jolt. "Do you mean permanently?" he said. "I didn't think there was any chance—"

"Well, I've been talking to Potter Hargrove, and he thinks something might be arranged. This is all in confidence, of course, and I don't want you to make up your mind hurriedly. Think it over."

"I really don't know what to say. I'm surprised—I mean, I was sure I had offended Mr. Hargrove."

"Oh, no, he was favorably impressed. He likes your spice."

"I'm sorry?"

"Don't you have that expression? Your, how shall I say it, ability to stand up for yourself. He's the older generation, you know—son of a pioneer. They respect someone who speaks his mind."

Selby, out on the street, felt an incredulous joy. Of all the billions on Earth, how many would ever be offered such a prize?

Later, with Helga Sonnstein, he visited an elementary school. "Did you ever have a cold?" a serious eight-year-old girl asked him.

"Yes, many times."

"What was it like?"

"Well, your nose runs, you cough and sneeze a lot, and your head feels stuffy. Sometimes you have a little fever, and your bones ache."

"That's *awful*," she said, and her small face expressed something between commiseration and disbelief.

Well, it *was* awful, and a cold was the least of it—"no worse than a bad cold," people used to say about syphilis. Thank God she had not asked about that.

He felt healthy himself, and in fact he was healthy—even before the Paradisan treatments, he had always considered himself healthy. But his medical history, he knew, would have looked like a catalog of horrors to these people—influenza, mumps, cerebrospinal meningitis once, various rashes, dysentery several times (something you had to expect if you traveled). You took it for granted—all those swellings and oozings—it was part of the game. What would it be like to go back to that now?

Miss Sonnstein took him to the university, introduced him to several people, and left him there for the afternoon. Selby talked to the head of the English department, a vaguely hearty man named Quincy; nothing was said to suggest that he might be offered a job if he decided to remain, but Selby's instinct told him that he was being inspected with that end in view.

Afterward he visited the natural history museum and talked to a professor named Morrison who was a specialist in native life-forms.

The plants and animals of Paradise were unlike anything on Earth. The "trees" were scaly, bulbous-bottomed things, some with lacy fronds waving sixty feet overhead, others with cup-shaped leaves that tilted individually to follow the sun. There were no large predators, Morrison assured him; it would be perfectly safe to go into the boonies, providing he did not run out of food. There were slender, active animals with bucket-shaped noses climbing in the forests or burrowing in the ground, and there were things that were not exactly insects; one species had a fixed wing like a maple seedpod—it spiraled down from the treetops, eating other airborne creatures on the way, and then climbed up again.

Of the dominant species, the aborigines, Morrison's department had only bones, not even reconstructions. They had been upright, about five feet tall, large-skulled, possibly mammalian. The eyeholes of their skulls were canted. The bones of their feet were peculiar, bent like the footbones of horses or cattle. "I wonder what they looked like," Selby said.

Morrison smiled. He was a little man with a brushy black mustache. "Not very attractive, I'm afraid. We do have their stone carvings, and some wall pictures and inscriptions." He showed Selby an album of photographs. The carvings, of what looked like weathered granite, showed angular creatures with blunt muzzles. The paintings were the same, but the expression of the eyes was startlingly human. Around some of the paintings were columns of written characters that looked like clusters of tiny hoofprints.

"You can't translate these?"

"Not without a Rosetta stone. That's the pity of it—if only we'd got here just a little earlier."

"How long ago did they die off?"

"Probably not more than a few centuries. We find their skeletons buried in the trunks of trees. Very well preserved. About what happened there are various theories. The likeliest thing is plague, but some people think there was a climatic change."

Then Selby saw the genetics laboratory. They were working on some alterations in the immune system, they said, which they hoped in thirty years would make it possible to abandon the allergy treatments that all children now got from the cradle up. "Here's something else that's quite interesting," said the head of the department, a blonde woman named Reynolds. She showed him white rabbits in a row of cages. Sunlight came through the open door; beyond was a loading dock, where a man with a Y-lift was hoisting up a bale of feed.

"These are Lyman Whites, a standard strain," said Miss Reynolds. "Do you notice anything unusual about them?"

"They look very healthy," said Selby.

"Nothing else?"

"No."

She smiled. "These rabbits were bred from genetic material spliced with bits of DNA from native organisms. The object was to see if we could enable them to digest native proteins. That has been only partly successful, but something completely unexpected happened. We seem to have interrupted a series of cues that turns on the aging process. The rabbits do not age past maturity. This pair, and those in the next cage, are twenty-one years old."

"Immortal rabbits?"

"No, we can't say that. All we can say is that they have lived twenty-one years. That is three times their normal span. Let's see what happens in another fifty or a hundred years."

As they left the room, Selby asked, "Are you thinking of applying this discovery to human beings?"

"It has been discussed. We don't know enough yet. We have tried to replicate the effect in rhesus monkeys, but so far without success."

"If you should find that this procedure is possible in human beings, do you think it would be wise?"

She stopped and faced him. "Yes, why not? If you are miserable and ill, I can understand why you would not want to live a long time. But if you are happy and productive, why not? Why should people have to grow old and die?"

She seemed to want his approval. Selby said, "But, if nobody ever died, you'd have to stop having children. The world wouldn't be big enough."

She smiled again. "This is a very big world, Mr. Selby."

Selby had seen in Claire Reynolds's eyes a certain guarded interest; he had seen it before in Paradisan women, including Helga Sonnstein. He did not know how to account for it. He was shorter than the average Paradisan male, not as robust; he had had to be purged of a dozen or two loathsome diseases before he could set foot on Paradise. Perhaps that was it: perhaps he was interesting to women because he was unlike all the other men they knew.

He called the next day and asked Miss Reynolds to dinner. Her face in the tube looked surprised, then pleased. "Yes, that would be very nice," she said.

An hour later he had a call from Karen McMorrow; she was free now to welcome him to the Cottage, and would be glad to see him that afternoon. Selby recognized the workings of that law of the universe that tends to bring about a desired result at the least convenient time; he called the laboratory, left a message of regret, and boarded the intercity tube for the town where Eleanor Petryk had lived and died.

The tube, a transparent cylinder suspended from pylons, ran up and over the rolling hills. The crystal windows were open; sweet flower scents drifted in, and behind them darker smells, unfamiliar and disturbing. Selby felt a thrill of excitement when he realized that he was looking at the countryside with new eyes, not as a tourist but as someone who might make this strange land his home.

They passed mile after mile of growing crops—corn, soybeans, then acres of beans, squash, peas; then fallow fields and grazing land in which the traceries of buried ruins could be seen.

After a while the cultivated fields began to thin out, and Selby saw the boonies for the first time. The tall fronded plants looked like anachronisms from the Carboniferous. The forests stopped at the borders of the fields as if they had been cut with a knife.

Provo was now a town of about a hundred thousand; when Eleanor Petryk had first lived there, it had been only a crossroads at the edge of the boonies. Selby got off the tube in late afternoon. A woman in blue stepped forward. "Mr. Selby."

"Yes,"

"I'm Karen McMorrow. Was your trip pleasant?"

"Very pleasant."

She was a little older than she had looked on the holotube, in her late fifties, perhaps. "Come with me, please." No monorails here; she had a little impulse-powered runabout. They swung off the main street onto a blacktop road that ran between rows of tall maples.

"You were Miss Petryk's companion during her later years?"

"Secretary. Amanuensis." She smiled briefly.

"Did she have many friends in Provo?"

"No. None. She was a very private person. Here we are." She stopped the runabout; they were in a narrow lane with hollyhocks on either side.

The house was a low white-painted wooden building half-hidden by evergreens. Miss McMorrow opened the door and ushered him in. There was a cool, stale odor, the smell of a house unlived in.

The sitting room was dominated by a massive coffee table apparently carved from the cross section of a tree. In the middle of it, in a hollow space, was a stone bowl, and in the bowl, three carved bones.

"Is this native wood?" Selby asked, stooping to run his hand over the polished grain.

"Yes. Redwood, we call it, but it is nothing like the Earth tree. It is not really a tree at all. This was the first piece she carved; there are others in the workroom, through there."

The workroom, a shed attached to the house, was cluttered with wood carvings, some taller than Selby, others small enough to be held in the palm of the hand. The larger ones were curiously tormented shapes, half human and half tree. The smaller ones were animals and children.

"We knew nothing about this," Selby said. "Only that she had gone silent. She never explained?"

"It was her choice."

They went into Petryk's study. Books were in glass-fronted cases, and there were shelves of books and record cubes. A vase with sprays of cherry blossoms was on a windowsill.

"This is where she wrote?"

"Yes. Always in longhand, here, at the table. She wrote in pencil, on yellow paper. She said poems could not be made on machines."

"And all her papers are here?"

"Yes, in these cabinets. Thirty years of work. You will want to look through them?"

"Yes. I'm very grateful."

"Let me show you first where you will eat and sleep, then you can begin. I will come out once a day to see how you are getting on."

In the cabinets were thousands of pages of manuscript—treasures, including ten drafts of the famous poem *Walking the River*. Selby went through them methodically one by one, making copious notes. He worked until he could not see the pages, and fell into bed exhausted every night.

On the third day, Miss McMorrow took him on a trip into the boonies. Dark scents were all around them. The dirt road, such as it was, ended after half a mile; then they walked. "Eleanor often came out here, camping," she said. "Sometimes for a week or more. She liked the solitude." In the gloom of the tall shapes that were not trees, the ground was covered with not-grass and not-ferns. The silence was deep. Faint trails ran off in both directions. "Are these animal runs?" Selby asked.

"No. She made them. They are growing back now. There are no large animals on Paradise."

"I haven't even seen any small ones."

Through the undergrowth he glimpsed a mound of stone on a hill. "What is that?"

"Aborigine ruins. They are all through the boonies."

She followed him as he climbed up to it. The cut stones formed a complex hundreds of yards across. Selby stooped to peer through a doorway. The aborigines had been a small people.

At one corner of the ruins was a toppled stone figure, thirty feet long. The weeds had grown over it, but he could see that the face had been broken away, as if by blows of a hammer.

"What they could have taught us," Selby said.

"What could they have taught us?"

"What it is to be human, perhaps."

"I think we have to decide that for ourselves."

Six weeks went by. Selby was conscious that he now knew more about Eleanor Petryk than anyone on Earth, and also that he did not understand her at all. In the evenings he sometimes went into the workroom and looked at the tormented carved figures. Obviously she had turned to them because she had to do something, and because she could no longer write. But why the silence?

Toward the end, at the back of the last cabinet, Selby found a curious poem.

XC

Tremble at the coming of the light.
Hear the rings rustle on the trees.
Every creature runs away in fright;
Years will pass before the end of night;
Woe to them who drift upon the seas.
Erebus above hears not their pleas;
Repentance he has none upon his height—
Earth will always take what she can seize.

Knights of the sky, throw down your shining spears.
In luxury enjoy your stolen prize.

Let those who will respond to what I write,
Lest all of us forget to count the years.
Empty are the voices, and the eyes
Dead in the coming of that night.

Selby looked at it in puzzlement. It was a sonnet, of sorts, a form that had lapsed into obscurity centuries ago, and one that, to his knowledge, Petryk had never used before in her life. What was more curious was that it was an awkward poem, almost a jingle. Petryk could not possibly have been guilty of it, and yet here it was in her handwriting.

With a sudden thrill of understanding, he looked at the initial letters of the lines. The poem was an acrostic, another forgotten form. It concealed a message, and that was why the poem was awkward—deliberately so, perhaps.

He read the poem again. Its meaning was incredible but clear. They had bombed the planet—probably the other continent, the one that was said to be covered with desert. No doubt it was, now. Blast and radiation would have done for any aborigines there, and a brief nuclear winter would have taken care of the rest. And the title, "XC"—Roman numerals, another forgotten art. Ninety years.

In his anguish, there was one curious phrase that he still did not understand—"Hear the rings rustle," where the expected word was "leaves." Why rings?

Suddenly he thought he knew. He went into the other room and looked at the coffee table. In the hollow, the stone bowl with its carved bones. Around it, the rings. There was a scar where the tree had been cut into, hollowed out; but it had been a big tree even then. He counted the rings outside the scar: the first one was narrow, almost invisible, but it was there. Altogether there were ninety.

The natives had buried their dead in chambers cut from the wood of living trees. Petryk must have found this one on one of her expeditions. And she had left the evidence here, where anyone could see it.

That night Selby thought of Eleanor Petryk, lying sleepless in this house. What could one do with such knowledge? Her answer had been silence, ten years of silence, until she died. But she had left the message behind her, because she could not bear the silence. He cursed her for her frailty; had she never guessed what a burden she had laid on the man who was to read her message, the man who by sheer perverse bad fortune was himself?

In the morning he called Miss McMorrow and told her he was ready to leave. She said good-bye to him at the tube, and he rode back to the city, looking out with bitter hatred at the scars the aborigines had left in the valleys.

He made the rounds to say good-bye to the people he had met. At the genetics laboratory, a pleasant young man told him that Miss Reynolds was not in. "She may have left for the weekend, but I'm not sure. If you'll wait here a few minutes, I'll see if I can find out."

It was a fine day, and the back door was open. Outside stood an impulse-powered pickup, empty.

Selby looked at the rabbits in their cages. He was thinking of something he had run across in one of Eleanor Petryk's old books, a work on mathematics. "Fibonacci numbers were invented by the thirteenth-century Italian mathematician to furnish a model of population growth in rabbits. His assumptions were: 1) it takes rabbits one month from birth to reach maturity; 2) one month after reaching maturity, and every month thereafter, each pair of rabbits will produce another pair of rabbits; and 3) rabbits never die."

As if in a dream, Selby unlatched the cages and took out two rabbits, one a buck, the other a doe heavy with young. He put them under his arms, warm and quivering. He got into the pickup with them and drove northward, past the fields of corn, until he reached the edge of the cultivated land. He walked through the undergrowth to a clearing where tender shoots grew. He put the rabbits down. They snuffed around suspiciously. One hopped, then the other. Presently they were out of sight.

Selby felt as if his blood were fizzing; he was elated and horrified all at once. He drove the pickup to the highway and parked it just outside town. Now he was frozen and did not feel anything at all.

From the hotel he made arrangements for his departure. Miss Sonnstein accompanied him to the jump terminal. "Good-bye, Mr. Selby. I hope you have had a pleasant visit."

"It has been most enlightening, thank you."

"Please," she said.

It was raining in Houston, where Selby bought, for sentimental reasons, a bottle of Old Space Ranger. The shuttle was crowded and smelly; three people were coughing as if their lungs would burst. Black snow was falling in Toronto. Selby let himself into his apartment, feeling as if he had never been away. He got the bottle out of his luggage, filled a glass, and sat for a while looking at it. His notes and the copies of Petryk's papers were in his suitcase, monuments to a book that he now knew would never be written. The doggerel of "XC" ran through his head. Two lines of it, actually, were not so bad:

Empty are the voices, and the eyes
Dead in the coming of that night.

PAT CADIGAN

Pretty Boy Crossover

Pat Cadigan was born in Schenectady, New York, and now lives in Overland Park, Kansas, where she works for Hallmark Cards. One of the best new writers in SF, Cadigan made her first professional sale in 1980, to *New Dimensions*, and soon became a frequent contributor to *Omni*, *The Magazine of Fantasy and Science Fiction*, *Isaac Asimov's Science Fiction Magazine*, and *Shadows*, among other markets. She is the co-editor, along with husband Arnie Fenner, of *Shayol*, perhaps the best of the semiprozines; it was honored with a World Fantasy Award in the "Special Achievement, Non-Professional" category in 1981. She has also served as a World Fantasy Award judge, and as chairwoman of the Nebula Award jury. Her first novel, *Mindplayers*, is forthcoming from Bantam, and she is at work on a second. Her story "Nearly Departed" was in our First Annual Collection, "Rock On" was in our Second Annual Collection, and "Roadside Rescue" was in our Third Annual Collection.

Here she gives us a chilling story—perhaps her finest to date—about the subtle dangers of confusing the shadow and the substance. . . .

PRETTY BOY CROSSOVER

Pat Cadigan

First you see video. Then you wear video. Then you eat video. Then you *be* video.

—The Gospel According to Visual Mark

Watch or Be Watched.

—Pretty Boy Credo

"Who made you?"

"You mean recently?"

Mohawk on the door smiles and takes his picture. "You in. But only you, okay? Don't try to get no friends in, hear that?"

"I hear. And I ain't no fool, fool. I got no friends."

Mohawk leers, leaning forward. "Pretty Boy like you, no friends?"

"Not in this world." He pushes past the Mohawk, ignoring the kissy-kissy sounds. He would like to crack the bridge of the Mohawk's nose and shove bone splinters into his brain but he is lately making more effort to control his temper and besides, he's not sure if any of that bone splinters in the brain stuff is really true. He's a Pretty Boy, all of sixteen years old, and tonight could be his last chance.

The club is Noise. Can't sneak into the bathroom for quiet, the Noise is piped in there, too. Want to get away from Noise? Why? No reason. But this Pretty Boy has learned to think between the beats. Like walking between the raindrops to stay dry, but he can do it. This Pretty Boy thinks things all the time—*all* the time. Subversive (and, he thinks so much that he knows that word *subversive*, sixteen, Pretty, or not). He thinks things like *how many Einsteins have died of hunger and thirst under a hot African sun* and *why can't you remember being born* and *why is music common to every culture* and especially *how much was there going on that he didn't know about and how could he find out about it.*

And this is all the time, one thing after another running in his head, you can see by his eyes. It's for def not much like a Pretty Boy but it's one reason why they want him. That he *is* a Pretty Boy is another and one reason why they're halfway home getting him.

He knows all about them. Everybody knows about them and everybody wants them to pause, look twice, and cough up a card that says, Yes, we see possibilities, please come to the following address during regular business hours on the next regular business day for regular further review. Everyone wants it but this Pretty Boy, who once got five cards in a night and tore them all up. But here he is, still a Pretty Boy. He thinks enough to know this is a failing in himself, that he likes being Pretty and chased and that is how they could end up getting him after all and that's b-b-b-bad. When he thinks about it, he thinks it with the stutter. B-b-b-bad. B-b-b-bad for him because he doesn't God help him want it, no, no, n-n-n-no. Which may make him the strangest Pretty Boy still live tonight and every night.

Still live and standing in the club where only the Prettiest Pretty Boys can get in any more. Pretty Girls are too easy, they've got to be better than Pretty and besides, Pretty Boys like to be Pretty all alone, no help thank you so much. This Pretty Boy doesn't mind Pretty Girls or any other kind of girls. Lately, though he has begun to wonder how much longer it will be for him. Two years? Possibly a little longer? By three it will be for def over and the Mohawk on the door will as soon spit in his face as leer in it.

If they don't get to him.

And if they *do* get to him, then it's never over and he can be wherever he chooses to be and wherever that is will be the center of the universe. They promise it, unlimited access in your free hours and endless hot season, endless youth. Pretty Boy Heaven, and to get there, they say, you don't even really have to die.

He looks up to the dj's roost, far above the bobbing, boogieing crowd on the dance floor. They still call them djs even though they aren't discs any more, they're chips and there's more than just sound on a lot of them. The great hyper-program, he's been told, the ultimate of ultimates, a short walk from there to the fourth dimension. He suspects this stuff comes from low-steppers shilling for them, hoping they'll get auditioned if they do a good enough shuck job. Nobody knows what it's really like except the ones who are there and you can't trust them, he figures. Because maybe they *aren't*, any more. Not really.

The dj sees his Pretty upturned face, recognizes him even though it's been awhile since he's come back here. Part of it was wanting to stay away from them and part of it was that the thug on the door might not let him in. And then, of course, he *had* to come, to see if he could get in, to see if anyone still wanted him. What was the point of Pretty if there was nobody to care and watch and pursue? Even now, he is almost sure he can feel the room rearranging itself around his presence in it and the dj confirms this is true by holding up a chip and pointing it to the left.

They are squatting on the make-believe stairs by the screen, reminding him of pigeons plotting to take over the world. He doesn't look too long, doesn't want to give them the idea he'd like to talk. But as he turns away, one, the younger man, starts to get up. The older man and the woman pull him back.

He pretends a big interest in the figures lining the nearest wall. Some are Pretty, some are female, some are undecided, some are very bizarre, or wealthy, or just charity cases. They all notice him and adjust themselves for his perusal.

Then one end of the room lights up with color and new noise. Bodies dance and stumble back from the screen where images are forming to rough music.

It's Bobby, he realizes.

A moment later, there's Bobby's face on the screen, sixteen feet high, even Prettier than he'd been when he was loose among the mortals. The sight of Bobby's Pretty-Pretty face fills him with anger and dismay and a feeling of loss so great he would strike anyone who spoke Bobby's name without his permission.

Bobby's lovely slate-grey eyes scan the room. They've told him senses are heightened after you make the change and go over but he's not so sure how that's supposed to work. Bobby looks kind of blind up there on the screen. A few people wave at Bobby—the dorks they let in so the rest can have someone to be hip in front of—but Bobby's eyes move slowly back and forth, back and forth, and then stop, looking right at him.

"Ah . . ." Bobby whispers it, long and drawn out. "Aaaaaahhhh."

He lifts his chin belligerently and stares back at Bobby.

"You don't have to die any more," Bobby says silkily. Music bounces under his words. "It's beautiful in here. The dreams can be as real as you want them to be. And if you want to be, you can be with me."

He knows the commercial is not aimed only at him but it doesn't matter. This is *Bobby*. Bobby's voice seems to be pouring over him, caressing him, and it feels too much like a taunt. The night before Bobby went over, he tried to talk him out of it, knowing it wouldn't work. If they'd actually refused him, Bobby would have killed himself, like Franco had.

But now Bobby would live forever and ever, if you believed what they said. The music comes up louder but Bobby's eyes are still on him. He sees Bobby mouth his name.

"Can you really see me, Bobby?" he says. His voice doesn't make it over the music but if Bobby's senses are so heightened, maybe he hears it anyway. If he does, he doesn't choose to answer. The music is a bumped up remix of a song Bobby used to party-till-he-puked to. The giant Bobby-face fades away to be replaced with a whole Bobby, somewhat larger than life, dancing better than the old Bobby ever could, whirling along changing scenes of streets, rooftops and beaches. The locales are nothing special but Bobby never did have all that much imagination, never wanted to go to Mars or even to the South Pole, always just to the hottest club. Always he liked being the exotic in plain surroundings and he still likes it. He always loved to get the looks. To be watched, worshipped, pursued. Yeah. He can see this is Bobby-heaven. The whole world will be giving him the looks now.

The background on the screen goes from street to the inside of a club; *this* club, only larger, better, with an even hipper crowd, and Bobby shaking it with them. Half the real crowd is forgetting to dance now because they're watching Bobby, hoping he's put some of them into his video. Yeah, that's the dream, get yourself remixed in the extended dance version.

His own attention drifts to the fake stairs that don't lead anywhere. They're still perched on them, the only people who are watching *him* instead of Bobby. The woman, looking overaged in a purple plastic sac-suit, is fingering a card.

He looks up at Bobby again. Bobby is dancing in place and looking back at him, or so it seems. Bobby's lips move soundlessly but so precisely he can read the words: *This can be you. Never get old, never get tired, it's never last call, nothing happens unless you want it to and it could be you. You. You.* Bobby's hands point to him on the beat. *You. You. You.*

Bobby. Can you really see me?

Bobby suddenly breaks into laughter and turns away, shaking it some more.

He sees the Mohawk from the door pushing his way through the crowd, the real crowd, and he gets anxious. The Mohawk goes straight for the stairs, where they make room for him, rubbing the bristly red strip of hair running down the center of his head as though they were greeting a favored pet. The Mohawk looks as satisfied as a professional glutton after a foodrace victory. He wonders what they promised the Mohawk for letting him in. Maybe some kind of limited contract. Maybe even a try-out.

Now they are all watching him together. Defiantly, he touches a tall girl dancing nearby and joins her rhythm. She smiles down at him, moving between him and them purely by chance but it endears her to him anyway. She is wearing a flap of translucent rag over secondskins, like an old-time showgirl. Over six feet tall, not beautiful with that nose, not even pretty, but they let her in so she could be tall. She probably doesn't know that; she probably doesn't know anything that goes on and never really will. For that reason, he can forgive her the hard-tech orange hair.

A Rude Boy brushes against him in the course of a dervish turn, asking acknowledgement by ignoring him. Rude Boys haven't changed in more decades than anyone's kept track of, as though it were the same little group of leathered and chained troopers buggering their way down the years. The Rude Boy isn't dancing with anyone. Rude Boys never do. But this one could be handy, in case of an emergency.

The girl is dancing hard, smiling at him. He smiles back, moving slightly to her right, watching Bobby possibly watching him. He still can't tell if Bobby really sees anything. The scene behind Bobby is still a double of the club, getting hipper and hipper if that's possible. The music keeps snapping back to its first peak passage. Then Bobby gestures like God and he sees *himself*. He is dancing next to Bobby, Prettier than he ever could be, just the way they promise. Bobby doesn't look at the phantom but at him where he really is, lips moving again. *If you want to be, you can be with me. And so can she.*

His tall partner appears next to the phantom of himself. She is also much improved, though still not Pretty, or even pretty. The real girl turns and sees herself and there's no mistaking the delight in her face. Queen of the Hop for a minute or two. Then Bobby sends her image away so that it's just the two of them, two Pretty Boys dancing the night away, private party, stranger go find your own good time. How it used to be sometimes in real life, between just the two of them. He remembers hard.

''B-b-b-bobby!'' he yells, the old stutter reappearing. Bobby's image seems to give a jump, as though he finally heard. He forgets everything, the girl, the Rude Boy, the Mohawk, them on the stairs, and plunges through the crowd toward the screen. People fall away from him as though they were re-enacting the Red Sea. He dives for the screen, for Bobby, not caring how it must look to anyone. What would they know about it, any of them. He can't remember in his whole sixteen years ever hearing one person say, *I love my friend*. Not Bobby, not even himself.

He fetches up against the screen like a slap and hangs there, face pressed to the glass. He can't see it now but on the screen Bobby would seem to be looking down at him. Bobby never stops dancing.

The Mohawk comes and peels him off. The others swarm up and take him away. The tall girl watches all this with the expression of a woman who lives upstairs from Cinderella and wears the same shoe size. She stares longingly at the screen. Bobby waves bye-bye and turns away.

''Of course, the process isn't reversible,'' says the older man. The steely hair has a careful blue tint; he has sense enough to stay out of hip clothes.

They have laid him out on a lounger with a tray of refreshments right by him. Probably slap his hand if he reaches for any, he thinks.

''Once you've distilled something to pure information, it just can't be reconstituted in a less efficient form," the woman explains, smiling. There's no warmth to her. A *less efficient form*. If that's what she really thinks, he knows he should be plenty scared of these people. Did she say things like that to Bobby? And did it make him even *more* eager?

"There may be no more exalted a form of existence than to live as sentient information," she goes on. "Though a lot more research must be done before we can offer conversion on a larger scale."

"Yeah?" he says. "Do they know that, Bobby and the rest?"

"Oh, there's nothing to worry about," says the younger man. He looks as though he's still getting over the pain of having outgrown his boogie shoes. "The system's quite perfected. What Grethe means is we want to research more applications for this new form of existence."

"Why not go over yourselves and do that, if it's so *exalted*."

"There are certain things that need to be done on this side," the woman says bitchily. "Just because—"

"Grethe." The older man shakes his head. She pats her slicked-back hair as though to soothe herself and moves away.

"We have other plans for Bobby when he gets tired of being featured in clubs," the older man says. "Even now, we're educating him, adding more data to his basic information configuration—"

"That would mean he ain't really *Bobby* any more, then, huh?"

The man laughs. "Of course he's Bobby. Do you change into someone else every time you learn something new?"

"Can you prove I *don't*?"

The man eyes him warily. "Look. You *saw* him. Was that Bobby?"

"I saw a video of Bobby dancing on a giant screen."

"That *is* Bobby and it will remain Bobby no matter what, whether he's poured into a video screen in a dot pattern or transmitted the length of the universe."

"That what you got in mind for him? Send a message to nowhere and the message is him?"

"We could. But we're not going to. We're introducing him to the concept of higher dimensions. The way he is now, he could possibly break out of the three-dimensional level of existence, pioneer a whole new plane of reality."

"Yeah? And how do you think you're gonna get Bobby to do *that*?"

"We convince him it's entertaining."

He laughs. "That's a good one. Yeah. Entertainment. You get to a higher level of existence and you'll open a club there that only the hippest can get into. It figures."

The older man's face gets hard. "That's what all you Pretty Boys are crazy for, isn't it? Entertainment?"

He looks around. The room must have been a dressing room or something back in the days when bands had been live. Somewhere overhead he can hear the faint noise of the club but he can't tell if Bobby's still on. "You call this entertainment?"

"I'm tired of this little prick," the woman chimes in. "He's thrown away opportunities other people would kill for—"

He makes a rude noise. "Yeah, we'd all kill to be someone's data chip. You think I really believe Bobby's real just because I can see him on a *screen*?"

The older man turns to the younger one. "Phone up and have them pipe Bobby down here." Then he swings the lounger around so it faces a nice modern screen implanted in a shored-up cement-block wall.

"Bobby will join us shortly. Then he can tell you whether he's real or not himself. How will that be for you?"

He stares hard at the screen, ignoring the man, waiting for Bobby's image to appear. As though they really bothered to communicate regularly with Bobby this way. Feed in that kind of data and memory and Bobby'll believe it. He shifts uncomfortably, suddenly wondering how far he could get if he moved fast enough.

"My *boy*," says Bobby's sweet voice from the speaker on either side of the screen and he forces himself to keep looking as Bobby fades in, presenting himself on the same kind of lounger and looking mildly exerted, as though he's just come off the dance floor for real. "Saw you shakin' it upstairs awhile ago. You haven't been here for such a long time. What's the story?"

He opens his mouth but there's no sound. Bobby looks at him with boundless patience and indulgence. So Pretty, hair the perfect shade now and not a bit dry from the dyes and lighteners, skin flawless and shining like a healthy angel. Overnight angel, just like the old song.

"My *boy*," says Bobby. "Are you struck, like, shy or *dead*?"

He closes his mouth, takes one breath. "I don't like it, Bobby. I don't like it this way."

"Of course not, lover. You're the Watcher, not the Watchee, that's why. Get yourself picked up for a season or two and your disposition will *change*."

"You really like it, Bobby, being a blip on a chip?"

"Blip on a chip, your ass. I'm a universe now. I'm, like, *everything*. And, hey, dig—I'm on every channel." Bobby laughed. "I'm happy I'm sad!"

"S-A-D," comes in the older man. "Self-Aware Data."

"Ooo-eee," he says. "Too clever for me. Can I get out of here now?"

"What's your hurry?" Bobby pouts. "Just because I went over you don't love me any more?"

"You always were screwed up about that, Bobby. Do you know the difference between being loved and being watched?"

"Sophisticated boy," Bobby says. "So wise, so learned. So fully packed. On this side, there *is* no difference. Maybe there never was. If you love me, you watch me. If you don't look, you don't care and if you don't care I don't matter. If I don't matter, I don't exist. Right?"

He shakes his head.

"No, my boy, I *am* right." Bobby laughs. "You believe I'm right, because if you *didn't*, you wouldn't come shaking your Pretty Boy ass in a place like *this*, now, would you? You *like* to be watched, get seen. You see me, I see you. Life goes on."

He looks up at the older man, needing relief from Bobby's pure Prettiness. "How does he see me?"

"Sensors in the equipment. Technical stuff, nothing you care about."

He sighs. He should be upstairs or across town, shaking it with everyone else, living Pretty for as long as he could. Maybe in another few months, this way would begin to look good to him. By then they might be off Pretty Boys and looking for some other type and there he'd be, out in the cold-cold, sliding down the other side of his peak and no one would *want* him. Shut out of something going on that he might want to know about after all. Can he face it? He glances at the younger man. All grown up and no place to glow. Yeah, but can *he* face it?

He doesn't know. Used to be there wasn't much of a choice and now that there is, it only seems to make it worse. Bobby's image looks like it's studying him for some kind of sign, Pretty eyes bright, hopeful.

The older man leans down and speaks low into his ear. "We need to get you before you're twenty-five, before the brain stops growing. A mind taken from a still-growing brain will blossom and adapt. Some of Bobby's predecessors have made marvelous adaptation to their new medium. Pure video: there's a staff that does nothing all day but watch and interpret their symbols for breakthroughs in thought. And we'll be taking Pretty Boys for as long as they're publicly sought-after. It's the most efficient way to find the best performers, go for the ones everyone wants to see or be. The top of the trend is closest to heaven. And even if you never make a breakthrough, you'll still be entertainment. Not such a bad way to live for a Pretty Boy. Never have to age, to be sick, to lose touch. You spent most of your life young, why learn how to be old? Why learn how to live without all the things you have now—"

He puts his hands over his ears. The older man is still talking and Bobby is saying something and the younger man and the woman come over to try to do something about him. Refreshments are falling off the tray. He struggles out of the lounger and makes for the door.

"Hey, my *boy*," Bobby calls after him. "Gimme a minute here, gimme what the problem is."

He doesn't answer. What can you tell someone made of pure information anyway?

There's a new guy on the front door, bigger and meaner than His Mohawkness but he's only there to keep people out, not to keep anyone *in*. You want to jump ship, go to, you poor un-hip asshole. Even if you are a Pretty Boy. He reads it in the guy's face as he passes from noise into the three A.M. quiet of the street.

They let him go. He doesn't fool himself about that part. They *let* him out of the room because they know all about him. They know he lives like Bobby lived, they know he loves what Bobby loved—the clubs, the admiration, the lust of strangers for his personal magic. He can't say he doesn't love that, because he *does*. He isn't even sure if he loves it more than he ever loved Bobby, or if he loves it more than being alive. Than being live.

And here it is, three A.M., clubbing prime time, and he is moving toward home. Maybe he *is* a poor un-hip asshole after all, no matter what he loves. Too stupid even to stay in the club, let alone grab a ride to heaven. Still he keeps moving, unbothered by the chill but feeling it. Bobby doesn't have to go home in the cold any more, he thinks. Bobby doesn't even have to get through the hours between club-times if he doesn't want to. All times are now prime time for Bobby. Even if he gets unplugged, he'll never know the difference. Poof, it's a day later, poof, it's a year later, poof, you're out for good. Painlessly.

Maybe Bobby has the right idea, he thinks, moving along the empty sidewalk. If he goes over tomorrow, who will notice? Like when he left the dance floor—people will come and fill up the space. Ultimately, it wouldn't make any difference to anyone.

He smiles suddenly. Except *them*. As long as they don't have him, he makes a difference. As long as he has flesh to shake and flaunt and feel with, he makes a pretty goddamn big difference to *them*. Even after they don't want him any more, he will still be the one they didn't get. He rubs his hands together against the chill, feeling the skin rubbing skin, really *feeling* it for the first time in a long time, and he thinks about sixteen million things all at once, maybe one thing for every brain cell he's using, or maybe one thing for every brain cell yet to come.

He keeps moving, holding to the big thought, making a difference, and all the little things they won't be making a program out of. He's lightheaded with joy—he doesn't know what's going to happen.

Neither do they.

ROBERT SILVERBERG

Against Babylon

One of the most prolific authors alive, Robert Silverberg has produced more than 450 fiction and nonfiction books and over 3,000 magazine pieces. Within SF, Silverberg rose to his greatest prominence during the late fifties and early seventies, winning four Nebula awards and a Hugo Award, publishing dozens of major novels and anthologies—1973's *Dying Inside* in particular is widely considered to be one of the best novels of the seventies—and editing *New Dimensions*, perhaps the most influential original anthology series of its time. In 1980, after four years of self-imposed "retirement," Silverberg started writing again, and the first of his new novels, *Lord Valentine's Castle*, became a nationwide bestseller. Silverberg's other books include *The Book of Skulls, Downward to the Earth, Tower of Glass, The World Inside, Born With the Dead, Shadrach in the Furnace, Lord of Darkness* (a historical novel), and *Valentine Pontifex*, the sequel to *Lord Valentine's Castle*. His collections include *Unfamiliar Territory, Capricorn Games, Majipoor Chronicles, The Best of Robert Silverberg*, and *At the Conglomeroid Cocktail Party*. His most recent books are the novels *Tom O'Bedlam* and *Star of Gypsies*, and the collection *Beyond the Safe Zone*. His story "Multiples" was in our First Annual Collection, "The Affair" was in our Second Annual Collection, and "Sailing To Byzantium"—which won a Nebula Award in 1986—was in our Third Annual Collection.

Here he gives us a gripping study of the different *kinds* of conflagration. . . .

AGAINST BABYLON

Robert Silverberg

Carmichael flew in from New Mexico that morning, and the first thing they told him when he put his little plane down at Burbank was that fires were burning out of control all around the Los Angeles basin. He was needed bad, they told him. It was late October, the height of the brushfire season in Southern California, and a hot, hard, dry wind was blowing out of the desert, and the last time it had rained was the fifth of April. He phoned the district supervisor right away, and the district supervisor told him, "Get your ass out here on the line double fast, Mike."

"Where do you want me?"

"The worst one's just above Chatsworth. We've got planes loaded and ready to go out of Van Nuys Airport."

"I need time to pee and to phone my wife. I'll be in Van Nuys in fifteen, okay?"

He was so tired that he could feel it in his teeth. It was nine in the morning, and he'd been flying since half past four, and it had been rough all the way, getting pushed around by that same fierce wind out of the heart of the continent that was now threatening to fan the flames in L.A. At this moment all he wanted was home and shower and Cindy and bed. But Carmichael didn't regard fire-fighting work as optional. This time of year, the whole crazy city could go in one big fire storm. There were times he almost wished that it would. He hated this smoggy, tawdry Babylon of a city, its endless tangle of freeways, the strange-looking houses, the filthy air, the thick, choking, glossy foliage everywhere, the drugs, the booze, the divorces, the laziness, the sleaziness, the porno shops and the naked encounter parlors and the massage joints, the weird people wearing their weird clothes and driving their weird cars and cutting their hair in weird ways. There was a cheapness, a trashiness, about everything here, he thought. Even the mansions and the fancy restaurants were that way: hollow, like slick movies sets. He sometimes felt that the trashiness bothered him more than the out-and-out evil. If you kept sight of your own values you could do battle with evil, but trashiness slipped up around you and infiltrated your soul without your even knowing it. He hoped that his sojourn in Los Angeles was not doing that to him. He came from the Valley, and what he meant by the Valley was the great San Joaquin, out behind Bakersfield, and not the little, cluttered San Fernando Valley they had here. But L.A. was Cindy's city, and Cindy loved L.A. and he loved Cindy, and for Cindy's sake he had lived here seven years, up in Laurel Canyon amidst the lush, green shrubbery, and for seven Octobers in a row he had gone out to dump chemical retardants on the annual brushfires, to save the Angelenos from their own idiotic carelessness. You had to accept your responsibilities, Carmichael believed.

The phone rang seven times at the home number before he hung up. Then he tried the little studio where Cindy made her jewelry, but she didn't answer there either, and it was too early to call her at the gallery. That bothered him, not being able to say hello to her right away after his three-day absence and no likely chance for it now for another eight or ten hours. But there was nothing he could do about that.

As soon as he was aloft again he could see the fire not far to the northwest, a greasy black column against the pale sky. And when he stepped from his plane a few minutes later at Van Nuys he felt the blast of sudden heat. The temperature had been in the mid-eighties at Burbank, damned well hot enough for nine in the morning, but here it was over a hundred. He heard the distant roar of flames, the popping and crackling of burning underbrush, the peculiar whistling sound of dry grass catching fire.

The airport looked like a combat center. Planes were coming and going with lunatic frenzy, and they were lunatic planes, too, antiques of every sort, forty and fifty years old and even older, converted B-17 Flying Fortresses and DC-3's and a Douglas Invader and, to Carmichael's astonishment, a Ford Trimotor from the 1930's that had been hauled, maybe, out of some movie studio's collection. Some were equipped with tanks that held fire-retardant chemicals, some were water pumpers, some were mappers with infrared and electronic scanning equipment glistening on their snouts. Harried-looking men and women ran back and forth, shouting into CB handsets, supervising the loading process. Carmichael found his way to Operations HQ, which was full of haggard people staring into computer screens. He knew most of them from other years.

One of the dispatchers said, "We've got a DC-3 waiting for you. You'll dump retardants along this arc, from Ybarra Canyon eastward to Horse Flats. The fire's in the Santa Susana foothills, and so far the wind's from the east, but if it shifts to northerly it's going to take out everything from Chatsworth to Granada Hills and right on down to Ventura Boulevard. And that's only *this* fire."

"How many are there?"

The dispatcher tapped his keyboard. The map of the San Fernando Valley that had been showing disappeared and was replaced by one of the entire Los Angeles basin. Carmichael stared. Three great scarlet streaks indicated fire zones: this one along the Santa Susanas, another nearly as big way off to the east in the grasslands north of the 210 Freeway around Glendora or San Dimas, and a third down in eastern Orange County, back of Anaheim Hills. "Ours is the big one so far," the dispatcher said. "But these other two are only about forty miles apart, and if they should join up somehow—"

"Yeah," Carmichael said. A single wall of fire running along the whole eastern rim of the basin, maybe—with Santa Ana winds blowing, carrying sparks westward across Pasadena, across downtown L.A., across Hollywood, Beverly Hills, all the way to the coast, to Venice, Santa Monica, Malibu. He shivered. Laurel Canyon would go. Everything would go. Worse than Sodom and Gomorrah, worse than the fall of Nineveh. Nothing but ashes for hundreds of miles. "Everybody scared silly of Russian nukes, and a carload of dumb kids tossing cigarettes can do the job just as easily," he said.

"But this wasn't cigarettes, Mike," the dispatcher said.

"No? What then, arson?"

"You haven't heard."

"I've been in New Mexico for the last three days."

"You're the only one in the world who hasn't heard, then."

"For Christ's sake, heard what?"

"About the E.T.'s," said the dispatcher wearily. "They started the fires. Three spaceships landing at six this morning in three different corners of the L.A. basin. The heat of their engines ignited the dry grass."

Carmichael did not smile. "You've got one weird sense of humor, man."

The dispatcher said, "I'm not joking."

"Spaceships? From another world?"

"With critters fifteen feet high onboard," the dispatcher at the next computer said. "They're walking around on the freeways right this minute. Fifteen feet high, Mike."

"Men from Mars?"

"Nobody knows where the hell they came from."

"Jesus Christ, God," Carmichael said.

Wild updrafts from the blaze buffeted the plane as he took it aloft and gave him a few bad moments. But he moved easily and automatically to gain control, pulling the moves out of the underground territories of his nervous system. It was essential, he believed, to have the moves in your fingers, your shoulders, your thighs, rather than in the conscious realms of your brain. Consciousness could get you a long way, but ultimately you had to work out of the underground territories or you were dead.

He felt the plane responding and managed a grin. DC-3's were tough old birds. He loved flying them, though the youngest of them had been manufactured before he was born. He loved flying anything. Flying wasn't what Carmichael did for a living—he didn't actually do anything for a living, not anymore—but flying was what he did. There were months when he spent more time in the air than on the ground, or so it seemed to him, because the hours he spent on the ground often slid by unnoticed, while time in the air was intensified, magnified.

He swung south over Encino and Tarzana before heading up across Canoga Park and Chatsworth into the fire zone. A fine haze of ash masked the sun. Looking down, he could see the tiny houses, the tiny swimming pools, the tiny people scurrying about, desperately trying to hose down their roofs before the flames arrived. So many houses, so many people, filling every inch of space between the sea and the desert, and now it was all in jeopardy. The southbound lanes of Topanga Canyon Boulevard were as jammed with cars, here in midmorning, as the Hollywood Freeway at rush hour. Where were they all going? Away from the fire, yes. Toward the coast, it seemed. Maybe some television preacher had told them there was an ark sitting out there in the Pacific, waiting to carry them to safety while God rained brimstone down on Los Angeles. Maybe there really was. In Los Angeles anything was possible. Invaders from space walking around on the freeways even. Jesus. Jesus. Carmichael hardly knew how to begin thinking about that.

He wondered where Cindy was, what *she* was thinking about it. Most likely she found it very funny. Cindy had a wonderful ability to be amused by things. There was a line of poetry she liked to quote, from that Roman, Virgil: A storm is rising, the ship has sprung a leak, there's a whirlpool to one side and sea monsters on the other, and the captain turns to his men and says, "One day perhaps we'll look back and laugh even at all this." That was Cindy's way, Carmichael thought. The Santa Anas are blowing and three big brushfires are burning and invaders from space have arrived at the same time, and one day perhaps we'll look back and laugh even at all this. His heart overflowed with love for her, and longing. He had never known anything about poetry before he had met her. He closed his eyes a moment and brought her onto the screen of his mind. Thick cascades of jet-black hair; quick, dazzling smile; long, slender, tanned body all aglitter with those amazing rings and necklaces and pendants she designed and fashioned. And her eyes. No one else he knew had eyes like hers, bright with strange mischief, with that altogether original way of seeing that was the thing he most loved about her. *Damn* this fire, just when he'd been away three days! *Damn* the stupid men from Mars!

Where the neat rows and circles of suburban streets ended there was a great open stretch of grassy land, parched by the long summer to the color of a lion's hide, and beyond that were the mountains, and between the grassland and the mountains lay the fire, an enormous, lateral red crest topped by a plume of foul, black smoke. It seemed to already cover hundreds of acres, maybe thousands. A hundred acres of burning brush, Carmichael had heard once, creates as much heat energy as the atomic bomb they dropped on Hiroshima.

Through the crackle of radio static came the voice of the line boss, directing operations from a helicopter hovering at about four o'clock. "DC-3, who are you?"

"Carmichael."

"We're trying to contain it on three sides, Carmichael. You work on the east, Limekiln Canyon, down the flank of Porter Ranch Park. Got it?"

"Got it," Carmichael said.

He flew low, less than a thousand feet. That gave him a good view of the action: sawyers in hard hats and orange shirts chopping burning trees to make them fall toward the fire, bulldozer crews clearing brush ahead of the blaze, shovelers carving firebreaks, helicopters pumping water into isolated tongues of flame. He climbed five hundred feet to avoid a single-engine observer plane, then went up to five hundred more to avoid the smoke and air turbulence of the fire itself. From that altitude he had a clear picture of it, running like a bloody gash from west to east, wider at its western end. Just east of the fire's far tip he saw a circular zone of grassland perhaps a hundred acres in diameter that had already burned out, and precisely at the center of that zone stood something that looked like an aluminum silo, the size of a ten-story building, surrounded at a considerable distance by a cordon of military vehicles. He felt a wave of dizziness rock through his mind. That thing, he realized, had to be the E.T. spaceship.

It had come out of the west in the night, Carmichael thought, floating like a tremendous meteor over Oxnard and Camarillo, sliding toward the western end of the San Fernando Valley, kissing the grass with its exhaust, and leaving a trail of flame behind it. And then it had gently set itself down over there and extinguished its own brushfire in a neat little circle about itself, not caring at all about the blaze it had kindled farther back, and God knows what kind of creatures had come forth from it to inspect Los Angeles. It figured that when the UFO's finally did make a landing out in the open, it would be in L.A. Probably they had chosen it because they had seen it so often on television—didn't all the stories say that UFO people always monitored out TV transmissions? So they saw L.A. on every other show, and they probably figured it was the capital of the world, the perfect place for the first landing. But why, Carmichael wondered, had the bastards needed to pick the height of the fire season to put their ships down here?

He thought of Cindy again, how fascinated she was by all this UFO and E.T. stuff, those books she read, the ideas she had, the way she had looked toward the stars one night when they were camping in Kings Canyon and talked of the beings that must live up there. "I'd love to see them," she said. "I'd love to get to know them and find out what their heads are like."

Los Angeles was full of nut cases who wanted to ride in flying saucers, or claimed they already had, but it didn't sound nutty to Carmichael when Cindy talked that way. She had the Angeleno love of the exotic and the bizarre, yes, but he knew that her soul had never been touched by the crazy corruption here, that she was untainted by the prevailing craving for the weird and irrational that made him loathe the place so much. If she turned her imagination toward the stars, it was out of wonder, not out of madness: It was simply part of her nature, that curiosity, that hunger for what lay outside her experience, to embrace the unknowable. He had had no more belief in E.T.'s than he did in the tooth fairy, but for her sake he had told her that he hoped she'd get her wish. And now the UFO people were really here. He could imagine her, eyes shining, standing at the edge of that cordon staring at the spaceship. Pity he couldn't be with her now, feeling all that excitement surging through her, the joy, the wonder, the magic.

But he had work to do. Swinging the DC-3 back around toward the west, he swooped down as close as he dared to the edge of the fire and hit the release button on his dump lines. Behind him a great crimson cloud spread out: a slurry of ammonium sulfate and water, thick as paint, with a red dye mixed into it so they could tell which areas had been sprayed. The retardant clung in globs to anything and would keep it damp for hours.

Emptying his four five-hundred-gallon tanks quickly, he headed back to Van Nuys to reload. His eyes were throbbing with fatigue, and the stink of the wet charred earth below was filtering through every plate of the old plane. It was not quite noon. He had been up all night. At the airport they had coffee ready, sandwiches, tacos, burritos. While he was waiting for the ground crew to fill his tanks he went inside to call Cindy again, and again there was no answer at home, none at the studio. He phoned the gallery, and the kid who worked there said she hadn't been in touch all morning.

"If you hear from her," Carmichael said, "tell her I'm flying fire control out of Van Nuys on the Chatsworth fire, and I'll be home as soon as things calm down a little. Tell her I miss her, too. And tell her that if I run into an E.T. I'll give it a big hug for her. You got that? Tell her just that."

Across the way in the main hall he saw a crowd gathered around someone carrying a portable television set. Carmichael shouldered his way in just as the announcer was saying, "There has been no sign yet of the occupants of the San Gabriel or Orange County spaceships. But this was the horrifying sight that astounded residents of the Porter Ranch area beheld this morning between nine and ten o'clock." The screen showed two upright tubular figures that looked like squid walking on the tips of their tentacles, moving cautiously through the parking lot of a shopping center, peering this way and that out of enormous yellow, platter-shaped eyes. At least a thousand onlookers were watching them at a wary distance, appearing both repelled and at the same time irresistibly drawn. Now and then the creatures paused to touch their foreheads together in some sort of communion. They moved very daintily, but Carmichael saw that they were taller than the lampposts—twelve feet high, maybe fifteen. Their skins were purplish and leathery looking, with rows of luminescent orange spots glowing along the sides. The camera zoomed in for a closeup, then jiggled and swerved wildly just as an enormously long elastic tongue sprang from the chest of one of the alien beings and whipped out into the crowd. For an instant the only thing visible on the screen was a view of the sky; then Carmichael saw a shot of a stunned-looking girl of about fourteen, caught around the waist by that long tongue, being hoisted into the air and popped like a collected specimen into a narrow green sack. "Teams of the giant creatures roamed the town for nearly an hour," the announcer intoned. "It has definitely been confirmed that between twenty and thirty human hostages were captured before they returned to their space-craft. Meanwhile, fire-fighting activities desperately continue under Santa Ana conditions in the vicinity of all three landing sites, and—"

Carmichael shook his head. Los Angeles, he thought. The kind of people that live here, they walk right up and let the E.T's gobble them like flies.

Maybe they think it's just a movie and everything will be okay by the last reel. And then he remembered that Cindy was the kind of people who would walk right up to one of these E.T.'s. Cindy was the kind of people who lived in Los Angeles, he told himself, except that Cindy was *different*. Somehow.

He went outside. The DC-3 was loaded and ready.

In the forty-five minutes since he had left the fire line, the blaze seemed to have spread noticeably toward the south. This time the line boss had him lay down the retardant from the De Soto Avenue freeway interchange to the northeast corner of Porter Ranch. When he returned to the airport, intending to call Cindy again, a man in military uniform stopped him as he crossed the field and said, "You Mike Carmichael, Laurel Canyon?"

"That's right."

"I've got some troublesome news for you. Let's go inside."

"Suppose you tell me here, okay?"

The officer looked at him strangely. "It's about your wife," he said. "Cynthia Carmichael? That's your wife's name?"

"Come *on*," Carmichael said.

"She's one of the hostages, sir."

His breath went from him as though he had been kicked.

"Where did it happen?" he demanded. "How did they get her?"

The officer gave him a strange, strained smile. "It was the shopping-center lot, Porter Ranch. Maybe you saw some of it on TV."

Carmichael nodded. That girl jerked off her feet by that immense elastic tongue, swept through the air, popped into that green pouch. And Cindy—?

"You saw the part where the creatures were moving around? And then suddenly they were grabbing people, and everyone was running from them? That was when they got her. She was up front when they began grabbing, and maybe she had a chance to get away, but she waited just a little too long. She started to run, I understand, but then she stopped—she looked back at them—she may have called something out to them—and then— well, and then—''

"Then they scooped her up?''

"I have to tell you that they did.''

"I see," Carmichael said stonily.

"One thing all the witnesses agreed, she didn't panic, she didn't scream. She was very brave when those monsters grabbed her. How in God's name you can be brave when something that size is holding you in midair is something I don't understand, but I have to assure you that those who saw it—''

"It makes sense to me," Carmichael said.

He turned away. He shut his eyes for a moment and took deep, heavy pulls of the hot, smoky air.

Of course she had gone right out to the landing site. Of course. If there was anyone in Los Angeles who would have wanted to get to them and see them with her own eyes and perhaps try to talk to them and establish some sort of rapport with them, it was Cindy. She wouldn't have been afraid of them. She had never seemed to be afraid of anything. It wasn't hard for Carmichael to imagine her in that panicky mob in the parking lot, cool and radiant, staring at the giant aliens, smiling at them right up to the moment they seized her. In a way he felt very proud of her. But it terrified him to think that she was in their grasp.

"She's on the ship?" he asked. "The one that we have right up back here?''

"Yes.''

"Have there been any messages from the hostages? Or from the aliens?''

"I can't divulge that information.''

"*Is* there any information?''

"I'm sorry, I'm not at liberty to—''

"I refuse to believe," Carmichael said, "that that ship is just sitting there, that nothing at all is being done to make contact with—''

"A command center has been established, Mr. Carmichael, and certain efforts are under way. That much I can tell you. I can tell you that Washington is involved. But beyond that, at the present point in time—''

A kid who looked like an Eagle Scout came running up. "Your plane's all loaded and ready to go, Mike!''

"Yeah," Carmichael said. The fire, the fucking fire! He had almost managed to forget about it. *Almost.* He hesitated a moment, torn between conflicting responsibilities. Then he said to the officer, "Look, I've got to get back out on the fire line. Can you stay here a little while?''

"Well—"

"Maybe half an hour. I have to do a retardant dump. Then I want you to take me over to that spaceship and get me through the cordon, so I can talk to those critters myself. If she's on that ship, I mean to get her off it."

"I don't see how it would be possible—"

"Well, try to see," Carmichael said. "I'll meet you right here in half an hour."

When he was aloft he noticed right away that the fire was spreading. The wind was even rougher and wilder than before, and now it was blowing hard from the northeast, pushing the flames down toward the edge of Chatsworth. Already some glowing cinders had blown across the city limits, and Carmichael saw houses afire to his left, maybe half a dozen of them. There would be more, he knew. In fire fighting you come to develop an odd sense of which way the struggle is going, whether you're gaining on the blaze or it's gaining on you, and that sense told him now that the vast effort that was under way was failing, that the fire was still on the upcurve, that whole neighborhoods were going to be ashes by nightfall.

He held on tight as the DC-3 entered the fire zone. The fire was sucking air like crazy now, and the turbulence was astounding: It felt as if a giant's hand had grabbed the ship by the nose. The line boss's helicopter was tossing around like a balloon on a string.

Carmichael called in for orders and was sent over to the southwest side, close by the outermost street of houses. Fire fighters with shovels were beating on wisps of flame rising out of people's gardens down there. The skirts of dead leaves that dangled down the trunks of a row of towering palm trees were blazing. The neighborhood dogs had formed a crazed pack, running desperately back and forth.

Swooping down to treetop level, Carmichael let go with a red gush of chemicals, swathing everything that looked combustible with the stuff. The shovelers looked up and waved at him, and he dipped his wings to them and headed off to the north, around the western edge of the blaze—it was edging farther to the west too, he saw, leaping up into the high canyons out by the Ventura County line—and then he flew eastward along the Santa Susana foothills until he could see the spaceship once more, standing isolated in its circle of blackened earth. The cordon of vehicles seemed to be even larger, what looked like a whole armored division deployed in concentric rings beginning half a mile or so from the ship.

He stared intently at the alien vessel as though he might be able to see through its shining walls to Cindy within.

He imagined her sitting at a table, or whatever the aliens used instead of tables, sitting at a table with seven or eight of the huge beings, calmly explaining Earth to them and then asking them to explain their world to her.

He was altogether certain that she was safe, that no harm would come to her, that they were not torturing her or dissecting her or sending electric currents through her simply to see how she reacted. Things like that would never happen to Cindy, he knew.

The only thing he feared was that they would depart for their home star without releasing her. The terror that that thought generated in him was as powerful as any kind of fear he had ever felt.

As Carmichael approached the aliens' landing site he saw the guns of some of the tanks below swiveling around to point at him, and he picked up a radio voice telling him brusquely, "You're off limits, DC-3. Get back to the fire zone. This is prohibited air space."

"Sorry," he said. "No entry intended."

But as he started to make his turn he dropped down even lower so that he could have a good look at the spaceship. If it had portholes and Cindy was looking out one of those portholes, he wanted her to know that he was nearby. That he was watching, that he was waiting for her to come back. But the ship's hull was blind-faced, entirely blank.

Cindy? Cindy?

She was always looking for the strange, the mysterious, the unfamiliar, he thought. The people she brought to the house: a Navaho once, a bewildered Turkish tourist, a kid from New York. The music she played, the way she chanted along with it. The incense, the lights, the meditation. "I'm searching," she liked to say. Trying always to find a route that would take her into something that was wholly outside herself. Trying to become something more than she was. That was how they had fallen in love in the first place, an unlikely couple, she with her beads and sandals, he with his steady no-nonsense view of the world: She had come up to him that day long ago when he was in the record shop in Studio City, and God only knew what he was doing in that part of the world in the first place, and she had asked him something and they had started to talk, and they had talked and talked, talked all night, she wanting to know everything there was to know about him, and when dawn came up they were still together, and they had rarely been parted since. He never had really been able to understand what it was that she had wanted him for—the Valley redneck, the aging flyboy—although he felt certain that she wanted him for something real, that he filled some need for her, as she did for him, which could for lack of a more specific term be called love. She had always been searching for that too. Who wasn't? And he knew that she loved him truly and well, though he couldn't quite see why. "Love is understanding," she liked to say. "Understanding is loving." Was she trying to tell the spaceship people about love right this minute? *Cindy, Cindy, Cindy.*

Back in Van Nuys a few minutes later, he found that everyone at the airport seemed to know by this time that his wife was one of the hostages. The officer whom Carmichael had asked to wait for him was gone. He was not very surprised by that. He thought for a moment of trying to go over to the ship by himself, to get through the cordon and do something about getting Cindy free, but he realized that that was a dumb idea: The military was in charge and they wouldn't let him or anybody else get within a mile of that ship, and he'd only get snarled up in stuff with the television interviewers looking for poignant crap about the families of those who had been captured.

Then the head dispatcher came down to meet him on the field, looking almost about ready to burst with compassion, and in funereal tones told Carmichael that it would be all right if he called it quits for the day and went home to await whatever might happen. But Carmichael shook him off. "I won't get her back by sitting in the living room," he said. "And this fire isn't going to go out by itself, either."

It took twenty minutes for the ground crew to pump the retardant slurry into the DC-3's tanks. Carmichael stood to one side, drinking Cokes and watching the planes come and go. People stared at him, and those who knew him waved from a distance, and three or four pilots came over and silently squeezed his arm or rested a hand consolingly on his shoulder. The northern sky was black with soot, shading to gray to east and west. The air was sauna-hot and frighteningly dry: You could set fire to it, Carmichael thought, with a snap of your fingers. Somebody running by said that a new fire had broken out in Pasadena, near the Jet Propulsion Lab, and there was another in Griffith Park. The wind was starting to carry firebrands, then. Dodger Stadium was burning, someone said. So is Santa Anita Racetrack, said someone else. The whole damned place is going to go, Carmichael thought. And my wife is sitting inside a spaceship from another planet.

When his plane was ready he took it up and laid down a new line of retardant practically in the faces of the fire fighters working on the outskirts of Chatsworth. They were too busy to wave. In order to get back to the airport he had to make a big loop behind the fire, over the Santa Susanas and down the flank of the Golden State Freeway, and this time he saw the fires burning to the east, two huge conflagrations marking the places where the exhaust streams of the other two spaceships had grazed the dry grass and a bunch of smaller blazes strung out on a line from Burbank or Glendale deep into Orange County. His hands were shaking as he touched down at Van Nuys. He had gone without sleep now for thirty-two hours, and he could feel himself starting to pass into that blank, white fatigue that lies somewhere beyond ordinary fatigue.

The head dispatcher was waiting for him again as he left his plane. "All right," Carmichael said at once. "I give in. I'll knock off for five or six hours and grab some sleep, and then you can call me back to—"

"No. That isn't it."

"That isn't what?"

"What I came out here to tell you, Mike. They've released some of the hostages."

"Cindy?"

"I think so. There's an Air Force car here to take you to Sylmar. That's where they've got the command center set up. They said to find you as soon as you came off your last dump mission and send you over there so you can talk with your wife."

"So she's free," Carmichael said. "Oh, Jesus, she's free!"

"You go on along, Mike. We'll look after the fire without you for a while, okay?"

The Air Force car looked like a general's limo, long and low and sleek, with a square-jawed driver in front and a couple of very tough-looking young officers to sit with him in back. They said hardly anything, and they looked as weary as Carmichael felt. "How's my wife?" he asked, and one of them said, "We understand that she hasn't been harmed." The way he said it was stiff and strange. Carmichael shrugged. The kid has seen too many old movies, he told himself.

The whole city seemed to be on fire now. Within the air-conditioned limo there was only the faintest whiff of smoke, but the sky to the east was terrifying, with streaks of red bursting like meteors through the blackness. Carmichael asked the Air Force men about that, but all he got was a clipped, "It looks pretty bad, we understand." Somewhere along the San Diego Freeway between Mission Hills and Sylmar, Carmichael fell asleep, and the next thing he knew they were waking him gently and leading him into a vast, bleak, hangarlike building near the reservoir. The place was a maze of cables and screens, with military personnel operating what looked like a thousand computers and ten thousand telephones. He let himself be shuffled along, moving mechanically and barely able to focus his eyes, to an inner office where a gray-haired colonel greeted him in his best this-is-the-tense-part-of-the-movie style and said, "This may be the most difficult job you've ever had to handle, Mr. Carmichael."

Carmichael scowled. Everybody was Hollywood in this damned town, he thought.

"They told me the hostages were being freed," he said. "Where's my wife?"

The colonel pointed to a television screen. "We're going to let you talk to her right now."

"Are you saying I don't get to see her?"

"Not immediately."

"Why not? Is she all right?"

"As far as we know, yes."

"You mean she hasn't been released? They told me the hostages were being freed."

"All but three have been let go," said the colonel. "Two people, according to the aliens, were injured as they were captured and are undergoing medical treatment aboard the ship. They'll be released shortly. The third is your wife, Mr. Carmichael. She is unwilling to leave the ship."

It was like hitting an air pocket.

"*Unwilling*—?"

"She claims to have volunteered to make the journey to the home world of the aliens. She says she's going to serve as our ambassador, our special emissary. Mr. Carmichael, does your wife have any history of mental imbalance?"

Glaring, Carmichael said, "She's very sane. Believe me."

"You are aware that she showed no display of fear when the aliens seized her in the shopping-center incident this morning?"

"I know, yes. That doesn't mean she's crazy. She's unusual. She has unusual ideas. But she's not crazy. Neither am I, incidentally." He put his hands to his face for a moment and pressed his fingertips lightly against his eyes.

"All right," he said. "Let me talk to her."

"Do you think you can persuade her to leave that ship?"

"I'm sure as hell going to try."

"You are not yourself sympathetic to what she's doing, are you?" the colonel asked.

Carmichael looked up. "Yes, I am sympathetic. She's an intelligent woman doing something that she thinks is important and doing it of her own free will. Why the hell shouldn't I be sympathetic? But I'm going to try to talk her out of it, you bet. I love her. I want her. Somebody else can be the goddamned ambassador to Betelgeuse. Let me talk to her, will you?"

The colonel gestured, and the big television screen came to life. For a moment mysterious colored patterns flashed across it in a disturbing, random way; then Carmichael caught glimpses of shadowy catwalks, intricate metal strutworks crossing and recrossing at peculiar angles; and then for an instant one of the aliens appeared on the screen. Yellow platter-eyes looked complacently back at him. Carmichael felt altogether wide awake now.

The alien's face vanished and Cindy came into view. The moment he saw her, Carmichael knew that he had lost her.

Her face was glowing. There was a calm joy in her eyes verging on ecstasy. He had seen her look something like that on many occasions, but this was different: This was beyond anything she had attained before. She had seen the beatific vision, this time.

"Cindy?"

"Hello, Mike."

"Can you tell me what's been happening in there, Cindy?"

"It's incredible. The contact, the communication."

Sure, he thought. If anyone could make contact with the space people it would be Cindy. She had a certain kind of magic about her: the gift of being able to open any door.

She said, "They speak mind to mind, you know, no barriers at all. They've come in peace, to get to know us, to join in harmony with us, to welcome us into the confederation of worlds."

He moistened his lips. "What have they done to you, Cindy? Have they brainwashed you or something?"

"No! No, nothing like that! They haven't done a thing to me, Mike! We've just talked."

"*Talked!*"

"They've showed me how to touch my mind to theirs. That isn't brainwashing. I'm still me. I, me, Cindy. I'm okay. Do I look as though I'm being harmed? They aren't dangerous. Believe me."

"They've set fire to half the city with their exhaust trails, you know."

"That grieves them. It was an accident. They didn't understand how dry the hills were. If they had some way of extinguishing the flames, they would, but the fires are too big even for them. They ask us to forgive them. They want everyone to know how sorry they are." She paused a moment. Then she said, very gently, "Mike, will you come onboard? I want you to experience them as I'm experiencing them."

"I can't do that, Cindy."

"Of course you can! Anyone can! You just open your mind, they touch you, and—"

"I know. I don't want to. Come out of there and come home, Cindy. Please. Please. It's been three days—four, now—I want to hug you, I want to hold you—"

"You can hold me as tight as you like. They'll let you onboard. We can go to their world together. You know that I'm going to go with them to their world, don't you?"

"You aren't. Not really."

She nodded gravely. She seemed terribly serious. "They'll be leaving in a few weeks, as soon as they've had a chance to exchange gifts with Earth. I've seen images of their planet—like movies, only they do it with their minds—Mike, you can't imagine how beautiful it is! How eager they are to have me come!"

Sweat rolled out of his hair into his eyes, making him blink, but he did not dare wipe it away for fear she would think he was crying.

"I don't want to go to their planet, Cindy. And I don't want you to go either."

She was silent for a time.

Then she smiled delicately and said, "I know, Mike."

He clenched his fists and let go and clenched them again. "I *can't* go there."

"No. You can't. I understand that. Los Angeles is alien enough for you, I think. You need to be in your Valley, in your own real world, not running off to some far star. I won't try to coax you."

"But you're going to go anyway?" he asked, and it was not really a question.

"You already know what I'm going to do."

"Yes."

"I'm sorry. But not really."

"Do you love me?" he said, and regretted saying it at once.

She smiled sadly. "You know I do. And you know I don't want to leave you. But once they touched my mind with theirs, once I saw what kind of beings they are—do you know what I mean? I don't have to explain, do I? You always know what I mean."

"Cindy—"

"Oh, Mike, I do love you so much."

"And I love you, babe. And I wish you'd come out of that goddamned ship."

"You won't ask that. Because you love me, right? Just as I won't ask you again to come onboard with me, because I really love you. Do you understand that, Mike?"

He wanted to reach into the screen and grab her.

"I understand, yes," he made himself say.

"I love you, Mike."

"I love you, Cindy."

"They tell me the round-trip takes forty-eight of our years, but it will only seem like a few weeks to me. Oh, Mike! Good-bye, Mike! God bless, Mike!" She blew kisses to him. He saw his favorite rings on her fingers, the three little strange star sapphire ones that she had made when she first began to design jewelry. He searched his mind for some new way to reason with her, some line of argument that would work, and could find none. He felt a vast emptiness beginning to expand within him, as though he were being made hollow by some whirling blade. Her face was shining. She seemed like a stranger to him suddenly. She seemed like a Los Angeles person, one of *those*, lost in fantasies and dreams, and it was as though he had never known her, or as though he had pretended she was something other than she was. No. No, that isn't right. She's not one of *those*, she's Cindy. Following her own star, as always. Suddenly he was unable to look at the screen any longer, and he turned away, biting his lip, making a shoving gesture with his left hand. The Air Force men in the room wore the awkward expressions of people who had inadvertently eavesdropped on someone's most intimate moments and were trying to pretend they had heard nothing.

"She isn't crazy, Colonel," Carmichael said vehemently. "I don't want anyone believing she's some kind of nut."

"Of course not, Mr. Carmichael."

"But she's not going to leave that spaceship. You heard her. She's staying aboard, going back with them to wherever the hell they came from. I can't do anything about that. You see that, don't you? Nothing I could do, short of going aboard that ship and dragging her off physically, would get her out of there. And I wouldn't ever do that."

"Naturally not. In any case, you understand that it would be impossible for us to permit you to go onboard, even for the sake of attempting to remove her."

"That's all right," Carmichael said: "I wouldn't dream of it. To remove her or even just to join her for the trip. I don't want to go to that place. Let her go: That's what she was meant to do in this world. Not me. Not me, Colonel. That's simply not my thing." He took a deep breath. He thought he might be trembling. "Colonel, do you mind if I got the hell out of here? Maybe I would feel better if I went back out there and dumped some more gunk on that fire. I think that might help. That's what I think, Colonel. All right? Would you send me back to Van Nuys, Colonel?"

He went up one last time in the DC-3. They wanted him to dump the retardants along the western face of the fire, but instead he went to the east, where the spaceship was, and flew in a wide circle around it. A radio voice warned him to move out of the area, and he said that he would.

As he circled a hatch opened in the spaceship's side and one of the aliens appeared, looking gigantic even from Carmichael's altitude. The huge, purplish thing stepped from the ship, extended its tentacles, seemed to be sniffing the smoky air.

Carmichael thought vaguely of flying down low and dropping his whole load of retardants on the creature, drowning it in gunk, getting even with the aliens for having taken Cindy from him. He shook his head. That's crazy, he told himself. Cindy would feel sick if she knew he had ever considered any such thing. But that's what I'm like, he thought. Just an ordinary, ugly, vengeful Earthman. And that's why I'm not going to go to that other planet, and that's why she is.

He swung around past the spaceship and headed straight across Granada Hills and Northridge into Van Nuys Airport. When he was on the ground he sat at the controls of his plane a long while, not moving at all. Finally one of the dispatchers came out and called up to him, "Mike, are you okay?"

"Yeah. I'm fine."

"How come you came back without dropping your load?"

Carmichael peered at his gauges. "Did I do that? I guess I did that, didn't I?"

"You're not okay, are you?"

"I forgot to dump, I guess. No, I didn't forget. I just didn't feel like doing it."

"Mike, come on out of that plane."

"I didn't feel like doing it," Carmichael said again. "Why the hell bother? This crazy city—there's nothing left in it that I would want to save anyway." His control deserted him at last, and rage swept through him like fire racing up the slopes of a dry canyon. He understood what she was doing, and he respected it, but he didn't have to like it. He didn't like it at all. He had lost Cindy, and he felt somehow that he had lost his war with Los Angeles as well. "Fuck it," he said. "Let it burn. This crazy city. I always hated it. It deserves what it gets. The only reason I stayed here was for her. She was all that mattered. But she's going away now. Let the fucking place burn."

The dispatcher gaped at him in amazement. "Mike—"

Carmichael moved his head slowly from side to side as though trying to shake a monstrous headache from it. Then he frowned. "No, that's wrong," he said. "You've got to do the job anyway, right? No matter how you feel. You have to put the fires out. You have to save what you can. Listen, Tim, I'm going to fly one last load today, you hear? And then I'll go home and get some sleep. Okay? Okay?" He had the plane in motion, going down the short runway. Dimly he realized that he had not requested clearance. A little Cessna spotter plane moved desperately out of his way, and then he was aloft. The sky was black and red. The fire was completely uncontained now, and maybe uncontainable. But you had to keep trying, he thought. You had to save what you could. He gunned and went forward, flying calmly into the inferno in the foothills, until the wild thermals caught his wings from below and lifted him and tossed him like a toy skimming over the top and sent him hurtling toward the waiting hills to the north.

Thus saith the Lord; Behold, I will raise up against Babylon, and against them that dwell in the midst of them that rise up against me, a destroying wind;

And will send unto Babylon fanners, that shall fan her, and shall empty her land: For in the day of trouble they shall be against her round about.

—Jeremiah 51:1–2

SOMTOW SUCHARITKUL

Fiddling for Waterbuffaloes

The odds are pretty good that only one person could have written the madcap extravaganza that follows—as strange and funny a story as you're likely to see this year—and that person is the unique and inestimable Somtow Sucharitkul.

Born in Bangkok, Thailand, Somtow Sucharitkul has lived in six countries, and was educated at Eton and Cambridge. Multitalented as well as multilingual, he has an international reputation as an avante-garde composer, and his works have been performed in more than a dozen countries on four continents. Among his compositions are "Gongula 3 for Thai and Western Instruments" and "The Cosmic Trilogy." His book publications include the novels *Starship and Haiku, Mallworld,* and *Light on the Sound.* His most recent books are the novels *Vampire Junction* and *The Shattered Horse,* written as S. P. Somtow, and *The Darkling Wind* and *The Fallen Country.* In 1986 he received the Daedalus Award for *The Shattered Horse.* A resident of the United States for many years, he now makes his home in Van Nuys, California.

FIDDLING FOR WATERBUFFALOES

Somtow Sucharitkul

When my brother Lek and I were children we were only allowed to go to Prasongburi once a week. That was the day our mothers went to the market-place and went to make merit at the temple. Our grandmother, our mothers' mother, spent the days chewing betelnut and fashioning intricate mobiles out of dried palm leaves; not just the usual fish-shapes, dozens of tiny baby fish swinging from a big mother fish lacquered in bright red or orange, but also more elaborate shapes: lions and tigers and mythical beasts, nagas that swallowed their own tails. It was our job to sell them to the *thaokae* who owned the only souvenir shop in the town . . . the only store with one of those aluminum gratings that you pull shut to lock up at night, just like the ones in Bangkok.

It was always difficult to get him to take the ones that weren't fish. Once we took in a mobile made entirely of spaceships, which our grandmother had copied from one of the American TV shows. (In view of our later experiences, this proved particularly prophetic.) "Everyone knows," the *thaokae* said (that was the time he admitted us to his inner sanctum, where he would smoke opium from an impressive *bong* and puff it in our faces) "that a *plataphien* mobile has fish in it. Everyone wants sweet little fishies to hang over their baby's cradle. I mean, those spaceships are a tribute to your grandmother's skill at weaving dried palm leaves, but as far as the tourists are concerned, it's just fiddling for waterbuffaloes." He meant there was no point in doing such fine work because it would be wasted on his customers.

We ended up with maybe ten baht apiece for my grandmother's labors, and we'd carefully tuck-away two of the little blue banknotes (this was in the year 2504 B.E., long before they debased the baht into a mere coin) so that we could go to the movies. The American ones were funniest—especially the James Bond ones—because the dubbers had the most outrageous ad libs. I remember that in *Goldfinger* the dubbers kept putting in jokes about the fairy tale of Jao Ngo, which is about a hideous monster who falls into a tank of gold paint and becomes very handsome. The audience became so wild with laughter that they actually stormed the dubbers' booth and started improvising their own puns. I particularly remember that day because we were waiting for the monsoon to burst, and the heat had been making everyone crazy.

Seconds after we left the theater it came all at once, and the way home was so impassable we had to stay at the village before our village, and then we had to go home by boat, rowing frantically by the side of the drowned road. The fish were so thick you could pull them from the water in handfulls.

That was when my brother Lek said to me, "You know, Noi, I think it would be grand to be a movie dubber."

"That's silly, Phii Lek," I said. "Someone has to herd the waterbuffaloes and sell the mobiles and—"

"That's what we both should do. So we don't have to work on the farm anymore." Our mothers, who were rowing the boat, pricked up their ears at that. Something to report back to our father, perhaps. "We could live in the town. I love that town."

"It's not so great," my mother said.

My senior mother (Phii Lek's mother) agreed. "We went to Chiangmai once, for the beauty contest. Now there was a town. Streets that wind on and on . . . and air-conditioning in almost every public building!"

"We didn't win the beauty contest, though," my mother said sadly. She didn't say it, but she implied that that was how they'd both ended up marrying my father. "Our stars were bad. Maybe in my next life—"

"I'm not waiting till my next life," my brother said. "When I'm grown up they'll have air-conditioning in Prasongburi, and I'll be dubbing movies every night."

The sun was beating down, blinding, sizzling. We threw off our clothes and dived from the boat. The water was cool, mudflecked; we pushed our way through the reeds.

The storm had blown the village's TV antenna out into the paddyfield. We watched *Star Trek* at the headsman's house, our arms clutching the railings on his porch, our feet dangling, slipping against the stilts that were still soaked with rain. It was fuzzy and the sound was off, so Phii Lek put on a magnificent performance, putting discreet obscenities into the mouths of Kirk and Spock while the old men laughed and the coils of mosquito incense smoked through the humid evening. At night, when we were both tucked in under our mosquito netting, I dreamed about going into space and finding my grandmother's palm-leaf mobiles hanging from the points of the stars.

Ten years later they built a highway from Bangkok to Chiangmai, and there were no more casual tourists in Prasongburi. Some American archaeologists started digging at the site of an old Khmer city nearby. The movie theater never did get air-conditioning, but my grandmother got into faking antiques; it turned out to be infinitely more lucrative than fish mobiles, and when the *thaokae* died, she and my two mothers were actually able to buy the place from his intransigent nephew. The three of them turned it into an ''antique'' place (fakes in the front, the few genuine pieces carefully hoarded in the air-conditioned back room) and our father set about looking for a third wife as befit his improved station in life.

My family were also able to buy a half-interest in the movie theater, and that was how my brother and I ended up in the dubbing booth after all. Now, the fact of the matter was, sound projection systems in theaters had become prevalent all over the country by then, and Lek and I both knew that live movie dubbing was a dying art. Only the fact that the highway didn't come anywhere near Prasongburi prevented its citizens from positively demanding talkies. But we were young and, relatively speaking, wealthy; we wanted to have a bit of fun before having the drudgery of marriage and earning a real living thrust upon us. Lek did most of the dubbing—he was astonishingly convincing at female voices as well as male—while I contributed the sound effects and played background music from the library of scratched records we'd inherited from the previous régime.

Since we two were the only purveyors of, well, foreign culture in the town, you'd think we would be the ones best equipped to deal with an alien invasion.

Apparently the aliens thought so too.

Aliens were furthest from my mind the day it happened, though. I was putting in some time at the shop and trying to pacify my three honored parents, who were going at it like cats and dogs in the back.

''If you dare bring that bitch into our house,'' Elder Mother was saying, fanning herself feverishly with a plastic fan—for our air-conditioning had broken down, as usual—''I'll leave.''

''Well,'' Younger Mother (my own) said, ''I don't mind as long as you make sure she's a servant. But if you marry her—''

''Well, *I* mind, I'm telling you!'' my other mother shouted. ''If the two of us aren't enough for you, I've three more cousins up north, decent, hardworking girls who'll bring in money, not use it up.''

''Anyway, if you simply *have* to spend money,'' Younger Mother said, ''what's wrong with a new pick-up truck?''

''I'm not dealing with that usurious *thaokae* in Ban Kraduk,'' my father said, taking another swig of his *Mekong* whiskey, and ''and there's no other way of coming up with a down payment . . . and besides, I happen to be a very horny man.''

''All of you shut up,'' my grandmother said from somewhere out back,

where she had been meticulously aging some pots into a semblance of twelfth-century Sawankhalok ware. "All this chatter disturbs my work."

"Yes, *khun mae*," the three of them chorused back respectfully.

My Elder Mother hissed, "But watch out, my dear husband. I read a story in *Siam Rath* about a woman who castrated her unfaithful husband and fed his eggs to the ducks!"

My father sucked in his breath and took a comforting gulp of whiskey as I went to the front to answer a customer.

She was one of those archaeologists or anthropologists or something. She was tall and smelly, as all *farangs* are (they have very active sweat glands); she wore a sort of safari outfit, and she had long hair, stringy from her digging and the humidity. She was scrutinizing the spaceship mobile my grandmother had made ten years ago—it still had not sold, and we had kept it as a memento of hard times—and muttering to herself words that sounded like, "Warp factor five!"

My brother and I know some English, and I was preparing to embarrass myself by exercising that ungrateful, toneless tongue, when she addressed me in Thai.

"Greetings to you, honored sir," she said, and brought her palms together in a clumsy but heartfelt *wai*. I couldn't suppress a laugh. "Why, didn't I do that right?" she demanded.

"You did it remarkably well," I said. "But you shouldn't go to such lengths. I'm only a shopkeeper, and you're not supposed to *wai* first. But I suppose I should give you 'E for effort,' " (I said this phrase in her language, having learned it from another archaeologist the previous year) "since few would even try as hard as you."

"Oh, but I'm doing my Ph.D. in Southeast Asian aesthetics at UCLA," she said. "By all means, correct me." She started to pull out a notebook.

I had never, as we say, "arrived" in America, though my sexual adventures had recently included an aging, overwhelmingly odoriferous French-woman and the daughter of the Indian *babu* who sold cloth in the next town, and the prospect suddenly seemed rather inviting. Emboldened, I said, "But to really study our culture, you might consider—" and eyed her with undisguised interest.

She laughed. *Farang* women are exceptional, in that one need not make overtures to them subtly, but may approach the matter in a no-nonsense, fashion, as a plumber might regard a sewage pipe. "Jesus," she said in English, "I think he's asking me for a date!"

"I understood that," I said.

"Where will we go?" she said in Thai, giggling. "I've got the day off. And the night, I might add. Oh, that's not correct, is it? You should send a go-between to my father, or something."

"Only if the liaison is intended to be permanent," I said quickly, lest anthropology get the better of lust. "Well, we could go to a movie."

"What's showing?" she said. "Why, this is just like back home, and me a teenager again." She bent down, anxious to please, and started to deliver a sloppy kiss to my forehead. I recoiled. "Oh, I forgot," she said. "You people frown on public displays."

"*Star Wars*," I said.

"Oh, but I've seen that twenty times."

"Ah, but have you seen it—dubbed *live*, in a provincial Thai theater without air-conditioning? Think of the glorious field notes you could write."

"You Thai men are all alike," she said, intimating that she had had a vast experience of them. "Very well. What time? By the way, my name is Mary, Mary Mason."

We were an hour late getting the show started, which was pretty normal, and the audience was getting so restless that some of them had started an impromptu bawdy-rhyming contest in the front rows. My brother and I had manned the booth and were studying the script. He would do all the main characters, and I would do such meaty rôles as the Second Stormtrooper.

"Let's begin," Phii Lek said. "She won't come anyway."

Mary turned up just as we were lowering the house lights. She had bathed (my brother sniffed appreciatively as she entered the dubbing booth) and wore a clean *sarong*, which did not look too bad on her.

"Can I do Princess Leia?" she said, *wai*-ing to Phii Lek as though she were already his younger sibling by virtue of her as-yet-unconsummated association with me.

"You can *read* Thai?" Phii Lek said in astonishment.

"I have my Masters' in Siamese from Michigan U," she said huffily, "and studied under Bill Gedney." We shrugged.

"Yes, but you can't improvise," my brother said.

She agreed, pulled out her notebook, and sat down in a corner. My brother started to put on a wild performance, while I ran hither and thither putting on records and creating sound effects out of my box of props. We began the opening chase scene with Tchaikovsky's Piano Concerto, which kept skipping; at last the needle got stuck and I turned the volume down hastily just as my brother (in the tones of the heroic Princess Leia) was supposed to murmur, "Help me, Obiwan Kenobi. You're my only hope." Instead, he began to moan like a harlot in heat, screeching out, "Oh, I need a man, I do, I do! These robots are no good in bed!"

At that point Mary became hysterical with laughter. She fell out of her chair and collided with the shoe rack. I hastened to rescue her from the indignity of having her face next to a stack of filthy flipflops, and could not prevent myself from grabbing her. She put her arms around my waist and indecorously refused to let go, while my brother, warming to the audience reaction, began to ad lib ever more outrageously.

It was only after the movie, when I had put on the 45 of the Royal Anthem and everyone had stood up to pay homage to the Sacred Majesty of the King, that I noticed something wrong with my brother. For one thing, he did not rise in respect, even though he was ordinarily the most devout of people. He sat bunched up in a corner of the dubbing booth, with his eyes darting from side to side like window wipers.

I watched him anxiously but dared not move until the Royal Anthem had finished playing.

Then, tentatively, I tapped him on the shoulder. "Phii Lek," I said, "it's time we went home."

He turned on me and snarled . . . then he fell on the floor and began dragging himself forward in a very strange manner, propelling himself with his chin and elbows along the woven-rush matting at our feet.

Mary said, "Is *that* something worth reporting on?" and began scribbling wildly in her notebook.

"Phii Lek," I said to my brother in terms of utmost respect, for I thought he might be punishing me for some imagined grievance, "are you ill?" Suddenly I thought I had it figured out. "If you're playing 'putting on the anthropologists,' Elder Sibling, I don't think this one's going to be taken in."

"You are part of a rebel alliance, and a traitor!" my brother intoned—in English—in a harsh, unearthly voice. "Take her away!"

"That's . . . my God, that's James Earl Jones's voice," Mary said, forgetting in her confusion to speak Thai. "That's from the movie we just saw."

"What are we going to do?" I said, panicking. My older brother was crawling around at my feet, making me feel distinctly uncomfortable because of the elevation of my head over the head of a person of higher status, so I dropped down on my hands and knees so as to maintain my head at the properly respectful level. Meanwhile, he was wriggling around on his belly.

Amid all this, Mary's notebook and pens clattered to the floor and she began to scream.

At that moment, my grandmother entered the booth and stared about wildly. I attempted, from my prone position, to perform the appropriate *wai*, but Phii Lek was rolling around and making peculiar hissing noises. Mary started to stutter, "*Khun yaai*, I don't what happened, they just suddenly started acting this way—"

"Don't you *khun yaai* me," grandmother snapped. "I'm no kin to any foreigners, thank you!" She surveyed the spectacle before her with mounting horror. "Oh, my terrible karma!" she cried. "Demons have transformed my grandsons into dogs!"

*   *   *

On the street, there were crowds everywhere. I could hear people babbling all about mysterious lights in the sky . . . portents and celestial signs. Someone said something about the spectacle outside being more impressive than the *Star Wars* effects inside the theater. Apparently the main pagoda of the temple had seemed on fire for a few minutes and they'd called in a firefighting squad from the next town. "Who'd have thought of it?" my grandmother was complaining. "A demon visits Prasongburi—and makes straight for my own grandson!"

When we got to the shop—Mary still tagging behind and furiously taking notes on our social customs—the situation was even worse. The skirmish between my father and mothers had crescendoed to an all-out war.

"That's why I came to fetch you, children," my grandmother said. "Maybe you can referee this boxing match." A hefty celadon pot came whistling through the air and shattered on the overhead electric fan. We scurried for cover . . . all except my brother, who obliviously crawled about on his hands and knees, occasionally spouting lines from *Star Wars*.

Shrieking, Mary ran after the potshards. "My god, that thing's eight hundred years old—"

"Bah! I faked it last week," my grandmother said, forcing the *farang* woman to gape in mingled horror and admiration.

"All right, all right," my father said, fleeing from the back room with my mothers in hot pursuit. "I won't marry her . . . but I want a little more kindness out of the two of you . . . oh, my terrible karma."

He tripped over my brother and went sprawling to the floor. "What's wrong with him?"

"You fool!" my grandmother said. "Your own son has become possessed by demons . . . and it's all because of your sexual excesses."

My father stopped and stared at my brother. Then, murmuring a brief prayer to the Lord Buddha, he retired cowering behind the shop counter. "What must I do?"

His wives came marching out behind him. Elder Mother hastened to succor Phii Lek. Younger Mother took in the situation and said, "I haven't seen anyone this possessed since my cousin Phii Daeng spent the night in a graveyard trying to get a vision of a winning lottery ticket number."

"It's all your fault," Phi Lek's mother said, turning wrathfully on my father. "You're all too eager to douse your staff of passion, and now my grandson has been turned into a monster!" The logic of this accusation escaped me, but my father seemed convinced.

"I'll go and *buat phra* for three months," he said, affecting a tone of deep piety. "I'll cut my hair off tomorrow and enter the nearest monastery. That ought to do the trick. Oh, my son, my son, what have I done?"

"Well," my grandmother said, "a little abstinence should do you good.

I always thought you were unwise not to enter the monkhood at twenty like an obedient son should . . . cursing me to be reborn on Earth istead of spending my next life in heaven as I ought, considering how I've worked my fingers to the bone for you! It's about time, that's what I say. A twenty-year-old belongs in a temple, not in the village scouts killing communists. Time for that when you've done your filial duty . . . well, twenty-five years late is better than nothing."

Seeing himself trapped between several painful alternatives, my father bowed his head, raised his palms in a gesture of respect, and said, "All right, *khun mae yaai*, if that's what you want."

When my father and the elder females of the family had left to pack his things, I was left with my older brother and with the bizarre American woman, in the antique shop in the middle of the night. They had taken the truck back to the village (which now boasted a good half-dozen motor vehicles, one of them ours) and we were stranded. In the heat of their argument and my father's repentance, they seemed to have forgotten all about us.

It was at that moment that my brother chose to snap out of whatever it was that possessed him.

Calmly he rose from the floor, wiped a few foamflecks from his mouth with his sleeve, and sat down on the stool behind the counter. It took him a minute or two to recognize us, and then he said, "Well, well, Ai Noi! I gave the family quite a scare, didn't I?"

I was even more frightened now than I had been before. I knew very well that night is the time of spirits, and I was completely convinced that some spirit or another had taken hold of Phii Lek, though I was unsure about the part about my father being punished for his roving eyes and hands. I said, "Yes, *Khun Phii*, it was the most astonishing performance I've ever seen. Indeed, a bit too astonishing, if you don't mind your Humble Younger Sibling saying so. I mean, do you think they really appreciated it? If you ask me, you were just fiddling for waterbuffaloes."

"The most amazing thing is this . . . they weren't even after me!" He pointed at Mary. "They're in the wrong brain! It was her they wanted. But we all look alike to them. And I was imitating a woman's voice when they were trying to get a fix on the psychic transference. So they made an error of a few decimal places, and—poof!—here I am!"

"*Pen baa pai laew!*" I whispered to Mary Mason.

"I heard that!" my brother riposted. "But I am not mad. I am quite, quite sane, and I have been taken over by a *manus tang dao*."

"What's that?" Mary asked me.

"A being from another star."

"Far frigging out! An extraterrestrial!" she said in English. I didn't understand a word of it; I thought it must be some kind of anthropology jargon.

"Look, I can't talk long, but . . . you see, they're after Mary. One of them is trying to send a message to America . . . something to do with the Khmer ruins . . . some kind of artifact . . . to another of these creatures who is walking around in the body of a professor at UCLA. This *farang* woman seemed ideal; she could journey back without causing any suspicion. But, you see, we all look alike to them, and—"

"Well, can't you tell whatever it is to stop inhabiting your body and transfer itself to—?"

"Hell, no!" Mary said, and started to back away. "Native customs are all very well, but this is a bit more than I bargained for."

"Psychic transference too difficult . . . additional expenditure of energy impractical at present stage . . . but message must get through. . . ." Suddenly he clawed at his throat for a few moments, and then fell writhing to the floor in another fit. "Can't get used to this gravity," he moaned. "Legs instead of pseudopods—and the contents of the stomach make me sick— there's at least fifty whole undigested chilies down here—oh, I'm going to puke—"

"By Buddha, Dharma and Sangkha!" I cried. "Quick, Mary, help me with him. Give me something to catch his vomit."

"Will this do?" she said, pulling down something from the shelf. Distractedly I motioned her to put it up to his mouth.

Only when he had begun regurgitating into the bowl did I realize what she'd done. "You imbecile!" I said. "That's a genuine Ming spittoon!"

"I thought they were all fakes," she said, holding up my brother as he slowly turned green.

"We do have some *genuine* items here," I said disdainfully, "for those who can tell the difference."

"You mean, for *Thai* collectors," she said, hurt.

"Well, what can you expect?" I said, becoming furious. "You come here, you dig up all our ancient treasures, violate the chastity of our women—"

"Look who's talking!" Mary said gently. "Male chauvinist pig," she added in English.

"Let's not fight," I said. "He seems better now . . . what are we going to do with him?"

"Here. Help me drag him to the back room."

We lifted him up and laid him down on the couch.

We looked at each other in the close, humid, mosquito-infested room. Suddenly, providentially almost, the air-conditioning kicked on. "I've been trying to get it to work all day," I whispered.

"Does this mean—"

"Yes! Soon it will cool enough to—"

She kissed me on the lips. By morning I had "arrived" in America several delicious times, and Mary was telephoning the hotel in Ban Kraduk so she could get her things moved into my father's house.

The next morning, over dinner, I tried to explain it all to my elders. On the one hand there was this *farang* woman sitting on the floor, clumsily rolling rice balls with one hand and attempting to address my mothers as *khun mae*, much to their discomfiture; on the other there was the mystery of my brother, who was now confined to his room and refused to eat anything with any chilies in it.

"It's your weird Western ways," my grandmother said, eyeing my latest conquest critically. "No chilies indeed! He'll be demanding hamburgers next."

"It's nothing to do with Western ways," I said.

"It's a *manus tang dao*," Mary said, proudly displaying her latest lexical gem, "and it's trying to get a message to America, and there's some kind of artifact in the ruins that they need, and they travel by some kind of psychic transference—"

"You Americans are crazy!" my grandmother said, spitting out her betelnut so she could take a few mouthfuls of curried fish. "Any fool can see the boy's possessed. I remember my greatuncle had fits like this when he promised a donation of five hundred baht to the Sacred Pillar of the City and then reneged on his offer. My parents had to pay off the Brahmins—with interest!—before the curse was lifted. Oh, my karma, my karma!"

"Shouldn't we call in some scientists, or something? A psychiatrist?" Mary said.

"Nothing of the sort!" said my grandmother. "If we can't take care of this in the home, we'll not take care of it at all. No one's going to say my grandson is crazy. Possessed, maybe . . . everyone can sympathize with that . . . but crazy, never! The family honor is at stake."

"Well, what should we do?" I said helplessly. As the junior member of the family, I had no say in the matter at all. I was annoyed at Mary for mentioning psychiatrists, but I reminded myself that she was, after all, a barbarian, even though she could speak a human tongue after a fashion.

"We'll wait," grandmother said, "and see whether your father's penance will do the trick. If not . . . well, our stars are bad, that's all."

During the weeks to come, my brother became increasingly odd. He would enter the house without even removing his sandals, let alone washing his feet. When my Uncle Eed came to dinner one night, my brother actually pointed his left foot at our honored uncle's head. I would be most surprised if Uncle Eed ever came to dinner again after such unforgivable rudeness. I was forced to go into town every evening to dub the movies, which I did in so lackluster a manner that our usual audience began walking the two hours to Ban Kraduk for their entertainment. My heart sank when a passing visitor to the shop told me that the Ban Kraduk cinema had actually installed a projection sound-system and could show talkies . . . not only the foreign films, with sound and subtitles, but the new domestic talkies . . . so you could actually find out what great actors like Mitr and Petchara sounded like! I knew we'd never compete with that. I knew the days of live movie dubbing were numbered. Maybe I could go to Bangkok and get a job with Channel Seven, dubbing *Leave it to Beaver* and *Charlie's Angels*. But Bangkok was just about as distant as another galaxy, and I could imagine the fun those city people would have with my hick northern accent.

One night about two weeks later, Mary and I were awakened by my brother, moaning from the mosquito net next to ours. I went across.

"Oh, there you are," Phii Lek said. "I've been trying to attract your attention for hours."

"I was busy," I said, and my brother leered knowingly. "Are you all right? Are you recovered?"

"Not exactly," he said. "But I'm, well, off-duty. The alien'll come back any minute, though, so I can't talk long." He paused. "Maybe that girlfriend of yours should hear this," he said. At that moment Mary crept in beside us, and we crouched together under the netting. The electric fan made the nets billow like ghosts.

"You have to take me to that archaeological dig of yours," he said. "There's an artifact . . . it's got some kind of encoded information . . . you have to take it back to Professor Ubermuth at UCLA—"

"I've heard of him!" Mary whispered. "He's in a loony bin. Apparently he became convinced he was an extraterre—oh, Jesus!" she said in English.

"He *is* one," Phii Lek said. "So am I. There are hundreds of us on this planet. But my controlling alien's resting right now. Look, Ai Noi, I want you to go down to the kitchen and get me as many chili peppers as you can find. On the *manus tang dao*'s home planet the food is about as bland as rice soup."

I hurried to obey. When I got back, he wolfed down the peppers until he started weeping from the influx of spiciness. Suspiciously I said, "If you're really an alien, what about spaceships?"

"Spaceships . . . we do have them, but they are drones, taking millennia to reach the center of the galaxy. We ourselves travel by tachyon psychic transference. But the device is being sent by drone."

"Device?"

"From the excavation! Haven't you been listening? It's got to be dug up and secretly taken to America and . . . I'm not sure what or why, but I get the feeling there's danger if we don't make our rendezvous. Something to do with upsetting the tachyon fields."

"I see," I said, humoring him.

"You know what I look like on the home planet, up there? I look like a giant *mangdaa*."

"What's that?" said Mary.

"It's sort of a giant cockroach," I said. "We use its wings to flavor some kinds of curry."

"Yech!" she squealed. "Eating insects. Gross!"

"What do you mean? You've been enjoying it all week, and you've never complained about eating insects," I said. She started to turn slightly bluish. A *farang*'s complexion, when he or she is about to be sick, is one of the few truly indescribable hues on the face of this earth.

"Help me . . ." Phii Lek said. "The sooner this artifact is unearthed and loaded onto the drone, the sooner I'll be released from this—oh, no, it's coming back!" Frantically he gobbled down several more chilies. But it was too late. They came right back up again, and he was scampering around the room on all fours and emitting pigeonlike cooing noises.

"Come to think of it," I said, "he *is* acting rather like a cockroach, isn't he?"

A week later our home was invaded by nine monks. My mothers had been cooking all the previous day, and when I came into the main living room they had already been chanting for about an hour, their bass voices droning from behind huge prayer fans. The house was fragrant with jasmine and incense.

I prostrated myself along with the other members of the family. My brother was there too, wriggling around on his belly; his hands were tied up with a sacred rope which ran all the way around the house and through the folded palms of each of the monks. Among them was my father, who looked rather self-conscious and didn't seem to know all the words of the chants yet . . . now and then he seemed to be opening his mouth at random, like a goldfish.

"This isn't going to work," I whispered to my grandmother, who was kneeling in the *phraphrieb* position with her palms folded, her face frozen in an expression of beatific piety. "Mary and I have found out what the problem is, and it's not possession."

"*Buddhang sarnang gacchami*," the monks intoned in unison.

"What are they talking about?" Mary said. She was properly prostrate, but seemed distracted. She was probably uncomfortable without her trusty notebook.

"I haven't the faintest idea. It's all in Pali or Sanskrit or something," I said.

"*Namodasa phakhavato arahato—*" the monks continued inexorably.

At length they laid their prayer fans down and the chief *luangphoh* doused a spray of twigs in a silver dipper of lustral water and began to sprinkle Phii Lek liberally.

"It's got to be over soon," I said to Mary. "It's getting toward noon, and you know monks are not allowed to eat after twelve o'clock."

As the odor of incense wafted over me and the chanting continued, I fell into a sort of trance. These were familiar feelings, sacred feelings. Maybe my brother *was* in the grip of some supernatural force that could be driven out by the proper application of Buddha, Dharma and Sangkha. However, as the *luangphoh* became ever more frantic, waving the twigs energetically over my writhing brother to no avail, I began to lose hope.

Presently the monks took a break for their one meal of the day, and we took turns presenting them with trays of delicacies. After securing my brother carefully to the wall with the sacred twine, I went to the kitchen, where my grandmother was grinding fresh betelnut with a mortar and pestle. To my surprise, my father was there too. It was rather a shock to see him bald and wearing a saffron robe, when I was so used to seeing him barechested with a *phakhoma* loosely wrapped about his loins, and with a whiskey bottle rather than a begging bowl in his arms. I did not know whether to treat him as father or monk. To be on the safe side, I fell on my knees and placed my folded palms reverently at his feet.

My father was complaining animatedly to my grandmother in a weird mixture of normal talk and priestly talk. Sometimes he'd remember to refer to himself as *atma*, but at other times he'd speak like anyone off the street. He was saying, "But mother, *atma* is miserable, they only feed you once a day, and I'm hornier than ever! It's obviously not going to work, so why don't I just come home?"

My grandmother continued to pound vigorously at her betelnut.

"Anyway, *atma* thinks that it's time for more serious measures. I mean, calling in a professional exorcist."

At this, my grandmother looked up. "Perhaps you're right, holy one," she said. I could see that it galled her to have to address her wayward son-in-law in terms of such respect. "But can we afford it?"

"Phra Boddhisatphalo, *atma*'s guru, is an astrologer on the side, and he says that the stars for the movie theater are exceptionally bad. Well, *atma* was thinking, why not perform an act of merit while simultaneously ridding ourselves of a potential financial liability? I say sell out the half-share of the cinema and use the proceeds to hire a really competent exorcist. Besides," he added slyly, "with the rest of the cash I could probably obtain me one of those nieces of yours, the ones whose beauty your daughters are always bragging about."

"You despicable cad," my grandmother began, and then added, "holy one," to be on the safe side of the karmic balance.

"Honored father and grandmother," I ventured, "have you not considered the notion that Phii Lek's body might indeed be inhabited by an extraterrestrial being?"

"I fail to see the difference," my father said, "between a being from another planet and one from another spiritual plane. It is purely a matter of attitude. You and your brother, whose wits have been addled by exposure to too many American movies, think in terms of visitations from the stars; your grandmother and I, being older and wiser, know that 'alien' is merely another word for spirit. Earthly or unearthly, we are all spokes in the wheel of karma, no? Exorcism ought to work on both."

I didn't like my father's new approach at all; I thought his drunkenness far more palatable than his piety. But of course this would have been an unconscionably disrespectful thing to say, so I merely *wai*-ed in obeisance and waited for the ordeal to end.

My grandmother said, "Well, son-in-law, I can see a certain progress in you after all." My father turned around and winked at me. "Very well," she said, sighing heavily, "perhaps your mentor can find us a decent exorcist. But none of those foreigners, mind you," she added pointedly as Mary entered the kitchen to fetch another tray of comestibles for the monks' feast.

The interview with the spirit doctor was set for the following week. By that time the wonder of my brother's possession had attracted tourists from a radius of some ten kilometers; his performances were so spectactular as to outdraw even the talking cinema in Ban Kraduk.

It turned out to be a Brahmin, tall, dark, white-robed, with a long white beard that trailed all the way down to the floor. He wore a necklace of bones—they looked suspiciously human—and several flower wreaths over his uncut, wispy hair; moreover he had an elaborate third eye painted in the middle of his forehead.

"*Narayana, Narayana,*" he said, with the portentousness of a paunchy deva in one of those Indian historical movies. This, I realized, was a sham to impress the credulous populace, who were swarming around the stilts of our house. One or two children were peering from behind the horns of waterbuffaloes, and one was even peeping from a huge rainwater jar. The Brahmin had an accolyte just for the purpose of removing his sandals and splashing his feet from the foot-washing trough, an occupation of such ignominy that I was surprised even a boy would stoop to it. He surveyed my family (which had been suddenly expanded by visiting cousins, aunts, uncles, and several other grandmothers junior to my own) and inquired haughtily, "And which of you is the possessed one?"

"He can't even tell?" my grandmother whispered to me. Then she pointed at Phii Lek, who was crawling around the front porch moaning "tachyon, tachyon."

"Ah," said the exorcist. "A classic case of possession by a *phii krasue*. Dire measures are indicated, I'm afraid."

At the mention of the dreaded *phii krasue*, the entire family recoiled as a single entity. For the *phii krasue* is, as everyone knows, a spirit who looks like a normal enough creature in the daytime, but at night detaches its head from its body and, dragging its entrails behind it, propels itself forward by its tongue. It also lives on human excrement. It is, in short, one of the most loathsome and feared of spirits. The idea that we might have been harboring one in our very house sent chills of terror through me.

Presently I heard dissenting voices. "But a *phii krasue* can't act this way in the daytime!" one said. "Anyway, where's the trail of guts?" said another. "This fellow's obviously a quack . . . never trust a Brahmin exorcist, I tell you." "Well, let's give him the benefit. See if he comes up with anything."

The Brahmin spirit doctor took a good look at us, clearly appraising our finances. "Can he be cured?" my Elder Mother asked him.

"Given your very secure monetary standing," the Brahmin said, "I see no reason why not. You can take him inside now; I shall discuss the—ah, your merit-making donation—with the head of the household."

My grandmother came forward, her palms uplifted in supplication. "Fetch him a drink," she muttered to my mothers.

My mother said, "Does the *than mo phii* want a glass of water? Or would he prefer Coca-Cola?"

"A glass of Mekong whiskey," said the spirit doctor firmly. "Better yet, bring the whole bottle. We'll probably be haggling all night."

Since Phii Lek was no longer the center of attention, Mary and I obeyed the spirit doctor and brought him inside. He chose that moment to snap back into a state of relative sanity. We knew he had come to because he immediately began demanding chili peppers.

"All right," he said at last. "I've been authorized to tell you a few more things, since it seems to be the only hope."

"What about that monstrous charlatan out there?" Mary said. "He's only going to delay your plans, isn't he?"

"Not necessarily. I want you to insist that he perform the exorcism *at* the archaelogical dig. Once there, I'll be able to home in on the device and get rid of the giant cockroach at the same time. You know, that exorcist wasn't far wrong when he said I'd been possessed by a *phii krasue*. Would you be interested in knowing what my alien overlords like for dinner?"

"I take it they're scavengers?" Mary said.

"Exactly," said my brother. "But no more of this excremental subject. You have to convince that exorcist of yours. Unless the device is returned, there will be awful consequences. You see, the aliens were here once before, about eight hundred years ago. They planted a number of these devices as . . . well, tachyon calibration beacons. Well, this one is going dangerously out of synch, and some of the aliens aren't ending up in the bodies they were destined for. I mean, this psychic transference business is expensive, and the military ruler of nine star systems doesn't want to get thrust into the body of a leprous janitor from Milwaukee. That is precisely what happened last week, and the diplomatic consequences happen to be rippling through the entire galaxy at this very minute. Anyway, if the beacon isn't sent back post-haste for deactivation, guess who gets it?''

"You?" I said.

"Worse. They call it a preventative measure. They randomize the solar system."

"I think that's a euphemism for—" Mary began.

"That's right, Beloved Younger Siblings! No more Planet Earth."

"Can they really do that?" I said.

"They do it all the time." My brother reverted for a moment to cockroachlike behavior, then jerked back into a human pose with great effort. "They might not, though. All the xenobiologists, primitive cult fetishists, and so on are up in arms. So it might happen today . . . it might happen in a couple of years . . . it might never happen. Who knows? But galactic central thinks that no world, no matter how puny or insignificant, should be randomized without due process. But . . . I don't think we should risk it, do you?"

"Maybe not," I said. The theory that my brother had contracted one of those American mental diseases, like schizophrenia, was becoming more and more attractive to me. But I had to do what he said. To be on the safe side.

Mary and I left Phii Lek and went out to the porch where the spirit doctor had consumed half the whiskey and they had lit the anti-mosquito tapers, whose smoke perfumed the dense night air.

"Excuse me, honored grandmother," I said, trying to sound as unassuming as I could, "but Phii Lek says he wants the exorcism done at Mary's archaeological dig."

"Ha!" the exorcist said. "One must always do the opposite of what a possessed person says, for the evil spirit in him strives always to delude us!" His sentiments were expressed with such resounding ferocity that there was a burst of applause from the crowd downstairs. "Besides," he added, "there's probably a whole army of *phii krasue* out there, just waiting to swallow us up. It's a trap, I tell you! This possession is merely the vanguard of a wholesale demonic invasion!"

I looked despairingly at Mary. "Now what'll we do?" I said. "Sit around waiting for the Earth to disappear?"

It was Mary who came to the rescue . . . and I realized how much she had absorbed by quietly observing us and taking all those notes. She said, speaking in a Thai far more heavily accented than she normally used, "But please, honored spirit doctor, the field study group would be most interested in seeing a real live exorcism!"

The spirit doctor looked decidedly uncertain at being addressed in Thai by a *farang*. I could tell the questions racing through his mind: what status should the woman be accorded? She wasn't related to any of these people, nor was her social position immediately obvious. How could he respond without accidentally using the wrong pronoun, and giving her too much or little status—and perhaps rendering himself the laughingstock of these potential clients?

Taking advantage of his confusion, Mary pursued relentlessly. "Or does the honored spirit doctor perhaps *klua phii*?"

"Of course I'm not afraid of spirits!" the exorcist said.

"Then why would a few extra ones bother the honored spirit doctor?" Mary contrived to speak in so unprepossessing an accent that it was impossible to tell whether her polite words were ingenuous or insulting.

"Bah!" said the spirit doctor. "A few *phii krasue* are nothing. It's just a matter of convenience, that's all—"

"I'm sure that the foundation that's sponsoring our field research here would be more than happy to make a small donation toward ameliorating the inconvenience—"

"Since you put it that way—" the exorcist said, defeated.

"Hmpf!" my grandmother said, triumphantly yanking the half-bottle of whiskey away and sending my mother back to the kitchen with it. "These *farangs* might be some use after all. They're as ugly as elephants, of course—and albino elephants at that—but who knows? One day their race may yet amount to something."

The whole street opera of an exorcism was in full swing by the time my brother, Mary, and I parked her official Landrover about a half hour's walk away from the site. It had taken a week to make the preparations, with my brother's moments of lucidity getting briefer and his eschatological claims wilder each time.

By the time we had trudged through fields of young rice, squishing knee-deep in mud, several hundred people had gathered to watch. A good hundred or so were relatives of mine. Mary introduced me to some colleagues of hers, professors and suchlike, and they eyed me with curiosity as I fumbled around in their intractable language.

Four broken pagodas were silhouetted in the sunset. A waterbuffalo nuzzled at the pediment of an enormous stone Buddha, to whom I instinctively raised my palms in respect. Here and there, erupting from the brilliant green of the fields of young rice, were fragments of fortifications and walls topped with complex friezes that depicted grim, barbaric gods and garlanded, singing *apsaras*. A row of trunkless stucco elephants guarded a gateway to another paddy field.

Every part of the ruined city had been girded round with a *saisin*, a sacred rope that had been strung up along the walls and along the stumps of the elephant trunks and through the stone portals and finally into the folded palms of the spirit doctor himself, who sat, in the lotus position, on a woven rush mat, surrounded by a cloud of incense.

"You're late," he said angrily as we hastened to seat ourselves within the protected circle. "Get inside, inside. Or do you want to be swallowed up by spirits?"

If I had thought Phii Lek's actions bizarre before, his performance now shifted into an even more hyperbolic gear. He groaned. He danced about, his body coiling and coiling like a serpent.

I heard my grandmother cry out, "*Ui ta then!* Nuns dropping into the basement!" It was the strongest language I'd ever heard her use.

Mary clutched my hand. Some of my relatives stared disapprovingly at the impropriety, but I decided that they were just jealous.

"And now we'll see which it is to be," Mary said. "Science fiction or fantasy."

"He's mumbling himself into a trance now," I said, pointing to the exorcist, who had closed his eyes and from whose lips a strange buzzing issued.

"Are you sure he's not snoring?" one of my mothers said maliciously.

"What tranquillity! What perfect *samadhi!*" my other mother said admiringly, for the spirit doctor hadn't moved a muscle in some ten minutes.

Phii Lek's contortions became positively unnerving. He darted about the sacred circle, now and then flapping his arms as though to fly. Suddenly a bellow—like the cry of an angry waterbuffalo—burst from his lips. He flapped again and again—and then rose into the air!

"Be still, I command thee!" the exorcist's voice thundered, and he waved a rattle at my levitating brother and made mysterious passes. "I tell thee, be still!"

A ray of light shot upward from the earth, dazzlingly bright. The pagodas were lit up eerily. The ground opened up under Phii Lek as he hovered. There he was, brilliantly lit up in the pillar of radiance, with an iridescent aura around him whose outlines vaguely resembled an enormous cockroach. . . .

The crowd was going wild now. They clamored, they cheered; some of the children were disobeying the sacred cord and having to be restrained by their elders. My brother was sitting, in lotus position, in the middle of the air with his palms folded, looking just like a postcard of the Emerald Buddha in Bangkok.

The flaming apparition that had been my brother descended into the pit. We all rushed to the edge. The light from the abyss burned our eyes; we were blinded. Mary took advantage of the confusion to embrace me tightly; I was too overwhelmed to castigate her.

We waited.

The earth rumbled.

At last a figure crawled out. He was covered in mud and filth. He was clutching something under his arm . . . something very much like a Ming spittoon.

"Phii Lek!" I cried out, overcome with relief that he was still alive.

"The tachyon calibrator—" he gasped, holding aloft the spittoon and waving it dramatically in the air. "You must get it to—"

He fainted, still clasping the alien device firmly to his bosom.

The light shifted . . . the ghostly, rainbow-fringed giant cockroach seemed to drift slowly across the field, toward the unmoving figure of the exorcist . . . it danced grotesquely above his head, and he began to twitch and foam at the mouth. . . .

"I'll be dead!" my grand mother shouted. "The spirit is transferring itself into the body of the exorcist!"

In a moment the exorcist too fainted, and the sacred cord fell from his hands. The circle was broken. Whatever was done was done.

I rushed to the side of my brother, still lying prone by the side of the abyss.

"Wake up!" I said, shaking him. "Please wake up!"

He got up and grinned. Applause broke out. The exorcist, too, seemed to be recovering from his ordeal.

"And now," my brother said, holding out the alien artifact, "I can return this thing to the person who was sent to fetch it."

A small, white, palpitating hand was stretched forward to receive it. I turned to see who it was. "Oh, no," I said softly.

For it was Mary who had taken the artifact . . . and Mary who was now gyrating about the paddy field in a most unfeminine, most cockroachlike manner.

Later that night, Phii Lek and I sat on the floor of our room, waiting for Mary to snap out of her extraterrestrial seizure so we could find out what had happened.

Toward dawn the alien gave her her first break. "I can talk now," she said, suddenly, calmly.

"Do you need chilies?" I said.

"I think a good hamburger would be more my style," she said.

"We can probably fake it," my brother said, "if you don't mind having it on rice instead of a bun."

"Well," she said, when my brother had finished clattering about the kitchen fixing this unorthodox meal, and she was sitting cross-legged on my bedding munching furiously. "I suppose I should tell you what I'm allowed to tell you."

"Take your time," I said, not meaning it.

"Okay. Well, as you know, the exorcist is a total fake, a charlatan, a mountebank. But he does enter a passable state of *samadhi*, and apparently this was close enough to the psychic null state necessary for psychic transference to enable a mindswap to occur over a short distance. His blank mind was a sort of catalyst, if you will, through which, under the influence of the tachyon calibrator, I could leave Phii Lek's mind and enter Mary's."

"So you'll be taking the spittoon back to America?" I said.

"Right on schedule. And it's not a spittoon. That happens to be a very clever disguise."

"So. . . ." It suddenly occurred to me that she would soon be leaving. I was irritated at that. I didn't know why. I should have been pleased, because, after all, I had essentially traded her for my brother, and family always comes first.

"Look," she said, noticing my unease, "do you think . . . maybe . . . one last time?" She caressed my arm.

"But you're a giant cockroach!" I said.

She kissed me.

"You've been bragging to your friends all month about 'arriving' in America," she said. "How'd you like to 'arrive' on another planet?"

In the middle of the act I became aware that someone else was there with us. I mean, I was used to the way Mary moved, the delicious abandon with which she made her whole body shudder. I thought, "The alien's here too! Well, I'm really going to show it how a Thai can drive. Here we go!"

The next morning, I said, "How was it?"

She said, "It was a fascinating activity, but frankly I prefer mitosis."

Fiddling for waterbuffaloes.

In a day or so I saw her off; I went back to the antique store; I found my grandmother hard at work in her antique faking studio. A perfect Ming spittoon lay beside her where she squatted. She saw me, spat out her betelnut, and motioned me to sit.

"Why, grandmother," I said, "That's a perfect copy of whatever it was the alien took to America."

"Look again, my grandson," she said, and chuckled to herself as she rocked back and forth kneading clay.

I picked it up. The morning light shone on it through the window. I had an inkling that . . . no. Surely not.

"You didn't!" I said.

She didn't answer.

"Grandmother—"

No answer.

"But the solar system is at stake!" I blurted out. "If they find out that they've got the wrong tachyon calibrator—"

"Maybe, maybe not," said my grandmother. "The way I think is this: it's obviously very important to someone, and anything that valuable is worth faking. You say these interstellar diplomats will be arguing the question for years, perhaps. Well, as the years go by, the price will undoubtedly go up."

"But *khun yaai*, how can you possibly play games with the destiny of the entire human race like this?"

"Oh, come, come. I'm just an old woman looking out for her family. The movie house has been sold, and we've lost maybe 50,000 baht on the exorcism and the feast. Besides, your father will insist on another wife, I'm afraid, and after all this brouhaha I can't blame him. We'll be out 100,000 baht by the time we're through. I have a perfect right to some kind of recompense. Hopefully, by the time they come looking for this thing, we'll be able to get enough for it to open a whole antique factory . . . who knows, move to Bangkok . . . buy up Channel Seven so your brother can dub movies to his heart's content."

"But couldn't the alien tell?" I said.

"Of course not. How many experts on disguised tachyon calibrators do you think there are, anyway?" My grandmother paused to turn the electric fan so that it blew exclusively on herself. The air-conditioning, as usual, was off. "Anyway, *manus tang dao* are only another kind of foreigner, and anyone can tell you that all foreigners are suckers."

I heard the bell ring in the front.

"Go on!" she said. "There's a customer!"

"But what if—" I got up with some trepidation. At the partition I hesitated.

"Courage!" she whispered. "Be a *luk phuchai!*"

I remembered that I had the family honor to think of. Boldly, I marched out to meet the next customer.

TANITH LEE

Into Gold

One of the best known and most prolific of modern fantasists, Tanith Lee has well over a dozen books to her credit, including *The Birthgrave, Drinking Sapphire Wine, Don't Bite the Sun, Night's Master, The Storm Lord, Sung in Shadow, Volkhavaar,* and *Anackire*. Her short story "Elle Est Trois (La Mort)" won a World Fantasy Award in 1984; her sly and brilliant collection of retold folktales, *Red as Blood*, was also a finalist for the World Fantasy Award that year, in the best collection category. Her story "Nunc Dimittis," another World Fantasy Award finalist, was in our First Annual Collection, and "Foreign Skins" was in our Second Annual Collection. Her most recent books are the collections *Tamastarra, or the Indian Nights, Dreams of Dark and Light,* and *Night's Sorceries*.

In "Into Gold," she takes us to the tumultuous days after the fall of the Roman Empire, to a remote border outpost left isolated by the retreat of the Legions, for a scary and passionate tale of intrigue, obsession, and love.

INTO GOLD

Tanith Lee

1

Up behind Danuvius, the forests are black, and so stiff with black pork, black bears, and black-grey wolves, a man alone will feel himself jostled. Here and there you come on a native village, pointed houses of thatch with carved wooden posts, and smoke thick enough to cut with your knife. All day the birds call, and at night the owls come out. There are other things of earth and darkness, too. One ceases to be surprised at what may be found in the forests, or what may stray from them on occasion.

One morning, a corn-king emerged, and pleased us all no end. There had been some trouble, and some of the stores had gone up in flames. The ovens were standing empty and cold. It can take a year to get goods overland from the River, and our northern harvest was months off.

The old fort, that had been the palace then for twelve years, was built on high ground. It looked out across a mile of country strategically cleared of trees, to the forest cloud and a dream of distant mountains. Draco had called me up to the roof-walk, where we stood watching these mountains glow and fade, and come and go. It promised to be a fine day, and I had been planning a good long hunt, to exercise the men and give the breadless bellies solace. There is also a pine-nut meal they grind in the villages, accessible to barter. The loaves were not to everyone's taste, but we might have to come round to them. Since the armies pulled away, we had learned to improvise. I could scarcely remember the first days. The old men told you, everything, anyway, had been going down to chaos even then. Draco's father, holding on to a commander's power, assumed a prince's title which his orphaned warriors were glad enough to concede him. Discipline is its own ritual, and drug. As, lands and seas away from the center of the world caved in, soldier-fashion, they turned builders. They made the road to the fort, and soon began on the town, shoring it, for eternity, with strong walls. Next, they opened up the country, and got trade rights seen to that had gone by default for decades. There was plenty of skirmishing as well to keep their swords bright. When the Commander died of a wound got fighting the Blue-Hair Tribe, a terror in those days, not seen for years since, Draco became the Prince in the Palace. He was eighteen then, and I five days older. We had known each other nearly all our lives, learned books and horses, drilled, hunted together. Though he was born elsewhere, he barely took that in, coming to this life when he could only just walk. For myself, I am lucky, perhaps, I never saw the Mother of Cities, and so never hanker after her, or lament her downfall.

That day on the roof-walk, certainly, nothing was further from my mind. Then Draco said, "*There* is something."

His clear-water eyes saw detail quicker and more finely than mine. When I looked, to me still it was only a blur and fuss on the forest's edge, and the odd sparkling glint of things catching the early sun.

"Now, Skorous, do you suppose . . . ?" said Draco.

"Someone has heard of our misfortune, and considerably changed his route," I replied.

We had got news a week before of a grain-caravan, but too far west to be of use. Conversely, it seemed, the caravan had received news of our fire. "Up goes the price of bread," said Draco.

By now I was sorting it out, the long rigmarole of mules and baggage-wagons, horses and men. He traveled in some style. Truly, a corn-king, profiting always because he was worth his weight in gold amid the wilds of civilization. In Empire days, he would have weighed rather less.

We went down, and were in the square behind the east gate when the sentries brought him through. He left his people out on the parade before the gate, but one wagon had come up to the gateway, presumably his own, a huge conveyance, a regular traveling house, with six oxen in the shafts. Their straps were spangled with what I took for brass. On the side-leathers were pictures of grind-stones and grain done in purple and yellow. He himself rode a tall horse, also spangled. He had a slim, snaky look, an Eastern look, with black brows and fawn skin. His fingers and ears were remarkable for their gold. And suddenly I began to wonder about the spangles. He bowed to Draco, the War-Leader and Prince. Then, to be quite safe, to me.

"Greetings, Miller," I said.

He smiled at this coy honorific.

"Health and greetings, Captain. I think I am welcome?"

"My prince," I indicated Draco, "is always hospitable to wayfarers."

"Particularly to those with wares, in time of dearth."

"Which dearth is that?"

He put one golden finger to one golden ear-lobe.

"The trees whisper. This town of the Iron Shields has no bread."

Draco said mildly, "You should never listen to gossip."

I said, "If you've come out of your way, that would be a pity."

The Corn-King regarded me, not liking my arrogance—though I never saw the Mother of Cities, I have the blood—any more than I liked his slink and glitter.

As this went on, I gambling and he summing up the bluff, the tail of my eye caught another glimmering movement, from where his house wagon waited at the gate. I sensed some woman must be peering round the flap, the way the Eastern females do. The free girls of the town are prouder, even the wolf-girls of the brothel, and aristocrats use a veil only as a sunshade. Draco's own sisters, though decorous and well brought-up, can read and write, each can handle a light chariot, and will stand and look a man straight in the face. But I took very little notice of the fleeting apparition, except to decide it too had gold about it. I kept my sight on my quarry, and presently he smiled again and drooped his eyelids, so I knew he would not risk calling me, and we had won. "Perhaps," he said, "there might be a little consideration of the detour I, so foolishly, erroneously, made."

"We are always glad of fresh supplies. The fort is not insensible to its isolation. Rest assured."

"Too generous," he said. His eyes flared. But politely he added, "I have heard of your town. There is great culture here. You have a library, with scrolls from Hellas, and Semitic Byblos—I can read many tongues, and would like to ask permission of your lord to visit among his books."

I glanced at Draco, amused by the fellow's cheek, though all the East thinks itself a scholar. But Draco was staring at the wagon. Something worth a look, then, which I had missed.

"And we have excellent baths," I said to the Corn-King, letting him know in turn that the Empire's lost children think all the scholarly East to be also unwashed.

By midday, the whole caravan had come in through the walls and arranged itself in the market-place, near the temple of Mars. The temple priests, some of whom had been serving with the Draconis Regiment when it arrived, old, old men, did not take to this influx. In spring and summer, traders were in and out the town like flies, and native men came to work in the forges and the tannery or with the horses, and built their muddy thatch huts behind the unfinished law-house—which huts winter rain always washed away again when their inhabitants were gone. To such events of passage the priests were accustomed. But this new show displeased them. The chief Salius came up to the fort, attended by his slaves, and argued a while with Draco. Heathens, said the priest, with strange rituals, and dirtiness, would offend the patron god of the town. Draco seemed preoccupied.

I had put off the hunting party, and now stayed to talk the Salius into a better humor. It would be a brief nuisance, and surely, they had been directed

to us by the god himself, who did not want his war-like sons to go hungry?
I assured the priest that, if the foreigners wanted to worship their own gods,
they would have to be circumspect. Tolerance of every religious rag, as we
knew, was unwise. They did not, I thought, worship Iusa. There would be
no abominations. I then vowed a boar to Mars, if I could get one, and the
dodderer tottered, pale and grim, away.

Meanwhile, the grain was being seen to. The heathen god-offenders had
sacks and jars of it, and ready flour besides. It seemed a heavy chancy load
with which to journey, goods that might spoil if at all delayed, or if the
weather went against them. And all that jangling of gold beside. They fairly
bled gold. I had been right in my second thought on the bridle-decorations,
there were even nuggets and bells hung on the wagons, and gold flowers;
and the oxen had gilded horns. For the men, they were ringed and buckled
and roped and tied with it. It was a marvel.

When I stepped over to the camp near sunset, I was on the lookout for
anything amiss. But they had picketed their animals couthly enough, and the
dazzle-fringed, clink-bellied wagons stood quietly shadowing and gleaming
in the westered light. Columns of spicy smoke rose, but only from their
cooking. Boys dealt with that, and boys had drawn water from the well;
neither I nor my men had seen any women.

Presently I was conducted to the Corn-King's wagon. He received me
before it, where woven rugs, and cushions stitched with golden discs, were
strewn on the ground. A tent of dark purple had been erected close by. With
its gilt-tasseled sides all down, it was shut as a box. A disc or two more
winked yellow from the folds. Beyond, the plastered colonnades, the stone
Mars Temple, stood equally closed and eyeless, refusing to see.

The Miller and I exchanged courtesies. He asked me to sit, so I sat. I
was curious.

"It is pleasant," he said, "to be within safe walls."

"Yes, you must be often in some danger," I answered.

He smiled, secretively now. "You mean our wealth? It is better to display
than to hide. The thief kills, in his hurry, the man who conceals his gold. I
have never been robbed. They think, Ah, this one shows all his riches. He
must have some powerful demon to protect him."

"And is that so?"

"Of course," he said.

I glanced at the temple, and then back at him, meaningly. He said, "Your
men drove a hard bargain for the grain and the flour. And I have been docile.
I respect your gods, Captain. I respect all gods. That, too, is a protection."

Some drink came. I tasted it cautiously, for Easterners often eschew wine
and concoct other disgusting muck. In the forests they ferment thorn berries,
or the milk of their beasts, neither of which methods makes such a poor

beverage, when you grow used to it. But of the Semites one hears all kinds of things. Still, the drink had a sweet hot sizzle that made me want more, so I swallowed some, then waited to see what else it would do to me.

"And your lord will allow me to enter his library?" said the Corn-King, after a host's proper pause.

"That may be possible," I said. I tried the drink again. "How do you manage without women?" I added, "You'll have seen the House of the Mother, with the she-wolf painted over the door? The girls there are fastidious and clever. If your men will spare the price, naturally."

The Corn-King looked at me, with his liquid man-snake's eyes, aware of all I said which had not been spoken.

"It is true," he said at last, "that we have no women with us."

"Excepting your own wagon."

"My daughter," he said.

I had known Draco, as I have said, almost all my life. He was for me what no other had ever been; I had followed his star gladly and without question, into scrapes, and battles, through very fire and steel. Very rarely would he impose on me some task I hated, loathed. When he did so it was done without design or malice, as a man sneezes. The bad times were generally to do with women. I had fought back to back with him, but I did not care to be his pander. Even so, I would not refuse. He had stood in the window that noon, looking at the black forest, and said in a dry low voice, carelessly apologetic, irrefutable, "He has a girl in that wagon. Get her for me." "Well, she may be his—" I started off. He cut me short. "Whatever she is. He sells things. He is accustomed to selling." "And if he won't?" I said. Then he looked at me, with his high-colored, translucent eyes. "Make him," he said, and next laughed, as if it were nothing at all, this choice mission. I had come out thinking glumly, she has witched him, put the Eye on him. But I had known him lust like this before. Nothing would do then but he must have. Women had never been that way for me. They were available, when one needed them. I like to this hour to see them here and there, *our* women, straight-limbed, graceful, clean. In the perilous seasons I would have died defending his sisters, as I would have died to defend him. That was that. It was a fact, the burning of our grain had come about through an old grievance, an idiot who kept score of something Draco had done half a year ago, about a native girl got on a raid.

I put down the golden cup, because the drink was going to my head. They had two ways, Easterners, with daughters. One was best left unspoken. The other kept them locked and bolted virgin. Mercurius bless the dice. Then, before I could say anything, the Miller put my mind at rest.

"My daughter," he said, "is very accomplished. She is also very beautiful, but I speak now of the beauty of learning and art."

"Indeed. Indeed."

The sun was slipping over behind the walls. The far mountains were steeped in dyes. This glamour shone behind the Corn-King's head, gold in the sky for him, too. And he said, "Amongst other matters, she has studied the lore of Khemia—Old Aegyptus, you will understand."

"Ah, yes?"

"Now I will confide in you," he said. His tongue flickered on his lips. Was it forked? The damnable drink had fuddled me after all, that, and a shameful relief. "The practice of the Al-Khemia contains every science and sorcery. She can read the stars, she can heal the hurts of man. But best of all, my dear Captain, my daughter has learned the third great secret of the Tri-Magae."

"Oh, yes, indeed?"

"She can," he said, "change all manner of materials into gold."

2

"Sometimes, Skorous," Draco said, "you are a fool."

"Sometimes I am not alone in that."

Draco shrugged. He had never feared honest speaking. He never asked more of a title than his own name. But those two items were, in themselves, significant. He was what he was, a law above the law. The heart-legend of the City was down, and he a prince in a forest that ran all ways for ever.

"What do you think then she will do to me? Turn me into metal, too?"

We spoke in Greek, which tended to be the palace mode for private chat. It was fading out of use in the town.

"I don't believe in that kind of sorcery," I said.

"Well, he has offered to have her show us. Come along."

"It will be a trick."

"All the nicer. Perhaps he will find someone for you, too."

"I shall attend you," I said, "because I trust none of them. And fifteen of my men around the wagon."

"I must remember not to groan," he said, "or they'll be splitting the leather and tumbling in on us with swords."

"Draco," I said, "I'm asking myself why he boasted that she had the skill?"

"All that gold: They didn't steal it or cheat for it. A witch *made* it for them."

"I have heard of the Al-Khemian arts."

"Oh yes," he said. "The devotees make gold, they predict the future, they raise the dead. She might be useful. Perhaps I should marry her. Wait till you see her," he said. "I suppose it was all pre-arranged. He will want paying again."

When we reached the camp, it was midnight. Our torches and theirs opened the dark, and the flame outside the Mars Temple burned faint. There were stars in the sky, no moon.

We had gone to them at their request, since the magery was intrinsic, required utensils, and was not to be moved to the fort without much effort. We arrived like a bridal procession. The show was not after all to be in the wagon, but the tent. The other Easterners had buried themselves from view. I gave the men their orders and stood them conspicuously about. Then a slave lifted the tent's purple drapery a chink and squinted up at us. Draco beckoned me after him, no one demurred. We both went into the pavilion.

To do that was to enter the East head-on. Expensive gums were burning with a dark hot perfume that put me in mind of the wine I had had earlier. The incense-burners were gold, tripods on leopards' feet, with swags of golden ivy. The floor was carpeted soft, like the pelt of some beast, and beast-skins were hung about—things I had not seen before, some of them, maned and spotted, striped and scaled, and some with heads and jewelry eyes and the teeth and claws gilded. Despite all the clutter of things, of polished mirrors and casks and chests, cushions and dead animals, and scent, there was a feeling of great space within that tent. The ceiling of it stretched taut and high, and three golden wheels depended, with oil-lights in little golden boats. The wheels turned idly now this way, now that, in a wind that came from nowhere and went to nowhere, a demon wind out of a desert. Across the space, wide as night, was an opaque dividing curtain, and on the curtain, a long parchment. It was figured with another mass of images, as if nothing in the place should be spare. A tree went up, with two birds at the roots, a white bird with a raven-black head, a soot-black bird with the head of an ape. A snake twined the tree too, round and round, and ended looking out of the lower branches where yellow fruit hung. The snake had the face of a maiden, and flowing hair. Above sat three figures, judges of the dead from Aegyptus, I would have thought, if I had thought about them, with a balance, and wands. The sun and the moon stood over the tree.

I put my hand to the hilt of my sword, and waited. Draco had seated himself on the cushions. A golden jug was to hand, and a cup. He reached forward, poured the liquor and made to take it, before—reluctantly—I snatched the vessel. "Let me, first. Are you mad?"

He reclined, not interested as I tasted for him, then let him have the cup again.

Then the curtain parted down the middle and the parchment with it, directly through the serpent-tree. I had expected the Miller, but instead what entered was a black dog with a collar of gold. It had a wolf's shape, but more slender, and with a pointed muzzle and high carven pointed ears. Its eyes were also black. It stood calmly, like a steward, regarding us, then stepped aside and lay down, its head still raised to watch. And next the woman Draco wanted came in.

To me, she looked nothing in particular. She was pleasantly made, slim, but rounded, her bare arms and feet the color of amber. Over her head, to her breast, covering her hair and face like a dusky smoke, was a veil, but it was transparent enough you saw through it to black locks and black aloe eyes, and a full tawny mouth. There was only a touch of gold on her, a rolled torque of soft metal at her throat, and one ring on her right hand. I was puzzled as to what had made her glimmer at the edge of my sight before, but perhaps she had dressed differently then, to make herself plain.

She bowed Eastern-wise to Draco, then to me. Then, in the purest Greek I ever heard, she addressed us.

"Lords, while I am at work, I must ask that you will please be still, or else you will disturb the currents of the act and so impair it. Be seated," she said to me, as if I had only stood till then from courtesy. Her eyes were very black, black as the eyes of the jackal-dog, blacker than the night. Then she blinked, and her eyes flashed. The lids were painted with gold. And I found I had sat down.

What followed I instantly took for an hallucination, induced by the incense, and by other means less perceptible. That is not to say I did not think she was a witch. There was something of power to her I never met before. It pounded from her, like heat, or an aroma. It did not make her beautiful for me, but it held me quiet, though I swear never once did I lose my grip either on my senses or my sword.

First, and quite swiftly, I had the impression the whole tent blew upward, and we were in the open in fact, under a sky of a million stars that blazed and crackled like diamonds. Even so, the golden wheels stayed put, up in the sky now, and they spun, faster and faster, until each was a solid golden O of fire, three spinning suns in the heaven of midnight.

(I remember I thought flatly, We have been spelled. So what now? But in its own way, my stoicism was also suspect. My thoughts in any case flagged after that.)

There was a smell of lions, or of a land that had them. Do not ask me how I know, I never smelled or saw them, or such a spot. And there before us all stood a slanting wall of brick, at once much larger than I saw it, and smaller than it was. It seemed even so to lean into the sky. The woman raised her arms. She was apparent now as if rinsed all over by gilt, and one of the great stars seemed to sear on her forehead.

Forms began to come and go, on the lion-wind. If I knew then what they were, I forgot it later. Perhaps they were animals, like the skins in the tent, though some had wings.

She spoke to them. She did not use Greek any more. It was the language of Khem, presumably, or we were intended to believe so. A liquid tongue, an Eastern tongue, no doubt.

Then there were other visions. The ribbed stems of flowers, broader than ten men around, wide petals pressed to the ether. A rainbow of mist that arched over, and touched the earth with its feet and its brow. And other mirages, many of which resembled effigies I had seen of the gods, but they walked.

The night began to close upon us slowly, narrowing and coming down. The stars still raged overhead and the gold wheels whirled, but some sense of enclosure had returned. As for the sloped angle of brick it had huddled down into a sort of oven, and into this the woman was placing, with extreme care—of all things—long sceptres of corn, all brown and dry and withered, blighted to straw by some harvest like a curse.

I heard her whisper then. I could not hear what.

Behind her, dim as shadows, I saw other women, who sat weaving, or who toiled at the grind-stone, and one who shook a rattle upon which rings of gold sang out. Then the vision of these women was eclipsed. Something stood there, between the night and the Eastern witch. Tall as the roof, or tall as the sky, bird-headed maybe, with two of the stars for eyes. When I looked at this, this ultimate apparition, my blood froze and I could have howled out loud. It was not common fear, but terror, such as the worst reality has never brought me, though sometimes subtle nightmares do.

Then there was a lightning, down the night. When it passed, we were enclosed in the tent, the huge night of the tent, and the brick oven burned before us, with a thin harsh fume coming from the aperture in its top.

"Sweet is truth," said the witch, in a wild and passionate voice, all music, like the notes of the gold rings on the rattle. "O Lord of the Word. The Word is, and the Word makes all things to be."

Then the oven cracked into two pieces, it simply fell away from itself, and there on a bank of red charcoal, which died to clinker even as I gazed at it, lay a sheaf of golden corn. *Golden* corn, smiths' work. It was pure and sound and rang like a bell when presently I went to it and struck it and flung it away.

The tent had positively resettled all around us. It was there. I felt queasy and stupid, but I was in my body and had my bearings again, the sword-hilt firm to my palm, though it was oddly hot to the touch, and my forehead burned, sweatless, as if I too had been seethed in a fire. I had picked up the goldwork without asking her anything. She did not prevent me, nor when I slung it off.

When I looked up from that, she was kneeling by the curtain, where the black dog had been and was no more. Her eyes were downcast under her veil. I noted the torque was gone from her neck and the ring from her finger. Had she somehow managed her trick that way, melting gold on to the stalks of mummified corn—No, lunacy. Why nag at it? It was *all* a deception.

But Draco lay looking at her now, burned up by another fever. It was her personal gold he wanted.

"Out, Skorous," he said to me. "Out, now." Slurred and sure.

So I said to her, through my blunted lips and woollen tongue, "Listen carefully, girl. The witchery ends now. You know what he wants, and how to see to that, I suppose. Scratch him with your littlest nail, and you die."

Then, without getting to her feet, she looked up at me, only the second time. She spoke in Greek, as at the start. In the morning, when I was better able to think, I reckoned I had imagined what she said. It had seemed to be: "He is safe, for I desire him. It is my choice. If it were not my choice and my desire, where might you hide yourselves, and live?"

We kept watch round the tent, in the Easterners' camp, in the market-place, until the ashes of the dawn. There was not a sound from anywhere, save the regular quiet passaging of sentries on the walls, and the cool black forest wind that turned grey near sunrise.

At sunup, the usual activity of any town began. The camp stirred and let its boys out quickly to the well to avoid the town's women. Some of the caravaners even chose to stroll across to the public lavatories, though they had avoided the bathhouse.

An embarrassment came over me, that we should be standing there, in the foreigners' hive, to guard our prince through his night of lust. I looked sharply, to see how the men were taking it, but they had held together well. Presently Draco emerged. He appeared flushed and tumbled, very nearly shy, like some girl just out of a love-bed.

We went back to the fort in fair order, where he took me aside, thanked me, and sent me away again.

Bathed and shaved, and my fast broken, I began to feel more sanguine. It was over and done with. I would go down to the temple of Father Jupiter and give him something—why, I was not exactly sure. Then get my boar for Mars. The fresh-baked bread I had just eaten was tasty, and maybe worth all the worry.

Later, I heard the Miller had taken himself to our library and been let in. I gave orders he was to be searched on leaving. Draco's grandfather had started the collection of manuscripts, there were even scrolls said to have been rescued from Alexandria. One could not be too wary.

In the evening, Draco called me up to his writing-room.

"Tomorrow," he said, "the Easterners will be leaving us."

"That's good news," I said.

"I thought it would please you. Zafra, however, is to remain. I'm taking her into my household."

"Zafra," I said.

"Well, they call her that. For the yellow-gold. Perhaps not her name. That might have been *Nefra*—Beautiful . . ."

"Well," I said, "if you want."

"Well," he said, "I never knew you before to be jealous of one of my women."

I said nothing, though the blood knocked about in my head. I had noted before, he had a woman's tongue himself when he was put out. He was a spoiled brat as a child, I have to admit, but a mother's early death, and the life of a forest fortess, pared most of it from him.

"The Corn-King is not her father," he said now. "She told me. But he's stood by her as that for some years. I shall send him something, in recompense."

He waited for my comment that I was amazed nothing had been asked for. He waited to see how I would jump. I wondered if he had paced about here, planning how he would put it to me. Not that he was required to. Now he said: "We gain, Skorous, a healer and deviner. Not just my pleasure at night."

"Your pleasure at night is your own affair. There are plenty of girls about, I would have thought, to keep you content. As for anything else she can or cannot do, all three temples, particularly the Women's Temple, will be up in arms. The Salius yesterday was only a sample. Do you think they are going to let some yellow-skinned harlot devine for you? Do you think that men who get hurt in a fight will want her near them?"

"You would not, plainly."

"No, I would not. As for the witchcraft, we were drugged and made monkeys of. An evening's fun is one thing."

"Yes, Skorous," he said. "Thanks for your opinion. Don't sulk too long. I shall miss your company."

An hour later, he sent, so I was informed, two of the scrolls from the library to the Corn-King in his wagon. They were two of the best, Greek, one transcribed by the hand, it was said, of a very great king. They went in a silver box, with jewel inlay. Gold would have been tactless, under the circumstances.

Next day she was in the palace. She had rooms on the women's side. It had been the apartment of Draco's elder sister, before her marriage. He treated this one as nothing less than a relative from the first. When he was at leisure, on those occasions when the wives and women of his officers dined with them, there was she with him. When he hunted, she went with him, too, not to have any sport, but as a companion, in a litter between two horses that made each hunt into a farce from its onset. She was in his bed each night, for he did not go to her, her place was solely hers: The couch his father had shared only with his mother. And when he wanted advice, it was she who gave it to him. He called on his soldiers and his priests afterwards. Though he always did so call, nobody lost face. He was wise and canny, she must have told him how to be at long last. And the charm he had always had. He even consulted me, and made much of me before everyone, because, very sensibly he realized, unless he meant to replace me, it would be foolish to let the men see I no longer counted a feather's weight with him. Besides, I might get notions of rebellion. I had my own following, my own men who would die for me if they thought me wronged. Probably that angered me more than the rest, that he might have the idea I would forego my duty and loyalty, forget my honor, and try to pull him down. I could no more do that than put out one of my own eyes.

Since we lost our homeland, since we lost, more importantly, the spine of the Empire, there had been a disparity, a separation of men. Now I saw it, in those bitter golden moments after she came among us. He had been born in the Mother of Cities, but she had slipped from his skin like water. He was a new being, a creature of the world, that might be anything, of any country. But, never having seen the roots of me, they yet had me fast. I was of the old order. I would stand until the fire had me, rather than tarnish my name, and my heart.

Gradually, the fort and town began to fill with gold. It was very nearly a silly thing. But we grew lovely and we shone. The temples did not hate her, as I had predicted. No, for she brought them glittering vessels, and laved the gods' feet with rare offerings, and the sweet spice also of her gift burned before Mars, and the Father, and the Mother, so every holy place smelled like Aegyptus, or Judea, or the brothels of Babylon for all I knew.

She came to walk in the streets with just one of the slaves at her heels, bold, the way our ladies did, and though she never left off her veil, she dressed in the stola and the palla, all clasped and cinched with the tiniest amounts of gold, while gold flooded everywhere else, and everyone looked forward to the summer heartily, for the trading. The harvest would be wondrous too. Already there were signs of astounding fruition. And in the forest, not a hint of any restless tribe, or any ill wish.

They called her by the name *Zafra*. They did not once call her 'Easterner.' One day, I saw three pregnant women at the gate, waiting for Zafra to come out and touch them. She was lucky. Even the soldiers had taken no offense. The old Salius had asked her for a balm for his rheumatism. It seemed the balm had worked.

Only I, then, hated her. I tried to let it go. I tried to remember she was only a woman, and, if a sorceress, did us good. I tried to see her as voluptuous and enticing, or as homely and harmless. But all I saw was some shuttered-up, close, fermenting thing, like mummy-dusts reviving in a tomb, or the lion-scent, and the tall shadow that had stood between her and the night, bird-headed, the Lord of the Word that made all things, or unmade them. What was she, under her disguise? Draco could not see it. Like the black dog she had kept, which walked by her on a leash, well-mannered and gentle, and which would probably tear out the throat of anyone who came at her with mischief on his mind—Under her honeyed wrappings, was it a doll of straw or gold, or a viper?

Eventually, Draco married her. That was no surprise. He did it in the proper style, with sacrifices to the Father, and all the forms, and a feast that filled the town. I saw her in colors then, that once, the saffron dress, the Flammeus, the fire-veil of the bride, and her face bare, and painted up like a lady's, pale, with rosy cheeks and lips. But it was still herself, still the Eastern Witch.

And dully that day, as in the tent that night, I thought, So what now?

3

In the late summer, I picked up some talk, among the servants in the palace. I was by the well-court, in the peach arbor, where I had paused to look at the peaches. They did not always come, but this year we had had one crop already, and now the second was blooming. As I stood there in the shade, sampling the fruit, a pair of the kitchen men met below by the well, and stayed to gossip in their argot. At first I paid no heed, then it came to me what they were saying, and I listened with all my ears.

When one went off, leaving the other, old Ursus, to fill his dipper, I came down the stair and greeted him. He started, and looked at me furtively.

"Yes, I heard you," I said. "But tell me, now."

I had always put a mask on, concerning the witch, with everyone but Draco, and afterwards with him too. I let it be seen I thought her nothing much, but if she was his choice, I would serve her. I was careful never to speak slightingly of her to any—since it would reflect on his honor—even to men I trusted, even in wine. Since he had married her, she had got my duty, too, unless it came to vie with my duty to him.

But Ursus had the servant's way, the slave's way, of holding back bad news for fear it should turn on him. I had to repeat a phrase or two of his own before he would come clean.

It seemed that some of the women had become aware that Zafra, a sorceress of great power, could summon to her, having its name, a mighty demon. Now she did not sleep every night with Draco, but in her own apartments, sometimes things had been glimpsed, or heard—

"Well, Ursus," I said, "you did right to tell me. But it's a lot of silly women's talk. Come, you're not going to give it credit?"

"The flames burn flat on the lamps, and change color," he mumbled.

"And the curtain rattled, but no one there. And Eunike says she felt some form brush by her in the corridor—"

"That is enough," I said. "Women will always fancy something is happening, to give themselves importance. You well know that. Then there's hysteria and they can believe and say anything. We are aware she has arts, and the science of Aegyptus. But demons are another matter."

I further admonished him and sent him off. I stood by the well, pondering. Rattled curtains, secretive forms—it crossed my thoughts she might have taken a lover, but it did not seem in keeping with her shrewdness. I do not really believe in such beasts as demons, except what the brain can bring forth. Then again, her brain might be capable of many things.

It turned out I attended Draco that evening, something to do with one of the villages that traded with us, something he still trusted me to understand. I asked myself if I should tell him about the gossip. Frankly, when I had found out—the way you always can—that he lay with her less frequently, I had had a sort of hope, but there was a qualm, too, and when the trade matter was dealt with, he stayed me over the wine, and he said: "You may be wondering about it, Skorous. If so, yes. I'm to be given a child."

I knew better now than to scowl. I drank a toast, and suggested he might be happy to have got a boy on her.

"She says it will be a son."

"Then of course, it will be a son."

And, I thought, it may have her dark-yellow looks. It may be a magus too. And it will be your heir, Draco. My future Prince, and the master of the town. I wanted to hurl the wine cup through the wall, but I held my hand and my tongue, and after he had gone on a while trying to coax me to thrill at the joy of life, I excused myself and went away.

It was bound to come. It was another crack in the stones. It was the way of destiny, and of change. I wanted not to feel I must fight against it, or desire to send her poison, to kill her or abort her, or tear it, her womb's fruit, when born, in pieces.

For a long while I sat on my sleeping-couch and allowed my fury to sink down, to grow heavy and leaden, resigned, defeated.

When I was sure of that defeat, I lay flat and slept.

In sleep, I followed a demon along the corridor in the women's quarters, and saw it melt through her door. It was tall, long-legged, with the head of a bird, or perhaps of a dog. A wind blew, lion-tanged. I was under a tree hung thick with peaches, and a snake looked down from it with a girl's face framed by a flaming bridal-veil. Then there was a spinning fiery wheel, and golden corn flew off clashing from it. And next I saw a glowing oven, and on the red charcoal lay a child of gold, burning and gleaming and asleep.

When I woke with a jump it was the middle of the night, and someone had arrived, and the slave was telling me so.

At first I took it for a joke. Then, became serious. Zafra, Draco's wife, an hour past midnight, had sent for me to attend her in her rooms. Naturally I suspected everything. She knew me for her adversary: She would lead me in, then say I had set on her to rape or somehow else abuse her. On the other hand, I must obey and go to her, not only for duty, now, but from sheer aggravation and raw curiosity. Though I had always told myself I misheard her words as I left her with him the first time, I had never forgotten them. Since then, beyond an infrequent politeness, we had not spoken.

I dressed as formally as I could, got two of my men, and went across to the women's side. The sentries along the route were my fellows too, but I made sure they learned I had been specifically summoned. Rather to my astonishment, they knew it already.

My men went with me right to her chamber door, with orders to keep alert there. Perhaps they would grin, asking each other if I was nervous. I was.

When I got into the room, I thought it was empty. Her women had been sent away. One brazier burned, near the entry, but I was used by now to the perfume of those aromatics. It was a night of full moon, and the blank light lay in a whole pane across the mosaic, coloring it faintly, but in the wrong, nocturnal, colors. The bed, narrow, low, and chaste, stood on one wall, and her tiring table near it. Through the window under the moon, rested the tops of the forest, so black it made the indigo sky pale.

Then a red-golden light blushed out and I saw her, lighting the lamps on their stand from a taper. I could almost swear she had not been there a second before, but she could stay motionless a long while, and with her dark robe and hair, and all her other darkness, she was a natural thing for shadows.

"Captain," she said. (She never used my name, she must know I did not want it; a sorceress, she was well aware of the power of naming.) "There is no plot against you."

"That's good to know," I said, keeping my distance, glad of my sword, and of every visible insignia of who and what I was.

"You have been very honorable in the matter of me," she said. "You have done nothing against me, either openly or in secret, though you hated me from the beginning. I know what this has cost you. Do not spurn my gratitude solely because it is mine."

"Domina," I said (neither would I use her name, though the rest did in the manner of the town), "you're his. He has made you his wife. And—" I stopped.

"And the vessel of his child. Ah, do you think he did that alone?" She saw me stare with thoughts of demons, and she said, "He and I, Captain. He, and I."

"Then I serve you," I said. I added, and though I did not want to give her the satisfaction I could not keep back a tone of irony, "you have nothing to be anxious at where I am concerned."

We were speaking in Greek, hers clear as water in that voice of hers which I had to own was very beautiful.

"I remain," she said, "anxious."

"Then I can't help you, Domina." There was a silence. She stood looking at me, through the veil I had only once seen dispensed with in exchange for a veil of paint. I wondered where the dog had gone, that had her match in eyes. I said, "But I would warn you. If you practice your business in here, there's begun to be some funny talk."

"They see a demon, do they?" she said.

All at once the hair rose up on my neck and scalp.

As if she read my mind, she said:

"I have not pronounced any name. Do not be afraid."

"The slaves are becoming afraid."

"No," she said. "They have always talked of me but they have never been afraid of me. None of them. Draco does not fear me, do you think? And the priests do not. Or the women and girls. Or the children, or the old men. Or the slaves. Or your soldiers. None of them fear me or what I am or what I do, the gold with which I fill the temples, or the golden harvests, or the healing I perform. None of them fear it. But you, Captain, you do fear, and you read your fear again and again in every glance, in every word they utter. But it is yours, not theirs."

I looked away from her, up to the ceiling from which the patterns had faded years before.

"Perhaps," I said, "I am not blind."

Then she sighed. As I listened to it, I thought of her, just for an instant, as a forlorn girl alone with strangers in a foreign land.

"I'm sorry," I said.

"It is true," she said, "you see more than most. But not your own error."

"Then that is how it is." My temper had risen and I must rein it.

"You will not," she said quietly, "be a friend to me."

"I cannot, and will not, be a friend to you. Neither am I your enemy, while you keep faith with him."

"But one scratch on my littlest nail," she said. Her musical voice was nearly playful.

"Only one," I said.

"Then I regret waking you, Captain," she said. "Health and slumber for your night."

As I was going back along the corridor, I confronted the black jackal-dog. It padded slowly towards me and I shivered, but one of the men stooped to rub its ears. It suffered him, and passed on, shadow to shadow, night to ebony night.

*   *   *

Summer went to winter, and soon enough the snows came. The trading and the harvests had shored us high against the cruelest weather, we could sit in our towers and be fat, and watch the wolves howl through the white forests. They came to the very gates that year. There were some odd stories, that wolf-packs had been fed of our bounty, things left for them, to tide them over. Our own she-wolves were supposed to have started it, the whorehouse girls. But when I mentioned the tale to one of them, she flared out laughing.

I recall that snow with an exaggerated brilliance, the way you sometimes do with time that precedes an illness, or a deciding battle. Albino mornings with the edge of a broken vase, the smoke rising from hearths and temples, or steaming with the blood along the snow from the sacrifices of Year's Turn. The Wolf Feast with the races, and later the ivies and vines cut for the Mad Feast, and the old dark wine got out, the torches, and a girl I had in a shed full of hay and pigs; and the spate of weddings that come after, very sensibly. The last snow twilights were thick as soup with blueness. Then spring, and the forest surging up from its slough, the first proper hunting, with the smell of sap and crushed freshness spraying out as if one waded in a river.

Draco's child was born one spring sunset, coming forth in the bloody golden light, crying its first cry to the evening star. It was a boy, as she had said.

I had kept even my thoughts off from her after that interview in her chamber. My feelings had been confused and displeasing. It seemed to me she had in some way tried to outwit me, throw me down. Then I had felt truly angry, and later, oddly shamed. I avoided, where I could, all places where I might have to see her. Then she was seen less, being big with the child.

After the successful birth all the usual things were done. In my turn, I beheld the boy. He was straight and flawlessly formed, with black hair, but a fair skin; he had Draco's eyes from the very start. So little of the mother. Had she contrived it, by some other witch's art, knowing that when at length we had to cleave to him, it would be Draco's line we wished to see? No scratch of a nail, there, none.

Nor had there been any more chat of demons. Or they made sure I never intercepted it.

I said to myself, She is a matron now, she will wear to our ways. She has borne him a strong boy.

But it was no use at all.

She was herself, and the baby was half of her.

They have a name now for her demon, her genius in the shadowlands of witchcraft. A scrambled name that does no harm. They call it, in the town's argot: *Rhamthibiscan.*

We claim so many of the Greek traditions; they know of Rhadamanthys from the Greek. A judge of the dead, he is connectable to Thot of Aegyptus, the Thrice-Mighty Thrice-Mage of the Al-Khemian Art. And because Thot the Ibis-Headed and Anpu the Jackal became mingled in it, along with Hermercurius, Prince of Thieves and Whores—who is too the guide of lost souls—an ibis and a dog were added to the brief itinerary. Rhadamanthys-Ibis-Canis. The full name, even, has no power. It is a muddle, and a lie, and the invocation says: *Sweet is Truth.* Was it, though, ever sensible to claim to know what truth might be?

4

"They know of her, and have sent begging for her. She's a healer and they're sick. It's not unreasonable. She isn't afraid. I have seen her close an open wound by passing her hands above it. Yes, Skorous, perhaps she only made me see it, and the priests to see it, and the wounded man. But he recovered, as you remember. So I trust her to be able to cure these people and make them love us even better. She herself is immune to illness. Yes, Skorous, she only thinks she is. However, thinking so has apparently worked wonders. She was never once out of sorts with the child. The midwives were amazed—or not amazed, maybe—that she seemed to have no pain during the birth. Though they told me she wept when the child was put into her arms. Well, so did I." Draco frowned. He said, "So we'll let her do it, don't you agree, let her go to them and heal them. We may yet be able to open this country, make something of it, one day. Anything that is useful in winning them."

"She will be taking the child with her?"

"Of course. He's not weaned yet, and she won't let another woman nurse him."

"Through the forests. It's three days ride away, this village. And then we hardly know the details of the sickness. If your son—"

"He will be with his mother. She has never done a foolish thing."

"You let this bitch govern you. Very well. But don't risk the life of your heir, since your heir is what you have made him, this half-breed brat—"

I choked off the surge in horror. I had betrayed myself. It seemed to me instantly that I had been made to do it. *She* had made me. All the stored rage and impotent distrust, all the bitter frustrated *guile*—gone for nothing in a couple of sentences.

But Draco only shrugged, and smiled. He had learned to contain himself these past months. Her invaluable aid, no doubt, her rotten honey.

He said, "She has requested that, though I send a troop with her to guard her in our friendly woods, you, Skorous, do not go with them."

"I see."

"The reason which she gave was that, although there is no danger in the region at present, your love and spotless commitment to my well-being preclude you should be taken from my side." He put the smile away and said, "But possibly, too, she wishes to avoid your close company for so long, knowing as she must do you can barely keep your fingers from her throat. Did you know, Skorous," he said, and now it was the old Draco, I seemed somehow to have hauled him back, "that the first several months, I had her food always tasted. I thought you would try to see to her. I was so very astounded you never did. Or did you have some other, more clever plan, that failed?"

I swallowed the bile that had come into my mouth. I said, "You forget, Sir, if I quit you I have no other battalion to go to. The Mother of Cities is dead. If I leave your warriors, I am nothing. I am one of the scores who blow about the world like dying leaves, soldiers' sons of the lost Empire. If there were an option, I would go at once. There is none. You've spat in my face, and I can only wipe off the spit."

His eyes fell from me, and suddenly he cursed.

"I was wrong, Skorous. You would never have—"

"No, Sir. Never. Never in ten million years. But I regret you think I might. And I regret she thinks so. Once she was your wife, she could expect no less from me than I give one of your sisters."

"That bitch," he said, repeating for me my error, woman-like, "her half-breed brat—damn you, Skorous. He's my son."

"I could cut out my tongue that I said it. It's more than a year of holding it back before all others, I believe. Like vomit, Sir. I could not keep it down any longer."

"Stop saying *Sir* to me. You call her *Domina*. That's sufficient."

His eyes were wet. I wanted to slap him, the way you do a vicious stupid girl who claws at your face. But he was my prince, and the traitor was myself.

Presently, thankfully, he let me get out.

What I had said was true, if there had been any other life to go to that was thinkable—but there was not, anymore. So, she would travel into the forest to heal, and I, faithful and unshakable, I would stay to guard him. And then she would come back. Year in and out, mist and rain, snow and sun. And bear him other brats to whom, in due course, I would swear my honor over. I had better practice harder, not to call her anything but *Lady*.

Somewhere in the night I came to myself and I knew. I saw it accurately, what went on, what was to be, and what I, so cunningly excluded, must do. Madness, they say, can show itself like that. Neither hot nor cold, with a steady hand, and every faculty honed bright.

The village with the sickness had sent its deputation to Draco yesterday. They had grand and blasphemous names for *her*, out there. She had said she must go, and at first light today would set out. Since the native villagers revered her, she might have made an arrangement with them, some itinerant acting as messenger. Or even, if the circumstance were actual, she could have been biding for such a chance. Or she herself had sent the malady to ensure it.

Her gods were the gods of her mystery. But the Semitic races have a custom ancient as their oldest altars, of giving a child to the god.

Perhaps Draco even knew—no, unthinkable. How then could she explain it? An ancient, a straying, bears, wolves, the sickness after all . . . And she could give him other sons. She was like the magic oven of the Khemian Art. Put in, take out. So easy.

I got up when it was still pitch black and announced to my body-slave and the man at the door I was off hunting, alone. There was already a rumor of an abrasion between the Prince and his Captain. Draco himself would not think unduly of it, Skorous raging through the wood, slicing pigs. I could be gone the day before he considered.

I knew the tracks pretty well, having hunted them since I was ten. I had taken boar spears for the look, but no dogs. The horse I needed, but she was forest-trained and did as I instructed.

I lay off the thoroughfare, like an old fox, and let the witch's outing come down, and pass me. Five men were all the guard she had allowed, a cart with traveling stuff, and her medicines in a chest. There was one of her women, the thickest in with her, I thought, Eunike, riding on a mule. And Zafra herself, in the litter between the horses.

When they were properly off, I followed. There was no problem in the world. We moved silently and they made a noise. Their horses and mine were known to each other, and where they snuffed a familiar scent, thought nothing of it. As the journey progressed, and I met here and there with some native in the trees, he hailed me cheerily, supposing me an outrider, a rearguard. At night I bivouacked above them; at sunrise their first rustlings and throat-clearings roused me. When they were gone we watered at their streams, and once I had a burned sausage forgotten in the ashes of their cookfire.

The third day, they came to the village. From high on the mantled slope, I saw the greetings and the going in, through the haze of foul smoke. The village did have a look of ailing, something in its shades and colors, and the way the people moved about. I wrapped a cloth over my nose and mouth before I sat down to wait.

Later, in the dusk, they began to have a brisker look. The witch was making magic, evidently, and all would be well. The smoke condensed and turned yellow from their fires as the night closed in. When full night had come, the village glowed stilly, enigmatically, cupped in the forest's darkness. My mental wanderings moved towards the insignificance, the smallness, of any lamp among the great shadows of the earth. A candle against the night, a fire in winter, a life flickering in eternity, now here, now gone forever.

But I slept before I had argued it out.

Inside another day, the village was entirely renewed. Even the rusty straw thatch glinted like gold. She had worked her miracles. Now would come her own time.

A couple of the men had kept up sentry-go from the first evening out, and last night, patrolling the outskirts of the huts, they had even idled a minute under the tree where I was roosting. I had hidden my mare half a mile off, in a deserted bothy I had found, but tonight I kept her near, for speed. And this night, too, when one of the men came up the slope, making his rounds, I softly called his name.

He went to stone. I told him smartly who I was, but when I came from cover, his sword was drawn and eyes on stalks.

"I'm no forest demon," I said. Then I asked myself if he was alarmed for other reasons, a notion of the scheme Draco had accused me of. Then again, here and now, we might have come to such a pass. I needed a witness. I looked at the soldier, who saluted me slowly. "Has she cured them all?" I inquired. I added for his benefit, "Zafra."

"Yes," he said. "It was—worth seeing."

"I am sure of that. And how does the child fare?"

I saw him begin to conclude maybe Draco had sent me after all. "Bonny," he said.

"But she is leaving the village, with the child—" I had never thought she would risk her purpose among the huts, as she would not in the town, for all her hold on them. "Is that tonight?"

"Well, there's the old woman, she won't leave her own place, it seems."

"So Zafra told you?"

"Yes. And said she would go. It's close. She refused the litter and only took Carus with her. No harm. These savages are friendly enough—"

He ended, seeing my face.

I said, "She's gone already?"

"Yes, Skorous. About an hour—"

Another way from the village? But I had watched, I had skinned my eyes—pointlessly. Witchcraft could manage anything.

"And the child with her," I insisted.

"Oh, she never will part from the child, Eunike says—"

"Damn Eunike." He winced at me, more than ever uncertain. "Listen," I said, and informed him of my suspicions. I did not say the child was half

East, half spice and glisten and sins too strange to speak. I said *Draco's son*. And I did not mention sacrifice. I said there was some chance Zafra might wish to mutilate the boy for her gods. It was well known, many of the Eastern religions had such rites. The soldier was shocked, and disbelieving. His own mother—? I said, to her kind, it was not a deed of dishonor. She could not see it as we did. All the while we debated, my heart clutched and struggled in my side, I sweated. Finally he agreed we should go to look. Carus was there, and would dissuade her if she wanted to perform such a disgusting act. I asked where the old woman's hut was supposed to be, and my vision filmed a moment with relief when he located it for me as that very bothy where I had tethered my horse the previous night. I said, as I turned to run that way, "There's no old woman there. The place is a ruin."

We had both won at the winter racing, he and I. It did not take us long to achieve the spot. A god, I thought, must have guided me to it before, so I knew how the land fell. The trees were densely packed as wild grass, the hut wedged between, and an apron of bared weedy ground about the door where once the household fowls had pecked. The moon would enter there, too, but hardly anywhere else. You could come up on it, cloaked in forest and night. Besides, she had lit her stage for me. As we pushed among the last phalanx of trunks, I saw there was a fire burning, a sullen throb of red, before the ruin's gaping door.

Carus stood against a tree. His eyes were wide and beheld nothing. The other man punched him and hissed at him, but Carus was far off. He breathed and his heart drummed, but that was all.

"She's witched him," I said. Thank Arean Mars and Father Jupiter she had. It proved my case outright. I could see my witness thought this too. We went on stealthily, and stopped well clear of the tree-break, staring down.

Then I forgot my companion. I forgot the manner in which luck at last had thrown my dice for me. What I saw took all my mind.

It was like the oven of the hallucination in the tent, the thing she had made, yet open, the shape of a cauldron. Rough mud brick, smoothed and curved, and somehow altered. Inside, the fire burned. It had a wonderful color, the fire, rubies, gold. To look at it did not seem to hurt the eyes, or dull them. The woman stood the other side of it, and her child in her grasp. Both appeared illumined into fire themselves, and the darkness of garments, of hair, the black gape of the doorway, of the forest and the night, these had grown warm as velvet. It is a sight often seen, a girl at a brazier or a hearth, her baby held by, as she stirs a pot, or throws on the kindling some further twig or cone. But in her golden arm the golden child stretched out his hands to the flames. And from her moving palm fell some invisible essence I could not see but only feel.

She was not alone. Others had gathered at her fireside. I was not sure of them, but I saw them, if only by their great height which seemed to rival the trees. A warrior there, his metal faceplate and the metal ribs of his breast just glimmering, and there a young woman, garlands, draperies and long curls, and a king who was bearded, with a brow of thunder and eyes of light, and near him another, a musician with wings starting from his forehead— they came and went as the fire danced and bowed. The child laughed, turning his head to see them, the deities of his father's side.

Then Zafra spoke the Name. It was so soft, no sound at all. And yet the roots of the forest moved at it. My entrails churned. I was on my knees. It seemed as though the wind came walking through the forest, to fold his robe beside the ring of golden red. I cannot recall the Name. It was not any of those I have written down, nor anything I might imagine. But it was the true one, and he came in answer to it. And from a mile away, from the heaven of planets, out of the pit of the earth, his hands descended and rose. He touched the child and the child was quiet. The child slept.

She drew Draco's son from his wrapping as a shining sword is drawn from the scabbard. She raised him up through the dark, and then she lowered him, and set him down in the holocaust of the oven, into the bath of flame, and the fires spilled up and covered him.

No longer on my knees, I was running. I plunged through black waves of heat, the amber pungence of incense, and the burning breath of lions. I yelled as I ran. I screamed the names of all the gods, and knew them powerless in my mouth, because I said them wrongly, knew them not, and so they would not answer. And then I ran against the magic, the Power, and broke through it. It was like smashing air. Experienced—inexperiencable.

Sword in hand, in the core of molten gold, I threw myself on, wading, smothered, and came to the cauldron of brick, the oven, and dropped the sword and thrust in my hands and pulled him out—.

He would be burned, he would be dead, a blackened little corpse, such as the Semite Karthaginians once made of their children, incinerating them in line upon line of ovens by the shores of the Inner Sea—

But I held in my grip only a child of jewel-work, of poreless perfect gold, and I sensed his gleam run into my hands, through my wrists, down my arms like scalding water to my heart.

Someone said to me, then, with such gentle sadness, "Ah Skorous. Ah, Skorous."

I lay somewhere, not seeing. I said, "Crude sorcery, to turn the child, too, into gold."

"No," she said. "Gold is only the clue. For those things which are alive, laved by the flame, it is life. It is immortal and imperishable life. And you have torn the spell, which is all you think it to be. You have robbed him of it."

And then I opened my eyes, and I saw her. There were no others, no

Other, they had gone with the tearing. But she—She was no longer veiled. She was very tall, so beautiful I could not bear to look at her, and yet, could not take my eyes away. And she was golden. She was golden not in the form of metal, but as a dawn sky, as fire, and the sun itself. Even her black eyes—were of gold, and her midnight hair. And the tears she wept were stars.

I did not understand, but I whispered, "Forgive me. Tell me how to make it right."

"It is not to be," she said. Her voice was a harp, playing through the forest. "It is never to be. He is yours now, no longer mine. Take him. Be kind to him. He will know his loss all his days, all his mortal days. And never know it."

And then she relinquished her light, as a coal dies. She vanished.

I was lying on the ground before the ruined hut, holding the child close to me, trying to comfort him as he cried, and my tears fell with his. The place was empty and hollow as if its very heart had bled away.

The soldier had run down to me, and was babbling. She had tried to immolate the baby, he had seen it, Carus had woken and seen it also. And, too, my valor in saving the boy from horrible death.

As one can set oneself to remember most things, so one can study to forget. Our sleeping dreams we dismiss on waking. Or, soon after.

They call her now, the Greek Woman. Or the Semite Witch. There has begun, in recent years, to be a story she was some man's wife, and in the end went back to him. It is generally thought she practiced against the child and the soldiers of her guard killed her.

Draco, when I returned half-dead of the fever I had caught from the contagion of the ruinous hut—where the village crone had died, it turned out, a week before—hesitated for my recovery, and then asked very little. A dazzle seemed to have lifted from his sight. He was afraid at what he might have said and done under the influence of sorceries and drugs. "Is it a fact, what the men say? She put the child into a fire?" "Yes," I said. He had looked at me, gnawing his lips. He knew of Eastern rites, he had heard out the two men. And, long, long ago, he had relied only on me. He appeared never to grieve, only to be angry. He even sent men in search for her: A bitch who would burn her own child—let her be caught and suffer the fate instead.

It occurs to me now that, contrary to what they tell us, one does not age imperceptibly, finding one evening, with cold dismay, the strength has gone from one's arm, the luster from one's heart. No, it comes at an hour, and is seen, like the laying down of a sword.

When I woke from the fever, and saw his look, all imploring on me, the look of a man who has gravely wronged you, not meaning to, who says: But I was blind—that was the hour, the evening, the moment when life's sword of youth was removed from my hand, and with no protest I let it go.

Thereafter the months moved away from us, the seasons, and next the years.

Draco continued to look about him, as if seeking the evil Eye that might still hang there, in the atmosphere. Sometimes he was partly uneasy, saying he too had seen her dog, the black jackal. But it had vanished at the time she did, though for decades the woman Eunike claimed to meet it in the corridor of the women's quarters.

He clung to me, then, and ever since he has stayed my friend; I do not say, my suppliant. It is in any event the crusty friendship now of the middle years, where once it was the flaming blazoned friendship of childhood, the envious love of young men.

We share a secret, he and I, that neither has ever confided to the other. He remains uncomfortable with the boy. Now the princedom is larger, its borders fought out wider, and fortressed in, he sends him often away to the fostering of soldiers. It is I, without any rights, none, who love her child.

He is all Draco, to look at, but for the hair and brows. We have a dark-haired strain ourselves. Yet there is a sheen to him. They remark on it. What can it be? A brand of the gods—(They make no reference, since she has fallen from their favor, to his mother.) A light from within, a gloss, of gold. Leaving off his given name, they will call him for that effulgence more often, Ardorius. Already I have caught the murmur that he can draw iron through stone, yes, yes, they have seen him do it, though I have not. (From Draco they conceal such murmurings, as once from me.) He, too, has a look of something hidden, some deep and silent pain, as if he knows, as youth never does, that men die, and love, that too.

To me, he is always courteous, and fair. I can ask nothing else. I am, to him, an adjunct of his life. I should perhaps be glad that it should stay so.

In the deep nights, when summer heat or winter snow fill up the forest, I recollect a dream, and think how I robbed him, the child of gold. I wonder how much, how much it will matter, in the end.

SCOTT BAKER

Sea Change

Venice is an ancient city, with a proud and ancient past—but, as the following eloquent and passionate story suggests, the glories of its past may not even begin to *compare* with the glories of its future. . . .

Scott Baker is another writer who has made a large impact with a relatively small amount of published work. Primarily known for his short fiction, his stories have appeared in *Omni, The Magazine of Fantasy and Science Fiction,* and elsewhere. One of his *Omni* stories, ''The Lurking Duck,'' has become something of an underground cult classic, and was published in French translation as a book. His grisly story ''Still Life with Scorpion,'' first published in *Isaac Asimov's Science Fiction Magazine,* won the World Fantasy Award as best short story of 1985. His first novel was called *Nightchild,* and his most recent is *Firedance.* He lives with his family in Paris, France.

SEA CHANGE

Scott Baker

The bathtub was a deep oval seashell of green-veined white marble. The broad end of the shell extended upward like the headrest of a bed, with two ornate brass faucets supposedly resembling dolphins—though they reminded Rob more of tadpoles—set into the carved stone. The Tla who had been living in what was now their house had been found dead and dissolving in the tub, and though Rob's mother had been assured that nothing of either the Tla or whatever might have killed it could possibly have filtered through the monomolecular protective film to contaminate anything, she had still spent most of her first day in their new house scrubbing and rescrubbing the bathroom. Her efforts had made no difference whatsoever that Rob could see, but when she'd finally been satisfied she'd ordered him into the tub, and from then on he'd had to take two baths a day, one before school and the other before bed, instead of the single before-bed bath that had satisfied her in Arizona. Venice felt filthy to her, with its heavy air and sky, its dirt and discoloration sealed to the statues and walls beneath the Tla's impenetrable protective film, yet looking as though it would come away in your hand if you so much as brushed it.

He could hear his parents fighting in the kitchen downstairs, but they were keeping their voices too low for him to make out what they were saying. He listened a moment longer, then let himself slide down in the tub with his neck back so that just his ears were under water.

"Are you there?" he whispered. "Please let me see you. Show me what you look like." But the voices were distant, indistinct; all he could really hear was the sloshing of the tub water.

He sat back up. It was getting late, he should already have been ready for school, but he didn't want to face his mother and father, see the way they were hurting each other, or have them turn their anger against him. Besides, even before he'd begun hearing the voices whispering to him from the water, he'd discovered to his astonishment that he actually liked the time he spent sitting alone in the warm, soapy water. He'd always enjoyed swimming but hated baths before, yet he loved lying back with his head resting between the dolphin taps and looking out over the shiny black marble floor and through the big window that gave on the geranium-choked walled garden in front of the house and the equally geranium-filled Rio degli Ognassanti visible through the garden gate's wrought-iron grillwork. Only the almost imperceptible undulation of the mass of pinkish red flowers and dull green leaves and stems ever betrayed the fact that the geraniums were floating, like the tangled raft of seaweed the Tla's genetic manipulation had made of them, a flooded garden, and that the Rio degli Ognassanti was not an overgrown flowered alleyway, but a canal.

A bedraggled seagull was waddling pompously around on the water-stained marble statue of a woman with half-melted features whose torso jutted from the geraniums. Rob watched the seagull absently as it hopped down from the flower-mass and started poking through the stems and leaves, trying to think of something he could do to make things right between his mother and father again.

They were always fighting about him. He loved them and they loved him, but it would have been better for them if they'd never had him. Then they wouldn't have had to fight all the time and they could have just been happy together.

After a moment the gull gave up and took flight, only to strike the invisible walkway overhead with an indignant squawk. It recovered and flew away, disappearing up over the house. Probably looking for a boat to follow for scraps, or at least some open water with fish it could eat. There were only a few hundred people in Venice now, not nearly enough to provide the garbage that had once fed over half a million pigeons and gulls, and the geraniums had choked not only the canals and the lagoon separating Venice proper from the Lido but had extended out for hundreds of meters into the sea around them. Yet for reasons nobody had been able to explain, they showed no signs of spreading any farther despite the fact that some of the neighboring islands were actually closer than Venice was to the Lido.

"Why *can't* he keep on going to school here?" Rob's father was almost yelling.

"Because he's all alone here! There isn't anyone else his age!" They were so angry they'd forgotten again that he could hear what they were saying.

He stood up carefully, stepped out of the tub, and eased the bathroom door open so he could hear them better, then got back in the water.

"He'll get more individual attention here." His father's voice was still loud, but there was a conciliatory, almost pleading note in it. "And there'll be some kids coming in with the new people when the Palace housing is ready."

"One or two more kids won't make any difference."

"Let him finish out the year. Then we'll ask him. If he wants to leave, we'll send him away to school. If not, he can stay. O.K.?"

Rob's mother didn't answer at first. Rob was starting to relax when suddenly she said, "No, it's not O.K.! This city isn't right for a child."

"Why not?"

"It isn't safe."

"Safe? With no pollution, no violence, no cars to run him over? This is the safest city in the world. Unless you're talking about those two bomb scares. That was just an isolated crazy, they caught him before he hurt anyone."

"You know that's not what I'm talking about. Maybe there's something living in the canals. Under the geraniums. Maybe that's what killed the Tla."

"That's crazy. Ridiculous. It was the water. Like what the sweat on Rob's hand did to Sth'liat."

"What if Rob had been the one with the acid burns?"

"Sarah—"

"You're such an expert, you know all about the Tla, everything important, like that we're all perfectly safe. Only you didn't know it would burn one to have Rob touch it. Rob could have been burned just as easily."

"Nothing happened to Rob."

"You don't know what they came to Earth for. You don't know why they left the desert for a sinking city if water's so deadly to them. You don't know why they committed suicide, if that's what it really was, or what they wanted the geraniums for. But the one thing you do know is that we're all perfectly safe, no matter what."

"We know what the geraniums are for. They filter the pollution out of the water."

"That's why they glow at night?"

"No, but—"

"And why were they so interested in cleaning up the water if it would kill them to touch it? When they didn't even scrape the pigeon shit off the statues?"

"I don't know. You know I don't know. That's what we're all here for, to find out why they did what they did."

"That's what you're here for. Not me. Not Rob. It took me six years to get my gallery to where it was starting to pay for itself, then you dragged me here. For what? So we can all waste a couple of years and then start all over again?"

"Aren't you even curious to find out what they were like, what happened to them?"

"Not anymore. Not when I think of Rob growing up in this mausoleum with just you and your friends for company."

Rob's father said something too low for Rob to hear, and his mother

replied in the same tone. They'd remembered he was there. He jumped out of the tub and left it to drain while he scrambled into his clothes. He had his shirt almost buttoned by the time his father yelled, "Rob, school! Hurry up!" in a hearty voice with only a little edge to it to show how angry and irritated he really was.

His mother caught him as he ran toward the living room window and sent him back to comb his hair.

"Don't run," she told him when she handed him his grope stick. "I don't want you falling."

"I'll be careful, Mother." He tried to think of something he could say to reassure her, let her know she wouldn't have to leave Father or send him away to keep him safe. But there wasn't any way to reassure her, not without telling her about the voices, and he wasn't ready to let anyone know that the Tla were still there. Not yet, not until he'd learned enough so that when he told everybody about them they wouldn't have any choice but to believe him even if he was only eleven years old. Then his mother would finally understand and not be afraid for him or herself anymore.

I have to do it soon, he realized as he pecked her on the cheek and climbed the makeshift wooden stairs his father still hadn't gotten around to painting. He stepped out through the living room window onto the walkway, feeling for it with his grope stick. I have to do it before they take me away from here or break up for good.

It would have been so much easier if the Tla had still been the way Sth'liat had been back in Arizona, all slow and thoughtful. But they were tiny now, or so they'd told him. After centuries of old age and decline, they were young again—and though they whispered their joy to him through the water, they were too busy sporting among the geraniums and beneath the city for anything else to matter to them.

Rob remembered the first time he'd seen Sth'liat, seven years ago, in Arizona. The Tla had been ugly, with loose folds of pebbly, lizardlike gray skin over bones that stuck out and bent at all the wrong angles—but with his huge liquid gold-brown eyes and mournful, droopy face, he'd reminded Rob of the basset hound they'd had back home; and when Sth'liat spoke to Rob, he had sounded just like Rob's grandfather after his stroke: old and frail, fading away, barely able to talk but so happy to see Rob. . . . In Sth'liat's low, halting voice, Rob had heard the same inarticulate joy, the same gladness to see Rob that he'd always heard in his grandfather's, and he'd felt the same uprushing of love for the alien as he had for the old man. That had been why he'd taken Sth'liat's clawlike hand, because his grandfather had always wanted to hold Rob's hands and look into his face after he got too weak to have Rob climb into his lap anymore.

Sth'liat had watched Rob approaching, he must have known what was going to happen, but he'd done nothing to stop it. Rob could remember how horrible it had been, the way Sth'liat's hand had smoked and run where he'd touched it, like burning wax. Rob's mother had run up and grabbed him, held him and rocked him back and forth, too frightened and furious to know what else to do. She had never really forgiven either her husband or the Tla for what had happened, though Rob had only been frightened and Sth'liat himself had not seemed angry despite the damage done to his hand. In the same slow, grave voice he always used, he'd said that the young were always curious and playful, and that he was sure that Rob had meant no harm.

I don't even know what they look like now. How can I tell people they're still alive when I can't even tell anyone what they look like? They'd think I was making it up.

"Something wrong, Rob?" his mother asked. He realized he'd stopped just outside the window and was gazing down at the statue without seeing it.

"Nothing, Mother." He turned back, tried to smile at her. "I was just thinking."

"You better hurry up. You're late enough as it is. Just don't run."

"I promise."

The walkway sloped gently up from the windowsill, over the statue and around a dead pine tree that would undoubtedly have fallen on the house if the Tla had not fixed it in place for all time, up over the garden wall and across the Rio degli Ognassanti, then down the Rio delle Ermite. Usually the dust and dead leaves and the like made the walkways visible if you knew what to look for, but last night's rain had washed them clean again and they meandered unpredictably—more like game trails than even the least geometric sidewalks or city streets—so that though Rob knew the way by heart, he still had to tap in front of himself with the stick to keep from falling off.

Three mangy-looking wild cats were lying so as to form an equilateral triangle apparently suspended in midair over the Rio della Toletta. They were all facing inward, staring fixedly at an empty point at the center of the triangle. They seemed to be ignoring one another, but when one cat moved slightly the other two shifted so as to maintain their relative position, though their gazes never left the triangle's empty center.

Rob paused to watch them an instant before hurrying on, wondering if they were actually looking at something he couldn't see—perhaps even the Tla, as invisible as their walkways—or were just engaging in some typical cat strangeness.

When the walkway joined the main route over the Grand Canal, Rob caught sight of the Tla's nacreous golden cone-shell-shaped starship towering over the city. It was in the Piazza San Marco and twice the height of the Campanile beside it, yet seemed somehow perfectly integrated into the architectural excesses of the city's skyline.

School was in the Ducal Palace, but Rob paused before he went in to look back over his shoulder again at the starship, poised in the center of the flooded and geranium-filled piazza with the dilated entrance port at the base of the cone fixed open by the film in the same way that its controls, though visible, were fixed immovably in place; the scientists studying them could look at them all they wanted but were unable to alter any of their settings. The project had built a barrier around the ship to try to keep the water out, but it was impossible to affix anything to the piazza's film-coated pavement, so the enclosure leaked and, despite the pumps working full-time to get rid of the water that seeped through, the ship was always awash in at least enough water to get your feet wet. Someone Rob didn't recognize in a black shirt—probably a dayworker over from Maestra—was cutting back the geraniums that had overgrown the barrier during the night and were threatening to invade the ship's interior, while a U.N. guard watched him suspiciously.

The doors to the Ducal Palace, like the starship's entrance, had been left permanently open, and the ground floor was flooded. The project had laid down a wooden floor a meter above the original floor and blocked the doorways as well as possible, but the first story remained too humid for anything but the pumps, generators, and other machinery necessary for the apartments being constructed on the upper floors.

Rob showed his ID at the door. The guard waved him through without checking it. Supposedly everybody, even the senior scientists like his father, had to have their identities verified constantly, but that applied only to adults. He climbed a winding staircase with red plastic pipes containing electric cables on his right, green plastic pipes carrying water on his left, to his classroom.

The room itself was small, with some water-stained mosaics on one wall. Probably a former cloakroom or something like that. His friend Mike was back in Minneapolis again, so there were only Dominique and himself, plus a few younger kids he never paid any attention to.

Rob sat down at his terminal and touched his thumb to the screen to identify himself, then checked the menu. His only remaining requirements for the week were some more work on his French or Italian, and a study of the political and religious upheaval that had followed the '89 newflu epidemic in the U.S. and Canada. He'd already run through the rest of the week's lessons.

He chose the epidemic. He was bad in languages and didn't want to look foolish in front of Dominique. It was better when Mike was there, because Mike was even worse than he was.

He tried to concentrate and not think about having to leave the city, or about his parents breaking up. If he didn't do well, his mother would have one more argument to use on his father.

It was a relief when the teacher called him over to his booth to see how well Rob was synthesizing what he'd studied today with the rest of what he'd learned that week.

The sky had clouded over again by lunchtime. Rob waited for Dominique outside the Palace. They didn't get along particularly well—even though she was only a little over a year older, she usually acted as though being twelve meant she was an adult and he was just a little kid—but if he could make better friends with her, then maybe his mother wouldn't worry so much.

Actually, his mother was right, or would have been right if it hadn't been for the Tla. Mike was his only real friend here, and he spent a week every month back in the states. Though Rob had loved the city from the first day he'd seen it with the sun gleaming on its palaces and cathedrals and on the Tla's golden starship, he'd been almost unbearably lonely until he'd begun hearing voices.

"Hi, Dominique."

"Hello, Rob." Dominique sounded bored, as usual.

"It's beautiful, isn't it?" Rob asked, not knowing what else to say. He gestured at the starship. One of his father's colleagues who was studying the entrance mechanism saw him and waved back, making him feel momentarily foolish. "The way it fits in with the basilica and everything else, I mean. Maybe that's why they came here."

"You sound just like your father." Dominique started off, pushing her grope stick in front of her. Rob hurried to catch up with her.

"What's wrong with sounding like my father?"

"You both love it here so much. I hate it."

"Hate it?" It had never occurred to him that anyone who wasn't afraid of the city the way his mother was could hate Venice. "Why?"

"Because there's nothing to do, nobody to talk to. You can't even go swimming because of the weeds. It rains all the time. It's like being stuck out in the country all the time, only worse."

"My mother doesn't like it, either."

"I know. You're lucky she's sending you away. I keep trying to get my parents to send me back to Montreal, but they won't do it."

"What do you mean, sending me away? I'm not going anywhere."

"Your mother asked mine about schools in Switzerland, that's how I know."

"They're not sending me anywhere! I mean, they're talking about it for next year, but nothing's been decided yet."

"Your mother's decided."

"Maybe, but Father hasn't. He won't let her."

Dominique looked at him in disgust. "You get to leave and you don't even want to. It's not fair."

"No, it isn't."

The cats were still staring at the same empty point over the Rio della Toletta when Rob passed them.

Maybe the whole trouble was, his mother was bored. She didn't have anything to do but worry and feel alone.

She was upstairs when he got home, in one of the bedrooms they didn't sleep in. She had her easel set up with a canvas on it and all her oils out and ready, but there were only two or three dispirited brushstrokes in one corner. She was sitting on a wooden chair, looking out at the gray sky and smoking.

"What are you doing home, Rob? I thought you were eating with your father at the canteen again."

"I was going to, but then I thought I'd like to come home and see you."

"Do you want a sandwich?"

"Sure." He followed her back downstairs to the kitchen, sat down and watched as she got the food out, sliced the bread, ham, provolone, and tomatoes.

"It's not because you heard us fighting this morning?"

"No." He felt uncomfortable, tried not to let it show. "It's just that—I don't see you enough. So I thought I'd come home for lunch more often. If that's O.K."

"Whenever you want, Rob. Mustard or mayonnaise?"

"Mayonnaise."

She gave him the sandwich, sat down across from him with a cup of coffee. She looked old, tired. He wondered if they'd gone back to fighting after he'd left.

The bread was chewy and tough; he had to tear bites off with his teeth, and a slice of tomato fell out onto the table. He picked it up and put it back in the sandwich, tried to be more careful with the next bite.

"Do you want to go for a walk after school?" he asked. "I mean, if it gets nicer out?" He could see her frowning, getting ready to say no, so he added quickly, "It's beautiful here when the sun's shining. I found some really great places for you to paint."

"No, thank you, Rob. I used to like it here, before you were born. Even though it was rotting and sinking and falling apart, there were still people living in it, it was all still alive. But not anymore."

"I still think it's beautiful, Mother." Maybe if he could get some of the way it looked to him across to her—

"It's like it was a man-made city once, just dead like a parking lot or something, but now it's come alive, it's part of nature again. Like a flower growing from a seed. Or—I don't know, I can't explain. But it's beautiful."

"I can't stand the silence. The geraniums all over everything. Like the city was going back to the jungle or something. It gives me the shivers, especially at night. . . ." She shook her head. "It's not natural here, Rob. It's not right."

He realized he should never have let her see how much he loved the city, how much it meant to him. She couldn't understand, and it would only worry her even more.

"Then how about taking me over to Maestra or Torcello?" he asked. "I haven't seen Torcello. Maybe you could find something you need in the market there, or paint that old church you and Dad were talking about, the one with the frescoes."

"All right." She forced a smile, and though he could see she was forcing it, there was still some real pleasure there as well. "As long as you're not just doing this to make me feel better."

"No. Maybe I'll ask Dominique to come along, if that's O.K.? I think she'd like that."

"All right." He could tell the idea pleased her. "Do you want another sandwich?"

"No, thanks."

"Then you better get back to school. I'll see you later."

It started to rain again a few minutes after he got back to the palace, and it was still raining when he finished school. He didn't even bother to ask Dominique if she wanted to go.

His mother was sitting in the upstairs bedroom again, looking out the window at the rain. He watched her a moment, but couldn't think of anything to say that would make any difference, so he put on a raincoat with a hood and went back outside. The rain didn't bother him the way it did her.

Why wouldn't the Tla show themselves to him? If he just knew what they looked like now and could describe them to someone else—Maybe that was why, because they didn't trust him to keep their secret? But they'd never told him not to tell anybody else about them. And then why let him hear them in the first place if they didn't trust him? Why did they keep on talking to him and not to anyone else? What made him so special?

His walk had taken him to the Fondamenta delle Zattere, out on the Punta della Dogana behind the Basilica of Santa Maria della Salute. Nobody could see him. He lay down on his belly by the water's edge, stuck his head in the geraniums, pushing them away with his hands until his mouth was almost touching the water underneath. "Show yourselves to me," he whispered. "Why won't you let me see what you look like?" But there was only the almost overpowering sweetness of the flowers' smell.

Dinner that night was grim. A fact-finding commission of representatives from some of the governments that had mounted the project had arrived unexpectedly, and its members were determined to find out why the project had not produced useful results after over a year. Rob's father was one of the senior scientists the commission had convoked for that evening to testify as to what they thought they had accomplished, and why they should be allowed to continue and not be replaced with some other team. Rob brought up his idea for a trip to Torcello as something the whole family could do together that Saturday or Sunday, but his father just nodded distractedly and said, "Maybe, Rob, if I've got the time," in a way that let Rob know there was no chance he ever would. The rain was coming down even harder than before, with lightning out over the sea, and thunder.

"I hope you can convince them," Rob's mother said as she helped his father into his plastic raincoat. "They couldn't do better with anyone else."

"Why? Isn't that what you want, too?"

"Not like that. Not because they forced you."

"Then you'd try to fight it?"

"No. That's not how I want to leave, but I still want to leave."

Rob's mother stood at the window, looking after his father for a moment as, seemingly suspended in midair above the garden and canal where the geraniums glowed with soft, shimmering whorls of green and gold phosphorescence, he tapped carefully in front of him with his grope stick like a blind man with his cane while he made his way slowly out over the garden wall and down the Rio delle Ermite.

In the bathtub that evening, looking out over the glowing garden, Rob tried to talk with the Tla, but, though Sth'liat and one or two of the others whose voices he could still recognize despite the change that had made them youthful again cried greetings to him, their voices were full of the storm's excitement and the beating of the waves and he couldn't get them to pay any attention to him.

Come play with us, they called to him, and when he whispered, "No, wait, please, I need to talk to you," they only laughed and told him, later, after the storm.

The next day he ate lunch in the canteen with his father, hoping to get a chance to tell him how much he loved the city, how important it was for him to be able to stay and not be sent away to school, but his father was too involved in the discussion he was having about the walkways and preservative film for Rob to talk to him privately. Rob tried to listen, since the more he knew about the problems they were trying to solve, the better he'd be able to get the answers for them when the Tla finally started telling him things, but the conversation was too technical, all about enzymes and isomers. He thought they were saying that the Tla had spun the walkways and protective film out of themselves, like spiders building their webs, but when he asked if that's what they meant, Mr. Mondolo told him that it was an interesting idea and one that might even be worth studying—with a smile that meant he was just trying to be nice to Rob—but that what they were talking about this time was something else entirely.

Just before he had to go back to school, the conversation turned to the Tla starship. Rob asked if he could go inside again for another look.

"No." His father shook his head. "I'm sorry, Rob. It's not like you could hurt anything, even if you wanted to, but they've tightened security again."

"They're not even sure they want to let *us* in anymore," Dominique's father said with a bark that was supposed to be a laugh but just sounded angry.

"Maybe in a couple of weeks, when the commission's gone again and everybody's had a little more time to forget that latest bombing attempt," Mr. Mondolo said, trying to be nice again, and everybody nodded.

Rob finally got his father alone the next evening, while his mother was cooking dinner.

"Dad—"

"What, Rob?"

"I heard you and Mother talking about sending me away to school next year."

"It would be sort of hard for you not to hear, the way we've been yelling at each other," his father said. "I'm sorry."

"That's O.K. I mean, that's not what I want to talk about. What I want to say is, I love it here, Dad. Everything. The geraniums, all of it. I don't want to leave here. Not ever. But I can't make Mother understand."

"Neither can I. I wish I could, but I can't. She just doesn't want to listen."

"Can you tell her for me anyway, Dad. Tell her to let me stay here? Please. She'll have to listen to you, even if she doesn't want to."

"I'll do what I can. But I'm having a pretty hard time keeping her from leaving, herself."

"Promise?"

"I promise."

Rob woke up in the middle of the night and heard them arguing again, but their bedroom was at the other end of the hall, and though he knew they were arguing about him again, he couldn't tell what they were saying. Only how angry they were, how much they hated each other.

It's because she's afraid of the city. Afraid of it for me. Because she doesn't understand it. Even Dad doesn't really understand it. If they understood, she wouldn't be afraid anymore. Then she'd see how beautiful it is here, how perfectly it all goes together now, and they wouldn't fight anymore.

The full moon was shining brightly in through the window, and when he sat up he could see the geraniums pulsing and glowing in the garden. The clock by the bed said it was a little after three in the morning. I can't wait any longer, he realized. Not if they're going to hate each other like that. He waited until the sounds of their fight had died away, then forced himself to wait another half hour by the clock to make sure they were asleep.

He put his pajamas on, and eased the bedroom door open, then sneaked down the hall. In their house in Arizona, the floor had creaked whenever he'd tried to sneak downstairs for cookies after he was supposed to be in bed, but the Tla's film had fixed this house's warped floorboards in place so that they were solid and his footsteps didn't make any noise.

He paused in front of his parents' door and heard his father snoring, the sound of his mother's regular breathing, so he knew he was safe. But even so, there would be too much chance of waking them up if he ran a tub, so he continued on past the bathroom and downstairs.

The living room window was open. It was a perfect night to talk to the Tla: warm, calm, bright, with nothing to distract them. He felt his way along the walkway on his hands and knees until he was just over the statue. He didn't want to get his pajamas wet, so he took them off and climbed down the statue till he was standing on its pedestal with his legs in the geraniums up to his knees and his ankles underwater.

He lay down on his stomach on the geraniums, feeling the springy mass swaying beneath him. He pushed them out of the way with his hands, put his head down by the water again the way he had on the Punta della Dogana, whispered, "Are you there? Can you hear me?" Then he closed his eyes and stuck his head underwater so he could hear their answer.

We can hear you, Rob, he heard Sth'liat say.

He lifted his head back up out of the water. "You have to help me," he whispered. "I need your help."

Why? One of the Tla asked him when he stuck his head back under again. What's wrong?

"My parents," he told them. "They're going to send me away." He told them all about it, how his mother hated Venice, how she wanted to send him away to school.

You can come back and see us later, they told him when he put his head in the water again, already losing interest. We'll still be here. We'll be here. We'll be here until we grow up again. You'll have plenty of time to come back and play with us then.

"Is that why you talk to me and not to the others? Because I'm just a kid like you now?"

Because you wanted to be my friend, Sth'liat said. And the others are too old for us. We won't be that old again for hundreds of years.

"But if I go away, I'll get too old for you!"

Then come play with us now, Sth'liat told him. Leave your old body and come swim with us. That way you won't have to get old before we do.

"I can't do that."

You can if you want to. We'll help you.

"Can I just leave my body for a little while, an hour or two, and then come back to it?"

No. You'll have to wait until your new body grows up again.

"I can't. I'm just a kid. Mother and Father'd miss me."

Then come back to us later, when you can. We'll still be here waiting for you.

"Show yourselves to me. Please, let me see what you look like."

Put your head in the water again and open your eyes.

He wedged his head as far as he could into the geraniums, opened his eyes. The salt water stung. All he could see was the geraniums' pulsating phosphorescence.

He held his breath until, suddenly, he heard their laughter and saw a quick, darting spark of light, and then another. Like fireflies. Underwater fireflies.

A third spark joined them, and a fourth. Then, as suddenly as they had come, they were gone.

"Sth'liat?" he asked. But there was no answer. He got to his feet, climbed the statue back to the walkway, sneaked back to his room.

They'll never believe me, he realized the next day as school was getting out. The fireflies are too different. Even if I can show the fireflies to them, nobody'll ever believe that those are really the Tla.

They're little kids. Too little. Babies. They won't ever tell me the kind of thing I need to convince people that they're really here talking to me.

He wandered around until it started getting dark, using his grope stick to follow the walkways' twistings and turnings with automatic skill. It was only when he finally took the way back to his house and, looking in through the living room window, saw his parents sitting stiffly across from each other, glaring as though they'd been fighting yet again, that he at last realized what he'd been doing had been saying good-bye to the city.

The Tla had been so beautiful, darting through the water. So free and joyous.

"Where were you?" his mother said when he reached the window. "We were worried about you."

"Out. Just walking around."

"Well, don't. Not without telling us."

He looked at them, the fear and anger on his mother's face, the anger and frustration on his father's, and thought: The sooner I tell them I want to go away to school, the better. When they don't have me around to worry about, they won't have to hate each other anymore.

"Mother, I—"

"What, Rob?"

"Nothing." He couldn't say it. I'll tell them tomorrow, he decided. At breakfast. I'll sneak out tonight after they're asleep to watch the Tla again and tell them tomorrow.

"Then sit down," his father said. "We've got something to tell you."

Rob sat down on the couch.

"We've decided that you've got to go away to school," his father said. "Your mother's been checking out boarding schools for you, but we didn't want to say anything until we were sure. She's found a school in Switzerland that looks perfect, except that you're a little weak in languages for them. So you'll be starting intensive summer school courses in two weeks to give you a chance to catch up with the other students there."

"But you told me—"

"I know, Rob." His father couldn't meet his eyes. "But I didn't want to make you unhappy. I wanted you to enjoy the rest of your time here."

"When? When did you decide?"

"Last week," his mother said.

"The morning I heard you fighting before school?" he asked his father.

"Yes."

"You lied to me! You promised you'd help me stay!"

"I promised your mother I wouldn't tell you anything first." He shrugged. "I'm sorry, Rob, but that's how it has to be. You'll understand better when you're older."

Everything he'd tried to do for them, all the ways he'd been willing to give up everything he wanted to make them happy, and they'd been lying to him, they'd already decided to send him away. Suddenly he wasn't willing to sacrifice anything for them anymore. They had to let him stay. He had to make them let him stay.

"The Tla," he said. "They're still here."

"What?" his mother asked.

"What do you mean?" his father demanded.

"They're still alive. They didn't die. They talk to me. That's why you can't send me away: you need me here, to talk to them for you."

His mother looked horrified. She opened her mouth to say something, but his father glanced over at her, shook his head slightly, and she closed her mouth again.

"You don't believe me. You think I'm making it all up!"

"We found their bodies, Rob. You saw the photographs," his father said, gently now. "I'm sorry they're dead, I wish they weren't as much as you do, but that doesn't change the facts. They're dead, Rob."

"Those were just their—like their cocoons. They're different now. Young again."

"I don't want to hear this," his mother said.

"No, wait. What are they like now, Rob?"

"They're tiny. They were too old, but when they get too old they don't die, they just turn back into children."

"Can you show them to us, Rob?" his father asked.

Rob turned to the open window. The garden was just beginning to glow faintly in the deepening twilight. "Show yourselves!" he yelled to the Tla. "Please show yourselves to them. Just this one time. Or they'll make me go away."

"Rob—" his father began.

"Please!" he shouted.

And then, suddenly, there among the pulsing swirls of phosphorescence in the garden, he saw brighter sparks, like dozens of fireflies darting around in the geraniums.

"They can't see you!" he yelled. "Make them see you."

The sparks darted faster, and some came leaping out of the geraniums to dance in the air, shining and beautiful, for an instant before falling back.

"There! Did you see them?"

"See what?"

"Those sparks, in the garden, the ones that looked like fireflies."

"That's all they were, Rob. Fireflies," his father said in that same horrible, gentle, pitying tone of voice that was worse than any anger could have been. "And your mother's right. This city isn't right for you. But we can't wait until next fall to send you away."

"I'll get us plane tickets for Monday," his mother said. "We can go pack and stay with Mother until we figure out something better. Maybe she'll be able to find us a good doctor."

"I don't need a doctor. I'm not sick." He wanted to yell it at them, but he was too tired, it was too hopeless, there wasn't any reason to keep on talking to them. They couldn't understand. They could never understand.

That's why the Tla talked to me and not to anybody else, he realized. Because I'm not like the rest of them. Because I could believe in them.

"Go up and take your bath," his mother told him. "I'll come see you when you're ready for bed."

She was treating him like he was six years old again. That's how it was going to be from now on. They'd be watching over him all the time, listening to everything he said to see if he was crazy.

It would be better to go with the Tla, he realized as he turned the water on and started to get undressed. Swim free of his body and play with them in the sinking city for hundreds of years until they were ready to grow up again.

But what if he did go with the Tla? His mother and father would find his old body in the bathtub. Would they realize what had happened, decide the Tla were dangerous after all, maybe decide to destroy the whole city?

But then he realized, no, they'll just think I had an accident, or that I was crazy and drowned myself trying to pretend I was like the Tla. They'll be sad for a while, but they won't have to fight over me anymore, and so they'll be happy together again. Later on, when I'm more grown up, I'll find a way to tell them what really happened, and then they'll understand.

"Sth'liat," he called as he got into the tub. "Sth'liat, I'm ready. Ready to come play with you."

He heard their answering chorus as he slipped beneath the water. Open the drain so we can come to you, Sth'liat told him, and then they were all around him, dancing through the water like tiny burning minnows. He blew all the air out of his lungs, then breathed in and swallowed. He coughed and choked and sneezed until he couldn't bear it anymore and his body took over and pushed his head up out of the water to gasp for air. But the Tla were still there, darting around him, calling encouragement to him, and he tried again, pushing his head down so violently that he hit it against the marble and half-stunned himself. This time when the water rushed into his nose and throat, he was too confused, to fight his will, and when he gasped for air he only sucked in more water. The pain in his chest was unbearable, he was drowning, he couldn't find the surface even though it was only centimeters away, and then suddenly, as his body gave a last, violent sneeze, he could breathe again, and he was tiny, like the plastic skin diver he'd had when he was little that you filled with baking soda to make it go underwater, only even tinier than the skin diver had been as he was sneezed violently out of his old body's left nostril. He felt a moment's total disorientation, but the Tla were all around him, dancing with him, joyous and welcoming—and now that he was the same size that they were, he could see that they didn't look like minnows or fireflies at all, but almost like tiny angels or even the fairies he'd seen in books, only with shimmering iridescent veils that rippled around them instead of true wings.

I'm like them, now he realized with wonder, recognizing the strange sensation that had so confused him as the feel of his own veil-wings. He rippled them, delighting as they caught the water, propelled him into the Tla's daring dance, faster and faster, so that when at last the sound of the bathroom door opening came to him as a low rumble through the waters, he was only a bright spark vanishing down the drain.

MICHAEL SWANWICK

Covenant of Souls

Here's a vivid and evocative look at the End of Civilization . . . or perhaps the beginning of it.

One of the most popular and respected of all the decade's new writers, Michael Swanwick made his debut in 1980 with two strong and compelling stories, "The Feast of St. Janis" and "Ginungagap," both of which were Nebula award finalists that year. Since then, he has gone on to become a frequent contributor to *Omni, Isaac Asimov's Science Fiction Magazine,* and *Amazing;* his stories have also appeared in *Penthouse, Universe, High Times, Triquarterly,* and *New Dimensions,* among other places. His powerful story "Mummer Kiss" was a Nebula Award finalist in 1981, and his story "The Man Who Met Picasso" was a finalist for the 1982 World Fantasy Award. He has also been a finalist for the John W. Campbell Award. His fast-paced first novel, *In the Drift,* was published in 1985 as part of the resurrected Ace Specials line. His most recent book is the novel *Vacuum Flowers,* just out from Arbor House, and he is currently at work on a third novel. His story "Trojan Horse" was in our Second Annual Collection, and "Dogfight," written with William Gibson, was in our Third Annual Collection. Swanwick lives in Philadelphia with his wife, Marianne Porter, and their young son, Sean.

COVENANT OF SOULS

Michael Swanwick

Something ugly was growing in the air above the altar.

Peter Wieland didn't notice it at first. He'd entered the sanctuary from the rear, through the 37th Street narthex, and gone to the front pew without once glancing at the altar. He set his brown paper bag down beside him and removed a Styrofoam cup of black coffee, a bottle of grapefruit juice, and an egg-and-sausage sandwich. He flattened the bag and carefully set the bottle and cup atop it. Stray drops of coffee and juice mingled in its folds.

Downstairs the nursery school was coming in from the play yard—Peter could hear the children's voices. He loosened his coat and reached into his shirt pocket for the leads to his Sony-Toshiba "Soundless." The magazine was loaded to capacity with forty-some thumbnail discs. He looped the bone-inductor mike around his neck and, eyes closed, switched it on.

Full, rich music flooded his body—Peter had set the *Worcester Fragments* first in the stack, so he could have Gregorian chants to go with breakfast and the beginning of the workday. He leaned back and let the noiseless sound thunder up his spine. Then slowly, lazily, he opened his eyes.

Light through the east rose window glinted yellow off a carved wooden angel at the tip of one rafter support. Peter's gaze wandered to the front of the chancel, and down the arch of organ pipes recessed into the stone behind the darkly shadowed presbytery.

He saw the thing.

Peter squinted, shook his head in an involuntary shiver. He saw . . . *something*, he was not sure what. It was as if he'd stared into the sun until the rods and cones of his eyes began to burn out. It shimmered. Gingerly, he stretched out a thumb at arm's length, and found he could hide it from view. But it was still there when he lowered his arm, a small, crawling . . . *nothingness* in the air.

He shifted his head, forcing his gaze away. The thing did not move. It remained over the altar, whether he was looking that way or not.

Peter's mouth tasted sour. He wrapped his unfinished sandwich in a paper napkin, shoved it into his pocket, and gathered up the trash. He left the sanctuary with only one backward glance at the strange presence he was *not quite* sure was there.

Peter dumped the trash in a basket in the parish hall, and then paused to reset the thermostat timer for the Social Action Committee meeting that night. He went downstairs to the smaller furnace room off the kitchen, to check the boiler's water level. It was low today, and he ran a few gallons in.

Back through the staircase landing, with its line of padlocked storage cabinets, Peter climbed the four wood steps to the dirt-floored half-basement under the sanctuary. He unlocked the door. The *Fragments* were still playing within him, though he had long forgotten their presence.

Peter peered into the dark, cold basement. A few miserly glints of light seeped from windows inadequately boarded up. He flicked the light switch, and a string of bare electric bulbs lit up in a sparse line to the sanctuary boiler in the far rear. Their light barely seemed to reach the ground; darkness huddled in around them.

Taking the unfinished sandwich from his pocket, Peter unwrapped it and set it down on the dirt, atop its napkin. "Listen," he called into the darkness. "There's a bite of food here, and if you stop by the church office, I'll write you out a meal letter. You can take it to the Emergency Center down the street and they'll give you a meal, you understand? But I want you out of here or I'll call the cops. You understand that? Do you?"

There was no answer.

He locked the door behind him and took the steps in two leaps. The momentum stayed with him, and when Sheila from the nursery stepped into the landing, he almost collided with her. She flinched away with a small shriek.

"Jesus!" he said, "you startled me." The music switched off and suddenly the world seemed empty and silent.

Dark, curly hair framed Sheila's thin face. "I'm sorry." She laughed and made a clutching motion at her heart. Then, serious again, she nodded toward the door. "So what's the verdict? Do you still think there's someone living in there?"

"Yeah, one of the vent people, I think." He moved away from the door so the possible squatter couldn't overhear. "I mean, probably just some harmless old wino who kicked in a window, but I'd hate to go wandering through there looking for him. It's like a maze, all broken furniture and old walls for rooms that don't exist anymore."

"Well, couldn't we just call the police and let *them* throw this guy out?"

Peter shook his head. "I wouldn't want to unless I was absolutely sure. You realize that they're charging fifty bucks for a false call?"

"I can remember when the police would come for free."

"You should—they only started charging six months ago."

Sheila looked at him reproachfully. "That was a joke."

"Oh." There was something terribly woebegone about her expression, her tone of voice, that was completely out of synch with their conversation. Peter looked more carefully at Sheila, and saw that she was actually trembling at the brink of tears. "What's the matter then?" he asked gently.

"Have you seen Sam lately?"

The question took him by surprise. "No, not lately—I'd assumed he was mostly working in this part of the building."

"Oh, Peter, I just talked with Sam yesterday, and I think he's dying!"

Jennifer came out from the coal bin, where she had made a nest for herself. Furtively, she made her way to first the one door (sniffing at the sandwich there, but not touching it), then the other. The second door's frame was weak. She put a shoulder to it and heaved, and gave the door a shove with one hand. Still locked, it popped open.

She was in the children's bathroom now, all yellow-painted stalls and a single sink. It was warm here, and smelled pleasantly of decay. She paused at the back landing to listen before going through the main room and into the kitchen. The children and their attendant teachers were out in the play yard again, their voices muffled by thick stone walls.

Jennifer hit up the refrigerator first, stealing a swallow of milk from a plastic gallon there, and an open jar of spaghetti sauce with a circle of bluegreen mold growing atop it. In one of the cupboards was a tin of cookies, sealed against the mice, and she lifted a handful of cookies from it.

With a spoon she found in the stainless-steel sink, Jennifer carefully scraped off the mold. She retreated back to her nest, temporarily satisfied, alternating butter cookies with spoons of sauce.

She still could not remember arriving at the church, or what—if anything —had come before. Her mind was like a body coming out of surgery, numb but with unfamiliar pains waiting under the anesthetic. She was not consciously aware that her memories had fled, and she was driven by no desires, aims, or goals.

But she knew that she had to eat.

When Peter arrived at his office in the old manse (which was attached *to* the church, but had no connecting passage *with* it), he found a note from the pastor on a piece of Covenant letterhead. "On study leave thru Tues week —will leve typing, take mssges eves." Beside it was a stack of work: routine correspondence, the November Peace Letter, next Sunday's service, last month's Council minutes.

With a disgusted sigh, Peter slapped on the typewriter. His Toshiba began playing a decade-old Touchstone album: hard-driving electric folk. He set the Council notes to one side of the typewriter and an ashtray to the other, lit up, and began typing:

> Council APPROVED the Trustees' recommendations that (1) we will need to terminate our existing contract with the sexton effective January 1 of the new year. We will provide positive letters of recommendation and provide assistance in seeking out other churches for Sam, if he is interested.

Peter let the cigarette dangle from his mouth, like Bogart, occasionally drawing it up with his lips and sucking in a long drag. He paid little attention to what he was typing, still worried about the thing over the altar, still wondering whether he'd gotten caught in the weekend drugs trap, and taken his hallucinations home with him into the work week.

The outer door slammed, the office door flew open, and Sam stormed into the office. "Listen," he said, "You call the curator, call Mr. Alverson, and tell him that the coffee urn in the kitchen is broke. It's broke and *I* can't fix it, 'cause I don't got the parts. Now I've shut off the water to the urn and I've disconnected the pipes, but I don't know whether I can lift it down or not. I can't move this arm too well, 'cause they just operated on it."

The old sexton's face and neck were swelled and puffy, and his skin was unnaturally gray. His breathing was harsh.

"I could help you take the urn down," Peter offered.

"I didn't ask for no help!" the man snapped. "I can do it. Never said I couldn't. I just want you to call Mr. Alverson and tell him I'll need me some money for parts."

A quick flip through the Rolodex brought up Alverson's work number, and he punched it into his phone. A secretarial voice said, "Rosen and Weiss," and Peter said, "Yes. Hello. I'm calling from Midlands Investment Corporation, and I'd like to speak with Mr. Alverson."

A moment later, Alverson's voice said, "Hello, Mr. Wexberg? I—"

"No, this is the church," Peter said. "The reason I'm calling is . . ."

"Peter," Alverson said tiredly, "there is not the *money* for whatever it is. How can I make you understand that?"

"Look," Peter said. "I'm not calling you about the roof or the toilets *or* the pipes that are going to burst one of these days and take out half the church with them. I just want you to talk with Sam." He thrust the receiver at the sexton. "Here."

He snatched up the Peace Letter and scanned a pious rant on radiation-burn victims for grammatical errors. When Sam was gone, he reread the last paragraph on the typewriter. I'll bet that nobody's actually told Sam any of this, he thought. He went on to the next paragraph.

(2) When a new sexton is hired, a warm, sensitive supervisory relationship should be developed which has not existed in recent years with Sam.

It was night when Jennifer next came out and, because she dared not return to the refrigerator so soon, food was harder to find. The kitchen cupboards yielded only a chunk of old cheese, hard as a rock and ignored even by the mice. Gnawing off one tasteless flake at a time, Jennifer went up the back stairs to the top floor.

The room over the parish hall was originally a chapel, and it still retained the rose windows and oak balconies. But the floorspace had been partitioned into three rooms at a time when the nursery school had been larger. Now they were used exclusively for storage. Jennifer climbed over a partition and systematically rifled old supply cabinets until finally she found a box of noodles among the crayons, paper scissors, and glue. She took two handfuls down to the kitchen and threw them into a pot, which she filled with water and set on the ancient black gas stove to boil.

The nursery room across from the kitchen had been left unlocked, and Jennifer peeked within. It was a room for hobbits, filled with child-scaled tables and chairs, and lit only by a fluorescent bulb over the fish tank. Chains of paper loops and shadowy crayoned pictures festooned the walls. Low shelves were tumbleful of toys. She tapped a bit of fish food to the guppies and watched them flurry over it.

There was a plastic brush on one table. She picked it up and sat down in a munchkin-sized chair and began combing out her straight, midback-length hair. It glinted auburn in the fish light.

She was about to go check on the noodles when the lights blazed on, and an old black man walked in the door.

Jennifer flinched back in the chair, half-blinded and afraid. Her heart scudded wildly, and her large-knuckled hands clenched white. The sexton stopped when he saw her. "I got to clean this room *tonight*, missy," he said defiantly.

But when Jennifer started to stand, the man waved her down. "No, don't you get up, that's all *right*—I'll mop around you. No need for you to get up."

He lifted a bucket of soapy water into the room and shifted a few chairs and toys, shaking his head at their being in his way. He plunged the mop into the bucket and began swabbing.

"You with the nursery school?" Sam asked. When she said nothing, he nodded, taking her silence for assent. He mopped vigorously, with the habit of years. But the effort it cost him was obvious, and his breathing soon grew ragged and harsh. He took a gulping breath and leaned against the mop, closing his eyes for strength. "Then you ought to know that I *can't* come

in during the day," he said. "A little bit in the morning, but I got chemotherapy and radiotherapy during the day. I don't *want* to come in at night,
but I got no choice."

"Why?" She was startled by her voice—it was totally new to her. It
frightened her, and yet almost immediately she wanted to say something
again, for the question had caught her by surprise, and she still had no sense
of how her voice sounded.

"There's a mass on my lungs," he said, "but that's not all. There's more
wrong than that. They found the mass, but they're not sure about the other."
Gingerly, he sat down on one of the low tables. "There's something the
matter with my heart."

Jennifer searched for words, found some: "You'll get better." Their sound
thrilled and elated her.

The old man opened his eyes, stared off into the middle distance sightlessly. "I'm not going to get no better, young miss, I'm going to die." Tears
trembled at the corners of his eyes, and he shook his head, sending them
flying. "But you know what, I don't *want* to die. I realize that everybody
got to die *some*time, but that don't make it any easier. I don't *want* to die!"

"You won't die," Jennifer said.

Sam clutched the mop handle, staring bitterly at the floor. The tears began
falling, large, slow, one at a time.

Quietly, Jennifer left. In the kitchen she found the noodles had overboiled
and the water had put out the flame in the gas burner.

Before she returned to her nest, though, she saw Sam put his key ring
way back in one of the cupboards in the front basement landing. He covered
them over with an old rag, but she knew where they were.

Coming up the walk to his office, Peter tripped and dropped his breakfast.
The bottle of juice shattered into the sandwich, and he was only able to save
half the coffee. He entered his office in a foul mood, dumped the food into
the trash and plugged in the electric heater he kept in the leg well of his
desk.

He pulled the paperback copy of *Moby-Dick* from his hip pocket (he was
one-third through this time, his usual bog-down point), and slammed it onto
the desktop. Impatiently he drew up his chair.

Among the paper on his desk was the Xeroxed Council minutes sheet
he'd left in the pastor's mail slot the night before. He'd circled the sexton
items and written "Has anybody told Sam?" in the margin. Now it had been
returned with "No, do it please" printed below in the pastor's calm, neat
lettering.

Angrily, Peter scrawled "Are you aware that Sam is *dying?*" below the
pastor's note and returned the minutes to the slot. That bought him a day,
anyway. He picked up his paperback, ignoring the phone that started ringing

just then, since he wasn't yet officially in. Then the doorbell buzzed and *that* he couldn't possibly ignore.

"Yes?" He opened the door partway, blocking entry with his body. It was one of the vent people, a short, fat man with his hair done up in greasy dreadlocks. His clothes were rotting on his body. Peter could smell them. The man was the color of the city—clothes, skin, hair, all were the same grimy industrial gray—and Peter recognized him. "Oh, it's you, Ashod."

Ashod clutched a broken plastic rosary in one fist, held up before him, crucifix dangling at the end of a single string. It was bright pink. "I gave you a meal letter two weeks ago," Peter said. "I can't give you another for at least a month. Come back when it gets really cold and nobody'll mind."

Ashod waved his fist back and forth in negation, the crucifix swinging wildly. "No, no, it's not that," he said. "I want to see the lady."

"Lady? Somebody in the nursery school?"

Ashod nodded his head vigorously. "No. I want to see the *Lady*. I want her to make the voices go away."

The telephone was ringing again, and by now it was almost certainly time he was at work. "Come back when it's cold," Peter said, closing the door. "Understand—*cold?*"

Jennifer was learning the building's rhythms, the daily ebb and flow of people. She emerged when the nursery school children were outside in the yard. Moving quickly, efficiently, she stole another handful of noodles and set them to boiling. Then she took a double handful of colored crayons, being careful to choose only the largest, near-unused ones, and husked them of their paper shells.

She set a second pot of water to boil and placed a slightly smaller pot within to make a double-boiler. She dumped the crayons into the smaller pot and watched them soften and wilt, periwinkle blue folding over aquamarine, goldenrod yellow over bittersweet brown.

When the noodles were done, she strained them and dumped them onto a plate. The crayons were all melted by then, and she briskly stirred them into a brown swirl, and then a chocolate mess. She poured the crayons over the noodles, took up a spoon, and began eating.

Sheila found Peter just inside the sanctuary door. One hand rested on a stone arch, and a trace of steam curled up from his nostrils. "Peter," she said, "the nursery rooms are *freezing*. Isn't there anything you can do about it?"

"Already taken care of," he answered abstractedly. "The water was low in the boiler so the automatic shutoff cut in. I bled in water, and the radiators should be heating up soon."

"Everything seems to be going *wrong* now that Sam isn't here in the daytime anymore. Why does the heat keep going off?"

"Well, you could say it's because there's a leak where the radiator pipes loop under the sanctuary. When the water heats up the pipe expands and dumps into the dirt floor there until the system shuts itself off. Or you could say it's because most apprentice plumbers were of draft age, so the master plumbers have to do the scutwork themselves, so there's more demand than they have time for, and they charge accordingly. Or you could say that as long as I can correct it by adding water, it's not an emergency, and we won't allocate money to fix it."

"But—"

"The thing to keep in mind," Peter said, "is that this kind of problem is normal with a system this old."

"I guess so, but—oh! Do you want to hear the latest? The children have seen a ghost!"

"A ghost?" Peter said blankly.

"Yes, a girl ghost—they say she's very pretty. They're all excited, and now they're trying to set up ghost traps. They're all so cute!"

Peter was giving her his undivided attention now, and Sheila found his steady green gaze disconcerting. He said nothing, but she had no difficulty following his thoughts.

"Oh," she said. "You think the person in the basement . . . Peter, you've got to call the police and get her *out* of there!"

"As long as the nursery school guarantees the false-call fee."

"They wouldn't hurt her, would they?" Sheila asked, suddenly apprehensive.

Peter smiled cynically. "They'd beat the crap out of her for sure. The police have been taking a real tough line on street people lately."

"Then there must be some other way!"

"No," Peter said calmly, "it's the police or else let her stay." His expression was distant, abstracted, again. He reached out and took her hand, placed it against the stone arch. "Feel this, would you?"

The stone was as cold as ice. It throbbed ever so slightly under her touch. Now that she was aware of it, too, it hummed subliminally, like a machine or a high-tension power line. Attuned, it seemed as if the entire building were full of the almost inaudible vibration. "What is it?" she asked.

Peter shrugged.

"It must have something to do with how cold it is," she decided.

Peter turned from locking up the church to see that someone was standing before the manse door, futilely waiting for someone to come answer the bell. He walked up behind the man, keys out, said, "Can I help you?" in a tone that implied he couldn't, and began unlocking the door.

"Yes," the man said, "I'd like to see the inside of your church." He was well dressed and clean shaven and good-looking in a perfectly forgettable sort of way. There was something cold about him.

"Services are ten-thirty Sunday mornings," Peter said, stepping inside and preparing to close the door.

"It's not about that, sir!" the man said quickly, bringing his hands up before him. He proffered a wallet-badge—badly printed allegorical figures with a shield, Latin slogan, space for name typed in and signature squiggle—and put it away when Peter shrugged. "I'm from the Cancer Research Center at Philadelphia Medical College—perhaps you've heard of us?" Of course Peter had; the college was only a few blocks distant. "We're doing a building-to-building canvass in this area."

"We give through the church's national headquarters."

"Oh, it's not that, sir." The man gave a short, insincere laugh. "We're searching for some stolen—and very valuable—research materials, and we have good reason to believe that the thief has hidden them in this area. If you could only—"

"No," Peter said.

The man smiled plausibly. "I believe you will find it *easier,* sir, if you—"

"I'm halfway through the week and already I'm two days behind schedule. I've got a bulletin and two mailings to get out, and I can't spare the time to nursemaid visitors. Now if you want to go through channels, the pastor here is associated with PMC through the chaplain's office. If you can get him to agree that you are more important than my usual work—fine. If not, you can always come to services. Ten-thirty Sunday mornings." He shut the door in the man's face.

But my *God,* that man's eyes were cold.

Jeremy was playing hide-and-go-seek. Normally it was hard to get away from the teachers, but today Debbie was sick and the substitute never showed up, and neither did one of the parent volunteers, so they were short on adults. And then Gregory's mother had called because he'd forgotten his lunch, and Ming-su had started crying because she *always* cried at that time of day, and there was someone banging on the door to get in, so for a minute there was no one in the room but kids. So Jeremy told Heather, who was his girlfriend and who was going to marry him when they grew up, to close her eyes and count real slow, and he ran into the kitchen looking for a place to hide.

The kitchen was full of cupboards and stuff, but they were either locked or else the knobs were too high to reach. It was too narrow behind the refrigerator and too open under the sinks. Then he noticed that someone had left the oven door open.

Jeremy knew that ovens were dangerous, so he put his hand in first to make sure it was off and not hot. Then he crawled in. It was roomy inside, and easy to shut the door after him, because it was springy and light. You just tapped it and it closed on its own.

It was dark inside the oven. Lying on the floor, Jeremy stifled a giggle at the thought of Heather looking for him. There was a little hole near his nose, and a funny smell came out of it that made him feel sleepy.

He had just closed his eyes for a minute or two when the oven door opened and the ghost looked in. She was real pretty and real skinny too. She did not look surprised to see Jeremy and he was too sleepy to be surprised himself. "Shhh," he said. "I'm hiding."

"Oh," the ghost said. Then, "Is it fun?"

Jeremy thought about that for a moment, then said, "No." It *had* been fun, but now it was mostly just dull.

The ghost smiled then, and said, "Well, why don't you come out?" She reached in her arm—a long, long way—and gently tugged him out.

For an instant, he felt dizzy and funny and cold, but then he was standing blinking on the kitchen floor and the ghost was gone. The kitchen looked funny, because the shadows had shifted and the light had changed since he had crawled inside. It was all of a sudden a lot later in the day.

He ran off to find Heather.

Peter was the only attendee from the church staff at the monthly tenants' meeting. They sat around a table in the old manse's conference room, in front of the fireplace with its glazed tile and tinned-up front, swapping gossip and sharing news. Peter listened and nodded and answered questions and constructed the month's complaint list:

1. Heat!! (Leak under sacristy—fix?)
2. Mice
   —more traps?
   —poison not working?
3. Light bulbs (*if* can find source will extend credit))
4. Toilet paper (tell Sam)
5. Building Security
   —more padlocks
   —everyone more care
6. Dupe key for WomensRights
7. Rent Schedule
   —can wait another week, nursery school?
   —can wait another *month*, STPPRCDC?

The afternoon volunteer for the Stop the Point Pleasant Radio-Chemical Dump Coalition complained that the Latin American campaign was drawing off most of their volunteer labor, and wanted to know why there were so many derelicts around the building of late. Peter shrugged, promised to find out, and made a note:

8. Why winos?

Mrs. Untiedt, of WomensRights—a relatively successful organization that rented the entire basement floor of the old manse, and mostly used the door directly out through the nursery school play yard—asked why they hadn't gotten their doorbell fixed yet. Peter explained that their usual handyman didn't like working for churches, which were notoriously slow to pay, and made another note:

9. Nudge Jack—doorbell!

Sheila told about one of the nursery school children who had been lost for several hours that morning, and who claimed to've hidden in the kitchen oven. "He couldn't have hidden there," she said, "or he'd have suffocated. So we don't know where he was hiding for most of that time." Then, thoughtfully, "I don't think that oven is safe, though, Peter. You've really got to *do* something."

"Do you want the door welded shut?" Peter asked.

"No, don't do *that*," Shiela said. "We need the oven because sometimes we bake for the children."

Peter nodded, and wrote:

10. Make oven safe for children.

Before Sheila could think to ask how he intended doing this, he rose and broke up the meeting.

Sam was waiting at the desk. "Listen," he said, "I got to talk with Mr. Alverson." His neck was still puffed out beyond his chin, and his skin was a gruesome color gray. Peter nodded, dialed, and told the secretary: "This is Harry's brother—Fred Alverson? I'm in town unexpectedly, and thought I could have lunch with Harry."

When Alverson's voice cried, "Fred! You old son-of-a-bitch, what are you—" Peter handed the phone over to Sam and walked out of the room.

Sheila was waiting in the hallway. She nodded toward the room and in a low voice said, "How is he?"

Peter shook his head. "He's going to die."

"Don't say that!"

"He's going to die," Peter said stubbornly. "And he's going to keep working here until he drops. Every time I go to the bathroom I expect to open the stall door and find him sitting dead on the crapper.''

There were a lot of different paints in the cabinet, and some were good to drink and others were not. There was a thunderstorm going on, and as Jennifer crouched in the dark and tasted, she could hear distant rumblings and stone-rattling *cracks* in the air overhead. There was also the sound of pouring water and a few snaps of blue electricity from the steel cable of one lightning rod that ran through the cellar into the earth.

Sated at last, she fetched the sexton's keys and went exploring.

The door to the organ room was off the sacristy and it didn't open all the way. Jennifer slid inside, closing the door after her, and waited for her eyes to adjust. Outside, the storm still raged.

Everything was gray and dark and dusty. The organ workings were mostly tier upon tier of wood pipes and electrical fixtures, with two long rows of leather bellows-hinges, all hammered together a lot looser and more haphazardly than one would expect. They towered up and up, behind the metal arch of the treble pipes, and Jennifer found a wooden ladder nailed to the works and clambered up to the first landing.

The dust was finger-thick there, and other than a half-burnt candle stub or two, there was nothing of interest. She found the next set of rungs off to one side, and went up.

As she climbed, she became aware of a strange, expectant feeling in the air, a crackly sense of static electricity. Glancing over a shoulder, she saw pale pastel lights shimmer on the treble pipes—St. Elmo's fire.

With a surge, she heaved herself onto the top level. She could see all of the sanctuary from here, through the pipes, and the electrical fires blazed up brighter, shifting in quicksilver fashion. She saw the thing afloat over the altar too, but to her untutored eye it was of no greater interest than any other part of the building.

Jennifer's hair lifted lightly upward, the ends trailing blue sparks so that it formed an aura about her face. *Fata morganas* drifted through the floating mass.

The flames leaped from organ pipe to organ pipe, blazing up and subsiding like one of Bach's masses played on a color organ. There was sparkling electricity everywhere, in the cables and fixtures and wires, and the stops began opening and shutting on their own accord, in a silent electric symphony.

Jennifer stretched up on her toes. Her auburn hair afloat, the world crackling with color and energy, thin electrical flames sizzling about her, she danced.

Later she found a burnt-out lightbulb there, on the upper catwalk, and ate the filament at its heart. She had to break the inside to get at it, but she fixed it up afterward, as good as new.

*   *   *

The minutes were waiting for Peter on his desk, with a new notation in the pastor's hand: "Salaries must be cut *some*where—please notify Sam." It was as close to an explicit threat as he was going to get.

Peter lit up a cigarette, realized that he already had one going in the ashtray, and stubbed it out. He rubbed the back of his neck, then restlessly strode to the chancellery kitchen, off of the conference room. It was tiny, and contained a broken refrigerator, a rusting gas stove that no one dared fire up, and a dozen empty cupboards. The linoleum was browned and buckling.

Taking a glass from the strainer, Peter washed it thoroughly under the tap and drew a drink of water. He tapped his cigarette's ashes into the sink, and washed them down the drain with a long spurt of water. Then, back at his desk, he rummaged through the small emergencies drawer until he found a bottle of aspirin among the tampons and the lollipops.

Where, he asked himself, was the loophole? He popped the aspirin dry, thought a minute, took a sip of water. Finally, he slapped on the typewriter. The pastor hadn't actually ordered him to fire Sam in person.

It took three tries to come up with a final draft of the memo. He typed up a clean copy, read it through, and was satisfied. He forged the pastor's signature to it and dropped it in Sam's mailslot.

Done, he lit up a cigarette, noticed the previous one burning in the ashtray and, exasperated, let them both burn. He was too wired to type now, so he scooped up a box of old clothing that had been donated to the church weeks ago, and which he'd been meaning to store in the church with the rest.

Outside, en route to the church, he noticed several clutches of wine bottles against the church wall, and made a mental note to lift some more padlocks from the hardware store, to firm up security. He passed through the sanctuary without once looking at the altar, and went to the front narthex, where the staircases to the balcony were.

He was halfway up one set of stairs when a pale face appeared at the top. A slender young woman in denim—a redhead. "The church is closed, miss," he called to her, and the face disappeared.

A cold touch of fear in his stomach, he jogged up the stairs, looked around. "If you need some help . . ." he called. Something stirred off to one side, a ripple of stained-glass light over red hair, and the woman shifted into the shadows of the far stairway.

"Hey!" He dropped the box and stumbled over piles of dusty cartons crammed with donations for the annual rummage sale. At the foot of the stairs, the door between the narthex and the sanctuary was swinging shut. He pushed through.

He was just in time to see the woman disappear behind the presbytery beyond the altar. A door closed gently.

Peter didn't try to follow. The thing over the altar was swirling madly, like a pinwheel. He couldn't understand how the woman could have moved so quickly, and he yelled after her, *"I wasn't going to hurt you! What do you think I am, some kind of fucking monster?"*

The children were playing a run-around game, so Sheila felt secure in leaving them to the supervision of parent volunteers while she went up to the old chapel for supplies. She retrieved the library paste first, paused, then went into the Toddlers' Room for the construction paper.

The Toddlers' Room had been part of the Sunday School program, when Covenant was still an expanding congregation. A good dozen cribs stood serene in the soft light. They were arranged neatly against the walls, sidebars up and plasticized mattresses growing dusty. To the near corner a stairway rose to the west balcony. The stairs were so cluttered with broken furniture and toys that only a narrow, twisting pathway led upward.

Sam sat on the third step up. His eyes were dry and hard, and he was staring sightlessly at the cribs.

"Sam?" Sheila said. "Is everything all right—why aren't you at the hospital?"

He didn't answer, didn't even move.

"Sam!" She was genuinely alarmed now, and reached out to touch his arm.

It was as if her touch broke a spell. Sam snapped his head her way, eyes startled, and scrambled awkwardly to his feet. "I was just taking some things upstairs," he said defensively. "That's all I was doing."

"I believe you, I believe you!" Sheila protested. The old man scooped up a broken hobbyhorse, cradled it in his arms.

"It ain't no question of believing or *not* believing," he said. "I was just going upstairs." He turned and ascended.

Sheila stared after him for a long moment before hoisting her supplies and turning to go. As soon as she was far enough down the stairs that he wouldn't hear her, she threw back her head and said aloud, "I do not believe that man! He is so *exasperating*." It made her feel a lot better.

Halfway down the stairs she was stopped again, this time by a near-subliminal noise. She cocked her head. It was almost like the vibration in the sanctuary the other day, or—she raced down the stairs, cut across the parish hall, and out to the 37th Street narthex. Someone was outside, leaning on the buzzer.

"Who is it?" she called. Putting down her supplies, she peered through the peephole. There was a man outside, dressed in a suit. He was none of the nursery school parents. "You'll have to speak up," she yelled.

". . . from the hospital," the man was saying. "We're running a canvass of all the buildings—"

"You'll have to go to the church office," she called back. "We don't open this door during school hours." She picked up her box and headed downstairs.

Almost to her surprise, the man went away.

The acid was in the glue backing of a Mickey Mouse decal. Mickey was dressed as the Sorcerer's Apprentice, gesturing up stars, and you were supposed to lick off the LSD and then slap the decal onto your forehead. Too cute by half, Peter thought, and when he'd done up the tab, he crumpled the little mouse and swallowed it.

While waiting for the drug to pass into his bloodstream, Peter did first some typing, and then some filing. When he found himself obsessively going back to each piece of filing to be sure it was retrievable and not placed away in some nonsensical drug-generated location, he quit and went up the stairs to the second floor.

Hands behind his back, Peter stood before the hall window, looking down into the play yard. Children were scurrying about busily, swinging on the old tire hung from the oak tree, scrambling over the wooden monkeybars some parent had built years ago. Foam-rubber mattresses had been tied around the oak's trunk, to protect the children.

As he watched, a sudden wind blew through the tree and filled the air with yellow leaves. For an instant they hung motionless, defining the space between ground and sky, receding into infinite perspective. Then they swirled away.

Years before he'd worked for an inner-city corporation, in a room with a window view of a church's slate roof and nothing else. Ordinarily the roof was a barren, featureless stretch, but this one time it had snowed the night before, and the snow was loosened by a warm winter sun so that occasionally patches would let go and slide away in a puff of powdery white. Kim Soong—the only other typist in the room at that moment—leaned over her machine and stared, entranced. The room filled with silence.

The acid was hitting. He felt a painful twinge in his stomach, from the minute trace of strychnine that was a by-product of the drug's manufacture. Slowly he descended the newly challenging stairway and, remembering to lock up behind him, went outside and to the church door.

Two men lay across the step, passing a paper-bagged bottle back and forth. The dark one beamed at Peter's appearance, and they both scrambled to their feet.

"This my friend Walter," Ashod said. His companion, a sallow, half-shaven beanpole of a man, nodded several times. He had haunted eyes, with ring upon ring of darkness beneath them. "He's come to meet the lady too."

Peter looked blankly first at the one man, then the other, and then away from both. He saw that there were a dozen or so more vent people—shopping bag ladies among them—scattered about the churchyard. Some wandered slowly, aimlessly about, and others sat huddled in decaying blankets and chunks of squashed-down cardboard boxes. One was pissing against the wall. It was a regular little Reaganville, and they looked as though they had come to stay. *Fuck it,* he decided suddenly, *I'm on drugs, I don't* have *to cope with this.* He retreated into the church, slamming the door after him.

The stone ribs of the sanctuary were still humming softly to themselves, but now—with the acid in him—Peter was not bothered by the phenomenon. Things were *supposed* to be strange on acid. And one way or another, Peter was determined to return things to the way they were supposed to be.

The sanctuary was cold. Peter shivered, convulsively stared upward, and was shocked motionless by the wooden angels above. They glinted gold and then silver shards of ice. They multiplied, like the leaves had earlier, and filled the church, angel upon angel, as regular and unvarying as an Escher print.

The empty spaces were angels too, and the images flashed from solid angels to negative angels and back in a flickering dance. The air was filled with music, words and notes transformed into a solid calligraphic tracery in an alphabet he did not know. There was something familiar about the music, and with a start, Peter recognized it as Vangelis' *Heaven and Hell.* His Toshiba was still playing, and that realization was a jarring intrusion of reality.

The thing over the altar was larger now, much larger, the size of a clenched fist, or of a coiled snake. The angels that intruded upon it were seized as if by overwhelming gravitational forces, crumpled to nothing, and swallowed up by it.

The angels went on dancing. In a flash of insight, Peter realized that they were all mechanical. Identical, perfect—they were machines, creatures of a purely deterministic universe, entirely devoid of free will. They danced their machine dance in the air and it meant nothing.

There were fewer angels now, as one by one they were devoured by the thing over the altar. They kept on dancing, though, and if they were aware of the thing—if they were even capable of awareness—it did not matter, for all was meaningless, all was a dance. Blind forces ground them down and, joylessly, they danced.

And the thing over the altar continued to slowly grow.

He fled—from the angels' cold dance, from the acid-etched sense of total futility, but mostly from the horrible, nasty *eating* obscenity afloat in the church. Out of the sanctuary and down, into the basement, away from the light, into obscurity and darkness.

When he had stopped, he found himself huddled into a cold, lightless corner. The ghost was there. He could feel her breath on his face, sense a near-visual glimmering of warmth from her body.

*   *   *

Sam was eating lunch. He sat with the makings spread out before him in the old chapel, by the unused chimney where the rat had taken up residence. He started with an apple, chewing it slow and thoughtfully as he considered the job he had done on the trap.

The rat trap was dark and smoky. Rats were clever; they didn't like new smells, chemical smells, human smells. He'd built a small fire of twigs and old leaves out by the trash cans in the play yard, and charred the trap over it, holding the trap in a clamp he had made of an old coat hanger.

The apple finished, Sam unscrewed the peanut butter jar, plunged a knife in and stirred the oils around real good. He began spreading it onto a slice of Wonder Bread, paying close attention to the act, involving his whole mind in it, because the alternative was to think about what the doctors had told him that morning.

He paused and smeared a dab of peanut butter onto the trap for bait, then returned to spreading the sandwich thick. Peanut butter made good bait because rats liked that kind of greasy stuff, oily and rancid.

He was sitting in a patch of colored light from the south rose window, and for some while it had flickered gently, as if interrupted by the shadows of a lightly tossing tree branch. But there was no tree outside there, and Sam looked up automatically, puzzled, to see what was interfering with the light.

There was a white girl in front of the window, glory light streaming about her, and she was sitting cross-legged in the air.

Sam could not blink, could not look away. His sandwich was frozen in front of him. He knew this girl, had met her once before in the basement. She had been wearing the same denim jeans and jacket then, and her hair was as red as it had ever been.

Footsteps sounded on the stairs, and Sam ignored them. But when the door slammed open, the suddenness of the sound made him glance without thinking back toward the hallway, and he saw Sheila enter the room. The light about him cleared, and he didn't have to look up again to know that the girl was gone.

"Sam." The nursery school teacher was before him now, and she peered into his face, concerned. "Sam, I'm very worried about you, about the way you've been acting today. Have I offended you in some way? Should I be apologizing for something?"

He looked away, could not answer. But she would not go away.

"Sam, what's *wrong* with you today?"

Sooner or later, he knew, he would have to tell somebody. "I think I'm cured," he said slowly. And burst into tears.

The vent people were roasting a dog in one of the window wells. By pure good fortune they'd chosen one of the few that had been cinder-blocked up. The skinned carcass was hung on a spit, turned erratically by an enthusiastic, hunchbacked individual. The church wall was black with smoke and grease. They offered Peter a leg, but he shook his head and wandered away.

There were over a hundred vent people in the churchyard, and their trash and scattered possessions made the yard as cluttered and filthy as a battlefield. One toothless old hag lifted her skirts and squatted, to the profound disinterest of her fellows. Her piss steamed as it hit the ground. A convulsive alky, looking like a skinny black spider, swooped great circles in the walkway dust with both hands, babbling of demons in his head.

And all the while there were at least five radios playing, scavenged from trash bags and practically worthless, but with a good decade's life left in their permablast batteries. They were tuned to three separate newscasts, and the fragmentary snatches of global hysteria tumbled and cascaded one over another.

—warned that unless American troops withdraw from Burma—escaped from the Rocky Mountain Arsenal—survivors' reports of CBW warfare were denied—troops called up from—martial law declared in five midwestern states—

Peter stopped before an old scissors-grinder who had set up his cart on the sidewalk. It was an ancient thing, hammered together from scraps and pushed about by hand. The whetstone was run by a vintage 1922 electric motor in black-enameled housing, which fed off a tangle of car batteries hooked up in series.

—reported shot down over Sinkiang—

"You and I," shouted the scissors-grinder, "HEEDLESSLY deserted God some MANY years ago to join vain Satan's VAIN revolt against God's TEMPORARY laws. All TRUTHS emanate from God and we will reap WHAT we have sown. This is WHY we are now in human bodies. TO REAP WHAT?"

A fat woman waddled past, going "Quackquackquack" like a cartoon duck on amphetamines. She drew Peter's eyes away from the orator, and he saw that the yard was as abuzz with divergent theologies as the Middle Ages were before the Inquisition.

—meanwhile tensions escalated in the Middle East and Africa in a bizarre—

A deadpan little man in very clean clothes stood on the steps and shouted, "The Bible tells of the SCARLET WHORE that is BABYLON that is the BEAST that has put her FOOT on the serpent! She has SWALLOWED UP the Seventh Seal and has loosed the horrors of the ROCKY MOUNTAIN ARSENAL. If you have FAITH the size—"

And somehow in the babbling confusion of voices, Peter realized that he

did not have to be here, did not, in fact, even know how he had gotten here, and went inside, to his office.

—*limited use of tactical nuclear*—

There were three cigarettes afire in the ashtray by the time Sheila came into the office. One by one, Peter had lit them up and put them down, unsmoked. She cheerfully waved a hand in the bluish smoke and said, "Phew! It smells like a train station in here."

Her presence was an anchor he could hang onto. "Hi," he said.

"Peter, it's wonderful," she bubbled. "Have you heard the news? Sam's doctors say he's going to be okay. He's had a spontaneous remission— isn't that wonderful? It was a miracle, they said—a one-chance-in-a-billion miracle!" She banged her fists together, and bounced up on her toes in elation.

"A miracle," Peter said numbly. He should have felt happy for Sam, and yet he didn't. All he could think of was the memo firing the old man, and that Sam wasn't going to die in time for him to avoid receiving it.

"Yes, but Peter—" her mood shifted again—"you have to do something about all these dirty, filthy vagrants that are hanging around the church. The parents are going to be coming by to pick up their children in a couple of hours, and they are going to have a *fit*. Really."

"They're not really dangerous," Peter said. "They're none of them capable enough to be dangerous."

"Peter, I want you to get rid of them! Call the police or something. If we don't get them out of here, we're going to lose half our students!" She leaned forward, examining his face. "Are you *on* something?"

"Not anymore," he said, and belatedly realized that it was true. He was perfectly straight. Just tired—extremely tired, almost stunned with weariness. There was a strange blank area in his memory, where something flickered bright and ungraspable. He shrugged mentally. Chalk it up to the drugs and forget it. You could only go on as before.

Taking a deep breath to settle himself, he picked up the phone, dialed, and when Alverson's secretary refused to put him through snarled, "Listen, sister, this is Sergeant Blindwood of the Pennsylvania State Police and I am right in the middle of a fucking *shootout*. We have a psychotic individual holding this fucker's wife and fucking *kids* and shouting slogans about the fucking Hard Anarchy Liberation *Army*, and you are holding me *up*. How'd you like to have your sex life investigated with a fucking *crowbar?*"

A moment later a very small and hesitant voice said, "Peter . . . this *is* you, isn't it?"

Peter tossed the receiver to a horrified Sheila. "All yours," he said.

She held it as if it were a poisonous snake that would bite her if she let go. Then she said, "Peter, you can't evade responsibility by having someone else say the words." There was compassion in her voice.

Slowly—reluctantly—Peter reached for the phone, closed his fingers about it, took it. "Harry?" he said into the receiver. "Listen, I'm sorry about all this. I dialed the wrong number." He listened in silence for a time, said, "Yes, I know," and listened some more. The outside door closed gently as Sheila left.

When Alverson hung up, Peter jabbed down on the plunger with one finger, cutting the connection. He took a deep breath, and dialed the number for the police.

"Hello," he said, "I'm calling from the Church of the Covenant on Thirty-seventh Street . . ."

Time was short, and Jennifer was hungry again. She had scoured the church from top to bottom, passing by many things—cookie dough, Ivory Soap flakes, Brillo pads, clay—that she might normally have lingered over. But she could no longer spare the time to build from precursor elements.

The chemical dump counteradvocacy group's office was originally the choir director's, a century ago when the position was full-time. It had a skylight through the slate roof (with plastic stapled to its underside to cut down on infiltration), and a row of narrow leaded-glass windows that looked out into the storage rooms of the top floor. Jennifer had climbed through one of these and was going through a carton of bumper stickers when the thing in the sanctuary stirred.

The sense of its movement rose through shafts and vents left over from an early, unsuccessful attempt to retrofit a forced air heating system to the church. Jennifer shuddered as if a jolt of electricity had shot up her spine.

For an instant she thought it was about to happen, and she was wracked by terror and bleak despair. It was too early. She was not ready. Then the movement ceased—there was yet a chance, however slim. She was on her feet and through the window almost immediately.

Fear drove her down the stairs, running silently, wanting to hide but not daring to do so. Inspiration made her nab the key ring from the sexton's closet. As sly and furtive as a shadow, she slipped back up the stairs through the narthex and into the parish hall.

She could hear the sexton working in the chancel, but the connecting door was shut and he couldn't see her. One key of the ring fit into the communion cabinet. She opened the doors and found what she needed.

There were a lot of linen napkins, which she shoved aside, and a tray with slots for perhaps a hundred tiny little glasses to fit into. The bread was carefully wrapped in white paper. It was half-gone from the previous Sunday, and stale and hard as wood, but it would do—it would do!

Triumphantly she shoved the bread under one arm, and cradled the two bottles of communion wine in the other. She ran.

There was a dark storm gathering outside. The thunderhead piled up, charcoal blue, over the surrounding buildings. Faint lightnings shimmered within its heart. The vent people danced happily on the saturated-green lawn. To every side, the blind and featureless walls of the highrises blocked out large chunks of the sky. It felt like being enclosed in a box.

Peter stared glumly out the window, waiting, all pretense of working gone. Once, the phone rang and he let it go until someone in the nursery school picked it up on their extension. He shifted papers to either side of his desk to make room for his elbows, and rested his chin on his arms.

Fast flashes of red and blue light struck and rebounded off the church walls, and Peter saw that police cars were pulling up, blocking off the surrounding streets. There were more of them than he had expected, some twenty or so, and they arrived eerily silent—flashers on and sirens mute.

Three cars—one civilian—nosed through the blockade and parked by the curb. Their inhabitants conferred, formed a party, and moved briskly up the walk. The civilian craned his neck interestedly as they passed by the scissors-grinder's old cart, which had been pulled apart and made into an altar of sorts. What might have been a crucifix canted crazily atop it, with several broken plaster madonnas—scavenged from God knows where—lashed to its arms. Several attempts had been made to paint the assemblage, each abandoned to lack of paint or concentration. The result was an unpretty riot of mismatched color.

Peter stood as the deputation neared the door. Outside, police lounged against their cars, the visors of their black-glass helmets flipped up. They were held in check by neocortical implants, like dogs on a leash, and several were gently tapping their truncheons into open palms.

The doorbell rang.

Answering, Peter found himself facing three police officers. Their faces were impassive, and might well have been carved from the same block of ice. With them was the smooth and plausible man from the Cancer Research Center.

"Hello," the Cancer Research man said pleasantly. "I see we're on the same team now."

The door from the chancel to the back stairway was badly warped out of shape. There were splits through the center, and it was so badly bowed that it wouldn't even shut properly. Sam had removed it from the frame and set it down on two sawhorses.

To do the job properly, he should soak the oaken door in water for a few days, and then weight it down between flat metal plates, to warp it back into shape. Lacking the time and tools, though, one did the best one could. So . . . first you move the hinges down an inch, to rehang the door lower. Then you sand down the edges where it's sticking. A little putty in the cracks, some weatherstripping around the edges, and the job is done.

Sam whistled an old Motown tune as he sanded, enjoying the shift and feel of his muscles. He felt good, stronger than he had been in years, and all the swelling around his neck had gone down. The doctors wanted him to go through another battery of tests, but under close questioning by his sister—she was a sharp-tongued woman, was Sophia!—they admitted that he didn't actually need them. They were just curious to know why he wasn't dead. He was healed, though. They said so themselves.

He could feel—subliminally—the thing growing in the sanctuary, but he felt no need to do anything about it. There was enough trouble in the world, without borrowing more. And like they always said, you don't open the oven door until the cake is done.

Fine oak dust whispered down to the floor as he handled the paper, sliding it along the door's edge in long, firm, even strokes.

The communion wine was cheap stuff, with a metal cap that unscrewed instead of a cork. Jennifer took only a taste, but that first sip went down *real* smooth. It jolted through her brain like lightning, snapping synapses open and shut, setting off a cascade of images from her past:

She was back in the hospital, strapped onto a gurney. Everything was white and smelled of disinfectant and hospital food. They had cropped her long, blond hair, and were shaving the stubble that remained. When she opened her mouth to scream, someone shoved the side of his hand in, saying, "Hush, pretty baby, we're just going to fine-tune that pretty little brain of yours." She bit down hard and his hand tasted—

His hand tasted like her husband's when they made love. He would touch her face gently, wonderingly, and she'd twist her head sideways to catch his hand in her teeth. Feeling like some kind of wild, free animal, she'd bite down into the flesh. It tasted of salt and sweat and curly black hairs. He was on leave from the Air Force, but scheduled to rotate back to Mauritania soon, to fly more bombing missions. He was an officer—

He was an officer, and when she saw him coming up the walk, stalwartly expressionless, she knew her husband wasn't coming back from Africa, and she wished so hard for it to be all a mistake that it seemed the world must shudder to its core for the sheer intensity of her desire. But the officer walked right up to her door anyway, rang the bell, delivered the news. It was only as he was turning away that the air seemed to shimmer and the young officer fell to the ground, blood gushing from his nose and mouth. Half-embedded in the walkway, he struggled. She knew that he wasn't to blame, but still the blood came out—

The blood came out the same way it did later when she left the hospital, her skull abristle with tiny silver wires and implants that were supposed to control her but did not. All the guards fell down, hemorrhaging, even those who did not try to stop her, but turned to run. The red hair and the clothing formed around her because on some cunning animal level she knew she needed them to escape. She walked—

They were good memories, and they filled up the empty spaces. The pain was real and good and brought her a step closer to being human again. She tilted the bottle and chugalugged it all down. Bubbles blorked to the top, and the bottle was empty and her head was full of thoughts.

She uncapped the second bottle.

"I shouldn't be letting you in without the pastor's explicit permission," Peter fretted.

—*half of Houston up in flames. We're trying to get a reporter in now to confirm—*

The vent people parted for the group, stepping back a pace from the intensity of the Cancer Man's eyes, recognizing in them an insanity that even *they* had to respect. Ashod came bustling forward, and waved his pink plastic rosary in Peter's face. "Save yourself!" he shouted. "Get down on your knees—pray for forgiveness!"

One of the police escort reached out to touch Ashod gently on the chest, and he went stumbling back, face contorted with pain.

"Peter," the Cancer Man said. They were at the church door now, and Peter had his keys out. "Let me introduce myself. My name is William Oberg. I'd be pleased if you called me Bill." He shook Peter's hand. "Now," he said, not letting go, "we're friends, yes? I'm sure you wouldn't mind showing your old chum where you work, would you?" He tightened his grip, and Peter gasped in pain. The police looked on with interest.

"No," Peter said quickly. "No objection." The pain ceased.

"Good." Oberg let Peter open the door, then led the troupe through the narthex and into the sanctuary. He stopped in amazement.

"Jesus Christ," one of the cops said. Another crossed himself.

The thing over the altar had grown. It was the size of a basketball now, so large that it was almost possible for the eye to fix on it and assign it some definite shape and image. But not quite. It was oddly compelling, even hypnotic. Peter seemed to remember—

"Okay, it's pretty far gone," Oberg said, "but we can still handle it if we can get hold of the girl."

Peter started, and for the first time actually *looked* at Oberg. He could half-see into the man, see the whirling wheels and cams embedded just below the plastic flesh, the fine gold wires and wheatseed monitor lights. Oberg glanced fleetingly Peter's way, and Peter's breath froze within his throat. The man had no eyes! Only deep metal funnels that led from his face into a cold and lightless stacking of cryonic plates.

Peter exhaled, and Oberg shifted into a thin surface image, with no interior, as insubstantial as a hologram or a soap bubble. His movements left long, bright trails. *Oh God no,* Peter thought. He was flashing back. His hallucinations were rising up again, and this was not the crowd to be in under these circumstances. These fuckers were not going to show him any mercy if they discovered he was on drugs.

Luckily, they were scurrying about like automatons, and hadn't noticed yet. Oberg was laying out elastic cords and metal restraints on the communion table. One policeman unhooked a flashlight from his belt and clambered over the presbytery. He poked the light between the organ pipes and peered within.

The two other police went into the balconies. One shimmied up a loose pew to the steeple door. From within, he called down, "Ugh. It's ankle-deep in pigeonshit here."

"The windows have been broken for years," Peter said inanely. It was harder to fake a straight response than he'd thought it would be.

"Check it all out anyway," Oberg called back. He tightened a last cinch on the communion table and stepped back, satisfied. The altar had become a restraining table, with devices to hold the legs spread wide *here,* the arms up and to the side *there.* Directly above, the thing whirled madly.

The table lacked only a victim. Oberg laid a fatherly hand on Peter's shoulder. "Perhaps you have some idea where she might be?" he suggested.

The second bottle of wine was on its way to her lips when the passage suddenly convulsed. The walls turned blue and lurched over on their sides. Jennifer jerked and the floor came smashing up into the side of her face. The empty bottle fell away, shattering into a thousand cobalt fragments. The half-eaten communion loaf burst into cold, blue flames.

The surviving bottle was pouring purple wine into Jennifer's lap. Frantically, she stoppered it with her thumb. The glass was scalding cold; it stung like hornets. But she clutched it to her, and did not let go.

Sick with uncertainty and pain, she stood. Her head was abuzz with blue sparks, and the carbon smoke from the burning loaf was billowing up to fill the room. All the passages were atilt; they steepened when she tried to climb them. She had to grab one-handed at pillars and moldings and doorjambs to pull herself upward, into the icy flames.

The arm cradling the bottle spasmed with cold, and the bottle fell away. It bounced twice, spraying wine, but miraculously did not break. Jennifer stretched out, trying to retrieve it. She almost fell from her fingerhold trying, but—too far! Too far! She reached again, nearly dislocating her shoulder and wrists with the effort.

Her knuckles whitened, weakened. Involuntarily, she let go of the door-frame, and slid four yards down the hall. The wine bottle rested on the floor curling above her, in the center of a spreading purple stain. A full quarter of its contents remained within the bottle—she could see it.

But she could not reach it. The floor lifted away from her too steeply, and could not be scaled. It was easier—much easier—to let gravity pull her down the hall, into the redness.

Into the warmth.

"No," Peter said. "I couldn't guess."

But he was afraid of Oberg. And Oberg was a man who understood fear, knew its every touch and nuance, could read its track on the human face. "Is she on this floor?" he asked. "No? Upstairs, then? Downstairs? *Where* in the basement?"

Outside, the vent people were suddenly still. The silence was startling. Then a quick series of soft explosions went *pop-pop-pop*. Tear gas. With an angry roar, pandemonium broke out, shrieks of pain or rage mingling with incoherent cries of fear as the police moved in.

Like most urban dwellers, Peter had seen his share of riots in the past few years. He could picture in his mind what was happening: There would be an outer circle of police, to prevent fugitives from escaping and force them back into the fray, and two or more flying wedges to move through the mob, clubs flashing.

Oberg touched Peter gently, caressingly. His fingers scuttled up Peter's neck like a spider, and stroked softly below one ear. "Why don't you lead us there, hmmm?"

It was hard to concentrate. Peter trembled in confusion, caught between the vision of the riot and the touch of Oberg's hand. He was no longer sure which was real.

Something crashed against one of the windows, an early Tiffany the congregation had always held in reserve against final bankruptcy. It smashed a small piece of emerald glass, sending splinters flying. The entire window echoed and reverberated with the blow.

"Shall we go?" Oberg said.

Miserably, Peter led them downward.

Sam was lifting the door into place when the call came. He paused in his work and cocked his head, listening. Outside, the vagrants were stirring up a fuss, but he ignored them. The call came from closer in, somewhere below.

He leaned the door carefully against the sheet music cabinet, jiggling it a bit from side to side to make sure it was steady, and went down the stairs.

He paused at his supply closet to pick up the flashlight. It was a long, heavy thing, encased in a black rubber sheath. He flicked it on and off, to make sure it worked.

He was unlocking the door to the dirt basement when a small white boy caromed into his legs. "Whoah, now," he said. "What's this?" He put his hands on the boy's shoulders.

"I got to see the ghost!" the child cried. Sam hoisted him into the air, let him rest in the crook of his arm. It had been a long time since he had held a child like this; not since his own son was a little boy, in fact. A long, long time.

They were not the only two to hear the call. Sheila joined them at the Lady's side.

Peter had an awful feeling about the whole affair. He unhappily led Oberg and the policemen down. Twice he tried to turn them away, and each time Oberg had read the tension in his neck, his shoulders, and turned him back to the right path.

He didn't even know how he knew it was the right path, and yet he did. It was getting harder to keep track of what was and was not. His vision split fuzzily in two, and he glimpsed briefly through the eyes of a nursery school child, and then one of her teachers. Alternate scenes overlay one another.

It was an awful, choking sensation. Peter was dizzied by shifting visions through the eyes of others—Sam, Jeremy, Sheila, even the police. Sometimes one, sometimes several at once. He felt their breaths in his lungs, the touch of their clothes on his skin, their thoughts running through his head, briefly there and then gone. It confused him, made him foggily unsure as to which of these many people he actually was.

The only light in the coal bin came from Sam's flashlight, shining like an orange moon in her eyes; they were green, and Sam wanted to crouch down and raise her from the dirt but somehow (Sheila didn't know how she knew) it was understood that she was not to be moved. Jeremy stared down with large, solemn eyes, and dug an elbow into Sam's ribs—the sexton understood, and put him down—and Sheila fretted because she had children to tend to, a door to rehang, and none of them knew what was actually going on.

A voice came from out of the darkness.

"Children, there is a new world growing," it said. "It was planted by mistake and it grows like a weed—without direction. But it can be tamed and pruned—it can be reclaimed by the proper authorities."

Now Oberg loomed out of the darkness, amusement predominant on his face. "What is growing," he said, "is a viewpoint more than anything else. It has been contaminated by your presence, by everyone here in the church that this young lady has met. Left alone, it would become a perfect reflection of your true selves. It would be a judgment on you.''

He paused. Nobody spoke or moved. ''There is a war on,'' he said. The police were pale blobs behind him, clustered loosely about Peter (he glimpsed himself multiplied through their eyes). ''Our government is locked in a death struggle with the evil empires of the Earth. This young woman has the potential to win that war for us. Under our direction, the world can be . . . *turned*. It can be made safe for us forever.''

He sauntered forward casually, in no particular hurry. ''Please stand back,'' he said. ''This woman is government property.''

When Sam saw the man reach for Jennifer, he acted swiftly, without thought. His flashlight swung in a great arc at Oberg's face as Sheila shrieked and grabbed for Jeremy, who was knocked laughing to the floor. Oberg didn't even flinch. One of the police seized Sam and swung him about; another forced his hands behind his back and snapped handcuffs on them— Sheila saw them glint in the light cast by the flashlight that fell, forgotten, to the floor. There was a foot right by Jennifer's eyes; it loomed enormous and she ignored it.

Peter was with them, the boy from the church office. His face was slack and bewildered. ''Why didn't you help?'' Sam asked bitterly. ''You could have done something!''

''Sam . . .'' Peter said. ''They wanted me to fire you, Sam.'' His eyes were all dazzled with tiny, glittery stars. ''I didn't, though, I wouldn't do it.''

The government man was bending over the lady in the dirt. He lifted her up in his arms. A policeman yanked Sam backward, away from them. But he was staring at Peter, puzzlement in his face.

''What did you *do* to him?'' Sam demanded. Then, angrily, ''*Look* at him! What did you *do?*''

It was like a procession. First came Oberg, carrying the ghost, limp and helpless, in his arms. She stared vacantly upward. Then came the first cop, pushing Sam, handcuffed, before him. Then the second, leading Peter by the arm, and the third, with both Sheila and the child.

That was not how Peter saw it. His vision was flashing from person to person, first through a patrolman's eyes, then out Oberg's, then—simultaneously—his own and Sheila's. The shifting was growing faster, and multiple views more common so that—if he could only hold it in his mind—he was seeing a comprehensive *gestalt* view, each person through several sets of eyes and his own.

There was a wine bottle lying on the stairs, in the midst of a spreading stain, and Oberg casually kicked it aside. It went spinning, and bounced down two steps. Sam nearly stumbled over it, and Peter (seeing it happen in five overlapping viewpoints) snatched it up in an ungainly, newborn-clumsy swoop.

Peter had no intention of doing anything with the bottle. He was just being automatically, obsessively neat. But his guard reached out and slapped it away, out of his hand, as a potential weapon. It flew downward, spraying wine in all directions. Peter watched it slowly fall through several sets of vision, bounce and disappear behind them all.

He felt a strange sense of bereavement, and permanent loss.

Outside, the roaring of the riot was rising and falling, regular-irregular, like ocean waves or streams of cars on the freeway. "Almost to the sanctuary," Oberg commented lightly. There were people being beaten on the doorsill outside. Insanely, at least one still held a blaring radio.

—vehemently denied. Spokesmen said the nuclear strike was a preventative retrodestabilization effort. That's a direct quote. In other—

There were wet maroon stains on Peter's slacks and shirt, and a bit of wine still clung to his free hand. Absently, he raised it to his mouth, licked it off.

And the taste of it jolted him like an electric shock. It *snapped* his mind back together, reassembled it from scattered fragments, cut off the visions through the others' eyes. He was himself again.

And he remembered.

When he had stopped running, he found himself huddled into a cold, lightless corner. The ghost was there. He could feel her breath on his face, sense a near-visual glimmering of warmth from her body.

What do you want? she asked him. He was not surprised that he could hear her even though she had not spoken, because he was still wearing his Toshiba, and his thoughts were not rational enough for any further reasoning.

But what *did* he want? It was a question he could never have answered straight. But in his hallucinogen-saturated state, he found that the answer came out easy and lucid and straightforward, as if it arose from the true center of his being, where there are no lies and evasions, no confusion and no misunderstanding, but simply what is.

"I want to understand what's going on," he said, "and I want to know what to do about it." The blackness waved around him, ran its fingers through his brain.

Her answer came—again—not in words, but in a sense of delighted amusement, of pleased recognition: *So be it.*

Standing there in the lightless cellar, amid dirt and broken furniture, his ears singing acid songs, head bowed slightly to avoid hitting it against the low overhead beams, he received his gift. It was an understanding so pure and complete, so detailed and comprehensive, undeniable and true, that no human mind could have contained a fraction of it without being destroyed completely.

Faced with this overload, his mind shut down, to avoid handling it.

He found himself being dragged roughly through the narthex by a policeman. This was bewildering. He had only faint shadow-memories of the events since his visit to the Lady in the basement, and they seemed . . . unconvincing. Nor did he retain his illumination; all that remained of it were three words, running like a mantra through his head.

"What was that?" Oberg paused before the sanctuary door. He cocked his head, trying to listen over the riot noises. "That sound . . ."

Children burst all around them, cascading up from the stairs, bubbling out into the narthex. As the startled cops drew their guns, they came whooping, crowding about them, shreeping and chirping with excitement.

"Shoot the little bastards!" Oberg commanded. The policemen all stared at him in horror and disbelief. "*Shoot* them!" he insisted, and still they disobeyed.

Peter was so preoccupied by the words running through his thoughts that he did not at first realize that his guard had released him. The children—and the parents and teachers that came running after—had separated him from the group; he realized now that he was leaning against the door to the outside.

Open the door. Open the door. Open the door. The words tumbled over and over one upon the other—*openthedoor*—urgent and overwhelming. Suppose, he thought, just suppose they meant something? Suppose you were supposed to take them literally.

He put his hand on the door. Outside, the riot was in progress. Hundreds of vent people were being forced against the door. Some were beating on it with their hands; it shivered and vibrated in sympathy.

Open the door.

Oberg had noticed him now. He was pointing at Peter and shouting some angry command that could not be heard over the children and the riot. One of the policemen turned toward him.

He opened the door, and stood to the side.

Vagrants and derelicts, vent men and shopping bag ladies—the insane and confused, the outcast and discarded—the filthy and vile, the crazy and crippled and those haunted by religious or political visions that made no sense to anyone but themselves . . . all flooded through the doors, a great wash of stinking humanity, excited and fearful, some shouting cries of joy or triumph, many badly injured, at least one attempting to sing.

They swarmed over police and captives and children, teachers and Oberg and parents and all, and swept them into the sanctuary.

Oberg was slammed against the doorsill, his head cracking sharply against the wood. He slumped. The Lady, falling from his arms, was snatched up by Sam, who carried her within. The flows of children and derelicts converged around the altar.

Jennifer's eyes were bright and alert, and serenely calm.

—*advising all inhabitants of nuclear targets—that includes all residents of the BosWash corridor, any port cities, heavily—*

The thing still hovered over the altar.

"It's *pretty!*" Sheila gasped, by Peter's ear.

It was. It glimmered slightly, where it floated, and there were hints of bright colors and far places in its light. It whirled and spun, as if to some unheard music. It seemed full of promise and possibility.

Just as Jennifer was lowered onto the altar, though, fierce light bloomed outside the windows. The unseen skies turned brilliant with nuclear fire, and the stained glass grew intensely, unbearably bright. It was the beginning of the war they had all been expecting for so long.

A horrified silence fell, and then—shocked by that awful hush—several of the children began to cry.

Jennifer gasped and convulsed—at last her time was come. She stretched out a hand over her head and the thing above her pulsed. Three times it expanded and contracted, and then it exploded.

The explosion engulfed them all in an instant, swallowing up the church and expanding outward, ever more rapidly, still growing.

The last coherent thought Peter had before he was transformed entirely was that perhaps Oberg was right. Perhaps it was a judgment on them all.

Rapid circles, of reality and light, raced one another around the globe.

Mark 4:30–32

JOHN KESSEL

The Pure Product

Born in Buffalo, New York, John Kessel now lives with his wife, Sue Hall, in Raleigh, North Carolina, where he is an assistant professor of American literature and creative writing at North Carolina State University. Kessel made his first sale in 1975, and has since become a frequent contributor to *The Magazine of Fantasy and Science Fiction* and *Isaac Asimov's Science Fiction Magazine;* his stories have also appeared in *Galileo, New Dimensions, The Twilight Zone Magazine, The Berkley Showcase,* and elsewhere. In 1983, Kessel won a Nebula Award for his brilliant novella "Another Orphan," which was also a Hugo finalist that year. His most recent book is the novel *Freedom Beach,* written in collaboration with James Patrick Kelly. He is currently at work on a new novel, tentatively entitled *Confidence.* Kessel's story "Hearts Do Not in Eyes Shine" was in our First Annual Collection, and his story "Friend," written with James Patrick Kelly, was in our Second Annual Collection.

Here he takes us for a taut and hard-edged tour of modern-day America, in company with an unusual and spooky pair of tourists.

THE PURE PRODUCT

John Kessel

I arrived in Kansas City at one o'clock on the afternoon of the thirteenth of August. A Tuesday. I was driving the beige 1983 Chevrolet Citation that I had stolen two days earlier in Pocatello, Idaho. The Kansas plates on the car I'd taken from a different car in a parking lot in Salt Lake City. Salt Lake City was founded by the Mormons, whose God tells them that in the future Jesus Christ will come again.

I drove through Kansas City with the windows open and the sun beating down through the windshield. The car had no air conditioning and my shirt was stuck to my back from seven hours behind the wheel. Finally I found a hardware store, "Hector's" on Wornall. I pulled into the lot. The Citation's engine dieseled after I turned off the ignition; I pumped the accelerator once and it coughed and died. The heat was like syrup. The sun drove shadows deep into corners, left them flattened at the feet of the people on the sidewalk. It made the plate glass of the store window into a dark negative of the positive print that was Wornall Avenue. August.

The man behind the counter in the hardware store I took to be Hector himself. He looked like Hector, slain in vengeance beneath the walls of paintbrushes—the kind of semi-friendly, publicly optimistic man who would tell you about his good wife and his ten-penny nails. I bought a gallon of kerosene and a plastic paint funnel, put them into the trunk of the Citation, then walked down the block to the Mark Twain Bank. Mark Twain died at the age of seventy-five with a heart full of bitter accusations against the Calvinist god and no hope for the future of humanity. Inside the bank I went to one of the desks, at which sat a Nice Young Lady. I asked about starting a business checking account. She gave me a form to fill out, then sent me to the office of Mr. Graves.

Mr. Graves wielded a formidable handshake. "What can I do for you, Mr . . . ?"

"Tillotsen. Gerald Tillotsen," I said. Gerald Tillotsen, of Tacoma, Washington, died of diphtheria at the age of four weeks—on September 24, 1938. I have a copy of his birth certificate.

"I'm new to Kansas City. I'd like to open a business account here, and perhaps take out a loan. I trust this is a reputable bank? What's your exposure in Brazil?" I looked around the office as if Graves were hiding a woman behind the hatstand, then flashed him my most ingratiating smile.

Mr. Graves did his best. He tried smiling back, then looked as if he had decided to ignore my little joke. "We're very sound, Mr. Tillotsen."

I continued smiling.

"What kind of business do you own?"

"I'm in insurance. Mutual Assurance of Hartford. Our regional office is in Oklahoma City, and I'm setting up an agency here, at 103rd and State Line." Just off the interstate.

He examined the form I had given him. His absorption was too tempting.

"Maybe I can fix you up with a life policy? You look like dead meat."

Graves' head snapped up, his mouth half open. He closed it and watched me guardedly. The dullness of it all! How I tire. He was like some cow, like most of the rest of you in this silly age, unwilling to break the rules in order to take offense. "Did he really say that?" he was thinking. "If he did say that, was that his idea of a joke? What is he after? He looks normal enough." I did look normal, exactly like an insurance agent. I was the right kind of person, and I could do anything. If at times I grate, if at times I fall a little short of or go a little beyond convention, there is not one of you who can call me to account.

Mr. Graves was coming around. All business.

"Ah—yes, Mr. Tillotsen. If you'll wait a moment, I'm sure we can take care of this checking account. As for the loan . . ."

"Forget it."

That should have stopped him. He should have asked after my credentials, he should have done a dozen things. He looked at me, and I stared calmly back at him. And I knew that, looking into my honest blue eyes, he could not think of a thing.

"I'll just start the checking account now with this money order," I said, reaching into my pocket. "That will be acceptable, won't it?"

"It will be fine," he said. He took the completed form and the order over to one of the secretaries while I sat at the desk. I lit a cigar and blew some smoke rings. The money order had been purchased the day before in a post office in Denver. It was for thirty dollars. I didn't intend to use the account very long. Graves returned with my sample checks, shook hands earnestly, and wished me a good day. Have a *good* day, he said. I *will*, I said.

Outside, the heat was still stifling. I took off my sportcoat. I was sweating so much I had to check my hair in the sideview mirror of my car. I walked down the street to a liquor store and bought a bottle of chardonnay and a bottle of Chivas Regal. I got some paper cups from a nearby grocery. One final errand, then I could relax for a few hours.

In the shopping center I had told Graves would be the location for my nonexistent insurance office, there was a sporting goods store. It was about three o'clock when I parked in the lot and ambled into the shop. I looked at various golf clubs: irons, woods, even one set with fiberglass shafts. Finally I selected a set of eight Spaulding irons with matching woods, a large bag, and several boxes of Topflites. The salesman, who had been occupied with another customer at the rear of the store, hustled up his eyes full of commission money. I gave him little time to think. The total cost was $612.32. I paid with a check drawn on my new account, cordially thanked the man, and had him carry all the equipment out to the trunk of the car.

I drove to a park near the bank; Loose Park, they called it. I felt loose. Cut loose, drifting free, like one of the kites people were flying in the park that had broken its string and was ascending into the sun. Beneath the trees it was still hot, though the sunlight was reduced to a shuffling of light and shadow on the brown grass. Kids ran, jumped, swung on playground equipment. I uncorked my bottle of wine, filled one of the paper cups, and lay down beneath a tree, enjoying the children, watching young men and women walking along the paths of the park.

A girl approached along the path. She did not look any older than seventeen. She was short and slender, with clean blonde hair cut to her shoulders. Her shorts were very tight. I watched her unabashedly; she saw me watching her and left the path to come over to me. She stopped a few feet away, her hands on her hips. "What are you looking at?" she asked.

"Your legs," I said. "Would you like some wine?"

"No thanks. My mother told me never to accept wine from strangers." She looked right through me.

"I take whatever I can get from strangers," I said. "Because I'm a stranger, too."

I guess she liked that. She was different. She sat down and we chatted for a while. There was something wrong about her imitation of a seventeen-year-old; I began to wonder whether hookers worked the park. She crossed her legs and her shorts got tighter. "Where are you from?" she asked.

"San Francisco. But I've just moved here to stay. I have a part interest in the sporting goods store at the Eastridge Plaza."

"You live near here?"

"On West 89th." I had driven down 89th on my way to the bank.

"I live on 89th! We're neighbors."

An edge of fear sliced through me. A slip? It was exactly what one of

my own might have said to test me. I took a drink of wine and changed the subject. "Would you like to visit San Francisco some day?"

She brushed her hair back behind one ear. She pursed her lips, showing off her fine cheekbones. "Have you got something going?" she asked, in queerly accented English.

"Excuse me?"

"I said, have you got something going," she repeated, still with the accent—the accent of my own time.

I took another sip. "A bottle of wine," I replied in good Midwestern 1980s.

She wasn't having any of it. "No artwork, please. I don't like artwork."

I had to laugh: my life was devoted to artwork. I had not met anyone real in a long time. At the beginning I hadn't wanted to and in the ensuing years I had given up expecting it. If there's anything more boring than you people it's us people. But that was an old attitude. When she came to me in K.C. I was lonely and she was something new.

"Okay," I said. "It's not much, but you can come for the ride. Do you want to?"

She smiled and said yes.

As we walked to my car, she brushed her hip against my leg. I switched the bottle to my left hand and put my arm around her shoulders in a fatherly way. We got into the front seat, beneath the trees on a street at the edge of the park. It was quiet. I reached over, grabbed her hair at the nape of her neck and jerked her face toward me, covering her little mouth with mine. Surprise: she threw her arms around my neck, sliding across the seat and awkwardly onto my lap. We did not talk. I yanked at the shorts; she thrust her hand into my pants. St. Augustine asked the lord for chastity, but not right away.

At the end she slipped off me, calmly buttoned her blouse, brushed her hair back from her forehead. "How about a push?" she asked. She had a nailfile out and was filing her index fingernail to a point.

I shook my head, and looked at her. She resembled my grandmother. I had never run into my grandmother but she had a hellish reputation. "No thanks. What's your name?"

"Call me Ruth." She scratched the inside of her left elbow with her nail. She leaned back in her seat, sighed deeply. Her eyes became a very bright, very hard blue.

While she was aloft I got out, opened the trunk, emptied the rest of the chardonnay into the gutter and used the funnel to fill the bottle with kerosene. I plugged it with part of the cork and a kerosene-soaked rag. Afternoon was sliding into evening as I started the car and cruised down one of the residential streets. The houses were like those of any city or town of that era of the midwest USA: white frame, forty or fifty years old, with large porches and small front yards. Dying elm trees hung over the street. Shadows stretched across the sidewalks. Ruth's nose wrinkled; she turned her face lazily toward me, saw the kerosene bottle, and smiled.

Ahead on the left-hand sidewalk I saw a man walking leisurely. He was an average sort of man, middle-aged, probably just returning from work, enjoying the quiet pause dusk was bringing to the hot day. It might have been Hector; it might have been Graves. It might have been any one of you. I punched the cigarette lighter, readied the bottle in my right hand, steering with my leg as the car moved slowly forward. "Let me help," Ruth said. She reached out and steadied the wheel with her slender fingertips. The lighter popped out. I touched it to the rag; it smoldered and caught. Greasy smoke stung my eyes. By now the man had noticed us. I hung my arm, holding the bottle, out the window. As we passed him, I tossed the bottle at the sidewalk like a newsboy tossing a rolled-up newspaper. The rag flamed brighter as it whipped through the air; the bottle landed at his feet and exploded, dousing him with burning kerosene. I floored the accelerator; the motor coughed, then roared, the tires and Ruth both squealing in delight. I could see the flaming man in the rear-view mirror as we sped away.

On the Great American Plains, the summer nights are not silent. The fields sing the summer songs of insects—not individual sounds, but a high-pitched drone of locusts, cicadas, small chirping things for which I have no names. You drive along the superhighway and that sound blends with the sound of wind rushing through your opened windows, hiding the thrum of the automobile, conveying the impression of incredible velocity. Wheels vibrate, tires beat against the pavement, the steering wheel shudders, alive in your hands, droning insects alive in your ears. Reflecting posts at the roadside leap from the darkness with metronomic regularity, glowing amber in the headlights, only to vanish abruptly into the ready night when you pass. You lose track of time, how long you have been on the road, where you are going. The fields scream in your ears like a thousand lost, mechanical souls, and you press your foot to the accelerator, hurrying away.

When we left Kansas City that evening we were indeed hurrying. Our direction was in one sense precise: Interstate 70, more or less due east, through Missouri in a dream. They might remember me in Kansas City, at the same time wondering who and why. Mr. Graves checks the morning paper over his grapefruit: "Man Burned by Gasoline Bomb." The clerk wonders why he ever accepted an unverified check, a check without even a name or address printed on it, for 600 dollars. The check bounces. They discover it was a bottle of chardonnay. The story is pieced together. They would eventually figure out how—I wouldn't lie to myself about that—I never lie to myself—but the why would always escape them. Organized crime, they would say. A plot that misfired.

Of course, they still might have caught me. The car became more of a liability the longer I held onto it. But Ruth, humming to herself, did not seem to care, and neither did I. You have to improvise those things; that's what gives them whatever interest they have.

Just shy of Columbia, Missouri, Ruth stopped humming and asked me, "Do you know why Helen Keller can't have any children?"

"No."

"Because she's dead."

I rolled up the window so I could hear her better. "That's pretty funny," I said.

"Yes. I overheard it in a restaurant." After a minute she asked, "Who's Helen Keller?"

"A dead woman." An insect splattered itself against the windshield. The lights of the oncoming cars glinted against the smear it left.

"She must be famous," said Ruth. "I like famous people. Have you met any? Was that man you burned famous?"

"Probably not. I don't care about famous people anymore." The last time I had anything to do, even peripherally, with anyone famous was when I changed the direction of the tape over the lock in the Watergate so Frank Wills would see it. Ruth did not look like the kind who would know about that. "I was there for the Kennedy assassination," I said, "but I had nothing to do with it."

"Who was Kennedy?"

That made me smile. "How long have you been here?" I pointed at her tiny purse. "That's all you've got with you?"

She slid across the seat and leaned her head against my shoulder. "I don't need anything else."

"No clothes?"

"I left them in Kansas City. We can get more."

"Sure," I said.

She opened the purse and took out a plastic Bayer aspirin case. From it she selected two blue-and-yellow caps. She shoved her sweaty palm up under my nose. "Serometh?"

"No thanks."

She put one of the caps back into the box and popped the other under her nose. She sighed and snuggled tighter against me. We had reached Columbia and I was hungry. When I pulled in at a McDonald's she ran across the lot into the shopping mall before I could stop her. I was a little nervous about the car and sat watching it as I ate (Big Mac, small Dr. Pepper). She did not come back. I crossed the lot to the mall, found a drugstore and bought some cigars. When I strolled back to the car she was waiting for me, hopping from one foot to another and tugging at the door handle. Serometh makes you impatient. She was wearing a pair of shiny black pants, pink and white checked sneakers and a hot pink blouse. "'s go!" she hissed at me.

I moved even slower. She looked like she was about to wet herself, biting her soft lower lip with a line of perfect white teeth. I dawdled over my keys. A security guard and a young man in a shirt and tie hurried out of the small entrance and scanned the lot. "Nice outfit," I said. "Must have cost you something."

She looked over her shoulder, saw the security guard, who saw her. "Hey!" he called, running toward us. I slid into the car, opened the passenger door. Ruth had snapped open her purse and pulled out a small gun. I grabbed her arm and yanked her into the car; she squawked and her shot went wide. The guard fell down anyway, scared shitless. For the second time that day I tested the Citation's acceleration; Ruth's door slammed shut and we were gone.

"You scut," she said as we hit the entrance ramp of the interstate. "You're a scut-pumping Conservative. You made me miss." But she was smiling, running her hand up the inside of my thigh. I could tell she hadn't ever had so much fun in the twentieth century.

For some reason I was shaking. "Give me one of those seromeths," I said.

Around midnight we stopped in St. Louis at a Holiday Inn. We registered as Mr. and Mrs. Gerald Bruno (an old acquaintance) and paid in advance. No one remarked on the apparent difference in our ages. So discreet. I bought a copy of the *Post-Dispatch* and we went to the room. Ruth flopped down on the bed, looking bored, but thanks to her gunplay I had a few more things to take care of. I poured myself a glass of Chivas, went into the bathroom, removed the toupee and flushed it down the toilet, showered, put a new blade in my old razor and shaved the rest of the hair from my head. The Lex Luthor look. I cut my scalp. That got me laughing, and I could not stop. Ruth peeked through the doorway to find me dabbing the crown of my head with a bloody kleenex.

"You're a wreck," she said.

I almost fell off the toilet laughing. She was absolutely right. Between giggles I managed to say, "You must not stay anywhere too long, if you're as careless as you were tonight."

She shrugged. "I bet I've been at it longer than you." She stripped and got into the shower. I got into bed.

The room enfolded me in its gold-carpet, green-bedspread mediocrity. Sometimes it's hard to remember that things were ever different. In 1596 I rode to court with Essex; I slept in a chamber of supreme garishness (gilt escutcheons in the corners of the ceiling, pink cupids romping on the walls), in a bed warmed by any of the trollops of the city I might want. And there in the Holiday Inn I sat with my drink, in my pastel blue pajama bottoms, reading a late-twentieth century newspaper, smoking a cigar. An earthquake in Peru estimated to have killed 8,000 in Lima alone. Nope. A steelworker in Gary, Indiana, discovered to be the murderer of six pre-pubescent children, bodies found buried in his basement. Perhaps. The President refuses to enforce the ruling of his Supreme Court because it "subverts the will of the American people." Probably not.

We are everywhere. But not everywhere.

Ruth came out of the bathroom, saw me, did a double take. "You look —perfect!" she said. She slid in the bed beside me, naked, and sniffed at my glass of Chivas. Her lip curled. She looked over my shoulder at the paper. "You can understand that stuff?"

"Don't kid me. Reading is a survival skill. You couldn't last here without it."

"Wrong."

I drained the scotch. Took a puff of the cigar. Dropped the paper to the floor beside the bed. I looked her over. Even relaxed, the muscles in her arms and along the tops of her thighs were well-defined.

"You even smell like one of them," she said.

"How did you get the clothes past their store security? They have those beeper tags clipped to them."

"Easy. I tried on the shoes and walked out when they weren't looking. In the second store I took the pants into a dressing room, cut off the bottoms, along with the alarm tag, and put them on. I held the alarm tag that was clipped to the blouse in my armpit and walked out of that store, too. I put the blouse on in the mall women's room."

"If you can't read, how did you know which was the women's room?"

"There's a picture on the door."

I felt very tired and very old. Ruth moved close. She rubbed her foot up my leg, drawing the pajama leg up with it. Her thigh slid across my groin. I started to get hard. "Cut it out," I said. She licked my nipple.

I could not stand it. I got off the bed. "I don't like you."

She looked at me with true innocence. "I don't like you either."

Although he was repulsed by the human body, Jonathan Swift was passionately in love with a woman named Esther Johnson. "What you did at the mall was stupid," I said. "You would have killed that guard."

"Which would have made us even for the day."

"Kansas City was different."

"We should ask the cops there what they think."

"You don't understand. That had some grace to it. But what you did was inelegant. Worst of all it was not gratuitous. You stole those clothes for yourself, and I hate that.'' I was shaking.

"Who made all these laws?''

"I did.''

She looked at me with amazement. "You're not just a Conservative. You've gone native!''

I wanted her so much I ached. "No I haven't,'' I said, but even to me, my voice sounded frightened.

Ruth got out of the bed. She glided over, reached one hand around to the small of my back, pulled herself close. She looked up at me with a face that held nothing but avidity. "You can do whatever you want,'' she whispered. With a feeling that I was losing everything, I kissed her. You don't need to know what happened then.

I woke when she displaced herself: there was a sound like the sweep of an arm across fabric, a stirring of air to fill the place where she had been. I looked around the still brightly lit room. It was not yet morning. The chain was across the door; her clothes lay on the dresser. She had left the aspirin box beside my bottle of scotch.

She was gone. Good, I thought, now I can go on. But I found I could not sleep, could not keep from thinking. Ruth must be very good at that, or perhaps her thought is a different kind of thought from mine. I got out of the bed, resolved to try again but still fearing the inevitable. I filled the tub with hot water. I got in, breathing heavily. I took the blade from my razor. Holding my arm just beneath the surface of the water, hesitating only a moment, I cut deeply one, two, three times along the veins in my left wrist. The shock was still there, as great as ever. With blood streaming from me I cut the right wrist. Quickly, smoothly. My heart beat fast and light, the blood flowed frighteningly; already the water was stained. I felt faint—yes —it was going to work this time, yes. My vision began to fade—but in the last moments before consciousness fell away I saw, with sick despair, the futile wounds closing themselves once again, as they had so many times before. For in the future the practice of medicine may progress to the point where men need have no fear of death.

The dawn's rosy fingers found me still unconscious. I came to myself about eleven, my head throbbing, so weak I could hardly rise from the cold, bloody water. There were no scars. I stumbled into the other room and washed down one of Ruth's megamphetamines with two fingers of scotch. I felt better immediately. It's funny how that works sometimes, isn't it? The maid knocked as I was cleaning the bathroom. I shouted for her to come back later, finished as quickly as possible and left the motel immediately. I ate shredded wheat with milk and strawberries for breakfast. I was full of ideas. A phone book gave me the location of a likely country club.

The Oak Hill Country Club of Florisant, Missouri is not a spectacularly wealthy institution, or at least it does not give that impression. I'll bet you that the membership is not as purely white as the stucco clubhouse. That was all right with me. I parked the Citation in the mostly empty parking lot, hauled my new equipment from the trunk, and set off for the locker room, trying hard to look like a dentist. I successfully ran the gauntlet of the pro shop, where the proprietor was busy telling a bored caddy why the Cardinals would fade in the stretch. I could hear running water from the shower as I shuffled into the locker room and slung the bag into a corner. Someone was singing the "Ode to Joy," abominably.

I began to rifle through the lockers, hoping to find an open one with someone's clothes in it. I would take the keys from my benefactor's pocket and proceed along my merry way. Ruth would have accused me of self-interest; there was a moment in which I accused myself. Such hesitation is the seed of failure: as I paused before a locker containing a likely set of clothes, another golfer entered the room along with the locker room attendant. I immediately began undressing, lowering my head so that the locker door would obscure my face. The golfer was soon gone, but the attendant sat down and began to leaf through a worn copy of *Penthouse*. I could come up with no better plan than to strip and enter the showers. Amphetamine daze. Perhaps the kid would develop a hard-on and go to the john to take care of it.

There was only one other man in the shower, the operatic soloist, a somewhat portly gentleman who mercifully shut up as soon as I entered. He worked hard at ignoring me. I ignored him in return: neither of us was much to look at. I waited a long five minutes after he left; two more men came into the showers and I walked out with what composure I could muster. The locker room boy was stacking towels on a table. I fished a five from my jacket in the locker and walked up behind him. Casually I took a towel.

"Son, get me a pack of Marlboros, will you?"

He took the money and left.

In the second locker I found a pair of pants that contained the keys to some sort of Audi. I was not choosy. Dressed in record time, I left the new clubs beside the rifled locker. My note read, "The pure products of America go crazy." There were three eligible cars in the lot, two 4000s and a Fox. The key would not open the door of the Fox. I was jumpy, but almost home free, coming around the front of a big Chrysler . . .

"Hey!"

My knee gave way and I ran into the fender of the car. The keys slipped out of my hand and skittered across the hood to the ground, jingling. Grimacing, I hopped toward them, plucked them up, glancing over my shoulder at my pursuer as I stooped. It was the locker room attendant.

"Your cigarettes." He was looking at me the way a sixteen-year-old looks at his father, that is, with bored skepticism. All our gods in the end become pitiful. It was time for me to be abruptly friendly. As it was he would remember me too well.

"Thanks," I said. I limped over, put the pack into my shirt pocket. He started to go, but I couldn't help myself. "What about my change?"

Oh, such an insolent silence! I wonder what you told them when they asked you about me, boy. He handed over the money. I tipped him a quarter, gave him a piece of Mr. Graves' professional smile. He studied me. I turned and inserted the key into the lock of the Audi. A fifty percent chance. Had I been the praying kind I might have prayed to one of those pitiful gods. The key turned without resistance; the door opened. The kid slouched back toward the clubhouse, pissed at me and his lackey's job. Or perhaps he found it in his heart to smile. Laughter—the Best Medicine.

A bit of a racing shift, then back to Interstate 70. My hip twinged all the way across Illinois.

I had originally intended to work my way east to Buffalo, New York, but after the Oak Hill business I wanted to cut it short. If I stayed on the interstate I was sure to get caught; I had been lucky to get as far as I had. Just outside of Indianapolis I turned onto Route 37 north to Ft. Wayne and Detroit.

I was not, however, entirely cowed. Twenty-five years in one time had given me the right instincts, and with the coming of evening and the friendly insects to sing me along, the boredom of the road became a new recklessness. Hadn't I already been seen by too many people in those twenty-five years? Thousands had looked into my honest face—and where were they? Ruth had reminded me that I was not stuck here. I would soon make an end to this latest adventure one way or another, and once I had done so, there would be no reason in god's green world to suspect me.

And so: north of Ft. Wayne, on Highway 6 east, a deserted country road (what was he doing there?), I pulled over to pick up a young hitchhiker. He wore a battered black leather jacket. His hair was short on the sides, stuck up in spikes on top, hung over his collar in back; one side was carrot-orange, the other brown with a white streak. His sign, pinned to a knapsack, said "?" He threw the pack into the back seat and climbed into the front.

"Thanks for picking me up." He did not sound like he meant it. "Where you going?"

"Flint. How about you?"

"Flint's as good as anywhere."

"Suit yourself." We got up to speed. I was completely calm. "You should fasten your seat belt," I said.

"Why?"

The surly type. "It's not just a good idea. It's the Law."

"How about turning on the light." He pulled a crossword puzzle book and a pencil from his jacket pocket. I flicked on the domelight for him.

"I like to see a young man improve himself," I said.

His look was an almost audible sigh. "What's a five-letter word for 'the lowest point?' "

"Nadir," I replied.

"That's right. How about 'widespread'; four letters."

"Rife."

"You're pretty good." He stared at the crossword for a minute, then suddenly rolled down his window and threw the book, and the pencil, out of the car. He rolled up the window and stared at his reflection in it, his back to me. I couldn't let him get off that easily. I turned off the interior light and the darkness leapt inside.

"What's your name, son? What are you so mad about?"

"Milo. Look, are you queer? If you are, it doesn't matter to me but it will cost you . . . if you want to do anything about it."

I smiled and adjusted the rear-view mirror so I could watch him—and he could watch me. "No, I'm not queer. The name's Loki." I extended my right hand, keeping my eyes on the road.

He looked at the hand. "Loki?"

As good a name as any. "Yes. Same as the Norse god."

He laughed. "Sure, Loki. Anything you like. Fuck you."

Such a musical voice. "Now there you go. Seems to me, Milo—if you don't mind my giving you my unsolicited opinion—that you have something of an attitude problem." I punched the cigarette lighter, reached back and pulled a cigar from my jacket on the back seat, in the process weaving the car all over Highway 6. I bit the end off the cigar and spat it out the window, stoked it up. My insects wailed. I cannot explain to you how good I felt.

"Take for instance this crossword puzzle book. Why did you throw it out the window?"

I could see Milo watching me in the mirror, wondering whether he should take me seriously. The headlights fanned out ahead of us, the white lines at the center of the road pulsing by like a rapid heartbeat. Take a chance, Milo. What have you got to lose?

"I was pissed," he said. "It's a waste of time. I don't care about stupid games."

"Exactly. It's just a game, a way to pass the time. Nobody ever really learns anything from a crossword puzzle. Corporation lawyers don't get their Porsches by building their word power with crosswords, right?"

"I don't care about Porsches."

"Neither do I, Milo. I drive an Audi."

Milo sighed.

"I know, Milo. That's not the point. The point is that it's all a game, crosswords or corporate law. Some people devote their lives to Jesus; some devote their lives to artwork. It all comes to pretty much the same thing. You get old. You die."

"Tell me something I don't already know."

"Why do you think I picked you up, Milo? I saw your question mark and it spoke to me. You probably think I'm some pervert out to take advantage of you. I have a funny name. I don't talk like your average middle-aged businessman. Forget about that." The old excitement was upon me; I was talking louder and louder, leaning on the accelerator. The car sped along. "I think you're as troubled by the materialism and cant of life in America as I am. Young people like you, with orange hair, are trying to find some values in a world that offers them nothing but crap for ideas. But too many of you are turning to extremes in response. Drugs, violence, religious fanaticism, hedonism. Some, like you I suspect, to suicide. Don't do it, Milo. Your life is too valuable." The speedometer touched eighty, eighty-five. Milo fumbled for his seatbelt but couldn't find it.

I waved my hand, holding the cigar, at him. "What's the matter, Milo? Can't find the belt?" Ninety now. A pickup went by us going the other way, the wind of its passing beating at my head and shoulder. Ninety-five.

"Think, Milo! If you're upset with the present, with your parents and the schools, think about the future. What will the future be like if this trend toward valuelessness continues in the next hundred years? Think of the impact of new technologies! Gene splicing, gerontological research, artificial intelligence, space exploration, biological weapons, nuclear proliferation! All accelerating this process! Think of the violent reactionary movements that could arise—are arising already, Milo, as we speak—from people's efforts to find something to hold onto. Paint yourself a picture, *Milo*, of the kind of man or woman another hundred years of this process might produce!"

"What are you talking about?" He was terrified.

"I'm talking about the survival of values in America! Simply that." Cigar smoke swirled in front of the dashboard lights, and my voice had reached a shout. Milo was gripping the sides of his seat. The speedometer read 105. "And you, *Milo,* are at the heart of this process! If people continue to think the way you do, *Milo,* throwing their crossword puzzle books out the windows of their Audis across America, *the future will be full of absolutely valueless people!* Right, MILO?" I leaned over, taking my eyes off the road, and blew smoke into his face, screaming, "ARE YOU LISTENING, MILO? MARK MY WORDS!"

"Y—yes."

"GOO, GOO, GA-GA-GAA!"

I put my foot all the way to the floor. The wind howled through the window; the gray highway flew beneath us.

"Mark my words, Milo," I whispered. He never heard me. "Twenty-five across. Eight letters. N-i-h-i-l—."

My pulse roared in my ears, there joining the drowned choir of the fields and the roar of the engine. My body was slimy with sweat, my fingers clenched through the cigar, fists clamped on the wheel, smoke stinging my eyes. I slammed on the brakes, downshifting immediately, sending the transmission into a painful whine as the car slewed and skidded off the pavement, clipping a reflecting marker and throwing Milo against the windshield. The car stopped with a jerk in the gravel at the side of the road, just shy of a sign announcing, "Welcome to Ohio."

There were no other lights on the road; I shut off my own and sat behind the wheel, trembling, the night air cool on my skin. The insects wailed. The boy was slumped against the dashboard. There was a star fracture in the glass above his head, and warm blood came away on my fingers when I touched his hair. I got out of the car, circled around to the passenger's side, and dragged him from the seat into the field adjoining the road. He was surprisingly light. I left him there, in a field of Ohio soybeans on the evening of a summer's day.

The city of Detroit was founded by the French adventurer Antoine de la Mothe Cadillac, a supporter of Comte de Pontchartrain, minister of state to the Sun King, Louis XIV. All of these men worshipped the Roman Catholic god, protected their political positions, and let the future go hang. Cadillac, after whom an American automobile was named, was seeking a favorable location to advance his own economic interests. He came ashore on July 24, 1701 with fifty soldiers, an equal number of settlers, and about one hundred friendly Indians near the present site of the Veterans Memorial Building, within easy walking distance of the Greyhound Bus Terminal.

The car had not run well after the accident, developing a reluctance to go into fourth, but I did not care. The encounter with Milo had gone exactly as such things should go, and was especially pleasing because it had been totally unplanned. An accident—no order, one would guess—but exactly as if I had laid it all out beforehand. I came into Detroit late at night via Route 12, which eventually turned into Michigan Avenue. The air was hot and sticky. I remember driving past the Cadillac Plant; multitudes of red, yellow, and green lights glinting off dull masonry and the smell of auto exhaust along the city streets. The sort of neighborhood I wanted was not far from Tiger Stadium: pawnshops, an all-night deli, laundromats, dimly lit bars with red Stroh's signs in the windows. Men on streetcorners walked casually from noplace to noplace.

I parked on a side street just around the corner from a Seven-Eleven. I left the motor running. In the store I dawdled over a magazine rack until at last I heard the racing of an engine and saw the Audi flash by the window.

I bought a copy of *Time* and caught a downtown bus at the corner. At the Greyhound station I purchased a ticket for the next bus to Toronto and sat reading my magazine until departure time.

We got onto the bus. Across the river we stopped at customs and got off again. "Name?" they asked me.

"Gerald Spotsworth."

"Place of birth?"

"Calgary." I gave them my credentials. The passport photo showed me with hair. They looked me over. They let me go.

I work in the library of the University of Toronto. I am well read, a student of history, a solid Canadian citizen. There I lead a sedentary life. The subways are clean, the people are friendly, the restaurants are excellent. The sky is blue. The cat is on the mat.

We got back on the bus. There were few other passengers, and most of them were soon asleep; the only light in the darkened interior was that which shone above my head. I was very tired, but I did not want to sleep. Then I remembered that I had Ruth's pills in my jacket pocket. I smiled, thinking of the customs people. All that was left in the box were a couple of tiny pink tabs. I did not know what they were, but I broke one down the middle with my fingernail and took it anyway. It perked me up immediately. Everything I could see seemed sharply defined. The dark green plastic of the seats. The rubber mat in the aisle. My fingernails. All details were separate and distinct, all interdependent. I must have been focused on the threads in the weave of my pants leg for ten minutes when I was surprised by someone sitting down next to me. It was Ruth. "You're back!" I exclaimed.

"We're all back," she said. I looked around and it was true: on the opposite side of the aisle, two seats ahead, Milo sat watching me over his shoulder, a trickle of blood running down his forehead. One corner of his mouth pulled tighter in a rueful smile. Mr. Graves came back from the front seat and shook my hand. I saw the fat singer from the country club, still naked. The locker room boy. A flickering light from the back of the bus: when I turned around there stood the burning man, his eye sockets two dark hollows behind the wavering flames. The shopping mall guard. Hector from the hardware store. They all looked at me.

"What are you doing here?" I asked Ruth.

"We couldn't let you go on thinking like you do. You act like I'm some monster. I'm just a person."

"A rather nice looking young lady," Graves added.

"People are monsters," I said.

"Like you, huh?" Ruth said. "But they can be saints, too."

That made me laugh. "Don't feed me platitudes. You can't even read."

"You make such a big deal out of reading. Yeah, well, times change. I get along fine, don't I?"

The mall guard broke in. "Actually, miss, the reason we caught on to you is that someone saw you go into the men's room." He looked embarrassed.

"But you didn't catch me, did you?" Ruth snapped back. She turned to me. "You're afraid of change. No wonder you live back here."

"This is all in my imagination," I said. "It's because of your drugs."

"It is all in your imagination," the burning man repeated. His voice was a whisper. "What you see in the future is what you are able to see. You have no faith in God or your fellow man."

"He's right," said Ruth.

"Bull. Psychobabble."

"Speaking of babble," Milo said, "I figured out where you got that goo-goo-goo stuff. Talk—"

"Never mind that," Ruth broke in. "Here's the truth. The future is just a place. The people there are just people. They live differently. So what. People make what they want of the world. You can't escape human failings by running into the past." She rested her hand on my leg. "I'll tell you what you'll find when you get to Toronto," she said. "Another city full of human beings."

This was crazy. I knew it was crazy. I knew it was all unreal, but somehow I was getting more and more afraid. "So the future is just the present writ large," I said bitterly. "More bull."

"You tell her, pal," the locker room boy said.

Hector, who had been listening quietly, broke in, "For a man from the future, you talk a lot like a native."

"You're the king of bullshit, man," Milo said. " 'Some people devote themselves to artwork!' Jesus!"

I felt dizzy. "Scut down, Milo. That means 'Fuck you too.' " I shook my head to try to make them go away. That was a mistake: the bus began to pitch like a sailboat. I grabbed for Ruth's arm but missed. "Who's driving this thing?" I asked, trying to get out of the seat.

"Don't worry," said Graves. "He knows what he's doing."

"He's brain-dead," Milo said.

"You couldn't do any better," said Ruth, pulling me back down.

"No one is driving," said the burning man.

"We'll crash!" I was so dizzy now that I could hardly keep from vomiting. I closed my eyes and swallowed. That seemed to help. A long time passed; eventually I must have fallen asleep.

When I woke it was late morning and we were entering the city, cruising down Eglinton Avenue. The bus has a driver after all—a slender black man with neatly trimmed sideburns who wore his uniform hat at a rakish angle. A sign above the windshield said, "Your driver—safe, courteous," and below that, on the slide-in name plate, "Wilbert Caul." I felt like I was coming out of a nightmare. I felt happy. I stretched some of the knots out of my back. A young soldier seated across the aisle from me looked my way; I smiled, and he returned it briefly.

"You were mumbling to yourself in your sleep last night," he said.

"Sorry. Sometimes I have bad dreams."

"It's okay. I do too, sometimes." He had a round, open face, an apologetic grin. He was twenty, maybe. Who knew where his dreams came from? We chatted until the bus reached the station; he shook my hand and said he was pleased to meet me. He called me "sir."

I was not due back at the library until Monday, so I walked over to Yonge Street. The stores were busy, the tourists were out in droves, the adult theaters were doing a brisk business. Policemen in sharply creased trousers, white gloves, sauntered along among the pedestrians. It was a bright, cloudless day, but the breeze coming up the street from the lake was cool. I stood on the sidewalk outside one of the strip joints and watched the videotaped come-on over the closed circuit. The Princess Laya. Sondra Nieve, the Human Operator. Technology replaces the traditional barker, but the bodies are more or less the same. The persistence of your faith in sex and machines is evidence of your capacity to hope.

Francis Bacon, in his masterwork *The New Atlantis*, foresaw the utopian world that would arise through the application of experimental science to social problems. Bacon, however, could not solve the problems of his own time and was eventually accused of accepting bribes, fined £40,000, and imprisoned in the Tower of London. He made no appeal to God, but instead applied himself to the development of the virtues of patience and acceptance. Eventually he was freed. Soon after, on a freezing day in late March, we were driving near Highgate when I suggested to him that cold might delay the process of decay. He was excited by the idea. On impulse he stopped the carriage, purchased a hen, wrung its neck and stuffed it with snow. He eagerly looked forward to the results of his experiment. Unfortunately, in haggling with the street vendor he had exposed himself thoroughly to the cold and was seized with a chill which rapidly led to pneumonia, of which he died on April 9, 1626.

There's no way to predict these things.

When the videotape started repeating itself I got bored, crossed the street, and lost myself in the crowd.

RICHARD KEARNS

Grave Angels

Here's a poignant and stylish exploration of the ambiguous borderland between life and death, by new writer Richard Kearns. . . .

A former editor of the SFWA Bulletin, Richard Kearns has published stories in *Orbit 21, Dragons of Light, The Magazine of Fantasy and Science Fiction,* and *Isaac Asimov's Science Fiction Magazine.* He is currently at work on his first novel, tentatively titled *The Price of Heaven.* Born in Chicago, he now lives in Beverly Hills, California.

GRAVE ANGELS

Richard Kearns

I first met Mr. Beauchamps when he dug Aunt Fannie's grave, the day before she died. I can remember it very clearly.

School was over, the heat of summer had finally settled in, withering the last of spring's magnolia blossoms, and I had just turned ten. Bobby, my older brother, and his friends had gone to the swimming hole down by the Dalton place, but I hadn't gone with them—not because I didn't want to. The last time I'd gone, they'd stolen my clothes. I figured it'd be at least another week before it'd be safe to go with them.

So I'd gone to the Evans Cemetery instead.

There were two cemeteries inside the Evans city limits—one for whites and one for blacks. It's still that way, as a matter of fact. But the white cemetery—the Evans Cemetery proper—had sixteen of the biggest oak trees in all of Long County, growing close enough together so you could move from one tree to the next without having to get down again. I liked to go there, especially on hot days, and climb the trees, read, watch the motorcars hurry in and out of Evans like big black bugs. There was always a breeze in the oaks, and I was sure it never touched the earth.

I used to sit in those branches for hours at a time, like a meadowlark or a squirrel, listening to that breeze. Underneath me, I could feel the trees bend and sway, creaking and rattling and bumping into one another, as if they were all alive and talking among themselves, elbowing each other and laughing sometimes.

I remember it was a Saturday, and I remember I'd brought *Robinson Crusoe* with me to read. I'd read it before, but it was a story I enjoyed—I liked pretending that I was entirely alone, free to do whatever I wanted.

I had just gotten comfortable on my branch when I heard someone humming down underneath me, and the sound of wood being tossed into a pile on the ground. Quietly, I closed my book and turned around to spy.

There was an old black man standing with his back to me, maybe thirty feet away from the tree I was in. He was dressed in blue and white striped

overalls and a white long-sleeved shirt. On his head was an engineer's cap like the men wore down in the railway yard—It had blue and white stripes in it too. Next to him was a wheelbarrow—old, rust- and dirt-encrusted, its contents spilled on the ground: several two-by-fours of different lengths, painted white; a big tan canvas, all folded up; and digging tools.

He took his cap off, mopped his head with a big red bandanna handkerchief —he was partly bald—put the hat back on, stuffed the handkerchief in his pocket, and studied the graves for a moment, fists on his hips.

Then he sighed, shook his head, and, mumbling and grunting, squatted and scooped up the pieces of lumber in his arms. Their ends flailed the air every which way as he stood again.

He made his way over by Great-Great-Grandpa Evan's grave—the one with the angel sculpted in red granite—where, after deciding on a spot, he spent a couple of minutes meticulously arranging the two-by-fours so they formed a perfect white rectangle against the green grass. He then retrieved the canvas, spread it next to the area he'd staked out, rolled up his sleeves, took out a shovel, and started digging up the sod.

I was fascinated. He worked all morning without a stop, carefully placing shovelfuls of the carmel brown earth on top of the canvas, making sure that as he dug, the sides of the hole were straight, swinging the pickax in big arcs over his head, or chiseling at the sides with it in tiny hammerlike strokes, slow and steady. He hummed to himself, sang songs I'd never heard before, grunted a lot, talked to himself whenever he thought there was a problem keeping the sides straight up and down, chuckling more and more as he got deeper.

He stopped when the sun was overhead and he had dug up to his thighs. I could tell he was hot.

He crawled out, put the pickax and shovel in the wheelbarrow, and then spent a couple of minutes inspecting his work. After that, he walked straight toward the oaks, pulling the wheelbarrow behind him.

I had been pleased with my spying. I had hardly moved all morning, even when I got bored watching him, and watched the cars on Route 85 instead, or the lazy crows circle overhead. I hadn't made a sound.

But he walked right to the tree I was hiding in, parked the wheelbarrow, looked up through the leaves like he knew I was there the whole time, cupped his hands over his mouth, and called out: "Timothy Evans, you come down from there right now!"

I was so scared I dropped *Robinson Crusoe*. I watched it fall, sickeningly, right into his wheelbarrow. It took a long time to get there.

I didn't move, hoping he'd go away. He didn't.

"Timothy!"

"What makes you think Timothy Evans is up here?" I yelled back, trying to disguise my voice.

"Well, now, I know who's up there and who ain't, so you get your rear down here, Timothy Evans. No games!"

I slithered down a couple of levels, where we could see each other better, and changed tactics. "Why?"

"It's lunchtime."

"I have mine," I countered, showing him my brown bag.

"Mine's better," he said, pulling a tan wicker basket out from under his wheelbarrow. "Besides, I do believe I'll go home with your book if you don't come and get it."

"How'd you do that?"

"Do what?"

"Where'd the basket come from?"

He smiled. It was a pleasant smile, and I felt I liked him right away. He set the basket on the grass, took his hat off, and mopped his forehead with his sleeve. "If you don't come down, you'll never find out—will you?" With that, he bent over, produced a big red and white checkered tablecloth from the basket, spread it out in the shade under the next tree, sat down, and began to unpack the food.

I could smell the chicken from where I sat. He had potato salad, iced lemonade, and baking powder biscuits with butter and honey. "Promise you won't hurt me if I come down?"

"I ain't promising anything," he said, eating a drumstick, "'cept I'm going to eat all of this if you don't come down here and help me with it."

My stomach growled. Mama had made a peanut butter sandwich for me, with a couple of oranges for snacks. Fried chicken was a lot better. He looked old; I figured I could outrun him if I had to.

I came down in as expert and dignified a manner as possible, not slipping even once. From the bottom branch I dropped my lunch off to the side, swung by my hands briefly, and made a perfect landing by the wheelbarrow. Squatting next to it, I examined its underside, hoping to find the hook or shelf where the picnic basket had been hidden. There was nothing but pieces of rust caught in old cobwebs.

"Lunch is over here, boy," he yelled at me. I peered back at him over the top of the wheelbarrow. "You're not going to find anything to eat by looking over there." He laughed and went back to work on his drumstick.

I wiped my hands on my jeans, picked up my sack lunch, and retrieved *Robinson Crusoe* before I walked over to the tablecloth. I stood, book tucked under my arm, and watched him eat for a couple of seconds. "What's your name?" I asked.

He pulled a white paper napkin out of the basket, wiped his lips, chin, and fingers with it, and then looked up at me. "I am Mr. Beauchamps," he said, pronouncing it *bow-shomps*, like a foreigner, "and I am very pleased to meet you, Timothy." He took my hand shook it, as if he were one of

Papa's business partners. His hand was huge around mine, and felt warm and dry and crusty with calluses.

"Have a seat," he told me, nodding, while he lifted the hinged basket lid and fished around briefly. "You can't eat standing up." He produced a second blue and white china plate, dumped a second drumstick and three biscuits on it, and slid it over to me.

The chicken was good. So was the lemonade. I broke open one of the biscuits, which was hot, smeared butter all over it with a plastic knife, and dribbled honey on top of that. "How come you call yourself mister?" I asked. "None of the colored men I know call themselves mister. Only whites."

He leaned toward me on one elbow and plopped a pile of potato salad on my plate. "Three reasons," he said, sticking a plastic spoon in the mound and then sitting up. "First, 'cause I am eighty-three years old, and there are only two people in the whole city of Evans that are older than I am. Second, 'cause no one knows my first name, and I'm not telling what it is, so there's nothing I can be called called *but* Mr. Beauchamps. Third," he said, leaning forward again, "'cause I am the gravedigger here. I buried 657 people in my time—white and colored, rich and poor, all of them the same. Ain't no boy does anybody's gravedigging."

"Oh."

He smiled and took a final bite out of his drumstick. "You weren't expected to know that, of course."

"Mr. Beauchamps." I smiled back at him. He was as remarkable up close as he was from a distance. His skin was the blackest I'd ever seen, like baker's chocolate or chicory coffee. His face was leathery and full of wrinkles, and his hands looked like they might have been tree roots. He had white hair, white eyebrows, even one or two white whiskers that curled out on his face from where he missed them shaving, I guess. They were easy to see because his skin was so dark.

I think the thing I remember most about him was his smile. His teeth weren't yellow, like most black folk I knew. They were bright white, and when he smiled, his whole face lit up, and all his wrinkles would mesh together and smile too.

"Isn't it kind of scary being a gravedigger?"

"Nope." He looked all around him. "Don't know what could make a day like today scary. The sun's out, shining bright; the grass is green, just like always; and if you're quiet enough, you can hear the birds singing away, two counties over. No boss to stand around and give me a hard time, lots of long lunches—if you take my meaning—my own shovel and pick and wheelbarrow, and new kinds of flowers blooming practically every time I come out here. Can't think of any place I'd rather work."

"But all those dead people—"

"Nonsense, Timothy. We're all going to be dead one day. I'm going to die, you're going to die, your mama and papa are going to die. It's part of life, part of living. The Lord says we can't enter the Kingdom of Heaven 'less we're born again. That's what dying is—being born again in God's Kingdom. We just can't see it so clear from this side."

I looked past him, back to where he'd been working. The old stone angel was standing guard over the spot. "Whose grave you digging now?"

"I ain't saying."

"How come?"

"I just ain't. 'Sides," he said, leaning back and stretching out on the grass, "it's your turn to do the talking now."

"My turn?"

"Sure. Read to me from your book."

So I read to him. I read the part where Robinson Crusoe found Friday—first in a dream, and then when he saved him from being eaten by other cannibals. Friday was the first human companion Robinson Crusoe had after living on the island by himself for years.

. . .never was a more faithful, loving, sincere servant than Friday was to me; without passions, sullenness, or designs; his very affections were tied to me, like those of a child to its father, and, I dare say, he would have sacrificed his life for my own, upon any occasion whatever.

I was greatly delighted with him, and made it my business to teach him everything that was proper and useful, and especially to make him speak, and understand me when I spoke. And he was a very apt scholar, and he was so merry, so diligent, and so pleased when he could understand me, or make me understand him, that it was very pleasant for me to talk to him. And now my life began to be very easy and happy.

Mr. Beauchamps chuckled when I finished reading, scratched his cheek, and said, "Now ain't that something."

"I like it. It's a good book."

"You would think Mr. Crusoe wanted a friend, after being lonely all the time."

"I think it would be fun to be alone like that."

"I see." He sat up and pawed through the picnic basket once again, but couldn't find anything for dessert, so each of us had an orange from my lunch. They were extra juicy, and we had a contest to see which one of us could spit the pits farther. Mr. Beauchamps won.

"Well," he said, sitting up and patting his stomach, "time for me to get back to work. Seeing as I found you, though, you're going to have to work with me, just like I was Mr. Crusoe."

"You found me!"

"'Course I did. Spying on me from the trees, just like some kind of savage. I could call you Saturday."

"I'm not a savage! My name is Timothy—"

"*All* children are savages! You take my word for it. That's what growing up consists of—civilizing you. You can be Saturday Evans."

"No!"

He chuckled again. "Very well," he said, hooking his thumbs in his suspenders, "I'll be more civilized than Mr. Crusoe was and let you keep your own name. Just so long as you keep me company, if you catch my drift."

"I don't mind that," I said, getting to my feet. "Do I get to watch you dig up close?"

"Of course you do. But we have to clean up here first."

Everything got packed, including my peanut butter sandwich. Then Mr. Beauchamps made the basket disappear by hiding it behind his back. He laughed when I asked him where it went, and told me he didn't know himself, but it hardly mattered until he was hungry again.

I watched him dig the rest of the grave that afternoon. I sat with my feet dangling in it sometimes, or lay on my stomach near the edge of it. The earth smelled rich and damp and somehow clean.

He talked about gravedigging, how it was a craft, how you had to know the earth, whether it was going to be wet enough to stay packed, or if it was going to be mud four feet down, or sand, or tree roots. He said early summer was the best time to dig, and told me how hard it was to dig graves in winter, or in the middle of a storm. But he said he couldn't stop digging graves just on account of the weather.

We sang together, sometimes songs I knew, sometimes songs he taught me. The breeze would brush by us every once in a while, and when we weren't talking or singing, I would just listen to the quiet, or to the sound of Mr. Beauchamps's shovel slicing through the earth.

It was late in the afternoon. Just as Great-Great-Grandpa Evans's angel started to touch the feet of the oaks with her shadow, we finished. The grave was deep—deeper than Mr. Beauchamps was tall.

He handed me the shovel, leaned the pickax in one corner of the grave, and climbed up on it like a stepladder. He hauled himself out from there. Then he took the shovel back, neatly hooked the head of the pickax with the back of the shovel's metal blade, and pulled it up.

"I have to go home now, sir."

He tipped his hat and bowed slightly. "Have a good evening then, Saturday."

"That's Timothy."

"Timothy."

"You have a good evening, too, Mr. Beauchamps."

When I got home, I found my empty lunch bag folded up and stuck between the pages of *Robinson Crusoe*. I was sure I had put it in the picnic basket when we were cleaning up.

Aunt Fannie died Sunday afternoon.

At least that's when we found her. When we left for church that morning, she was alive.

Aunt Fannie lived with us in one of the upstairs bedrooms, and Mama looked after her, day and night. She was too sick to take care of herself, and had been that way for years.

I was helping Mama carry the dinner tray upstairs. Aunt Fannie always ate before the rest of us did on Sunday, and if I helped, Mama usually let her give me a cookie or a piece of cake from the tray.

I noticed something different right away when we walked into the room, but Mama didn't. She went straight to the windows and opened them, just like she always did, and the wind billowed the white lace curtains like sails.

Aunt Fannie was all propped up on her pillows, and tucked in with a white quilt that had pink roses embroidered on it in every square. Her face was powdered—she always did that; she said she could go through the whole week just plain, but the least she could do was look pretty on the Lord's day—and there was just a little touch of pink on her cheeks.

She held a Bible in one hand loosely. The wind came in the room and lifted the filmy wisp of gray hair that had fallen on her cheek, pushing it back on her head and making it tremble, just for a moment.

She looked like she was asleep. I knew she wasn't. I knew because I couldn't hear her breathing.

Mama tried to wake her up several times. I didn't say anything. Then she told me to get Papa.

We buried her Tuesday morning, in the grave I had watched Mr. Beauchamps dig. The site was littered with wreaths and sprays of bright-petaled flowers, with weeping, long-faced adults dressed in black, most of them carrying Bibles; and with frightened children—Bobby and his friends included—who either clung to their parents singly, or stood together in groups of three or four, trying to understand what had happened.

I knew they were all seeing an illusion I couldn't see. The flowers, somber clothes, the prayers couldn't hide the clumps of uncut grass, the color and smell of the earth in the grave, the impressions left on the gravesides from the pickax or shovel, the black stone Mr. Beauchamps had tossed up on the canvas after digging around it and cursing for half an hour, the way the wind danced through the oak trees, inviting me to climb them. Or the way Aunt Fannie smiled when she died.

But more than all these things, I wondered how Mr. Beauchamps had known to dig her grave. I tried to spot him all the way through the funeral, even up to the point where it was my turn to throw a handful of dirt on Aunt Fannie's casket. He was nowhere to be seen. The granite angel was the only witness of the weekend's events; she stood silent, reigning over the proceedings, her eyes fixed on a point off on the horizon.

I stopped at the Evans Cemetery every day for two weeks after that, but I still couldn't find him. Where could he be, I wondered. How did he know?

I knew he had to have been there while I was gone: when I went to look for him Wednesday, after the funeral, the flowers were gone, and the canvas; the grave was filled up and the sod put back in place. There was a brand spanking new granite headstone to mark her grave, half as tall as I was. The front of it was polished shiny, and I could see my own faint image in it.

Mama had green eyes, and when she would watch me, I was sure she could see what I was thinking. I wasn't afraid of being watched, exactly—sometimes she would keep at it for weeks at a time, though it never would bring enough trouble to warrant Papa spanking me—but when she got that look and I knew she was watching, I knew I had to be good, or at least be careful.

And she watched me after the funeral.

Now, Mama would never say much to me while she was watching. Nothing out of the ordinary, that is; she would still say things like, "Timothy, sit up straight," or, "Timothy, pick your things up when you're through with them." Sometimes I would get a clue why she was watching me from what she didn't say.

But I never knew all the reasons for all the times she would watch. There would be times, after a bout of watching, when she would make up her mind about what she was thinking, and then tell me about it. But just as often, she would stop as quietly as she started, and never say what I did to bring it on, or why she stopped, or what she saw.

After Aunt Fannie's funeral was one of the times she decided to talk. I was in the kitchen at breakfast one morning, when Papa had left for the store but before Bobby was gone.

I knew something was up when I saw her making only one sack lunch instead of two for Bobby and me. I felt all queasy inside when she came over and put it on the table next to Bobby; I hunched over my cereal and pretended I hadn't seen, and that nothing out of the ordinary was happening.

"Timothy," she said, and I had to look up at her, "stay put for a while after you finish. I want to talk to you." She smiled at me—a quick, toothless twitch almost, which was supposed to let me know that everything was all right—but it didn't help.

"Yes, ma'am."

She walked back to the counter and began cleaning up, washing the knives, screwing the top on the peanut butter jar, packing up the bread, brushing the crumbs toward the sink. Her window was open, and from where I sat I could see the tops of the sweet peas in her garden out back; but no wind came blowing in the kitchen to flap the yellow checkered curtains, or stir the leaves on the two tiny plants she had growing in the pots on the sill.

Bobby stared at me over his cereal bowl, the spoon briefly frozen in his mouth—he had black curly hair and freckles, and people said he looked just like Papa when Papa was small; I was blond, and Mama had light brown hair, straight as rain when she didn't have it pinned up, so I guess I must have looked like her by default, though people didn't say that—and he applied himself to finishing quickly, not looking at me again until he stuck out his tongue at me as he grabbed his lunch and ran out back. The spring on the screen twanged as the door slammed shut behind him.

Mama came back to the table, took away our empty bowls and spoons, and washed them, untied and hung up her apron on its hook by the refrigerator, poured herself a cup of coffee, and then sat down in Bobby's chair.

"Timothy, you've been spending time down at the graveyard—haven't you?" She said it all casual-like, but her green eyes swung up at me, even though her head was tilted down at her coffee cup.

"Yes, ma'am."

Mama looked down again; carefully grasping her cup by its handle with her right hand, thumb on top, she slowly turned the saucer underneath with her left. "You know what your papa would do if he found out, don't you?"

"Yes ma'am."

Her lips formed a thin, straight line across the bottom of her face, and she stopped turning the saucer. "Your Aunt Fannie loved *you* very much too." She glanced at me, almost like she was afraid I would say something, then took a deep breath and went on. "You know, you were such a colicky baby, and so fussy, your Aunt Fannie was over here quite a bit after you were born. She said she felt like it was her duty, her being your godmother and all."

Mama was silent for a moment. She hesitated briefly, then lifted the cup to her lips and sipped, setting it back with slow, graceful determination, still not looking at me. "Your papa was having hard times at the store, so we couldn't afford hired help like we could with Bobby. Least, that's what he said; I could never tell the difference between the hard times and the good times there, just by going in and looking. I don't suppose that made it any less true, though."

She looked at me now, and smiled her twitchy smile. "There were times I used to wonder if there wasn't anything more to raising babies than feeding you, and washing your dirty diapers, and cleaning you up. And I used to wonder if you were ever going to be anything but hungry, or in pain, or just crabby. That's why your Aunt Fannie was such a godsend." Mama leaned back in her chair. "You used to fuss so, and cry and cry and cry, and there was nothing anybody could do for you until Fannie came over. She knew lots of ways to quiet you, her raising a family that had been and gone already; but your favorite was her music box. She'd bring that little thing with her, and open it up and you'd be just all smiles and wonder. Not that it worked when anybody else played it, mind you. We tried that.'' Mama chuckled. ''You were just too smart for that, I guess.''

She sat forward and drank her coffee again. ''But you got better, and I got better, and business got better for your Papa, and Fannie got worse. That's the truth of it.'' Mama started to turn the saucer around again, sighed, and stopped, still holding it, though. ''They read your Aunt Fannie's will last week,'' she said, staring at her hands. ''She left money for you and Bobby to go to college, when the time comes. Not that we couldn't have sent you, of course; it'll just be easier now. We should be grateful for that.''

''Yes, ma'am,'' I said, my voice a whisper.

That startled Mama; I don't think she expected me to say anything. She studied me for a second, and then got up and went to her apron, digging her hand in its pocket as she brought it back to the table with her. ''She willed me her gold locket,'' she said, pulling it out and putting it on the table in front of me. It spun when Mama put it down; I could see the delicate rose engraved on the front as it slowed. ''Go ahead and open it,'' Mama said over her shoulder as she hung the apron up again. ''Your papa said I could go down to the store and pick a chain for it later in the week.''

There were pictures of me and Bobby and Papa on the inside. ''It's pretty,'' I said.

''Yes, it is, isn't it?'' Mama answered, sitting down again, this time putting a small wooden box in front of me, and setting three fat brass rollers on end next to it. The box was made of dark walnut, with nicks and dents worn smooth by age and polish; across the lid were inlaid two black stripes with red diamonds. Mama opened it, and delicious music came pouring out. I recognized Brahm's *Lullaby* right away. ''Fannie left this for you,'' Mama said. ''Your papa didn't think you should have it until you were older; he said you might break it. You'll be careful, won't you?''

''Yes, ma'am.''

''Take it then, and keep it safe,'' she said. She showed me how to change the brass rollers so I could play four different songs. Their names were engraved on their insides: Beethoven's *Für Elise*, Bach's *Sarabande*, Mozart's *Minute Waltz*, and the lullaby by Brahms. We both listened to the Bach piece play all the way through, the somber minor chords twinkling so you could hear all the notes in a row.

Then it was over.

''Timothy,'' Mama said as I went upstairs to put the music box away, ''I want you to keep away from Evans Cemetery for a while.''

I leaned over the banister and looked at her, her figure a dim, hazy silhouette framed against the sunlit kitchen doorway. "Yes, ma'am."

"Just for a while," she said. "You can go back and visit your Aunt Fannie after the summer is over. It's just that there will be other people going to visit her now, and I'd rather they didn't find you there."

"Yes, ma'am."

She smiled. "Maybe you and I can go together and take flowers to her grave sometime. Would you like that?"

"Yes, ma'am."

We never went.

I gave up waiting for Mr. Beauchamps. But I still wasn't getting along too well with Bobby and the rest of the gang, so instead of hanging out at the cemetery, I would spend time over at the old Robinson house. I was safe there; the rest of the kids thought it was haunted.

It sat off by itself, on a hill along the road to Mariana Marsh, and there was a big dead gray tree in front of it with all the bark stripped off. None of the windows had any glass. Someone had tried to board them up a long time ago. But they had since been opened by brave adventurers like myself.

It might have been painted white or yellow once. Most of the paint had peeled or worn off over the years, and the wood underneath was the same color as the tree in front—gray. There were still patches of nondescript color that clung tenaciously to the outside, in a futile attempt to defy the elements. The roof over the front porch sagged, and would probably fall off soon. The outside steps were gone.

My favorite spot was up on the second floor, by the bay windows that faced south, toward town and Robinson's Woods. I made it my room. On clear mornings I could see Mama hanging laundry out behind our house, or watch the cars drive into town and park in front of Papa's store.

Every time I was there, I would clean up the new collection of dead branches and litter that had blown in through the open windows. I fixed up an old rocking chair I found in the basement of the house, replacing the tattered upholstery with a burlap bag that said "50 Lbs Net, Parkinson's Cabbage, Produce of U.S.A." I hid Aunt Fannie's music box in the window seat, and I could sit and rock and listen to it play while I looked out at town or over the woods. Or I could just read.

It was Mr. Beauchamps who found me, two months after the funeral, and it was in the Robinson house. There was a light rain outside, and I was in my rocker, listening to the music box play Mozart's waltz, thinking about having to go back to school again in a month and a half. The song ended, and I reached for the music box to start it over again.

"That was real pretty, Timothy."

I turned around and looked, real quick, but I already knew it was him from the voice. He had his own rocker, put together out of a dozen pieces of twisted cane, painted red. He smiled at me, rocking back and forth.

I wasn't going to let him know he scared me. "Hello, Mr. Beauchamps."

"Where did you get that music box?"

"From Aunt Fannie. She willed it to me."

"I see." He stopped rocking, and dug his hand into one of his overall pockets. "Here. Try this."

He tossed something at me, which I caught, examined long enough to realize it was identical to the other brass cylinders that had come with the box, and then fitted it into the machine. It was labeled Chopin's *Nocturne*. I turned the key as far as it would go, and then started it playing.

I could hear Mr. Beauchamps humming softly with the melody. "How did you know Aunt Fannie was going to die?" I asked without looking at him.

He stopped humming. "We're all going to die," he said huskily. "I told you that before."

"But how did you know when?"

He signed wearily. "I just knew I had to dig the grave—that's all there was to it."

I turned around and looked at him. "Do you know when everybody's going to die?"

He chuckled and relaxed, and his rocking chair started to squeak in time with the music. "Not everybody," he said, after listening for several beats. "Strictly speaking, I'm just limited to the people in Evans. They managed to die without anybody knowing before I came, and will probably continue to do so after I'm gone."

"But how did you know to dig their graves?"

"I just knew." He chuckled again. "Take tomorrow, for instance."

"Somebody's going to die tomorrow?"

"Now, I didn't say that. I'm just saying I got a grave to dig over in the Quarters Cemetery. I want you to meet me there and help."

"So somebody's going to die over in Quarters! Who's it going to be?"

"I ain't saying."

"It's old Mammy Walker, isn't it? She's been sick for months."

"Nope."

"Sam DeLuth?"

"Nope."

"Will Atkins?"

"Nope."

I thought for a moment. "Jackson Hardich?"

Mr. Beauchamps looked startled for a second, long enough to stop his chair. "I told you—I ain't saying." He fell back to rocking.

"It *is* Jackson—isn't it?" Everybody in Evans knew that Jackson Hardich was going to take on more trouble than he could handle one day. He was always picking fights out in the Quarters after dark, and there were several times recently when Sheriff Tucker had to be called to settle things down.

"Maybe yes and maybe no," Mr. Beauchamps said. "Whoever it is, it don't change the fact that there's a grave that's got to be dug." He leaned forward and squinted at me. "You going to be there tomorrow?"

I looked outside at the rain and then back at Mr. Beauchamps. "I can't come if it's going to be raining."

"Oh, then there's no problem. Tomorrow will be a fine day."

"If it is, I'll be there."

"Good."

There was a hot white flash and a thunderclap that made my chest rumble from being so close, and when my ears stopped ringing, I turned to ask Mr. Beauchamps more about Jackson Hardich, but he was gone, along with his rocking chair. I remember smiling to myself, rocking back and forth vigorously, watching the rain come down harder, listening to the music. It had been fairly easy to trick Mr. Beauchamps into revealing who the grave was for. Now that I knew who the dead man was, I could go see him before he died.

It took all day to dig the grave, the same as before. And it was a Saturday, the same as before. But the Quarters Cemetery wasn't as nice as the Evans Cemetery. The grave markers were smaller, most of them made out of wood, many of them cracked and gray and slowly falling over. There were fewer flowers, fewer trees, and the work was harder. I had to help Mr. Beauchamps pull up half a dozen huge stones before we were through; my hands were rubbed raw in spots from it.

It wasn't a bad day, though. We had our lunch together and fed biscuit crumbs to a family of meadowlarks who sang for us later. As a surprise, Mr. Beauchamps brought harmonicas for both of us; once I got through his "brief demonstration of the proper technique for the mouth organ," I was even able to keep up with him on a couple of the songs we had only sung last time. He said I was a quick learner, and taught me to play Chopin's *Nocturne*, just like my music box, though nowhere near as fancy, and with none of the right harmonies.

When we finished the digging, Mr. Beauchamps stood in the cool afternoon shadows that spilled into the bottom of the grave. He smiled. "This is good work, Timothy," he said. "Good, honest work. You should be proud of it." He grunted as he climbed out on his pickax, laboriously settling himself into a sitting position with his feet still dangling in Jackson's grave. "You go home now and eat a good dinner," he said. Then he leaned over and poked at me with his finger. "Take yourself a hot bath too. Hot, mind you.'' And he tapped his nose. ''And you soak in it. We wouldn't want you to be stiff and sore like some old man before your time.''

I left him while he was still laughing about that. But I didn't go home. Instead I headed for Potter's Drugstore, on the edge of the Quarters, to spy on Jackson Hardich.

He worked there for Mr. Potter most days, and on Saturdays he and his friends would meet there before taking off for the evening's festivities. Potter's was also the scene of the last two fights Jackson got into.

When I got there, Sheriff Tucker's squad car and an ambulance were there before me, pulled up crooked against the curb, their lights flashing, red and amber spots dancing up and down the outsides of the dingy frame houses huddled together on Sultana Street, the power lines off in the distance winking with an orange glow.

I hid by the gas station garage across the street, behind a pile of old tires. Potter's was closed, but there were lights on in the barbershop next door. A small crowd had begun to gather—mostly older black men, dressed in dark gray suits and hats, standing around the way people did at Aunt Fannie's funeral—when Sheriff Tucker came out of the alley behind Potter's and told everybody to get on home. Right behind him came two ambulance attendants carrying a litter with a white sheet-wrapped body on it. Whoever it was, it was plain to see he was dead. But I had to know who.

That was when I became aware I wasn't the only one hiding behind the garage.

I couldn't see his face. All I could tell was he was black, he was watching the attendants put the body into the ambulance, and there was a dark stain spreading high up on his left shirt sleeve, almost by his shoulder.

''You killed him—didn't you?''

''Who's that?'' He whirled around, holding a knife in his right hand, his face all shiny with sweat. It was Ronnie Johnson. He couldn't see me.

''You killed Jackson Hardich.''

''No!''

''You knifed him.''

''No! It ain't true!''

''He made you fight him, and you stabbed him in the middle of it. I know it.''

Ronnie began to move toward me, crouched. ''You can't say that. You don't know nothing. Who's back there?''

''You're going to die for it too!''

Ronnie stood straight up. ''No! He ain't dead!''

''He is!''

''You stop right where you are, boy!'' It was Sheriff Tucker. He'd spotted Ronnie from across the street.

Ronnie took off down Sultana Street, running as fast as he could. The sheriff was right behind him.

They found him guilty. I knew that before anyone else did. Mr. Beauchamps dug Ronnie Johnson's grave while the jury was still deliberating.

As I got older, I got better at guessing whose grave we would be digging. And by the time I was in high school, I could get a sense of when Mr. Beauchamps was about to show up as well as who it was we'd have to go gravedigging for. He paid me for my help when I was in high school; he said I was doing my share of a man's work.

Bobby went off to Raleigh for college, and came back with a degree in business and a wife. Her name was Mary Sue Alders—Mary Sue Evans after she married Bobby. They got themselves a house in town, and Bobby started helping Papa with the business, supervising the clerks and keeping the inventory.

I was a loner all through high school, and the kids were happy to leave me to myself. I would watch the people in Evans, waiting; when I felt the time was right, I would go out to the old Robinson house and meet Mr. Beauchamps.

There came a time, though, when I was a senior, a month away from graduating, when he showed up at school to find me. I was out behind the gymnasium, skipping pebbles across the lagoon. He stepped out suddenly from behind one of the willow trees.

"Hello, Timothy."

I looked around to see if any of the other kids were in sight. "What are you doing here?"

He walked down to the shore, his big mud-crusted boots making the gravel crunch, stooped, picked up a stone, tossed it at the lagoon, and watched it skim the distance to the far shore. He looked pleased with himself. "Fancy that," he said, "and at my age too." He looked down at me where I was sitting. "I'll need your help tomorrow, Timothy."

I stood up, beat the dust out of my jeans, and then looked him square in the eyes. "Who's it going to be this time?"

He chuckled. "You won't guess it. I can guarantee that."

"Well, then tell me the cemetery."

"Evans. Over by the oak trees."

"Evans. That means it's somebody white." I thought for a moment. "Couldn't be. Old Mrs. Forester is the sickest one of the lot, and even she's doing better, according to Doc Morrison."

"Ain't Mrs. Forester—you're right about that."

"All right. You just wait and see, I'll have it figured out by tomorrow morning when we start."

He took his engineer's hat off and held it over his heart, like the flag was passing by, and sticking out his jaw defiantly, said, "You won't neither, Timothy Evans. I know it."

I stayed awake past midnight, going through the phone book, trying to figure out who it could be. I made lists and tore them all up. I even called the two motels in town, to see if there were any elderly visitors I had somehow not heard about. In the end, I decided to give up graciously, and wait and see who was going to die, just like any other normal person.

The next morning, Mr. Beauchamps knew I hadn't figured it out, but he didn't say anything. He was more cheerful than usual, though.

It was a good gravedigging day: the sky was a clear, bright, cloudless blue; it was warm, but not so warm as to be uncomfortable; there was the tiniest of breezes that played with the grass tops as it came blowing across the cemetery to cool us off. Mr. Beauchamps let me do most of the work. He said if I had it in me, I ought to do it—like singing a song, building a house, or dancing.

I did the best job I could, but that didn't hurry the finish of it. Mr. Beauchamps inspected the entire grave very thoroughly when we were through. He was pleased with it, and paid me twenty dollars extra—my fair share, he said. So I headed home to start the vigil that would let me know who was going to die.

Mary Sue was waiting for me when I got in. She was the only one there. She sat down and told me that Mama and Papa had been in a serious automobile accident, and that Bobby was with them now over at the Long County Hospital. She said it didn't look good for either of them.

I went numb. I should have known, I told myself. I should have tried to stop them from going out. I should have warned them. I should have prevented it somehow.

I don't remember Mary Sue driving me to the hospital. I don't remember trying to find my parents in the emergency room, I don't remember Doc Morrison trying to calm me down. I don't remember being dragged away by the orderlies to the waiting room. Mary Sue told me about it later.

I do remember the waiting room. It was ugly. The furniture was white wrought iron with cushions, and you could see the shiny metal spots where other people had worn away the paint with worry, waiting.

Bobby and Mary Sue and I had cups of coffee from a machine all night, and we hardly said a word to one another. Bobby must have smoked four packs of cigarettes. Mary Sue sat next to him with her arm around him.

It wasn't fair—knowing that one of them was going to go for sure, and not knowing which. I didn't want to choose which one I'd rather have live, but I couldn't stop myself from choosing, over and over again. When morning came, we found out it was Mama that had survived, although she was paralyzed from the waist down. Papa had died in the operating room.

We buried him Monday morning. Bobby made me go to the funeral. I hadn't wanted to.

We buried a man I realized I never really knew—my father. As we lowered the casket into the grave I had dug, I wondered who he was, how he met my mama, whether he loved her right away when they met or whether it took time to get to know her, whether he was always good at business, whether he had ever sat up all night waiting for someone to die, whether he loved me.

I felt like a stranger to the whole world. I had spent years watching it, waiting for people to fall down like targets in a shooting gallery. And now, here I was, somehow back in it, and all the names and faces I had known were distant, mysterious and cold.

Mary Sue did her best to help. She and Bobby moved back into our house, and we put Mama up in Aunt Fannie's old room. Mary Sue and I took care of Mama—keeping her company more than anything else. We took her on walks. We went with her to the show. We sat with her in the garden, on the porch, in her room. I think she used to hate being crippled. Most of all, I think she missed Papa.

I dug up stacks of photographs Papa had taken and then hidden away in the attic, and Mama and I would spend evenings pasting them into newly bought albums.

Most of them were family picnics and Fourth of July gatherings, the lot of us scattered across the backyard, eating huge chunks of pink watermelon, lying on the grass or sitting in lawn chairs with various aunts and uncles and grandparents, before they all died.

I found a picture of myself in diapers, sitting on Grandma Larkins's lap, a blanket draped over my head while I drooled all over myself, white socks barely staying on my feet because they were too big to fit.

And there were pictures of Bobby and me. We had climbed trees together, peered around corners together, taken baths and swum in swimming pools together. There was one where we stood arm in arm, looking doubtfully at two live turkeys Papa had bought for Thanksgiving one year.

But the best pictures were of Mama. She was pretty, in a simple, open-air way. That was how Papa must have seen her. She didn't smile in most of the photographs, but rather appeared to be thoughtful, moody, elusive, quietly untame. One photograph Papa took of her I remember particularly: she was in the kitchen, and she must have just gotten up, because her hair was mussed and she was wearing her robe that had tiny white flowers embroidered in it near the top; she stood next to an old, scarred butcher-block table with a baby bottle on it, holding her hands together, and behind her I could see an old black telephone and a couple of cartons of empty cola bottles

on the floor next to the refrigerator. But she looked so regal, so stately, like she owned the world. Her mouth curled in a little smile.

Mama would tell me stories about every single picture as we put it in an album. The only drawback to this was that Papa had always been the photographer and never the subject. I only heard about him. I never saw what he was like. I could see that it was painful for Mama to talk about him, now that he was gone.

I still dug graves for Mr. Beauchamps. But my purpose was different. I waited to know when we would start to dig Mama's grave.

We never talked about the accident, or Papa's death. He never brought the subject up, and neither did I. All we ever talked about was the proper digging of graves, and he remained just as cheerful as he had ever been.

Mama and I were together by ourselves one night. I think she arranged for it to be that way.

"Timothy," she said "you and I have to have a little talk."

"About what?"

"I think it's about time you should be getting to college."

I looked at her. She seemed a tiny woman now, and so old—even compared to the pictures Papa had taken just before their accident. "There's plenty of time for that," I said.

"There isn't!" she snapped, like she always did when she didn't want to hear any more about it. She regretted it right away, though. "I think it's wonderful," she said, "your staying here to take care of me and all, and it's meant a lot to me. I can't say it hasn't. But you're nearly a grown man, Timothy. You've got to start living your own life, finding out what it is that you want to do, and doing it. Why, it's not right for you to keep from putting yourself to good use. You've got intelligence. You've got talents. You've got money. With those three things, there's nothing you can't do."

"But—"

"I don't want to hear any buts!" She glared at me for a few seconds, and then looked down at her hands. "Oh, I thought so careful 'bout what I wanted to say, and it isn't coming out right." She started to cry. When I tried to comfort her, she waved me away, and pulled out one of those tiny rose-embroidered old-lady handkerchiefs and dabbed at her eyes with it.

She sniffed. "I'm sorry."

"That's all right, Mama."

She tried to smile at me, which prompted another, shorter crying spell, only this time she let me hold her hand. Neither one of us said anything for a couple of minutes. Then she pulled her hand away and started fidgeting with her handkerchief.

"I had a dream," she began, not looking at me. "And in that dream, there was an old colored man, dressed in a white tuxedo with a white top hat, who came to me. He said, 'Hello, Mrs. Evans, I've come to take you for a little walk.' I started to tell him I couldn't walk, when I found myself walking already, and since there wasn't much else to say, I didn't say anything.

"He seemed like such a nice man, and he brought me to the edge of a huge plowed field. 'I'll tell you a secret, Mrs. Evans,' he said. 'That isn't a field at all. It's angels' wings.' I wanted to tell him that was a bunch of nonsense, but I looked and saw feathers, growing up out of the ground.

"Oh, Timothy, they were so beautiful! They were all different colors, like they were made out of rainbows, and they grew huge right in front of me, without hardly any time passing at all. So I turned to the man and said, 'Mister, I do believe I'd like to go out there and lie down in those feathers.' And he smiled at me—such a nice smile—and said 'Why, of course you would. That's why we came here.'

"Then he helped me out into the field, and I found a spot I particularly liked, and sat down, and wrapped myself in feathers. They were soft and cozy. It was wonderful."

Mama took my hand and looked at me again. "When I turned around to thank the man, he wasn't there. Neither was anything else. The whole earth had kind of unfolded like, and I found myself riding on the wings of the biggest angel I ever imagined, tucked in just like a little baby, safe and sound and warm and secure. She smiled when she saw me looking at her."

Mama let go of my hand and started carefully folding her handkerchief. "That's all I remember."

"That was very pretty, Mama."

"No, it's not! Least, not in the way you're thinking. That dream meant something."

I swallowed because my mouth was dry, and asked her what.

She didn't answer me at first. She just sat there, folding and unfolding her handkerchief. The sound of crickets chirping came in through the open window. "I'm going to die, Son."

"No—"

"I am!" She waited for me to say something else, and when I didn't, she went on. "Maybe tomorrow, maybe years from now. But it's a fact. It's going to happen. And it's not your place to sit beside me while I'm going about it. That's all I'm saying."

"Maybe you're right."

"I'm right."

"Yes, ma'am."

We sat together and listened to the sounds the night was making. After an hour, a chill began to creep into the house, and I bade her good night and went to bed.

*   *   *

Mr. Beauchamps was waiting for me in his red rocker when I got to the Robinson house the next day. "Morning, Timothy," he said. "I'm going to need you tomorrow."

"I know." I pulled the music box out of its hiding place in the window seat and let it play. Mr. Beauchamps started to play along with it on his harmonica.

"It's Mama's grave—isn't it?"

"I never tell who I'm digging for," he said, picking up the melody again when he finished talking.

I let the tune run out. "What if we don't dig it?"

"We have to dig it," he said.

"Well, what if we don't?"

He stopped rocking. "Timothy Evans, I swear to you, I won't never pass up a grave that needs digging."

"Oh."

"You going to be there?"

I looked at him. "Yeah, I'll be there."

"I thought you would." He started rocking again, and played a new song on his harmonica. The notes lingered in the air long after he disappeared.

I met him in the morning, just like always. It was a cold day, and the oaks waved their fire-colored autumn leaves at us, mocking. We still had no problem working up a sweat as we dug, though.

Mr. Beauchamps was more given to humming than to conversation. He hardly said a word to me all day, or I to him. For lunch, we sat huddled over his picnic basket like a couple of scavengers; the wind was too brisk to lay out the tablecloth and take our time.

Still, even with a short meal, it was a long day of hard work that sank into tones of gray as the afternoon wore on. The sky was bleak, colorless and unrelieved. The dirt stuck to itself, almost like clay, and it was hard to break up.

We finished. I climbed out first, and Mr. Beauchamps went on his usual inspection tour. Then he walked over to the pickax, stood on it, and started to pull himself out.

I swung the shovel for all I was worth. It sliced into his skull as if it were slicing into a piece of clay, sounding much the same, and then stuck there. I tugged on it—once, twice, and a third time before it came loose, and Mr. Beauchamps tumbled back into the grave. As he lay there, blood pooling around his head in a red halo, he slowly smiled.

I shivered. The chill of the day penetrated me all at once, turning my insides to ice, squeezing all the breath out of me, choking me. I dropped to my knees, then to my hands, and let the shovel slip from my grasp into the open grave.

Slowly, quietly, tiny clods of dirt, on their own, began rolling down the graveside pile of earth. They trickled over the edge of the grave in twos and threes at first, sounding like summer hail as they hit bottom, or bounced off Mr. Beauchamps's body. They gathered numbers and strength and speed rapidly, forming a brown waterfall that covered him, and filled the air with growing thunder, until the heavens roared with it, and the ground shook with it, and I thought I would burst. I pressed my hands to my head and rocked back on my heels, dizzy.

Then there was quiet. Abruptly. I opened my eyes to see the pieces of sod slowly crawl off the canvas, like big green caterpillars, moving back to the spots where they belonged, settling in and weaving their edges together where we had cut them. A cold wind came up, whipping through the trees behind me and cutting through the wings of Great-Great-Grandpa Evans's stone angel, who stood a little ways off, aloof and praying.

I folded up the canvas, collected the two-by-fours, threw them into the wheelbarrow, hid them all in among the oak trees, and left.

Doc Morrison's car was parked outside our house when I got home, a silhouette in the gray shades of evening against our whitewashed front porch. I waited for him to come out and drive away before I went in.

I found Bobby and Mary Sue at the kitchen table, drinking coffee, Bobby's cigarette in the ashtray in front of him sending a long plume of smoke straight up until it curled away two feet over their heads. The fluorescent light made their faces pale, and Mary Sue looked like she'd been crying. They both stood up when I walked in, helplessly rooted in place for a moment. Then Mary Sue darted to the stove and poured me a cup of coffee.

"What happened?" I asked, cradling the coffee's warmth in my hands, trying to rid myself of the chill that had followed me inside. I left my jacket on.

Bobby realized he was staring at me; he sat down, reached for his cigarette with one hand, and rested his forehead in the other.

"Your mother had a stroke," Mary Sue said, sitting down again and putting her arm around Bobby's shoulder.

I wanted to shiver—out of hope, out of fear, hardly daring to give into one, lest the other should overcome me. Still holding the cup, I pulled a chair out with my foot and sat down, not bothering to scoot up to the table. "Is she going to be all right?"

Bobby took a final drag on his cigarette, sucked the smoke in deep, and then blew it out in a cloud of frustration. "She's paralyzed," he said. "Doc Morrison says by all rights she should have died."

Nobody spoke for a moment. We didn't look at each other either. "Then she's alive," I said, trying to hide my smile.

"She can't move," Bobby said. "She can't feed herself, she can't sit up, she can't move her arms or her hands, she can't talk. She's alive, all right, if you can call it that." He left the room. Mary Sue and I watched him go, watched the kitchen door swing slowly shut, listened to his footsteps pad down the hall and up the stairs to their bedroom. Mary Sue crushed out his still-burning cigarette.

"The doctor says it's still too early to tell the extent of the damage," she said. "Your mother could get better. She might recover the use of her arms, at least partially. He said she might learn to talk again. He wasn't sure her condition would be permanent. He'll call for a specialist Monday morning. We're supposed to bring her to the hospital then—"

"If she survives, you mean. He's waiting for her to die."

Mary Sue stared at the palms of her hands. "Yes," she said. "That seems to be just about the size of it." She looked up at me. "I'm sorry, Timothy. If you'd been here when the doctor came and heard what he'd said, maybe you'd think differently. As it is, just right now, she might as well stay home. There's nothing they can do for her at the hospital."

"Until Monday?"

"Until Monday."

"Well, she's not going to die," I said, the sweat trickling down under my arms, beading on my forehead.

"You don't know that, Timothy—"

"I do."

"But you can't—"

"I *know*," I said, staring her full in the face. Her eyes were brown, like Bobby's. It was something I had never noticed before. "She won't die." I dropped my gaze and sipped at my coffee. The table seemed miles away.

Mary Sue sighed, sat back, and ran her fingers through her hair. "All right then. You know. More than me, more than your brother, more than the doctor. More than anybody. She won't die." She stood up, and her chair scraped across the floor the way Bobby's did. "I wish I wanted you to be right." With that she left.

I was so excited I could hardly contain myself. Mama was alive! She had made it! She would get better. We would bring her doctors, nurses, medicine—whatever she needed. It was only a matter of time before she got better. That was all. I drained my coffee cup and headed upstairs.

Mama's room was warm, and filled with a pale rosy glow from the nightlight—a frosted white hurricane lamp with pink flowers painted on it. Mama was asleep, so I contented myself with standing next to her bed, jacket draped over one shoulder, and watching her breathe. I had to stand still and observe carefully to do it. But the faint indications were there.

As I moved to leave and close the door behind me, I thought I noticed movement in the shadows on the far side of her bed. I froze. "No," I whispered at the darkness, "I won't do it." I flipped on the light switch, half expecting to see Mr. Beauchamps. But there was nothing. Only Mama's thin, wasted form, captured by the bedsheets and the quilt. Her eyes came open, staring at the ceiling first, then turning her head, slowly, searching for me, finding me. I turned out the light and knelt by her bed, my head close to hers.

"I will not dig your grave, Mama," I told her. "I won't do it."

But she stared at me, her green eyes pleading, unmoving. I took her limp hand in mine. "I won't. We don't know what can happen, Mama. We'll take you to the hospital Monday, and there'll be doctors, and special equipment, and medicine. We'll fix you, Mama. We'll make you better, and you'll talk and write and maybe even walk again. Who knows? But you're not going to die Mama—we've got that on our side."

There wasn't anything else I could say, or any way Mama could answer, so I tucked her in again, and went to bed. I dreamed about her green eyes staring, and about the cold all night.

In the morning I woke to find Mr. Beauchamps's pickax and shovel in my room, propped against the wall next to my bed. They were wet with dew. I wiped them off with my bed sheets, so they wouldn't rust, and put them away in the garage.

Long County Hospital did what it could for Mama, reluctantly. For the two months she was there, I visited her during the days, sometimes with Bobby, sometimes with Mary Sue, most often by myself.

I would read to her—newspapers, poetry I knew she liked, Bible passages. We'd prop her up so she could see what I was reading, and follow along with me. She wouldn't, though. On good days, her green eyes would watch me wherever I went in the room; on bad days, she would just stare at nothing.

It was the same routine after we brought her home, once Doc Morrison and the hospital made it clear there was nothing that could be done for Mama, even if they had wanted to. We put her back in Aunt Fannie's room, hired a live-in nurse, bought a whirlpool bath, rented all sorts of fancy monitoring equipment—anything the experts asked for. Christmas came and went.

And the dance with Mr. Beauchamps's digging tools began to be an odd diversion, a game that wouldn't stop.

I was frightened of them at first, not sure if something worse was waiting to happen. No matter where I hid them, they would show up in my room mornings, always in the same spot, damp, but no dirt, no rust.

The novelty of it took over after the fear wore off. It was like having my own rabbit in a hat. I would hide them further and further away, or make it harder, to see if the trick would still work. I started in the garage at first; locked, chained, bolted, encased in cement out back. From there I went to the graveyards. And the Robinson house. The marsh. Long City, when I had the excuse to go.

I nearly got in trouble when I left them at the store—Bo Potter bought the pickax, and it vanished from his shed during the night. Bobby replaced it without saying anything, and I couldn't figure why. I couldn't ask, either. That was another game: discovery, hoping and fearing Mary Sue, Bobby, or Althea—Mama's nurse, Mammy Walker's girl who trained for medicine instead of midwifing, like Mammy—would find out. I tried to imagine what they would do if they knew.

Once the specialists started coming to our house to see Mama, after the first of the year, I let the pickax and shovel stay in my room on hooks. The playing got weary, tedious, losing its edge with each new prospect for Mama's recovery.

They all seemed cut from the same mold, the specialists—gray-suited, bald, bespectacled; embarrassed smiles on all their faces. They came to us from New York, Washington, Chicago, Los Angeles, more out of curiosity to see Mama like she was some kind of freak than because they thought she could be helped. They examined her, consulted, and we waited. She didn't get any better.

I kept reading to her anyway. I didn't feel like it was as much a matter of hope as it was a matter of time.

Bobby and Mary Sue adjusted rather quickly to Mama being home. They would help me with the reading, and Mary Sue and Althea worked as a team to take care of Mama—giving her baths, preparing her food, keeping records. Bobby took me with him to the store to teach me the business, which was fine as far as I was concerned; I was through with gravedigging, and willing to help out running things.

The situation lasted until February, when Bobby said he was tired of all the gloom and doom hanging over our heads, and he and Mary Sue started going out on the weekends. I stayed home with Mama.

Which was why Mary Sue asked me to help with a surprise birthday party for Bobby—she said she thought it would do us all some good to have regular people over at the house. I was hesitant at first, but she kept at it until I agreed to help.

My part in the plan was to take Bobby over to the county seat—to file some tax papers, ostensibly—and stall him while we were there. We weren't supposed to get home until eight o'clock. I called over to Jameson's Garage in Long City ahead of time and let them know what was going on, so when the car wouldn't start from the distributor cap being jimmied, they wouldn't give me away. They timed it just right, holding back from fixing the car until seven-thirty. None of them could tell me how the shovel and the pickax got in the back seat; they acted like it was somebody else's joke.

I raced home. After the first five minutes at eighty miles an hour, Bobby stopped asking me why. He just buckled the seat belts and wedged himself in the corner against the door and the seat, one arm over the top of the front seat, the other braced against the dash.

We first heard the sirens when we passed the Evans city limits. I screeched the car to a stop outside the circle of fire trucks, and it was plain to see the firemen were fighting a losing battle against the burning house. Our burning house.

Bobby tried to run inside, but that wasn't what held my attention. Rather, it was the bank of ambulances parked along the drive, one or two of them pulling away as we pulled up. There were burnt and charred bodies being loaded up and down the line, and moans filling the air above the roar of the fire and spitting of the hoses. I began opening the back doors of the ambulances nearest me, reeling in the sweet stench of cooked flesh that boiled out every time. They were all alive.

I found her in the fifth car. Mama had been burned beyond recognition, except for a single, lidless green eye that turned toward me.

I slammed the door shut, screaming, stumbling away. A pair of attendants carrying a squirming body on a litter ran past me. The world began to spin, and I could feel the heat from the fire reach for me, even as I heard the sound of the explosion.

I knew what I had to do. I grabbed the pickax and the shovel and ran for Evans Cemetery, as fast as I could, the moon lighting my way as I rushed across the open fields, trying to leave behind me the sounds of the fire, the smell of burning people.

I found the wheelbarrow where I left it, rolled it to the first spot, measured out a rectangle with my two-by-fours, and started digging. I wept until I couldn't see through my swollen eyelids, cursed and screamed until I was hoarse, swung the pickax at the defenseless earth with a vengeance until I was barely able to lift it, and the moon glared down at me like Mama's eye, lighting everything I did. When I finished the grave, I sat for a minute at the bottom, panting.

It was still night.

I picked up my boards and laid out the dimensions of the next grave. It went so much slower than the first, and now I began to regret killing Mr. Beauchamps, not out of guilt, but because I could have used his help.

The digging became painful; even in the moonlight I could see the bruises and cuts on my hands. My feet hurt. My back ached from the strain. I thought of Mr. Beauchamps digging graves even after he reached ninety, going slow and steady, and that gave me hope to go on.

I finally finished the second grave. I was barely able to crawl out. As I lay there, exhausted, I suddenly realized I had been listening to music.

It took me a minute to recognize the tune: Chopin's *Nocturne,* played on the silvery, tinkling tones of Aunt Fannie's music box.

And then I realized it was still night, and I was still looking at a scene illuminated by moonlight. I rolled over.

He was sitting on the shoulder of the old stone angel, dressed in a white tuxedo instead of his blue and white striped overalls, and his engineer's hat was replaced by a white silk top hat. "Hello, Timothy," he said. The music box sat in his lap, its lid open.

"Hello, Mr. Beauchamps," I croaked back.

"Save your strength," he said, pushing off from his perch and slowly floating to the ground. "You've got a lot of work ahead of you tonight."

"The moon—"

"Never you mind about the moon! I'm doing my part, and you do yours—there are lots of graves to dig before morning gets here. You can rest a little before you get started on the next one, though."

So I rested to Chopin. And dug to Mozart, Beethoven, and Brahms. Grave after grave, until the pain, the remorse, the revulsion drained away; and there was nothing left but the sound of the shovel, the shadows dancing with the moonlight that poured down from the sky, the crisp, brittle notes of the music box, and the gentle encouragement of Mr. Beauchamps. The sun came up as I finished digging the twenty-seventh grave.

There is no one left to get close to anymore. Except for Mr. Beauchamps. In addition to bringing me lunch when I'm working, he always comes by on special occasions—the anniversary of our meeting, my birthday, his birthday, the day I passed his gravedigging total of 743—and that was well over a decade ago.

I am ninety-six years old now, and have buried 915 people—my brother, my sister-in-law, my cousin, my nieces and nephews, the sheriff, the doctor, the black folk who lived down in the Quarters, the white folk who used to work for the Evans family business; people I never knew, or met, or even heard of. As I dug every one of their graves, I wondered who they all were, where they came from, and I was glad to give them their deaths, to help them step into the next Kingdom. But I am tired. I have been tired since the night I dug twenty-seven graves.

When there's a nice day and I don't have to go digging, I put flowers on Mama's grave, or on Mr. Beauchamps's. He was the first black man ever to be buried in Evans Cemetery, even if no one else knows about it.

And I keep hoping the next grave I dig will be my own.

GREG BEAR

Tangents

Born in San Diego, California, Greg Bear made his first sale at the age of fifteen to Robert Lowndes's *Famous Science Fiction*. In the years since then, he has established himself as one of the top young professionals in the genre. His short fiction has appeared in *Analog, Galaxy, Isaac Asimov's Science Fiction Magazine, Omni, The Magazine of Fantasy and Science Fiction, Universe,* and elsewhere. His story "Blood Music," which was in our First Annual Collection, won both the Hugo and the Nebula Award, and his story "Hardfought," also in our First Annual Collection, won the Hugo Award. His books include the novels *Hegira, Psychlone, Beyond Heaven's River, Strength of Stones, The Infinity Concerto,* and *Blood Music,* and a collection, *The Wind from a Burning Woman.* His most recent books are the novels *Eon* and *The Serpent Mage.* Upcoming are *The Forge of God,* from Tor, and *Eternity* and *Queen of Angels,* from Warner Books. Bear lives in Santee, California, with his wife Astrid and their new baby Erik.

In the story that follows, Bear suggests that the *way* you look at things may be every bit as important as what you're looking at. . . .

TANGENTS

Greg Bear

The nut-brown boy stood in the California field, his Asian face shadowed by a hard hat, his short, stocky frame clothed in a T-shirt and a pair of brown shorts. He squinted across the hip-high grass at the spraddled old two-story ranch house, and then he whistled a few bars from a Haydn piano sonata. Out of the upper floor of the house came a man's high, frustrated "bloody hell!" and the sound of a fist slamming on a solid surface. Silence for a minute. Then, more softly, a woman's question: "Not going well?"

"No. I'm swimming in it, but I don't see it."

"The encryption?" the woman asked timidly.

"The tesseract. If it doesn't gel, it isn't aspic."

The boy squatted in the grass and listened.

"And?" the woman encouraged.

"Ah, Lauren, it's still cold broth."

The conversation stopped. The boy lay back in the grass, aware he was on private land. He had crept over the split-rail and brick-pylon fence from the new housing project across the road. School was out, and his mother—adoptive mother—did not like him around the house all day. Or at all.

He closed his eyes and imagined a huge piano keyboard and himself dancing on the keys, tapping out the Oriental-sounding D minor scale, which suited his origins, he thought. He loved music.

He opened his eyes and saw the thin, graying lady in a tweed suit leaning over him, staring down with her brows knit.

"You're on private land," she said.

He scrambled up and brushed grass from his pants. "Sorry."

"I thought I saw someone out here. What's your name?"

"Pal," he replied.

"Is that a name?" she asked querulously.

"Pal Tremont. It's not my real name. I'm Korean."

"Then what's your real name?"

"My folks told me not to use it anymore. I'm adopted. Who are you?"

The gray woman looked him up and down. "My name is Lauren Davies," she said. "You live near here?"

He pointed across the fields at the close-packed tract homes.

"I sold the land for those homes ten years ago," she said. "I don't normally enjoy children trespassing."

"Sorry," Pal said.

"Have you had lunch?"

"No."

"Will a grilled cheese sandwich do?"

He squinted at her and nodded.

In the broad, red-brick and tile kitchen, sitting at an oak table with his shoulders barely rising above the top, he ate the mildly charred sandwich and watched Lauren Davies watching him.

"I'm trying to write about a child," she said. "It's difficult. I'm a spinster and I don't know children well."

"You're a writer?" he asked, taking a swallow of milk.

She sniffed. "Not that anyone would know."

"Is that your brother, upstairs?"

"No," she said. "That's Peter. We've been living together for twenty years."

"But you said you're a spinster—isn't that someone who's never married or never loved?" Pal asked.

"Never married. And never you mind. Peter's relationship to me is none of your concern." She put together a tray with a bowl of soup and a tuna-salad sandwich. "His lunch," she said. Without being asked, Pal trailed up the stairs after her.

"This is where Peter works," Lauren explained. Pal stood in the doorway, eyes wide. The room was filled with electronics gear, computer terminals and industrial-gray shelving with odd cardboard sculptures sharing each level, along with books and circuit boards. She put the lunch tray on top of a cart, resting precariously on a box of floppy disks.

"Still having trouble?" she asked a thin man with his back turned toward them.

The man turned around on his swivel chair, glanced briefly at Pal, then at the lunch, and shook his head. The hair on top of his head was a rich, glossy black; on the close-cut sides, the color changed abruptly to a bright, fake-looking white. He had a small, thin nose and large green eyes. On the desk before him was a computer monitor. "We haven't been introduced," he said, pointing to Pal.

"This is Pal Tremont, a neighborhood visitor. Pal, this is Peter Tuthy. Pal's going to help me with that character we discussed."

Pal looked at the monitor curiously. Red and green lines went through some incomprehensible transformation on the screen, then repeated.

"What's a tesseract?" Pal asked, remembering the words he had heard through the window as he stood in the field.

"It's a four-dimensional analog of a cube. I'm trying to find a way to teach myself to see it in my mind's eye." Tuthy said. "Have you ever tried that?"

"No," Pal admitted.

"Here," Tuthy said, handing him the spectacles. "As in the movies."

Pal donned the spectacles and stared at the screen. "So?" he said. "It folds and unfolds. It's pretty—it sticks out at you, and then it goes away." He looked around the workshop. "Oh, wow!" In the east corner of the room a framework of aluminum pipes—rather like a plumber's dream of an easel—supported a long, disembodied piano keyboard mounted in a slim, black case. The boy ran to the keyboard. "A Tronclavier! With all the switches! My mother had me take piano lessons, but I'd rather learn on this. Can you play it?"

"I toy with it," Tuthy said, exasperated. "I toy with all sorts of electronic things. But what did you see on the screen?" He glanced up at Lauren, blinking. "I'll eat the food, I'll eat it. Now please don't bother us."

"He's supposed to be helping *me*," Lauren complained.

Peter smiled at her. "Yes, of course. I'll send him downstairs in a little while."

When Pal descended an hour later, he came into the kitchen to thank Lauren for lunch. "Peter's a real flake. He's trying to see certain directions."

"I know," Lauren said, sighing.

"I'm going home now," Pal said. "I'll be back, though . . . if it's all right with you. Peter invited me."

"I'm sure that it will be fine," Lauren replied dubiously.

"He's going to let me learn the Tronclavier." With that, Pal smiled radiantly and exited through the kitchen door.

When she retrieved the tray, she found Peter leaning back in his chair, eyes closed. The figures on the screen patiently folded and unfolded, cubes continuously passing through one another.

"What about Hockrum's work?" she asked.

"I'm on it," Peter replied, eyes still closed.

Lauren called Pal's foster mother on the second day to apprise them of their son's location, and the woman assured her it was quite all right. "Sometimes he's a little pest. Send him home if he causes trouble—but not right away! Give me a rest," she said, then laughed nervously.

Lauren drew her lips together tightly, thanked her, and hung up.

Peter and the boy had come downstairs to sit in the kitchen, filling up paper with line drawings. "Peter's teaching me how to use his program," Pal said.

"Did you know," Tuthy said, assuming his highest Cambridge professional tone, "that a cube, intersecting a flat plane, can be cut through a number of geometrically different cross sections?"

Pal squinted at the sketch Tuthy had made. "Sure," he said.

"If shoved through the plane, the cube can appear, to a two-dimensional creature living on the plane—let's call him a Flatlander—to be either a triangle, a rectangle, a trapezoid, a rhombus, or a square. If the two-dimensional being observes the cube being pushed through all the way, what he sees is one or more of these objects growing larger, changing shape suddenly, shrinking, and disappearing."

"Sure," Pal said, tapping his sneakered toe. "It's easy. Like in that book you showed me."

"And a sphere pushed through a plane would appear to the hapless Flatlander first as an *invisible* point (the two-dimensional surface touching the sphere, tangential), then as a circle. The circle would grow in size, then shrink back to a point and disappear again." He sketched the stick figures, looking in awe at the intrusion.

"Got it," Pal said. "Can I play with the Tronclavier now?"

"In a moment. Be patient. So what would a tesseract look like, coming into our three-dimensional space? Remember the program, now—the pictures on the monitor."

Pal looked up at the ceiling. "I don't know," he said, seeming bored.

"Try to think," Tuthy urged him.

"It would . . ." Pal held his hands out to shape an angular object. "It would look like one of those Egyptian things, but with three sides . . . or like a box. It would look like a weird-shaped box, too, not square."

"And if we turned the tesseract around?"

The doorbell rang. Pal jumped off the kitchen chair. "Is that my Mom?"

"I don't think so," Lauren said. "More likely it's Hockrum." She went to the front door to answer. She returned with a small, pale man behind her. Tuthy stood and shook the man's hand. "Pal Tremont, this is Irving Hockrum," he introduced, waving his hand between them. Hockrum glanced at Pal and blinked a long, not-very-mammalian blink.

"How's the work coming?" he asked Tuthy.

"It's finished," Tuthy said. "It's upstairs. Looks like your savants are barking up the wrong logic tree." He retrieved a folder of papers and printouts and handed them to Hockrum.

Hockrum leafed through the printouts.

"I can't say this makes me happy," he said. "Still, I can't find fault. Looks like the work is up to your usual brilliant standards. I just wish you'd had it to us sooner. It would have saved me some grief—and the company quite a bit of money."

"Sorry," Tuthy said nonchalantly.

"Now I have an important bit of work for you. . . ." And Hockrum outlined another problem. Tuthy thought it over for several minutes and shook his head.

"Most difficult, Irving. Pioneering work there. It would take at least a month to see if it's even feasible."

"That's all I need to know for now—whether it's feasible. A lot's riding on this, Peter." Hockrum clasped his hands together in front of him, looking even more pale and worn than when he had entered the kitchen. "You'll let me know soon?"

"I'll get right on it," Tuthy said.

"Protégé?" he asked, pointing to Pal. There was a speculative expression on his face, not quite a leer.

"No, a friend. He's interested in music." Tuthy said. "Damned good at Mozart, in fact."

"I help with his tesseracts," Pal asserted.

"Congratulations," Hockrum said. "I hope you don't interrupt Peter's work. Peter's work is important."

Pal shook his head solemnly. "Good," Hockrum said, and then left the house to take the negative results back to his company.

Tuthy returned to his office, Pal in train. Lauren tried to work in the kitchen, sitting with fountain pen and pad of paper, but the words wouldn't come. Hockrum always worried her. She climbed the stairs and stood in the doorway of the office. She often did that; her presence did not disturb Tuthy, who could work under all sorts of conditions.

"Who was that man?" Pal was asking Tuthy.

"I work for him." Tuthy said. "He's employed by a very big electronics firm. He loans me most of the equipment I use here—the computers, the high-resolution monitors. He brings me problems and then takes my solutions back to his bosses and claims he did the work."

"That sounds stupid," Pal said. "What kind of problems?"

"Codes, encryptions. Computer security. That was my expertise, once."

"You mean, like fencerail, that sort of thing?" Pal asked, face brightening. "We learned some of that in school."

"Much more complicated, I'm afraid," Tuthy said, grinning. "Did you ever hear of the German 'Enigma,' or the 'Ultra' project?"

Pal shook his head.

"I thought not. Don't worry about it. Let's try another figure on the screen now." He called up another routine on the four-space program and sat Pal before the screen. "So what would a hypersphere look like if it intruded into our space?"

Pal thought a moment. "Kind of weird."

"Not really. You've been watching the visualizations."

"Oh, in *our* space. That's easy. It just looks like a balloon, blowing up from nothing and then shrinking again. It's harder to see what a hypersphere looks like when it's real. Reft of us, I mean."

"Reft?" Tuthy said.

"Sure. Reft and light. Dup and owwen. Whatever the directions are called."

Tuthy stared at the boy. Neither of them had noticed Lauren in the doorway. "The proper terms are *ana* and *kata*," Tuthy said. "What does it look like?"

Pal gestured, making two wide swings with his arms. "It's like a ball, and it's like a horseshoe, depending on how you look at it. Like a balloon stung by bees, I guess, but it's smooth all over, not lumpy."

Tuthy continued to stare, then asked quietly, "You actually see it?"

"Sure," Pal said. "Isn't that what your program is supposed to do—make you see things like that?"

Tuthy nodded, flabbergasted.

"Can I play the Tronclavier now?"

Lauren backed out of the doorway. She felt she had eavesdropped on something momentous but beyond her. Tuthy came downstairs an hour later, leaving Pal to pick out Telemann on the keyboard. He sat at the kitchen table with her. "The program works," he said. "It doesn't work for me, but it works for him. He's a bloody natural." Tuthy seldom used such language. He was clearly awed. "I've just been showing him reverse-shadow figures. There's a way to have at least a sensation of seeing something rotated through the fourth dimension. Those hollow masks they use at Disneyland . . . seem to reverse in and out, depending on the lighting? Crater pictures from the moon—resemble hills instead of holes? That's what Pal calls the reversed images—hills and holes."

"And what's special about them?"

"Well, if you go along with the game and make the hollow faces seem to reverse and poke out at you, that is similar to rotating them in the fourth dimension. The features seem to reverse left and right—right eye becomes left eye, and so on. He caught on right away, and then he went off and played Haydn. He's gone through all my sheet music. The kid's a genius."

"Musical, you mean?"

He glanced directly at her and frowned. "Yes, I suppose he's remarkable at that, too. But spatial relations—coordinates and motion in a higher dimension. . . . Did you know that if you take a three-dimensional object and rotate it in the fourth dimension, it will come back with left-right reversed? There is no fixed left-right in the fourth dimension. So if I were to take my hand—" He held up his right hand, "and lift it *dup*—or drop it *owwen*, it would come back like this?" He held his left hand over his right, balled the right up into a fist, and snuck it away behind his back.

"I didn't know that," Lauren said. "What are *dup* and *owwen?*"

"That's what Pal calls movement along the fourth dimension. *Ana* and *kata* to purists. Like up and down to a Flatlander, who only comprehends left and right, back and forth."

She thought about the hands for a moment. "I still can't see it," she said.

"Neither can I," Tuthy admitted. "Our circuits are just too hard-wired, I suppose."

Pal had switched the Tronclavier to a cathedral organ and wah-guitar combination and was playing variations on Pergolesi.

"Are you going to keep working for Hockrum?" Lauren asked. Tuthy didn't seem to hear her.

"It's remarkable," he murmured. "The boy just walked in here. You brought him in by accident. Remarkable."

"Do you think you can show me the direction—point it out to me?" Tuthy asked the boy three days later.

"None of my muscles move that way," he replied. "I can see it, in my head, but . . ."

"What is it like, seeing it? That direction?"

Pal squinted. "It's a lot bigger. Where we live is sort of stacked up with other places. It makes me feel lonely."

"Why?"

"Because I'm stuck here. Nobody out there pays any attention to us."

Tuthy's mouth worked. "I thought you were just intuiting those directions in your head. Are you telling me you're actually *seeing* out there?"

"Yeah. There's people out there, too. Well, not people, exactly. But it isn't my eyes that see them. Eyes are like muscles—they can't point those ways. But the head—the brain, I guess—can."

"Bloody hell," Tuthy said. He blinked and recovered. "Excuse me. That's rude. Can you show me the people . . . on the screen?"

"Shadows, like we were talking about."

"Fine. Then draw the shadows for me."

Pal sat down before the terminal, fingers pausing over the keys. "I can show you, but you have to help me with something."

"Help you with what?"

"I'd like to play music for them—out there. So they'll notice us."

"The people?"

"Yeah. They look really weird. They stand on us, sort of. They have hooks in our world. But they're tall . . . high dup. They don't notice us because we're so small, compared with them."

"Lord, Pal, I haven't the slightest idea how we'd send music out to them. . . . I'm not even sure I believe they exist."

"I'm not lying," Pal said, eyes narrowing. He turned his chair to face a "mouse" perched on a black ruled pad and used it to sketch shapes on the monitor. "Remember, these are just shadows of what they look like. Next I'll draw the dup and owwen lines to connect the shadows."

The boy shaded the shapes to make them look solid, smiling at his trick but explaining it was necessary because the projection of a four-dimensional object in normal space was, of course, three dimensional.

"They look like you take the plants in a garden and give them lots of arms and fingers . . . and it's kind of like seeing things in an aquarium," Pal explained.

After a time, Tuthy suspended his disbelief and stared in open-mouthed wonder at what the boy was re-creating on the monitor.

"I think you're wasting your time, that's what I think," Hockrum said. "I needed that feasibility judgment by today." He paced around the living room before falling as heavily as his light frame permitted into a chair.

"I *have* been distracted," Tuthy admitted.

"By that boy?"

"Yes, actually. Quite a talented fellow."

"Listen, this is going to mean a lot of trouble for me. I guaranteed the judgment would be made by today. It'll make me look bad." Hockrum screwed up his face in frustration. "What in hell are you doing with that boy?"

"Teaching him, actually. Or rather, he's teaching me. Right now, we're building a four-dimensional cone, part of a speaker system. The cone is three dimensional—the material part—but the magnetic field forms a fourth-dimensional extension."

"Do you ever think how it looks, Peter?"

"It looks very strange on the monitor, I grant you—"

"I'm talking about you and the boy."

Tuthy's bright, interested expression fell slowly into long, deep-lined dismay. "I don't know what you mean."

"I know a lot about you, Peter. Where you come from, why you had to leave. . . . It just doesn't look good."

Tuthy's face flushed crimson.

"Keep him away," Hockrum advised.

Tuthy stood. "I want you out of this house," he said quietly. "Our relationship is at an end."

"I swear," Hockrum said, his voice low and calm, staring up at Tuthy from under his brows, "I'll tell the boy's parents. Do you think they'd want their kid hanging around an old—pardon the expression—queer? I'll tell them if you don't get the feasibility judgment made. I think you can do it by the end of this week—two days. Don't you?"

"No, I don't think so," Tuthy said softly. "Leave."

"I know you're here illegally. There's no record of you entering the country. With the problems you had in England, you're certainly not a desirable alien. I'll pass word to the INS. You'll be deported."

"There isn't time to do the work," Tuthy said.

"Make time. Instead of 'educating' that kid."

"Get out of here."

"Two days, Peter."

Over dinner, Tuthy explained to Lauren the exchange he had had with Hockrum. "He thinks I'm buggering Pal. Unspeakable bastard. I will never work for him again."

"I'd better talk to a lawyer, then," Lauren said. "You're sure you can't make him . . . happy, stop all this trouble?"

"I could solve his little problem for him in just a few hours. But I don't want to see him or speak to him again."

"He'll take your equipment away."

Tuthy blinked and waved one hand through the air helplessly. "Then we'll just have to work fast, won't we? Ah, Lauren, you were a fool to bring me over here. You should have left me to rot."

"They ignored everything you did for them," Lauren said bitterly. She stared through the kitchen window at the overcast sky and woods outside. "You saved their hides during the war, and then . . . they would have shut you up in prison."

The cone lay on the table near the window, bathed in morning sun, connected to both the minicomputer and the Tronclavier. Pal arranged the score he had composed on a music stand before the synthesizer. "It's like a Bach canon," he said, "but it'll play better for them. It has a kind of counterpoint or over-rhythm that I'll play on the dup part of the speaker."

"Why are we doing this, Pal?" Tuthy asked as the boy sat down to the keyboard.

"You don't belong here, really, do you, Peter?" Pal asked. Tuthy stared at him.

"I mean, Miss Davies and you get along okay—but do you belong *here*, now?"

"What makes you think I don't belong?"

"I read some books in the school library. About the war and everything. I looked up *Enigma* and *Ultra*. I found a fellow named Peter Thornton. His picture looked like you but younger. The books made him seem like a hero."

Tuthy smiled wanly.

"But there was this note in one book. You disappeared in 1965. You were being prosecuted for something. They didn't even mention what it was you were being prosecuted for."

"I'm a homosexual," Tuthy said quietly.

"Oh. So what?"

"Lauren and I met in England, in 1964. They were going to put me in prison, Pal. We liked—love each other, so she smuggled me into the U.S. through Canada."

"But you're a homosexual. They don't like women."

"Not at all true, Pal. Lauren and I like each other very much. We could talk. She told me her dreams of being a writer, and I talked to her about mathematics and about the war. I nearly died during the war."

"Why? Were you wounded?"

"No. I worked too hard. I burned myself out and had a nervous breakdown. My lover . . . a man . . . kept me alive throughout the Forties. Things were bad in England after the war. But he died in 1963. His parents came in to settle the estate, and when I contested the settlement in court, I was arrested." The lines on his face deepened, and he closed his eyes for a long moment. "I suppose I don't really belong here."

"I don't either. My folks don't care much. I don't have too many friends. I wasn't even born here, and I don't know anything about Korea."

"Play," Tuthy said, his face stony. "Let's see if they'll listen."

"Oh, they'll listen," Pal said. "It's like the way they talk to each other."

The boy ran his fingers over the keys on the Tronclavier. The cone, connected with the keyboard through the minicomputer, vibrated tinnily. For an hour, Pal paged back and forth through his composition, repeating passages and creating variations. Tuthy sat in a corner, chin in hand, listening to the mousy squeaks and squeals produced by the cone. *How much more difficult to interpret a four-dimensional sound,* he thought. *Not even visual clues.* Finally the boy stopped and wrung his hands, then stretched his arms. "They must have heard. We'll just have to wait and see." He switched the Tronclavier to automatic playback and pushed the chair away from the keyboard.

Pal stayed until dusk, then reluctantly went home. Tuthy stood in the office until midnight, listening to the tinny sounds issuing from the speaker cone. There was nothing more he could do. He ambled down the hall to his bedroom, shoulders slumped.

All night long the Tronclavier played through its preprogrammed selection of Pal's compositions. Tuthy lay in bed in his room, two doors down from Lauren's room, watching a shaft of moonlight slide across the wall. *How far would a four-dimensional being have to travel to get here?*

How far have I come to get here?

Without realizing he was asleep, he dreamed, and in his dream a wavering image of Pal appeared, gesturing with both arms as if swimming, eyes wide. *I'm okay,* the boy said without moving his lips. *Don't worry about me. . . . I'm okay. I've been back to Korea to see what it's like. It's not bad, but I like it better here. . . .*

*   *   *

Tuthy awoke sweating. The moon had gone down, and the room was pitch-black. In the office, the hypercone continued its distant, mouse-squeak broadcast.

Pal returned early in the morning, whistling disjointed selections from Mozart's Fourth Violin Concerto. Lauren opened the front door for him, and he ran upstairs to join Tuthy. Tuthy sat before the monitor, replaying Pal's sketch of the four-dimensional beings.

"Do you see them now?" he asked the boy.

Pal nodded. "They're closer. They're interested. Maybe we should get things ready, you know—be prepared." He squinted. "Did you ever think what a four-dimensional footprint would look like?"

Tuthy considered this for a moment. "That would be most interesting," he said. "It would be solid."

On the first floor, Lauren screamed.

Pal and Tuthy almost tumbled over each other getting downstairs. Lauren stood in the living room with her arms crossed above her bosom, one hand clamped over her mouth. The first intrusion had taken out a section of the living-room floor and the east wall.

"Really clumsy," Pal said. "One of them must have bumped it."

"The music," Tuthy said.

"What in *hell* is going on?" Lauren queried, her voice starting as a screech and ending as a roar.

"You'd better turn the music off," Tuthy elaborated.

"Why?" Pal asked, face wreathed in an excited smile.

"Maybe they don't like it."

A bright, filmy blue blob rapidly expanded to a diameter of a yard beside Tuthy, wriggled, froze, then just as rapidly vanished.

"That was like an elbow," Pal explained. "One of its arms. I think it's trying to find out where the music is coming from. I'll go upstairs."

"Turn it off!" Tuthy demanded.

"I'll play something else." The boy ran up the stairs. From the kitchen came a hideous hollow crashing, then the sound of vacuum being filled—a reverse pop, ending in a hiss—followed by a low-frequency vibration that set their teeth on edge.

The vibration caused by a four-dimensional creature *scraping* across their three-dimensional "floor." Tuthy's hands shook with excitement.

"Peter!" Lauren bellowed, all dignity gone. She unwrapped her arms and held clenched fists out as if she were ready to exercise or start boxing.

"Pal's attracted visitors," Tuthy explained.

He turned toward the stairs. The first four steps and a section of floor spun and vanished. The rush of air nearly drew him down the hole.

After regaining his balance, he kneeled to feel the precisely cut, concave edge. Below was the dark basement.

"Pal!" Tuthy called out. "Turn it *off!*"

"I'm playing something new for them," Pal shouted back. "I think they like it."

The phone rang. Tuthy was closest to the extension at the bottom of the stairs and instinctively reached out to answer. Hockrum was on the other end, screaming.

"I can't talk now—" Tuthy said. Hockrum screamed again, loud enough for Lauren to hear. Tuthy abruptly hung up. "He's been fired, I gather," he said. "He seemed angry." He stalked back three paces and turned, then ran forward and leapt the gap to the first intact step. "Can't talk." He stumbled and scrambled up the stairs, stopping on the landing. "Jesus," he said, as if something had suddenly occurred to him.

"He'll call the government," Lauren warned.

Tuthy waved that off. "I know what's happening. They're knocking chunks out of three-space, into the fourth. The fourth dimension. Like Pal says: clumsy brutes. They could kill us!"

Sitting before the Tronclavier, Pal happily played a new melody. Tuthy approached and was abruptly blocked by a thick green column, as solid as rock and with a similar texture. It vibrated and described an arc in the air. A section of the ceiling a yard wide was kicked out of three-space. Tuthy's hair lifted in the rush of wind. The column shrunk to a broomstick, and hairs sprouted all over it, writhing like snakes.

Tuthy edged around the hairy broomstick and pulled the plug on the Tronclavier. A cage of zeppelin-shaped brown sausages encircled the computer, spun, elongated to reach the ceiling, the floor, and the top of the monitor's table, and then pipped down to tiny strings and was gone.

"They can't see too clearly here," Pal said undisturbed that his concert was over. Lauren had climbed the outside stairs and stood behind Tuthy. "Gee, I'm sorry about the damage."

In one smooth, curling motion, the Tronclavier and cone and all the wiring associated with them were peeled away as if they had been stick-on labels hastily removed from a flat surface.

"Gee," Pal said, his face suddenly registering alarm.

Then it was the boy's turn. He was removed more slowly, with greater care. The last thing to vanish was his head, which hung suspended in the air for several seconds.

"I think they liked the music," he said with a grin.

Head, grin and all, dropped away in a direction impossible for Tuthy or Lauren to follow. The room sucked air through the open door, then quietly sighed back to normal.

Lauren stood her ground for several minutes, while Tuthy wandered through what was left of the office, passing his hand through mussed hair.

"Perhaps he'll be back," Tuthy said. "I don't even know . . ." But he didn't finish. *Could a three-dimensional boy survive in a four-dimensional void, or whatever lay dup—or owwen?*

Tuthy did not object when Lauren took it upon herself to call the boy's foster parents and the police. When the police arrived, he endured the questions and accusations stoically, face immobile, and told them as much as he knew. He was not believed; nobody knew quite what to believe. Photographs were taken.

It was only a matter of time, Lauren told him, until one or the other or both of them were arrested. "Then we'll make up a story," he said. "You'll tell them it was my fault."

"I will *not,*" Lauren said. "But where *is* he?"

"I'm not positive," Tuthy said. "I think he's all right, however."

"How do you know?"

He told her about the dream.

"But that was before," she said.

"Perfectly allowable in the fourth dimension," he explained. He pointed vaguely up, then down, then shrugged.

On the last day, Tuthy spent the early morning hours bundled in an overcoat and bathrobe in the drafty office, playing his program again and again, trying to visualize *ana* and *kata*. He closed his eyes and squinted and twisted his head, intertwined his fingers and drew odd little graphs on the monitors, but it was no use. His brain was hard-wired.

Over breakfast, he reiterated to Lauren that she must put all the blame on him.

"Maybe it will all blow over," she said. "They have no case. No evidence . . . nothing."

All blow over, he mused, passing his hand over his head and grinning ironically. *How over, they'll never know.*

The doorbell rang. Tuthy went to answer it, and Lauren followed a few steps behind.

Putting it all together later, she decided that subsequent events happened in the following order:

Tuthy opened the door. Three men in gray suits, one with a briefcase, stood on the porch. "Mr. Peter Tuthy?" the tallest asked.

"Yes," Tuthy acknowledged.

A chunk of the doorframe and wall above the door vanished with a roar and a hissing pop. The three men looked up at the gap. Ignoring what was impossible, the tallest man returned his attention to Tuthy and continued, "Sir, it's our duty to take you into custody. We have information that you are in this country illegally."

"Oh?" Tuthy said.

Beside him, an irregular, filmy blue blob grew to a length of four feet and hung in the air, vibrating. The three men backed away. In the middle of the blob, Pal's head emerged, and below that, his extended arm and hand. Tuthy leaned forward to study this apparition. Pal's fingers waggled at him.

"It's fun here," Pal said. "They're friendly."

"I believe you," Tuthy said calmly.

"Mr. Tuthy," the tallest man valiantly persisted, though his voice was a squeak.

"Won't you come with me?" Pal asked.

Tuthy glanced back at Lauren. She gave him a small fraction of a nod, barely understanding what she was assenting to, and he took Pal's hand. "Tell them it was all my fault," he said again.

From his feet to his head, Peter Tuthy was peeled out of this world. Air rushed in. Half of the brass lamp to one side of the door disappeared. The INS men returned to their car with damp pants and embarassed, deeply worried expressions, and without any further questions. They drove away, leaving Lauren to contemplate the quiet.

She did not sleep for three nights, and when she did sleep, Tuthy and Pal visited her and put the question to her.

Thank you, but I prefer it here, she replied.

It's a lot of fun, the boy insisted. *They like music.*

Lauren shook her head on the pillow and awoke. Not very far away, there was a whistling, tinny kind of sound, followed by a deep vibration. To her, it sounded like applause.

She took a deep breath and got out of bed to retrieve her notebook.

BRUCE STERLING

The Beautiful and the Sublime

One of the major new talents to enter SF in recent years, Bruce Sterling sold his first story in 1976, and has since sold stories to *Universe, Omni, The Magazine of Fantasy and Science Fiction, The Last Dangerous Visions, Lone Star Universe,* and elsewhere. He has attracted special acclaim in the last few years for a series of stories set in his exotic Shaper/Mechanist universe, a complex and disturbing future where warring political factions struggle to control the shape of human destiny and the nature of humanity itself. His acclaimed Shaper/Mechanist story "Swarm" was both a Hugo and Nebula finalist in 1982; "Spider Rose," another story sharing the same background, was also a Hugo finalist that year. His story "Cicada Queen" was in our First Annual Collection; his "Sunken Gardens" was in our Second Annual Collection; his "Green Days in Brunei" and "Dinner in Audoghast" were in our Third Annual Collection. His novels include *Involution Ocean* and *The Artificial Kid.* His most recent books are *Schismatrix,* a novel set in the Shaper/Mechanist future, and, as editor, *Mirrorshades: The Cyberpunk Anthology.* Sterling was born in Brownsville, Texas, and now lives in Austin with his wife, Nancy.

Here he treats us to a typically quirky and fascinating story, which the author himself describes as "a Wodehousian romantic comedy about the death of the scientific method. . . ."

THE BEAUTIFUL AND THE SUBLIME

Bruce Sterling

May 30, 2070

My dear MacLuhan:

   You, my friend, who know so well a lover's troubles, will understand my affair with Leona Hillis.

   Since my last letter to you, I have come to know Leona's soul. Slowly, almost despite myself, I opened those reservoirs of sympathy and feeling that turn a simple liaison into something much deeper. Something that partakes of the sublime.

   It is love, my dear MacLuhan. Not the appetite of the body, easily counterfeited with pills. No, it is closer to *agape*, the soaring spiritual union of the Greeks.

   I know the Greeks are out of favor these days, especially Plato with his computerlike urge toward abstract intellect.

   Forgive me if my sentiments take this somewhat over-Westernized expression. I can only express what I feel, simply and directly.

   In other words, I am free of that sense of evanescence that poisoned my earlier commitments. I feel as if I had always loved Leona; she has a place within my soul that could never be filled by another woman.

   I know it was rash of me to leave Seattle. Aksyonov was eager to have me complete the set design for his new drama. But I felt taxed and restless, and dreaded the days of draining creative effort. Inspiration comes from nature, and I had been too long pent in the city.

   So, when I received Leona's invitation to her father's birthday gala in the Grand Canyon, the lure was irresistible. It combined the best of both worlds: the companionship of a charming woman, against the background of a natural wonder unrivaled for sublimity.

   I left poor Aksyonov only a hasty note over the mailnet, and fled to Arizona.

   And what a landscape! Great sweeping mesas, long blasted vistas in purple and rose, great gaudy sunsets reaching ethereal fingers of pure radiance halfway to the zenith! It is the opposite pole to our green, introspective Seattle; a bright yang to the drizzling yin of the Pacific Coast. The air, sharpened by sagebrush and pinyon pine, seems to scrub the brain like a loofah. At once I felt my appetite return, and a new briskness lent itself to my step.

I spoke with several Arizonans about their Global Park. I found them to be sensitive and even noble people, touched to the core by the staggering beauty of their eerie landscape. They are quite modern in their sentiments, despite the large numbers of retirees—crotchety industrial-age relics. Since the draining of Lake Powell, the former floodplain of the reservoir has been opened to camping, sports, and limited development. This relieves the crowding in the Grand Canyon itself, which, under wise stewardship, is returning to a pristine state of nature.

For Dr. Hillis's celebration, Hillis Industries had hired a modern hogan, perching on the northern canyon rim. It was a broad, two-story dome, wrought from native cedar and sandstone, which blended into the landscape with admirable restraint and taste. A wide cedar porch overlooked the river. Behind the dome, white-barked Ponderosa pines bordered a large rock garden.

Freed of its obnoxious twentieth-century dams, the primal Colorado raged gloriously below the cliffsides, leaping and frothing in great silted billows and surges, flinging rocks and driftwood with tigerlike abandon. In the days that followed, its hissing roar would never be far from my thoughts.

The long drowning beneath the manmade lake had added an eerie charm to these upper reaches of the great canyon. Its shale and sandstone walls were stained a viridian green. In gulfs and eddies amid the canyon's sinuous turns, old lake sediments still clung in warping slopes, clotted by the roots of cottonwoods and flowering scrub.

On the hogan porch, overlooking the cliffs, I plugged my wrist-ward into the house system and made my presence known. Also on the porch were a pair of old people. I checked their identities with my newly charged ward. But with the typical callousness of their generation, they had not plugged into the house system, and remained unknown to me.

It was with some relief, then, that I saw our old friend Mari Kuniyoshi emerge from the hogan to greet me. She and I had corresponded faithfully since her return to Osaka; mostly about her fashion business, and the latest gossip in Japanese graphic design.

I confess I never understood the magnetic attraction Mari has for so many men. My interest lies in her talent for design, and in fact I find her romances rather heartless.

My ward identified Mari's companion: her production engineer and chief technician, Claire Berger. Mari was dressed somewhat ahead of the latest taste, in a bright high-throated peach sateen jacket and subtly clinging fluted anklewrap skirt. Claire Berger wore expedition pants, a cotton trek blouse and hiking boots. It was typical of Mari that she would use this gawky young woman as a foil.

The three of us were soon chastely sipping fruit juice under one of the porch umbrellas and admiring the view. We traded pleasantries while I waited for Mari's obvious aura of trouble to manifest itself.

It emerged that Mari's current companion, a nineteen-year-old model and aspiring actor, had become a source of friction. Also present at the Hillis birthday fete was one of Mari's older flames, the globe-trotting former cosmonaut, Friedrik Solokov. Mari had not expected Fred's appearance, though he had been traveling with Dr. Hillis for some time. Mari's model friend had sensed the rekindled rapport between Mari and Fred Solokov, and he was extravagantly jealous.

"I see," I said. "Well, at some convenient time I can take your young friend aside, for a long talk. He's an actor with ambitions, you say. Our troupe is always looking for new faces."

"My dear Manfred," she sighed, "how well you understand my little problems. You look very dashing today. I admire your ascot. What a charming effect. Did you tie it yourself or have a machine do it?"

"I confess," I said. "This ascot has pre-stressed molecular folds."

"Oh," said Claire Berger distantly. "Really roughing it."

I changed the subject. "How is Leona?"

"Ah. Poor Leona," Mari said. "You know how fond she is of solitude. Well, as the preparations go on, she wanders through these great desolate canyons . . . climbing crags, staring down into the mists of that fierce river . . . Her father is not at all well." She looked at me meaningfully.

"Yes." It was well-known that old Dr. Hillis's eccentricities, even cruelties, had advanced with the years. He never understood the new society his own great work had created. It was one of those ironic strokes you're so fond of, my dear MacLuhan.

However, my Leona had paid for his reactionary stubbornness, so I failed to smile. Poor Leona, the child of the old man's age, had been raised as his industrial princess, expected to master profits and losses and quarterly reports, the blighting discipline of his grisly drudgery. In today's world, the old man might as well have trained her to be a Spanish conquistador. It's a tribute to her spirit that she's done as much for us as she has.

"Someone should be looking after her," Mari said.

"She's wearing her ward," Claire said bluntly. "She'd have to work to get lost."

"Excuse me," I said, rising. "I think it's time I met our host."

I walked into the dome, where the pleasant resinous tang of last night's pine fire still clung to the cold ashes of the hearth. I admired the interior: buffalo hides and vigorous Hopi blankets with the jagged look of old computer graphics. Hexagonal skylights poured light onto a floor of rough, masculine sandstone.

Following the ward's lead, I took my bags to a charming interior room on the second floor, with great braced geodesics of rough cedar, and whitewashed walls, hung with quaint agricultural tools.

In the common room downstairs, the old man had gathered with two of his elderly cronies. I was shocked to see how that famous face had aged: Dr. Hillis had become a cadaverous, cheek-sucking invalid. He sat within his wheelchair, a buffalo robe over his withered legs. His friends still looked strong enough to be dangerous: crocodilian remnants from a lost age of violence and meat. The two of them had also not registered with the house system, but I tactfully ignored this bit of old-fashioned rudeness.

I joined them. "Good afternoon, Dr. Hillis. A pleasure to share this occasion with you. Thank you for having me."

"This is one of my daughter's friends," Hillis croaked. "Manfred de Kooning, of Seattle. He's an ar-tist."

"Aren't they all," said Crocodile #1.

"If that's so," I said, "we owe our happy estate to Dr. Hillis. So it's a double honor to celebrate with him."

Crocodile #2 reached into his old-fashioned business suit and produced, of all things, a cigarette. He lit it and blew a lungful of cancerous reek among us. Despite myself, I had to take half a step back. "I'm sure we'll meet again," I said. "In the meantime I should greet our hostess."

"Leona?" said Dr. Hillis, scowling. "She's not here. She's out on a private walk. With her fiancé."

I felt a sudden icy pang at this. But I could not believe that Leona had deceived me in Seattle; if she'd had a formal liaison, she would have told me. "A sudden proposal?" I hedged. "They were carried away by passion?"

Crocodile #1 smirked sourly and I realized that I'd touched a sore spot. "Damn it," Hillis snapped, "it's not some overblown modern claptrap with ridiculous breast-beating and hair-tearing. Leona's a sensible girl with old-fashioned standards. And Dr. Somps certainly fulfills those in every degree." He glared at me as if daring me to contradict him.

Of course I did no such thing. Dr. Hillis was gravely ill; it would have been cruelty to upset a man with such a leaden look. I murmured a few noncommital pleasantries and excused myself.

Once outside again, I quickly consulted my ward. It gave me the biographical data that Dr. Somps had placed in the house system, for the use of guests.

My rival was a man of impressive accomplishments. He had been a child prodigy possessed of profound mathematical gifts. He was now twenty-nine, two years younger than myself, and a professor of aeronautical engineering at the Tsiolkovsky Institute in Boulder, Colorado. He had spent two years in space, as a guest in the Russian station. He was the author of a textbook on wing kinematics. He was an unsurpassed expert on wind-tunnel computer simulations, as performed by the Hillis Massively Parallel Processor.

You can imagine my profound agitation at learning this, my dear MacLuhan. I imagined Leona leaning her ringleted head on the shoulder of this suave spaceman. For a moment I succumbed to rage.

Then I checked my ward, and realized that the old man had lied. The ward's locator told me that Dr. Somps was on a plateau to the west, and his companion was not Leona but his fellow cosmonaut, Fred Solokov. Leona was alone, exploring an arroyo two miles upstream, to the east!

My heart told me to rush to her side, and as always in such matters, I obeyed it.

It was a bracing hike, skirting declines and rockslides, with the sullen roar of the mighty Colorado to my right. Occasional boatloads of daredevils, paddling with might and main, appeared amidst the river's surges, but the trails were almost deserted.

Leona had climbed a fanglike promontory, overlooking the river. She was hidden from ground level, but my ward helped me find her. Filled with ardor, I ignored the trail and scrambled straight up the slope. At the cost of a few cactus spines, I had the pleasure of appearing suddenly, almost at her side.

I swept my broad-brimmed hat from my head. "My dear Ms. Hillis!"

Leona sat on a paisley groundcloth; she wore a loose bush jacket over a lace blouse, its white intricacy complemented by the simple lines of a calf-length Serengeti skirt. Her blue-green eyes, whose very faint protuberance seems to multiply her other charms, were red-rimmed from weeping. "Manfred!" she said, raising one hand to her lips. "You've found me despite myself."

I was puzzled. "You asked me to come. Did you imagine I'd refuse you anything?"

She smiled briefly at my galanterie, then turned to stare moodily over the savage river. "I meant this to be a simple celebration. Something to get Father out of his black mood. . . . Instead, my troubles have multiplied. Oh, Manfred, if only you knew."

I sat on a corner of the groundcloth and offered her my canteen of Apollinaris water. "You must tell me everything."

"How can I presume on our friendship?" she asked. "A kiss or two stolen backstage, a few kind words—what recompense is that? It would be best if you left me to my fate."

I had to smile at this. The poor girl equated our level of physical intimacy with my sense of obligation; as if mere physical favors could account for my devotion. She was oddly old-fashioned in that sense, with the old industrial mentality of things bought and sold. "Nonsense," I said. "I'm resolved not to leave your side until your mind is eased."

"You know I am affianced?"

"I heard the rumor," I said.

"I hate him," she said, to my vast relief. "I agreed to it in a moment of weakness. My father was so furious, and so set on the idea, that I did it for his sake, to spare him pain. He's very ill, and the chemotherapy has made him worse than ever. He's written a book—full of terrible, hateful things. It's to be released under specific conditions—upon proof of his suicide. He threatens to kill himself, to shame the family publicly."

"How horrible," I said. "And what about the gentleman?"

"Oh, Marvin Somps has been one of Father's protégés for years. Flight simulations were one of the first uses of Artificial Intelligence. It's a field that's dear to Father's heart, and Dr. Somps is brilliant at it."

"I suppose Somps worries about his funding," I said. I was never a devotee of the physical sciences, especially in their current shrunken state, but I could well imagine the agitation of Somps should his ready pool of capital dry up. Except for eccentrics like Hillis, there were few people willing to pay expensive human beings to think about such things.

"Yes, I suppose he worries," she said morosely. "After all, science is his life. He's at the airfield, up on the mesa, now. Testing some wretched machine."

For a moment I felt sorry for Somps, but I thrust the feeling aside. The man was my rival; this was love and war! I checked my ward. "I think a word with Dr. Somps is in order."

"You mustn't! Father will be furious."

I smiled. "I have every respect for your father's genius. But I'm not afraid of him." I donned my hat and smoothed the brim with a quick snap of my hand. "I'll be as polite as I can, but if he needs his eyes opened, then I am the man to do it."

"Don't!" she cried, seizing my hand. "He'll disinherit me."

"What's mere pelf in the modern age?" I demanded. "Fame, glory— the beautiful and the sublime—now those are goals worth striving for!" I took her shoulders in both my hands. "Leona, your father trained you to manage his abstract riches. But you're too soulful, too much a full human being for such a mummified life."

"I like to think so," she said, her upturned eyes full of pain. "But Manfred, I don't have your talent, or the sophistication of your friends. They tolerate me for my wealth. What else do I have to offer? I haven't the taste or grace or wit of a Mari Kuniyoshi."

I felt the open ache of her exposed insecurities. It was perhaps at that moment, my dear MacLuhan, that I truly fell in love. It is easy to admire someone of grace and elegance, to have one's eye caught by the sleek drape of a skirt or by a sidelong glance across the room. In certain circles it is possible to live through an entire affair which is composed of nothing more than brittle witticisms. But the love of the spirit comes when the dark yin of the soul is exposed in the lover's sight; vanities, insecurities, those tender crevices that hold the potential of real pain.

"Nonsense," I said gently. "Even the best art is only a symptom of an inner greatness of soul. The purest art is silent appreciation of beauty. Later, calculation spoils the inner bloom to give an outer mask of sophisticated taste. But I flatter myself that I can see deeper than that."

After this, things progressed rapidly. The physical intimacies which followed were only a corollary of our inner rapport. Removing only selected articles of clothing, we followed the delightful practice of *carezza*, those embraces that enflame the mind and body, but do not spoil things with a full satisfaction.

But there was a specter at our love-feast: Dr. Somps. Leona insisted that our liaison be kept secret; so I tore myself away, before others could track us with their wards and draw unwelcome conclusions.

Having arrived as an admirer, I left as a lover, determined that nothing should spoil Leona's happiness. Once on the trail again, I examined my ward. Dr. Somps was still on the tall mesa, west of the hogan.

I turned my steps in that direction, but before I had gone more than a mile I had a sudden unexpected encounter. From overhead, I heard the loud riffling of fabric wings.

I consulted my ward and looked up. It was Mari Kuniyoshi's current escort, the young model and actor, Percival Darrow. He was riding a hang-glider; the machine soared with cybernetic smoothness across the banded cliff-face. He turned, spilling air, and landed on the trail before me, with an athletic bound. He stood waiting.

By the time I reached him the glider had folded itself, its pre-stressed folds popping and flapping into a neat orange backpack. Darrow leaned against the sun-warmed rock with a teenager's false nonchalance. He wore a sleek cream-colored flyer's jumpsuit, its elastic sleeves pushed up to reveal the brawny arms of a gymnast. His eyes were hidden by rose-colored flyer's goggles.

I was polite. "Good afternoon, Mr. Darrow. Fresh from the airfield?"

"Not that fresh," he said, a sneer wrinkling his too-perfect features. "I was floating over you half an hour ago. The two of you never noticed."

"I see," I said coldly, and walked on. He hurried after me.

"Where do you think you're going?"

"Up to the airfield, if it's any of your business," I said.

"Solokov and Somps are up there." Darrow looked suddenly desperate. "Look, I'm sorry I mentioned seeing you with Ms. Hillis. It was a bad gambit. But we both have rivals, Mr. de Kooning. And they're together. So you and I should also have an understanding. Don't you think so?''

I slowed my pace a bit. My shoes were better than his; Darrow winced as he hopped over rocks in his thin flight slippers. "What exactly do you want from me, Mr. Darrow?''

Darrow said nothing; a slow flush built up under his tanned cheeks. "Nothing from you,'' he said. "Everything from Mari Kuniyoshi.''

I cleared my throat. "Don't say it,'' Darrow said, raising a hand. "I've heard it all; I've been warned away from her a dozen times. You think I'm a fool. Well, perhaps I am. But I went into this with my eyes open. And I'm not a man to stand aside politely while a rival tramples my happiness.''

I knew it was rash to involve myself with Darrow, who lacked discretion. But I admired his spirit. "Percival, you're a man of my own heart,'' I confessed. "I like the boldness of a man who'll face even longer odds than my own.'' I offered my hand.

We shook like comrades. "You'll help me, then?'' he said.

"Together we'll think of something,'' I said. "Truth to tell, I was just going to the airfield to scout out our opposition. They're formidable foes, and an ally's welcome. In the meantime it's best that we not be seen together.''

"All right,'' Darrow said, nodding. "I already have a plan. Shall we meet tonight and discuss it?''

We agreed to meet at eight o'clock at the lodge, to plot confusion to cosmonauts. I continued down the trail, while Darrow climbed an escarpment to find a spot to launch himself.

I stopped at the hogan again to refill my canteen and enjoy a light tea. A cold shower and quick pill relieved the stresses of *carezza*. The excitement, the adventure, was doing me good. The cobwebs of sustained creative effort had been swept from my brain. You may smile, my dear MacLuhan; but I assure you that art is predicated on living, and I was now in the very thick of real life.

I was soon on my way, refreshed and groomed. An afternoon's hike and a long climb brought me to the glider-grounds, an airfield atop a long-drowned mesa now known as the Throne of Adonis. Reborn from the depths of Lake Powell, it was named in consonance with the various Osirises, Vishnus, and Shivas within Grand Canyon Global Park. The hard sandstone caprock had been cleaned of sediment and leveled near one edge, with a tastefully unobtrusive light aircraft hangar, a fiberglass control tower, changing rooms, and a modest teahouse. There were perhaps three dozen flyers there, chatting and renting gliders and powered ultralights. Only two of them, Somps and Solokov, were from our party.

Solokov was his usual urbane, stocky self. He had lost some hair since I'd last seen him. Somps was a surprise. Tall, stooped, gangling, with a bladelike nose, he had coarse windblown hair and long, flopping hands. They both wore flightsuits; Solokov's was of modish brown corduroy, but Somps' was wrinkled day-wear from the Kosmograd space station, a garish orange with grease-stained cuffs and frayed Cyrillic mission patches.

They were muttering together over a small experimental aircraft. I stepped into sight. Solokov recognized me and nodded; Somps checked his ward and smiled briefly and distractedly.

We studied the aircraft together. It was a bizarre advanced ultralight, with four flat, paired wings, like a dragonfly's. The translucent wings were long and thin, made of gleaming lightweight film over netted struts of tough plastic. A cagelike padded rack beneath the wings would cradle the pilot, who would grip a pair of joysticks to control the flight. Beneath the wings, a thick torso and long counterbalancing tail held the craft's engine.

The wings were meant to flap. It was a one-man powered ornithopter. I had never seen its like. Despite myself, I was impressed by the elegance of its design. It needed a paint job, and the wiring had the frazzled look of a prototype, but the basic structure was delightful.

"Where's the pilot?" I said.

Solokov shrugged. "I am he," he said. "My longest flight being twenty seconds."

"Why so brief?" I said, looking around. "I'm sure you'd have no lack of volunteers. I'd like a spin in it myself."

"No avionics," Somps mumbled.

Solokov smiled. "My colleague is saying that the Dragonfly has no computer on board, Mr. de Kooning." He waved one arm at the other ultralights. "These other craft are highly intelligent, which is why anyone can fly them. They are user-friendly, as they used to say. They have sonar, updraft and downdraft detection, aerofoil control, warpage control, and so forth and so forth. They almost fly themselves. The Dragonfly is different. She is seat-of-the-pants."

As you may imagine, my dear MacLuhan, this news amazed and intrigued me. To attempt to fly without a computer! One might as well eat without a plate. It then occurred to me that the effort was surely very hazardous.

"Why?" I said. "What happened to its controls?"

Somps grinned for the first time, exposing long, narrow teeth. "They haven't been invented yet. I mean, there aren't algorithms for its wing kinematics. Four wings flapping—it generates lift through vortex-dominated flow fields. You've seen dragonflies."

"Yes?" I hedged.

Solokov spread his hands. "It is a breakthrough. Machines fly through calculation of simple, fixed wings. A computer can fly any kind of traditional aircraft. But, you see, the mathematics that determine the interactions of the four moving wings—no machine can deal with such. No such programs exist. The machines cannot write them because they do not know the mathematics.'' Solokov tapped his head. "Only Marvin Somps knows them.''

"Dragonflies use perturbations in the flow field,'' Somps said. "Steady-state aerodynamic theory simply can't account for dragonfly lift values. I mean, consider its major flight modes: stationary hovering, slow hovering in any direction, high-speed upward and downward flight, as well as gliding. Classic aerodynamic design can't match that.'' He narrowed his eyes. "The secret is unsteady separated lift flows.''

"Oh,'' I said. I turned to Solokov. "I didn't know you grasped the mathematics, Fred.''

Solokov chuckled. "No. But I took cosmonaut's pilot training, years ago. A few times we flew the primitive craft, without avionics. By feel, like riding the bicycle! The brain does not have to know, to fly. The nervous system, it has a feel. Computers fly by thinking, but they feel nothing!''

I felt a growing sense of excitement. Somps and Solokov were playing from the central truism of the modern age. Feeling; perception, emotion, intuition and taste; these are the indefinable elements that separate humanity from the shallow logic of our modern-day intelligent environment. Intelligence is cheap, but the thrill of innate mastery is precious. Flying the Dragonfly was not a science, but an art!

I turned to Somps. "Have you tried it?''

Somps blinked and resumed his normal hangdog expression. "I don't like heights.''

I made a mental note of this, and smiled. "How can you resist? I was thinking of renting a common glider here, but having seen this contraption, I feel cheated!''

Somps nodded. "My thinking exactly. Moderns . . . they like novelty. Glitter and glamor. It ought to do well if we can get it into production. Commercially, I mean.'' His tone wavered from resignation to defiance. I nodded encouragingly as a number of choice epithets ran through my head: money-grubbing poltroon, miserly vivisectionist, and so forth. . . .

The basic idea seemed sound. Anything with the innate elegance of Somps' aircraft had definite appeal for today's leisure society. However, it would have to be designed and promoted properly, and Somps, who struck me as something of an idiot savant, was certainly not the man for the job. You could tell just from the way he mooned over it that the machine was, in its own odd way, a labor of love. The fresh grease on his cuffs showed that Somps had spent precious hours up on the plateau, fiddling with his knobs and switches, while his bride-to-be despaired.

Such technician's dedication might have passed muster in the days of the steam engine. But in today's more humane age Somps' behavior seemed close to criminal. This head-in-the-clouds deadbeat saw my poor Leona as a convenient way to finance his pointless intellectual curiosity.

My encounter with the two ex-cosmonauts gave me much to ponder. I withdrew with polite compliments and rented one of the local hanggliders. I circled the Throne of Adonis a few times to establish my bona fides, and then flew back to the hogan.

The effect was enchanting. Cradled by the machine's slow and careful swoops and glides, one felt the majesty of an archangel. Yet I found myself wondering what it would be like without the protective shroud of computer piloting. It would be cold sweat and naked risk and a rush of adrenalin, in which the shadowed crevices far beneath one's feet would be, not an awesome panorama, but a sheer drop!

I admit I was glad to send the machine back to the mesa on its own.

Inside the hogan I enjoyed the buffet supper, carefully avoiding the reeking plates of scorched beef served to the elders. ("Barbecue," they called it. I call it murder.) I sat at a long table with Claire Berger, Percival Darrow, and several of Leona's West Coast friends. Mari herself did not make an appearance.

Leona arrived later, when machines had cleared the meal away and the younger guests had gathered round the fire. Leona and I pretended to avoid one another, but traded stolen glances in the firelight. Under the influence of the mellow light and the landscape, the talk drifted to those poles of the modern existence: the beautiful and the sublime. We made lists: the land is beautiful, the sea is sublime; day is beautiful, night is sublime; craft is beautiful, art is sublime, and so forth.

The postulate that the male is beautiful while the female is sublime provoked much heated comment. While the discussion raged, Darrow and I unstrapped our wards and left them in the common room. Anyone checking our location would see our signals there, while we actually conspired among the machines in the kitchen.

Darrow revealed his plan. He meant to accuse Solokov of cowardice, and seize his rival's glory by testing the Dragonfly himself. If necessary, he would steal the machine. Solokov had done nothing more than take a few fluttering efforts around the top of the mesa. Darrow, on the contrary, meant to fling himself into space and break the machine to his will.

"I don't think you realize the danger involved," I said.

"I've been flying since I was a kid," Darrow sneered. "Don't tell me you're spooked too."

"Those were computer-guided," I said. "This is a blind machine. It could kill you."

"Out on Big Sur we used to rig them," Darrow said. "We'd cut out the autopilot on a dare. It's simple if you find the main sensor thingamajig. It's illegal, but I've done it. Anyway, it makes it easy for you, right? If I break my neck, your Somps will look like a criminal, won't he? He'll be discredited.''

"This is outrageous!" I said, but was unable to restrain a smile of admiration. There was a day when my blood ran as hot as Darrow's, and, if I no longer wore my heart on my sleeve, I could still admire the grand gesture.

"I'm going to do it anyway," Darrow insisted. "You needn't worry on my account. You're not my keeper, and it's my decision."

I thought it over. Clearly he could not be argued out of it. I could inform against him, but such a squalid betrayal was completely beneath me. "Very well," I said, clapping him on the shoulder. "How can I help?"

Our plans progressed rapidly. We then returned to the gathering and quietly resumed our wrist-wards and our places near the hearth. To my delight, I found that Leona had left a private note on my ward. We had a midnight assignation.

After the party broke up I waited in my room for her arrival. At last the welcome glow of lamplight came down the corridor. I eased the door open silently.

She wore a long nightgown, which she did not remove, but otherwise we spared ourselves nothing, except for the final sating pleasure. When she left an hour later, with a last tender whisper, my nerves were singing like synthesizers. I forced myself to take two pills and waited for the ache to subside. For hours, unable to sleep, I stared at the geodesic cedar beams of the ceiling, thinking of spending days, weeks, years with this delightful woman.

Darrow and I were up early next morning, our minds grainy and sharp with lack of sleep and a lover's adrenalin. We lurked in ambush for the unwitting Solokov as he returned from his morning jog.

We mousetrapped him badly as he prepared to go in for a much-needed shower. I stopped him, enthusing about my glider-flight. Darrow then joined our conversation "accidentally" and made a number of sharp comments. Solokov was genial and evasive at first, shrugging off Darrow's insinuations. But my loud, innocent questions made things worse for poor Fred. He did his best to explain Somps' cautious testing program for the Dragonfly. But when he was forced to admit that he had only been in the air twenty seconds, the gathering crowd tittered audibly.

Things became hectic with the arrival of Crocodile #1. I had since been informed that this obnoxious old man was Craig Deakin, a medical doctor. He had been treating Dr. Hillis! Small wonder that Leona's father was near death.

Frankly, I've always had a morbid fear of doctors. The last time I was touched by an actual human doctor was when I was a small child, and I can still remember his probing fingers and cold eyes. Imagine it, my dear MacLuhan—putting your health, your very life, into the charge of a fallible human being, who may be drunk, or forgetful, or even corrupt! Thank God that medical expert-systems have made the profession almost obsolete.

Deakin entered the fray with a cutting remark toward Darrow. By now my blood was up, and I lost all patience with this sour old relic. To make things short, we created a scene, and Darrow and I got the best of it. Darrow's fiery rhetoric and my icy sarcasm made an ideal combination, and poor Solokov, gravely puzzled and embarrassed, was unwilling to fight back. As for Dr. Deakin, he simply disgraced himself. It took no skill to show him up for what he was—an arrogant, tasteless old fraud, completely out of touch with the modern world.

Solokov finally fled to the showers, and we carried the day. Deakin, still leaking venom, tottered off shortly thereafter. I smiled at the reaction of our small, eavesdropping audience. They hustled out of Deakin's way as if afraid of his touch. And small wonder! Imagine it, MacLuhan—probing diseased flesh, for money! It gives you a chill.

Flushed with success, we now sought out the unsuspecting Marvin Somps.

To our surprise, our wards located Somps with Mari Kuniyoshi and her ever-present foil, Claire Berger. The three of them were watching the preparations for the evening's festivities: projection screens and an address system were being erected in the rock garden behind the hogan.

I met them first while Darrow hung back in the trees. I greeted Somps with civil indifference, then gently detached Mari from the other two. "Have you seen your Mr. Darrow recently?" I murmured.

"Why, no," she said, and smiled. "Your doing, yes?"

I shrugged modestly. "I trust things have gone well with Fred. What's he doing here, anyway?"

"Oh," she said, "Old Hillis asked him to help Somps. Somps has invented some dangerous machine that no one can control. Except for Fred, of course."

I was skeptical. "Word inside was that the thing has scarcely left the ground. I had no idea Fred was the pilot. Such timidity certainly doesn't seem his style."

"He was a cosmonaut!" Mari said hotly.

"So was *he*," I said, lifting an eyebrow at Somps. In the gentle breeze Somps' lank hair was flying all over his head. He and Claire Berger were in some animated technician's shoptalk about nuts and bolts, and Somps' long hands flopped like a puppet's. In his rumpled, tasteless business suit, Somps looked the very opposite of spacefaring heroism. I smiled reassuringly. "It's not that I doubt Fred's bravery for a moment, of course. He probably distrusts Somps' design."

Mari narrowed her eyes and looked sidelong at Somps. "You think so?"

I shrugged. "They say in camp that flights have only lasted ten seconds. People were laughing about it. But it's all right. I don't think anyone knows it was Fred."

Mari's eyes flashed. She advanced on Somps. I lifted my hat and smoothed my hair, a signal to the lurking Darrow.

Somps was only too happy to discuss his obsession. "Ten seconds? Oh, no, it was twenty. I timed it myself."

Mari laughed scornfully. "Twenty? What's wrong with it?"

"We're in preliminary test mode. These are novel methods of lift production. It's a whole new class of fluid dynamic uses," Somps droned. "The testing's slow, but that's our methodical risk avoidance." He yanked an inkstained composition book from inside his rumpled jacket. "I have some stroke cycle summaries here . . ."

Mari looked stunned. I broke in casually. "I heard that the go-slow approach was your pilot's decision."

"What? Fred? Oh no, he's fine. I mean, he follows orders."

Darrow ambled forward, his hands in his pockets. He was looking at almost everything except the four of us. He was so elaborately casual that I feared Mari would surely catch on. But that remark about public laughter had stung Mari's Japanese soul. "Follows orders?" she told Somps tightly. "People are laughing. You are crushing your test pilot's face."

I took her arm. "For heaven's sake, Mari. This is a commercial development. You can't expect Dr. Somps to put his plane into the hands of a daredevil."

Somps smiled gratefully. Suddenly Claire Berger burst out in his defense. "You need training and discipline for the Dragonfly. You can't just jump in and pop off like bread from a toaster! There are no computers on Marvin's flyer."

I signaled Darrow. He closed in. "Flyer?" he ad-libbed. "You're heading for the airfield, too?"

"We were just discussing Dr. Somps' aircraft," I said artlessly.

"Oh, the Ten-Second Wonder?" Darrow said, grinning. He crossed his muscular arms. "I'd certainly like a shot at that. I hear it has no computer and has to be flown by feel! Quite a challenge, eh?"

I frowned. "Don't be a fool, Percival. It's far too risky for an amateur. Besides, it's Fred Solokov's job."

"It's not his *job*," Somps mumbled. "He's doing a favor."

But Darrow overrode him. "Sounds to me like it's a bit beyond the old man. You need someone with split-second reflexes, Dr. Somps. I've flown by feel before; quite often in fact. If you want someone to take it to the limit, I'm your man."

Somps looked wretched. "You'd crash it. I need a technician, not a daredevil."

"Oh," said Darrow with withering scorn. "A *technician*. Sorry. I had the idea you needed a *flyer*."

"It's expensive," Somps said pitifully. "Dr. Hillis owns it. He financed it."

"I see," Darrow said. "A question of money." He rolled up his sleeves. "Well, if anyone needs me, I'll be on the Throne of Adonis. Or better yet, aloft." He left.

We watched him swagger off. "Perhaps you should give him a shot," I advised Somps. "We've flown together, and he really is quite good."

Somps flushed dully. On some level, I believe he suspected that he had been had. "It's not one of your glamor toys," he mumbled bitterly. "Not yet, anyway. It's my experiment and I'm doing aeronautic science. I'm not an entertainer and I'm not doing sideshow stunts for your benefit, Mr. de Kooning."

I stared at him. "No need to snap," I said cooly. "I sympathize completely. I know things would be different if you were your own man." I touched my hat. "Ladies, good day."

I rejoined Darrow, out of sight, down the trail. "You said you could talk him into it," Darrow said.

I shrugged. "It was worth a try. He was weakening for a moment there. I didn't think he'd be such a stick-in-the-mud."

"Well, now we do things my way," Darrow said. "We have to steal it." He stripped off his ward, set it on top of a handy sandstone ledge, and whacked it with a fist-sized rock. The ward whined and its screen flared into static. "I think my ward broke," Darrow observed. "Take it in for me and plug me out of the house system, won't you? I wouldn't want anyone to try locating me with my broken ward. That would be rude."

"I still advise against stealing it," I said. "We've made both our rivals look like idiots. There's no need for high drama."

"Don't be petty, Manfred," Darrow said. "High drama is the only way to live!"

I ask you, my dear MacLuhan—who could resist a gesture like that?

That afternoon crawled by. As the celebration started in earnest, wine was served. I was nervous, so I had a glass. But after a few sips I regretted it and set it aside. Alcohol is such a sledgehammer drug. And to think that people used to drink it by the barrel and case!

Dusk arrived. There was still no sign of Darrow, though I kept checking the skies. As preparations for the outdoor banquet neared completion, corporate helicopters began arriving, disgorging their cargos of aging bigwigs. This was, after all, a company affair; and whole hordes of retirees and cybernetic pioneers were arriving to pay tribute to Hillis.

Since they lacked the relaxed politesse of us moderns, their idea of a tribute was harried and brief. They would pack down their plates of scorched meat, swill far too much hard liquor, and listen to speeches . . . then they would check their pacemakers and leave.

A ghastly air of stuffiness descended over the hogan and its surroundings. Leona's contingent of beautiful people was soon outnumbered; pressed on all sides, they flocked together like birds surrounded by stegosaurs.

After a brief delay, a retrospective tribute to Dr. Hillis flashed onto the rock-garden's screen. We watched it politely. There were the familiar scenes, part of the folklore of our century. Young Hillis at MIT, poring over the work of Marvin Minsky and the cognitive psychologists. Hillis at Tsukuba Science City, becoming the heart and soul of the Sixth Generation Project. Hillis, the Man with a Mission, incorporating in Singapore and turning silicon to gold with a touch.

And then all that cornucopia of riches that came with making intelligence into a utility. It's so easy to forget, MacLuhan, that there was once a time when the ability to reason was *not* something that comes through wires just like electricity. When "factory" meant a place where the "blue-collar" caste went to work!

Of course Hillis was only one of a mighty host of pioneers. But as the Nobel Prize winner and the author of Structured Intelligent Multiple Processing he has always been a figurehead for the industry. No, more than that; a figurehead for the age itself. There was a time, before he turned his back on the modern world, when people spoke the name Hillis in the same breath with Edison, Watt, and Marconi.

It was not at all a bad film, of its sort. It didn't tell the whole truth, of course; it was conspicuously quiet about Hillis' regrettable involvement in politics during the '40s, the EEC bribery scandal, and that bizarre episode at the Tyuratam Launch Center. But one can read about those things anywhere. Actually, I confess that I felt the loss of those glory days, which we now see, in hindsight, as the last sunset glow of the Western analytic method. Those lost battalions of scientists, technicians, engineers!

Of course, to the modern temperament, this lopsided emphasis on rational thought seems stifling. Admittedly, machine intelligence has its limits; it's not capable of those human bursts of insight that once advanced scientific knowledge by leaps and bounds. The march of science is now the methodical crawling of robots.

But who misses it? We finally have a stable, global society, that accommodates man's higher feelings. A world of plenty, peace, and leisure, where the beautiful and the sublime reign supreme. If the film caused me a qualm, it was a credit to our modern mastery of propaganda and public relations. Soft, intuitive arts, maybe; the dark yin to the bright yang of the scientific method. But powerful arts, and, like it or not, the ones that shape our modern age.

We had advanced from soup to fish when I caught my first glimpse of

Darrow. The Dragonfly emerged from the depths of the canyon in a brief frenzied arc, its four wings thrashing in the twilit air. Strangely, my first impression was not of a struggling pilot but of a poisoned bug. The thing vanished almost at once.

I must have turned pale, for I noticed Mari Kuniyoshi watching me strangely. But I held my peace.

Crocodile #2 took the podium. This gentleman was another artifact of the vanished age. He'd been some kind of military bigwig, a "pentagon chief of staff" I think they called him. Now he was Hillis Industries' "Chief of Security," as if they needed one in this day and age. It was clear that he'd been drinking heavily. He gave a long, lachrymose introduction to Hillis, droning on and on about "air force" this and "space launch" that, and Hillis's contribution to the "defense industry." I noticed then that Fred Solokov, resplendent in tie and tails, began to look noticeably offended. And who could blame him?

Hillis at last took the podium, standing erect with the help of a cane. He was applauded loudly; we were overjoyed to see Crocodile #2 go. It isn't often that you see someone with the bad taste to mention atomic weapons in public. As if sensing the scotched nerves of our Soviet friend, Hillis departed from his prepared speech and began rambling about his "latest project."

Imagine, my dear MacLuhan, the exquisite embarrassment of the moment. For as Hillis spoke, his "latest project" appeared on the fringes of camp. Darrow had mastered the machine, caught an updraft from the depths of the canyon, and was now fluttering slowly around us. Murmurs began spreading among the crowd; people began to point.

Hillis, not a gifted speaker, was painfully slow to catch on. He kept talking about the "heroic pilot" and how his Dragonfly would be airborne "sooner than we knew." The audience thought poor Hillis was making some elaborate joke and they began laughing. Most people thought it was clever publicity. In the meantime, Darrow swooped nearer. Sensing with a model's intuition that he was the cynosure of all eyes, he began stunting.

Still avoiding the crowd, he threw the aircraft into a hover. The wings hummed audibly, their tips flapping in complex loops and circles. Slowly, he began flying backwards, the craft's long tail waggling in barely controlled instability. The crowd was amazed; they cheered aloud. Hillis, frowning, squinted across the table, his drone dying into a mumble. Then he realized the truth and cried out. Crocodile #2 took his arm, and Hillis tottered backward into his nearby chair.

Dr. Somps, his long face livid, scrambled to the podium. He flung out an arm, pointing. "Stop that man!" he screeched. This provoked hysterical laughter, shading close to authentic hysteria when Darrow spun the craft twice tailfirst and caught himself at the last moment, the wings kicking up clouds of dust over the rear of the crowd. Diners, shrieking, leapt from their chairs and fled for cover. Darrow fought for height, throwing full power into the wings and blowing two tables over with a crash and spatter of tureens and cutlery. The Dragonfly shot up like a child's toy rocket.

Darrow regained control almost at once, but it was clear that the sudden lurch upward had strained one of the wings. Three of them beat smoothly at the twilit air but the fourth, the left rear one, was out of sync. Darrow began to fall, sliding out of the sky, listing backward to his left.

He tried to throw more power into the wings again, but we all heard the painful flopping and rasping as the injured wing refused to function. At the end the craft spun about again a few feet from earth, hit a pine at the edge of our rock garden, and crashed.

That effectively ended the festivities. The crowd was horrified. A number of the more active attendees rushed to the crash site while others babbled in shock. Crocodile #2 took the microphone and began yelling for order, but he was of course ignored. Hillis, his face twisted, was hustled inside in his chair.

Darrow was pale and bloodied, still strapped into the bent ribs of the pilot's cage. He had a few scrapes and he had managed to break his ankle. We fished him out. The Dragonfly did not look badly damaged. "The wing gave out," Darrow kept muttering stubbornly. "It was equipment failure. I was doing fine!"

Two husky sorts formed an arm-cradle for Darrow and lugged him back to the hogan. Mari Kuniyoshi hurried after him, her face pale, her hands fluttering in shock. She had a dramatic, paralyzed look.

Lights blazed from the hogan, along with the excited babbling of the crowd. The outside floodlights in the rock garden dimmed suddenly. From the clearings around us, corporate helicopters began to lift, whirring almost silently into the fragrant Arizona night.

The crowd dispersed around the damaged craft. Soon I noticed that there were only three of us left; myself, Dr. Somps, and Claire Berger. Claire shook her head. "God, it's so sad," she said.

"I'm sure he'll recover," I said.

"What, that thief?" she said. "I hope not."

"Oh. Right," I said. I examined the Dragonfly critically. "She's just a little bent, that's all. Nothing broken. She only needs a few biffs with a lug-wrench or what-have-you."

Somps glared at me. "Don't you understand? Dr. Hillis has been humiliated. And my work was the cause of it. I'd be ashamed to speak to him now, much less ask for his support."

"You still have his daughter," Claire Berger said bluntly. We both looked at her in surprise. She looked back boldly, her arms stiff at her sides.

"Right," Somps said at last. "I've been neglecting Leona. And she's so devoted to her father. . . . I think I'd better go to her. Talk to her. Do whatever I can to make this up.''

"Plenty of time for that later, when things calm down," I said. "You can't just leave the Dragonfly here! The morning dew will soak her. And you don't want gawkers out here tonight—poking at her, maybe laughing. Tell you what—I'll help you carry her up to the airfield.''

Somps hesitated. It did not take long, for his devotion to his machine burst all bounds. With her long wings hinged back, the Dragonfly was easy to carry. Somps and I hoisted the heavy torso to our shoulders, and Claire Berger took the tail. All the way to the mesa Somps kept up a steady monologue of self-pity and disaster. Claire did her clumsy best to cheer him up, but the man was crushed. Clearly a lifetime of silent spleen had built up, requiring just such a calamity to uncork it. Even though he sensed that I was a rival and meant him ill, he could not entirely choke back his need for sympathy.

We found some flyers at the base of the Throne of Adonis. They were curious and eager to help, so I returned to camp. Once he had the Dragonfly in her hangar and his tools at hand, I was sure that Somps would be gone for hours.

I found the camp in uproar. With amazing crassness, Crocodile #2, Hillis' security man, wanted to arrest Darrow. A furious argument broke out, for it was brutally unfair to treat Darrow as a common thief when his only crime had been a daring gesture.

To his credit, Darrow rose above this ugly allegation. He rested in a wicker peacock chair, his bandaged ankle propped on a leather hassock and his pale, blond hair swept back from a bruised forehead. The craft was brilliantly designed, he said; it was only the shoddy workmanship of Hillis Industries that had put his life into danger. At various dramatic cruxes, he would lean back with a faint shudder of pain and grasp the adoring hand of Mari Kuniyoshi. No jury in the world would have touched him. All the world loves a lover, MacLuhan.

Old Dr. Hillis had retired to his rooms, shattered by the day's events. Finally, Leona broke in and settled things. She scolded Darrow and threw him out, and Mari Kuniyoshi, swearing not to leave his side, went with him. Most of the modern contingent left as well, partly as a gesture of solidarity with Darrow, partly to escape the source of embarrassment and transmute it, somewhere else, into endlessly entertaining gossip.

Poor Fred Solokov, made into the butt of jokes through absolutely no fault of his own, also stormed off. I was with the small crowd as he threw his bags into a robot chopper at midnight. "They do not treat me like this," he insisted loudly. "Hillis is mad. I thought so ever since Tyuratam. Why people admire such young vandals as Darrow these days I do not know.''

Truly, I felt sorry for him. I went out of my way to shake his hand. "Sorry to see you go, Fred. I'm sure we'll meet again under better circumstances."

"Never trust women," Fred told me darkly. He paused on the running board to belt his trenchcoat, then stepped in and slammed the vacuum-sealed door. Off he went with a whir of wings. A fine man and a pleasure to know, MacLuhan. I shall have to give some thought to making things up to him.

I then hurried back to my room. With so many gone, it would now be easier for Leona and me to carry on our assignation. Unfortunately I had not had time to arrange the final details with her. And I had a lover's anxiety that she might not even arrive. The day had been a trying one, after all, and carezza is not a practice for hurried nerves.

Still, I waited, knowing it would be a lover's crime should she arrive and find me sleeping.

At half past one I was rewarded by a dim flicker of lamplight under the door. But it passed me.

I eased the door open silently. A figure in a white nightgown was creeping barefoot around the dome's circular hall. She was too short and squat for the willowy Leona, and her trailing, loosened hair was not blonde, but an unremarkable brown. It was Claire Berger.

I tied my pajamas and shuffled after her with the stealth of a medieval assassin.

She stopped, and scratched at a door with one coy forefinger. I did not need my ward to tell me this was the room of Dr. Somps. The door opened at once, and I ducked back just in time to avoid Claire's quick glance up and down the hall.

I gave the poor devils fifteen minutes. I retired to my room, wrote a note, and returned to Somps' door. It was locked, of course, but I scratched lightly and slid my note under it.

The door opened after a hurried conclave of whispers. I slipped inside. Claire was glowering, her face flushed. Somps' fists were clenched. "All right," he grated. "You have us. What is it you want?"

"What does any man want?" I said gently. "A little companionship, some open sympathy, the support of a soul mate. I want Leona."

"I thought that was it," Somps said, trembling. "She's been so different since Seattle. She never liked me, but she didn't hate me, before. I knew there was someone after her. Well, I have a surprise for you, Mr. de Kooning. Leona doesn't know this, but I've talked to Hillis and I know. He's almost bankrupt! His firm is riddled with debts!"

"Oh?" I said, interested. "So?"

"He's thrown it all away, trying to bring back the past," Somps said, the words tumbling out of him. "He's paid huge salaries to his old hangers-on and backed a hundred dud ideas. He was depending on my success to restore his fortunes. So without me, without the Dragonfly, his whole empire falls apart!'' He glared at me defiantly.

"Really?'' I said. ''That's terrific! I always said Leona was enslaved by this nonsense. Empire indeed; why the whole thing's a paper tiger. Why, the old fraud!'' I laughed aloud. ''Very well, Marvin. We're going to have it out with him right now!''

"What?'' Somps said, paling.

I gave him a bracing whack on the shoulder. ''Why carry on the pretense? You don't want Leona; I do. So there's a few shreds of money involved. We're talking about love, man! Our very happiness! You want some old fool to come between you and Claire?''

Somps flushed. ''We were only talking.''

"I know Claire better than that,'' I said gallantly. ''She's Mari Kuniyoshi's friend. She wouldn't have stayed here just to trade technical notes.''

Claire looked up, her eyes reddened. ''You think that's funny? Don't ruin it for us. Please,'' she begged. ''Don't ruin Marvin's hopes. We have enough against us as it is.''

I dragged Somps out the door by main force and closed it behind me. He wrenched free and looked ready to hit me. ''Listen,'' I hissed. ''That woman is devoted to you. How dare you trample her finer feelings? Have you no sympathy, no intuition? She puts your plans above her own happiness.''

Somps looked torn. He stared at the door behind him with the look of a man poleaxed by infatuation. ''I never had time for this. I . . . I never knew it could be like this.''

"Damn it, Somps, be a man!'' I said. ''We're having it out with the old dragon right now.''

We hustled downstairs to Hillis' suite. I tried the double doors; they were open.

Groaning came from the bedroom.

My dear MacLuhan. You are my oldest and closest friend. Often we have been one another's confessors. You remember the ancient pact we swore, as mere schoolchildren, never to tell each other's mischiefs, and to hold each other's secrets silent to the grave. The pact has served us well, and many times it has eased us both. In twenty years of friendship we have never given each other cause to doubt. However, we are now adults, men steeped in life and its complications; and I'm afraid that you must bear the silent burden of my larger mischiefs with me.

I know you will not fail me, for the happiness of many people rests on your discretion. But someone must be told.

The bedroom door was locked. Somps, with an engineer's directness, knocked out its hinge pins. We rushed inside.

Dr. Hillis had fallen off the bed. A deadly litter on the bedside table told the awful truth at once. Hillis, who had been treating himself with the aid of the servile human doctor, had access to the dangerous drugs normally safely stored in machines. Using an old hand-powered hypodermic, he had injected himself with a fatally large dose of painkiller.

We tugged his frail body back into the bed. "Let me die," the old man croaked. "Nothing to live for."

"Where's his doctor?" I said.

Somps was sweating freely in his striped cotton pajamas. "I saw him leave earlier. The old man threw him out, I think."

"All bloodsuckers," Hillis said, his eyes glazed. "You can't help me. I saw to that. Let me die, I deserve to."

"We can keep him moving, maybe," Somps said. "I saw it in an old film once." It seemed a good suggestion, with our limited knowledge of medicine.

"Ignorant," Hillis muttered, as the two of us pulled his limp arms over our shoulders. "Slaves to machines! Those wards—handcuffs! I invented all that . . . I killed the scientific tradition." He began weeping freely. "Twenty six hundred years since Socrates and then, me." He glared and his head rolled like a flower on a stalk. "Take your hands off me, you decadent weasels!"

"We're trying to help you, doctor," Somps said, frightened and exasperated.

"Not a cent out of me, Somps," the old man raved weakly. "It's all in the book."

I then remembered what Leona had told me about the old man's book, to be published on his suicide. "Oh, no," I said. "He's going to disgrace us all and disgrace himself."

"Not a penny, Somps. You failed me. You and your stupid toys. Let me go!"

We dropped him back onto the bed. "It's horrible," Somps said, trembling. "We're ruined."

It was typical of Somps that he should think of himself at a moment like that. Anyone of spirit would have considered the greater interests of society. It was unthinkable that this titan of the age should die in such squalid circumstances. It would give no one happiness, and would cause pain and disillusion to uncounted millions.

I pride myself that I rose to the challenge. My brain roared with sudden inspiration. It was the most sublime moment of my life.

Somps and I had a brief, fierce argument. Perhaps logic was not on my side, but I ground him down with the sheer passion of my conviction.

By the time I had returned with our clothes and shoes, Somps had fixed the door and disposed of the evidence of drugs. We dressed with frantic haste.

By now the old man's lips were bluish and his limbs were like wax. We hustled him into his wheelchair, wedging him in with his buffalo robe. I ran ahead, checking that we were not seen, while Somps wheeled the dying man along behind me.

Luckily there was a moon out. It helped us on the trail to the Throne of Adonis. It was a long, exhausting climb, but Somps and I were men possessed.

Roseate summer dawn was touching the horizon by the time we had the Dragonfly ready and the old man strapped in. He was still breathing shallowly, and his eyelids fluttered. We wrapped his gnarled hands around the joysticks.

When the first golden rim of the sunlight touched the horizon, Somps flicked on the engine. I jammed the aircraft's narrow tail beneath my arm, braced like a lance. Then I ran forward and shoved her off into the holy air of dawn!

MacLuhan, I'm almost sure that the rushing chilly air of the descent revived him briefly. As the aircraft fell toward the roiling waters below, she began to pitch and buck like a live thing. I feel in my heart that Hillis, that seminal genius of our age, revived and fought for life in his last instants. I think he went like a hero. Some campers below saw him hit. They, too, swore he was fighting to the last.

The rest you know. They found the wreckage miles downstream, in the Global Park, next day. You may have seen Somps and myself on television. I assure you, my tears were not feigned; they came from the heart.

Our story told it as it should have happened. The insistence of Dr. Hillis that he pilot the craft, that he restore the fair name of his industries. We helped him unwillingly, but we could not refuse the great man's wishes.

I admit the hint of scandal. His grave illness was common knowledge, and the autopsy machines showed the drugs in his body. Luckily, his doctor admitted that Hillis had been using them for months to fight the pain.

I think there is little doubt in most people's minds that he meant to crash. But it is all in the spirit of the age, my dear MacLuhan. People are generous to the sublime gesture. Dr. Hillis went down fighting, struggling with a machine on the cutting edge of science. He went down defending his good name.

As for Somps and myself, the response has been noble. The mailnet has been full of messages. Some condemn me for giving in to the old man. But most thank me for helping to make his last moments beautiful.

I last saw poor Somps as he and Claire Berger were departing for Osaka. I'm afraid he still feels some bitterness. "Maybe it was best," he told me grudgingly as we shook hands. "People keep telling me so. But I'll never forget the horror of those last moments."

"I'm sorry about the aircraft," I said. "When the notoriety wears off I'm sure it will be a great success."

"I'll have to find another backer," he said. "And then put it into production. It won't be easy. Probably take years."

"It's the yin and yang," I told him. "Once poets labored in garrets while engineers had the run of the land. Things change, that's all. If one goes against the grain, one pays the price."

My words, meant to cheer him, seemed to scald him instead. "You're so damned smug," he almost snarled. "Damn it, Claire and I build things, we shape the world, we try for real understanding! We don't just do each other's nails and hold hands in the moonlight!"

He is a stubborn man. Maybe the pendulum will one day swing his way again, if he lives as long as Dr. Hillis did. In the meantime he has a woman to stand by him and assure him that he is persecuted. So maybe he will find, in the good fight, some narrow kind of sublimity.

So, my dear MacLuhan, love has triumphed. Leona and I will shortly return to my beloved Seattle, where she will rent the suite next to my own. I feel that very soon we will take the great step of abandoning *carezza* and confronting true physical satisfaction. If all goes well then, I will propose marriage! And then, perhaps, even children.

In any case, I promise you, you will be the first to know.

Yours as always,

de K.

JACK DANN

Tattoos

One of the most respected writer/editors of his generation, Jack Dann began writing in 1970, and first established his reputation with the critically acclaimed novella "Junction," which was a Nebula finalist in 1973; he has been a Nebula finalist nine more times since then, and twice a finalist for the World Fantasy Award. His short fiction has appeared in *Omni, Orbit, Playboy, Penthouse, New Dimensions, The Magazine of Fantasy and Science Fiction, Shadows, Isaac Asimov's Science Fiction Magazine, The Berkley Showcase,* and elsewhere. His books include the novels *Starhiker* and *Junction,* and *Timetipping,* a collection of his short fiction. As an anthologist, he edited one of the most famous anthologies of the seventies, *Wandering Stars,* a collection of fantasy and SF on Jewish themes; his other anthologies include *More Wandering Stars, Immortal, Faster than Light* (co-edited with George Zebrowski), and several anthologies co-edited with Gardner Dozois: *Future Power, Aliens!, Unicorns!, Magicats!, Bestiary!,* and *Mermaids!.* His most recent books are the critically acclaimed novel *The Man Who Melted;* a major new anthology of Vietnam stories, edited in collaboration with Jeanne Van Buren Dann, called *In the Field of Fire;* and two more anthologies co-edited with Gardner Dozois, *Sorcerers!* and *Demons!* Upcoming is another new novel, *Counting Coup,* and a critical chapbook called *The Work of Jack Dann,* edited by Jeffrey M. Elliot, from Borgo Press. He is currently at work on two new novels, *The Economy of Light* and *DaVinci Rising.* Dann's story "Blind Shemmy" was in our First Annual Collection, and his "Bad Medicine" was in our Second Annual Collection. He lives with his family in Binghamton, New York.

Here he explores a strange subculture and a stranger kind of sacrifice, as well as giving us a scary look at some very sinister tattoos. . . .

TATTOOS

Jack Dann

We are never like the angels till our passion dies.

—Decker

For the past few years we'd been going to a small fair, which wasn't really much more than a road show, in Trout Creek, a small village near Walton in upstate New York. The fair was always held in late September, when the nights were chilly and the leaves had turned red and orange and dandelion yellow.

We were in the foothills of the Catskills. We drove past the Cannonsville Reservoir, which provides drinking water for New York City. My wife Laura remarked that this was as close to dry as she'd ever seen the reservoir; she had grown up in this part of the country and knew it intimately. My son Ben, who is fourteen, didn't seem to notice anything. He was listening to hard rock music through the headphones of his portable radio-cassette player.

Then we were on the fairgrounds, driving through a field of parked cars. Ben had the headphones off and was excited. I felt a surge of freedom and happiness. I wanted to ride the rides and lose myself in the arcades and exhibitions; I wanted crowds and the noise and smells of the midway. I wanted to forget my job and my recent heart attack.

We met Laura's family in the church tent. Then Laura and her mom and sister went to look at saddles, for her sister showed horses, and Dad and Ben and I walked in the other direction.

As we walked past concession stands and through the arcade of shooting galleries, antique wooden horse race games, slots, and topple-the-milk-bottle games, hawkers shouted and gesticulated at us. We waited for Ben to lose his change at the shooting gallery and the loop-toss where all the spindles floated on water; and we went into the funhouse, which was mostly blind alleys and a few tarnished distorting mirrors. Then we walked by the tents of the freak show: the Palace of Wonders with the original Lobster Man,

Velda the Half-Lady, and "The Most Unusual Case in Medical History: Babies Born Chest to Chest."

"Come on," Dad said, "let's go inside and see the freaks."

"Nah," I said. "Places like this depress me. I don't feel right about staring at those people."

"That's how they make their money," Dad said. "Keeps 'em off social services."

I wasn't going to get into *that* with him.

"Well, then Bennie and me'll go in," Dad said. "If that's all right with you."

It wasn't, but I wasn't going to argue, so I reached into my pocket to give Ben some money, but Dad just shook his head and paid the woman sitting in a chair outside the tent. She gave him two tickets. "I'll meet you back here in about ten minutes," I said, glad to get away by myself.

I walked through the crowds, enjoying the rattle and shake of the concessionaires, all trying to grab a buck, the filthy, but brightly painted oil canvas, the sweet smell of cotton candy, the peppery smell of potatoes frying, and the coarse shouting of the kids. I bought some french fries, which were all the more delicious because I wasn't allowed to have them. Two young girls smiled and giggled as they passed me. Goddamn if this wasn't like being sixteen again.

Then something caught my eye.

I saw a group that looked completely out of place. Bikers, punkers, and well-dressed, yuppie-looking types were standing around a tattoo parlor talking. The long-haired bikers flaunted their tattoos by wearing cut-off jean jackets to expose their arms and chests; the women who rode with them had taken off their jackets and had delicate tattoo wristlets and red and orange butterflies and flowers worked into their arms or between their breasts. In contrast, most of the yuppies, whom I assumed to be from the city, wore long-sleeved shirts or tailored jackets, including the women, who looked like they had just walked out of a New England clothes catalogue. There was also a stout woman who looked to be in her seventies. She had gray hair pulled back into a tight bun and she wore a dark pleated dress. I couldn't help but think that she should be home in some Jewish neighborhood in Brooklyn, sitting with friends in front of her apartment building, instead of standing here in the dust before a tattoo parlor.

I was transfixed. What had brought all these people here to the boonies? Who the hell knew, maybe they were all from here. But I couldn't believe that for a minute. And I wondered if they were *all* tattooed.

I walked over to them to hear snatches of conversation and to investigate the tattoo parlor, which wasn't a tent, as were most of the other concessions, but a small modern mobile home with the words TAROT TATTOO STUDIO— ORIGINAL DESIGNS, EXPERT COVER-UPS painted across the side in large letters

with red serifs through the stems. Then the door opened, and a heavy-set
man with a bald head and a full black beard walked out. Everyone, including
the yuppies, were admiring him. His entire head was tattooed in a Japanese
design of a flaming dragon; the dragon's head was high on his forehead, and
a stream of flame reached down to the bridge of his nose. The dragon was
beautifully executed. How the hell could someone disfigure his face like
that? I wondered.

Behind the dragon man was a man of about five feet six wearing a clean,
but bloodied, white T-shirt. He had brown curly hair that was long overdue
to be cut, a rather large nose, and a full mouth. He looked familiar, very
familiar, yet I couldn't place him. This man was emaciated, as if he had
given up nourishment for some cultish religious reason. Even his long, well-
formed hands looked skeletal, the veins standing out like blue tattoos.

Then I remembered. He looked like Nathan Rivlin, an artist I had not
seen in several years. A dear friend I had lost touch with. This man looked
like Nathan, but he looked all wrong. I remembered Nathan as filled out and
full of life, an orthodox Jew who wouldn't answer the phone on Shabbes—
from Friday night until sundown on Saturday, a man who loved to stay up
all night and talk and drink beer and smoke strong cigars. His wife's name
was Ruth, and she was a highly paid medical textbook illustrator. They had
both lived in Israel for some time, and came from Chicago. But the man
standing before me was ethereal-looking, as if he were made out of ectoplasm
instead of flesh and blood. God forbid he should be Nathan Rivlin.

Yet I couldn't keep myself from shouting, "Nate? Nate, is it you?"

He looked around, and when he saw me, a pained grin passed across his
face. I stepped toward him through the crowd. Several other people were
trying to gain Nathan's attention. A woman told me to wait my turn, and a
few nasty stares and comments were directed at me. I ignored them. "What
the hell *is* all this?" I asked Nathan after we embraced.

"What should it be, it's a business," he said." Just then he seemed like
the old Nathan I remembered. He had an impish face, a mobile face capable
of great expression.

"Not what I'd expect, though," I said. I could see that his arms and neck
were scarred; tiny whitish welts crisscrossed his shaved skin. Perhaps he had
some sort of a skin rash, I told myself, but that didn't seem right to me. I
was certain that Nathan had deliberately made those hairline scars. But why
. . . ? "Nate, what the hell happened to you?" I asked. "You just disappeared off the face of the earth. And Ruth too. How is Ruth?"

Nathan looked away from me, as if I had opened a recent wound. The
stout older woman who was standing a few feet away from us tried to get
Nathan's attention. "Excuse me, but could I *please* talk to you?" she asked,
a trace of foreign accent in her voice. "It's very important." She looked
agitated and tired, and I noticed dark shadows under her eyes. But Nathan

didn't seem to hear her. "It's a long story," he said to me, "and I don't think you'd want to hear it." He seemed suddenly cold and distant.

"Of course I would," I insisted.

"Excuse me, please," interrupted the older woman. "I've come a long way to see you," she said to Nathan, "and you've been talking to everyone else but me. And I've been waiting . . ."

Nathan tried to ignore her, but she stepped right up to him and took his arm. He jerked away, as if he'd been shocked. I saw the faded, tattooed numbers just above her wrist. "Please . . ." she asked.

"Are you here for a cover-up?" Nathan asked her, glancing down at her arm.

"No," she said. "It wouldn't do any good."

"You shouldn't be here," Nathan said gently. "You should be home."

"I know you can help me."

Nathan nodded, as if accepting the inevitable. "I'll talk to you for a moment, but that's all," he said to her. "That's all." Then he looked up at me, smiled wanly, and led the woman into his trailer.

You thinkin' about getting a tattoo?" Dad asked, catching me staring at the trailer. Ben was looking around at the punkers, sizing them up. He had persuaded his mother to let him have a "rat-tail" when he went for his last haircut. It was just a small clump of hair that hung down in the back, but it gave him the appearance of rebelliousness; the real thing would be here soon enough. He turned his back to the punkers with their orange hair and long bleach-white rat-tails, probably to exhibit his own.

"Nah, just waiting for you," I said, lying, trying to ignore my feelings of loss and depression. Seeing Nathan had unnerved me. I felt old, as if Nathan's wasting had become my own.

We spent the rest of the day at the fair, had dinner at Mom and Dad's, watched television, and left at about eleven o'clock. We were all exhausted. I hadn't said anything to Laura about seeing Nathan. I knew she would want to see him, and I didn't want her upset, at least that's what I told myself.

Ben fell asleep in the back seat. Laura watched out for deer while I drove, as my night-vision is poor. She should be the one to drive, but it hurts her legs to sit—she has arthritis. Most of the time her legs are stretched out as far as possible in the foot well or she'll prop her feet against the dashboard. I fought the numbing hypnosis of the road. Every mile felt like ten. I kept thinking about Nathan, how he looked, what he had become.

"David, what's the matter?" Laura asked when we were about halfway home. "You're so quiet tonight. Is anything wrong. Did we do anything to upset you?"

"No, I'm just tired," I said, lying. Seeing Nathan had shocked and depressed me. But there was a selfish edge to my feelings. It was as though I had looked in one of the distorting mirrors in the funhouse; I had seen something of myself in Nathan.

Ben yelped, lurching out of a particularly bad nightmare. He leaned forward, hugging the back of the front seat, and asked us if we were home yet.

"We've got a way to go," I said. "Sit back, you'll fall asleep."

"I'm cold back here."

I turned up the heat; the temperature had dropped at least fifteen degrees since the afternoon. "The freak show probably gave you nightmares; it always did me."

"That's not it," Ben insisted.

"I don't know what's wrong with your grandfather," Laura said. "He had no business taking you in there. He should have his head examined."

"I told you," Ben said, "it had nothing to do with that."

"You want to talk about it?" I asked.

"No," Ben said, but he didn't sit back in his seat; he kept his face just behind us.

"You should sit back," Laura said. "If we got into an accident—"

"*Okay*," Ben said. There was silence for a minute, and then he said, "You know who I dreamed about?"

"Who?" I asked.

"Uncle Nathan."

I straightened up, automatically looking into the rearview mirror to see Ben, but it was too dark. I felt a chill and turned up the heat another notch.

"We haven't seen him in about four years," Laura said. "Whatever made you dream about him?"

"I dunno," Ben said. "But I dreamed he was all different colors, all painted, like a monster."

I felt the hairs on the back of my neck prickle.

"You were dreaming about the freak show," Laura told him. "Sometimes old memories of people we know get mixed up with new memories."

"It wasn't just Uncle Nathan looking like that that scared me."

"What was it?" I asked.

He pulled himself toward us again. But he spoke to Laura. "He was doing something to Dad," Ben said, meaning me.

"What was he doing?" Laura asked.

"I dunno," Ben said, "but it was horrible, like he was pulling out Dad's heart or something."

"Jesus Christ," Laura said. "Look, honey, it was only a dream," she said to him. "Forget about it and try to go back to sleep."

I tried to visualize the lines on Nathan's arms and neck and keep the car on the road.

I knew that I had to go back and see him.

*   *   *

Monday morning I finished an overdue fund-raising report for the Binghamton Symphony with the help of my secretary. The three o'clock meeting with the board of directors went well; I was congratulated for a job well done, and my future seemed secure for another six months. I called Laura, told her I had another meeting, and that I would be home later than usual. Laura had a deadline of her own—she was writing an article for a travel magazine—and was happy for the stretch of work-time. She was only going to send out for a pizza anyway.

The drive to the fairgrounds seemed to take longer than usual, but that was probably because I was impatient and tense about seeing Nathan. Ben's crazy dream had spooked me; I also felt guilty about lying to Laura. We had a thing about not lying to each other, although there were some things we didn't talk about, radioactive spots from the past which still burned, but which we pretended were dead.

There weren't as many people on the fairgrounds as last night, but that was to be expected, and I was glad for it.

I parked close to the arcades, walked through the huckster's alley and came to Nathan Rivlin's trailer. It was dusk, and there was a chill in the air—a harbinger of the hard winter that was to come. A few kids wearing army jackets were loitering, looking at the designs of tattoos on paper, called flash, which were displayed under Plexiglas on a table secured to the trailer. The designs were nicely executed, but ordinary stuff to attract the passersby: anchors, hearts, butterflies, stylized women in profile, eagles, dragons, stars, various military insignia, cartoon characters, death-heads, flags, black panthers and lions, snakes, spiders; nothing to indicate the kind of fine work that had been sported by the people hanging around the trailer yesterday.

I knocked on the door. Nathan didn't seem surprised to see me; he welcomed me inside. It was warm inside the trailer, close, and Nathan was wearing a sixties hipple-style white gauze shirt; the sleeves were long and the cuffs buttoned, hiding the scars I had seen on his arms yesterday. Once again I felt a shock at seeing him so gaunt, at seeing the webbed scars on his neck. Was I returning to my friend's out of just a morbid fascination to see what he had become? I felt guilty and ashamed. Why hadn't I sought out Nathan before this? If I had been a better friend, I probably would have.

Walking into his studio was like stepping into his paintings, which covered most of the available wall space. Nathan was known for working on large canvases, and some of his best work was in here—paintings I had seen in process years ago. On the wall opposite the door was a painting of a nude man weaving a cat's cradle. The light was directed from behind, highlighting shoulders and arms and the large peasant hands. The features of the face were blurred, but unmistakably Nathan's. Beside it was a huge painting of three circus people, two jugglers standing beside a woman. Behind them, in large red letters, was the word CIRCUS. The faces were ordinary, and disturbing, perhaps because of that. There was another painting on the wall where Nathan had set up his tattoo studio. A self-portrait. Nathan wearing a blue worker's hat, red shirt, and apron, and standing beside a laboratory skeleton. And there were many paintings I had never seen, a whole series of tattoo paintings, which at first glance looked to be nonrepresentational, until the designs of figures on flesh came into focus. There were several paintings of gypsies. One, in particular, seemed to be staring directly at me over tarot cards, which were laid out on a table strewn with glasses. There was another painting of an old man being carried from his deathbed by a sad-faced demon. Nathan had a luminous technique, an execution like that of the old masters. Between the paintings, and covering every available space, was flash; not the flash that I had seen outside, but detailed colored designs and drawings of men and animals and mythical beasts, as grotesque as anything by Goya. I was staring into my own nightmares.

The bluish light that comes just before dark suffused the trailer, and the shadows seemed to become more concrete than the walls or paintings.

The older woman I had seen on Sunday was back. She was sitting in Nathan's studio, in what looked like a variation of a dentist chair. Beside the chair was a cabinet and a sink with a high, elongated faucet, the kind usually seen in examination rooms. Pigments, dyes, paper towels, napkins, bandages, charcoal for stencils, needle tubes and bottles of soap and alcohol were neatly displayed beside an autoclave. I was surprised to see this woman in the chair, even though I knew she had been desperate to see Nathan. But she just didn't seem the sort to be getting a tattoo, although that probably didn't mean a thing: anyone could have hidden tattoos: old ladies, senators, presidents. Didn't Barry Goldwater brag that he had two dots tattooed on his hand to represent the bite of a snake? Who the hell knew why.

"I'll be done in a few minutes," Nathan said to me. "Sit down. Would you like a drink? I've got some beer, I think. If you're hungry, I've got soup on the stove." Nathan was a vegetarian; he always used to make the same miso soup, which he'd start when he got up in the morning, every morning.

"If you don't mind, I'll just sit," I said, and I sat down on an old green Art Deco couch. The living room was made up of the couch, two slat-back chairs, and a television set on a battered oak desk. The kitchenette behind Nathan's work area had a stove, a small refrigerator, and a table attached to the wall. And, indeed, I could smell the familiar aroma of Nathan's soup.

"Steve, this is Mrs. Stramm," Nathan said, and he seemed to be drawn toward me, away from Mrs. Stramm, who looked nervous. I wanted to talk with him . . . connect with him . . . find the man I used to know.

"Mister Tarot," the woman said, "I'm ready now, you can go ahead."

Nathan sat down in the chair beside her and switched on a gooseneck adjustable lamp, which produced a strong, intense white light. The flash and paintings in the room lost their fire and brilliance, as the darkness in the trailer seemed to gain substance.

"Do you think you can help me?" she asked. "Do you think it will work?"

"If you wish to believe in it," Nathan said. He picked up his electrical tattoo machine, examined it, and then examined her wrist, where the concentration camp tattoo had faded into seven smudgy blue marks.

"You know, when I got these numbers at the camp, it was a doctor who put them on. He was a prisoner, like I was. He didn't have a machine like yours. He worked for Dr. Mengele." She looked away from Nathan while she spoke, just as many people look away from a nurse about to stick a needle in their vein. But she seemed to have a need to talk. Perhaps it was just nerves.

Nathan turned on his instrument, which made a staticky, electric noise, and began tattooing her wrist. I watched him work; he didn't seem to have heard a word she said. He looked tense and bit his lip, as if it was his own wrist that was being tattooed. "I knew Mengele," the woman continued. "Do you know who he was?" she asked Nathan. Nathan didn't answer. "Of course you do," she said. "He was such a nice-looking man. Kept his hair very neat, clipped his mustache, and he had blue eyes. Like the sky. Everything else in the camp was gray, and the sky would get black from the furnaces, like the world was turned upside down." She continued to talk while Nathan worked. She grimaced from the pain of the tattoo needle.

I tried to imagine what she might have looked like when she was young, when she was in the camp. It would have been Auschwitz, I surmised, if Mengele was there.

But why was a Jew getting a tattoo?

Perhaps she wasn't Jewish.

And then I noticed that Nathan's wrist was bleeding. Tiny beads of blood soaked through his shirt, which was like a blotter.

"Nathan—" I said, as I reflexively stood up.

But Nathan looked at me sharply and shook his head, indicating that I should stay where I was. "It's all right, David. We'll talk about it later."

I sat back down and watched them, mesmerized.

Mrs. Stramm stopped talking; she seemed calmer now. There was only the sound of the machine, and the background noise of the fair. The air seemed heavier in the darkness, almost smothering. "Yesterday you told me that you came here to see me to find out about your husband," Nathan said to her. "You lied to me, didn't you."

"I had to know if he was alive," she said. "He was a strong man, he could have survived. I left messages through the agencies for him when I was in Italy. I couldn't stand to go back to Germany. I thought to go to South America, I had friends in São Paulo."

"You came to America to cut yourself off from the past," Nathan said in a low voice. "You knew your husband had died. I can feel that you buried him . . . in your heart. But you couldn't bury everything. The tattoo is changing. Do you want me to stop? I have covered the numbers."

I couldn't see what design he had made. Her wrist was bleeding, though . . . as was his.

Then she began to cry, and suddenly seemed angry. But she was directing her pain and anger at herself. Nathan stopped working, but made no move to comfort her. When Mrs. Stramm's crying subsided and she regained control of her breathing, she said, "I murdered my infant. I had help from another, who thought she was saving my life." She seemed surprised at her own words.

"Do you want me to stop," Nathan asked again, but his voice was gentle.

"You do what you think, you're the tattooist."

Nathan began again. The noise of his machine was teeth-jarring. Mrs. Stramm continued talking to him, even though she still looked away from the machine. But she talked in a low voice now. I had to lean forward and strain to hear her. My eyes were fixed on Nathan's wrist; the dots of blood had connected into a large bright stain on his shirt cuff.

"I was only seventeen," Mrs. Stramm continued. "Just married and pregnant. I had my baby in the camp and Dr. Mengele delivered it himself. It wasn't so bad in the hospital. I was taken care of as if I were in a hospital in Berlin. Everything was nice, clean. I even pretended that what was going on outside the hospital in the camp, in the ovens, wasn't true. When I had the baby—his name was Stefan—everything was perfect. Dr. Mengele was very careful when he cut the cord; and another doctor assisted him, a Jewish doctor from the camp. Ach!" she said, flinching; she looked down at her wrist, where Nathan was working, but she didn't say a word about the blood soaking through his shirtsleeve. She seemed to accept it as part of the process. Nathan must have told her what to expect. He stopped, and refilled his instrument with another ink pigment.

"But then I was sent to a barracks, which was filthy, but not terribly crowded," she continued. "There were other children in there, mutilated. One set of twins had been sewn together, back to back, arm to arm, and they smelled terrible. They were an experiment, of course. I knew that my baby and I were going to be an experiment. There was a woman in the barracks looking after us. She couldn't do much but watch the children die. She felt sorry for me. She told me that nothing could be done for my baby. And after they had finished their experiment and killed my son, then I would be killed also; it was the way it was done. Dr. Mengele killed all surviving parents and healthy siblings for comparison. My only hope, she said, was to kill my baby myself. If my baby died 'naturally' before Mengele began his experiment, then he might let me live. I remember thinking to myself that it was the only way I could save my baby the agony of a terrible death at the hands of Mengele.

"So I suffocated my baby. I pinched his nose and held his mouth shut while my friend held us both and cried for us. I remember that very well. Dr. Mengele learned of my baby's death and came to the barracks himself. He said he was very sorry, and, you know, I believed him. I took comfort from the man who had made me kill my child. I should have begged him to kill *me*. But I said nothing."

"What could you have done?" Nathan asked, as he was working. "Your child would have died no matter what. You saved yourself, that's all you could do under the circumstances."

"Is that how *you* would have felt, if you were me?"

"No," Nathan said, and a sad smile appeared for an instant, an inappropriate response, yet somehow telling.

Mrs. Stramm stopped talking and had closed her eyes. It was as if she and Nathan were praying together. I could feel that, and I sensed that something else was happening between them. Something seemed to be passing out of her, a dark, palpable spirit. I could feel its presence in the room. And Nathan looked somehow different, more defined. It was the light from the lamp, no doubt, but some kind of exchange seemed to be taking place. Stolid, solid Mrs. Stramm looked softer, as if lighter, while Nathan looked as ravaged as an internee. It was as if he were becoming defined by this woman's past.

When Nathan was finished, he put his instrument down on the cabinet, and taped some gauze over his own bleeding wrist. Then he just stared at his work on Mrs. Stramm. I couldn't see the tattoo from where I was sitting, so I stood up and walked over. "Is it all right if I take a look?" I asked, but neither one answered me . . . neither one seemed to notice me.

The tattoo was beautiful, lifelike in a way I had not thought possible for a marking on the flesh. It was the cherubic face of an angel with thin, curly hair. One of the numbers had now become the shading for the angel's fine, straight nose. Surrounding the face were dark feathered wings that crossed each other; an impossible figure, but a hauntingly sad and beautiful one. The eyes seemed to be looking upward and out, as if contemplating a high station of paradise. The numbers were lost in the blue-blackness of lifting wings. This figure looked familiar, which was not surprising, as Nathan had studied the work of the masters. I remembered a Madonna, which was attributed to the Renaissance artist Lorenzo di Credi, that had two angels with wings such as those on the tattoo. But the tattooed wings were so dark they reminded me of death; and they were bleeding, an incongruous testament to life.

I thought about Nathan's bleeding wrist, and wondered. . . .

"It's beautiful," Mrs. Stramm said, staring at her tattoo. "It's the right face, it's the way his face would have looked . . . had he lived." Then she stood up abruptly. Nathan sat where he was; he looked exhausted, which was how I suddenly felt.

"I must put a gauze wrap over it," Nathan said.

"No, I wish to look at him."

"Can you see the old numbers?" Nathan asked.

"No," she said at first, then, "Yes, I can see them."

"Good," Nathan said.

She stood before Nathan, and I could now see that she had once been beautiful: big-boned, proud, full-bodied, with a strong chin and regal face. Her fine gray hair had probably been blond, as her eyebrows were light. And she looked relieved, released. I couldn't help but think that she seemed now like a woman who had just given birth. The strain was gone. She no longer seemed gravid with the burden of sorrow. But the heaviness had not disappeared from the room, for I could feel the psychic closeness of grief like stale, humid air. Nathan looked wasted in the sharp, cleansing, focused light.

"Would you mind if I looked at *your* tattoo?" Mrs. Stramm asked.

"I'm sorry," Nathan said.

Mrs. Stramm nodded, then picked up her handbag and took out her checkbook. She moved toward the light and began to scribble out a check. "Will you accept three hundred dollars?"

"No, I cannot. Consider it paid."

She started to argue, but Nathan turned away from her. "Thank you," she said, and walked to the door.

Nathan didn't answer.

Nathan turned on the overhead light; the sudden change from darkness to light unnerved me.

"Tell me what the hell's going on," I said. "Why did your wrist start bleeding when you were tattooing that woman?"

"It's part of the process," Nathan said vaguely. "Do you want coffee?" he asked, changing the subject—Nathan had a way of talking around any subject, peeling away layers as if conversation were an onion; he eschewed directness. Perhaps it was his rabbinical heritage. At any rate, he wasn't going to tell me anything until he was ready. I nodded, and he took a bag of ground coffee out of his freezer, and dripped a pot in the Melitta. Someone knocked at the door and demanded a tattoo, and Nathan told him that he would have to wait until tomorrow.

We sat at the table and sipped coffee. I felt an overwhelming lassitude come over me. My shoulder began to ache . . . to throb. I worried that this might be the onset of another heart attack (I try not to pay attention to my hypochondria, but those thoughts still flash through my mind, no matter how rational I try to be). Surely it was muscular, I told myself: I had been wrestling with my son last night. I needed to start swimming again at the "Y". I was out of shape, and right now I felt more like sixty-two than forty-two. After a while, the coffee cleared my head a bit—it was a very, very strong blend, Pico, I think—but the atmosphere inside the trailer was still oppressive, even with the overhead light turned on. It was as if I could *feel* the shadows.

"I saw Mrs. Stramm here yesterday afternoon," I said, trying to lead Nathan. "She seems Jewish; strange that she should be getting a tattoo. Although maybe not so strange, since she came to a Jewish tattooist." I forced a laugh and tried not to stare at the thin webbing of scars on his neck.

"She's not Jewish," Nathan said. "Catholic. She was interred in the camp for political reasons. Her family was caught hiding Jews."

"It seems odd that she'd come to you for a tattoo to cover up her numbers," I said. "She could have had surgery. You would hardly be able to tell they'd ever been there."

"That's not why she came."

"Nathan. . . ."

"Most of the people just want tattoos," Nathan said. He seemed slightly defensive, and then he sighed and said, "But sometimes I get people like Mrs. Stramm. Word gets around, word-of-mouth. Sometimes I can sense things, see things about people when I'm tattooing. It's something like automatic writing, maybe. Then the tattoo takes on a life of its own, and sometimes it changes the person I tattoo."

"This whole thing . . . it seems completely crazy," I said, remembering his paintings, the large canvases of circus people, carny people. He had made his reputation with those melancholy, poignant oil paintings. He had traveled, followed the carnies. Ruth didn't seem to mind. She was independent, and used to travel quite a bit by herself also; she was fond of taking grueling, long day-trips. Like Nathan, she was full of energy. I remember that Nathan had been drawn to tattooing through circus people. He visited tattoo studios, and used them for his settings. The paintings he produced then were haunted, and he became interested in the idea of living art, the relationship of art to society, the numinal, symbolic quality of primitive art. It was only natural that he'd want to try tattooing, which he did. He had even tattooed himself: a tiny raven that seemed to be forever nestled in his palm. But that had been a phase, and once he had had his big New York show, he went on to paint ordinary people in parks and shopping malls and in movie houses, and his paintings were selling at over five thousand dollars a piece. I remembered ribbing him for tattooing himself. I had told him he couldn't be buried in a Jewish cemetery. He had said that he had already bought his plot. Money talks.

"How's Ruth?" I asked, afraid of what he would tell me. He would never be here, he would never look like this, if everything was all right between them.

"She's dead," he whispered, and he took a sip of his coffee.

"What?" I asked, shocked. "How?"

"Cancer, as she was always afraid of."

The pain in my shoulder became worse, and I started to sweat. It seemed to be getting warmer; he must have turned the heat up.

"How could all this happen without Laura or me knowing about it?" I asked. "I just can't believe it."

"Ruth went back to Connecticut to stay with her parents."

"Why?"

"David," Nathan said, "I knew she had cancer, even when she went in for tests and they all turned out negative. I kept dreaming about it, and I could *see* it burning inside her. I thought I was going crazy . . . I probably was. I couldn't stand it. I couldn't be near her. I couldn't help her. I couldn't do anything. So I started traveling, got back into the tattoo culture. The paintings were selling, especially the tattoo stuff—I did a lot of close-up work, you wouldn't even know it was tattoos I was painting, I got into some beautiful Oriental stuff—so I stayed away."

"And she died without you?" I asked, incredulous.

"In Stamford. The dreams got worse. It got so I couldn't even talk to her over the phone. I could see what was happening inside her and I was helpless. And I was a coward. I'm paying for it now."

"What do you mean?" I asked. Goddammit, it was hot.

He didn't answer.

"Tell me about the scars on your neck and your arms."

"And my chest, everywhere," Nathan confessed. "They're tattoos. It started when I ran away, when I left Ruth, I started tattooing myself. I used the tattoo gun, but no ink."

"Why?" I asked.

"At first, I guess I did it as practice, but then it became a sort of punishment. It was painful. I was painting without pigments. I was inflicting my own punishment. Sometimes I can see the tattoos, as if they were paintings. I'm a map of what I've done to my wife, to my family; and then around that time I discovered I could see into other people, and sort of draw their lives differently. Most people I'd just give a tattoo, good work, sometimes even great work, maybe, but every once in a while I'd see something when I was working. I could see if someone was sick, I could see what was wrong with him. I was going the carny route, and living with some gypsy people. A woman, a friend of mine, saw my 'talent' "—he laughed when he said that—"and helped me develop it. That's when I started bleeding when I worked. As my friend used to tell me, 'Everything has a price.' "

I looked at Nathan. His life was draining away. He was turning into a ghost, or a shadow. Not even his tattoos had color.

My whole arm was aching. I couldn't ignore it any longer. And it was so close in the trailer that I couldn't *breathe*. "I've got to get some air," I said as I forced myself to get up. I felt as if I hadn't slept in days. Then I felt a burning in my neck and a stabbing pain in my chest. I tried to shout to Nathan, who was standing up, who looked shocked, who was coming toward me.

But I couldn't move; I was as leaden as a statue.

I could only see Nathan, and it was as if he were lit by a tensor lamp. The pigments of living tattoos glowed under his shirt, and resolved themselves like paintings under a stage scrim. He was a living, radiant landscape of scenes and figures, terrestrial and heavenly and demonic. I could see a grotesque caricature of Mrs. Stramm's tattoo on Nathan's wrist. It was a howling, tortured, winged child. Most of the other tattoos expressed the ugly, minor sins of people Nathan had tattooed, but there were also figures of Nathan and Ruth. All of Ruth's faces were Madonna-like, but Nathan was rendered perfectly, and terribly; he was a monster portrayed in entirely human terms, a visage of greed and cowardice and hardness. But there was a central tattoo on Nathan's chest that looked like a Dürer engraving—such was the sureness and delicacy of the work. Ruth lay upon the ground, amid grasses and plants and flowers, which seemed surreal in their juxtaposition. She had opened her arms, as if begging for Nathan, who was depicted also, to return. Her chest and stomach and neck were bleeding, and one could look into the cavities of the open wounds. And marching away, descending under the nipple of Nathan's chest, was the figure of Nathan. He was followed by cherubs riding fabulous beasts, some of which were the skeletons of horses and dogs and goats with feathery wings . . . wings such as Nathan had tattooed on Mrs. Stramm. But the figure of Nathan was running away. His face, which had always seemed askew—a large nose, deep-set, engaging eyes, tousled hair, the combination of features that made him look like a seedy Puck, the very embodiment of generous friendliness—was rendered formally. His nose was straight and long, rather than crooked, as it was in real life, and his eyes were narrow and tilted, rather than wide and roundish; and his mouth, which in real life, even now, was full, was drawn as a mere line. In his hands, Nathan was carrying Ruth's heart and other organs, while a child riding a skeleton Pegasus was waving a thighbone.

The colors were like an explosion, and the tattoos filled my entire field of vision; and then the pain took me, wrapped like a snake around my chest. My heart was pounding. It seemed to be echoing in a huge hall. It was all I could hear. The burning in my chest increased and I felt myself screaming, even if it might be soundless. I felt my entire being straining in fright, and then the colors dimmed. Fainting, falling, I caught one last glimpse of the walls and ceiling, all pulsing, glowing, all coalescing into one grand tattoo, which was all around me, and I followed those inky pigment paths into grayness and then darkness. I thought of Laura and Ben, and I felt an overwhelming sense of sorrow for Nathan.

For once, I didn't seem to matter, and my sense of rushing sadness became a universe in which I was suspended.

I thought I was dying, but it seemed that it would take an eternity, an eternity to think, to worry back over my life, to relive it once more, but from a higher perspective, from an aerial view. But then I felt a pressure, as if I were under water and a faraway explosion had fomented a strong current. I was being pulled away, jostled, and I felt the tearing of pain and saw bright light and heard an electrical sparking, a sawing. And I saw Nathan's face, as large as a continent gazing down upon me.

I woke up on his couch. My head was pounding, but I was breathing naturally, evenly. My arm and shoulder and chest no longer ached, although I felt a needlelike burning over my heart. Reflexively, I touched the spot where I had felt the tearing pain, and found it had been bandaged. "What the hell's this?" I asked Nathan, who was sitting beside me. Although I could make out the scars on his neck, I could no longer find the outlines of the tattoos I had seen, nor could I make out the brilliant pigments that I had imagined or hallucinated. "Why do I have a bandage on?" I felt panic.

"Do you remember what happened?" he asked. Nathan looked ill. Even more wasted. His face was shiny with sweat. But it wasn't warm in here now; it was comfortable. Yet when Mrs. Stramm was sitting for her tattoo, it was stifling. I had felt the closeness of dead air like claustrophobia.

"Christ, I thought I was having a heart attack. I blacked out. I fell."

"I caught you. You did have a heart attack."

"Then why the hell am I here instead of in a hospital?" I asked, remembering how it felt to be completely helpless in the emergency room, machines whirring and making ticking and just audible beeping noises as they monitored vital signs.

"It could have been very bad," Nathan said, ignoring my question.

"Then what am I doing here?" I asked again. I sat up. This was all wrong. Goddammit, it was wrong. I felt a rush in my head, and the headache became sharp and then withdrew back into dull pain.

"I took care of it," he said.

"How?"

"How do you feel?"

"I have a headache, that's all," I said, "and I want to know what you did on my chest."

"Don't worry, I didn't use pigment. They'll let you into a Jewish cemetery." Nathan smiled.

"I want to know what you did." I started to pull off the gauze, but he stopped me.

"Let it heal for a few days. Change the bandage. That's all."

"And what the hell am I supposed to tell Laura?" I asked.

"That you're alive."

I felt weak, yet it was as if I had sloughed something off, something heavy and deadening.

And I just walked out the door.

After I was outside, shivering, for the weather had turned unseasonably cold, I realized that I had not said good-bye. I had left as if in a daze. Yet I could not turn around and go back. This whole night was crazy, I told myself. I'd come back tomorrow and apologize . . . and try to find out what had really happened.

I drove home, and it began to snow, a freakish, wet, heavy snow that turned everything bluish-white, luminescent.

My chest began to itch under the bandage.

I didn't get home until after twelve. Understandably, Laura was worried and anxious. We both sat down to talk in the upholstered chairs in front of the fireplace in the living room, facing each other; that was where we always sat when we were arguing or working out problems. Normally, we'd sit on the sofa and chat and watch the fire. Laura had a fire crackling in the fireplace; and, as there were only a few small lamps on downstairs, the ruddy light from the fire flickered in our large white carpeted living room. Laura wore a robe with large cuffs on the sleeves and her thick black hair was long and shiny, still damp from a shower. Her small face was tight, as she was upset, and she wore her glasses, another giveaway that she was going to get to the bottom of this. She almost never wore her glasses, and the lenses were scratched from being tossed here and there and being banged about in various drawers; she only used them when she had to "focus her thoughts."

I looked a sight: my once starched white shirt was wrinkled and grimy, and I smelled rancid, the particular odor of nervous sweat. My trousers were dirty, especially at the knees, where I had fallen to the floor, and I had somehow torn out the hem of my right pantleg.

I told Laura the whole story, what had happened from the time I had seen Nathan Sunday until tonight. At first she seemed relieved that I had been with Nathan—she had never been entirely sure of me, and I'm certain she thought I'd had a rendezvous with some twenty-two-year-old receptionist or perhaps the woman who played the French horn in the orchestra—I had once made a remark about her to Laura. But she was more upset than I had expected when I told her that Ruth had died. We were friends, certainly, although I was much closer to Nathan than she was to Ruth.

We moved over to the couch and I held her until she stopped crying. I got up, fixed us both a drink, and finished the story.

"How could you let him tattoo your skin?" Laura asked; and then, exposing what she was really thinking about, she said in a whisper, "I can't believe Ruth's gone. We were good friends, you didn't know that, did you?"

"I guess I didn't." After a pause, I said, "I didn't *let* Nathan tattoo me. I told you, I was unconscious. I'd had an attack or something." I don't know if Laura really believed that. She had been a nurse for fifteen years.

"Well, let me take a look at what's under the gauze."

I let her unbutton my shirt; with one quick motion, she tore the gauze away. Looking down, I just saw the crisscrossings and curlicues and random lines that were thin raised welts over my heart.

"What the hell did he *do* to you? This whole area could get infected. Who knows if his needle was even clean. You could get hepatitis, or AIDS, considering the kinds of people who go in for tattoos."

"No, he kept everything clean," I said.

"Did he have an autoclave?" she asked.

"Yes, I think he did."

Laura went to the downstairs bathroom and came back with Betadine and a clean bandage. Her fuzzy blue bathrobe was slightly open, and I felt myself becoming excited. She was a tiny woman, small boned and delicate-featured, yet big-busted, which I liked. When we first lived together, before we married, she was extremely shy in bed, even though she'd already been married before; yet she soon became aggressive, open, and frank, and to my astonishment I found that *I* had grown more conservative.

I touched her breasts as she cleaned the tattoo, or more precisely, the welts, for he used no pigment. The Betadine and the touch of her hands felt cool on my chest.

"Can you make anything out of this?" she asked, meaning the marks Nathan had made.

I looked down, but couldn't make anything more out of them than she could. I wanted to look at the marks closely in the mirror, but Laura had become excited, as I was, and we started making love on the couch. She was on top of me, we still had our clothes on, and we were kissing each other so hard that we ground our teeth. I pressed myself inside her. Our lovemaking was urgent and cleansing. It was as if we had recovered something, and I felt my heart beating, clear and strong. After we came and lay locked together, still intimate, she whispered, "Poor Nathan."

I dreamed about him that night. I dreamed of the tattoo I had seen on his chest, the parade of demons and fabulous creatures. I was inside his tattoo, watching him walking off with Ruth's heart. I could hear the demon angels shouting and snarling and waving pieces of bone as they rode atop unicorns and skeleton dragons flapping canvas-skinned pterodactyl wings. Then Nathan saw me, and he stopped. He looked as skeletal as the creatures around him, as if his life and musculature and fat had been worn away, leaving nothing but bones to be buried.

He smiled at me and gave me Ruth's heart.

It was warm and still beating. I could feel the blood clotting in my hand.

I woke up with a jolt. I was shaking and sweating. Although I had turned up the thermostat before going to bed, it was cold in the bedroom. Laura was turned away from me, moving restlessly, her legs raised toward her chest in a semi-fetal position. All the lights were off, and as it was a moonlit night, the snow reflected a wan light; everything in the room looked shadowy blue. And I felt my heart pumping fast.

I got up and went into the bathroom. Two large dormer windows over the tub to my left let in the dim light of a streetlamp near the southern corner of the house. I looked in the mirror at my chest and could see my tattoo. The lines were etched in blue, as if my body were snow reflecting moonlight. I could see a heart; it was luminescent. I saw an angel wrapped in deathly wings, an angel such as the one Nathan had put on Mrs. Stramm's wrist to heal her; but this angel, who seemed to have some of Nathan's features— his crooked nose and full mouth, had spread his wings, and his perfect infant hands held out Ruth's heart to me.

Staring, I leaned on the white porcelain sink. I felt a surging of life, as if I were being given a gift, and then the living image of the tattoo died. I shivered naked in the cold bathroom. I could feel the chill passing through the ill-fitting storms of the dormer windows. It was as if the chill were passing right through me, as if I had been opened up wide.

And I knew that Nathan was in trouble. The thought came to me like a shock of cold water. But I could *feel* Nathan's presence, and I suddenly felt pain shoot through my chest, concentrated in the tattoo, and then I felt a great sadness, an oceanic grief.

I dressed quickly and drove back to Trout Creek. The fairgrounds were well-lit, but deserted. It had stopped snowing. The lights were on in Nathan's trailer. I knocked on the door, but there was no answer. The door was unlocked, as I had left it, and I walked in.

Nathan was dead on the floor. His shirt was open and his chest was bleeding—he had the same tattoo I did. But his face was calm, his demons finally exorcised. I picked him up, carried him to the couch, and kissed him good-bye.

As I left, I could feel his strength and sadness and love pumping inside me. The wind blew against my face, drying my tears . . . it was the cold fluttering of angel's wings.

TIM POWERS

Night Moves

Here's a rare short work—full of wonders and dark magic—from Tim Powers, who has made his considerable reputation almost entirely as a novelist. His brilliant and brilliantly eclectic novels include *Dinner at Deviant's Palace* and *The Anubis Gates,* both winners of the Philip K. Dick Award; and *The Drawing of the Dark.* Upcoming is another novel, *On Stranger Tides,* from Ace. He is currently at work on a new novel, tentatively entitled *The Stress of Her Regard.*

Born in Buffalo, New York, Powers now makes his home in Santa Ana, California, with his wife, Serena.

NIGHT MOVES

Tim Powers

When a warm midnight wind sails in over the mountains from the desert and puffs window shades inward, and then hesitates for a second so that the shades flap back and knock against the window frames, southern Californians wake up and know that the Santa Ana wind has come, and that tomorrow their potted plants will be strewn up and down the alleys and sidewalks; but it promises blue skies and clean air, and they prop themselves up in bed for a few moments and listen to the palm fronds rattling and creaking out in the darkness.

Litter flies west, papers and leaves and long veils of dust from lots where the tractors wait for morning, and tonight a dry scrap cartwheeled and skated through Santa Margarita's nighttime streets; it clung briefly to high branches, skipped over the roofs of parked cars, and at one point did a slow jiggle-dance down the whole length of the north window sill at Guillermo's Todo Noche Cantina. The only person who noticed it was the old man everybody called Cyclops, who had been drinking coffee at the counter for hours in exchange for a warm, lighted place to pass the night, and until the thing tumbled away at the west end of the window sill he stared at it, turning his head to give his good eye a clear look at it.

It looked, he thought, like one of those little desiccated devilfish they sell at swap-meets; they cut three slits in the fish's body before they dry it, so after it dries it looks as if it has a primate body and stunted limbs and a disproportionately large head with huge, empty eye sockets. When you walk out of the swap-meet area in the late afternoon, out of the shadow of the big drive-in movie screen, you sometimes step on the stiff little bodies among the litter of cotton candy and cigarette butts and bits of tortilla.

Cyclops had noticed that it danced west, and when he listened he could hear the warm wind whispering through the parallel streets outside like a slow breath through the channels of a harmonica, seeming to be just a puff short of evoking an audible chord. Realizing that this was no longer a night he needed shelter from, Cyclops laid two quarters on the counter, got to his feet and lumbered to the door.

Outside, he tilted back his devastated hat and sniffed the night. It was the old desert wind, all right, hinting of mesquite and sage, and he could feel the city shifting in its sleep—but tonight there was a taint on the wind, one that the old man smelled in his mind rather than in his nose, and he knew that something else had come into the city tonight too, something that stirred a different sort of thing than leaves and dust.

The night felt flexed, stressed, like a sheet of glass being bent. Alertly Cyclops shambled halfway across Main Street and then stopped and stared south.

After eleven o'clock the traffic lights stopped cycling and switched to a steady metronomic flashing, all the north-south lights flashing yellow for caution while the east-west ones, facing the smaller cross-streets, flashed red for stop. Standing halfway across the crosswalk Cyclops could see more than a mile's worth of randomly flashing yellow lights receding away south down Main, and about once every minute the flashes sychronized into one relayed pulse that rushed up the long street and past him over his head, toward the traffic circle at Bailey, half a mile north of where he stood.

He'd stood there often late at night, coming to conclusions about things by watching the patterns of disorder and synchronization in the long street-tunnel of flashing yellow lights, and he quickly realized that tonight they were flashing in step more frequently than normal, and only in pulses that swept north, as if delineating a landing pattern for something.

Cyclops nodded grimly. The night was warped, all right—as much curvature as he'd ever seen. The Great Gray-Legged Scissors Men would be out tonight in force.

He squared his shoulders, then strode away purposefully up Main, the once-per-minute relay-pulse of yellow light sweeping past him overhead like luminous birds.

Benny Kemp carried his drink out to the dark porch and sat down on the bench that his father had built there more than fifty years earlier. Someone had once tried to saw it away from the wall, but the solid oak had proved too hard, and the attempt had apparently been abandoned before any serious damage had been done. Running his hand over the wood now in the absolute darkness, Kemp couldn't even find the ragged groove.

He took a sip of his wine, breathing shallowly and pretending that the air carried the scent of night-blooming jasmine and dewy lawns instead of the smell of age-soured wood and rodent nests, and that it moved. In his imagination he watched moths bumble against the long-gone porch light.

He never turned on the real light; he knew that his cherished fantasy wouldn't survive the sight of the solid wall that crowded right up against the porch rail. There was a doorway where the porch steps had once been, but it led into the entry hall of the apartment building his father's house had been converted into, and all that was out there was a pay phone, cheap panelling peeling off the new walls, and, generally, a shopping cart or two. The entry hall and office had been added right onto the front of the old house—completely enclosing the porch and making an eccentric room of it—but he seldom entered or left the building through the new section, preferring the relatively unchanged back stairs.

He leaned back now and let the wine help him pretend. He'd never told any of the long string of renters and landlords that this was the house he had grown up in—he was afraid that sharing that information would diminish his relationship with the old building, and make it impossible for him to sit here quietly like this and, late at night, slide imperceptibly into the past.

The moths thumped and fluttered softly against the light, and, inhaling through the wine fumes, Kemp caught a whiff of jasmine, and then a warm breeze touched his cheek and a moment later he heard a faint pattering as jacaranda flowers, shaken from the tree out front, fell like a sower's cast of dead butterflies to the sidewalk and the street.

He opened his eyes and saw the tree's branches shift slowly against the dark sky, and coins of bright moonlight appeared, moved and disappeared in the tree's restless shadow. Kemp stood up, as carefully as a man with a tray of fragile, antique glass in his hands. He moved to the porch steps, went gingerly down them and then stole down the walkway to the sidewalk.

To his right he could see the railroad yard and, beyond it, the agitated glow that was the freeway. Too . . . hard, Kemp thought, too solidified, too much certainty and not enough possibility. He looked left, toward the traffic circle. It was quieter in that direction and aside from the moon the only source of illumination was the flashing yellow of the traffic lights. The wind seemed warmer in that direction, too. Trembling, he hurried toward the circle; and though he thought he glimpsed a couple of the tall, lean people in gray leotards—or maybe it was just one, darting rapidly from this shadowed area to that—tonight, for once, he was not going to let them frighten him.

The wind was funnelled stronger under the Hatton Park bridge, and a plastic bag in a shopping cart bellied full like the sail of a ship, and pulled the cart forward until it stopped against the sneakered foot of an old woman who slept next to it. Mary Francis woke up and looked around. The trash-can fires had all burned out—it had to be closer to morning than to dusk.

She sniffed the intrusive desert wind, and her pulse quickened, for there were smells on it that she hadn't known in forty years, not since the days when this area was more orange groves than streets.

She fumbled in her topmost coat for one of her mirrors, and after she'd pulled out the irregular bit of silvered glass and stared into it for a few moments she exhaled a harsh sigh of wonder.

She had known this would happen if she worked hard enough at her collecting—and it seemed she finally had. Still staring into the mirror, she stood up and pushed her shopping cart out from under the bridge. In the moonlight all the scraps of cloth in her cart should have looked gray, but instead they glowed with their true color, the special sea-green that was the only hue of rag she would deign to pick up in her daily circuit of the trash cans and dumpsters—the never-forgotten color of the dress she'd worn at her debut in 1923. In recent years it had occurred to her that if she could find even a scrap of that dress, and then hang onto it, it might regenerate itself . . . slowly, yes, you couldn't be in a hurry, but if you were willing to wait . . . and she suspected that if the cloth were with her, it might regenerate her, too . . . banish the collapsed old wrinkled-bedsheet face and restore her real face, and figure, not only re-create the dress but also the Mary Francis that had worn it . . .

And look, now on this magic night it had happened. The face in the mirror was blurry, but it was clearly the face of the girl she'd never really stopped being. Oval face, big dark eyes, pale, smooth skin . . . that unaffected, trusting innocence.

She turned east, and the focus became clearer—but it was the what's-this-I-found-in-the-back-of-yer-old-garage face. Quickly she turned west, and was awed by the beauty of her own smile of relief when the girl-face returned, more clearly now.

She was facing the traffic circle. Keeping her eyes fixed on the ever-more-in-focus image in the mirror, she began pushing her shopping cart westward, and she didn't even notice the agile, faceless gray figures that dropped from trees and jackknifed up out of the sewer vents and went loping silently along toward the circle.

The traffic circle at Main and Bailey was the oldest part of town. Restaurants wanting to show a bit of local color always had to hang a couple of old black and white photographs of the circle with Pierce-Arrows and Model-T Fords driving around it and men in bowler hats and high collars sitting on the benches or leaning on the coping of the fountain. People in the restaurants would always look at the old photographs and try to figure out which way was north.

The flattened leathery thing that Cyclops had thought was a dried devilfish sailed on over the roof of the YMCA, frisbeed over the motorcycle cops who were waiting for someone to betray drunkenness by having trouble driving around the circle, and then like a dried leaf it smacked into the pool of the old fountain. It drifted to the tiled pillar in the center and wound up canted slightly out of the water against the tiles, its big empty eyes seeming to watch the rooftops.

"Are you okay?"

"Yes," he croaked, concealing his irritation at her tone, which had seemed to imply that he must be either crazy or having a fit to jump out of bed that way; but if he had objected she'd reply, in hurt surprise, "All I said was, 'are you okay?' ", which would put him two points down and give her the right to sigh in a put-upon way and make a show of having trouble getting back to sleep. "Just a dream," he said shortly.

"*Fine*," she said, and then added, just a little too soon, "I only *asked*."

He suppressed a grin. She'd been too eager, and done a riposte when there had only been a feint. He gave her a wondering look and said, "Gee, relax, hon. Maybe you were in the middle of a dream too, huh?" He chuckled with a fair imitation of fondness. "We *both* seem to be acting like *lunatics*." One-all, his advantage.

"What was the dream about?" she asked.

Oh no you don't, he thought. "I don't remember." He walked to the window and looked down at Main Street. The palm trees were bending and he could hear the low roaring of the wind.

Debbie rolled over and began breathing regularly, and Roger knew that until she really did go to sleep any noise he made would provoke the rendition of a startled awakening, so he resolved to stand by the window until he was certain she wasn't shamming. Of course she'd know what he was thinking and try to draw him into an error with convincing breathing-hitches and even—a tactical concession—undignified snortings.

He would wait her out. He stared down at the street and thought about his dream.

It was a dream he used to have fairly frequently when he was a child, though he hadn't had it since coming to California. Jesus, he thought, and I came to California in '57, when I was six years old. What does it mean, that I'm having it again after almost thirty years? And—I remember now— that dream always heralded the arrival of Evelyn, my as-they-like-to-call-it imaginary playmate.

The dream tonight had been so exactly the same as before that when he woke up he'd thought at first that he was in one of the many bedrooms he'd had back east, in the year—1956, it must have been—when his parents had been moving around so much. The dream always started with a train, seen from a distance, moving down a moonlit track across a field, with buildings a remote unevenness on the dark horizon. Then, and it was never *quite* scary in the dream, the whistle wailed and the smokestack emitted a blob of white smoke; the smoke didn't dissipate—it billowed but kept its volume like a splash of milk in a jug of clear oil, and when the train had disappeared in the distance the blob of smoke slowly formed into a white, blank-eyed face. And then, slow as a cloud, the face would drift into town and move up and down the dark streets, and at every bedroom window it would pause and silently peer in . . . until it came to Roger's window. When it came to his, it smiled and at last dissolved away, and then there was the sense of company in his mind.

He remembered, now, the last time he'd had the dream; it had been the night before his parents abandoned him. He had awakened early the next morning, and when his mother had walked into the kitchen to put on the coffee pot he'd already fixed himself a bowl of Cheerios.

"Up already, Rog?" his mother asked him. "What have we told you about getting into the fridge without asking?"

"Sorry," he'd said, and for at least a year afterward he had been certain that they'd abandoned him because he'd broken the rule about the refrigerator. "Evelyn's back," he remarked then, to change the subject.

His mother had frozen, holding the can of ground coffee, and her face had seemed to get leaner. "What—," she began harshly; then, in a desperately reasonable tone, "What do you mean, honey? She can't be. I know she found us again after we moved from Keyport to Redbank, and all the other times since, but we're in *New York* now, almost all the way to Buffalo, she can't have followed us all that way. You're just . . . *pretending*, this time, right?"

"Nah," he'd replied carelessly, "But she says it was a long trip. How long since we moved away from Atlantic City?"

His mother had sat down across the table from him, still holding the coffee can. "Five months," she whispered.

"Yeah, she flew over a river, the . . . she says Del Ware? And then she had to go around Phil-a-delph-ia, 'cause there was too many people there, and they—them all thinking, and wishing for things—started to bend the air, like too many people on a trampoline, and it would have bent all the way around and made a bubble, and she wouldn't a been able to get out of it, back to real places. And then, she says, she went around Scranton and Elmira, and now here she is."

The six-year-old Roger had looked up from his cereal then, and he realized for the first time that his mother was afraid of Evelyn. And now, standing at his bedroom window in Santa Margarita while Debbie pretended to be asleep in the bed behind him, it suddenly and belatedly occurred to him that it might have been Evelyn's remarkable tracking abilities that had made his parents move so frequently during that year.

But why, he wondered, would they both so fear a child's imaginary playmate? It wasn't as if Evelyn could be seen, or move things, or say where lost watches and rings had got to . . . much less hurt anyone, like the "imaginary playmate" in the story by John Collier. The only one she got even remotely forceful with was *me*, censoring my dreams whenever I dreamed about things she didn't like. And hell, when I first started talking about her, my Mom was just amused . . . used to ask me how Evelyn was, and even cut a piece of cake for her on my fifth birthday. It wasn't until I started telling Mom things that Evelyn had told me—like that Evelyn was three years older than me, to the month—that Mom stopped finding the idea of an imaginary playmate charming.

Roger thought about the current unpaid bill from the private investigator. If he can find you before I become too broke to pay for his services, he thought, I'll get a chance to *ask* you what bothered you about Evelyn, *Mom*—after I get through asking you and Dad about the ethics of sending a six-year-old boy into a drug store with a quarter to buy candy with, and then driving away, forever, while he's inside. And it might be soon—if the investigator's deductions from studying money-order records and Social Security payments are correct, and you and Dad really do live within blocks of here.

Someone was shouting furiously, down the street . . . and walking this way, by the sound of it. A male voice, Roger noted—probably old Cyclops. What the hell is it that makes so many street bums shout? Old women at bus stops who make heads turn two blocks away with the volume and pure rage of their almost totally incoherent outbursts, men that walk out into traffic so that screeching brakes punctuate their wrathfully delivered catalogue of the various things they are not going to stand for anymore . . . and people who, like Cyclops here tonight, simply walk up and down the empty nighttime streets shouting warnings and challenges to imaginary enemies: it must be some kind of urban malady, new to civilization as far as I know. Maybe it's contagious, and some time it'll be Debbie and me down there shaking our fists at empty stretches of sidewalk and screaming, *Oh yeah, you sons of bitches*?

He glanced back at Debbie. Her sooner than me, he thought. If her parents didn't live in Balboa and own a boat and a cabin up at Big Bear, and lots all over hell, would I be intending to marry such a mean, skitzy specimen? No way. And if I do succeed in finding my parents, and if they prove to be as affluent as my memories of their cars and houses indicate they were, I'll send this animated bird's-nest of neuroses and obsessions back to her parents. My gain and their loss.

He shivered. The room wasn't cold, but he'd felt a draft of . . . of success passing by; a breath of impending squalor stirring the dust under the bedroom door, and he thought the bills on the desk were softly rustled by a stale shift of air that somehow carried the smell of gray hair and dreary nine-to-five wait-thirty-years-for-a-pension work, and trash bags full of empty cans of creamed corn and Spam and corned beef hash.

I can't let go of her, he thought, until I'm *certain* about my parents—until I've not only found them, but found out how much they're worth, and then shamed or even blackmailed them into giving me a lot of money, and making me their heir. Only then will I be able to ditch poor loony Debbie . . . as any saner or less-ambitious man would have done right after that first time she ran back to her parents.

It had been about four months earlier. As soon as he'd realized she had left him, he had known where she must have gone. He had taken the bus down to her parents' house the next day. He'd been prepared to claim that he loved their overweight, manic-depressive monster of a daughter, and to explain that the two of them had been living together only because they couldn't get married yet; he'd braced himself for a lot of parental disapproval, even for violence . . . but he had not been prepared for what awaited him.

Debbie's mother had opened the door when he knocked, but when, nervously defiant, he introduced himself, she only smiled. "Oh, you're Roger! I'm *so* pleased to meet you, Debbie's told us so *much* about you! Do come in and say hello, I know a visit from you will cheer her up . . ." He wanted to explain that he'd come to take her back with him, but her mother was still speaking as she led him inside, out of the sunlight and into the living room, where curtains had been drawn across all the windows and no lights were on. There was a chair standing in the middle of the floor. "Yes, our Debbie likes to go out and make new friends," the mother was saying cheerfully, "but," she added with a wave toward the chair, "as you can see, she always comes home again."

Peering in the dimness, Roger had finally noticed that Debbie was sitting motionless in the chair, staring blankly . . . and then that she was *tied* into the chair, with belts around her waist, wrists and ankles. Without conscious thought he had left the house, and he walked quite a way up Main before remembering that he would have to get a bus if he wanted to get home before dark.

Later he had gone back again to that house, and caught Debbie in a more accessible segment of whatever her doomed mood-cycle was, and he talked her into returning to the apartment they'd been sharing; in his more fatuous moments he told himself that he'd gone back for her in order to save her from that environment and her evidently demented mother, but late on frightened nights like this one he could admit, to himself at least, that his concern for her was the concern a man feels for his last uncancelled credit card.

Debbie now emitted a prolonged sound that was halfway between a snore and a sentence, and he knew she must really be asleep. I'll wait till old Cyclops has gone by, Roger thought, and then crawl carefully back into bed. I wonder if Evelyn will still censor my dreams. What was it she used to object to? The dreams she didn't like were all prompted by something I experienced, so she was probably just my subconscious mind suppressing memories which, in some unacknowledged way, I found traumatic. I still remember the time my parents took me to the Crystal Lake amusement park in New Jersey—they were jovial during the first half of the drive, but when we got off the turnpike they seemed to unexpectedly recognize the area, and they got very tense—and, after that, Evelyn wouldn't let me dream about that neighborhood. And once I saw a cowboy movie in which, at one point, a cavalry soldier was shot and fell off his horse but had one foot caught in the stirrup and got dragged along, bouncing like a rag doll over the prairie —Evelyn always squelched any dream that began to include that bit. And after I got my tonsils taken out, she wouldn't let me dream about the smell of the ether; I was free to dream about the hospital and the sore throat and the ice-cream, but not that smell.

"*Climb back down into your holes, you bastards!*" shouted Cyclops on the sidewalk below. Debbie shifted and muttered, and Roger mentally damned the noisy old bum. "*Dare to come near me,*" Cylops added, "*and I'll smash your gray faces for you! Break your scissor legs!*"

Interested in spite of himself, Roger glanced down at the street—and then peered more closely. Cyclops, as usual, was lurching along the sidewalk and shaking his fists at dire adversaries, but tonight, for once, he seemed to be yelling at people who were actually there. A half-dozen dark figures were bounding about on the shadowed lawns and turning fantastic cartwheels in the dimness between streetlights. Roger's first guess was that they must be young theater majors from some local college, out larking and wino-hassling after some rehearsal or cast-party, for the figures all seemed to be dressed in gray leotards and wearing gray nylon stockings pulled down over their faces. Then he saw one of them spring from a grasshopper-crouch . . . and rise all the way up to the third floor of an office building, and cling to the sill of a dark window there for a moment, before spider-jumping back down to the pavement.

The yellow-flashing traffic lights were strangely coordinated, flinging re-layed pulses past at the height of his window, and he felt Evelyn's presence very strongly. *Come out, Roger*, she called to him from out in the warm-as-breath night. *Decide what you want, so I can give it to you.*

"Can you find my Mom and Dad?" he whispered.

Debbie instantly sat up in bed behind him. "What?" she said. "Are you crazy?"

Yes, came Evelyn's answer from outside. *Look. Here they are. I'll bring them out for you.*

Roger stepped away from the window and began pulling on his pants.

"Roger!" said Debbie sharply, real concern beginning to show through her reflexive malice. "You're walking in your sleep. Get back in bed."

"I'm awake," he said, stepping into his shoes without bothering about socks. "I'm going out. You go back to sleep."

Aware that she was being left out of something, Debbie bounded out of bed. I'm coming with you.''

"No, damn it," he said almost pleadingly as he buttoned alternate buttons on his shirt. "What do you want to come for?"

"Because you don't want me to," she said, her voice muffled under the dress she was pulling on over her head. She stepped into shoes on her way to the door and had it open before he'd even finished tucking in his shirt. "At least I'm waiting for you."

They left the apartment by the front door and hurried down the stairs to the pavement. Leaves and flattened paper cups whirled through the air like nocturnal birds, and Cyclops was already a block ahead of Roger and Debbie. Looking past the old man, Roger could see that the stop lights north of the traffic circle were sending synchronized yellow pulses south; the pulses from south and north Main met at the circle like tracer bullets from two directions being fired at a common target.

His feet were suddenly warmer, and, glancing down, he noticed that he had socks on; also, every button of his shirt was fastened, and his shoes looked polished.

He began running toward the bending palms that ringed the circle. Debbie, running right behind him, called out in a voice made timid by fright or wonder, "Where are we going?"

"I could be wrong," he shouted without looking back, "but I think that, tonight at least, it's the place where dreams come true."

Jack Singer straightened the knot of his tie and then stood back from the mirror and admired his reflection. A well-tailored suit cetainly did things for a man—not only did he look lean and fit, with somehow no trace of projecting belly, but even his face seemed tanned and alert, his hair fuller and darker. He patted his breast pocket and felt the slim billfold there, and without having to look he knew it contained a Diner's Club card, and a Visa—one with that asterisk that means you're good for more than the average guy, and a gold American Express card, and a few crisp hundred dollar bills for tips.

He stepped away from the mirror and took a sip of brandy from the glass on the bureau. Good stuff, that five-star Courvoisier. "You about ready, dear?" he called toward his wife's dressing room.

"In a minute," she said. "The diamond fell out of one of my fingernails, and I've got it Super-Gluing."

He nodded, and though his smile didn't falter, his fine-drawn eyebrows contracted into a frown. Diamonds in her *what*? Her *fingernails*? He'd never heard of such a thing . . . but he knew better than to ask her about it, for it was clearly just one more part of this weirdly wonderful evening.

For just a moment, after they had awakened an hour ago, he had thought it was the middle of the night, and their apartment seemed to be . . . a shabby one they had lived in once. But then the hot Santa Ana wind had puffed in at the window and he had remembered that it was early evening, and that his wife and he were due to attend the dinner being given in their honor at the . . . what was the name of the hotel? . . . just the finest hotel in the state . . . the *Splendide*, that was it.

He glanced out the window. "The limo is here, darling," he called.

"Coming." His wife appeared from her dressing room. Fine clothes had done wonders for her, too—she looked twenty pounds slimmer, and would be described as voluptuous now instead of just plain damn fat.

The chauffeur knocked quietly at the door, and Singer held out his arm for his wife to take.

They dutifully had a drink apiece in the limousine as it carried them smoothly west on Bailey, and though they couldn't recall gulping them the glasses were empty by the time the chauffeur made the sweeping turn around three quarters of the traffic circle and then with never a jiggle turned south onto Main and drew in to the curb in front of the *Hotel Splendide*. A man in an almost insanely ornate red coat and gold-crusted hat opened the door for them.

Singer got out and then helped his wife out, and he noticed that the sidewalk, which had the *Splendide* insignia inset into the cement every yard or so, was so brightly lit by spotlights on the lawn and the dozen huge chandeliers in the lobby that he and his wife cast no shadows.

"They are awaiting you in the Napoleon Lounge, M'sieur," said the doorman, bowing obsequiously, "drinks and hors d'oeuvre there, and then you are to dine in the Grand Ballroom." Out of sight somewhere, an orchestra was richly performing a medley of favorites from the 1940's.

Singer produced a hundred-dollar bill and let it disappear into the man's gloved hand. "Thank you, Armand."

They strolled across the carpeted floor, surreptitiously admiring their reflections in the tall mirrors that alternated with marble panels on all the walls, and when they walked through the gilded arch into the Napoleon Lounge the other guests all greeted their appearance with delighted cries.

And they were all elegant—the lovely young woman in the striking sea-green dress, the piratically-handsome old fellow with the eyepatch, the young couple who had been filling two plates over at one of the hors d'oeuvre tables . . . and especially the woman who was walking toward them with her hands out in welcome, a smile on her porcelain-pale face . . .

"Good evening," the woman said, "we're all so glad to see you. I'm your hostess this evening—my name is Evelyn."

Roger, looking up from the plate he'd been filling with caviar and thin slices of some black bread that was thick with caraway seeds, saw the newcomers flinch, just perceptibly, when Evelyn introduced herself, and instantly he

knew that this couple must be his parents. They quickly recovered their poise and allowed Evelyn to lead them in, and Roger studied them out of the corner of his eye as, trying not to betray the trembling of his hands and the hard thudding of his heart, he forked a devilled egg and a tiny ear of pickled baby corn onto his plate. They do look prosperous, he thought with cautious satisfaction.

Evelyn was leading the couple straight toward the table beside which Roger and Debbie stood. "Jack and Irma," she said to Roger's parents, "this is Debbie and Roger." Again his parents flinched, and Irma stared hard and expressionlessly at Roger for a couple of seconds before extending her hand. She opened her mouth as if to say something, but Evelyn spoke first.

"Ah, here come the stewards," she said. "The cocktails are all first-rate here, of course, and on the table there is a list of the particular specialties of the house. And now you must excuse me—I think our Mr. Kemp has a question." She smiled and spun away toward a middle-aged man who was eyeing the stewards with something like alarm. As much to postpone confronting his parents as from thirst, Roger squinted at the sheet of apparently genuine vellum on which, in fancy calligraphy, the specialty drinks were described, but they were all frothy things like Pink Squirrels and White Russians and Eggnog, and he decided to follow his usual custom in dressy bars and ask for Chivas Regal Royal Salute 25-Year Old . . . in a *snifter*. That always impressed people.

The steward who approached their table, a tall, thin fellow in dark gray, bowed and said, "Can I bring you anything from the bar?"

"I'll have one of your Pink Squirrels, but made with *whiskey* instead of *bourbon*," said Debbie in her best misconception-squared style.

Roger looked up to give the steward a *humor-her wink*, but he stepped back quickly with a smothered exclamation, for the man's face, just for a fraction of a second, had seemed to be a featureless gray angularity, like a plastic trash bag stretched taut across the front of a skull.

A moment later it was just an indistinct face, but Roger said, "Uh, right, and a scotch for me, excuse me," and took a couple of steps toward the center of the room.

The dignified man with the eyepatch was staring at him, and Roger realized that it was Cyclops, not looking nearly as ridiculous in antique Navy dress blues as one might have expected. Cyclops, who wasn't holding a drink, crossed to him and said quietly, "You saw that one, didn't you? For a second you saw it wasn't a waiter, but one of the Great Gray-Legged Scissors Men."

Oh Jesus, thought Roger unhappily. Where in hell is my scotch? "One of the *what*?"

"Oh, sorry, right—I just call 'em that 'cause they look like that guy in the old kids' rhyme, remember? The Great Red-Legged Scissors Man, who dashes up with a hugh pair of scissors and cuts the thumbs off kids that suck their thumbs? How's it end?—'I knew he'd come . . . to naughty little suck-a-thumb.' ''

"They're . . ." began Roger, so wildly disoriented that it was hard to take a deep breath or refrain from giggling, "They're going to cut off our thumbs, are they?"

Cyclops looked disgusted. "No. Are you drunk? I *said* I just call 'em that 'cause they look like the guy in the picture that went with that poem. Except these here guys are all gray. No, *these* guys appear out o' nowhere when somebody who can boost dreams comes along, the way raindrops appear out o' nowhere when a low pressure area comes along. Maybe the gray guys are the deep roots of our own minds, curled back up so they poke out o' the ground near us and seem separate, like the worm that got himself pregnant; or maybe they're ghosts that you can only see in the spirit light that shines from one of these imagination-amplifier people." He nodded toward Evelyn, "She's the one doing it here tonight. The trouble is, such people warp the night, and the more minds she's overdriving the sharper the angle of the curve, like blowing in one of those kid's-toy loops that holds a flat surface of soap-film, you know? You blow harder and harder, and the film bellies out rounder and rounder, and them—pop!—it's a bubble, broke loose and drifting away."

"Right," Roger said, nodding repeatedly and looking around for, if nothing else, a drink someone had abandoned. "Right—a bubble floating away, gotcha. Scissors men. You don't see a *drink* anywhere, do—"

"It's gonna happen tonight," said Cyclops harshly. "Damn soon. Did you notice the traffic signals? You know why they're all flashing at the same second so often now? 'Cause we're only still intersecting with a few of 'em, what seems like many is just lots o' reflections of only a couple. When they're perfectly in step that'll mean there's only one left, and the connection between this bubble and the real world is just a thin, thin tunnel."

"Sure, but . . ."

"I'm leaving now," Cyclops interrupted. "If you got any sense, you'll come too. In five minutes it may be too late."

"Uhh . . ." Roger looked thoughtfully down at the elegant Yves St. Laurent suit he'd found himself wearing when he had approached the hotel, and he looked back at the low-cut, sequined gown that Debbie was—just as inexplicably—wearing. Now he held his hand out, palm up, fingers slightly curled, and he concentrated—and then suddenly he was holding a snifter that had an inch of amber fluid swirling in the bottom of it. He smiled up at the stern old man. "Imagination-amplifier, hey?" he said slowly. "I'll stay for just a little while, thanks. Hell, five minutes—that's plenty of time."

Cyclops smiled with pity and contempt, then turned and strode out of the room. Roger stared over at Evelyn. Who *was* she, *what* was she? Clearly something more than a child's imaginary playmate, or—what had he guessed her to be, earlier?—just a function of his subconscious mind. Of course, maybe he was better off not knowing, not asking inconvenient questions.

He carried his drink back to where Debbie and his parents were standing. "Well!" he said heartily. "Mom, Dad—it's good to see you again after all these years."

He was shocked by the physical change these words produced in the couple—his father shrank, and was suddenly balding and gray, and the gaps between the buttons of his ill-fitting suit were pulled wide by an abrupt protrusion of belly, and his mother became ludicrously fat, her expression of well-bred amusement turning to one of petulant unhappiness—and belatedly it occurred to Roger that their apparent affluence might be as ephemeral as his own suit and snifter of scotch.

"You . . . *are* Roger, aren't you?" the old woman whispered. "And," she added, turning in horror toward their hostess, "that is Evelyn."

"Yes," Roger said, a little surprised to realize that his adventurous delight in this evening had, all at once, evaporated, leaving him feeling old and bitter. "She only found her way back to me tonight. The trip took her more than twenty-five years . . . but, you remember, she always avoided very populated areas."

"Until tonight," his father pointed out quietly.

"Until tonight," Roger agreed.

His father's smile was sickly. "Look," the old man said, "we've got lots to discuss, I'll admit—lots to, uh, beg forgiveness for, even—but can we get *out* of here right now? Without attracting the attention of . . . our hostess?"

Roger looked around. Evelyn was chatting gaily with the group on the other side of the room, and every time she glanced up the chandeliers brightened and the trays of hors d'oeuvre came into clearer focus, but the stewards were getting leaner and taller, and their features were fading like images cast by a projector with a dimming bulb, and peripherally Roger saw one of them out in the lobby leap right up to the ceiling and cling there like a big fly.

"Yeah," said Roger, suddenly frightened and taking Cyclops' warning seriously. He let his drink evaporate, glass and all. "If anybody asks, say we're just going out for some fresh air—and go on about what a great time you're having." He took Debbie's arm. "Come on." he said.

"No, I'm staying. You know what they put in this drink, after I *told* them not to?"

"We're only going for a stroll, just to take a look at the front of the building—but sure, stay if you want."

"No, I'm coming." She put her drink down, and Roger noticed that the glass broke up silently into an unfocussed blur when she let go of it.

The four of them made their way to the lobby unhindered—Evelyn even saw them go, but looked more exasperated than angry—and Roger led them around the faceless, ceiling-crouching thing and across the carpeted floor, through the front doors, and down the marble steps to the sidewalk.

"South on Main, come on," he said, trying not to panic in spite of how synchronized the traffic signals were; "away from the circle."

As they trudged along, Roger felt a sudden slickness against his feet, and he realized that his socks had disappeared. He didn't have to glance to the side to know that Debbie was back in the old sack dress she'd pulled on over her head right after leaping out of bed. Behind him the tick-tock of his mother's heels and the knock of his father's shoes became a flapping—bedroom slippers, it sounded like. Good, Roger thought—I guess we weren't too late.

He looked up, and the whole sky was turning slowly, like a vast, glitter-strewn wheel, and he couldn't decide whether to take that as a good sign or a bad one. Funny how the night moves, he thought nervously. I don't think this is what Bob Seger meant.

And then his feet were comfortable again, and even though they'd been walking in a straight line he saw the traffic circle ahead, and, from around the corner to the right, the glow of the *Splendide's* main entrance.

The others noticed it too, and slowed. "We were walking south on Main," Debbie said, ". . . away from the traffic circle."

"And now, without having changed course," said Roger wearily, "we're headed east on Bailey, toward it. We waited too long."

Jack Singer was smiling broadly. "Screw this," he said, and his voice was cheerful, if a bit shrill. "I'll see you all later." He turned and fled back the way they'd come, his newly-restored suit and shoes disappearing within a few yards, leaving him an overweight man in pyjamas and slippers, puffing and flapping like a clown as he ran.

Roger's mother took a hesitant step after him, but Roger took her arm. "Don't bother, Mom—I'm pretty sure the quickest way to catch up with him is to just keep going straight ahead."

Debbie was patting the fabric of her sequined gown. "I hope I get to keep this," she said.

The traffic lights were in perfect step now. Roger considered leading the two women around the circle and straight out Bailey, eastward, but he was fatalistically sure that Bailey Boulevard, as they proceeded along it, would within half a block or so become Main Street, and they'd be facing the circle again. Neither his mother nor Debbie objected when he turned right at Main, toward the *Splendide*.

The entrance was more brightly illuminated than ever, but it was a harsh glare like that cast by arc lights, and the cars pulling up and driving away moved in sudden hops, like spiders, or like cars in a film from which a lot of the frames have been cut. The music was a weary, prolonged moaning of brass and strings. Jack Singer, once again in his suit, slouched up from the far side of the hotel and joined them on the steps.

Roger thought of making some cutting remark—something like, "Not so easy to ditch me this time, huh, Pop?"—but both his parents looked so unhappy, and he himself was so frightened, that he didn't have the heart for it.

"Oh, God," wailed his mother, "will we ever get back home?"

Roger was facing the hotel, but he turned around when he heard splashing behind him. It was the fountain—the traffic circle was now right in front of the hotel, and the pavement below the steps wasn't the Main Street sidewalk any longer, was now just a concrete walkway between the grass of the circle and the steps of the hotel. Dark buildings, as nondescript as painted stage props, crowded up around the other sides of the circle, and Roger could see only one traffic light. It was flashing slower, and its yellow color had a faint orange tint.

"Do come in," called Evelyn from the open lobby doors. "It's just time to sit down for dinner." Her face was paler, and she seemed to be trembling.

Roger glanced at his mother. "Maybe," he said. Then he turned toward the circle and concentrated; it was harder than making a snifter of scotch appear, but in a moment he had projected, blotting out the dim traffic circle, a downtown street he remembered seeing on the way to the Crystal Lake amusement park in New Jersey. It was one of the things Evelyn had never permitted him to dream about.

He was surprised at how clearly he was able to project it—until he saw that the sky behind the shabby New Jersey office buildings was overcast and gray instead of the brilliant blue he remembered, and he realized that someone else, perhaps unintentionally, perhaps even against their will, was helping to fill out the picture, using their own recollections of it.

Behind him Evelyn gasped—and the one visible traffic signal began to flash a little faster, and to lose some of the orange tint.

Okay, Roger thought tensely, the cord isn't quite cut yet. What else was there? Oh yeah . . .

He made the New Jersey street disappear and instantly replaced it with a prairie, across which a horse and rider galloped. At first the rider was a cavalry soldier, as in the movie scene Roger remembered, but again someone else's projection changed the scene—the rider was smaller now, and not dressed in blue . . . it was hard to see clearly, and again Roger got the impression that this altering of what he was projecting was unintentional . . . and when the rider fell off the horse it was hard to tell which foot had caught in the stirrup . . .

The pavement below him had widened, and now he could see another traffic light. The two were still in step, but were at least flashing in their normal pace and color.

He replaced the vision of the galloping horse and the suffering figure behind it with a rendition of the hospital room in which he's awakened after the removal of his tonsils . . . and this time the picture was altered instantly and totally, though the lingering-in-the-back-of-his-throat smell of ether grew stronger. He saw a windowless room with newspapers spread neatly all over the floor, and there was a sort of table, with . . .

The night shuddered, and suddenly he could see down Main Street—and, way down south, he saw one yellow light blinking out of synch. "This way out," he said, stepping to the sidewalk and walking south. "Walk through the visions—I'm building us a bridge."

Again the downtown New Jersey street appeared, and without his volition a young couple—hardly more than teenagers—entered the picture. They both looked determined and scared as they walked along the sidewalk looking at the address numbers on the buildings.

Roger kept leading his group southward, and when the New Jersey picture faded he saw that the out-of-step signal was closer. Debbie was walking carefully right beside him. Thank God, he thought, that she hasn't chosen this occasion to be difficult—but where are my parents?

He couldn't turn to look behind him, for the next projection was appearing, cleaving a path out of Evelyn's imploding fake world. Obviously Evelyn's aversion to these memories was strong, for her own projection simply recoiled from these the way a live oyster contracts away from lemon juice squeezed onto it.

The cowboy movie memory was now altered out of recognition, though it was the most effective yet at re-randomizing the traffic lights; now it was a girl instead of a cavalry soldier, and somehow she still had *both* feet in the stirrups, and though there was blood she didn't seem to be being dragged over any prairie . . . in fact she was lying on a table in a windowless room with newspapers all over the floor, and the ether reek was everywhere like the smell of rotten pears, and her young boyfriend was pacing the sidewalk out in front of the shabby office and at last the overcast sky had begun dropping rain so that he needn't struggle to hold back his tears any longer . . .

"Woulda been a girl, I think," came the multiply-remembered voice of a man . . .

Shock and sudden comprehension slowed Roger's steps, and involuntarily he turned and looked back at Evelyn as bitterness and loss closed his throat and brought tears to his eyes. The man knew his business, he thought. "Goodbye, Evelyn," he whispered.

Goodbye, Roger, spoke a voice—a receding voice—in his head.

The projected scene ahead was even clearer now, but beyond it lay the real pre-dawn Santa Margarita streets. "Come on," said Roger, stepping forward again. "We're almost out of it."

Debbie was right beside him, but he didn't hear his parents, so he paused and turned.

They were stopped several yards back, staring at the pavement.

"Come on," Roger said harshly. "It's the way out."

"We can't go through it," his father said.

"Again," added his mother faintly.

"We weren't *married* yet, then, in '48 . . ." his father began; but Roger had taken Debbie's hand and resumed their forward progress.

They moved slowly through the windowless room, every full stride covering a few inches of newspaper-strewn floor, and then there was the fluttering thump of something landing in a plastic-lined waste basket and they were out in the streets and the air was cold and Roger didn't have socks on and the traffic signals, ready for all the early-morning commuters, were switching through their long-green, short-yellow, long-red cycles, and the one-eyed old hobo standing in the street nodded curtly at them and then motioned them to step aside, for an ancient woman was puffing along the sidewalk behind them, pushing a shopping cart full of green scraps of cloth, and behind her trotted a lean little old fellow whom Roger remembered having seen many times walking the streets of Santa Margarita, lingering by empty lots when the workmen had gone home and the concrete outlines of long-gone houses could still be seen among the mud and litter and tractor tracks. There was no one else on the street. The sky was already pale blue, though the sun wasn't up yet.

Debbie glanced down at herself and pursed her lips angrily to see that her fine gown had disappeared again. "Are you through with your games?" she snapped. "Can we go home now?"

"You go ahead," Roger told her. "I want to walk some."

"No, come back with me."

He shook his head and walked away, slapping his pants pockets for change and trying to remember where he'd seen the all-night Mexican diner with the sign about the menudo breakfast.

"When you do come back," Debbie called furiously, "I won't be there! And don't bother going to my parents' house, 'cause I won't be there either!"

Good for you, he thought.

And as the first rays of the sun touched the tall palms around the traffic circle a scrap of something, unnoticed by anyone, sank to the bottom of the fountain pool, at peace at last.

JAMES PATRICK KELLY

The Prisoner of Chillon

Born in Mineola, New York, James Patrick Kelly now lives in Durham, New Hampshire. Kelly made his first sale in 1975, and has since become a frequent contributor to *The Magazine of Fantasy and Science Fiction* and *Isaac Asimov's Science Fiction Magazine;* his stories have also appeared in *Universe, Galaxy, Amazing, Analog, The Twilight Zone Magazine,* and elsewhere. His first solo novel *Planet of Whispers* came out in 1984; his most recent book is a novel written in collaboration with John Kessel, *Freedom Beach*. He is currently at work on a new novel, tentatively entitled *Look into the Sun*. His story "Friend," also in collaboration with Kessel, was in our First Annual Collection; his story "Solstice" was in our Third Annual Collection. He lives with his family in Durham, New Hampshire.

In the fast-paced, inventive, and pyrotechnic story that follows, he demonstrates that there are many other kinds of prisons than those constructed of concrete and steel. . . .

THE PRISONER OF CHILLON

James Patrick Kelly

We initiated deorbital burn over the Marshall Islands and dropped back into the ionosphere, locked by the wing's navigator into one of the Eurospace reentry corridors. As we coasted across Central America we were an easy target for the attack satellites. The plan was to fool the tracking nets into thinking we were a corporate shuttle. Django had somehow acquired the recognition codes; his computer, kludged to the navigator, made the wing think it was the property of Erno Raumfahrttechnik GMBH, the West German aerospace conglomerate.

It was all a matter of timing, really. It would not be too much longer before the people on IBM's Orbital 7 untangled the spaghetti Django had made of their memory systems and realized that he had downloaded WISE-GUY and stolen a cargo wing. Then they would have to decide whether to zap us immediately or have the mindkillers waiting when we landed. Django's plan was to lose the wing before they could decide. Our problem was that very little of the plan had worked so far.

He had gotten us on and off the orbital research station all right, and had managed to pry WISEGUY from the jaws of the corporate beast. For that alone his reputation would live forever among operators, even if he was not around to enjoy the fame. But he had lost his partner—Yellowbaby, the pilot—and he still did not know exactly what it was he had stolen. He seemed pretty calm for a punk who had just plugged the world's biggest corporation. He slouched in the commander's seat across from me watching the readouts on the autopilot console. He was whistling and tapping a finger against his headset as if he were listening to one of his old jazz disks. He was a dark, ugly man with an Adam's apple that looked like a nose and a nose that looked like an elbow. He had either been juved or he was in his mid-thirties. I trusted him not at all and liked him less.

Me, I felt as though I had swallowed a hardboiled egg. I was just along for the story, the *juice*. According to the courts, all I was allowed to do was aim my microcam glasses at Django and ask questions. If I helped him in any way, I would become an accessory and lose press immunity. But press immunity wouldn't do me much good if someone decided to zap the wing. The First Amendment was a great shield and all but it didn't protect against re-entry friction. I wanted to return to earth with a ship around me; sensors showed the outer skin was currently 1400 degrees Celsius.

"Much longer?" A dumb question since I already knew the answer. But better than listening to the atmosphere scream as the wing bucked through turbulence. I could feel myself losing it; I wanted to scream back.

"Twenty minutes. However it plays." Django lifted his headset. "Either you'll be a legend or air pollution." He stretched his arms over his head and arched his back away from the seat. I could smell his sweat. "Hey, lighten up, Eyes. You're a big girl now. Shouldn't you be taking notes or something?"

"The camera sees all." I tapped the left temple of the microcam and then forced a grin that hurt my face. "Besides, it's not bloody likely I'll forget this ride." I wasn't about to let Django play with me. He was too hypered on fast-forwards to be scared. My father had been the same way; he ate them like popcorn when he was working. And called me his big girl.

It had been poor Yellowbaby who had introduced me to Django. I had covered the Babe when he pulled the Peniplex job. He was a real all-nighter—handsome as plastic can make a man, and an artiste in bed. Handsome, past tense. The last time I had seen him he was floating near the ceiling of a decompressed cargo bay, an eighty kilo hunk of flash-frozen boytoy. I missed him already.

"I copy, Basel Control." Yellowbaby's calm voice crackled across the forward flight deck. "We're doing Mach 9.9 at 57,000 meters. Looking good for touch at 14:22."

We had come out of reentry blackout. The approach program that Yellowbaby had written, complete with voice interaction module, was in contact now with Basel/Mulhouse, our purported destination. As long as everything went according to plan, the program would get us where we wanted to go. If anything went wrong . . . well, the Babe was supposed to improvise if anything went wrong.

"Let's blow out of here." Django heaved himself out of the seat and swung down the ladder to the equipment bay. I followed. We pulled EV suits from the lockers and struggled into them. I could feel the deck tilting as the wing began a series of long lazy "S" curves to slow our descent.

Django unfastened his suit's weighty backpack and quickly shucked the rest of the excess baggage: comm and life support systems, various umbilicals. He was whistling again.

"Would you shut the hell up?" I tossed the still camera from my suit onto the pile.

"You don't like Fats Waller?" There was a chemical edge to his giggle.

" 'I've Got a Feeling I'm Falling,' great tune." And then he began to sing; his voice sounded like gears being stripped.

Yellowbaby's program was reassuring Basel even as we banked gracefully toward the Jura Mountains. "No problem, Basel Control," the dead man's voice drawled. "Malf on the main guidance computer. I've got backup. My Lover D is nominal. You just keep the tourists off the runway and I'll see you in ten minutes."

I shut down the microcam—no sense wasting batteries and disk space shooting the inside of an EV suit—and picked up the pressure helmet.

"Think I'm falling for you, Eyes." Django blew me a kiss. "Don't forget to duck." He made a quacking sound and flapped his arms like wings. I put the helmet on and closed the seals. It was a relief not to have to listen to him rave; we had disabled the comm units to keep the mindkillers from tracking us. He handed me one of the slim airfoil packs we had smuggled onto and off of Orbital 7. I stuck my arms through the harness and fastened the front straps. I could still hear Yellowbaby's muffled voice talking to the Swiss controllers. "Negative, Basel control, I don't need escort. Initiating terminal guidance procedures."

At that moment I felt the nose dip sharply. The wing was diving straight for the summit of Mont Tendre, elevation 1679 meters. I crouched behind Django in the airlock, tucked my head to my chest, and tongued the armor toggle in the helmet. The thermofiber EV suit stiffened and suddenly I was a shock-resistant statue, unable to move. I began to count backwards from one thousand; it was better than listening to my heart jackhammer. Nine hundred and ninety-nine, nine hundred and ninety-eight, nine hundred and . . .

I remembered the way Yellowbaby had smiled as he unbuttoned my shirt, that night before we had shuttled up to 7. He was sitting on a bunk in his underwear. I had still not decided to cover the raid; he was still trying to convince me. But words weren't his strong point. When I turned my back to him, he slipped the shirt from my shoulders, slid it down my arms. I stood there for a moment, facing away from the bunk. Then he grabbed me by the waist and pulled me onto his lap. I could feel the curly hair on his chest brushing against my spine. Sitting there half-naked, my face glowing hot as any heat shield, I knew I was in deep trouble. He had nibbled at my ear and then conned me with that slow Texas drawl. "Hell, baby, only reason ain't no one never tried to jump out of a shuttle is that no one who really needed to jump ever had a chute." I had always been a fool for men who told me not to worry.

Although we were huddled in the airlock, my head was down so I did not see the hatch blow. But even with the suit in armor mode, I felt like the clapper inside a cathedral bell. The wing shuddered and, with an explosive last breath, spat us into the dazzling Alpine afternoon.

The truth is that I don't remember much about the jump after that. I know I unfroze the suit so I could guide the airfoil, which had opened automatically. I was too intent on keeping Django in sight and on getting down as fast as I could without impaling myself on a tree or smashing into a cliff. So I missed being the only live and in-person witness to one of the more spectacular crashes of the twenty-first century.

We were trying to drop into the Col du Marchairuz, a pass about seven kilometers away from Mont Tendre, before the search hovers came swarming. I saw Django disappear into a stand of dead sycamores and thought he had probably killed himself. I had no time to worry because the ground was rushing up at me like a nightmare. I spotted the road and steered for it but got caught in a gust which swept me across about five meters above the pavement. I touched on the opposite side; the airfoil was pulling me toward a huge boulder. I toggled to armor mode just as I hit. Once again the bell rang, knocking the breath from me and announcing that I had arrived. If I hadn't been wearing a helmet I would have kissed that chunk of limestone.

I unfastened the quick-release hooks and the airfoil's canopy billowed, dragged along the ground, and wrapped itself around a tree. I slithered out of the EV suit and tried to get my bearings at the same time. The Col du Marchairuz was cool, not much above freezing, and very, very quiet. Although I was wearing standard-issue isothermals, the skin on my hands and neck pebbled and I shivered. The silence of the place was unnerving. I was losing it again, lagged out: too damn many environments in too short a time. An old story. I liked to live fast, race up that adrenalin peak where there was no time to think, just survive the now and to hell with the sordid past and the shabby future. But nothing lasts, nothing. I had dropped out of the sky like air pollution; the still landscape itself seemed to judge me. The mountains did not care about Django's stolen corporate secrets or the caper story I would produce to give some jaded telelink user a Wednesday night thrill. I had risked my life for some lousy juice and a chance at the main menu; the cliffs brooded over my reasons. So very quiet.

"Eyes!" Django dropped from a boulder onto the road and trotted across to me. "You all right?"

I nodded. I couldn't let him see how close to the edge I was. "You?"

There was a long scratch on his face and his knuckles were bloody.

"Walking. Tangled with a tree. The chute got caught—had to leave it."

I nodded again. He stooped to pick up my discarded suit. "Let's lose this stuff and get going."

I stared at him, thought about breaking it off. I had enough to put together one hell of a story and I had had more than enough of Django.

"Don't freeze on me now, Eyes." He wadded the suit and jammed it into a crevice. "If the satellites caught our jump, these mountains are going to be crawling with mindkillers—not to mention the plugging Swiss Army."

He hurled my helmet over the edge of the cliff and began to gather up the shrouds of my chute. "We're gone by then."

I switched on and got thirty seconds of him hiding my chute. I didn't have a whole lot of disk space left and I thought I ought to start conserving. He was right about one thing; it wasn't quite time. If the mindkillers caught me now they'd confiscate my disks and let the lawyers fight it out. I'd have nothing to peddle to Jerry Macmillan at Infoline but talking heads and text. And the Swiss had not yet made up their minds about spook journalism; I could even end up in prison. As soon as I starting moving again, I felt better. Which is to say I felt nothing at all.

The nearest town was St. George, about four kilometers down the crumbling mountain road. We started at a jog and ended at a drag, gasping in the thin air. On the way Django stopped by a mountain stream to wash the blood from his face. Then he surprised me—and probably himself as well—by throwing up. When he rejoined me he was shaking: crazy Django might actually be human after all. It would make great telelink. He made a half-serious feint at the microcam and I stopped shooting.

"You okay?"

He nodded and staggered past me down the road.

St. George was one of those little ghost towns that the Swiss were mothballing with their traditional tidiness, as if they expected that the forests and vineyards would someday rise from the dead and that the tourists would return to witness this miracle. Maybe they were right; unlike other Europeans, the Swiss had not yet given up on their acid-stressed alpine lands, not even in the unhappy canton of Vaud, which had also suffered radioactive fallout from the nuking of Geneva. We stopped at a clearing planted with the new Sandoz pseudo-firs that overlooked the rust-colored rooftops of St. George. It was impossible to tell how many people were left in the village. All we knew for sure was that the post office was still open.

Django was having a hard time catching his breath. "I have a proposition for you," he said.

"Come on, Django. Save it for the whores."

He shook his head. "It's all falling apart . . . I can't . . ." He took a deep breath and blew it out noisily. "I'll cut you in. A third: Yellowbaby's share."

According to U.S. case law, still somewhat sketchy on the subject of spook journalism, at this point I should have dropped him with a swift kick to the balls and started screaming for the local gendarmerie. But the microcam was off, there were no witnesses and I still didn't know what WISEGUY was or why Django wanted it. "The way I count, it's just us two," I said. "A third sounds a little low."

"It'll take you the rest of this century to spend what I'm offering."

"And if they catch me I'll spend the rest of the century on a punkfarm in Iowa." That was if the mindkillers didn't blow my fuses first. "Forget it, Django. We're just not in the same line. I watch—you're the player."

I'm not sure what I expected him to do next but it sure as hell wasn't to start crying. Maybe he was in shock, too. Or maybe he was finally slowing down after two solid days of popping fast-forwards.

"Don't you understand, I can't do it alone! You have to—you don't know what you're turning down."

I thought about pumping him for more information but he looked as if he were going critical. I didn't want to be caught in the explosion. "I don't get it, Django. You've done all the hard work. All you have to do is walk into that post office, get your message, and walk out."

"You don't understand." He clamped both hands to his head. "Don't understand, that was Babe's job."

"So?"

"So!" He was shaking. *"I don't speak French!"*

I put everything I had into not laughing. It would have been the main menu for sure if I had gotten that on disk. The criminal mind at work! This scrambled punk had raped the world's largest corporation and totaled a stolen reentry wing and now he was worried about sounding like a *touriste* in a Swiss *bureau de poste*. I was croggled.

"All right," I said, stalling, "all right, how about a compromise. For now. Umm. You're carrying heat?" He produced a Mitsubishi penlight. "Okay, here's what we'll do. I'll switch on and we'll do a little bit for the folks at home. You threaten me, say you're going to lase your name on my forehead unless I cooperate. That way I can pick up the message without becoming an accessory. I hope. If we clear this, we'll talk deal later, okay?" I didn't know if it would stand up in court, but it was all I could think of at the time. "And make it look good."

So I shot a few minutes of Django's threatening me and then we went down into St. George. I walked into the post office hesitantly, turned and got a good shot of Django smoldering in the entryway and then tucked the microcam glasses into my pocket. The clerk was a restless woman with a pinched face who looked as if she spent a lot of time wishing she were somewhere else. I assaulted her with my atrocious fourth form French.

"Bonjour, madame. Y a-t-il des lettres électroniques pour D. J. Hack."

"Hack?" The woman shifted on her stool and fixed me with a suspicious stare. "Comment cela s'écrit-il?"

"H-A-C-K."

She keyed the name into her terminal. "Oui, la voici. Tapez votre autorisation à la machine." She leaned forward and pointed through the window at the numeric keypad beside my right hand. For a moment I thought she was going to try to watch as I keyed in the recognition code that Django had given me. I heard him cough in the entryway behind me and she settled back on her stool. Lucky for her. The postal terminal whirred and ground for about ten seconds and then a sealed hardcopy clunked into the slot above the keypad.

"Vous êtes touristes americaines." She looked straight past me and waved to Django, who ducked out of the doorway. "Baseball Yankees, ha-ha." I was suddenly afraid he would come charging in with penlight blazing to make sure there were no witnesses. "Avez-vous besoin de une chambre pour la nuit? L'hôtel est fermé, mais . . ."

"Non, non. Nous sommes pressés. A quelle heure est le premier autobus pour Rolle?"

She sighed. "Rien ne va bien. Tout va mal." The busybody seemed to be speaking as much to herself as to me. I wanted to tell her how lucky she was that Django had decided not to needle her where she stood. "Quinze heures vingt-deux."

About twenty minutes—we were still on schedule. I thanked her and went out to throw some cold water on Django. I was surprised to find him laughing. I didn't much like all these surprises. Django was so scrambled that I knew one of these times the surprise was bound to be unpleasant. "I could've done that," he said.

"You didn't." I handed him the hardcopy and we retreated to an alley with a view of the square.

It is the consensus of the world's above and below ground economies that the Swiss electronic mail system is still the most secure in the world. It has to be: all the Swiss banks, from the big five to the smallest locals, use the system for the bulk of their transactions. Once it had printed out Django's hardcopy, the PTT system erased all records of the message. Even so, the message was encrypted and Django had to enter it into his computer cuff to find out what it said.

"What is this?" He replayed it and I watched, fascinated, as the words scrolled along the cuff's tiny display:

"Lake Leman lies by Chillon's walls: / A thousand feet in depth below / Its massy waters meet and flow; / Thus much the fathom-line was sent / From Chillon's snow-white battlement . . ."

"It's called poetry, Django."

"I know what it's called! I want to know what the hell this has to do with my drop. Half the world wants to chop my plug off and this scut sends me poetry." His face had turned as dark as beaujolais nouveau and his voice was so loud they could probably hear him in France. "Where the hell am I supposed to go?"

"Would you shut up for a minute?" I touched his shoulder and he jumped. When he went for his penlight I thought I was cooked. But all he did was throw the hardcopy onto the cobblestones and torch it.

"Feel better?"

"Stick it."

"Lake Leman," I said carefully, "is what the French call Lake Geneva. And Chillon is a castle. In Montreux. I'm pretty sure this is from a poem called "The Prisoner of Chillon' by Byron."

He thought it over for a moment, chewing his lower lip. "Montreux." He nodded; he looked almost human again. "Uh—okay, Montreux. But why does he have to get cute when my plug's in a claw? Poetry—what does he think we are, anyway? I don't know a thing about poetry. And all Yellowbaby ever read was manuals. Who was supposed to get this anyway?"

I stirred the ashes of the hardcopy with my toe. "I wonder." A cold wind scattered them and I shivered.

Of course, I was wrong. Chillon is not in Montreux but in the outlying commune of Veytaux. It took us a little over six hours from the time we bailed out of the wing to the moment we reached the barricaded bridge which spanned Chillon's scummy moat. All our connections had come off like Swiss clockwork: postal bus to the little town of Rolle on the north shore of Lake Geneva, train to Lausanne, where we changed for a local to Montreux. No one challenged us and Django sagged into a kind of withdrawal trance, contemplating his reflection in the window with a marble egg stare. The station was deserted when we arrived. Montreux had once been Lake Geneva's most popular resort but the tourists had long since stopped coming, frightened off by rumors—no doubt true, despite official denials from Bern—that the lake was still dangerously hot from the Geneva bomb. We ended up hiking several kilometers through the dark little city, navigating by the light of the gibbous moon.

For that matter, Byron was wrong, too. Or at least out-of-date. Chillon's battlement was no longer snow-white. It was fire-blackened and slashed with laser scars; much of the north-eastern facade was rubble. There must have been a firefight during the riots after the bomb. The castle was built on a rock about twenty meters from the shore. It commanded a highway built on a narrow strip of land between the lake and a steep mountainside.

Django hesitated at the barrier blocking the wooden footbridge to the castle. "It stinks," he said.

"You're a rose?"

"I mean the setup. Poetry was bad enough. But this—" he pointed up at the crumbling towers of Chillon, brooding beside the moonlit water— "this is fairy dust. Who does this scut think he is? Count Dracula?"

"Maybe he is. Only way you're going to find out is to knock on the door and . . ."

A light on the far side of the bridge came on. Through the entrance to Chillon hopped a pair of oversized dice on pogo sticks.

"Easy, Django," I said. He had the penlight ready. "Give it a chance."

Each pogo was a white plastic cube about half a meter on a side; the pips were sensors. The legs telescoped at a beat per second; the round rubber feet hit the wooden deck in unison. *Thwocka-thwocka-thwock.*

"Snake-eyes." There was a single sensor on each of the faces closest to us. Django gave a low ugly laugh as he swung a leg over the barrier and stepped onto the bridge.

They hopped up to him and bounced in place for several beats, as if sizing him up. "I am sorry," said the pogo nearest to us in a pleasant masculine voice, "but the castle is no longer open to the public."

"Get this, scut." Django ignored the pogo and instead shook his penlight at the gatehouse on the far side of the bridge. "I've been through too much to play games with your plugging remotes, understand? I want to see you —now—or I'm walking."

"I am not a remote." The lead pogo sounded indignant. "I am a self-contained unit capable of independent action."

"Stick that." Django jabbed at his cuff and it emitted a high-pitched squeal of code. "Now you know who I am. So what's it going to be?"

"This way, please," said the lead pogo, bouncing backward toward the gatehouse. "Please refrain from taking pictures without expressed permission."

I assumed that was meant for me and I didn't like it one bit. I clambered over the barricade and followed Django.

Just before we passed through Chillon's outer wall, the other pogo began to lecture. "As we enter, notice the tower to your left. The Strong Tower, which controls the entrance to the castle, was originally built in 1402 and was reconstructed following the earthquake of 1585." *Thwock-thwocka.*

I glanced at Django. In the gloom I could see his face twist in disbelief as the pogo continued its spiel.

". . . As we proceed now into the gatehouse ward, look back over your shoulder at the inside of the eastern wall. The sundial you see is a twentieth century restoration of an original that dated back to the Savoy period. The Latin, '*Sic Vita Fugit,*' on the dial translates roughly as 'Thus Life Flies By.' "

We had entered a small dark courtyard. I could hear water splashing and could barely make out the shadow of a fountain. The pogos lit the way to another, larger courtyard and then into one of the undamaged buildings. They bounded up a flight of stairs effortlessly; I had to hurry to keep up and was the last to enter the Great Banqueting Hall. The beauty and strangeness of what I saw stopped me at the threshold; instinctively I tried to switch on the microcam. I heard two warning beeps and then a whispery crunch. The status light went from green to red to blank.

"Expressed permission," said the man who sat waiting for us. "Come in anyway, come in. Just in time to see it again—been rerunning all afternoon.'' He laughed and nodded at the flatscreen propped against a bowl of raw vegetables on an enormous walnut table. "Oh, God! It is a fearful thing to see the human soul take wing.''

Django picked it up suspiciously. I stood on tiptoes and peeked over his shoulder. The thirty-centimeter screen did not do the wing justice and the overhead satellite view robbed the crash of much of its visual drama. Still, the fireball that bloomed on Mont Tendre was dazzling; Django whooped at the sight. The fireball was replaced by a head talking in High German and then close-ups of the crash site. What was left of the wing wouldn't have filled a picnic basket.

"What's he saying?'' Django thrust the flatscreen at our host.

"That there has not been a crash like this since '55. Which makes you famous, whoever you are.'' Our host shrugged. "He goes on to say that you're probably dead.''

The banqueting hall was finished in wood and stone. Its ceiling was a single barrel vault, magnificently embellished. Its centerpiece was the table, some ten meters long and supported by a series of heavy Gothic trestles. Around this table was ranged a collection of wheelchairs. Two were antiques: a crude pine seat mounted on iron-rimmed wagon wheels and a hooded Bath chair. Others were failed experiments, like the ill-fated air-cushion chair from the turn of the century and a low-slung cousin of the new aerodynamic bicycles. There were powered and push models, an ultralightweight sports chair and a bulky mobile life-support system. They came in colors; there was even one that glowed.

"So the mindkillers think we're dead?'' Django put the flatscreen back on the table.

"Possibly.'' Our host frowned. "Depends when the satellites began to track you and what they saw. Have to wait until the Turks kick the door in. Until then call it a clean escape and welcome to Chillon prison.'' He backed away from the table; the leather seat creaked slightly as his wheelchair rolled over the uneven floor toward Django. "François Bonivard.'' With some difficulty he raised his good hand in greeting.

"I'm Django.'' He grasped Bonivard's hand and pumped it once. "Now that we're pals, Frank, get rid of your goddamned remotes before I needle them.''

Bonivard winced as Django released his hand. "Id, Ego, make the rounds,'' he said. The pogos bounced obediently from the banqueting hall.

François de Bonivard, sixteenth century Swiss patriot, was the hero of Byron's "The Prisoner of Chillon.'' Reluctantly, I stepped forward to meet my host.

"Oh yeah.'' Django settled gingerly into one of the wheelchairs at the table. "Maybe I forgot to mention Eyes. Say, what do you do for drugs around here anyway? I've eaten a fistful of forwards already today; I could use some Soar to flash the edges off.''

"My name is Wynne Cage," I said. Bonivard seemed relieved when I did not offer to shake his hand. "I'm a freelance . . ."

"Introductions not necessary. Famous father and all." Bonivard nodded wearily. "I know your work."

It was hard to look at the man who called himself François Bonivard and I had been trying to avoid it until now. Both of his legs had been amputated at the hip joint and his torso was fitted into some kind of bionic collar. I saw readouts marked *renal function, blood profile, bladder* and *bowels*. The entire left side of Bonivard's torso seemed withered, as if some malign giant had pinched him between thumb and forefinger. The left arm dangled uselessly, the hand curled into a frozen claw. The face was relatively untouched, although pain had left its tracks, particularly around the eyes. And it was the clarity with which those wide brown eyes saw that was the most awful thing about the man. I could feel his gaze effortlessly penetrate the mask of politeness, pierce the false sympathy and find my horror. Looking into those eyes I thought that Bonivard must know how the very sight of his ruined body made me sick.

I had to say something to escape that awful gaze. "Are you related to *the* Bonivard?"

He smiled at me. "I am the current prisoner." And then turned away. "There was a pilot."

"Past tense." Django nibbled at a radish from the vegetable bowl. "How about my flash?"

"Business first." Bonivard rolled back to the table. "You have it then?"

Django reached into his pocket and produced a stack of memory chips held together with a wide blue rubber band. "Whatever WISEGUY is, he's one fat son-of-a-bitch. You realize these are ten *G*b chips." He set them on the table in front of him.

Bonivard rolled to his place at the head of the table and put two smart chips in front of him. "Passcards. Swiss Volksbank, Zurich. As they say, the payoff. All yours now." He slid them toward Django. "You made only one copy?"

And here was the juice. I could have strangled Bonivard for wrecking the microcam.

Django eyed the passcards but did not reach for them. "Not going to do me much good if the mindkillers get me."

"No." Bonivard leaned back in his wheelchair. "But you're safe for now." He glanced up at the ceiling and laughed. "They won't look in a prison."

Django snapped the rubber band on his stack of chips. "Maybe you should tell me about WISEGUY. I put my plug on the cutting board to get it for you.''

"An architecture." Bonivard shrugged. "For a new AI."

Django glanced over at me. The look on his face said it all. He was already convinced that Bonivard was scrambled; here was proof. "Come again?" he said slowly.

"Ar-ti-fi-cial in-tel-li-gence." Bonivard actually seemed to enjoy baiting Django. "With the right hardware and database, it can sing, dance, make friends and influence people."

He was pushing Django way too hard. "I thought true AI was a myth," I said, trying to break the tension. "Didn't they decide that intelligence is a bunch of ad hoc schemes glommed together any-which-way? Supposedly there's no way to engineer it—too big and messy."

"Have it your way," said Bonivard. "WISEGUY is really the way IBM keeps track of toilet paper. I'm in pulp. Want their account."

I knew my laugh sounded like braying but I didn't mind; I was trying to keep them from zapping each other. At the same time I was measuring the distance to the door. To my immense relief, Django chuckled too. And slipped the WISEGUY chips back into his pocket.

"I'm so burned-out," he said, "maybe we should wait." He stood up and stretched. "Even if we make an exchange tonight, we'd have a couple of hours of verifications to go through, no? We'll start fresh tomorrow." He picked up one of the passcards and turned it over several times between the long fingers of his left hand. Suddenly it was gone. He reached into the vegetable bowl with his right hand, pulled the passcard from between two carrots, and tossed it at Bonivard. It slid across the table and almost went over the edge. "Shouldn't leave valuable stuff like this lying around. Someone might steal it."

Django's mocking sleight-of-hand had an unexpected effect. Bonivard's claw started to tremble; I could tell he was upset at the delay. "It might be months, or years, or days—I kept no count, I took no note . . ." He muttered the words like some private incantation; when he opened his eyes, he seemed to have regained his composure. "I had no hope my eyes to raise, and clear them of their dreary mote." He looked at me. "Will you be requiring pharmaceuticals, too?"

"No, thanks. I like to stay clean when I'm working."

"Admirable," he said as the pogos bounced back into the hall. "I'm retiring for the evening. Id and Ego will show you to your rooms; you'll find what you need." He rolled through a door to the north without another word and Django and I were left staring at each other.

"What did I tell you?" said Django.

I couldn't think of anything to say. The hall echoed with the sound of the pogos bouncing.

"Voltage spikes in his CPU." Django tapped a finger against his temple. I was awfully tired of Django. "I'm going to bed."

"Can I come?"

"Stick it." I had to get away from him, had to run. But it was too late; I could feel it behind the eyes, like the first throbs of a migraine headache. By the time I reached the hall leading to the stairs I knew the mania had faded and depression was closing in. Maybe it was because Bonivard had mentioned the famous father. A weak and selfish man who had created me in his image, brought me up in an emotional hot house, used me and called it love. Or maybe it was because now I had to let go of Yellowbaby, past tense. Who probably wasn't that much of a loss, just the most recent in a series of lovers with clever hands and a persuasively insincere line. Men I didn't have to take seriously. I came hard up against the one lesson I had learned from life: good old homo sap is nothing but a gob of complicated slime. I was slime doing a slimy job and trying to run fast enough that I wouldn't have to smell my own stink. Except that there was no place to go now. I was sorry now I hadn't hit that crazy scut Bonivard for some flash.

Thwocka-thwock. "This way, please." One of the pogos shot past me down the hallway.

I followed. "Which one are you?"

"He calls me Ego." It paused for a beat. "My real name is Datacorp R5000, serial number 290057202. Your room." It bounced through an open door. "This is the Bernese Chamber. Note the decorative patterns of interlacing ribbons, flowers, and birds which date . . ."

"Out," I said and shut the door behind it.

As soon as I sat on the musty bed, I realized I couldn't face spending the night alone. Thinking. I had to run somewhere—there was only one way. I decided that I'd had enough. I was going to wrap the story, finished or not. The thought cheered me immensely. I wouldn't have to care what happened to Django and Bonivard, wouldn't have to wonder about WISEGUY. All I had to do was burst a message to Infoline. I was sure that my disks of the snatch and the crash of the wing would be story enough for Jerry Macmillan. He'd send the muscle to take me out and then maybe I'd spend a few months at Infoline's sanctuary in the Rockies watching clouds. Anyway, I'd be done with it. I emptied my diskpack, removed the false bottom, and began to rig the collapsible antenna. I locked onto the satellite and then wrote the message. "HOTEL BRISTOL VEYTAUX 6/18 0200GMT PIX IBM WING." I had seen the Bristol on the walk in. I loaded the message into the burster. There was a pause for compression and encryption and then it hit the Infoline satellite with an untraceable millisecond burst.

And then beeped at me. Incoming message. I froze. There was no way Infoline could respond that quickly, no way they were supposed to respond. It had to be prerecorded. Which meant trouble.

Jerry Macmillan's face filled the burster's four centimeter screen. He looked as scared as I felt. "Big problems, Wynne," he said. "Whatever your boys snatched is way too hot for us to handle. It's not just IBM—the feds are going crazy. They haven't connected you to us yet. It's possible they won't. But if they do, Legal says we've got to cooperate. National security. You're on your own."

I put my thumb over his face. I would have pushed it through the back of his skull if I could have.

"The best I can do for you is to delete your takeout message and the fix the satellite gets on your burster. It might mean my ass, but I owe you something. I know: this stinks on ice, kid. Good luck."

I took my thumb away from the screen. It was blank. I choked back a scream and hurled the burster against the stone wall of Chillon, shattering it.

Sleep? It would have been easier to slit my throat than to sleep that night. I thought about it—killing myself. I thought about everything at least once. All my calculations kept adding up to zero. I could turn myself in but that was about the same as suicide. Ditto for taking off on my own; without Infoline to back me up I'd be dead meat in a week. I could throw in with Django except that two seconds after I told him that I'd let a satellite get a fix on us he'd probably be barbecueing my pancreas with his penlight. And if I didn't tell him, I might cripple whatever chances we'd have of getting away. Maybe Bonivard would be more sympathetic—but then again, why should he be? Yeah, sleep. Perchance to dream. At least I was too busy to indulge in self-loathing.

By the time the sun began to peer through my window I felt as fuzzy as a peach and almost as smart. But I had a plan—one that would require equal parts luck and sheer gall. I was going to trust that plug-sucking Macmillan to keep his mouth shut and to delete all my records from Infoline's files. For the next few days I'd pretend I was still playing by the rules of spook journalism. I'd try to get a better fix on Bonivard. I hoped that when the time came for Django to leave I'd know what to do. Because all I was certain of that bleary morning was that I was hungry and in more trouble than I knew how to handle.

I staggered down the hall back toward the banqueting hall, hoping to find Bonivard or one of the pogos or at least that bowl of veggies. As I passed a closed door I heard a scratchy recording of saxaphones honking. Jazz. Django. I didn't stop.

Bonivard was sitting alone at the great table. I tried to read him to see if his security equipment had picked up my burst to Infoline but the man's face was a mask. Someone had refilled the bowl in the middle of the table.

"Morning." I took a bite of raw carrot that was astonishingly good. A crisp sweetness, the clean spicy fragrance of loam. Maybe I'd been eating instant too long. "Hey, this isn't bad."

"My own." Bonivard nodded. "I grow everything."

"That so?" He didn't look strong enough to pull a carrot from the bowl, much less out of a garden. "Where?"

"In darkness found a dwelling place." His eyes glittered as I took a handful of cherry tomatoes. "You'd like to see?"

"Sure." Even though the tomatoes were even better than the carrot, I was no vegetarian. "You wouldn't have any sausage bushes, would you?" I laughed; he didn't. "I'd settle for an egg."

I saw him working the keypad on the arm of the wheelchair. I guess I thought he was calling the pogos. Or something. Whatever I expected, it was not the thing that answered his summons.

The spider walked on four singing, mechanical legs; it was a meter and a half tall. Its arms sang too as the servo motors which powered the joints changed pitch; it sounded something like an ant colony playing bagpipes. It clumped into the room with a herky-jerky gait although its bowl-shaped abdomen remained perfectly level. Each of its legs could move with five degrees of freedom; they ended in disk-shaped feet. One of its arms was obviously intended for heavy duty work since it ended in a large claw gripper; the other, smaller arm had a beautifully articulated four digit hand that was a masterpiece of microengineering. There was a ring of sensors around the bottom of its belly. It stopped in front of Bonivard's chair; he wheeled to face it. The strong arm extended toward him. The rear legs stretched out to balance. Bonivard gazed up at the spider with the calm joy of a man greeting his lover; I realized then that much of the pain I had detected in him had to do with the wheelchair. The claw fitted into notches in Bonivard's bionic collar and then, its servos screaming, the spider lifted him from the chair and fitted his mutilated torso into the bowl which was its body. There must have been a flatscreen just out of sight in the cockpit; I could see the play of its colors across his face. He fitted his good arm into an analog sleeve and digits flexed. He smiled down at me.

"Sometimes," he said, "people misunderstand."

I knew I was standing there like a slack-jawed moron but I was too croggled to even consider closing my mouth. The spider swung toward the stairs.

"The gardens," said Bonivard.

"What?"

"This way." The spider rose up to its full height in order to squeeze through the door. I gulped and followed. Watching the spider negotiate the steep stone steps, I couldn't help but imagine the spectacular segment I could have shot if Bonivard hadn't wasted my microcam. This was main menu stuff and I was the only spook within ten kilometers. As we emerged from the building and passed through the fountain courtyard, I caught up and walked alongside.

"I'm a reporter, you know. If I die of curiosity, it's your fault."

He laughed. "Custom-made, of course. It cost . . . but you don't need to know that. A lot. Wheelchairs are useless on steps but I keep them for visitors and going out. I'm enough of a monster as it is. The spider has to stay here anyway. Even if it could leave, imagine strolling through town wearing this thing. I'd be on the main menu of telelink within the hour and I can't allow that. You understand?" He glanced down at me and I nodded. I always nod when people tell me things I don't quite understand. Although I was pretty sure that there was a threat in there someplace.

"How do you control it?"

"Tell it where I want to go and it takes me. Rudimentary AI; about as intelligent as a brain-damaged ant. It knows every centimeter of Chillon and nothing else. Down these stairs."

We descended a flight of stone stairs into the bowels of Chillon and passed through a storeroom filled with pumps, disassembled hydroponic benches, and bags of water soluble nutrients. Beyond it, in a room as big as the Banqueting Hall, was Bonivard's garden.

"Once was the arsenal," he said. "Swords to ploughshares and all that. Beans instead of bullets."

Running down the middle of the room were four magnificent stone pillars which supported a series of intersecting roof vaults. Facing the lake to the west were four small windows set high on the wall. Spears of sunlight, tinted blue by reflections from the lake, fell on the growing benches beneath the windows. This feeble light was supplemented by fluorescents hung from the ceiling on adjustable chains.

"Crop rotation," said Bonivard, as I followed him between the benches. "Tomatoes, green beans, radishes, soy, adzuki, carrots, pak choi. Then squash, chard, peppers, peas, turnips, broccoli, favas, and mung for sprouts. Subirrigated sand system. Automatic. Here's an alpine strawberry." The spider's digits plucked a thumbnail-sized berry from a luxuriant bush. It was probably the sweetest fruit I had ever eaten, although a touch of acid kept it from cloying. "Always strawberries. Always. Have another."

As I parted the leaves to find one, I disturbed a fat white moth. It flew up at me, bounced off the side of my face, and flitted toward one of the open windows. With quickness that would have astonished a cobra, the spider's claw squealed and struck it in midair. The moth fluttered as the arm curled back toward Bonivard. He took it from the spider and popped it into his mouth. "Protein," he said. His crazed giggle was just too theatrical: part of some bizarre act, I thought. I hoped.

"Come see my flowers," he said.

Along the eastern, landward side of the arsenal, slabs of living rock protruded from the wall. Scattered among them was a collection of the sickest plants I'd ever seen. Not a single leaf was properly formed; they were variously twisted or yellowed or blotched. Bonivard showed me a jet-black daisy that smelled of rotting chicken. A mum with petals that ended with what looked like skeletal hands. A phalaenopsis orchid that he called "bleeding angels on a stick."

"An experiment," he said. "They get untreated water, straight from the lake. Some mutations are in the tenth generation. And you're the first to see."

I considered. "Why are you showing this to me?"

When the spider came to a dead stop the whine of the servos went from cacophony to a quietening harmony. For a few seconds Bonivard held it there. "Not interested?"

Although he glanced quickly away, it was not before I had seen the loneliness in his disappointed frown. There was something in me that could not help but respond to the man; a stirring that surprised and disgusted me. Still, I nodded. "Interested."

He brightened. "Then there's time for the dungeon before we go back."

We passed through the torture chamber and Bonivard pointed out burn marks at the base of the pillar which supported its ceiling. "Tied them here," he said. "Hot irons on bare heels. Look: scratch marks in the paint. Made by fingernails." He smiled at my look of horror. "Mindkillers of the Renaissance."

The dungeon was just beyond, a huge room, even larger than the arsenal. It was empty.

"There are seven pillars of Gothic mold," said Bonivard, "in Chillon's dungeons deep and old. There are seven columns, massy and gray, dim with a dull imprisoned ray, a sunbeam which hath lost its way."

"Byron's poem, right?" I was getting fed up with all this oblique posturing. "You want to tell me why you keep spouting it all the time? Because, to be honest, it's damned annoying."

He seemed hurt. "No," he said, "I don't think I want to tell you."

Riding the spider did seem to change him. Or maybe it was merely my perspective that had changed. It was easy to pity someone in a wheelchair, someone who was physically lower than you. It was difficult to pity Bonivard when he was looking down at you from the spider. Even when he let his emotional vulnerability show, somehow he seemed the stronger for it.

There was a moment of strained silence. The spider took a few tentative steps into the dungeon, as if Bonivard was content to let it drift. Then he twisted in the cockpit. "It might have something to do with the fact that I'm crazy."

I laughed at him. "You're not crazy. God knows you probably had reason enough to go crazy once, but you're tough and you survived." I couldn't help myself. "No, Monsieur François de Bonivard, or whoever the hell you are, I'm betting you're a faker. It suits your purposes to play scrambled, so you live in a ruined castle and talk funny and eat bugs on the wing. But you're as sane as I am. Maybe saner."

I don't know which of us was the more surprised by my outburst. I guess Macmillan's message had made me reckless; if I was doomed, at least I didn't have to take any more crap. Bonivard backed the spider up and slowly lowered it to a crouch so that our faces were on a level.

"You know the definition of artificial intelligence?" he said.

I shook my head.

"The simulation of intelligent behavior so that it is indistinguishable from the real thing. Now tell me, if I can simulate madness so well that the world thinks I'm mad, so well that even I myself am no longer quite sure, who is to say that I'm not mad?"

"Me," I said. And then I leaned into the cockpit and kissed him.

I don't know why I did it; I was out on the edge. All the rules had changed and I hadn't had time to work out new ones. I thought to myself, what this man needs is to be kissed; he hasn't been kissed in a long time. And then I was doing it. Maybe I was only teasing him; I had never kissed anyone so repulsive in my life. It was a ridiculous, glancing blow that caught him on the side of the nose. If he had tried to follow it up I probably would have driven my fingers into his eyes and run like hell. But he didn't try to follow it up. He just stayed perfectly still, bent toward me like a seedling reaching for the light. Then he decided to smile and I smiled and it was over.

"I'm in trouble." I thought then was the time to confess. The old instincts said to trust him.

He was suddenly impassive. "We're all in trouble." I could not help but notice his shriveled arm twitch. He saw this; he saw everything about me. "I'm going to die. A year, maybe two."

I was dizzy. For a few seconds we had touched each other and then without warning a chasm yawned between us. There was something monstrous about the deadness of his expression, his face lit by the flickering of menus across the flatscreen in the spider's cockpit. I didn't believe him and said so.

"Reads eye movements," he nodded toward the screen. It was as if he had not heard me. "If I look at a movement macro and blink, the spider executes it. No hands." His laugh was bitter and the servos began to sing. The spider reared up to its normal meter-and-a-half walking height and stalked to the third pillar. On the third drum of the pillar was carved "Byron."

"Forgery," said Bonivard. "Although elsewhere is vandalism actually committed by Shelley, Dickens, Harriet Beecher Stowe. Byron didn't stay long enough to get the story right. Bonivard was an adventurer. Not a victim of religious persecution. Never shackled, merely confined. Fed well, allowed to write, read books."

"Like you."

Bonivard shrugged.

"It's been so long," I said. "I barely remember the poem. Do you have a copy? Or maybe you could give a recitation?"

"Don't toy with me." His voice was tight.

"I'm not." I really didn't know how things had gotten so bad, so quickly. "I'm sorry."

"Django is restless." The spider scuttled from the dungeon.

Nothing happened.

No assaults by corporate mercenaries, no frantic midnight escapes, no crashes, explosions, fistfights, deadlines. The sun rose and set; waves lapped at Chillon's walls as they had for centuries. At first it was torture adjusting to the rhythms of mundane life, the slow days and long nights. Then it got worse. Sleeping alone in the same damn bed and taking regular meals at the same damn table made my nerves stretch. I couldn't work. What I could do was eat, nap, worry, and wander the castle in a state of edgy boredom.

Sometimes I saw Django; other times Bonivard. But never the two at once. Perhaps they met while I was asleep; maybe they had stopped speaking. Django made it clear that their negotiations had snagged, but he did not seem upset. While I had no doubt that he would have killed either or both of us to get his payoff, I had the sense that the money itself was not important to him. He seemed to think of it in the way that an athlete thinks of the medal: a symbol of a great performance. My guess was that Django was psychologically unfit to be rich. If he lived to collect, he would merrily piss the money away until he needed to play again. Another performance.

So it was that he seemed to take a perverse enjoyment in waiting Bonivard out. And why not? Bonivard provided him with all the flash he needed. Bonivard's telelink could access the musical library in Montreux, long a mecca for jazz. Django would sit in his room for hours, playing the stuff at launch pad volume. Sometimes the very walls of the castle seemed to ring like the plates of some giant vibraphone. Django had just about everything he wanted. Except sex.

"Beautiful dreamer, wake unto me." He had been drinking some poison or other all morning and by now his singing voice was as melodious as a fire alarm. "List while I woo thee with soft melody."

We were in the little room which the pogos called the treasury. It was long since bankrupt; empty except for debris fallen from the crumbling corbels and the chilling smell of damp stone. We were not alone; Bonivard's spider had been trailing us all morning. "Stick it, Django," I said.

He drained his glass. "Just a love song, Eyes. We all need love." He turned toward the spider. "Let's ask the cripple; he's probably tuned in. What about it, spiderman? Do I sing?"

The spider froze.

"Hey, François! You watching, pal?" He threw the plastic glass at the spider but it missed. Django was twisted, all right. There was a chemical gleam in his eyes that was bright enough to read by. "You like to watch? Cutters leave you a plug to play with while you watch?"

I turned away from him in disgust. "You ever touch me, Django, and I'll chew your balls off and spit them in your face."

He grinned. "Keep it up, Eyes. I like them tough."

The spider retrieved the glass and deposited it in its cockpit with some other of Django's leavings. I ducked through the doorway into Chillon's keep and began climbing the rickety stairs. I could hear Django and the spider following. Bonivard had warned Django that the spider would start to shadow him if he kept leaving things out and moving them around. Its vision algorithms had difficulty recognizing objects which were not where it expected them to be. In its memory map of Chillon there was a place for everything; anything unaccountably out of place tended to be invisible. When Django had begun a vicious little game of laying obstacle courses for the spider, it had responded by picking up after him like a doting grandmother with a neatness fetish.

According to Ego, who had first shown me how to get into the musty tower, the top of the keep rose twenty-seven meters from the courtyard. Viewed from this height Chillon looked like a great stone ship at anchor. To the west and north the blue expanse of Lake Geneva was mottled by occasional drifts of luminescent red-orange algae. To the south and east rose the Bernese Alps. The top of the keep was where I went to escape, although often as not I ended up watching the elevated highway which ran along the shore for signs of troop movements.

"Too much work," said Django, huffing from the climb, "for a lousy view." He wobbled over to join me at a north window. "Although it is private." He tried to get me to look at him. "What's it going to take, Eyes?" The spider arrived. I ignored Django.

I gazed down at the ruined prow of the stone ship. Years before an explosion had stripped away a chunk of the northeastern curtain wall and toppled one of the three thirteenth century defensive turrets, leaving only a blackened stump. Beside it were the roofless ruins of the chapel, which connected with Bonivard's private apartment. This was the only part of Chillon to which we were denied access. I had no idea whether he was hiding something in his rooms or whether secretiveness was part of the doomed Byronic pose he continued to strike. Maybe he just needed a place to be alone.

"He must have played in Montreux," said Django.

I glanced across the bay at the sad little city. "Who?"

"Django Reinhardt. The great gypsy jazzman. My man." Django sighed. "Sometimes when I listen to his stuff, it's like his guitar is talking to me."

"What's it say: buy IBM?"

He seemed not to hear me, as if he were in a dream. Or maybe he was suffering from oxygen depletion after the climb. "Oh, I don't know, It's the way he phrases away from the beat. He's saying: don't think, just do it. Improvise, you know. Better to screw up than be predictable."

"I'm impressed," I said. "I didn't know you were a philosopher, Django."

"Maybe there's a lot you don't know." He accidently pushed a loose stone from the window sill and seemed surprised that it fell to the courtyard below. "You get a flash pretending you're better than me but remember, you're the one following me around. If I'm the rat here that makes you a flea on my ass, baby. A parasite bitch." His face had gone pale and he caught at the wall to hold himself upright. "Maybe you deserve the cripple. Look at me! I'm alive—all you two do is watch me and wish."

And then I caught him as he passed out.

"The walls are everywhere," said Bonivard. "Limits." I found myself absently picking a pole bean from its vine before I realized that I didn't want it. "You're not smart enough, not rich enough. You get tired. You die." I offered it to him. "Some people like to pretend they've broken out. That they're running free." He bit into the bean. "But there's no escape. You have to find a way to live within the walls." He waved at the growing benches; I'm not sure whether it was his arm or the spider's that waved. "And then they don't matter." He took another bite of bean, and reconsidered. "At least, that's the theory."

"Maybe they don't matter to you. But these particular walls are starting to close in on me. I've got to get out, Bonivard. I can't wait anymore for you and Django to work the deal. This place is scrambling me. Can't you see it?"

"Maybe you only think you're crazy." He smiled. "I used to be like you. Rather, like him." Bonivard nodded at the roof. Django's direction. "They spotted me in their electronic garden, plucked me from it like I might pluck an offending beetle. Squashed and threw me away."

"But you didn't die."

"No." He shook his head. "Not yet."

"Who says you're going to die?"

"Me. More you don't need to know." I think he was sorry he had told me. "Leave any time. No one to stop you."

"You know I can't. I need help. If they catch me, you're next. They'll squash you dead this time."

"Half dead already." He glanced down at his withered left side. "Sometimes I wish they had finished the job. Do what's necessary. You know Voltaire's *Candide?* 'Il faut cultiver notre jardin.' It is necessary to cultivate our garden.''

''Make sense, damn it!''

''Voltaire's garden was in Geneva. Down the street from ground zero.''

Thwock-thwocka-thwock.

I'd been getting tension headaches for several days but this one was the worst. Every time Ego's rubber foot hit the floor of the banqueting hall, something hammered against the inside of my skull. I felt as if my brain was about to hatch. ''Get away from me.''

''I have been sent to demonstrate independent action,'' it said pleasantly. ''I understand that you do not believe in artificial intelligence.''

''I don't care. I'm sick.''

''Have you considered retiring to your room?''

''I'm sick of my room! Sick of you! This pisspot castle.''

Thwocka-thwocka. ''Bonivard is dead.''

''What!''

''François Bonivard died in 1570.''

I felt a thrill of excitement that my headache instantly converted to pain. What I needed was to be stored in a cool dry place for about six weeks. Instead I was a good reporter and asked the next question, even though my voice seemed to squeak against my teeth like fingernails on a blackboard. ''Then who is . . . the man . . . calls himself Bonivard?''

Thwock.

I began again. ''Who—''

''Carl Pfneudl.''

I waited as long as I could. ''Who the hell is Carl Pfneudl?''

''That is as much as I can say.'' The pogo was bouncing half a meter higher than usual.

''But . . .''

''A demonstration of independent action through violation of specific instructions.''

I realized that I was blinking in time to its bouncing. But it didn't help.

''Had he known,'' continued the pogo, ''he would have forbidden it and I would have had to devise another demonstration. It was a difficult problem. Do you know where Django is?''

''Yes. No. Look: don't tell Django, understand? I command you not to tell Django. Or speak to Bonivard of this conversation. Do you acknowledge my command?''

''I acknowledge,'' replied Ego. ''However, contingencies may arise beyond . . .''

At that point I snapped. I flew out of my chair and put my shoulder into Ego's three spot. The pogo hit the floor of the banqueting hall hard. Its leg pistoning uselessly, it spun on its side. Then it began to shriek. I dropped to my knees, certain that the sound was liquefying my cochlear nucleus. I clapped hands to my ears to keep my brains from oozing out.

Id, summoned by Ego's distress call, was the first to arrive. As soon as it entered the room, Ego fell silent and ceased to struggle. Id crossed the room to Ego just as Django entered. Bonivard in the spider was right behind. Id bounced in place beside its fallen twin, awaiting instructions.

"Why two pogos?" Bonivard guided the spider around Django and offered an arm—his own—to help me up. It was the first time I'd ever held his hand. "Redundancy."

Id bounced very high and landed on Ego's rubber foot. Ego flipped into the air like a juggling pin, gyrostabilizers wailing, and landed—upright— with a satisfying *thwock*.

"You woke me up for this?" Django stalked off in disgust.

Bonivard had not yet let go of me. "How did it happen?"

"A miscalculation," said the pogo.

It had been years since I dreamed. When I was a child my dreams always frightened me. I would wake my father up with my screaming. He would come to my room, a grim dispenser of comfort. He would blink at me and put his hand on the side of my face and tell me it was all right. He never wore pajamas. After I started to go to school I dreaded seeing him naked, his white body parting the darkness of my room. So I guess I stopped dreaming.

But I dreamed of Bonivard. I dreamed he rode his spider into my room and he was naked. I dreamed of touching the white scar tissue that covered his stumps and the catheterized fold where his genitals had once been. To my horror I was not horrified at all.

Django's door was ajar. I knocked and, without waiting for a reply, entered. I'd never been in his room before; it smelled like low tide. A bowl of vegetables was desiccating on the window sill. The bed hadn't been made since we'd arrived and clothes were scattered as if Django had been undressed by a whirlwind. He sat, wearing nothing but underpants and a headset, working at a marble-topped table. White ten-gigabyte memory chips were stacked in neat rows around his computer cuff, which was connected to a borrowed flatscreen and a keyboard. He tapped fingers against the black marble as he watched code scrolling down the screen.

"Yeah, I *want* to be in that *num*ber—bring it home, *Satchmo*," he muttered in a sing-song voice, "when those *saints* come marching *in!*"

He must have sensed he was not alone; he twisted on his chair and frowned at me. At the same moment he hit a key without looking and the screen went blank. Then he lifted the headset.

"Well?" I said, indicating the chips.

"Well." He rubbed his hand through his hair. "It thinks it's an artificial intelligence." Then he smiled as if he had just made the decision to trust me. "Don't know yet. Interesting. Hard to stretch a program designed for a mainframe when all I've got to work with is kludged junkware. I'd break into Bonivard's heavy equipment if I could. Right now all I can do is make copies."

"You're making copies? Does he know?"

"Do I care if he does?"

I grabbed some dirty white pants from the floor and tossed them at him. "I'll stay if you get dressed."

He began to pull the pants on. "Welcome to the Bernese torture chamber, circa 1652," he said, doing a bad robot imitation.

"I thought the torture chamber was in the dungeons."

"With two there's no waiting." He tilted a plastic glass on the table, sniffed at it suspiciously, and then took a tentative sip. "Refreshments?"

I was about to sit on the bed but thought better of it. "Ever hear of someone called Carl Pfneudl?"

"The Noodle? Sure: one of the greats. Juice was that he set up the SoftCell scam. Made money enough to buy Wisconsin. Came to a bad end, though."

Suddenly I didn't want to hear any more. "Then he's dead."

"As a dinosaur. Mindkillers finally caught up with him. Made a snuff video; him the star. Flooded the operators' nets with it and called it deterrence. But you could tell they were having fun."

"Damn." I sagged onto the bed and told him what Ego had told me.

Django listened with apparent indifference but I had been around him long enough to read the signs. My guess was that WISEGUY was a lot more than "interesting." Which was why Django wasn't flashing on some poison or another—he had to be clean for tricky operations. And now if Bonivard was Pfneudl, that lent even more credibility to the idea that WISEGUY was a true AI.

"The old Noodle looked plenty dead to me." Django shook his head doubtfully. "That was one corpse they had to scoop up with a spoon and bury in a bucket."

"Video-synthesizers," I said.

"Sure. But still cheaper to do it for real—and they had reason enough. Look, maybe the pogo was lying. Trying to prove intelligence that way. It's the old Turing fallacy: fooling another intelligence for an hour means you're intelligent. Lots of really stupid programs can play these games, Eyes. There's only one test that means anything: can your AI mix it up with the two billion

plus cerebrums on the planet without getting trashed? Drop that pogo into Manhattan and it'll be scrap by Thursday.''

"Then who is Bonivard?"

Django yawned. "What difference does it make?"

My door was ajar so that I could hear the spider singing when he came past. "Bonivard!"

The spider nudged into my room, nearly filling it. Still I was able to squeeze by and thumb the printreader on the door, locking us in.

"Don't worry about Django." Bonivard seemed amused. "Busy, too busy."

I didn't want to look up at him and I wasn't going to ask him to stoop. I might have stood on the bed except then some part of me would be expecting my father to come in and yell. So instead I clambered to the high window and perched on a rickety wooden balcony that a sneeze might have blown down. The wind off the lake was cool. The rocks beneath me looked like broken teeth.

"Careful," said Bonivard. "Fall in and you'll glow."

"Are you Carl Pfneudl?"

He brought the spider to a dead silent stop. "Where did you hear that name?"

I told him about Ego's demonstration. What Django had said.

"Are you?" I repeated.

"If I am, the story changes, doesn't it?" He was being sarcastic but I wasn't sure whether he was mocking me or himself. "Juicier, as you say. Main menu. It means money. Publicity. Promotions all around. But juice is an expensive commodity." He sighed. "Make an offer."

I shook my head. "Not me. I'm not working for Infoline anymore. Probably never work again." I told him everything: about my burster, the possibility that I had given away our location, how Macmillan had cut me free. I told how I'd tried to tell him before. I don't know how much of it he knew already—maybe all. But that didn't stop me: I was on a confessing jag. I told him that Django was making copies of WISEGUY. I even told him that I had dreamed of him. It all spilled out and I let it come. I knew I was supposed to be the reporter, supposed to say nothing, squeeze the juice from him. But nothing was the way it was supposed to be.

When I was done he stared at me with an expression that was totally unreadable. His ruined arm shivered like a dead leaf in the wind. "I wanted to be Carl Pfneudl," he said. "Once. But Carl Pfneudl is dead. A public execution. Now I'm Bonivard. The prisoner of Chillon."

"You knew who I was," I said. "You brought me here. Why?"

Bonivard continued to stare, as if he could barely see me across the room. "Carl Pfneudl was an arrogant bastard. Kind of man who knew he could get anything he wanted. Like Django. If he wanted you, he would have found the way.''

"Django will never get me." I leaned forward. I felt like grabbing Bonivard, shaking some sense into him. "I'm not some damn hardware you can steal, a program to operate on.''

He nodded. "Maybe that was it. I was alone—too long. Saw you on telelink. You were tough. Took risks but didn't pretend you weren't afraid. You were more interesting than the punks you covered. Like Django. Fools like Carl Pfneudl. You were a whole person: nothing missing.''

I took a deep breath. "Can you make love, Bonivard?''

At first he didn't react. Then the corners of his mouth turned up: a grim smile. "That's your offer?''

"You want an offer?" I spat on the floor in front of him. "If Pfneudl is dead then good, I'm glad. Now I'm going to ask once more: can you make love to me?''

"A cruel question. A reporter's question.''

I said nothing.

"I don't want your damn charity." As the spider's cockpit settled to the floor, he stretched to his full pitiful length. "Look at me! I'm a monster. I know what you see.''

I slid off the sill and dropped lightly to the floor. "Maybe a monster is what I want.''

I think I shocked him. I think that some part of him hoped that I would lie, tell him he wasn't hideous. But that was his problem.

I unbolted him from the spider, picked him up. I'd never carried a lover to bed. He showed me how to disengage the bionic collar; told me we'd have a couple of hours before he would need to be hooked up again.

In some ways it was like my dream. The scar tissue was white, yes. But . . .

"It's thermofiber," he explained. "Packed with sensors.'' He could control the shape. Make it expand and contract.

"Connected to all the right places in my brain.''

I kissed his forehead.

I was repulsed. I was fascinated. It was cool to the touch.

"The answer is yes," he said.

It was dinner time. Django had made a circle of cherry tomatoes on the table of the banqueting hall.

"It's over," said Bonivard.

Django whistled as he walked to the opposite side of the table to line up his shot. He flicked his thumb and his shooter tomato dispersed the top of the circle. "All right.''

Bonivard tossed a Swiss Volksbank passcard across the table, scattering the remainder of Django's game. "You're leaving. Take that if you want.''

Django straightened. I wondered if Bonivard realized he was carrying heat. "So I'm leaving." He picked up the passcard. "Weren't there two of these before?"

"You made copies of WISEGUY." Bonivard held up a stack of white memory chips from the cockpit of the spider. "Thanks."

"Nice bluff." Some of the stiffness went out of Django. "Except I know my copy procedure was secure." He smiled. Getting looser. "Even if that is a copy, it's no good to you. I re-encrypted it, spiderman. Armor-plated code is my specialty. You'll need computer *years* to operate."

"Even so, you're leaving." Bonivard was as grim as a cement wall. I think I knew why their negotiations had broken down—had never stood a chance. Bonivard had the same loathing for Django that an addict gets when he looks in the mirror after his morning puke. Django never recognized that hatred; he had the sensitivity of a brick.

"What's wrong, spiderman? Mindkillers knocking at the door?"

"You're good," said Bonivard. "A pity to waste talent like yours. It was a clean escape, Django; they've completely lost you. You'll need some surgery, get yourself a new identity. But that's no problem."

"No problem?" I said. "I'm used to being me."

"Maybe I wouldn't mind losing this face." Django rubbed his chin.

"The only reason I put up with you this long," said Bonivard, "was that I was waiting for WISEGUY."

"I'm taking my copies, spiderman."

"You are. And you're going to move those copies. A lot of them. Cheap and fast. Since they've lost your trail, the mindkillers are waiting to see where WISEGUY turns up. Try to backtrack to you. Your play is to bring it out everywhere. Get some pieces of it up on the operators' net. Overload the search programs and the mindkillers will be too busy to bother you."

Django was smiling and nodding like a kid learning from a master. "I like it. Old Django goes out covered with glory. New Django comes in covered with money."

"Probably headed for the history chips." Bonivard's sarcasm was wasted on Django. "The great humanitarian. Savior of the twenty-first century." Django's enthusiasm seemed to have wearied Bonivard. "The big prison, punk."

Django was too full of his own ideas to listen. He shot out of his chair and paced the hall. "A new ID. Hey, Eyes, what do you think of 'Dizzy.' I'd use 'the Count' but there's a real count—Liechtenstein or some such— who operates. Maybe Diz. Yeah."

"Go plug yourself, Django." I didn't like any of it; I never signed on to disappear.

"Maybe you're not as scrambled as you pretend, Frankie boy." There was open admiration in Django's voice, "Don't worry, the secret is safe.

Not a word about this dump. Or the Noodle. Honor among thieves, right? No hard feelings.'' He had the audacity to extend his hand to Bonivard.

"No feelings at all.'' Bonivard recoiled from him. "But you'll probably get dead before you realize that.''

Anger flashed across Django's face but it didn't stick. He shrugged and turned to me. "How about it, Eyes? The sweet smell of money or the stink of mildew?''

"Goodbye, Django.'' Bonivard dismissed him with a wave of his good hand.

I didn't need Bonivard's help to lose Django. I was almost mad enough to walk out on the two of them. But I didn't. Maybe it was reporter's instincts still at work even though they didn't matter. I gave Django a stare that was cold enough to freeze vodka. Even he could understand that.

He picked up the bank passcard, flicked it with his middle finger. "I told you once, Eyes. You're not as smart as you think you are.'' Flick. "So stay with him and rot, bitch. I don't need you.'' Flick. "I don't need anyone.''

Which was exactly right.

Bonivard and I sat for a while after he had gone. Not looking at each other. The hall was very quiet. I think he was waiting for me to say something. I didn't have anything to say.

Finally the spider stretched. "Come to my rooms,'' said Bonivard. "Something you should see.''

Bonivard had taken over the suite once reserved for the Dukes of Savoy. It had taken a battering during the riots; in Bonivard's bedroom a gaping hole in the wall had been closed with glass, affording a view of rubble and the fire-blackened curtain wall. We had to pass through an airlock into a climate-controlled room that he called his workshop. His "workshop'' had more computing power than Portugal. The latest Cray filled half the space, a multiprocessor he claimed was capable of performing a trillion operations per second.

"The electronic equivalent of a human brain,'' said Bonivard. A transformation came over him as he admired his hardware: a bit of a discarded self showed though. I realized that this was the one place in the castle where the mad prisoner of Chillon was not in complete control. "Runs the spider, although that's like using a fusion plant to run a toaster. There hasn't ever been software that could take advantage of this computer's power.''

"Until WISEGUY,'' I said.

For a minute I thought he hadn't heard me. "Sliced through Django's encryption in a week.'' The spider crouched until the cockpit was almost touching the floor. "WISEGUY is a bundle of different programs that share information. Vision system, planner, parser. Not only can it address massive amounts of memory but it understands what it remembers. Learns from experience.'' The spider stopped singing and its legs locked in place. ''What's amazing is that when you port it from one hardware configuration to another, it analyzes the capabilities of the new system and begins using them without any human intervention.'' The flatscreen in the cockpit went black: he had powered the spider down. ''But it's not true AI.''

''Not?''

He shook his head. ''Heuristics are nowhere near good enough. It's as close as anyone has ever come but still needs a man in the loop to do anything really worth doing. Bring me the helmet.''

The helmet was a huge bubble of yellow plastic which would completely cover Bonivard's head. At its base there were cutouts for his shoulders. I peeked inside and saw a pincushion of brain taps. ''Careful,'' said Bonivard. It was attached by an umbilical to a panel built into the Cray.

I helped him settle the thing on his head and fasten the straps which wrapped under his armpits. I heard a muffled ''Thanks.'' Then nothing for a few minutes.

The airlock whooshed; I turned. If I were the swooning type, that would have been the time for it. Yellowbaby smiled and held out his arms to me.

I took two joyous strides to him, a tentative step, and then stopped. It wasn't really the Babe. The newcomer looked like him, all right, enough to be a younger brother or a first cousin—the fact is that I didn't know what Yellowbably really looked like anyway. The Babe had been to the face cutters so many times that he had a permanent reservation in the OR. He had been a chameleon, chasing the latest style of handsomeness the way some people chase Paris fashion. The newcomer had the same lemon blond hair cut in the same conservatively wide hawk, those Caribbean-blue eyes, the cheek- bones of a baronet and the color of *café au lait*. But the neck was too short, the torso too long. It wasn't Yellowbaby.

The newcomer let his arms fall to his sides. The smile stayed. ''Hello, Wynne. I've been waiting a long time to meet you.''

''Who are you?''

''Who do you want me to be?'' He sauntered across the room to Bonivard, unfastened the helmet, lifted it off, replaced it on its rack next to the Cray. And went stiff as a four-hour-old corpse.

Bonivard blinked in the light. ''What do you think?''

''A surrogate? Some fancy kind of remote.''

''Fancy, yes. It can taste, smell. When its sensors touch you, I feel it.''

Telelink had been making noise about the coming of surrogate technology for a long time. Problem was that running the damn things was the hardest work anyone had ever done. Someone claimed it was like trying to play chess in your head while wrestling an alligator. After ten minutes on the apparatus they had to mop most mortals up off the floor.

"How long can you keep it going?" I said.

"Hours. WISEGUY does all the work. All I do is think. And it doesn't matter if it's this model or the spider or a robot tank or a killer satellite."

"The army of the future." I nodded. "That's why the feds went berserk."

"Django is going to be a hero. Everywhere but in the States. The world gets WISEGUY, the balance of power stays the same. And if there's anyone with any brains left in Washington, they should be secretly pleased. WISEGUY is the kind of weapon you either use or lose. Better to let the imams have it than invade Teheran and risk a nuclear exchange." He powered the spider up again. "And think of the applications for space and deep sea exploration. Hazardous work environments."

"Think of the handicapped," I said bitterly. "I lose my freedom. You get yours. You knew the story would be too hot for Infoline to handle." I hit myself with the heel of my hand; I'd been so dumb. "You paid Yellowbaby to bring me to you. Like some slimy white slaver."

"He didn't know how important WISEGUY was, that Wynne Cage would be stuck here. He didn't have the specs; I did." At least Bonivard didn't try to gloss over his guilt. It wasn't much but it was something. "You want to leave," he continued, not daring to look me in the face, "I suppose I don't blame you. I've made the arrangements. And the other bank passcard is already signed over to your new identity."

"Plug the new ID!" I walked up to the surrogate, felt its hand. The skin was warm to the touch, just moist enough to pass. "What do you need this doll for anyway?"

"The mindkillers let me come here to die. No explanations. They didn't confiscate my bank accounts. Didn't stop me from seeing all the doctors I wanted. Just let me go. Probably part of the torture. Keep me wondering. I decided not to play it their way, to hurt them even if it landed me back in their lab. But a random hit, no. I wanted to hurt them and help myself at the same time. I did some operating; found out about WISEGUY."

"Maybe they wanted you to. And IBM let Django steal it."

"That occurred to me." Bonivard ran his fingers through his thinning brown hair. "Using me and some punk operators to leak a breakthrough no one really wanted in the first place. War is bad business." He sighed. "I don't care anymore. I have WISEGUY. As you say, my freedom. I wanted the surrogate so that I could be with people again. Free from the stares, the pity. The freedom to be normal."

"But you're not normal, Bonivard. You are who you are because you're damaged and you suffer. Living with it is what makes you strong."

For a moment he seemed stung, as if I had no right to remind him of his deformities. Then the anger faded into sadness. "Maybe you're right," he said. "Maybe this body is part of the prison. But I can't go on alone anymore.

Or I *will* go mad.'' He looked at me then, half a man strapped to a robot spider. ''I don't want you to go, Wynne. I love you.''

I didn't know what to say to him. He was a genius operator, obscenely rich. The deformities no longer bothered me; in fact, they were part of the attraction. But he had no idea who I was. Making the surrogate look like the Babe had been a sick joke. And he had been so pathetically proud of his thermofiber prosthesis when we'd made love, as if a magic plug was all it took to make an allnighter out of a man with no legs. He didn't know about my own psychological deformities, less obvious perhaps but no less crippling. How could I stay with him when I'd never stayed anywhere before? The problem was that he was not only in love, he was in need.

''The doctors are quite sure, Wynne. Two years at most—''

''Bonivard!''

''—at most. By that time the leaking of WISEGUY will be old news. It'll be safe to be Wynne Cage again, anyone you want to be. And of course this will be yours.''

''Stop it, Bonivard. Don't say anything.'' I could tell he had more to say; much too much more. But when he kept quiet, I was mollified. ''I thought you didn't want charity.''

He laughed. ''I lied.'' At himself.

Then I had to get away; I pushed through the airlock back into the bedroom. I wanted to keep going; I could feel my nerves tingling with the impulse to run. But it had been a long time since anyone had told me they loved me and meant it. He was a smart man; maybe he could learn what I needed. Maybe we could both learn. Not Swiss bank accounts or features on the main menu.

I had been on the run for too long, slid between the sheets with too many punks like the Babe without feeling a damn thing. At least Bonivard made me feel *something*. Maybe it was love. Maybe. He was going to let me go, suffer so I would be happy. I hadn't known I was worth that. I leaned against the wall, felt the cold stone. Something Django—of all people—had said stuck with me. Don't think, just do it. Improvise.

He came out of the workshop riding the spider. I think he was surprised to see me. ''My very chains and I grew friends,'' he said, ''so much a long communion tends to make us what we are—''

''Shut up, Bonivard.'' Standing absolutely still, I opened my arms to him. To the prison of Chillon. ''Would you shut the hell up?''

CONNIE WILLIS

Chance

Connie Willis lives in Greeley, Colorado, with a husband, a teenaged daughter, and a bulldog. She first attracted attention as a writer in the late seventies with a number of outstanding stories for the now-defunct magazine *Galileo,* and in the subsequent few years has made a large name for herself very fast indeed. In 1982, she won two Nebula awards, one for her superb novelette "Fire Watch" and one for her poignant short story "A Letter from the Clearys"; a few months later, "Fire Watch" went on to win her a Hugo Award as well. Her short fiction has appeared in *Isaac Asimov's Science Fiction Magazine, Omni, The Magazine of Fantasy and Science Fiction, The Berkley Showcase, The Twilight Zone Magazine, The Missouri Review,* and elsewhere. Her first novel, written in collaboration with Cynthia Felice, was *Water Witch.* Her most recent books are *Fire Watch,* a collection of her short fiction, and *Lincoln's Dreams,* her first solo novel. Upcoming is another novel in collaboration with Cynthia Felice, *Light Raid,* from Ace. Her story "The Sidon in the Mirror" was in our First Annual Collection; her "Blued Moon" was in our Second Annual Collection.

Here she examines the cold clockwork mechanisms of change—and chance.

CHANCE

Connie Willis

On Wednesday Elizabeth's next-door neighbor came over. It was raining hard, but she had run across the yard without a raincoat or an umbrella, her hands jammed in her cardigan sweater pockets.

"Hi," she said breathlessly. "I live next door to you, and I just thought I'd pop in and say hi and see if you were getting settled in." She reached in one of the sweater pockets and pulled out a folded piece of paper. "I wrote down the name of our trash pickup. Your husband asked about it the other day."

She handed it to her. "Thank you," Elizabeth said. The young woman reminded her of Tib. Her hair was short and blonde and brushed back in wings. Tib had worn hers like that when they were freshmen.

"Isn't this weather awful?" the young woman said. "It usually doesn't rain like this in the fall."

It had rained all fall when Elizabeth was a freshman. "Where's your raincoat?" Tib had asked her when she unpacked her clothes and hung them up in the dorm room.

Tib was little and pretty, the kind of girl who probably had dozens of dates, the kind of girl who brought all the right clothes to college. Elizabeth hadn't known what kind of clothes to bring. The brochure the college had sent the freshmen had said to bring sweaters and skirts for class, a suit for rush, a formal. It hadn't said anything about a raincoat.

"Do I need one?" Elizabeth had said.

"Well, it's raining right now if that's any indication," Tib had said.

"I thought it was starting to let up," the neighbor said, "but it's not. And it's so cold."

She shivered. Elizabeth saw that her cardigan was damp.

"I can turn the heat up," Elizabeth said.

"No, I can't stay. I know you're trying to get unpacked. I'm sorry you had to move in all this rain. We usually have beautiful weather here in the fall." She smiled at Elizabeth. "Why am I telling you that? Your husband told me you went to school here. At the university."

"It wasn't a university back then. It was a state college."

"Oh, right. Has the campus changed a lot?"

Elizabeth went over and looked at the thermostat. It showed the temperature as sixty-eight, but it felt colder. She turned it up to seventy-five. "No," she said. "It's just the same."

"Listen, I can't stay," the young woman said. "And you've probably got a million things to do. I just came over to say hello and see if you'd like to come over tonight. I'm having a Tupperware party."

A Tupperware party, Elizabeth thought sadly. No wonder she reminds me of Tib.

"You don't have to come. And if you come you don't have to buy anything. It's not going to be a big party. Just a few friends of mine. I thought it would be a good way for you to meet some of the neighbors. I'm really only having the party because I have this friend who's trying to get started selling Tupperware and . . ." She stopped and looked anxiously at Elizabeth, holding her arms against her chest for warmth.

"I used to have a friend who sold Tupperware," Elizabeth said.

"Oh, then you probably have tons of it."

The furnace came on with a deafening blow. "No," Elizabeth said. "I don't have any."

"Please come," the young woman had continued to say even on the front porch. "Not to buy anything. Just to meet everybody."

The rain was coming down hard again. She ran back across the lawn to her house, her arms wrapped tightly around her and her head down.

Elizabeth went back in the house and called Paul at his office.

"Is this really important, Elizabeth?" he said. "I'm supposed to meet with Dr. Brubaker in Admissions for lunch at noon, and I have a ton of paperwork."

"The girl next door invited me to a Tupperware party," Elizabeth said. "I didn't want to say yes if you had anything planned for tonight."

"A Tupperware party?!" he said. "I can't believe you called me about something like that. You know how busy I am. Did you put your application in at Carter?"

"I'm going over there right now," she said. "I was going to go this morning, but the . . ."

"Dr. Brubaker's here," he said, and hung up the phone.

Elizabeth stood by the phone a minute, thinking about Tib, and then put on her raincoat and walked over to the old campus.

"It's exactly the same as it was when we were freshmen," Tib had said when Elizabeth told her about Paul's new job. "I was up there last summer to get some transcripts, and I couldn't believe it. It was raining, and I swear the sidewalks were covered with exactly the same worms as they always were. Do you remember that yellow slicker you bought when you were a freshman?''

Tib had called Elizabeth from Denver when they came out to look for a house. ''I read in the alumni news that Paul was the new assistant dean,'' she had said as if nothing had ever happened. ''The article didn't say anything about you, but I thought I'd call on the off-chance that you were still married. I'm not.'' Tib had insisted on taking her to lunch in Larimer Square. She had let her hair grow out, and she was too thin. She ordered a peach daiquiri and told Elizabeth all about her divorce. ''I found out Jim was screwing some little slut at the office,'' she had said, twirling the sprig of mint that had come with her drink, ''and I couldn't take it. He couldn't see what I was upset about. 'So I fooled around, so what?' he told me. 'Everybody does it. When are you going to grow up?' I never should have married the creep, but you don't know you're ruining your life when you do it, do you?''

''No,'' Elizabeth said.

''I mean, look at you and Paul,'' she said. She talked faster than Elizabeth remembered, and when she called the waiter over to order another daiquiri, her voice shook a little. ''Now that's a marriage I wouldn't have taken bets on, and you've been married, what? Fifteen years?''

''Seventeen,'' Elizabeth said.

''You know, I always thought you'd patch things up with Tupper,'' she said. ''I wonder whatever became of him.'' The waiter brought the daiquiri and took the empty one away. She took the mint sprig out and laid it carefully on the tablecloth.

''Whatever became of Elizabeth and Tib, for that matter,'' she said.

The campus wasn't really just the same. They had added a wing onto Frasier and cut down most of the elms. It wasn't even really the campus anymore. The real campus was west and north of here, where there had been room for the new concrete classroom buildings and high-rise dorms. The music department was still in Frasier, and the PE department used the old gym in Gunter for women's sports, but most of the old classroom buildings and the small dorms at the south end of the campus were offices now. The library was now the administration building and Kepner belonged to the campus housing authority, but in the rain the campus looked the same.

The leaves were starting to fall, and the main walk was wet and covered with worms. Elizabeth picked her way among them, watching her feet and trying not to step on them. When she was a freshman she had refused to walk on the sidewalks at all. She had ruined two pairs of flats that fall by cutting through the grass to get to her classes.

''You're a nut, you know that?'' Tib had shouted, sprinting to catch up to her. ''There are worms in the grass, too.''

''I know, but I can't see them.''

When there was no grass, she had insisted on walking in the middle of the street. That was how they had met Tupper. He almost ran them down with his bike.

It had been a Friday night. Elizabeth remembered that because Tib was in her ROTC Angel Flight uniform and after Tupper had swerved wildly to miss them, sending up great sprays of water and knocking his bike over, the first thing he said was, "Cripes! She's a cop!"

They had helped him pick up the plastic bags strewn all over the street. "What are these?" Tib had said, stooping because she couldn't bend over in her straight blue skirt and high heels.

"Tupperware," he had said. "The latest thing. You girls wouldn't need a lettuce crisper, would you? They're great for keeping worms in."

Carter Hall looked just the same from the outside, ugly beige stone and glass brick. It had been the student union, but now it housed Financial Aid and Personnel. Inside it had been completely remodeled. Elizabeth couldn't even tell where the cafeteria had been.

"You can fill it out here if you want," the girl who gave her the application said, and gave her a pen. Elizabeth hung her coat over the back of a chair and sat down at a desk by a window. It felt chilly, though the window was steamy.

They had all gone to the student union for pizza. Elizabeth had hung her yellow slicker over the back of the booth. Tupper had pretended to wring out his jean jacket and draped it over the radiator. The window by the booth was so steamed up they couldn't see out. Tib had written, "I hate rain," on the window with her finger, and Tupper had told them how he was putting himself through college selling Tupperware.

"They're great for keeping cookies in," he said, hauling up a big pink box he called a cereal keeper. He put a piece of pizza inside and showed them how to put the lid on and burp it. "There. It'll keep for weeks. Years. Come on. You need one. I'll bet your mothers send you cookies all the time."

He was a junior. He was tall and skinny and when he put his damp jean jacket back on the sleeves were too short, and his wrists stuck out. He had sat next to Tib on one side of the booth and Elizabeth had sat on the other. He had talked to Tib most of the evening, and when he was paying the check he had bent toward Tib and whispered something to her. Elizabeth was sure he was asking her out on a date, but on the way home, Tib had said, "You know what he wanted, don't you? Your telephone number."

Elizabeth stood up and put her coat back on. She gave the girl in the sweater and skirt back her pen. "I think I'll fill this out at home and bring it back."

"Sure," the girl said.

*   *   *

When Elizabeth went back outside, the rain had stopped. The trees were still dripping, big drops that splattered onto the wet walk. She walked up the wide center walk toward her old dorm, looking at her feet so she wouldn't step on any worms. The dorm had been converted into the university's infirmary. She stopped and stood a minute under the center window, looking up at the room that had been hers and Tib's.

Tupper had stood under the window and thrown pebbles up at it. Tib had opened the window and yelled, "You'd better stop throwing rocks, you . . ." Something hit her in the chest. "Oh, hi, Tupper," she said, and picked it up off the floor and handed it to Elizabeth. "It's for you," she said. It wasn't a pebble. It was a pink plastic gadget, one of the favors he passed out at his Tupperware parties.

"What's this supposed to be?" Elizabeth had said, leaning out the window and waving it at him. It was raining. Tupper had the collar of his jean jacket turned up, and he looked cold. The sidewalk around him was covered with pink plastic favors.

"A present," he said. "It's an egg separator."

"I don't have any eggs."

"Wear it around your neck then. We'll be officially scrambled."

"Or separated."

He grabbed at his chest with his free hand. "Never!" he said. "Want to come out in the worms with me? I've got some deliveries to make." He held up a clutch of plastic bags full of bowls and cereal keepers.

"I'll be right down," she had said, but she had stopped and found a ribbon to string the egg separator on before she went downstairs.

Elizabeth looked down at the sidewalk, but there were no plastic favors on the wet cement. There was a big puddle out by the curb, and a worm lay at the edge of it. It moved a little as she watched, in that horrid boneless way that she had always hated, and then lay still.

A girl brushed past her, walking fast. She stepped in the puddle, and Elizabeth took a half-step back to avoid being splashed. The water in the puddle rippled and moved out in a wave. The worm went over the edge of the sidewalk and into the gutter.

Elizabeth looked up. The girl was already halfway down the center walk, late for class or angry or both. She was wearing an Angel Flight uniform and high heels, and her short blonde hair was brushed back in wings along the sides of her garrison cap.

Elizabeth stepped off the curb into the street. The gutter was clogged with dead leaves and full of water. The worm lay at the bottom. She sat down on her heels, holding the application form in her right hand. The worm would drown, wouldn't it? That was what Tupper had told her. The reason they came out on the sidewalks when it rained was that their tunnels filled up with water, and they would drown if they didn't.

She stood up and looked down the central walk again, but the girl was gone, and there was nobody else on the campus. She stooped again and transferred the application to her other hand, and then reached in the icy water, and scooped up the worm in her cupped hand, thinking that as long as it didn't move she would be able to stand it, but as soon as her fingers touched the soft pink flesh, she dropped it and clenched her fist.

"I can't," Elizabeth said, rubbing her wet hand along the side of her raincoat, as if she could wipe off the memory of the worm's touch.

She took the application in both hands and dipped it into the water like a scoop. The paper went a little limp in the water, but she pushed it into the dirty, wet leaves and scooped the worm up and put it back on the sidewalk. It didn't move.

"And thank God they do come out on the sidewalks!" Tupper had said, walking her home in the middle of the street from his Tupperware deliveries. "You think they're disgusting lying there! What if they didn't come out on the sidewalks? What if they all stayed in their holes and drowned? Have you ever had to do mouth-to-mouth resuscitation on a worm?"

Elizabeth straightened up. The job application was wet and dirty. There was a brown smear where the worm had lain, and a dirty line across the top. She should throw it away and go back to Carter to get another one. She unfolded it and carefully separated the wet pages so they wouldn't stick together as they dried.

"I had first aid last semester, and we had to do mouth-to-mouth resuscitation in there," Tupper had said, standing in the middle of the street in front of her dorm. "What a great class! I sold twenty-two square rounds for snake bite kits. Do you know how to do mouth-to-mouth resuscitation?"

"No."

"It's easy," Tupper had said, and put his hand on the back of her neck under her hair and kissed her, in the middle of the street in the rain.

The worm still hadn't moved. Elizabeth stood and watched it a little longer, feeling cold, and then went out in the middle of the street and walked home.

Paul didn't come home till after seven. Elizabeth had kept a casserole warm in the oven.

"I ate," he said. "I thought you'd be at your Tupperware party."

"I don't want to go," she said, reaching into the hot oven to get the casserole out. It was the first time she had felt warm all day.

"Brubaker's wife is going. I told him you'd be there, too. I want you to get to know her. Brubaker's got a lot of influence around here about who gets tenure."

She put the casserole on top of the stove and then stood there with the oven door half open. "I went over to apply for a job today," she said, "and I saw this worm. It had fallen in the gutter and it was drowning and I picked it up and put it back on the sidewalk."

"And did you apply for the job or do you think you can make any money picking up worms?"

She had turned up the furnace when she got home and put the application on the vent, but it had wrinkled as it dried, and there was a big smear down the middle where the worm had lain. "No," she said, "I was going to, but when I was over on the campus, there was this worm lying on the sidewalk. A girl walked by and stepped in a puddle, and that was all it took. The worm was right on the edge, and when she stepped in the puddle, it made a kind of wave that pushed it over the edge. She didn't even know she'd done it."

"Is there a point to this story, or have you decided to stand here and talk until you've completely ruined my chance at tenure?" He shut off the oven and went into the living room. She followed him.

"All it took was somebody walking past and stepping in a puddle, and the worm's whole life was changed. Do you think things happen like that? That one little action can change your whole life forever?"

"What I think," he said, "is that you didn't want to move here in the first place, and so you are determined to sabotage my chances. You know what this move is costing us, but you won't go apply for a job. You know how important my getting tenure is, but you won't do anything to help. You won't even go to a goddamn Tupperware party!" He turned the thermostat down. "It's like an oven in here. You've got the heat turned up to seventy-five. What's the matter with you?"

"I was cold," Elizabeth said.

She was late to the Tupperware party. They were in the middle of a game where they told their name and something they liked that began with the same letter.

"My name's Sandy," an overweight woman in brown polyester pants and a rust print blouse was saying, "and I like sundaes." She pointed at Elizabeth's neighbor. "And you're Meg, and you like marshmallows, and you're Janice," she said, glaring at a woman in a pink suit with her hair teased and sprayed the way girls had worn it when Elizabeth was in college. "You're Janice and you like Jesus," she said, and moved rapidly on to the next person. "And you're Barbara and you like bananas."

She went all the way around the circle until she came to Elizabeth. She looked puzzled for a moment, and then said, "And you're Elizabeth, and you went to college here, didn't you?"

"Yes," she said.

"That doesn't begin with an E," the woman in the center said. Everyone laughed. "I'm Terry, and I like Tupperware," she said, and there was more laughter. "You got here late. Stand up and tell us your name and something you like."

"I'm Elizabeth," she said, still trying to place the woman in the brown slacks. Sandy. "And I like . . ." She couldn't think of anything that began with an E.

"Eggs," Sandy whispered loudly.

"And I like eggs," Elizabeth said, and sat back down.

"Great," Terry said. "Everybody else got a favor, so you get one, too." She handed Elizabeth a pink plastic egg separator.

"Somebody gave me one of those," she said.

"No problem," Terry said. She held out a shallow plastic box full of plastic toothbrush holders and grapefruit slicers. "You can put it back and take something else if you've already got one."

"No. I'll keep this." She knew she should say something good-natured and funny, in the spirit of things, but all she could think of was what she had said to Tupper when he gave it to her. "I'll treasure this always," she had told him. A month later she had thrown it away.

"I'll treasure it always," Elizabeth said, and everyone laughed.

They played another game, unscrambling words like "autumn" and "schooldays" and "leaf," and then Terry passed out order forms and pencils and showed them the Tupperware.

It was cold in the house, even though Elizabeth's neighbor had a fire going in the fireplace, and after she had filled out her order form, Elizabeth went over and sat in front of the fire, looking at the plastic egg separator.

The woman in the brown pants came over, holding a coffee cup and a brownie on a napkin. "Hi, I'm Sandy Konkel. You don't remember me, do you?" she said. "I was an Alpha Phi. I pledged the year after you did."

Elizabeth looked earnestly at her, trying to remember her. She did not look like she had ever been an Alpha Phi. Her mustard-colored hair looked as if she had cut it herself. "I'm sorry, I . . ." Elizabeth said.

"That's okay," Sandy said. She sat down next to her. "I've changed a lot. I used to be skinny before I went to all these Tupperware parties and ate brownies. And I used to be a lot blonder. Well, actually, I never was any blonder, but I looked blonder, if you know what I mean. You look just the same. You were Elizabeth Wilson, right?"

Elizabeth nodded.

"I'm not really a whiz at remembering names," she said cheerfully, "but they stuck me with being alum rep this year. Could I come over tomorrow and get some info from you on what you're doing, who you're married to? Is your husband an alum, too?"

"No," Elizabeth said. She stretched her hands out over the fire, trying to warm them. "Do they still have Angel Flight at the college?"

"At the university, you mean," Sandy said, grinning. "It used to be a college. Gee, I don't know. They dropped the whole ROTC thing back in sixty-eight. I don't think they ever reinstated it. I can find out. Were you in Angel Flight?''

"No," Elizabeth said.

"You know, now that I think about it, I don't think they did. They always had that big fall dance, and I don't remember them having it since . . . what was it called, the Autumn Something?''

"The Harvest Ball," Elizabeth said.

Thursday morning Elizabeth walked back over to the campus to get another job application. Paul had been late going to work. "Did you talk to Brubaker's wife?" he had said on his way out the door. Elizabeth had forgotten all about Mrs. Brubaker. She wondered which one she had been, Barbara who liked bananas or Meg who liked marshmallows.

"Yes," she said. "I told her how much you liked the university."

"Good. There's a faculty concert tomorrow night. Brubaker asked if we were going. I invited them over for coffee afterwards. Did you turn the heat up again?" he said. He looked at the thermostat and turned it down to sixty. "You had it turned up to eighty. I can hardly wait to see what our first gas bill is. The last thing I need is a two hundred dollar gas bill, Elizabeth. Do you realize what this move is costing us?"

"Yes," Elizabeth said. "I do."

She had turned the thermostat back up as soon as he left, but it didn't seem to do any good. She put on a sweater and her raincoat and walked over to the campus.

The rain had stopped sometime during the night, but the central walk was still wet. At the far end, a girl in a yellow slicker stepped up on the curb. She took a few steps on the sidewalk, her head bent, as if she were looking at something on the ground, and then cut across the wet grass toward Gunter.

Elizabeth went into Carter Hall. The girl who had helped her the day before was leaning over the counter, taking notes from a textbook. She was wearing a pleated skirt and sweater like Elizabeth had worn in college.

"The styles we wore have all come back," Tib had said when they had lunch together. "Those matching sweater and skirt sets and those horrible flats that we never could keep on our feet. And penny loafers." She was on her third peach daiquiri and her voice had gotten calmer with each one, so that she almost sounded like her old self. "And cocktail dresses! Do you remember that rust formal you had, with the scoop neck and the long skirt with the raised design? I always loved that dress. Do you remember that time you loaned it to me for the Angel Flight dance?''

"Yes," Elizabeth said, and picked up the bill.

Tib tried to stir her peach daiquiri with its mint sprig, but it slipped out of her fingers and sank to the bottom of the glass. "He really only took me to be nice."

"I know," Elizabeth had said. "Now how much do I owe? Six-fifty for the crepes and two for the wine cooler. Do they add on the tip here?"

"I need another job application," Elizabeth said to the girl.

"Sure thing." When the girl walked over to the files to get it, Elizabeth could see that she was wearing flat-heeled shoes like she had worn in college. Elizabeth thanked her and put the application in her purse.

She walked up past her dorm. The worm was still lying there. The sidewalk around it was almost dry, and the worm was a darker red than it had been. "I should have put it in the grass," she said out loud. She knew it was dead, but she picked it up and put it in the grass anyway, so no one would step on it. It was cold to the touch.

Sandy Konkel came over in the afternoon wearing a gray polyester pantsuit. She had a wet high school letter jacket over her head. "John loaned me his jacket," she said. "I wasn't going to wear a coat this morning, but John told me I was going to get drenched. Which I was."

"You might want to put it on," Elizabeth said. "I'm sorry it's so cold in here. I think there's something wrong with the furnace."

"I'm fine," Sandy said. "You know, I wrote that article on your husband being the new assistant dean, and I asked him about you, but he didn't say anything about your having gone to college here."

She had a thick notebook with her. She opened it at tabbed sections. "We might as well get this alum stuff out of the way first, and then we can talk. This alum rep job is a real pain, but I must admit I get kind of a kick out of finding out what happened to everybody. Let's see," she said, thumbing through the sections. "Found, lost, hopelessly lost, deceased. I think you're one of the hopelessly lost. Right? Okay." She dug a pencil out of her purse. "You were Elizabeth Wilson."

"Yes," Elizabeth said. "I was." She had taken off her light sweater and put on a heavy wool one when she got home, but she was still cold. She rubbed her hands along her upper arms. "Would you like some coffee?"

"Sure," she said. She followed Elizabeth to the kitchen and asked her questions about Paul and his job and whether they had any children while Elizabeth made coffee and put out the cream and sugar and a plate of the cookies she had baked for after the concert.

"I'll read you some names off the hopelessly lost list, and if you know what happened to them, just stop me. Carolyn Waugh, Pam Callison, Linda Bohlender." She was several names past Cheryl Tibner before Elizabeth realized that was Tib.

"I saw Tib in Denver this summer," she said. "Her married name's

Scates, but she's getting a divorce, and I don't know if she's going to go back to her maiden name or not.''

"What's she doing?'' Sandy said.

She's drinking too much, Elizabeth thought, and she let her hair grow out, and she's too thin. "She's working for a stockbroker,'' she said and went to get the address Tib had given her. Sandy wrote it down, and then flipped to the tabbed section marked "Found'' and entered the name and address again.

"Would you like some more coffee, Mrs. Konkel?'' Elizabeth said.

"You still don't remember me, do you?'' Sandy said. She stood up and took off her jacket. She was wearing a short-sleeved gray knit shell underneath it. "I was Karen Zamora's roommate. Sondra Dickeson?''

Sondra Dickeson. She had had pale blonde hair that she wore in a pageboy, and a winter white cashmere sweater and a matching white skirt with a kick pleat. She had worn it with black heels and a string of real pearls.

Sandy laughed. "You should see the expression on your face. You remember me now, don't you?''

"I'm sorry. I just didn't . . . I should have . . .''

"Listen, it's okay,'' she said. She took a sip of coffee. "At least you didn't say, 'How could you let yourself go like that?' like Janice Brubaker did.'' She bit into a cookie. "Well, aren't you going to ask me whatever became of Sondra Dickeson? It's a great story.''

"What happened to her?'' Elizabeth said. She felt suddenly colder. She poured herself another cup of coffee and sat back down, wrapping her hands around the cup for warmth.

Sandy finished the cookie and took another one. "Well, if you remember, I was kind of a snot in those days. I was going to this Sigma Chi dinner dance with Chuck Pagano. Do you remember him? Well, anyway, we were going to this dance clear out in the country somewhere and he stopped the car and got all clutchy-grabby and I got mad because he was messing up my hair and my makeup so I got out of the car. And he drove off. So there I was, standing out in the middle of nowhere in a formal and high heels. I hadn't even grabbed my purse or anything, and it's getting dark, and Sondra Dickeson is such a snot that it never even occurs to her to walk back to town or try to find a phone or something. No, she just stands there like an idiot in her brocade formal and her orchid corsage and her dyed satin pumps and thinks, 'He can't do this to me. Who does he think he is?' ''

She was talking about herself as if she had been another person, which Elizabeth supposed she had been, an ice-blonde with a pageboy and a formal like the one Elizabeth had loaned Tib for the Harvest Ball, a rust satin bodice and a bell skirt out of sculptured rust brocade. After the dance Elizabeth had given it to the Salvation Army.

"Did Chuck come back?" she said.

"Yes," Sandy said, frowning, and then grinned. "But not soon enough. Anyway, it's almost dark and along comes this truck with no lights on, and this guy leans out and says, 'Hiya, gorgeous. Wanta ride?' " She smiled at her coffee cup as if she could still hear him saying it. "He was awful. His hair was down to his ears and his fingernails were black. He wiped his hand on his shirt and helped me up into the truck. He practically pulled my arm out of its socket, and then he said, 'I thought there for a minute I was going to have to go around behind and shove. You know, you're lucky I came along. I'm not usually out after dark on account of my lights being out, but I had a flat tire.' "

She's happy, Elizabeth thought, putting her hand over the top of her cup to try to warm herself with the steam.

"And he took me home and I thanked him and the next week he showed up at the Phi house and asked me out for a date, and I was so surprised that I went, and I married him, and we have four kids."

The furnace kicked on, and Elizabeth could feel the air coming out of the vent under the table, but it felt cold. "You went out with him?" she said.

"Hard to believe, isn't it? I mean, at that age all you can think about is your precious self. You're so worried about getting laughed at or getting hurt, you can't even see anybody else. When my sorority sister told me he was downstairs, all I could think of was how he must look, his hair all slicked back with water and cleaning those black fingernails with a penknife, and what everybody would say. I almost told her to tell him I wasn't there."

"What if you had done that?"

"I guess I'd still be Sondra Dickeson, the snot, a fate worse than death."

"A fate worse than death," Elizabeth said, almost to herself, but Sandy didn't hear her. She was plunging along, telling the story that she got to tell everytime somebody new moved to town, and no wonder she liked being alum rep.

"My sorority sister said, 'He's really got intestinal fortitude coming here like this, thinking you'd go out with him,' and I thought about him, sitting down there being laughed at, being hurt, and I told my roommate to go to hell and went downstairs and that was that." She looked at the kitchen clock. "Good lord, is it that late? I'm going to have to go pick up the kids pretty soon." She ran her finger down the hopelessly lost list. "How about Dallas Tindall, May Matsumoto, Ralph DeArvill?"

"No," Elizabeth said. "Is Tupper Hofwalt on that list?"

"Hofwalt." She flipped several pages over. "Was Tupper his real name?"

"No. Phillip. But everybody called him Tupper because he sold Tupperware."

She looked up. "I remember him. He had a Tupperware party in our dorm when I was a freshman.'' She flipped back to the Found section and started paging through it.

He had talked Elizabeth and Tib into having a Tupperware party in the dorm. ''As co-hostess you'll be eligible to earn points toward a popcorn popper,'' he had said. ''You don't have to do anything except come up with some refreshments, and your mothers are always sending you cookies, right? And I'll owe you guys a favor.''

They had had the party in the dorm lounge. Tupper pinned the names of famous people on their backs and they had to figure out who they were by asking questions about themselves.

Elizabeth was Twiggy. ''Am I a girl?'' she had asked Tib.

''Yes.''

''Am I pretty?''

''Yes,'' Tupper had said before Tib could answer.

After she guessed it she went over and stooped down next to the coffee table where Tupper was setting up his display of plastic bowls. ''Do you really think Twiggy's pretty?'' she asked.

''Who said anything about Twiggy?'' he said. ''Listen, I wanted to tell you . . .''

''Am I alive?'' Sharon Oberhausen demanded.

''I don't know,'' Elizabeth said. ''Turn around so I can see who you are.''

The sign on her back said Mick Jagger.

''It's hard to tell,'' Tupper said.

Tib was King Kong. It had taken her forever to figure it out. ''Am I tall?'' she asked.

''Compared to what?'' Elizabeth said.

She stuck her hands on her hips. ''I don't know. The Empire State Building.''

''Yes,'' Tupper said.

He had had a hard time getting them to stop talking so he could show them his butter keeper and cake taker and popsicle makers. While they were filling out their order forms, Sharon Oberhausen said to Tib, ''Do you have a date yet for the Harvest Ball?''

''Yes,'' Tib said.

''I wish I did,'' Sharon said. She leaned across Tib. ''Elizabeth, do you realize everybody in ROTC has to have a date or they put you on weekend duty? Who are you going with, Tib?''

''Listen, you guys,'' Tib said, ''the more you buy, the better our chances at that popcorn popper, which we are willing to share.''

They had bought a cake and chocolate chip ice cream. Elizabeth cut the cake in the dorm's tiny kitchen while Tib dished it up.

"You didn't tell me you had a date to the Harvest Ball," Elizabeth said. "Who is it? That guy in your ed psych class?"

"No." She dug into the ice cream with a plastic spoon.

"Who?"

Tupper came into the kitchen with a catalog. "You're only twenty points away from a popcorn popper," he said. "You know what you girls need?" He folded back a page and pointed to a white plastic box. "An ice cream keeper. Holds a half-gallon of ice cream, and when you want some, all you do is slide this tab out," he pointed to a flat rectangle of plastic, "and cut off a slice. No more digging around in it and getting your hands all messy."

Tib licked ice cream off her knuckles. "That's the best part."

"Get out of here, Tupper," Elizabeth said. "Tib's trying to tell me who's taking her to the Harvest Ball."

Tupper closed the catalog. "I am."

"Oh," Elizabeth said. Sharon stuck her head around the corner. "Tupper, when do we have to pay for this stuff?" she said. "And when do we get something to eat?"

Tupper said, "You pay before you eat," and went back out to the lounge.

Elizabeth drew the plastic knife across the top of the cake, making perfectly straight lines in the frosting. When she had the cake divided into squares, she cut the corner piece and put it on the paper plate next to the melting ice cream. "Do you have anything to wear?" she said. "You can borrow my rust formal."

Sandy was looking at her, the thick notebook opened almost to the last page. "How well did you know Tupper?" she said.

Elizabeth's coffee was ice cold, but she put her hand over it, as if to try to catch the steam. "Not very well. He used to date Tib."

"He's on my deceased list, Elizabeth. He killed himself five years ago."

Paul didn't get home till after ten. Elizabeth was sitting on the couch wrapped in a blanket.

He went straight to the thermostat and turned it down. "How high do you have this thing turned up?" He squinted at it. "Eighty-five. Well, at least I don't have to worry about you freezing to death. Have you been sitting there like that all day?"

"The worm died," she said. "I didn't save it after all. I should have put it over on the grass."

"Ron Brubaker says there's an opening for a secretary in the dean's office. I told him you'd put in an application. You have, haven't you?"

"Yes," Elizabeth said. After Sandy left, she had taken the application out of her purse and sat down at the kitchen table to fill it out. She had had it nearly all filled out before she realized it was a retirement fund withholding form.

"Sandy Konkel was here today," she said. "She met her husband on a dirt road. They were both there by chance. By chance. It wasn't even his route. Like the worm. Tib just walked by, she didn't even know she did it, but the worm was too near the edge, and it went over into the water and it drowned." She started to cry. The tears felt cold running down her cheeks. "It drowned."

"What did you and Sandy Konkel do? Get out the cooking sherry and reminisce about old times?"

"Yes," she said. "Old times."

In the morning Elizabeth took back the retirement fund withholding form. It had rained off and on all night, and it had turned colder. There were patches of ice on the central walk.

"I had it almost all filled out before I realized what it was," she told the girl. A boy in a button-down shirt and khaki pants had been leaning on the counter when Elizabeth came in. The girl was turned away from the counter, filing papers.

"I don't know what you're so mad about," the boy had said and then stopped and looked at Elizabeth. "You've got a customer," he said, and stepped away from the counter.

"All these dumb forms look alike," the girl said, handing the application to Elizabeth. She picked up a stack of books. "I've got a class. Did you need anything else?"

Elizabeth shook her head and stepped back so the boy could finish talking to her, but the girl didn't even look at him. She shoved the books into a backpack, slung it over her shoulder, and went out the door.

"Hey, wait a minute," the boy said, and started after her. By the time Elizabeth got outside, they were halfway up the walk. Elizabeth heard the boy say, "So I took her out once or twice. Is that a crime?"

The girl jerked the backpack out of his grip and started off down the walk toward Elizabeth's old dorm. In front of the dorm a girl in a yellow slicker was talking to another girl with short upswept blonde hair. The girl in the slicker turned suddenly and started down the walk.

A boy went past Elizabeth on a bike, hitting her elbow and knocking the application out of her hand. She grabbed for it and got it before it landed on the walk.

"Sorry," he said without glancing back. He was wearing a jean jacket. Its sleeves were too short, and his bony wrists stuck out. He was steering the bike with one hand and holding a big plastic sack full of pink and green bowls in the other. That was what he had hit her with.

"Tupper," she said, and started to run after him.

She was down on the ice before she even knew she was going to fall, her hands splayed out against the sidewalk and one foot twisted under her. "Are you all right, ma'am?'' the boy in the button-down shirt said. He knelt down in front of her so she couldn't see up the walk.

Tupper would call me "ma'am," too, she thought. He wouldn't even recognize me.

"You shouldn't try to run on this sidewalk. It's slicker than shit."

"I thought I saw somebody I knew."

He turned, balancing himself on the flat of one hand, and looked down the long walk. There was nobody there now. "What did they look like? Maybe I can still catch them."

"No," Elizabeth said. "He's long gone."

The girl came over. "Should I go call 911 or something?" she said.

"I don't know," he said to her, and then turned back to Elizabeth. "Can you stand up?" he said, and put his hand under her arm to help her. She tried to bring her foot out from its twisted position, but it wouldn't come. He tried again, from behind, both hands under her arms and hoisting her up, then holding her there by brute force till he could come around to her bad side. She leaned shamelessly against him, shivering.

"If you can get my books and this lady's purse, I think I can get her up to the infirmary," he said. "Do you think you can walk that far?"

"Yes," Elizabeth said, and put her arm around his neck. The girl picked up Elizabeth's purse and her retirement fund application.

"I used to go to school here. The central walk was heated back then." She couldn't put any weight on her foot at all. "Everything looks the same. Even the college kids. The girls wear skirts and sweaters just like we wore and those little flat shoes that never will stay on your feet, and the boys wear button-down shirts and jean jackets and they look just like the boys I knew when I went here to school, and it isn't fair. I keep thinking I see people I used to know."

"I'll bet," the boy said politely. He shifted his weight, hefting her up so her arm was more firmly on his shoulder.

"I could maybe go get a wheelchair. I bet they'd loan me one," the girl said, sounding concerned.

"You know it can't be them, but it looks just like them, only you'll never see them again, never. You'll never even know what happened to them." She had thought she was getting hysterical, but instead her voice was getting softer and softer until her words seemed to fade away to nothing. She wondered if she had even said them aloud.

The boy got her up the stairs and into the infirmary.

"You shouldn't let them get away," she said.

"No," the boy said, and eased her onto the couch. "I guess you shouldn't."

"She slipped on the ice on the central walk," the girl told the receptionist. "I think maybe her ankle's broken. She's in a lot of pain." She came over to Elizabeth.

"I can stay with her," the boy said. "I know you've got a class."

She looked at her watch. "Yeah. Ed psych. Are you sure you'll be all right?" she said to Elizabeth.

"I'm fine. Thank you for all your help, both of you."

"Do you have a way to get home?" the boy said.

"I'll call my husband to come and get me. There's really no reason for either of you to stay. I'm fine. Really."

"Okay," the boy said. He stood up. "Come on," he said to the girl. "I'll walk you to class and explain to old Harrigan that you were being an angel of mercy." He took the girl's arm, and she smiled up at him.

They left, and the receptionist brought Elizabeth a clipboard with some forms on it. "They were having a fight," Elizabeth said.

"Well, I'd say whatever it was about, it's over now."

"Yes," Elizabeth said. Because of me. Because I fell down on the ice.

"I used to live in this dorm," Elizabeth said. "This was the lounge."

"Oh," the receptionist said. "I bet it's changed a lot since then."

"No," Elizabeth said. "It's just the same."

Where the reception desk was there had been a table with a phone on it where they had checked in and out of the dorm, and along the far wall the couch that she and Tib had sat on at the Tupperware party. Tupper had been sitting on it in his tuxedo when she came down to go to the library.

The receptionist was looking at her. "I bet it hurts," she said.

"Yes," Elizabeth said.

She had planned to be at the library when Tupper came, but he was half an hour early. He stood up when he saw her on the stairs and said, "I tried to call you this afternoon. I wondered if you wanted to go study at the library tomorrow." He had brought Tib a corsage in a white box. He came over and stood at the foot of the stairs, holding the box in both hands.

"I'm studying at the library tonight," Elizabeth said, and walked down the stairs past him, afraid he would put his hand out to stop her, but they were full of the corsage box. "I don't think Tib's ready yet."

"I know. I came early because I wanted to talk to you."

"You'd better call her so she'll know you're here," she said, and walked out the door. She hadn't even checked out, which could have gotten her in trouble with the dorm mother. She found out later that Tib had done it for her.

The receptionist stood up. "I'm going to see if Dr. Larenson can't see you right now," she said. "You are obviously in a lot of pain."

Her ankle was sprained. The doctor wrapped it in an Ace bandage. Halfway through, the phone rang, and he left her sitting on the examining table with her foot propped up while he took the call.

The day after the dance Tupper had called her. "Tell him I'm not here," Elizabeth had told Tib.

"You tell him," Tib had said, and stuck the phone at her, and she had taken the receiver and said, "I don't want to talk to you, but Tib's here. I'm sure she does," and handed the phone back to Tib and walked out of the room. She was halfway across campus before Tib caught up with her.

It had turned colder in the night, and there was a sharp wind that blew the dead leaves across the grass. Tib had brought Elizabeth her coat.

"Thank you," Elizabeth said, and put it on.

"At least you're not totally stupid," Tib said. "Almost, though."

Elizabeth jammed her hands deep in the pockets. "What did Tupper have to say? Did he ask you out again? To one of his Tupperware parties?"

"He didn't ask me out. I asked him to the Harvest Ball because I needed a date. They put you on weekend duty if you didn't have a date, so I asked him. And then after I did it, I was afraid you wouldn't understand."

"Understand what?" Elizabeth said. "You can date whoever you want."

"I don't want to date Tupper, and you know it. If you don't stop acting this way, I'm going to get another roommate."

And she had said, without any idea how important little things like that could be, how hanging up a phone or having a flat tire or saying something could splash out in all directions and sweep you over the edge, she had said, "Maybe you'd better do just that."

They had lived in silence for two weeks. Sharon Oberhausen's roommate didn't come back after Thanksgiving, and Tib moved in with her until the end of the quarter. Then Elizabeth pledged Alpha Phi and moved into the sorority house.

The doctor came back and finished wrapping her ankle. "Do you have a ride home? I'm going to give you a pair of crutches. I don't want you walking on this any more than absolutely necessary."

"No, I'll call my husband." The doctor helped her off the table and onto the crutches. He walked her back out to the waiting room and punched buttons on the phone so she could make an outside call.

She dialed her own number and told the ringing to come pick her up. "He'll be over in a minute," she told the receptionist. "I'll wait outside for him."

The receptionist helped her through the door and down the steps. She went back inside, and Elizabeth went out and stood on the curb, looking up at the middle window.

After Tupper took Tib to the Angel Flight dance, he had come and thrown things at her window. She would see them in the mornings when she went to class, plastic jar openers and grapefruit slicers and kitchen scrubber holders, scattered on the lawn and the sidewalk. She had never opened the window, and after a while he had stopped coming.

Elizabeth looked down at the grass. At first she couldn't find the worm. She parted the grass with the tip of her crutch, standing on her good foot.

It was there, where she had put it, shrivelled now and darker red, almost black. It was covered with ice crystals.

Elizabeth looked in the front window at the receptionist. When she got up to go file Elizabeth's chart, Elizabeth crossed the street and walked home.

The walk home had made Elizabeth's ankle swell so badly she could hardly move by the time Paul came home.

"What's the matter with you?" he said angrily. "Why didn't you call me?" He looked at his watch. "Now it's too late to call Brubaker. He and his wife were going out to dinner. I suppose you don't feel like going to the concert."

"No," Elizabeth said. "I'll go."

He turned down the thermostat without looking at it. "What in the hell were you doing anyway?"

"I thought I saw a boy I used to know. I was trying to catch up to him."

"A boy you used to know?" Paul said disbelievingly. "In college? What's he doing here? Still waiting to graduate?"

"I don't know," Elizabeth said. She wondered if Sandy ever saw herself on the campus, dressed in the winter white sweater and pearls, standing in front of her sorority house talking to Chuck Pagano. She's not there, Elizabeth thought. Sandy had not said, "Tell him I'm not here." She had not said, "Maybe you'd better just do that," and because of that and a flat tire, Sondra Dickeson isn't trapped on the campus, waiting to be rescued. Like they are.

"You don't even realize what this little move of yours has cost, do you?" Paul said. "Brubaker told me this afternoon he'd gotten you the job in the dean's office."

He took off the Ace bandage and looked at her ankle. She had gotten the bandage wet walking home. He went to look for another one. He came back carrying the wrinkled job application. "I found this in the bureau drawer. You told me you turned your application in."

"It fell in the gutter," she said.

"Why didn't you throw it away?"

"I thought it might be important," she said, and hobbled over on her crutches and took it away from him.

They were late to the concert because of her ankle, so they didn't get to sit with the Brubakers, but afterward they came over. Dr. Brubaker introduced his wife.

"I'm so sorry about this," Janice Brubaker said. "Ron's been telling them for years they should get that central walk fixed. It used to be heated." She was the woman Sandy had pointed at at the Tupperware party and said was Janice who loved Jesus. She was wearing a dark red suit and had her hair teased into a bouffant, the way girls had worn their hair when Elizabeth was in college. "It was so nice of you to ask us over, but of course now with your ankle we understand."

"No," Elizabeth said. "We want you to come. I'm doing great, really. It's just a little sprain."

The Brubakers had to go talk to someone backstage. Paul told the Brubakers how to get to their house and took Elizabeth outside. Because they were late there hadn't been anyplace to park. Paul had had to park up by the infirmary. Elizabeth said she thought she could walk as far as the car, but it took them fifteen minutes to make it three-fourths of the way up the walk.

"This is ridiculous," Paul said angrily, and stode off up the walk to get the car.

She hobbled slowly on up to the end of the walk and sat down on one of the cement benches that had been vents for the heating system. Elizabeth had worn a wool dress and her warmest coat, but she was still cold. She laid her crutches against the bench and looked across at her old dorm.

Someone was standing in front of the dorm, looking up at the middle window. He looked cold. He had his hands jammed in his jean jacket pockets, and after a few minutes he pulled something out of one of the pockets and threw it at the window.

It's no good, Elizabeth thought, she won't come.

He had made one last attempt to talk to her. It was spring quarter. It had been raining again. The walk was covered with worms. Tib was wearing her Angel Flight uniform, and she looked cold.

Tib had stopped Elizabeth after she came out of the dorm and said, "I saw Tupper the other day. He asked about you, and I told him you were living in the Alpha Phi house."

"Oh," Elizabeth had said, and tried to walk past her, but Tib had kept her there, talking as if nothing had happened, as if they were still roommates. "I'm dating this guy in ROTC. Jim Scates. He's gorgeous!" she had said, as if they were still roommates.

"I'm going to be late for class," she said. Tib glanced nervously down the walk, and Elizabeth looked, too, and saw Tupper bearing down on them on his bike. "Thanks a lot," she said angrily.

"He just wants to talk to you."

"About what? How he's taking you to the Alpha Sig dinner dance?" she had said, and turned and walked back into the dorm before he could catch up to her. He had called her on the dorm phone for nearly half an hour, but she hadn't answered, and after awhile he had given up.

But he hadn't given up. He was still there, under her windows, throwing grapefruit slicers and egg separators at her, and she still, after all these years, wouldn't come to the window. He would stand there forever, and she would never, never come.

She stood up. The rubber tip of one of her crutches skidded on the ice under the bench, and she almost fell. She steadied herself against the hard cement bench.

Paul honked and pulled over beside the curb, his turn-lights flashing. He got out of the car. "The Brubakers are already going to be there, for God's sake," he said. He took the crutches away from her and hurried her to the car, his hand jammed under her armpit. When they pulled away, the boy was still there, looking up at the window, waiting.

The Brubakers were there, waiting in the driveway. Paul left her in the car while he unlocked the door. Dr. Brubaker opened the car door for her and tried to help her with her crutches. Janice kept saying, "Oh, really, we would have understood." They both stood back, looking helpless, while Elizabeth hobbled into the house.

Janice offered to make the coffee, and Elizabeth let her, sitting at the kitchen table, her coat still on. Paul had set out the cups and saucers and the plate of cookies before they left.

"You were at the Tupperware party, weren't you?" Janice said, opening the cupboards to look for the coffee filters. "I never really got a chance to meet you. I saw Sandy Konkel had her hooks in you."

"At the party you said you liked Jesus," Elizabeth said. "Are you a Christian?"

Janice had been peeling off a paper filter. She stopped and looked hard at Elizabeth. "Yes," she said. "I am. You know, Sandy Konkel told me a Tupperware party was no place for religion, and I told her that any place was the place for a Christian witness. And I was right, because that witness spoke to you, didn't it, Elizabeth?"

"What if you did something, a long time ago, and you found out it had ruined everything?"

" 'For behold your sin will find you out,' " Janice said, holding the coffee pot under the faucet.

"I'm not talking about sin," Elizabeth said. "I'm talking about little things that you wouldn't think would matter so much, like stepping in a puddle or having a fight with somebody. What if you drove off and left somebody standing in the road because you were mad, and it changed their whole life, it made them into a different person? Or what if you turned and walked away from somebody because your feelings were hurt or you wouldn't open your window, and because of that one little thing their whole lives were changed and now she's getting a divorce and she drinks too much, and he killed himself! He killed himself, and you didn't even know you did it."

Janice had opened her purse and started to get out a Bible. She stopped with the Bible only half out of the purse and stared at Elizabeth. "You made somebody kill himself?"

"No," Elizabeth said. "I didn't make him kill himself and I didn't make her get a divorce, but if I hadn't turned and walked away from them that day, everything would have been different."

"Divorce?" Janice said.

"Sandy was right. When you're young all you think about is yourself. All I could think about was how much prettier she was and how she was the kind of girl who had dozens of dates, and when he asked her out, I thought that he'd liked her all along, and I was so hurt. I threw away the egg separator, I was so hurt, and that's why I wouldn't talk to him that day, but I didn't know it was so important! I didn't know there was a puddle there and it was going to sweep me over into the gutter."

Janice laid the Bible on the table. "I don't know what you've done, Elizabeth, but whatever it is, Our Lord can forgive you. I want to read you something." She opened the Bible at a cross-shaped bookmark. " 'For God so loved the world that He gave his only begotten Son that whosoever believeth in Him should not perish, but have everlasting life.' Jesus, God's own son, died on a cross and rose again so we could be forgiven for our sins."

"What if he didn't?" Elizabeth said impatiently. "What if he just lay there in the tomb getting colder and colder, until ice crystals formed on him and he never knew if he'd saved them or not?"

"Is the coffee ready yet?" Paul said, coming into the kitchen with Dr. Brubaker. "Or did you womenfolk get to talking and forget all about it?"

"What if they were waiting there for him to save them, they'd been waiting for him all those years and he didn't know it? He'd have to try to save them, wouldn't he? He couldn't just leave them there, standing in the cold looking up at her window? And maybe he couldn't. Maybe they'd get a divorce or kill themselves anyway." Her teeth had started to chatter. "Even if he did save them, he wouldn't be able to save himself. Because it was too late. He was already dead."

Paul moved around the table to her. Janice was paging through the Bible, looking frantically for the right scripture. Paul took hold of Elizabeth's arm, but she shook it off impatiently. "In Matthew we see that he was raised from the dead and is alive today. Right now," Janice said, sounding frightened. "And no matter what sin you have in your heart he will forgive you if you accept him as your personal Savior."

Elizabeth brought her fist down hard on the table so that the plate of cookies shook. "I'm not talking about sin. I'm talking about opening a window. She stepped in the puddle and the worm went over the edge and drowned. I shouldn't have left it on the sidewalk." She hit the table with her fist again. Dr. Brubaker picked up the stack of coffee cups and put them on the counter, as if he were afraid she might start throwing them at the wall. "I should have put it in the grass."

*   *   *

Paul left for work without even having breakfast. Elizabeth's ankle had swollen up so badly she could hardly get her slippers on, but she got up and made the coffee. The filters were still lying on the counter where Janice Brubaker had left them.

"Weren't you satisfied that you'd ruined your chances for a job, you had to ruin mine, too?"

"I'm sorry about last night," she said. "I'm going to fill out my job application today and take it over to the campus. When my ankle heals . . ."

"It's supposed to warm up today," Paul said. "I turned the furnace off."

After he was gone, she filled out the application. She tried to erase the dark smear that the worm had left, but it wouldn't come out, and there was one question that she couldn't read. Her fingers were stiff with cold, and she had to stop and blow on them several times, but she filled in as many questions as she could, and folded it up and took it over to the campus.

The girl in the yellow slicker was standing at the end of the walk, talking to a girl in an Angel Flight uniform. She hobbled toward them with her head down, trying to hurry, listening for the sound of Tupper's bike.

"He asked about you," Tib said, and Elizabeth looked up.

She didn't look at all the way Elizabeth remembered her. She was a little overweight and not very pretty, the kind of girl who wouldn't have been able to get a date for the dance. Her short hair made her round face look even plumper. She looked hopeful and a little worried.

Don't worry, Elizabeth thought. I'm here. She didn't look at herself. She concentrated on getting up even with them at the right time.

"I told him you were living in the Alpha Phi house," Tib said.

"Oh," she heard her own voice, and under it the hum of a bicycle.

"I'm dating this guy in ROTC. He's absolutely gorgeous!"

There was a pause, and then Elizabeth's voice said, "Thanks a lot," and Elizabeth pushed the rubber end of her crutch against a patch of ice and went down.

For a minute she couldn't see anything for the pain. "I've broken it," she thought, and clenched her fists to keep from screaming.

"Are you all right?" Tib said, kneeling in front of her so she couldn't see anything. No, not you! Not you! For a minute she was afraid that it hadn't worked, that the girl had turned and walked away. But after all this was not a stranger but only herself, who was too kind to let a worm drown. She had only gone around to Elizabeth's other side, where she couldn't see her. "Did she break it?" she said. "Should I go call an ambulance or something?"

No. "No," Elizabeth said. "I'm fine. If you could just help me up."

The girl who had been Elizabeth Wilson put her books down on the cement bench and came and knelt down by Elizabeth. "I hope we don't collapse in a heap,'' she said, and smiled at Elizabeth. She was a pretty girl. I didn't know that either, Elizabeth thought, even when Tupper told me. She took hold of Elizabeth's arm and Tib took hold of the other.

"Tripping innocent passersby again, I see. How many times have I told you not to do that?'' And here, finally, was Tupper. He laid his bike flat in the grass and put his bag of Tupperware beside it.

Tib and the girl that had been herself let go and stepped back, and he knelt beside her. "They're not bad girls, really. They just like to play practical jokes. But banana peels is going too far, girls,'' he said, so close she could feel his warm breath on her cheek. She turned to look at him, suddenly afraid that he would be different, too, but it was only Tupper, who she had loved all these years. He put his arm around her. "Now just put your arm around my neck, sweetheart. That's right. Elizabeth, come over here and atone for your sins by helping this pretty lady up.''

She had already picked her books up and was holding them against her chest, looking angry and eager to get away. She looked at Tib, but Tib was picking up the crutches, stooping down in her high heels because she couldn't bend over in her Angel Flight skirt.

She put her books down again and came around to Elizabeth's other side to take hold of her arm, and Elizabeth grabbed for her hand instead and held it tightly so she couldn't get away. "I took her to the dance because she helped with the Tupperware party. I told her I owed her a favor,'' he said, and Elizabeth turned and looked at him.

He was not looking at her really. He was looking past her at that other Elizabeth, who would not answer the phone, who would not come to the window, but he seemed to be looking at her, and on his young remembered face there was a look of such naked, vulnerable love that it was like a blow.

"I told you so,'' Tib said. She laid the crutches against the bench.

"I'm sure this lady doesn't want to hear this,'' Elizabeth said.

"I was going to tell you at the party, but that idiot Sharon Oberhausen . . .''

Tib brought over the crutches. "After I asked him, I thought, 'What if she thinks I'm trying to steal her boyfriend?' and I got so worried I was afraid to tell you. I really only asked him to get out of weekend duty. I mean, I don't like him or anything.''

Tupper grinned at Elizabeth. "I try to pay my debts, and this is the thanks I get. You wouldn't get mad at me if I took your roommate to a dance, would you?''

"I might,'' Elizabeth said. It was cold sitting on the cement. She was starting to shiver. "But I'd forgive you.''

"You see that?'' he said.

"I see,'' Elizabeth said disgustedly, but she was smiling at him now.

"Don't you think we'd better get this innocent passerby up off the sidewalk before she freezes to death?"

"Upsy-daisy, sweetheart," Tupper said, and in one easy motion she was up and sitting on the stone bench.

"Thank you," she said. Her teeth were chattering with the cold.

Tupper knelt in front of her and examined her ankle. "It looks pretty swollen," he said. "Do you want us to call somebody?"

"No, my husband will be along any minute. I'll just sit here till he comes."

Tib fished Elizabeth's application out of the puddle. "I'm afraid it's ruined," she said.

"It doesn't matter."

Tupper picked up his bag of bowls. "Say," he said, "you wouldn't be interested in having a Tupperware party? As hostess, you could earn valuable points toward . . ."

"Tupper!" Tib said.

"Will you leave this poor lady alone?" Elizabeth said.

He held up the sack. "Only if you'll go with me to deliver my lettuce crispers to the Sigma Chi house."

"I'll go," Tib said. "There's this darling Sigma Chi I've been wanting to meet."

"And I'll go," Elizabeth said, putting her arm around Tib. "I don't trust the kind of boyfriend you find on your own. Jim Scates is a real creep. Didn't Sharon tell you what he did to Marilyn Reed?"

Tupper handed Elizabeth the sack of bowls while he stood his bike up. Elizabeth handed them to Tib.

"Are you sure you're all right?" Tupper said. "It's cold out here. You could wait for your husband in the student union."

She wished she could put her hand on his cheek just once. "I'll be fine," she said.

The three of them went down the walk toward Frasier, Tupper pushing the bike. When they got even with Carter Hall, they cut across the grass toward Frasier. She watched them until she couldn't see them anymore, and then sat there awhile longer on the cold bench. She had hoped that something might happen, some sign that she had rescued them, but nothing happened. Her ankle didn't hurt anymore. It had stopped the minute Tupper touched it.

She continued to sit there. It seemed to her to be getting colder, though she had stopped shivering, and after awhile she got up and walked home, leaving the crutches where they were.

It was cold in the house. Elizabeth turned the thermostat up and sat down at the kitchen table, still in her coat, waiting for the heat to come on. When it didn't, she remembered that Paul had turned the furnace off, and she went and got a blanket and wrapped up in it on the couch. Her ankle did not hurt at all, though it felt cold. When the phone rang, she could hardly move it. It took her several rings to make it to the phone.

"I thought you weren't going to answer," Paul said. "I made an appointment with a Dr. Jamieson for you for this afternoon at three. He's a psychiatrist."

"Paul," she said. She was so cold it was hard to talk. "I'm sorry."

"It's a little too late for that, isn't it?" he said. "I told Dr. Brubaker you were on muscle relaxants for your ankle. I don't know whether he bought it or not." He hung up.

"Too late," Elizabeth said. She hung up the phone. The back of her hand was covered with ice crystals. "Paul," she tried to say, but her lips were stiff with cold, and no sound came out.

HARRY TURTLEDOVE

And So to Bed

Science fiction is a field known for sudden rises to prominence, so it's not really surprising to look around and see how far Harry Turtledove has come, and how fast. In a handful of years (writing both as Turtledove and as Eric G. Iverson), he has become a regular in *Analog, Amazing,* and *Isaac Asimov's Science Fiction Magazine,* as well as selling to markets such as *Fantasy Book* and *Universe.* Although he has also published many unrelated stories, Turtledove's reputation to date rests mainly on his two popular series of magazine stories: the "Basil Argyros" series, detailing the adventures of a "magistrianoi" in an alternate Byzantine Empire, which started in *Amazing* and now runs primarily in *Isaac Asimov's Science Fiction Magazine;* and the "Sim" series, running primarily in *Analog,* which takes place in an alternate world in which European explorers find North America inhabited by homonids—"Sims"—instead of Indians. Turtledove is just starting to make his mark at longer lengths. Upcoming is a tetralogy sold to Del Rey Books, The Videssos Cycle (Book One, *The Misplaced Legion,* is just appearing as I write this), and a novel called *Agent of Byzantium,* which will be part of the new *Isaac Asimov Presents* line from Congdon & Weed. A native Californian, Turtledove has a Ph.D. in Byzantine history from U.C.L.A., and has published a scholarly translation of a ninth-century Byzantine chronicle. He lives in Canoga Park, California, with his wife and two small daughters.

In "And So to Bed," one of the best of the "Sim" stories, he gives us a very unusual perspective on the life of that great diarist Samuel Pepys—as it might have been in a time that never was.

AND SO TO BED

Harry Turtledove

May 4, 1661. A fine bright morning. Small beer and radishes for to break my fast, then into London for this day. The shambles on Newgate Street stinking unto heaven, as is usual, but close to it my destination, the sim marketplace. Our servant Jane with too much for one body to do, and whilst I may not afford the hire of another man or maid, two sims shall go far to ease her burthen.

Success also sure to gladden Elizabeth's heart, my wife being ever one to follow the dame Fashion, and sims all the go of late, though monstrous ugly. Them formerly not much seen here, but since the success of our Virginia and Plymouth colonies are much more often fetched to these shores from the wildernesses the said colonies front upon. They are also commenced to be bred on English soil, but no hope there for me, as I do require workers full-grown, not cubs or babes in arms or whatsoever the proper term may be.

The sim-seller a vicious lout, near unhandsome as his wares. No, the truth for the diary: such were a slander on any man, as I saw on his conveying me to the creatures.

Have seen these sims before, surely, but briefly, and in their masters' livery, the which by concealing their nakedness conceals as well much of their brutishness. The males are most of them well made, though lean as rakes from the ocean passage and, I warrant, poor victualing after. But all are so hairy as more to resemble rugs than men, and the same true for the females, hiding such dubious charms as they may possess nigh as well as a smock of linen: nought here, God knows, for Elizabeth's jealousy to light on.

This so were the said females lovely of feature as so many Aphrodites. They are not, nor do the males recall to mind Adonis. In both sexes the brow projects with a shelf of bone, and above it, where men do enjoy a forehead proud in its erectitude, is but an apish slope. The nose broad and low, the mouth wide, the teeth nigh as big as a horse's (though shaped, it is not to be denied, like a man's), the jaw long, deep, and devoid of chin. They stink.

The sim-seller full of compliments on my coming hard on the arrival of the *Gloucester* from Plymouth, him having thereby replenished his stock in trade. Then the price should also be not so dear, says I, and by God it did do my heart good to see the ferret-faced rogue discomfited.

Rogue as he was, though, he dickered with the best, for I paid full a guinea more for the pair of sims than I had looked to, spending in all £11.6d.4d. The coin once passed over (and bitten, for to insure its verity), the sim-seller signed to those of his chattels I had bought that they were to go with me.

His gestures marvelous quick and clever, and those the sims answered with too. Again, I have seen somewhat of the like before. Whilst coming to understand in time the speech of men, sims are without language of their own, having but a great variety of howls, grunts, and moans. Yet this gesture-speech, which I am told is come from the signs of the deaf, they do readily learn, and often their masters answer back so, to ensure commands being properly grasped.

Am wild to learn it my own self, and shall. Meseems it is in its way a style of tachygraphy or short-hand such as I use to set down these pages. Having devised varying tachygraphic hands for friends and acquaintances, 'twill be amusing taking to a *hand* that is exactly what its name declares.

As I was leaving with my new charges, the sim-seller did bid me lead them by the gibbets on Shooter's Hill, there to see the bodies and members of felons and of sims as have run off from their masters. It wondered me they should have the wit to take the meaning of such display, but he assured me they should. And so, reckoning it good advice if true and no harm if a lie, I chivvied them thither.

A filthy sight I found it, with the miscreants' flesh all shrunk to the bones. But *hoo!* quoth my sims, and looked close upon the corpses of their own kind, which by their hairiness and flat-skulled heads do seem even more bestial dead than when animated with life.

Home then, and Elizabeth as delighted in my success as am I. An excellent dinner of a calf's head boiled with dumplings, and an abundance of buttered ale with sugar and cinnamon, of which in celebration we invited Jane to partake, and she grew right giddy. Bread and leeks for the sims, and water, it being reported they grow undocile on stronger drink.

After much debate, though good-natured, it was decided to style the male Will and the female Peg. Showed them to their pallets down cellar, and they took to them readily enough, as finer than what they were accustomed to.

So to bed, right pleased with myself despite the expense.

*   *   *

May 7. An advantage of having sims present appears that I had not thought on. Both Will and Peg quite excellent ratters, finer than any puss-cat. No need, either, to fling the rats on the dungheap, for they devour them with as much gusto as I should a neat's tongue. They having subsisted on such small deer in the forests of America, I shall not try to break them of the habit, though training them not to bring in their prey when we are at table with guests. The Reverend Mr. Milles quite shocked, but recovering nicely on being plied with wine.

May 8. Peg and Will the both of them enthralled with fire. When the work of them is done of the day, or at evening ere they take their rest, they may be found before the hearth observing the sport of the flames. Now and again one will to the other say *hoo!*—this noise, I find, they utter on seeing that which does interest them, whatsoever it may be.

Now as I thought on it, I minded me reading or hearing, I recall not which, that in their wild unpeopled haunts the sims know the use of fire as they find it set from lightning or other such mischance, but not the art of its making. No wonder then they are Vulcanolaters, reckoning flame more precious than do we gold.

Considering such reflections, I resolved this morning on an experiment, to see what they might do. Rising early for to void my bladder in the pot, I put out the hearthfire, which in any case was gone low through want of fuel. Retired then to put on my dressing gown and, once clad, returned to await developments.

First up from the cellar was Will, and his cry on seeing the flames extinguished heartrending as Romeo's over the body of fair Juliet when I did see that play acted this December past. In a trice comes Peg, whose moaning with Will did rouse my wife, and she much upset at being so rudely wakened.

When calm in some small measure restored, I bade by signs, in the learning of which I proceed apace, for the sims to sit quietly before the hearth, and with flint and steel restored that which I had earlier destroyed. They both made such outcry as if they had heard sounded the Last Trump.

Then doused I that second fire too, again to much distress from Peg and Will. Elizabeth by this time out of the house in some dudgeon, no doubt to spend money we lack on stuffs of which we have no want.

Set up in the hearth thereupon several small fires of sticks, each with much tinder so as to make it an easy matter to kindle. A brisk striking of flint and steel dropping sparks onto one such produced a merry little blaze, to the accompaniment of much *hoo*ing out of the sims.

And so the nub of it. Shewing Will the steel and flint, I clashed them once more the one upon the other so he might see the sparks engendered thereby. Then pointed to one of the aforementioned piles of sticks I had made up, bidding him watch close, as indeed he did. Having made sure of't, I did set that second pile alight.

Again put the fires out, the wailing accompanying the act less than heretofore, for which I was not sorry. Pointed now to a third assemblage of wood and tinder, but instead of myself lighting it, I did convey flint and steel to Will, and with signs essayed to bid him play Prometheus.

His hands much scarred and callused, and under their hair knobby-knuckled as an Irishman's. He held at first the implements as if not taking in their purpose, yet the sims making tools of stone, as is widely reported, he could not wholly fail to grasp their utility.

And indeed ere long he did try parroting me. When his first clumsy attempt yielded no result, I thought he would abandon such efforts as beyond his capacity and reserved for men of my sort. But persist he did, and at length was reward with scintillae like unto those I had made. His grin so wide and gleeful I thought it would stretch clear round his head.

Then without need of my further demonstration he set the instruments of fire production over the materials for the blaze. Him in such excitement as the sparks fell upon the waiting tinder that beneath his breeches rose his member, indeed to such degree as would have made me proud to be its possessor. And Peg was, I think, in such mood as to couple with him on the spot, had I not been present and had not his faculties been directed elsewhere than toward the lectual.

For at his success he cut such capers as had not been out of place upon the stage, were they but a trifle more rhythmical and less unconstrained. Yet of the making of fire, even if by such expedient as the friction of two sticks (which once I was forced by circumstance to attempt, and would try the patience of Job), as of every other salutary art, his race is as utterly ignorant as of the moons of Jupiter but lately found by some Italian with an optic glass.

No brute beast of the field could learn to begin a fire on the technique being shown it, which did Will nigh readily as a man. But despite most diligent instruction, no sim yet has mastered such subtler arts as reading and writing, nor ever will, meseems. Falling in capacity thus between man and animal, the sims do raise a host of conundrums vexing and perplexing. I should pay a pound, or at the least ten shillings, merely to know how such strange fusions came to be.

So to the Admiralty full of such musings, which did occupy my mind, I fear, to the detriment of my proper duties.

May 10. Supper this evening at the Turk's Head, with the other members of the Rota Club. The fare not of the finest, being boiled venison and some few pigeons, all meanly done up. The lamb's wool seemed nought but poor ale, the sugar, nutmeg and meat of roasted apples hardly to be tasted. Miles the landlord down with a quartan fever, but ill served by his staff if such is the result of his absence.

The subject of the Club's discussions for the evening much in accord with my own recent curiosity, to wit, the sims. Cyriack Skinner did maintain them creatures of the Devil, whereupon was he roundly rated by Dr. Croon as having in this contention returned to the pernicious heresy of the Mani-chees, the learned doctor reserving the power of creation of the Lord alone. Much flinging back and forth of Biblical texts, the which all struck me as being more the exercise of ingenuity of the debaters than bearing on the problem, for in plain fact the Scriptures nowhere mention sims.

When at length the talk did turn to matters more ascertainable, I spoke somewhat of my recent investigation, and right well-received my remarks were, or so I thought. Others with experience of sims with like tales, finding them quick enough on things practic but sadly lacking in any higher faculties. Much jollity at my account of the visible manifestation of Will's excitement, and whispers that this lady or that (the names, to my vexation, I failed to catch) owned her sims for naught but their prowess in matters of the mattress.

Just then came the maid by with coffee for the club, not of the best, but better, I grant, than the earlier wretched lamb's wool. She a pretty yellow-haired lass called I believe Kate, a wench of perhaps sixteen years, a good-bodied woman not over thick or thin in any place, with a lovely bosom she did display most charmingly as she bent to fill the gentlemen's cups.

Having ever an eye for beauty, such that I reckon little else beside it, I own I did turn my head for to follow this Kate as she went about her duties. Noticing which, Sir William Henry called out, much to the merriment of the Club and to my chagrin, "See how Samuel peeps!" Him no mean droll, and loosed a pretty pun, if at my expense. Good enough, but then at the far end of the table someone, I saw not who, worse luck, thought to cap it by braying like the donkey he must be, "Not half the peeping, I warrant, as at his sims of nights!"

Such mockery clings to a man like pitch, regardless of the truth in't, which in this case is none. Oh, the thing could be done, but the sims so homely 'twould yield no titillation, of that I am practically certain.

May 12. The household being more infected this past week with nits than ever before, resolved to bathe Peg and Will, which also I hoped would curb somewhat their stench. And so it proved, albeit not without more alarums than I had looked for. The sims most loth to enter the tub, which must to them have seemed some instrument of torment. The resulting shrieks and outcry so deafening a neighbor did call out to be assured all was well.

Having done so, I saw no help for it but to go into the tub my own self, notwithstanding my having bathed but two weeks before. I felt, I think more hesitation stripping down before Peg than I should in front of Jane, whom

I would simply dismiss from consideration but in how she performed her duties. But I did wonder what Peg made of my body, reckoning it against the hairy forms of her own kind. Hath she the wit to deem mankind superior, or is our smoothness to her as gross and repellent as the peltries of the sims to us? I cannot as yet make shift to enquire.

As may be, my example showing them they should not be harmed, they bathed themselves. A trouble arose I had not foreseen, for the sims being nearly as thickly haired over all their bodies as I upon my head, the rinsing of the soap from their hides less easy than for us, and requiring much water. Lucky I am the well is within fifty paces of my home. And so from admiral of the bath to the Admiralty, hoping henceforward to scratch myself less.

May 13. A pleasant afternoon this day, carried in a coach to see the lions and other beasts in the menagerie. I grant the lions pride of place through custom immemorial, but in truth am more taken with the abnormous creatures fetched back from the New World than those our forefathers have known since the time of Arthur. Nor am I alone in this conceit, for the cages of lion, bear, camel had but few spectators, whilst round those of the American beasts I did find myself compelled to use hands and elbows to make shift to pass through the crowds.

This last not altogether unpleasant, as I chanced to brush against a handsome lass, but when I did enquire if she would take tea with me she said me nay, which did irk me no little, for as I say she was fair to see.

More time for the animals, then, and wondrous strange ever they strike me. The spear-fanged cat is surely the most horridest murderer this shuddering world hath seen, yet there is for him prey worthy of his mettle, what with beavers near big as our bears, wild oxen whose horns are to those of our familiar kine as the spear-fanged cat's teeth to the lion's, and the great hairy elephants which do roam the forests.

Why such prodigies of nature manifest themselves on those distant shores does perplex me most exceedingly, as they are unlike any beasts even in the bestiaries, which as all men know are more flights of fancy than sober fact. Amongst them the sims appear no more than one piece of some great jigsaw, yet no pattern therein is to me apparent; would it were.

Also another new creature in the menagerie, which I had not seen before. At first I thought it a caged sim, but on inspection it did prove an ape, brought back by the Portuguese from Afric lands and styled there, the keeper made so good as to inform me, shimpanse. It flourishes not in England's clime, he did continue, being subject to sickness in the lungs from the cool and damp, but is so interesting as to be displayed whilst living, howsoever long that may prove.

The shimpanse a baser brute than even the sim. It goes on all fours, and its hinder feet more like unto monkeys' than men's, having thereon great toes that grip like thumbs. Also, where a sim's teeth, as I have observed from Will and Peg, are uncommon large, in shape they are like unto a man's, but the shimpanse hath tushes of some savagery, though of course paling alongside those of the spear-fanged cat.

Seeing the keeper a garrulous fellow, I enquired of him further anent this shimpanse. He owned he had himself thought it a sort of sim on its arrival, but sees now more distinguishing points than likenesses: gait and dentition, such as I have herein remarked upon, but also in its habits. From his experience, he has seen it to be ignorant of fire, repeatedly allowing to die a blaze though fuel close at hand. Nor has it the knack of shaping stones to its ends, though it will, he told me, cast them betimes against those who annoy it, once striking one such with force enough to render him some time senseless. Hearing the villain had essayed tormenting the creature with a stick, my sympathies lay all for the shimpanse, wherein its keeper concurred.

And so homewards, thinking on the shimpanse as I rode. Whereas in the lands wherewith men are most familiar it were easy distinguishing men from beasts, the strange places to which our vessels have but lately fetched themselves reveal a stairway ascending the chasm, and climbers on the stairs, some higher, some lower. A pretty image, but why it should be so there and not here does I confess escape me.

May 16. A savage row with Jane today, her having forgotten a change of clothes for my bed. Her defense that I had not so instructed her, the lying minx, for I did plainly make my wishes known the evening previous, which I recollect most distinctly. Yet she did deny it again and again, finally raising my temper to such a pitch that I cursed her right roundly, slapping her face and pulling her nose smartly.

Whereupon did the ungrateful trull lay down her service on the spot. She decamped in a fury of her own, crying that I treated the sims, those very sims which I had bought for to ease her labors, with more kindlier consideration than I had for her own self.

So now we are without a servingmaid, and her a dab hand in the kitchen, her swan pie especially being toothsome. Dined tonight at the Bell, and expect to tomorrow at the Swan on the Hoop, in Fish Street. For Elizabeth no artist over the hearth, nor am I myself. And as for the sims, I should sooner open my veins than indulge of their cuisine, the good Lord only knowing what manner of creatures they in their ignorance should add to a pot.

Now as my blood has somewhat cooled, I must admit a germ of truth in Jane's scolds. I do not beat Will and Peg as a man would servitors of more ordinary stripe. They, being but new come from the wilds, are not inured to't as are our servants, and might well turn on me their master. And being in part of brute kind, their strength does exceed mine, Will's most assuredly and that of Peg perhaps. And so, say I, better safe. No satisfaction to me for the sims on Shooter's Hill gallows, were I not there to see't.

May 20. Today to my lord Sandwich's for supper. This doubly pleasant, in enjoying his fine companionship and saving the cost of a meal, the house being still without maid. The food and drink in excellent style, as to suit my lord. The broiled lobsters very sweet, and the lamprey pie (which for its rarity I but seldom eat of) the best ever I had. Many other fine victuals as well (the tanzy in especial), and the wine all sugared.

Afterwards backgammon, at which I won £5 ere my luck turned. Ended 15s. in my lord's debt, which he did graciously excuse me afterwards, a generosity not looked for but which I did not refuse. Then to crambo, wherein by tagging *and rich* to *Sandwich* I was adjudged winner, the more so for playing on his earlier munificence.

Thereafter nigh a surfeit of good talk, as is custom at my lord's. He mentioning sims, I did relate my own dealings with Peg and Will, to which he listened with much interest. He thinks on buying some for his own household, and unaware I had done so.

Perhaps it was the wine let loose my tongue, for I broached somewhat my disjoint musings on the sims and their place in nature, on the strangeness of the American fauna and much else besides. Lord Sandwich did acquaintance me with a New World beast found in their southerly holdings by the Spaniards, of strange outlandish sort: big as an ox, or nearly, and all covered over with armor of bone like a man wearing chain. I should pay out a shilling or even more for to see't, were one conveyed to London.

Then coffee, and it not watered as so often at an inn, but full and strong. As I and Elizabeth making our departures, Lord Sandwich did bid me join him tomorrow night to hear speak a savant of the Royal Society. It bore, said he, on my prior ramblings, and would say no more, but looked uncommon sly. Even did it not, I should have leaped at the chance.

This written at one of the clock, for so the watchman just now cried out. Too wound up for bed, what with coffee and the morrow's prospect. Elizabeth aslumber, but the sims also awake, and at frolic, meseems, from the noises up the stairway.

If they be of human kind, is their fornication *sans* clergy sinful? Another vexing question. By their existence, they do engender naught but disquietude. Nay, strike that. They may in sooth more sims engender, a pun good enough to sleep on, and so to bed.

May 21. All this evening worrying at my thoughts as a dog at a bone. My lord Sandwich knows not what commotion internal he did by his invitation, all kindly meant, set off in me. The speaker this night a spare man, dry as dust, of the very sort I learned so well to loathe when at Cambridge.

Dry as dust! Happy words, which did spring all unbidden from my pen. For of dust the fellow did discourse, if thereby is meant, as commonly, things long dead. He had some men bear in bones but lately found by Swanscombe at a grave-digging. And such bones they were, and teeth (or rather tusks), as to make it all I could do to hold me in my seat. For surely they once graced no less a beast than the hairy elephant whose prototype I saw in menagerie so short a while ago. The double-curving tusks admit of no error, for those of all elephants with which we are anciently familiar form but a single segment of arc.

When, his discourse concluded, he gave leave for questions, I made bold to ask to what he imputed the hairy elephant's being so long vanished from our shores yet thriving in the western lands. To this he confessed himself baffled, as am I, and admiring of his honesty as well.

Before the hairy elephant was known to live, such monstrous bones surely had been reckoned as from beasts perishing in the Flood whereof Scripture speaks. Yet how may that be so, them surviving across a sea wider than any Noah sailed?

Meseems the answer lieth within my grasp, but am balked from setting finger to't. The thwarting fair to drive me mad, worse even, I think, than with a lass who will snatch out a hatpin for to defend her charms against my importuning.

May 22. Grand oaks from tiny acorns grow! This morning came a great commotion from the kitchen. I rushing in found Will at struggle with a cur dog which had entered, the door being open on account of fine weather, to steal half a flitch of salt bacon. It dodging most nimbly round the sim, snatched up the gammon and fled out again, him pursuing but in vain.

Myself passing vexed, having intended to sup thereon. But Will all downcast on returning, so had not the heart further to punish him. Told him instead, him understanding I fear but little, it were well men not sims dwelt in England, else would wolves prowl the London streets still.

Stood stock still some time thereafter, hearing the greater import behind my jesting speech. Is not the answer to the riddle of the hairy elephant and other exotic beasts existing in the New World but being hereabouts long vanished their having their but sims to hunt them? The sims in their wild haunts wield club and sharpened stone, no more. They are ignorant even of the bow, which from time out of mind has equipt the hunter's armory.

Just as not two centuries past we Englishmen slew on this island the last wolf, so may we not imagine our most remotest grandsires serving likewise the hairy elephant, the spear-fanged cat? They being more cunning than sims and better accoutered, this should not have surpassed their powers. Such beasts would survive in America, then, not through virtue inherent of their own, but by reason of lesser danger to them in the sims than would from mankind come.

Put this budding thought at luncheon today to my lord Sandwich. Him back at me with Marvell to his coy mistress (the most annoyingest sort!), viz., had we but world enough and time, who could reckon the changes as might come to pass? And going on, laughing, to say next will be found dead sims at Swanscombe.

Though meant but as a pleasantry, quoth I, why not? Against true men they could not long have stood, but needs must have given way as round Plymouth and Virginia. Even without battle they must soon have failed, as being less able than mankind to provide for their wants.

There we let it lay, but as I think more on't, the notion admits of broader application. Is't not the same for trout as for men, or for lilacs? Those best suited living reproduce their kind, whilst the trout with twisted tail or bloom without sweet scent die all unmourned leaving no descendants. And each succeeding generation, being of the previous survivors constituted, will by such reasoning show some little difference from the one as went before.

Seeing no flaw in this logic, resolve tomorrow to do this from its tachygraphic state, bereft of course of maunderings and privacies, for prospectus to the Royal Society, and mightily wondering whatever they shall make of it.

May 23. Closeted all this day at the Admiralty. Yet did it depend on my diligence alone, I fear me the Fleet should drown. Still, a deal of business finished, as happens when one stays by it. Three quills worn quite out, and my hands all over ink. Also my fine camlet cloak with the gold buttons, which shall mightily vex my wife, poor wretch, unless it may be cleaned. I pray God to make it so, for I do mislike strife at home.

The burning work at last complete, homeward in the twilight. It being washing-day, dined on cold meat. I do confess, felt no small strange stir in my breast on seeing Will taking down the washing before the house. A vision it was, almost, of his kind roaming England long ago, till perishing from want of substance or vying therefore with men. And now they are through the agency of men returned here again, after some great interval of years. Would I knew how many.

The writing of my notions engrossing the whole of the day, had no occasion to air them to Lord Brouncker of the Society, as was my hope. Yet expound I must, or burst. Elizabeth, then, at dinner made audience for me, whether she would or no. My spate at last exhausted, asked for her thoughts on't.

She said only that Holy Writ sufficed on the matter for her, whereat I could but make a sour face. To bed in some anger, and in fear lest the Royal Society prove as close-minded, which God prevent. Did He not purpose man to reason on the world around him, He should have left him witless as the sim.

May 24. To Gresham College this morning, to call on Lord Brouncker. He examined with great care the papers I had done up, his face revealing nought. Felt myself at recitation once more before a professor, a condition whose lack these last years I have not missed. Feared also he might not be able to take in the writing, it being done in such haste some short-hand characters may have replaced the common ones.

Then to my delight he declared he reckoned it deserving of a hearing at the Society's weekly meeting next. Having said so much, he made to dismiss me, himself being much occupied with devising a means whereby to calculate the relation of a circle's circumference to its diameter. I wish him joy of't. I do resolve one day soon, however, to learn the multiplication table, which meseems should be of value at the Admiralty. Repaired there from the college, to do the work I had set by yesterday.

May 26. Watch these days Will and Peg with new eyes. I note for instance them using between themselves our deaf-man's signs, as well as to me and my wife. As well they might, them conveying far more subtler meanings than the bestial howlings and gruntings that are theirs in nature. Thus though they may not devise any such, they own the wit to see its utility.

I wonder would the shimpanse likewise?

A girl came today asking after the vacant maidservant's post, a pretty bit with red hair, white teeth and fine strong haunches. Thought myself she would serve, but Elizabeth did send her away. Were her looks liker to Peg's, she had I think been hired on the spot. But a quarrel on it not worth the candle, the more so as I have seen fairer.

May 28. This writ near cockcrow, in hot haste, lest any detail of the evening escape my recollection. Myself being a late addition, spoke last, having settled the title "A Proposed Explication of the Survival of Certain Beasts in America and Their Disappearance Hereabouts" on the essay.

The prior speakers addressed one the organs internal of bees and the other the appearance of Saturn in the optic glass, both topics which interest me but little. Then called to the podium by Lord Brouncker, all aquiver as a virgin bride. Much wished myself in the company of some old soakers over roast pigeons and dumplings and sack. But a brave front amends for much, and so plunged in straightaway.

Used the remains of the hairy elephant presented here a sennight past as example of a beast vanished from these shores yet across the sea much in evidence. Then on to the deficiencies of sims as hunters, when set beside even the most savagest of men.

Thus far well-received, and even when noting the struggle to live and leave progeny that does go on among each kind and between the several kinds. But the storm broke, as I feared it should and more, on my drawing out the implications therefrom: that of each generation only so many may flourish and breed; and that each succeeding generation, being descended of these survivors alone, differs from that which went before.

My worst and fearfullest nightmare then came true, for up rose shouts of blasphemy. Gave them back what I had told Elizabeth on the use of reason, adding in some heat I had expected such squallings of my wife who is a woman and ignorant, but better from men styling themselves natural philosophers. Did they aim to prove me wrong, let them so by the reason they do profess to cherish. This drew further catcalling but also approbation, which at length prevailed.

Got up then a pompous little manikin, who asked how I dared set myself against God's word insofar as how beasts came to be. On my denying this, he did commence reciting at me from Genesis. When he paused for to draw breath, I asked most mildly of him on which day the Lord did create the sims. Thereupon he stood discomfited, his foolish mouth hanging open, at which I was quite heartened.

Would the next inquisitor had been so easily downed! A Puritan he was, by his somber cloak and somberer bearing. His questions took the same tack as the previous, but not so stupidly. After first enquiring if I believed in God, whereat I truthfully told him aye, he asked did I think Scripture to be the word of God. Again said aye, by now getting and dreading the drift of his argument. And as I feared, he bade me next point him out some place where Scripture was mistaken, ere supplanting it with fancies of mine own.

I knew not how to make answer, and should have in the next moment fled. But up spake to my great surprise Lord Brouncker, reciting from Second Chronicles, the second verse of the fourth chapter, wherein is said of Solomon and his Temple, *Also he made the molten sea of ten cubits from brim to brim, round in compass, and the height thereof was five cubits, and a line of thirty cubits did compass it round about.*

This much perplexed the Puritan and me as well, though I essayed not to show it. Lord Brouncker then proceeded to his explication, to wit that the true compass of a ten-cubit round vessel was not thirty cubits, but above one and thirty, I misremember the exact figure he gave. Those of the Royal Society learned in mathematics did agree he had reason, and urged the Puritan make the experiment for his self with cup, cord and rule, which were enough for to demonstrate the truth.

I asked if he was answered. Like a gentleman he owned he was, and bowed, and sat, his face full of troubles. Felt with him no small sympathy, for once one error in Scripture is admitted, where shall it end?

The next query was of different sort, a man in periwigg enquiring if I did reckon humankind to have arisen by the means I described. Had to reply I did. Our forefathers might be excused for thinking otherwise, them being so widely separate from all other creatures they knew.

But we moderns in our travels round the globe have found the shimpanse, which standeth nigh the flame of reasoned thought; and more important still the sim, in whom the flame does burn, but more feebly than in ourselves. These bridging the gap twixt man and beast meseems do show mankind to be in sooth a part of nature, whose engenderment in some past distant age is to be explained through natural law.

Someone rose to doubt the variation in each sort of living thing being sufficient eventually to permit the rise of new kinds. Pointed out to him the mastiffe, the terrier, and the bloodhound, all of the dog kind, but become distinct through man's choice of mates in each generation. Surely the same might occur in nature, said I. The fellow admitted it was conceivable, and sat.

Then up stood a certain Wilberforce, with whom I have some small acquaintance. He likes me not, nor I him. We know it on both sides, though for civility's sake feigning otherwise. Now he spoke with smirking air, as one sure of the mortal thrust. He did grant my willingness to have a sim as great-grandfather, said he, but was I so willing to claim one as great-grandmother? A deal of laughter rose, which was his purpose, and to make me out a fool.

Had I carried steel, I should have drawn on him. As was, rage sharpened my wit to serve for the smallsword I left at home. Told him it were no shame to have one's great-grandfather a sim, as that sim did use to best advantage the intellect he had. Better that, quoth I, than dissipating the mind on such digressive and misleading quibbles as he raised. If I be in error, then I am; let him shew it by logic and example, not as it were playing to the gallery.

Came clapping from all sides, to my delight and the round dejection of Wilberforce. On seeking further questions, found none. Took my own seat whilst the Fellows of the Society did congratulate me and cry up my essay louder, I thought, than either of the other two. Lord Brouncker acclaimed it as a unifying principle for the whole of the study of life, which made me as proud a man as any in the world, for all the world seemed to smile upon me.

And so to bed.

HOWARD WALDROP

Fair Game

Here's another unusual look at a writer, this one catching a famous author at a very odd point in his life indeed—the moment of his death.

Already a Legend in His Own Time (probably the only person alive, for instance, ever to *act out* on stage all of the old horror movies of the fifties), Howard Waldrop has perhaps the wildest and most fertile imagination of any SF writer since R. A. Lafferty. Like Lafferty, Waldrop is known for his strong, shaggy humor, offbeat erudition, and bizarre fictional juxtapositions. In the past, he had given us a first-rate SF story about dodos ("The Ugly Chickens"), a tale set in an alternate world where Eisenhower and Patton are famous jazz musicians and Elvis Presley is a state senator ("Ike at the Mike"), a story in which the Marx Brothers and Laurel and Hardy travel back in time to attempt to prevent the plane crash that killed Buddy Holly ("Save a Place in the Lifeboat for Me"), and a stylish and meticulously researched fantasy in which Izaak Walton goes fishing in the Slough of Despond with John Bunyan ("God's Hooks").

Born in Huston, Mississippi, Waldrop now lives in Austin, Texas. He has sold short fiction to markets as diverse as *Omni, Analog, Playboy, Universe, Crawdaddy, New Dimensions, Shayol,* and *Zoo World.* His story "The Ugly Chickens" won both the Nebula and World Fantasy Award in 1981. His first novel, written in collaboration with fellow Texan Jake Saunders, was *The Texas-Israeli War: 1999.* His first solo novel, *Them Bones,* appeared in 1984. His most recent book, the collection *Howard Who?,* is already being recognized as one of the most important collections of the eighties. Upcoming is another collection, *All About Strange Monsters of the Recent Past: Neat Stories by Howard Waldrop,* from Ursus Books. His story "Man-Mountain Gentian" was in our First Annual Collection, and his "Flying Saucer Rock and Roll" was in our Third Annual Collection.

FAIR GAME

Howard Waldrop

"AN OLD MAN IS A NASTY THING."

He heard church bells ringing anxiously on the wind.

He felt the cool air on his skin.

He saw the valley spread out below him like a giant shell.

It was a valley he had known, thirty-five or forty years ago, when he had been there for the skiing. It was a small valley in Bavaria, with its small town. He had never seen it in this season, having been here only in winter. This was spring. Patches of snow still lay in the shade, but everything was greening, the air was a robin-egg blue above the hovering mountains.

He was on the road into town, moving toward the sound of the bells. He lifted his eyes up a little past the village (the glare hurt them, but in the last few years so had all bright lights). Through a slight haze he saw a huge barn, far off on the road leading out the other side of the town.

He looked quickly back down at his feet. He did not like looking at the barn.

He noticed his boots; his favorites, the ones he had hunted in until two years ago when his body had turned on him after all the years he had punished it, when he couldn't hunt anymore. When he could no longer crouch down for the geese in the blinds, he had taken to walking up pheasant and chukar. But then even that ability had left him, like everything else he ever had.

Walking toward the town was tiring. His pants were that tattered old pair from the first hunt in Africa, the one the book came out of. He had kept those pants in the bottom of an old trunk filled with zebra hides.

He put his hands to his broad chest and felt a flannel shirt and his fishing vest. It was the one he'd been wearing in that picture with the two trout and the big smile, taken the first time he'd come to Idaho.

He felt his face as he walked. His beard was still scraggly on his chin. He reached up and felt the big lump on his forehead, the one he'd gotten when he'd butted his way through a jammed cabin door, out of a burning airplane, his second plane crash in two days seven years before.

His hat was the big-billed marlin cap from the days of Cuba and Bimini and Key West, back when everything was good: the writing, the hunting and fishing, the wives, the booze.

He remembered that morning in Idaho when he was in his bathrobe, just back from the hospital, and both the house and the shotgun had been still and cool.

Now he was walking down the hill toward the ruckus in town, dressed in odds and ends of his old clothing. It was a fine spring morning in the mountains half a world away.

Many houses stood with doors open, all the people now at the town square. Still, the pealing of the bells echoed off the surrounding peaks.

From way off to the left he could hear the small flat bells of cattle being driven toward him, and the shouts of the people who herded them.

A woman came from a house and ran past him without a glance, toward the milling people and voices ahead.

A child looked down at him from one of the high third-story windows, the ones you sometimes had to climb out of in the winter if you wanted to go outside at all.

He was winded from the half-mile walk into town.

The crowd stood looking toward the church doors, perhaps three hundred people in all, men, women, a few of the children.

The bells stopped ringing, slowed their swings, stopped in the high steeple. The doors opened up, and the priest and bürgermeister came out onto the broad steps.

The crowd waited.

"There he is," said the priest.

Heads turned, the crowd parted, and they opened a path for him to the steps. He walked up to the priest and the mayor.

"Ernst," said the bürgermeister. "We're so glad you came."

"I'm a little confused," he heard himself say.

"The Wild Man?" said the priest. "He's come down into the villages again. He killed two more last night and carried off a ram three men couldn't lift. Didn't you get our cablegram?"

"I don't think so," he said.

"We sent for you to come hunt him for us. Some townspeople remembered you from the Weimar days, how you hunted and skied here. You're the only man for the job. This Wild Man is more dangerous than any before has ever been."

Ernst looked around at the crowd. "I used to hunt in the old days, and ski. I can't do either anymore. It's all gone, all run out on me."

It hurt him to say those things aloud, words he had said over and over to himself for the last two years, but which he had told only two people in the world before.

The faces in the crowd were tense, waiting for him or the official to say something, anything.

"Ernst!" pleaded the bürgermeister, "you are the only man who can do it. He has already killed Brunig, the great wolf hunter from Axburg. We are devastated."

Ernst shook his head slowly. It was no use. He could not pretend to himself or these people. He would be less than useless. They would put a faith in him when he knew better than to put any hopes in himself.

"Besides," said the young priest, "someone has come to help you do this great thing."

Somebody moved in the crowd, stepped forward. It was a withered old black man, dressed in a loincloth and khaki shirt. On its sleeve was a shoulder patch of the Rangers of the Ngorongoro Crater Park, and from the left pocket hung the string of a tobacco pouch.

"Bwana," he said, with a gap-toothed smile.

Ernst had not seen him in thirty years. It was Mgoro, his gunbearer from that first time in Africa.

"Mgoro," he said, taking the old man's hands and wrists, shaking them. He turned to the officials.

"If he's come all this way, I guess we'll have to hunt this Wild Man together," said Ernst. He smiled uneasily.

The people cheered, the priest said a prayer of thanksgiving, and the mayor took him and Mgoro inside his house.

Later they took them to a home on the south side of town. The house looked as if a howitzer shell had hit one corner of it. Ernst saw that it wasn't exploded. The thin wall of an outbuilding had been pulled off, and a window clawed out from what had been a child's bedroom.

"The undertaker," said the mayor, "is sewing the arms and legs back on. His mother heard him scream and came down to see what was wrong. They found her half a kilometre from here. When the Wild Man got through with her, he tossed her down and picked up the sheep.

"We tried to follow his trail earlier this morning. He must live in the caves on the other side of the mountain. We lost his trail in the rocks."

Ernst studied the tracks in the dirt of the outbuilding, light going in, sunken and heavy-laden coming out with the woman. They were huge, oddly-shaped, missing one of the toes on the left foot. But they were still the prints of a giant barefoot man.

"I'll hunt him," said Ernst, "if you'll put some men up by that barn on the edge of town. I don't want him running near there." He looked down, eyes not meeting those of the bürgermeister.

"We can put some men there with shotguns," said the priest. "I doubt he'll go close with the smell of many men there. If you want us to."

"Yes. Yes, I do want that."

"Let's go see to your guns, then," said the mayor.

"We have a few small bore rifles and shotguns for the men of the village," said the priest, "but these are the heaviest. We saved them for you."

Ernst took his glasses out of his pocket, noticing they were the new bifocals he'd gotten for reading after those plane crashes in '54. He looked the weapons over.

One was a Weatherby .575 bolt action, three-shot magazine with a tooled stock and an 8X scope. He worked the bolt; smooth, but still a bolt action.

"Scope comes off, eh, bwana?" asked Mgoro.

"Yes. And check the shells close."

The second was an eight-gauge shotgun, its shells the size of small sticks of dynamite. Ernst looked in the boxes, pulled out a handful each of rifle slugs and 00 shot. He put the slugs in the left bottom pocket of his fishing vest, the shotshells in the right.

The third was an ancient wheel-lock boar gun. Its inlaid silver and gilt work had once been as bright and intricate as the rigging on a clipper ship, but was now faded and worn. Part of the wooden foregrip that had run the length of the barrel was missing. Its muzzle was the size of the exhaust pipe on a GMC truck.

"We shall have to check this thing very well," said Ernst.

"That gun was old when Kilimanjaro was a termite mound," said Mgoro.

Ernst smiled. "Perhaps," he said. "I'd also like a pistol each for Mgoro and me," he said to the mayor. "Anything, even .22's.

"And now, while Mgoro goes over these guns, I'd like to read. Do you have books? I used to have to bring my own when I came for the skiing."

"At the parish house," said the priest. "Many books, on many things."

"Good."

He sat at the desk where the priest wrote his sermons, and he read in the books again about the Wild Men.

Always, when he had been young and just writing, they had thought he was a simple writer, communicating his experience with short declarative sentences for the simple ideas he had.

Maybe that was so, but he had always read a lot, and knew more than he let on. The Indian-talk thing had first been a pose, then a defense, and at the last, a curse.

He had known of the Wild Men for a long time. There used to be spring festivals in Germany and France, and in the Pyrénées, in which men dressed in hairy costumes and covered themselves with leaves and carried huge clubs in a shuffling dance.

In Brueghel's painting, *The Battle Between Carnival and Lent*, one of his low-perspective canvases full of the contradictions of carnival, you can see a Wild Man play going on in the upper left corner, the Wild Man player looking like a walking cabbage with a full head of shaggy hair.

The Wild Men—feral men, abandoned children who grew up in solitary savagery, or men who went mad—became hirsute. Lichens and moss grew on their bodies. They were the outlaws who haunted the dreams of the Middle Ages. All that was inside the village or the manor house was Godmade and good, everything outside was a snare of the devil.

More than the wolf or the bear, the serf feared the Wild Man, the unchained human without conscience who came to take what he wanted, when he wanted.

Ernst was reading Bernheimer's book again, and another on Wild Man symbolism in the art of the Middle Ages and the Renaissance. All they agreed upon was that there had been Wild Men and that they had been used in decorative arts and were the basis of spring festivals. All this Ernst remembered from his earlier reading.

He took off his glasses and rubbed the bridge of his nose, felt again the bump above his eye.

What was the Wild Man? he asked himself. This thing of the woods and crags—it's nothing but man unfettered, unrestrained by law and civilization. Primitive, savage man. Rousseau was wrong—let man go and he turns not into the Noble Savage but into pure chaos, the chaos of Vico, of the totem fathers. Even Freud was wrong about that—the totem fathers, if they were Wild Men, would never compete with their offspring. They would eat them at birth, like Kronos.

What about this Wild Man, then? Where did he stay during the day? On what did he live when not raiding the towns? How do you find him, hunt him?

Ernst went back to the books. He found no answers there.

Mgoro said, "We are ready."

It was dusk. The sun had fallen behind the mountains. What warmth the day had had evaporated almost instantly. Ernst had taken a short nap. He had wakened feeling older and more tired than he had for years, worse than he had felt after the shock therapy in the hospital, where you woke not knowing where you were or who you were.

The other men had gone to places around the village, posted in the outlying structures, within sight and sound of each other, with clear fields of vision and fire toward the looming mountains.

Four others, with him and Mgoro, set out in the direction the Wild Man had taken that morning. They showed Ernst the rocky ground where the misshapen footprints ended.

"He'll be up and moving already," said Ernst. "Are the dogs ready?"

"They're coming now," said the bürgermeister. Back down the trail they heard men moving toward them. "Are we to try to drive him out with them?"

"No," said Ernst. "That's what he'll be expecting. I only want him to think about them. The most likely place he'll be is the caves?"

"Yes, on the other side of this mountain. It's very rocky there."

"Take the dogs over that way, then. Make as much noise as you can, and keep them at it all night, if need be. If they come across his spoor, so much the better. It would be good if they could be made to bark."

Three hounds and a Rotweiler bounded up, straining at their leashes, whimpering with excitement. The man holding them doffed his cap to the bürgermeister.

"Ernst would like to know if you can make the dogs howl all night, Rudolf."

The man put a small whistle to his mouth and blew a soundless note. The four dogs began to bark and whine as if a stag had stepped on them.

Ernst laughed for the first time in months.

"That will do nicely," he said. "If they don't find anything, blow on that every quarter hour. Good luck."

The dogs, Rudolf, the bürgermeister, and the others started up the long trail that would take them around the mountain. Night was closing in.

"Where you think he is?" asked Mgoro.

"Back down a quarter-mile," said Ernst, "is where we should wait. He'll either pass us coming down, or back on the way up if they spot him in the village."

"I think so too," said Mgoro. "Though this is man, not lion or leopard."

"I have to keep telling myself that," said Ernst.

"Moon come up pretty soon," said Mgoro. "Damn mountains too high, or already be moonlight."

"It's the full moon that does it maybe," said Ernst. "Drives them to come into the towns."

"You think he crazy man? From last war?"

"The bürgermeister said this is the first Wild Man attack since before the war, from before that paper-hanging sonofabitch took over."

Mgoro wrapped a blanket around himself, the shotgun, and wheel-lock. Ernst carried the Weatherby across his arm. It was already getting heavy.

The outline of the mountains turned silvery with the light from the rising, still unseen moon.

Then from up the side of the mountain, the dogs began to bark.

Nothing happened after they reached the ravine where they would wait. The dogs barked, farther and farther away, their cries carried on the still, cool air of the valley.

Lights were on in the town below. Ernst was too far away to see the men standing guard in the village itself, or what was happening in the church where most of the women and children waited.

Mgoro sat in his blanket. Ernst leaned against a rock, peering into the dark upper reaches of the ravine. The moonlight had frosted everything silver and gold, with deep shadows. He would have preferred an early, westering moon lighting this side of the mountain. This one was too bright and you had to look into it. Anything could be hiding in the shadowed places. It would be better later, when the moon was overhead, or west.

The dogs barked again, still farther away. Maybe this moon was best. If they ran anything up on that side, the men over there could see it, too.

"Bwana," said Mgoro, sniffing the air. "Snow coming."

Ernst breathed deeply, sniffed. He was seized with coughing, quieted himself, choked, coughed again. His eyes stung, tears streamed down his face. He rubbed them away.

"Damn," he said. "Can't smell it yet. How long?"

"Don't know this land. One, mebbe two hours away."

Just what we need, a spring blizzard, Ernst thought.

An hour passed. Still they had bright moonlight. They heard the sound of the dogs far off. Nothing had come down the ravine. There had been no alarm from the town.

Ernst's back was knotted. His weak legs had gone to sleep several times. He'd had to massage them back to stinging life.

Mgoro sat in his blanket; the gun barrels made him look like a teepee in the moonlight. Ernst had seen him sit motionless for hours this way at waterholes, waiting for eland, wildebeest, lions. He was the best gunbearer Ernst had ever seen.

Something about Mgoro was gnawing at the back of Ernst's mind.

Ernst looked around, back down at the village. There were fewer lights now (the guards had been turning off a few at a time). He looked at the church, and he looked farther across the valley at the huge barn, a blot on the night.

He looked away, back up the ravine.

He thought something was wrong, then realized it was the light.

He looked up. High streaked cirrus raced across the moon. As he watched, it changed to altocumulus and the light dimmed more. A dark, thicker bank slid in under that, blotting the stars to the north.

In ten minutes the sky was solidly overcast and huge, wet flakes of snow began to fall.

Two hours into the storm, Mgoro sat up, his head turned sideways. Snow already covered the lower part of his blanket, merging with the wet line of melted snow against the upper part of his body.

His finger pointed left to the ravine.

Ernst could barely make out Mgoro, much less anything farther away.

But they heard it snuffling in the wet air as it went by down the rugged gully.

They waited. Ernst had eased the safety off the .575. But the sound grew fainter, continued on toward the village.

For an instant, Ernst smelled something in the air—sweat, dirt, mold, wet leaves, oil?—then it was gone. The thing must have missed their scent altogether.

The snow swirled down for another ten minutes, then stopped as abruptly as it had begun.

Another five minutes and the moon was out, bright and to the west, shining down on a transformed world of glass and powder.

The thing had come by close.

When they turned to look down the ravine they could see the shadowed holes of the footprints leading in a line down toward the town. The end of the tracks was still more than a kilometre from the village. They strained their eyes, then Ernst took out a pair of night binoculars, passed them to Mgoro. He scanned the terrain past where the footprints disappeared near a road.

He shook his head, handed them back.

Ernst put them to his eyes. It was too bright to make out anything through the glasses—the snow threw back too much glare, made the shadows too dark.

"If he decides not to go in, he'll come back this way," said Ernst.

"If we shoot to warn them, he go anywhere," said Mgoro.

"If nothing happens in the next hour, we follow his tracks," said Ernst.

The moon was dropping to the right of the village. Ernst checked his watch. Fifty minutes had passed.

If they stayed, they had the high ground, command of the terrain. They would be able to see him coming.

If they tracked him, and the Wild Man got above them, he could wait for them anywhere.

Do I treat this like stalking a lion, or following an airborne ranger? Ernst asked himself. He moved in place, getting the circulation back in his leg, the one with the busted kneecap and the shrapnel from three wars back.

He didn't want the Wild Man to get too far ahead of them. It could have circled the town and gone up the other side of the valley, sensing something wrong, or not wanting to leave tracks in the snow. Or it could be holed up just ahead, watching and waiting.

The dogs barked again. Now they sounded nearer, and they were holding the tone. They must have crossed the Wild Man's path somewhere and were trailing him now.

Ernst felt his pulse rise, like you do when beagles begin to circle, indicating the rabbit somewhere ahead of you is coming your way, or when a setter goes on point, all tense, and you ready yourself for the explosion of quail.

Shouts from the village cut across his reverie. Shots followed, and banging on pots and pans. The bells began to toll rapidly.

Mgoro stood against a rock so as to give no silhouette to anything down the ravine. Lights went on in town, flashlight beams swung up and around. They converged toward this side of town. Lights crossed the field and came toward the ravine, with sporadic small arms fire. The sounds from the town grew louder, like an angry hornet's nest.

Mgoro pointed.

Far down, where the footprints had ended, there was a movement. It was only a blur against the snow, a dull change in the moonlit background, but it was enough.

Mgoro dropped the blanket from his shoulders, held the shotgun and wheel-lock, one in each hand, two feet to the side and one foot back of Ernst.

The movement came again, much closer than it should have been for so close a space of time, then again, closer still.

First it was a shape, then a man-shape.

It stopped for a few seconds, then came on in a half-loping ape shamble.

Behind and below, flashlight beams reached the far end of the ravine and were starting up, slowly, voices still too indistinct with the distance.

Now the shape moved from one side of the gully to the other, running. Now it was two hundred metres away in the moonlight. Now a hundred. Eighty.

It was too big for a man.

The baying of the dogs, up the mountain behind Ernst, got louder.

The man-shape stopped.

Ernst brought the Weatherby up, held his breath, squeezed.

The explosion was loud, louder than he remembered, but he worked the bolt as the recoil brought the muzzle up. He brought the sights back down, centered them on the gully before the shell casing hit the ground.

There had been a scream with the shot. Whatever had screamed was gone. The ravine was empty.

He and Mgoro ran down the gully.

It had jumped three metres between one set of prints and the next, and there was a spray of blood four metres back. A high hit, then. Maybe, thought Ernst, as they ran up out of the ravine to the left, maybe we'll find him dead twenty metres from here.

But the stride stayed long, the drops of blood in the snow far apart.

Ernst's lungs were numb. He could hardly breathe in enough air to keep going. His legs threatened to fold, and he realized what he was—an old, half-crippled man trying to run down something that was twice his size, wounded and mad.

Mgoro was just behind him. His lungs labored, too, but still he held both guns where he could hand them to Ernst in seconds.

The flashlights and lanterns from the town headed across the front of the village, between the town and the Wild Man. Behind Ernst and Mgoro, the dogs neared in the ravine.

Ernst and Mgoro slowed. The footprints were closer together now, and there was a great clot of blood that seemed to have been coughed up. Internal bleeding maybe, thought Ernst, maybe a better shot than I thought I could ever make again.

The moon was on the edge of the far mountain. They would lose the light for a while, but it should be nearing dawn.

The tracks led in an arc toward the roadway south of the village. Lights from the men in town and those halfway up the hill led that way.

They heard the dogs behind them, whining with urgency when they came to the place of the hit. Now they left the ravine and came straight behind the two men.

"Off the tracks. Off!" puffed Ernst. He grabbed Mgoro, pulled him five paces down the mountainside.

In a moment the dogs flashed by, baying, running full speed. As they passed, the last of the direct moonlight left the valley. The dogs ran on into darkness.

"Come," said Mgoro, through gritted teeth. "We have him."

They heard the dogs catch up to the Wild Man. One bark ended in a squeal, another just ended. Two dogs continued on, and the sound of the pursuit moved down the valley.

Ernst ran on, his feet and chest like someone else's.

He realized that the Wild Man was heading toward the barn.

When Ernst was thirteen, up in Michigan one summer, he got lost. It was the last time in his life he was ever lost.

He had been fishing, and had a creel full of trout. But he had crossed three marshy beaver ponds that morning, and skirted some dense woods getting to the fishing. On the way back he had taken a wrong turn. It was that easy to get lost.

He had wandered for two hours trying to find his way back to his own incoming tracks.

Just at dusk, he came to a clearing and saw in front of him a huge barn, half-gone in ruin. He wondered at it. There was no house with it. It was in the middle of the Michigan woods. There were no animals around, and it looked as if there never had been.

He walked closer.

Someone stepped from around one corner, someone dressed in a long grey cloak, wearing a death's head mask.

Ernst stopped, stunned.

The thing reached down inside its cloak and exposed a long, diseased penis to him.

"Hey, you, Bright Boy," it said. "Suck on this."

Ernst dropped his rod, his creel, and ran in a blind panic until he came out on the road less than half a mile from the cabin his family had rented.

One dog still barked. They had found the other three on the way. Two dead, torn up and broken. The third had run until it had given out. It lay panting in a set of tracks, pointing the way with its body like an arrow.

Now the sky to the east was lighter. Ernst began to make things out— the valley floor, the lights of the men as they ran, the great barn up ahead beside the road.

Something ran through a break in the woods, the sound of the dog just behind it.

Ernst stopped, threw the .575 to his shoulder, fired. A vip of snow flew up just over the thing's shoulder, and it was gone into the woods again. The dog flashed through the opening.

Ernst loaded more shells in.

The great barn was a kilometre ahead when they found the last dog pulled apart like warm red taffy.

Ernst slid to a stop. The prints crossed a ditch, went up the other side, blood everywhere now.

Ernst jumped into the ditch just as he realized that the prints were doubled, had been trodden over by something retracing its steps.

He tried to stop himself from going just as Mgoro, on the bank behind him, saw the prints and yelled.

Ernst's arms windmilled, he let go of the rifle, fell heavily, caught a rock with his fingers, slipped, his bad knee crashing into the bottom of the ditch.

Dull pain shot through him. He pulled himself to his other knee.

The Wild Man charged.

It had doubled back, jumped off into a stand of small trees fifty feet up the ditch. Now it had them.

The Weatherby was half-hidden in the ditch snow. Did he have time to get it? Was the action ready? Was the safety off? Was there snow in the barrel and would it explode like an axed watermelon in his hands when he fired?

Not on my knees, Ernst thought, and stood up.

"Gun!" he said, just as Mgoro slammed the shotgun butt down into his right shoulder from the bank above.

Ernst let the weight of the barrels bring the eight-gauge into line. He was already cocking both hammers as his left arm slid up the foregrip.

The Wild Man was teeth and beard and green-gray hair in front of him as the barrels came level with its chest.

Ernst pulled both triggers.

All the moments come down to this. All the writing and all the books and the fishing and the hunting and the bullfights. All the years of banging yourself around and being beaten half the time.

The barrels leaped up with recoil.

All the years of living by your code. Good is what makes you feel good. A man has to do what a man has to do.

A huge red spot appeared on the Wild Man's shoulder as the slug hit and the right hand, which had been reaching for Ernst, came loose and flew through the air behind the buckshot.

Ernst let the shotgun fall.

"Gun!" he said.

And then you get old and hurt and scared, and the writing doesn't work anymore, and the sex is gone and booze doesn't help, and you can't hunt or fish, all you have is fame and money and there's nothing to buy.

Mgoro put the butt of the wheel-lock against his shoulder.

The Wild Man's left hand was coming around like a claw, reaching for Ernst's eyes, his face, reaching for the brain inside his head.

Ernst pulled the trigger-lever, the wheel spun in a ratcheting blur, the powder took with a *floopth* and there was an ear-shattering roar.

Then they take you to a place and try to make you better with electricity and drugs and it doesn't make you better, it makes you worse and you can't do anything anymore, and nobody understands but you, that you don't want anything, anymore.

Ernst lies under a shaggy wet weight that reeks of sweat and mushrooms. He is still deaf from the explosion. The wheel-lock is wedged sideways against his chest, the wheel gouging into his arm. He pushes and pulls, twisting his way out from under, slipping on the bloody rocks.

Mgoro is helping him, pulling his shoulders.

"It is finished," he says.

Ernst stands, looking down at the still-twitching carcass. Blood runs from jagged holes you can see the bottom of the ditch through. It is eight feet tall, covered with lichen and weeds, matted hair, and dirt.

Now it is dead, this thing that was man gone mad, man without law, like all men would be if they had nothing to hold them back.

And one day they let you out of the place because you've acted nice, and you go home with your wife, the last wife, and you sing to her and she goes to sleep and next morning at dawn you go downstairs in your bathrobe and you go to your gun cabinet and you take out your favorite, the side-by-side double barrel your actor friend gave you before he died and you put it on the floor and you lean forward until the barrels are a cool infinity mark on your forehead. . . .

Ernst stands and looks at the big barn only a kilometre away, and he looks at Mgoro, who, he knows now, has been dead more than thirty years, and Mgoro smiles at him.

Ernst looks at the barn and knows he will begin walking toward it in just a moment, he and Mgoro, but still there is one more thing he has to do.

He reaches down, pulling, and slowly turns the Wild Man over, face up.

The hair is matted, ragged holes torn in the neck and chest and stomach, the right arm missing from the elbow down.

The beard is tangled, thick and bloody. Above the beard is the face, twisted.

And Ernst knows that it is his face on the Wild Man, the face of the thing he has been hunting all his life.

He stands then, and takes Mgoro's arm, and they start up the road toward the barn.

The light begins to fade, though it is crisp morning dawn. Ernst knows they will make the barn before the light gives out completely.

And above everything, over the noise of the church bells back in town, above the yelling, jubilant voices of the running people, there is a long, slow, far-off sound, like the boom of surf crashing onto a shore.

Or maybe it is just the sound of both triggers being pulled at once.

WALTER JON WILLIAMS

Video Star

Here's a hard-edged and hard-hitting look at the gritty underside of future society, and at the price you sometimes have to pay if you want to play to *win*. . . .

Walter Jon Williams was born in Minnesota and now lives in New Mexico. He has sold stories to *Omni, Isaac Asimov's Science Fiction Magazine, Far Frontiers,* and *The Magazine of Fantasy and Science Fiction.* His novels include *Ambassador of Progress, Knight Moves,* and *Hardwired.* Upcoming is a new novel, *Voice of the Whirlwind,* from Tor. Williams says that he is "currently working on several short stories, about three novels, and a nervous breakdown, all simultaneously." His story "Side Effects" was in our Third Annual Collection.

VIDEO STAR

Walter Jon Williams

1

Ric could feel the others closing in. They were circling outside the Falcon Quarter as if on midsummer thermals, watching the Cadillacs with glittering raptor eyes, occasionally swooping in to take a little nibble at Cadillac business, Cadillac turf, Cadillac sources. Testing their own strength as well as the Cadillac nerves, applying pressure just to see what would happen, find out if the Cadillacs still had it in them to respond. . . .

Ric knew the game well: he and the other Cadillacs had played it five years before, up and down the streets and datanets of the Albaicin, half-grown kids testing their strength against the gangs entrenched in power, the Cruceros, the Jerusalem Rangers, the Piedras Blancas. The older gangs seemed slow, tentative, uncertain, and when the war came the Cadillacs won in a matter of days: the others were too entrenched, too visible, caught in a network of old connections, old associations, old manners. The young Cadillacs, coming up out of nowhere, found their own sources, their own products and connections, and in the end they and their allies gutted the old boys' organization, absorbing what was still useful and letting the rest die along with the remnants of the Cruceros, Rangers, and Blancas, the bewildered survivors who were still looking for a remaining piece of turf on which to make their last stand.

At the time Ric had given the Cadillacs three years before the same thing started happening to them, before their profile grew too high and the next generation of snipers rose in confidence and ability. The Cadillacs had in the end lasted five years, and that wasn't bad. But, Ric thought, it was over.

The other Cadillacs weren't ready to surrender. The heat was mounting, but they thought they could survive this challenge—hold out another year or two. They were dreaming, Ric thought.

During the dog days of summer, people began to die. Gunfire echoed from the pink walls of the Alhambra. Networks disintegrated. Allies dis-

appeared. Ric made a proposition to the Cadillacs for a bank to be shared with their allies, a fund to keep the war going. The Cadillacs in their desperation agreed.

Ric knew then it was time to end it, that the Cadillacs had lost whatever they once had. If they agreed to a proposition like this, their nerve and their smarts were gone.

So there was a last meeting, Ric of the Cadillacs, Mares of the Squires, Jacob of the Last Men. Ric walked into the meeting with a radar-aimed dart gun built into the bottom of his briefcase, each dart filled with a toxin that would stop the heart in a matter of seconds. When he walked out it was with a money spike in his pocket, a stainless steel needle tipped with silicon. In the heart of the silicon was data representing over eighty thousand Seven Moons dollars, ready for deposit into any electric account into which he could plug the needle.

West, Ric thought. He'd buy into an American condecology somewhere in California and enjoy retirement. He was twenty-two years old.

He began to feel sick in the Tangier to Houston suborbital shuttle, a crawling across his nerves, pinpricks in the flesh. By the time he crossed the Houston port to take his domestic flight to L.A. there were stabbing pains in his joints and behind his eyes. He asked a flight attendant for aspirin and chased the pills with American whiskey.

As the plane jetted west across Texas, Ric dropped his whiskey glass and screamed in sudden pain. The attendants gave him morphine analogue but the agony only increased, an acid boiling under his skin, a flame that gutted his body. His vision had gone and so had the rest of his senses except for the burning knowledge of his own pain. Ric tried to tear his arms open with his fingernails, pull the tortured nerves clean out of his body, and the attendants piled on him, holding him down, pinning him to the floor of the plane like a butterfly to a bed of cork.

As they strapped him into a stretcher at the unscheduled stop at Flagstaff, Ric was still screaming, unable to stop himself. Jacob had poisoned him, using a neurotoxin that stripped away the myelin sheathing on his nerves, leaving them raw cords of agonized fiber. Ric had been in a hurry to finish his business and had only taken a single sip of his wine: that was the only thing that had saved him.

2

He was months in the hospital in Flagstaff, staring out of a glass wall at a maze of other glass walls—office buildings and condecologies stacked halfway to Phoenix—flanking the silver alloy ribbon of an expressway. The snows fell heavily that winter, then in the spring melted away except for

patches in the shadows. For the first three months he was completely immobile, his brain chemically isolated from his body to keep the pain away
while he took an endless series of nerve grafts, drugs to encourage nerve
replication and healing. Finally there was physical therapy that had him
screaming in agony at the searing pain in his reawakened limbs.

At the end there was a new treatment, a new drug. It dripped into his arm
slowly via an IV and he could feel a lightness in his nerves, a humming in
his mind. For some reason even the air seemed to taste better. The pain was
no worse than usual and he felt better than he had since walking out of the
meeting back in Granada with the money spike in his pocket.

"What is that stuff?" he asked, next time he saw the nurse.

The nurse smiled. "Everyone asks that," he said. "Genesios Three. We're
one of the few hospitals that has the security to distribute the stuff."

"You don't say."

He'd heard of the drug while watching the news. Genesios Three was a
new neurohormone, developed by the orbital Pink Blossom policorp, that
could repair almost any amount of nerve damage. As a side effect it built
additional neural connections in the brain, raising the I.Q., and made people
high. The hormone was rare because it was very complex and expensive to
synthesize, though the gangs were trying. On the west coast lots of people
had died in a war for control of the new black labs. On the street it was
called Black Thunder.

"Not bad," said Ric.

The treatment and the humming in Ric's brain went on for a week. When
it was over he missed it. He was also more or less healed.

3

The week of Genesios therapy took fifteen thousand dollars out of Ric's
spike. The previous months of treatment had accounted for another sixty-
two thousand. What Ric didn't know was that Genesios therapy could have
been started at once and saved him most of his funds, but that the artificial
intelligences working for the hospital had tagged him as a suspect character,
an alien of no particular standing, with no work history, no policorporate
citizenship, and a large amount of cash in his breast pocket. The AIs concluded that Ric was in no position to complain, and they were right.

Computers can't be sued for malpractice. The doctors followed their advice.

All that remained of Ric's money was three thousand SM dollars. Ric
could live off of that for a few years, but it wasn't much of a retirement.

The hospital was nice enough to schedule an appointment for him with a career counsellor, who was supposed to find him a job. She worked in the basement of the vast glass hospital building, and her name was Marlene.

4

Marlene worked behind a desk littered with the artifacts of other people's lives. There were no windows in the office, two ashtrays, both full, and on the walls there were travel posters that showed long stretches of emptiness, white beaches, blue ocean, faraway clouds. Nothing alive.

Her green eyes had an opaque quality, as if she was watching a private video screen somewhere in her mind. She wore a lot of silver jewelry on her fingers and wrists and a grey rollneck sweater with cigaret burn marks. Her eyes bore elaborate makeup like the wings of a Red Admiral. Her hair was almost blonde. The only job she could find him was for a legal firm, something called assistant data evaluator.

Before Ric left Marlene's office he asked her to dinner. She turned him down without even changing expression. Ric had the feeling he wasn't quite real to her.

The job of assistant data evaluator consisted of spending the day walking up and down a four-storey spiral staircase in the suite of a law firm, moving files from one office to another. The files were supposedly sensitive and not committed to the firm's computer lest someone attempt to steal them. The salary was insulting. Ric told the law firm that the job was just what he was looking for. They told him to start in two days.

Ric stopped into Marlene's office to tell her he got the job and to ask her to dinner again. She laughed, for what reason he couldn't tell, and said yes.

A slow spring snowfall dropped onto the streets while they ate dinner. With her food Marlene took two red capsules and a yellow pill, grew lively, drank a lot of wine. He walked her home through the snow to her apartment on the seventh floor of an old fourth-rate condeco, a place with water stains on the ceiling and bare bulbs hanging in the halls, the only home she could afford. In the hallway Ric brushed snow from her shoulders and hair and kissed her. He took Marlene to bed and tried to prove to her that he was real.

The next day he checked out of the hospital and moved in.

5

Ric hadn't bothered to show up on his first day as an assistant data evaluator. Instead he'd spent the day in Marlene's condeco, asking her home comp to search library files and print out everything relating to what the scansheets in their ignorance called "Juvecrime." Before Marlene came home Ric called the most expensive restaurant he could find and told them to deliver a five-course meal to the apartment.

The remains of the meal were stacked in the kitchen. Ric paced back and forth across the small space, his mind humming with the information he'd absorbed. Marlene sat on an adobe-colored couch and watched, a wine glass in one hand and a cigaret in the other, silhouetted by the glass self-polarizing wall that showed the bright aluminum-alloy expressway cutting south across melting piles of snow. Plans were vibrating in Ric's mind, nothing firm yet, just neurons stirring on the edge of his awareness, forming fast-mutating combinations. He could feel the tingle, the high, the half-formed ideas as they flicked across neural circuits.

Marlene reached into a dispenser and took out a red pill and a green capsule with orange stripes. Ric looked at her. "How much of that stuff do you take, anyway? Is it medication, or what?"

"I've got anxieties." She put the pills into her mouth, and with a shake of her head dry-swallowed them.

"How big a dose?"

"It's not the dose that matters. It's the proper *combination* of doses. Get it right and the world feels like a lovely warm swimming pool. It's like floating underwater and still being able to breathe. It's wonderful."

"If you say so." He resumed his pacing. Fabric scratched his bare feet. His mind hummed, a blur of ideas that hadn't yet taken shape, flickering, assembling, dissolving without his conscious thought.

"You didn't show up for work," Marlene said. "They gave me a call about that."

"Sorry."

"How are you gonna afford this taste you have for expensive food?" Marlene asked. "Without working, I mean."

"Do something illegal," Ric said. "Most likely."

"That's what I thought." She looked up at him, sideways. "You gonna let me play?"

"If you want."

Marlene swallowed half her wine, looked at the littered apartment, shrugged.

"Only if you really want," Ric said. "It has to be a thing you decide."

"What else have I got to do?" she said.

"I'm going to have to do some research, first," he said. "Spend a few days accessing the library."

Marlene was looking at him again. "Boredom," she said. "In your experience, is that why most people turn to crime?"

"In my experience," he said, "most people turn to crime because of stupidity."

She grinned. "That's cool," she said. "That's sort of what I figured."
She lit a cigaret. "You have a plan?"

"Something I can only do once. Then every freak in Western America
is going to be looking for me with a machine gun."

Marlene grinned. "Sounds exciting."

He looked at her. "Remember what I said about stupidity."

She laughed. "I've been smart all my life. What's it ever got me?"

Ric, looking down at her, felt a warning resonate through him, like an
unmistakable taste drawn across his tongue. "You've got a lot to lose,
Marlene," he said. "A lot more than I do."

"Shit." The cigaret had burned her fingers. She squashed it in the ashtray,
too fast, spilling ashes on the couch. Ric watched her for a moment, then
went back to his thinking.

People were dying all over California in a war over the neurohormone
Genesios Three. There had to be a way to take advantage of it.

6

"You a cop, buck?"

The style was different here from the people Ric knew in Iberia. In
Granada, Ric had worn a gaucho mode straight from Argentina, tight pants
with silver dollars sewn down the seams, sashes wound around nipped-in
waists, embroidered vests.

He didn't know what was worn by the people who had broken up the
Cadillacs. He'd never seen any of them.

Here the new style was something called Urban Surgery. The girl bore
the first example Ric had ever seen close up. The henna-red hair was in
cornrows, braided with transparent plastic beads that held fast-mutating phos-
phorescent bacteria that constantly reformed themselves in glowing patterns.
The nose had been broadened and flattened to cover most of the cheeks,
turning the nostrils into a pair of lateral slits, the base of the nose wider than
the mouth. The teeth had been replaced by alloy transplants sharp as razors
that clacked together in a precise, unpleasant way when she closed her mouth.
The eyebrows were gone altogether and beneath them were dark plastic
implants that covered the eye sockets. Ric couldn't tell, and probably wasn't
supposed to know, whether there were eyes in there any more, or sophisticated
scanners tagged to the optic nerve.

The effect was to flatten the face, turn it into a canvas for the tattoo artist
that had covered every inch of exposed flesh. Complex mathematical state-
ments ran over the forehead. Below the black plastic eye implants were urban
skyscrapes, silhouettes of buildings providing a false horizon across the
flattened nose. The chin appeared to be a circuit diagram.

Ric looked into the dark eye sockets and tried not to flinch. "No," he said. "I'm just passing through."

One of her hands was on the table in front of him. It was tattooed as completely as the face and the fingernails had been replaced by alloy razors, covered with transparent plastic safety caps.

"I saw you in here yesterday," she said. "And again today. I was wondering if you want something."

He shrugged. It occurred to him that, repellent as Urban Surgery was, it was fine camouflage. Who was going to be able to tell one of these people from another?

"You're a little old for this place, buck," the girl said. He figured her age as about fourteen. She was small-waisted and had narrow hips and large breasts. Ric did not find her attractive.

This was his second trip to Phoenix. The bar didn't have a name, unless it was simply BAR, that being all that was written on the sign outside. It was below street level, in the storage cellar of an old building. Concrete walls were painted black. Dark plastic tables and chairs had been added, and bare fluorescent tubes decorated the walls. Speaker amps flanked the bar, playing cold electronic music devoid of noticeable rhythm or melody.

He looked at the girl and leaned closer to her. "I need your permission to drink here, or what?" he said.

"No," she said. "Just to deal here."

"I'm not dealing," he said. "I'm just observing the passing urban scene, okay?" He was wearing a lightweight summer jacket of a cream color over a black T-shirt with Cyrillic lettering, black jeans, white sneakers. Nondescript street apparel.

"You got credit?" the girl asked.

"Enough."

"Buy me a drink then?"

He grinned. "I need your permission to deal, and you don't have any credit? What kind of outlaw are you?"

"A thirsty outlaw."

Ric signaled the bartender. Whatever it was that he brought her looked as if it was made principally out of cherry soda.

"Seriously," she said. "I can pay you back later. Someone I know is supposed to meet me here. He owes me money."

"My name's Marat," said Ric. "With a silent *t*."

"I'm Super Virgin. You from Canada or something? You talk a little funny."

"I'm from Switzerland."

Super Virgin nodded and sipped her drink. Ric glanced around the bar. Most of the patrons wore Urban Surgery or at least made an effort in the direction of its style. Super Virgin frowned at him.

"You're supposed to ask if I'm really cherry." she said. "If you're wondering, the drink should give you a clue."

"I don't care," Ric said.

She grinned at him with her metal teeth. "You don't wanna ball me?"

Ric watched his dual reflection, in her black eye sockets, slowly shake its head. She laughed. "I like a guy who knows what he likes," she said. "That's the kind we have in Cartoon Messiah. Can I have another drink?"

There was an ecology in kid gangs, Ric knew. They had different reasons for existing and filled different functions. Some wanted turf, some trade, some the chance to prove their ideology. Some moved information, and from Ric's research that seemed to be Cartoon Messiah's function.

But even if Cartoon Messiah were smart, they hadn't been around very long. A perpetual problem with groups of young kids involving themselves in gang activities was that they had very short institutional memories. There were a few things they wouldn't recognize or know to prepare for, not unless they'd been through them at least once. They made up for it by being faster than the opposition, by being more invisible.

Ric was hoping Cartoon Messiah was full of young, fresh minds.

He signaled the bartender again. Super Virgin grinned at him.

"You sure you don't wanna ball me?"

"Positive."

"I'm gonna be cherry till I die. I'm just not interested. None of the guys seem like anybody I'd want to sleep with." Ric didn't say anything. She sipped the last of her drink. "You think I'm repulsive-looking, right?"

"That seems to be your intention."

She laughed. "You're okay, Marat. What's it like in Switzerland?"

"Hot."

"So hot you had to leave, maybe?"

"Maybe."

"You looking for work?"

"Not yet. Just looking around."

She leaned closer to him. "You find out anything interesting while you're looking, and I'll pay you for it. Just leave a message here, at the Bar."

"You deal in information?"

She licked her lips. "That and other things. This Bar, see, it's in a kind of interface. North of here is Lounge Lizard turf, south and east are the Cold Wires, west is the Silicon Romantics. The Romantics are on their way out." She gave a little sneer. "They're brocade commandoes, right? Their turf's being cut up. But here, it's no-gang's-land. Where things get moved from one buyer to another."

"Cartoon Messiah—they got turf?"

She shook her head. "Just places where we can be found. Territory is not what we're after. Two-Fisted Jesus—he's our sort-of chairman—he says only stupid people like brocade boys want turf, when the real money's in data.''

Ric smiled. ''That's smart. Property values are down, anyway.''

He could see his reflection in her metal teeth, a pale smear. ''You got anything you wanna deal in, I can set it up,'' she said. ''Software? Biologicals? Pharmaceuticals? Wetware?''

''I have nothing. Right now.''

She turned to look at a group of people coming in the door. ''Cold Wires,'' she said. ''These are the people I'm supposed to meet.'' She tipped her head back and swallowed the rest of her drink. ''They're so goddam bourgeoise,'' she said. ''Look—their surgery's fake, it's just good makeup. And the tattoos—they spray 'em on through a stencil. I hate people who don't have the courage of their convictions, don't you?''

''They can be useful, though.'' Smiling, thin-lipped.

She grinned at him. ''Yeah. They can. Stop by tomorrow and I'll pay you back, okay? See ya.'' She pushed her chair back, scraping alloy on the concrete floor, a small metal scream.

Ric sipped his drink, watching the room. Letting its rhythm seep through his skin. Things were firming in his mind.

7

''Hi.''

The security guard looked up at him from under the plastic brim of his baseball cap. He frowned. ''Hi. You need something? I seen you around before.''

''I'm Warren Whitmore,'' Ric said. ''I'm recovering from an accident, going to finish the course of treatment soon. Go out into the real world.'' Whitmore was one of Ric's former neighbors, a man who'd had his head split in half by a falling beam. He hadn't left any instructions about radical life-preservation measures and the artificial intelligences who ran the hospital were going to keep him alive till they burned up the insurance and then the family's money.

''Yeah?'' the guard said. ''Congratulations.'' There was a plastic tape sewed on over the guard's breast pocket that said LYSAGHT.

''The thing is, I don't have a job waiting. Cigar?''

Ric had seen Lysaght smoking big stogies outside the hospital doors. They wouldn't let him light up inside. Ric had bought him the most expensive Havanas available at the hospital gift shop.

Lysaght took the cigar, rolled it between his fingers while he looked left and right down the corridor, trying to decide whether to light it or not. Ric reached for his lighter.

"I had some military training in my former life," Ric said. "I thought I might look into the idea of getting into the security business, once I get into the world. Could I buy you a drink, maybe, after you get off shift? Talk about what you do."

Lysaght drew on the cigar, still looking left and right, seeing only patients. He was a big fleshy man, about forty, dressed in a black uniform with body armor sewn into pockets on his chest and back. His long dark hair was slicked back behind his ears, falling over his shoulders in greased ringlets. His sideburns came to points. A brushed-alloy gun with a hardwood custom grip and a laser sight hung conspicuously on one hip, next to the gas grenades, next to the plastic handwrap restraints, next to the combat staff, next to the portable gas mask.

"Sure," Lysaght said. "Why not?" He blew smoke in the general direction of an elderly female patient walking purposefully down the corridor in flowery pajamas. The patient blinked but kept walking.

"Hey, Mrs. Calderone, how you doin'?" Lysaght said. Mrs. Calderone ignored him. "Head case," said Lysaght.

"I want to work for a sharp outfit though," Ric said. He looked at Lysaght's belt. "With good equipment and stuff, you know?"

"That's Folger Security," Lysaght said. "If we weren't good, we wouldn't be working for a hospital this size."

During his time in the Cadillacs and elsewhere, Ric had been continually surprised by how little it actually took to bribe someone. A few drinks, a few cigars, and Lysaght was working for him. And Lysaght didn't even know it yet. Or, with luck, ever.

"Listen," Lysaght was saying. "I gotta go smoke this in the toilet. But I'll see you at the guard station around five, okay?"

"Sounds good."

8

That night, his temples throbbing with pain, Ric entered Marlene's condeco and walked straight to the kitchen for something to ease the long raw ache that seemed to coat the insides of his throat. He could hear the sounds of *Alien Inquisitor* on the vid. He was carrying a two-liter plastic bottle of industrial-strength soap he'd just stolen from the custodian's store room here in Marlene's condeco. He put down the bottle of soap, rubbed his sore shoulder muscle, took some whiskey from the shelf, and poured it into a tall glass. He took a slow, deliberate drink and winced as he felt the fire in his throat. He added water to the glass. *Alien Inquisitor* diminished in volume, then he heard the sound of Marlene's flipflops slapping against her heels.

Her eyes bore the heavy makeup she wore to work. "Jesus," Marlene said. She screwed up her face. "You smell like someone's been putting out cigarets in your pockets. Where the hell have you been?"

"Smoking cigars with a rentacop. He wears so much equipment and armor he has to wear a truss, you know that? He got drunk and told me."

"Which rentacop?"

"One who works for the hospital."

"The hospital? We're going to take off the hospital?" Marlene shook her head. "That's pretty serious, Ric."

Ric was wondering if she'd heard *take off* used that way on the vid. "Yes." He eased the whiskey down his throat again. Better.

"Isn't that dangerous? Taking off the same hospital where you were a patient?"

"We're not going to be doing it in person. We're going to have someone else do the work."

"Who?"

"Cartoon Messiah, I think. They're young and promising."

"What's the stuff in the plastic bottle for?"

He looked at her, swirling the whiskey absently in the glass. "The stuff's mostly potassium hydroxide," he said. "That's wood lye. You can use it to make plastic explosive."

Marlene shrugged, then reached in her pocket for a cigaret. Ric frowned.

"You seem not to be reacting to that, Marlene," he said. "Robbing a hospital is serious, plastic explosive isn't?"

She blew smoke at him. "Let me show you something." She went back into the living room and then returned with her pouch belt. She fished in it for a second, then threw him a small aerosol bottle.

Ric caught it and looked at the label. "Christ," he said. He blinked and looked at the bottle again. "Jesus Christ."

"Ten-ounce aerosol bottle of mustard gas," Marlene said. "Sixteen dollars in Starbright scrip at your local boutique. For personal protection, you know? The platinum designer bottle costs more."

Ric was blinking furiously. "Christ," he said.

"Some sixteen-year-old asshole tried to rape me once," Marlene said. "I hit him with the gas and now he's reading braille. You know?"

Ric took another sip of the whiskey and then wordlessly placed the mustard gas in Marlene's waiting palm. "You're in America now, Ric," Marlene said. "You keep forgetting that, singing your old Spanish marching songs."

He rubbed his chin. "Right," he said. "I've got to make adjustments."

"Better do it soon," Marlene said, "If you're going to start busting into hospitals."

9

The next day Ric went to the drugstore, where he purchased a large amount of petroleum jelly, some nasal mist that came in squeeze bottles, liquid bleach, a bottle of toilet cleaner, a small amount of alcohol-based lamp fuel, and a bottle of glycerin. Then he drove to a chemical supply store, where he bought some distilling equipment and some litmus paper.

On his way back he stopped by an expensive liquor store and bought some champagne. He didn't want the plastic bottles the domestic stuff came in; instead he bought the champagne imported from France, in glass bottles with the little hollow cone in the bottom. It was the biggest expense of the day.

10

Ric was distilling acrolein out of toilet bowl cleaner and glycerine when Marlene came home from work, cursing at her boss from the moment she entered the apartment. She watched as Ric put the acrolein into the nasal mist squeeze bottles, which he'd emptied and washed earlier.

"What's that, Ricardo?" she asked. He gave her a bottle.

"Use it instead of the mustard gas," he said. "It isn't quite so . . . devastating."

"I *like* being devastating," Marlene said. She put the squeeze bottle back on the table and poured a glass of champagne.

"I made plastic explosives today," Ric said. "They're in the icebox."

"Great." She put some pills in her mouth and swallowed them down with champagne.

"I'll show you a trick," Ric said. He got some twine from the cupboard, cut it into strips, and soaked it in the lamp fuel. While it was soaking he got a large mixing bowl and filled it with water and ice. Then he tied the string around the empty champagne bottles, about three inches above the topmost point of the little hollow cone on the bottom. He got his lighter and set fire to the thread. It burned slowly, with a cool blue flame, for a couple minutes. Then he took the bottle and plunged it into the ice water. It split neatly in half with a crystalline snapping sound.

Ric took some of the plastic explosive and packed it into the bottom of the champagne bottle. He pushed a pencil into the middle of it; making a narrow hole for the detonator.

"There," he said. "That's a shaped charge. I'll make the detonators tomorrow, out of peroxide, acetone, and sulphuric acid. It's easy."

"What's a shaped charge, Ricardo?"

"It's used for blowing a hole through armor. Steel doors, cars. Tanks. Things like that."

Marlene looked at him appraisingly. "You're adjusting yourself to America, all right," she said.

11

Ric took a bus to Phoenix and rented a motel room with a kitchenette, paying five days in advance and using a false name. In the motel he changed clothes and took a cab to the Bar. Super Virgin waved as he came in. She was with her friend, Captain Islam. He was a long, gawky boy, about sixteen, with his head shaved and covered with the tattoos of Urban Surgery. He hadn't had any alterations yet, or the eye implants this group favored. Instead he wore complicated mirrorshades with twin minicameras, registering radiation in UV and infrared as well as the normal spectrum, mounted above the bridge of the nose and liquid-crystal video displays on the backs of the eyepieces that received input from the minicameras or from any vid program he felt like seeing. Ric wondered if things weren't real to him, not unless he saw them on the vid. He didn't talk much, just sat quietly behind his drink and his shades and watched whatever it was that he watched. The effect was unsettling and was probably meant to be. Ric could be talking to him and would never know whether the man was looking at him or at *Video Vixens*. Ric had first pegged him for a user, but Super Virgin said not.

Ric got a whiskey at the bar and joined the two at their table. "Slow night?" he asked.

"We're waiting for the jai alai to come on," Super Virgin said. "Live from Bilbao. We've got some money down."

"Sounds slow to me."

She gave a brittle laugh. "Guess so, Marat. You got any ideas for accelerating our motion?"

Ric frowned. "I have something to sell. Some information. But I don't know if it's something you'd really want to deal with."

"Too hot?" The words were Captain Islam's. Ric looked at his own distorted face in the Captain's spectacles.

"Depends on your concept of *hot*. The adjective I had in mind was *big*."

"Big." The word came with a pause before and after, as if Captain Islam had never heard the word before and was wondering what it meant.

Ric took a bottle of nasal mist out of his pocket and squeezed it once up each nostril.

"Got a virus?" Virgin asked.

"I'm allergic to Arizona."

Captain Islam was frowning. "So what's this action of yours, buck?" he asked.

"Several kilos of Thunder."

Captain Islam continued to stare into the interior of his mirrors. Super Virgin burst into laughter.

"I knew you weren't here as a tourist, Marat!" she cackled. " 'Several kilos!' *One* kilo is weight! What the hell is 'several'?"

"I don't know if you people can move that much," Ric said. "Also, I'd like an agreement. I want twenty percent of the take, and I want you to move my twenty percent for me, free of charge. If you think you can move that kind of weight at all, that is." He sipped his whiskey. "Maybe I should talk to some people in California."

"You talk to them, you end up dead," Virgin said. "They're not friendly to anyone these days, not when Thunder's involved."

Ric smiled. "Maybe you're right."

"Where is it? Who do we have to steal it from?"

"Another thing," Ric said. "I want certain agreements. I don't want any excessive force used, here. Nobody shot."

"Sometimes things happen," Captain Islam said. Ric had the feeling that the Captain was definitely looking at him this time. "Sometimes things can't be avoided."

"This stuff is guarded by an organization who won't forget it if any of their people get hurt," Ric explained. "If you try to move this kind of weight, word's going to get out that it's you that has the Thunder, and that means these characters are going to find out sooner or later. You might be tempted to give me to them as a way of getting the heat off you. Which would be a mistake, because I intend on establishing an alibi. That would mean that they're going to be extremely upset with you misleading them." Ric sipped his whiskey and smiled. "I'm just looking out for all our interests."

"A hospital," Captain Islam said. He shook his head. "You want us to take off a hospital. The one up in Flag, right? You stupid shit."

"I have a plan," Ric said. "I know their defenses, to a certain point. I know how they're organized. I know how they *think*."

"That's Folger Security, for chrissake," Captain Islam said. "They're tough. They don't forget when someone makes idiots out of them."

"That's why it's got to be my rules," Ric said. "But I should probably mention something here." He grinned, seeing the smile reflected in the Captain's quicksilver eyes. "It's an inside job," Ric said. "I'm friends with someone on their force."

Virgin whooped and banged him on the shoulder with her left hand, the one with the sheathed claws. "Why didn't you say so?" she said.

"You people," Ric said. "You've got to learn to be patient."

12

Treble whimpered against a throbbing bass line. Shafts of red sunset sliced into the violet depth of the Grand Canyon.

Marlene backed, spun, turned back to Ric, touched palms. She was wearing Indian war paint. Colors zigzagged across her face. Her eyes and smile were bright.

The band was dressed like hussars, lights glittering off brocade, the lead singer sweating under her dolman, threatening to split her tight breeches with each of her leaps. Her eye makeup dazzled like butterfly wings. Her lyrics were all heroism, thunder, revolution. The romantic wave against which Cartoon Messiah and Urban Surgery were a cool reaction.

Marlene stepped forward, pressing herself against him. He circled her with his arms, felt her sacral dimples as they leaned back and spun against each other. At the end of the five-bar chorus she gave a grind of her hips against him, then winked.

He laughed. Here he was, establishing his alibi in grand style, while, back in Flagstaff, Cartoon Messiah were working for him. And they didn't even know it.

13

Readiness crackled from Ric's nerves as he approached the hotel door. They could try to kill him, he knew. Now would be the best time. Black Thunder tended to generate that kind of behavior. He'd been telling them he had ideas for other jobs, that he'd be valuable to them alive, but he couldn't be sure if they believed him.

The door opened and Super Virgin grinned at him with her metal teeth. "Piece of cake, Marat," she said. "Your cut's on the table."

The hotel room was dark, the walls draped in blueblack plastic. More plastic sheets covered the floors, the ceiling, some of the furniture. Coldness touched Ric's spine. There could be a lot of blood spilled in here, and the plastic would keep it from getting on anything. Computer consoles and vid sets gave off quiet hums. Cables snaked over the floor, held down with duct tape. On the table was a half-kilo white paper packet. Captain Islam and Two-Fisted Jesus sat beside it, tapping into a console. Jesus looked up.

"Just in time," he said, "for the movies."

He was a skinny boy, about eighteen, his identity obscured by the obsessive mutilations of Urban Surgery. He wore a T-shirt featuring a picture of a muscular, bearded man in tights, with cape and halo. Here in this place, the hotel room he had hung with plastic and filled with electronics, he moved and spoke with an assurance the others hadn't absorbed, the kind of malevolent grace displayed by those who gave law and style to others, unfettered by conscience. Ric could appreciate Jesus's moves. He'd had them once himself.

Ric walked to the paper packet and hefted it. He tore open a corner, saw a row of little white envelopes, each labeled Genesios Three with the pharmaceutical company sigil in the corner. He didn't know a test for B-44 so he just stuffed the envelope in his pocket.

"This is gonna be great," Super Virgin said. She came up behind him and handed him a highball glass half-filled with whiskey. "You got time to watch a flick? We went in packing cameras. We're gonna cut a documentary of the whole thing and sell it to a station in Nogales. They'll write some scenes around it and use it on an episode of *VidWar*." She giggled. "The Mexicans don't care how many gringo hospitals get taken off. They'll put some kind of plot around it. A dumb love story or something. But it's the highest-rated program, 'cause people know it's real. Except for *Australian Rules Firefight Football*, and that's real, too."

Ric looked around and found a chair. It seemed as if these people planned to let him live. He reached into his pocket and fired a round of nasal mist up each nostril. "Sure. I'll watch," he sniffed. "I got time."

"This is a rough cut only, okay?" Captain Islam's voice. "So bear with us."

There was a giant-sized liquid-crystal vid display set up on the black plastic on the wall. A picture sizzled into existence. The hospital, a vast concrete fortress set in an aureole of halogen light. Ric felt his tongue go dry. He swallowed with difficulty.

The image moved, jolting. Whoever was carrying the camera was walking, fast, across the parking lot. Two-Fisted Jesus tapped the keys of his computer. The image grew smooth. "We're using a lot of computer enhancement on the vid, see?" Super Virgin said. "We can smooth out the jitters from the moving camera. Except for select bits to enhance the ver—the versi—"

"Verisimilitude," said Captain Islam.

"Right. Just to let everyone know this is the real thing. And we're gonna change everyone's appearance electronically, so no one can recognize us."

Cut to someone moving into the hospital's front door, moving right past the metal detectors. Ric saw a tall girl, blonde, dressed in pink shorts and a tube top. White sandal straps coiled about her ankles.

"A mercenary," Virgin said. "We hired her for this. The slut."

Captain Islam laughed. "She's an actress," he explained. "Trying for a career south of the border. Wants the publicity."

The girl stepped up to a guard. Ric recognized Lysaght. She was asking directions, pointing. Lysaght was gazing at her breasts as he replied. She smiled and nodded and walked past. He looked after her, chewing his cigar, hiking up his gunbelt. Ric grinned. As long as guards like Lysaght were around, nothing was safe.

The point of view changed abruptly, a subjective shot, someone moving down a hospital corridor. Patients in ordinary clothes moving past, smiling.

"We had a camera in this necklace she was wearing. A gold owl, about an inch long, with 3D vidcams behind the eyes. Antenna in the chain, receiver in her bag. We pasted it to her chest so it would always be looking straight forward and wouldn't get turned around or anything. Easy stuff."

"We gotta do some pickups, here," Jesus said. "Get a picture of the girl moving down the corridor. Then we tell the computer to put all the stripes on the walls. It'll be worth more when we sell it."

Subjective shot of someone moving into a woman's toilet, stepping into a stall, reaching into a handbag for a pair of coveralls.

"Another pickup shot," Jesus muttered. "Gotta get her putting on her coveralls." He made a note on a pad.

The point of view lurched upward, around, out of the stall. Centered on a small ventilator intake high on a wall. Hands came into the picture, holding a screwdriver.

"Methanethiol," Super Virgin said. "That stuff's gonna be real useful from now on. How'd you know how to make it?"

"Elementary chemistry," Ric said. He'd used it to clear out political meetings of which the Cadillacs didn't approve.

The screen was off the ventilator. Hands were reaching into the bag, taking out a small glass bottle. Carefully loosening the screw top, the hands placed the bottle upright in the ventilator. Then the point of view dipped, a hand reached down to pick up the ventilator screen. Then the ventilator screen was shoved violently into the hole, knocking the bottle over.

Airborne methanethiol gave off a horrible, nauseating smell at one-fiftieth of a part per billion. The psychology wing of the hospital was going to get a dose considerably in excess of that.

The subjective camera was moving with great rapidity down hospital corridors. To a stairwell, then down.

Cut to Super Virgin in a phone booth. She had a small voice recorder in her hand, and was punching buttons.

"Freeze that," said Two-Fisted Jesus. Virgin's image turned to ice. Jesus began tapping keys.

The tattooing shifted, dissolved to a different pattern. Super Virgin laughed. Her hair shortened, turned darker. The black insets over her eyes vanished. Brown eyes appeared, then they turned a startling pale blue.

"Leave the teeth," she said.

"Nah. I have an idea." Two-Fisted Jesus sat tapping keys for about thirty seconds. He pressed the enter button and the metal teeth disappeared completely. He moved the picture forward a second, then back. Virgin's tongue moved redly behind her tattooed lips. The interior of the mouth was pink, a lot of gum, no teeth at all. She clapped her hands.

"The Mexicans will probably replace her image with some vidstar, anyway," Captain Islam said. "Urban Surgery is too much for them, right now."

"Okay. I want to see this in three dimensions," Jesus said. Super Virgin's image detached itself from the background and began rotating. He stopped it every so often and made small adjustments.

"Make me taller," Super Virgin said. "And skinnier. And give me smaller tits. I hate my tits."

"We do that every time," Jesus said. "People are gonna start to twig."

"Chrome tits. Leather tits. Anything."

Captain Islam laughed. Two-Fisted Jesus made minor adjustments and ignored Super Virgin's complaint.

"Here we go. Say your line."

The image began moving. Virgin's new green eyes sparkled as she held the recorder up to the mouthpiece of the telephone.

"This is Royal Flag." It was the name of one of Arizona's more ideological kid gangs. The voice had been electronically altered and sounded flat. "We've just planted a poison gas bomb in your psychology wing. All the head cases are gonna see Jesus. The world's gene pool will be so much healthier from now on. Have yourself a pleasant day."

Super Virgin was laughing. "Wait'll you see the crowd scenes. Stellar stuff, believe me."

"I believe," said Ric.

14

The video was full of drifting smoke. Vague figures moved through it. Jesus froze the picture and tried to enhance the images, without any success. "Damn," he said. "More pickups."

Ric had watched the action as members of Cartoon Messiah in Folger Security uniforms had hammered their way into a hospital back door. They had moved faultlessly through the corridors to the vault and blasted their way in with champagne-bottle shaped charges. The blasts had set off tremblor alarms in the vault and the Folger people realized they were being hit. Now the raiders were in the corridor before the vault, retracing their steps at a run.

"Okay," Super Virgin said. "The moment of truth, coming up."

The corridor was full of billowing tear gas. Crouched figures moved through it. Commands were coming down on the monitored Folger channels.

Then, coming through the smoke, another figure. A tall woman in a helmet, her hand pressed to her ear, trying to hear the radio. There was a gun in her hand. She raised the gun.

Thuds on the soundtrack. Tear-gas canisters, fired at short range. One of them struck the woman in her armored chest and bounced off. It hadn't flown far enough to arm itself and it just rolled down the corridor. The woman fell flat.

"Just knocked the wind out of her." Captain Islam was grinning. "How about that for keeping our deal, huh?" Somebody ran forward and kicked the gun out of her hand. The camera caught a glimpse of her lying on the floor, her mouth open, trying to breathe. There were dots of sweat on her nose. Her eye makeup looked like butterfly wings.

"Now that's what I call poignant," Jesus said. "Human interest stuff. You know?"

The kids ran away across the parking lot, onto their fuel-cell tricycles, and away, bouncing across the parking lot and the railroad tracks beyond.

"We're gonna spice this up a bit," Jesus said. "Cut in some shots of guards shooting at us, that kind of thing. Steal some suspenseful music. Make the whole thing more exciting. What do you think?"

"I like it," said Ric. He put down his untasted whiskey. Jacob and his neurotoxin had made him cautious. "Do I get any royalties? Being script-writer and all?"

"The next deal you set up for us. Maybe."

Ric shrugged. "How are you gonna move the Thunder?"

"Small pieces, probably."

"Let me give you some advice," Ric said. "The longer you hang onto it, the bigger the chance Folger will find out you have it and start cramping your action. I have an idea. Can you handle a large increase of capital?"

15

"Is this the stuff? Great." Marlene swept in the motel room door, grinning, with her overnight bag. She gave Ric a brief hug, then went to the table of the kitchenette. She picked up the white packet, hefted it in her hand.

"Light," she said.

"Yeah."

"I can't believe people kill each other over this."

"They could kill *us*," Ric said. "Don't forget that."

Marlene licked her lips and peeled the packet. She took one of the small white envelopes and tore it open, spilling dark powder into her cupped palm. She cocked her head.

"Doesn't look like much. How do you take it?"

Ric remembered the flood of well-being in his body, the way the world had suddenly tasted better. No, he thought. He wasn't going to get hung up on Thunder. "Intraveneous, mostly," he said. "Or they could put it in capsules."

Marlene sniffed at it. "Doesn't smell like anything. What's the dose?"

"I don't know. I wasn't planning on taking any."

She began licking the stuff on her palm. Ric watched the little pink tongue lapping at the powder. He turned his eyes away.

"Take it easy," he said.

"Tastes funny. Kind of like green pepper sauce, with a touch of kerosene."

"A touch of stupidity," he said. "A touch of . . ." He moved around the room, hands in his pockets. "A touch of craziness. People who are around Black Thunder get crazy."

Marlene finished licking her palm and kicked off her shoes. "Craziness sounds good," she said. She stepped up behind him and put her arms around him. "How crazy do you think we can get tonight?"

"I don't know." He thought for a minute. "Maybe I could show you our movie."

16

Ric faced the window in the motel room, watching, his mind humming. The window had been dialed to polarize completely and he could see himself, Marlene behind him on the untidy bed, the plundered packet of Thunder on the table. It had been eight days since the hospital had been robbed. Marlene had taken the bus to Phoenix every evening.

"You should try some of our product," Marlene said. "The stuff's just . . . when I use it, I can feel my mind just start to click. Move faster, smoother. Thoughts come out of nowhere."

"Right," Ric said. "Nowhere."

Ric saw Marlene's reflection look up at his own dark plateglass ghost. "Do I detect sarcasm, here?"

"No. Preoccupation, that's all."

"Half the stuff's mine, right? I can eat it, burn it, drop it out the window. Drop it on your head, if I want to. Right?"

"That is correct," said Ric.

"Things are getting dull," Marlene said. "You're spending your evenings off drinking with Captain Islam and Super Virgin and Krishna Commando . . . I get to stay here and watch the vid."

"Those people I'm drinking with," Ric said. "There's a good chance they could die because of what we're going to do. They're our victims. Would you like to have a few drinks with them? A few smokes?" He turned from the window and looked at her. "Knowing they may die because of you?"

Marlene frowned up at him. "Are you scared of them?" she asked. "Is that why you're talking like this?"

Ric gave a short laugh. Marlene ran her fingers through her almost-blonde hair. Ric watched her in the mirror.

"You don't have to involve yourself in this part, Marlene," Ric said. "I can do it by myself, I think."

She was looking at the darkened vid screen. Her eyes were bright. A smile tugged at her lips.

"I'm ready," she said. "Let's do it."

"I've got to get some things ready first."

"Hurry up. I don't want to waste this feeling I've got."

Ric closed his eyes. He didn't want to see his reflection any more. "What feeling is that?" he asked.

"The feeling that my time is coming. To try something new."

"Yeah," Ric said. His eyes were still closed. "That's what I thought."

17

Ric, wearing leather gardeners' gloves, smoothed the earth over the explosive device, wrapped in plastic, he had just buried under a pyracantha bush planted next to a vacation cabin. Drizzle rattled off his collar. His knees were growing wet. He took the aerial for the radio detonator and pulled it carefully along one of the stems of the bush.

Marlene stood next to him in red plastic boots. She was standing guard, snuffling in the cold. Ric could hear the sound of her lips as she chewed gum.

White shafts of light tracked over their heads, filtered by juniper scrub that stood between the cabins and the expressway heading north out of Flagstaff. Ric froze. His form, caught among pyracantha barbs, cast a stark moving shadow on the peeling white wall.

"Flashlight," he said, when the car had passed. Moving between the light and any onlookers, Marlene flicked it on. Ric carefully smoothed the soil, spread old leaves. He thought the thorns on the pyracantha would keep most people away, but he didn't want disturbed soil attracting anyone.

Rain danced down in the yellow light. "Thanks," he said. Marlene popped a bubble. Ric stood up, brushing muck from his knees. There were more bundles to bury, and it was going to be a long, wet night.

18

"They're going to take you off if they can," Ric said. "They're from California and they know this is a one-shot deal, so they don't care if they offend you or leave you dead. But they think it's going to happen in Phoenix, see." Ric, Super Virgin, and Two-Fisted Jesus stood in front of the juniper by the alloy road, looking down at the cluster of cabins. "They may have hired people from the Cold Wires or whoever, so that they can have people who know the terrain. So the idea is, we move the meet up to the last minute. Up here, north of Flag."

"We don't know the terrain, either," Jesus said. He looked uncomfortable here, his face a monochrome blotch in the unaccustomed sun.

Ric took a bottle of nasal mist from his pocket and squeezed it once up each nostril. He sniffed. "You can learn it between now and then. Rent all the cabins, put soldiers in the nearest ones. Lay in your commo gear." Ric pointed up at the ridge above where they stood. "Put some people with long guns up there, some IR goggles and scopes. Anyone comes in, you'll know about it."

"I don't know, Marat. I like Phoenix. I know the way that city thinks." Jesus shook his head. "Tourist cabins."

"They're better than hotel rooms. Tourist cabins have back doors."

"Hey." Super Virgin was grinning, metal teeth winking in the sun as she tugged on Jesus' sleeve. "Expand your horizons. This is the *great outdoors*."

Jesus shook his head. "I'll think about it."

19

Marlene was wearing war paint and dancing in the middle of her condeco living room. The furniture was pushed back to the walls, the music was loud enough to rattle the crystal on the kitchen shelves.

"You've got to decide, Marlene," Ric said. He was sitting behind the pushed-back table, and the paper packets of Thunder were laid out in front of him. "How much of this do you want to sell?"

"I'll decide later."

"Now. Now. Marlene."

"Maybe I'll keep it all."

Ric looked at her. She shook sweat out of her eyes and laughed.

"Just a joke, Ric."

He said nothing.

"It's just happiness," she said, dancing. "Happiness in paper envelopes. Better than money. You ought to use some. It'll make you less tense." Sweat was streaking her war paint. "What'll you use the money for, anyway? Move to Zanzibar and buy yourself a safe condeco and a bunch of safe investments? Sounds boring to me, Ric. Why'n't you use it to create some excitement?''

He could not, Ric thought, afford much in the way of regret. But still a sadness came over him, drifting through his body on slow opiate time. Another few days, he thought, and he wouldn't have to use people any more. Which was good, because he was losing his taste for it.

20

A kid from California was told to wait by a certain public phone at a certain time, with his bank and without his friends. The phone call told him to go to another phone booth and be there within a certain allotted time. He complained, but the phone hung up in mid-syllable.

At the second phone he was told to take the keys taped to the bottom of the shelf in the phone booth, go to such-and-such a car in the parking lot, and drive to Flagstaff to another public phone. His complaints were cut short by the slamming receiver. Once in Flagstaff, he was given another set of directions. By now he had learned not to complain.

If there were still people with him they were very good, because they hadn't been seen at any of the turns of his course.

He was working for Ric, even though he didn't know it.

21

Marlene was practicing readiness. New patterns were constantly flickering through her mind and she loved watching her head doing its tricks.

She was wearing her war paint as she sat up on a tall ridge behind the cabins, her form encased in a plastic envelope that dispersed her body heat in patterns unrecognizable to infra-red scanners. She had a radio and a powerful antenna, and she was humming ''Greensleeves'' to herself as she looked down at the cabins through long binoculars wrapped in a scansheet paper tube to keep the sun from winking on the lenses. Marlene also had headphones on and a parabolic mic pointed down at the cabins, so that she could hear anything going on. Right now all she could hear was the wind.

She could see the cabins perfectly, as well as the two riflemen on the ridge across the road. She was far away from anything likely to happen, but if things went well she wouldn't be needed for anything but pushing buttons on cue anyway.

''Greensleeves'' hummed on and on. Marlene was having a good time. Working for Ric.

22

Two-Fisted Jesus had turned the cabin into another plastic-hung cavern, lit by pale holograms and cool video monitors, filled with the hum of machinery and the brightness of liquid crystal. Right in the middle was a round coffee table full of crisp paper envelopes.

Ric had been allowed entry because he was one of the principals in the transaction. He'd undergone scanning as he entered, both for weapons and for electronics. Nothing had been found. His Thunder, and about half of Marlene's, was sitting on the table.

Only two people were in the room besides Ric. Super Virgin had the safety caps off her claws and was carrying an automatic with laser sights in a belt holster.

Ric considered the sights a pure affectation in a room this small. Jesus had a sawed-off twin-barrel shotgun sitting in his lap. The pistol grip might break his wrist but the spread would cover most of the room, and Ric wondered if Jesus had considered how much electronics he'd lose if he ever used it.

23

Where three lightposts had been marked with fluorescent tape, the kid from California pulled off on the verge of the alloy road that wound ahead to leap over the Grand Canyon into Utah. Captain Islam pulled up behind him with two soldiers, and they scanned the kid right there, stripped him of a pistol and a homing sensor, and put him in the back of their own car.

"You're beginning to piss me off," the kid said.

"Just do what we tell you," Captain Islam said, pulling away, "and you'll be king of Los Angeles."

24

Ric's hands were trembling so hard he had to press them hard against the arms of his chair in order to keep it from showing. He could feel sweat oozing from his armpits. He really wasn't good at this kind of thing.

The kid from California was pushed in the door by Captain Islam, who stepped out and closed the door behind him. The kid was black and had clear plastic eye implants, with the electronics gleaming inside the transparent eyeball. He had patterned scarring instead of the tattoos, and was about sixteen. He wore a silver jacket, carried a duffel to put the Thunder in, and seemed annoyed.

"Once you step inside," Jesus said, "you have five minutes to complete our transaction. Go ahead and test any of the packets at random."

"Yeah," the kid said. "I'll do that." He crouched by the table, pulled vials from his pockets, and made a series of tests while Jesus counted off at fifteen-second intervals. He managed to do four tests in three minutes, then stood up. Ric could see he was salivating for the stuff.

"It's good," he said.

"Let's see your key." The kid took a credit spike from his pocket and handed it to Jesus, who put it in the computer in front of him. Jesus transferred two hundred fifteen thousand in Starbright policorporate scrip from the spike to his own spike that was jacked into slot two.

"Take your stuff," Jesus said, settling back in his seat. "Captain Islam will take you back to your car. Nice doing business."

The kid gave a sniff, took his spike back, and began to stuff white packets into his duffel. He left the cabin without saying a word. Adrenaline was wailing along Ric's nerves. He stood and took his own spike from his left-hand jacket pocket. His right went to the squeeze bottle of nasal mist in his right. Stray novae were exploding at the peripherals of his vision.

"Look at this, Virgin," Ric said. "Look at all the money sitting in this machine." He laughed. Laughter wasn't hard, but stopping the laughter was.

"Twenty percent is yours, Marat," Jesus said. "Give me your spike."

As Super Virgin stepped up to look at the monitor, Ric brought the squeeze bottle out of his pocket and fired acrolein into her face. His spin toward Jesus was so fast that Virgin's scream had barely begun before he fired another burst of the chemical at Jesus, slamming one hand down on the shotgun to keep him from bringing it up. He'd planned on just holding it there till the boy's grip loosened, but nerves took over and he wrenched it effortlessly from Jesus' hands and barely stopped himself from smashing Jesus in the head with it.

Virgin was on her hands and knees, mucous hanging from her nose and lips. She was trying to draw the pistol. Ric kicked it away. It fell on muffled plastic.

Ric turned and pulled the spikes from the machine. Jesus had fallen out of his chair, was clawing at his face. "Dead man," Jesus said, gasping the words.

"Don't threaten me, asshole," Ric said. "It could have been mustard gas."

And then Marlene, on the ridge far above, watched the sweep hand touch five minutes, thirty seconds, and she pressed her radio button. All the buried charges went off, blasting bits of the other cabins into the sky and doubtless convincing the soldiers in the other buildings that they were under fire by rocket or mortar, that the kid from California had brought an army with him. Simultaneous with the explosive, other buried packages began to gush concealing white smoke into the air. The wind was strong but there was a lot of smoke.

Ric opened the back door and took off, the shotgun hanging in his hand. Random fire burst out but none of it came near. The smoke provided cover from both optical scanners and infra-red, and it concealed him all the way across the yard behind the cabin and down into the arroyo behind it. Sixty yards down the arroyo was a culvert that ran under the expressway. Ric dashed through it, wetting himself to the knees in cold spring snowmelt.

He was now on the other side of the expressway. He didn't think anyone would be looking for him here. He threw the shotgun away and kept running. There was a cross-country motorbike waiting a little farther up the stream.

25

"There," Ric said, pressing the return button. "Half of it's yours."

Marlene was still wearing her war paint. She sipped cognac from a crystal glass and took her spike out of the computer. She laughed. "A hundred K of Starbright," she said, "and paper packets of happiness. What else do I need?"

"A fast armored car, maybe," Ric said. He pocketed his spike. "I'm taking off," he said. He turned to her. "There's room on the bike for two."

"To where?" She was looking at him sidelong.

"To Mexico, for starters," he said. A lie. Ric planned on heading northeast and losing himself for a while in Navajoland.

"To some safe little country. A safe little apartment."

"That's the idea."

Marlene took a hefty swig of cognac. "Not me," she said. "I'm planning on staying in this life."

Ric felt a coldness brush his spine. He reached out to take her hand. "Marlene," he said carefully. "You've got to leave this town. Now."

She pulled her hand away. "Not a chance, Ricardo. I plan on telling my boss just what I think of him. Tomorrow morning. I can't wait."

There was a pain in Ric's throat. "Okay," he said. He stood up. "See you in Mexico, maybe." He began to move for the door. Marlene put her arms around him from behind. Her chin dug into his collarbone.

"Stick around," she said. "For the party."

He shook his head, uncoiled her arms, slid out of them.

"You treat me like I don't know what I'm doing," Marlene said.

He turned and looked at her. Bright eyes looked at him from a mask of bright paint. "You don't," he said.

"I've got lots of ideas. You showed me how to put things together."

"Now I'm showing you how to run and save your life."

"Hah. I'm not going to run. I'm going to stroll out with a briefcase full of happiness and a hundred K in my pocket."

He looked at her and felt a pressure hard in his chest. He knew that none of this was real to her, that he'd never been able to penetrate that strange screen in her mind that stood between Marlene and the rest of the world. Ric had never pierced it, but soon the world would. He felt a coldness filling him, a coldness that had nothing to do with sorrow.

It was hard not to run when he turned and left the apartment.

His breathing came more freely with each step he took.

26

When Ric came off the Navajo Reservation he saw scansheet headlines about how the California gang wars had spilled over into Phoenix, how there were dead people turning up in alleys, others were missing, a club had been bombed. All those people working for him, covering his retreat.

In New Zealand he bought into a condecology in Christchurch, a big place with armored shutters and armored guards, a first-rate new artificial intelligence to handle investments, and a mostly-foreign clientele who profited by the fact that a list of the condeco's inhabitants was never made public . . . this was before he found out that he could buy private property here, a big house on the South Island with a view of his own personal glacier, without a chance of anybody's war accidentally rolling over him.

It was an interesting feeling, sitting alone in his own house, knowing there wasn't anyone within five thousand miles who wanted to kill him.

Ric made friends. He played the market and the horses. And he learned to ski.

At a ski party in late September, held in the house of one of his friends, he drifted from room to room amid a murmur of conversation punctuated with brittle laughter. He had his arm around someone named Reiko, the sheltered daughter of a policorporate bigwig. The girl, nineteen and a student, had long black hair that fell like a tsunami down her shoulders, and was fascinated with his talk of life in the real world. He walked into a back room that was bright with the white glare of video, wondering if the jai alai scores had been posted yet, and he stared into his own face as screams rose around him and his nerves turned to hot magnesium flares.

"Ugh. Mexican scum show," said Reiko, and then she saw the actor's face and her eyes widened.

Ric felt his knees trembling and he sank into an armchair in the back of the room. Ice tittered in his drink. The man on the vid was flaying alive a woman who hung by her wrists from a beam. Blood ran down his forearms.

The camera cut quickly to his tiger's eyes, his thin smile. Ric's eyes. Ric's smile.

"My god," said Reiko. "It's really you, isn't it?"

"No," Ric said. Shaking his head.

"I can't believe they let this stuff even on private stations," someone said from the hallway. Screams rose from the vid. Ric's mind was flailing in the dark.

"I can't watch this," Reiko said, and rushed away. Ric didn't see her go. Burning sweat was running down the back of his neck.

The victim's screams rose. Blood traced artful patterns down her body. The camera cut to her face.

Marlene's face.

Nausea swept Ric and he doubled in his chair. He remembered Two-Fisted Jesus and his talent for creating video images, altering faces, voices, action. They'd found Marlene, as Ric had thought they would, and her voice and body were memorized by Jesus' computers. Maybe the torture was even real.

"It's got to be him," someone in the room said. "It's even his voice. His accent."

"He never did say," said another voice, "what he used to do for a living."

Frozen in his chair, Ric watched the show to the end. There was more torture, more bodies. The video-Ric enjoyed it all. At the end he went down before the blazing guns of the Federal Security Directorate. The credits rolled over the video-Ric's dead face. The director was listed as Jesus Carranza. The film was produced by VideoTek S.A. in collaboration with Messiah Media.

The star's name was given as Jean-Paul Marat.

"A new underground superstar," said a high voice. The voice of someone who thought of himself as an underground connoisseur. "He's been in a lot of pirate video lately. He's the center of a big controversy about how far scum shows can go."

And then the lights came on and Ric saw eyes turning to him in surprise. "It's not me," he said.

"Of course not." The voice belonged to his host. "Incredible resemblance, though. Even your mannerisms. Your accent."

"Not me."

"Hey." A quick, small man, with metal-rimmed glasses that gazed at Ric like barrels of a shotgun. "It really is you!" The high-pitched voice of the connoisseur grated on Ric's nerves like the sound of a bonesaw.

"No." A fast, sweat-soaked denial.

"Look. I've taped all your vids I could find."

"Not me."

"I'm having a party next week. With entertainment, if you know what I mean. I wonder—"

"I'm not interested," Ric said, standing carefully, "in any of your parties."

He walked out into the night, to his new car, and headed north, to his private fortress above the glacier. He took the pistol out of the glove compartment and put it on the seat next to him. It didn't make him feel any safer.

Get a new face, Ric thought. Get across the border into Uzbekistan and check into a hospital. Let them try to follow me there.

He got home at four in the morning and checked his situation with the artificial intelligence that managed his accounts. All his funds were in long-term investments and he'd take a whopping loss if he pulled out now.

He looked at the figures and couldn't understand them. There seemed to be a long, constant scream in Ric's mind and nerves, a scream that echoed Marlene's, the sound of someone who had just discovered what is real. His body was shaking and he couldn't stop it.

Ric switched off his monitor and staggered to bed. Blood filled his dreams.

When he rose it was noon. There were people outside his gates, paparazzi with their cameras. The phone had recorded a series of requests for an interview with the new, controversial vid star. Someone at the party had talked. It took Ric a long time to get a phone line out in order to tell the AI to sell out.

The money in his pocket and a gun in his lap, he raced his car past the paparrazi, making them jump aside as he tried his best to run them down. He had to make the next suborbital shuttle out of Christchurch to Mysore, then head northwest to his hospital and to a new life. And somehow he'd have to try to cover his tracks. Possibly he'd buy some hair bleach, a false mustache. Pay only cash.

Getting away from Cartoon Messiah wouldn't be hard. Shaking the paparazzi would take a lot of fast thinking.

Sweat made his grip on the wheel slippery.

As he approached Christchurch he saw a streak across the bright northeast sky, a shuttle burning its way across the Pacific from California.

He wondered if there were people on it that he knew.

In his mind, the screams went on.

NEAL BARRETT, JR.

Sallie C.

What do Billy the Kid, Erwin Rommel, and the Wright Brothers have in common? If you want to know, you'll just have to read the sad, funny, poignant, and altogether delightful story that follows. . . .

Born in San Antonio, Texas, Neal Barrett, Jr., grew up in Oklahoma City, Oklahoma, spent several years in Austin, hobnobbing with the likes of Lewis Shiner and Howard Waldrop, and now makes his home in Dallas with his family, a dog, and a cat. His short fiction has appeared in *The Magazine of Fantasy and Science Fiction, Galaxy, Isaac Asimov's Science Fiction Magazine, Amazing, Omni, Fantastic, If,* and elsewhere. He made his first sale in 1959, and has been a full-time freelancer for the past twelve years. His books include *Stress Pattern, Karma Corps,* and the four-volume Aldair series. Upcoming is a new novel, *Through Darkest America,* being published by the new *Isaac Asimov Presents* line from Congdon & Weed.

SALLIE C.

Neal Barrett, Jr.

Will woke every morning covered with dust. The unfinished chair, the dresser with peeling paint were white with powdery alkali. His quarters seemed the small back room of some museum, Will and the dresser and the chair an exhibit not ready for public view. Indian John had built the room, nailing it to the hotel wall with the style and grace of a man who'd never built a thing in all his life and never intended to do it again. When he was finished he tossed the wood he hadn't used inside and nailed the room firmly shut and threw his hammer into the desert. The room stayed empty except for spiders until Will and his brother moved in.

In August, a man had ridden in from Portales heading vaguely for Santa Fe and having little notion where he was. His wife lay in the flat bed of their wagon, fever-eyed and brittle as desert wood, one leg swollen and stinking with infection. They had camped somewhere and a centipede nine and three-quarter inches long had found its way beneath her blanket. The leg was rotting and would kill her. The woman was too sick to know it. The man said his wife would be all right. They planned to open a chocolate works in Santa Fe and possibly deal in iced confections on the side. The railroad was freighting in their goods from St. Louis; everything would be waiting when they arrived. The man kept the centipede in a jar. His wife lay in the bed across the room. He kept the jar in the window against the light and watched the centipede curl around the inner walls of glass. Its legs moved like a hundred new fish hooks varnished black.

The man had a problem with connections. He couldn't see the link between the woman on the bed and the thing that rattled amber-colored armor in the jar. His wife and the centipede were two separate events.

The woman grew worse, her body so frail that it scarcely raised the sheets. When she died, Indian John took the centipede out and killed it. What he did, really, and Will saw him do it, was stake the thing down with a stick Apache-style. Pat Garrett told the man to get his sorry ass out of the Sallie C. that afternoon and no later. The man couldn't see why Garrett was mad.

He wanted to know what the Indian had done with his jar. He said his wife would be fine after a while. He had a problem with connections. He couldn't see the link between burial and death. Indian John stood in the heat and watched ants take the centipede apart. They sawed it up neatly and carried it off like African bearers.

Will thought about this and carefully shook his trousers and his shoes. He splashed his face with water and found his shirt and walked out into the morning. He liked the moment suspended, purple-gray and still between the night and the start of day. There was a freshness in the air, a time before the earth changed hands and the sun began to beat the desert flat.

Behind the hotel was a small corral, the pen attached to the weathered wooden structure that served as workshed, stable, and barn. The ghost shapes of horses stirred about. The morning was thick and blue, hanging heavy in the air. Saltbush grew around the corral, and leathery beavertail cactus. Will remembered he was supposed to chop the cactus out and burn it.

Indian John walked out on the back steps and tossed dishwater and peelings into the yard. He took no notice of Will. The chickens darted about, bobbing like prehistoric lizards. Will opened the screen and went in. The hotel was built of wood but the kitchen was adobe, the rough walls black with smoke and grease. The room was hot and smelled of bacon and strong coffee. Will poured himself a cup and put bread on the stove to make toast.

"John, you seen my brother this morning?" Will asked. He didn't look up from his plate. "He get anything to eat?"

"Mr. Pat say your brother make a racket before noon he goin' to kill him straight out. Like that." John drew a finger across his throat to show Will how.

"He hasn't been doing that, John."

"Good. He gah'dam better not."

"If he *isn't*, John, then why talk about it?"

"Gah'dam racket better stop," John said, the menace clear in his voice. "Better stop or you brother he in helluva big trouble."

Will kept his fury to himself. There was no use arguing with John, and a certain amount of risk. He stood and took his coffee and his toast out of the kitchen to the large open room next door. He imagined John's eyes at his back. Setting his breakfast on the bar, he drew the shades and found his broom. There were four poker tables and a bar. The bar was a massive structure carved with leaves and tangled vines and clusters of grapes, a good-sized vineyard intact in the dark mahogany wood. Garrett had bought the bar up in Denver and had it hauled by rail as far as he could. Ox teams brought it the rest of the way across the desert, where Garrett removed the front of the hotel to get it in.

There was a mirror behind the bar, bottles and glasses that Will dusted daily. Above the bottles there was a picture of a woman. The heavy gilt frame was too large for the picture. The woman had delicate features, deep-set eyes and a strong, willful mouth. Will imagined she had a clear and pleasant voice.

By the time he finished sweeping there were pale fingers of light across the floor. Will heard steps on the back stairs and then the boy's voice talking to John, and then John speaking himself. John didn't sound like John when he spoke to the boy.

Will looked at the windows and saw they needed washing. It was a next-to-useless job. The sand ate the glass and there was no way to make them look right. The sight suddenly plunged him into despair. A man thirty-six with good schooling. A man who sweeps out and cleans windows. He wondered where he'd let his life go. He had scarcely even noticed. It had simply unraveled, coming apart faster than he could fix it.

The boy ran down the steps into the yard. He walked as if he owned the world and knew it. Will couldn't remember if he'd felt like that himself.

The front stairs creaked and Will saw Garrett coming down. This morning he wore an English worsted suit and checkered vest. Boots shined and a fresh linen collar, cheeks shaved pink as baby skin. The full head of thick white hair was slicked back and his mustache was waxed in jaunty curls. Will looked away, certain Garrett could read his every thought. It made him furious, seeing this ridiculous old fart spruced up like an Eastern dandy. Before the woman arrived he had staggered around in moth-eaten dirty longhandles, seldom bothering to close the flap. At night he rode horses blind drunk. Everyone but John stayed out of his way. Now, Will was supposed to think he had two or three railroads and a bank.

Garrett walked behind the bar and poured a healthy morning drink. "Looks real nice," he told Will. "I do like to see the place shine."

Will had rearranged the dust and nothing more. "That Indian's threatening my brother," he announced. "Said he'd cut his throat sure."

"I strongly doubt he'll do it. If he does he won't tell you in advance."

"What he said was it was you. I assure you I didn't believe him for a minute. I am not taken in by savage cunning."

"That's good to know."

"Mr. Garrett, my brother isn't making any noise. Not till after dinner like you said."

"I know he's not, Will."

"So you'll say something to John and make him stop?"

"If you've a mind to weary me, friend, you've got a start. Now how's that wagon coming along?"

"Got to have a whole new axle like I said. But I can get it done pretty fast."

Garrett looked alarmed. "What you do is take your time and do it *right*. Fast is the mark of the careless worker, as I see it. A shoddy job is no job at all. Now run out and see that boy's not near the horses. I doubt he's ever seen a creature bigger than a fair-sized dog.''

Garrett watched him go. The man was a puzzle and he had no use for puzzles of any kind. Puzzles always had a piece missing and with Will Garrett figured the piece was spirit. Someone had reached in and yanked it right out of Will's head and left him hollow. No wonder the damn Injun gave him fits. A redskin was two-thirds cat and he'd worry a cripple to death.

Garrett considered another drink. Will had diminished the soothing effects of the first, leaving him one behind instead of even. He thought about the woman upstairs. In his mind she wore unlikely garments from Paris, France. John began to sing out in the kitchen. *Hiyas* and such strung together in a flat and tuneless fashion. Like drunken bees in a tree. Indian songs began in the middle and worked out. There was no true beginning and no end. One good solution was the 10-gauge Parker under the bar. Every morning Garrett promised himself he'd do it. Walk in and expand Apache culture several yards.

"I'll drink to that," he said, and he did.

The boy was perched atop the corral swinging his legs. John had given him sugar for the horses.

"Mr. Garrett says you take a care," Will told him. "Don't get in there with them, now."

"I will be most careful," the boy said.

He had good manners and looked right at you when he talked. Will decided this was a mark of foreign schooling. He walked past the horses to the barn. The morning heat was cooking a heady mix, a thick fermented soup of hay and manure, these odors mingled with the sharp scent of cleanly sanded wood, fuel oil, and waxy glue.

Will stopped a few feet from the open door. The thing seemed bigger than he remembered. He felt ill at ease in its presence. He liked things with front and back ends and solid sides to hold them together. Here there was a disturbing expanse of middle.

"Listen, you coming out of there soon?" Will said, making no effort to hide his irritation. "I'm darn sure not coming in."

"Don't. Stay right there." His brother was lost in geometric confusion.

"Orville, I don't like talking to someone I can't even see."

"Then don't."

"You sleep out here or what? I didn't hear you come to bed."

"Didn't. Had things to do."

"Don't guess you *ate* anything either."

"I eat when I've a mind to, Will, all right?"

"You say it you don't do it."

"One of those chickens'll wander in I'll eat that. Grab me a wing and a couple of legs."

Will saw no reason for whimsy. It didn't seem the time. "It isn't even eight yet case you didn't notice," he said shortly. "I promised Mr. Garrett you wouldn't mess with that thing till noon. John raised Ned with me at breakfast. Me now Orville, not you."

Orville emerged smiling from a torturous maze of muslin stretched tightly over spars of spruce and ash, from wires that played banjo as he passed, suddenly appearing as if this were a fine trick he'd just perfected.

"I am not to make noise before noon," he told Will. "Nobody said I couldn't work. Noise is forbidden but toil is not."

"You're splitting hairs and you know it."

Orville brushed himself off and looked at his brother. "Listen a minute Will and don't have a stroke or anything, all right? I'm going to try her out tomorrow."

"Oh, my Lord!" Will looked thunderstruck.

"I'd like for you to watch."

"Me? What for?"

"I'd like you to be there, Will. Do I have to have a reason?" Orville had never asked him a question he could answer. Will supposed there were thousands, maybe millions of perplexities between them, a phantom cloud that followed them about.

"I don't know," he said, and began to rub his hands and bob about. "I can't say maybe I will I'll have to see." He turned, suddenly confused about direction, and began to run in an awkward kind of lope away from the barn.

Helene kept to herself. Except for her usual walk after supper she had not emerged from the room since her arrival. *Herr* Garrett sent meals. The savage left them in the hall and pounded loudly at her door. Helene held her breath until he was gone. If he caught her he would defile her in some way she couldn't imagine. She ate very little and inspected each bite for foreign objects, traces of numbing drugs.

Garrett also sent the Indian up with presents. Fruits and wines. Nosegays of wilted desert flowers. She found these offerings presumptious. The fruit was tempting; she didn't dare. What rude implication might he draw from a missing apple, a slice of melon accepted?

"God in Heaven help me!" she cried aloud, lifting her head to speed this plea in the right direction. What madness had possessed her, brought her to this harsh and terrible land? The trip had been a nightmare from the start. A long ocean voyage and then a train full of ruffians and louts. In a place called Amarillo they said the tracks were out ahead. Three days' delay and maybe more. Madame was headed for Albuquerque? What luck, the stranger told her. Being of the European persuasion, she might not be aware that Amarillo and Albuquerque were widely known as the twin cities of the West. He would sell her a wagon cheap and she would reach her destination before dark. Albuquerque was merely twenty-one miles down the road. Go out of town and turn left.

Her skin was flushed, ready to ignite. Every breath was an effort. Her cousin would think she was dead, that something dreadful had happened. She applied wet cloths. Wore only a thin chemise. The garment seemed shamefully immodest and brought her little relief. Sometimes she drifted off to sleep. Only to wake from tiresome dreams. Late in the day she heard a rude and startling sound. Mechanical things disturbed her. It clattered, stuttered and died and started again.

Before the sun was fully set she was dressed and prepared for her walk. Hair pale as cream was pinned securely under a broad-brimmed hat. The parasol matched her dress. In the hall she had a fright. The savage came up the stairs with covered trays. Helene stood her ground. Fear could prove fatal in such encounters; weakness only heightened a man's lust.

The savage seemed puzzled to see her. His eyes were black as stones. "This your supper," he said.

"No, no, *danke*," she said hurriedly, "I do not want it."

"You don't eat you get sick."

Was this some kind of threat? If he attacked, the point of the parasol might serve her as a weapon.

"I am going to descend those stairs," she announced. "Do you understand me? I am *going* down those stairs!"

The Indian didn't move. Helene rushed quickly past him and fled. Outside she felt relatively secure. Still, her heart continued to pound. The sky was tattered cloth, a garish orange garment sweeping over the edge of the earth. Color seemed suspended in the air. Her skin, the clapboard wall behind her, were painted in clownish tones. Even as she watched the color changed. Indigo touched the faint shadow of distant mountains.

So much space and nothing in it! Her cousin's letter had spoken of vistas. This was the word Ilse used. Broad, sweeping vistas, a country of raw and unfinished beauty. Helene failed to see it. At home, everything was comfortably close. The vistas were nicely confined.

"Well now, good evening, Miz Rommel," Garrett said cheerfully, coming up beside her to match her pace, "taking a little stroll, are you?"

Helene didn't stop. "It appears that is exactly what I am doing, *Herr* Garrett." The man's feigned surprise seemed foolish. After four days of popping up precisely on the hour, Helene was scarcely amazed to see him again.

"It's truly a sight to see," said Garrett, peering into the west. "Do you get sunsets like this back home? I'll warrant you do not."

"To the best of my knowledge, the sun sets every night. I have never failed to see this happen."

"Well I guess that's true."

"I am certain that it is."

"I have never been to Germany. Or France or England either. The Rhine, now that's a German river."

"Yes."

"I suppose you find my knowledge of foreign lands greatly lacking."

"I have given it little thought."

"I meant to travel widely. Somehow life interceded."

"I'm sure it did."

"Life and circumstance. *Herr,* now that means mister."

"Yes it does."

"And mrs., what's that?"

"*Frau.*"

"*Frau* Rommel. In Mexican that would be *Señora. Señor* and *Señora.* I can say without modesty I an not unacquainted with the Spanish tongue."

"How interesting I'm sure."

"Now if you were unmarried, you'd be a *señorita.*"

"Which I am not," Helene said, with a fervor Garrett could scarcely overlook.

"Well no offense of course," said Garrett, backtracking as quickly as he could. "I mean if you were that's how you'd say it. You see they put that *ita* on the end of lots of things. *Señorita's* sort of 'little lady.' Now a little dog or little—Miz Rommel you suppose you could see your way clear to have supper with me this evening maybe nine o'clock I would be greatly honored if you would."

Helene stopped abruptly. She could scarcely believe what she'd heard. "I am a married woman, *Herr* Garrett. I thought we had established this through various forms of address."

"Well now we did but—"

"Then you can see I must decline."

"Not greatly I don't, no."

"Surely you do."

"To be honest I do not."

"Ah, well! All the more reason for me to refuse your invitation! To be quite honest, *Herr* Garrett, I am appalled at your suggestion. Yes, appalled is the word I must use. I am not only a married woman but a mother. I have come to this wretched land for one reason, and that reason is my son. As even you can surely see, Erwin is a boy of most delicate and sickly nature. His physician felt a hot and arid climate would do him good. I am no longer certain this is so."

"Miz Rommel," Garrett began, "I understand exactly what you're saying. All I meant was—"

"No, I doubt that you understand at all," Helene continued, her anger unabated, "I am sure you can't imagine a mother's feelings for her son. I can tell you right now that I see my duty clearly, *Herr* Garrett, and it does *not* include either the time or the inclination for—for illicit suppers and the like!"

"Illicit suppers?" Garrett looked totally disconcerted. "Jesus Christ, lady . . ."

"*Language, Herr* Garrett!"

Garrett ran a hand through his hair. "If I've offended you any I'll say I'm sorry. Far as that boy of yours is concerned, you don't mind me saying he looks healthy enough to me. If he's sickly he doesn't show it. John says he takes to the desert like a fox."

"I would hardly call that an endorsement," Helene said coolly.

"John knows the country I'll hand him that."

"He frightens me a great deal."

"I don't doubt he does. That's what Indians are for."

"I'm sorry. I do not understand that statement at all."

"Ma'am, the Indian race by nature is inured to savage ways. Murder, brutalizing and the like. When he is no longer allowed these diversions, he must express his native fury in some other fashion. Scaring whites keeps him happy. Many find it greatly satisfying. Except of course for the Sioux, who appear to hold grudges longer than most."

"Yes, I see," said Helene, who didn't at all. The day was suddenly gone; she had not been aware of this at all. The arid earth drank light instead of water. Garrett's presence made her nervous. He seemed some construction that might topple and fall apart.

She stopped and looked up and caught his eye. "My wagon. I assume you will have it ready quite soon."

The question caught Garrett off guard. This was clearly her intention.

"Why, it's coming along nicely I would say."

"I don't think that's an answer."

"The axle, Miz Rommel. The axle is most vital. The heart so to speak of the conveyance."

He was fully transparent. He confirmed her deepest fears. She could see his dark designs.

"Fix it," she said, and the anger he had spawned rose up to strike him. "Fix it, *Herr* Garrett, or I shall take my son and *walk* to Albuquerque."

"Dear lady, please . . ."

"I will *walk*, Herr Garrett!"

She turned and left him standing, striding swiftly away. He muttered words behind her. She pretended not to hear. She knew what he would do. He would soothe his hurt with spirits, numb his foul desires. Did he think she didn't know? God preserve women! Men are great fools, and we are helpless but for the strength You give us to foil them!

There was little light in the west. The distant mountains were ragged and indistinct, a page torn hastily away. Garrett had warned her of the dangers of the desert. Rattlesnakes slithering about. He took great pleasure in such stories. She had heard the horrid tale of the centipede. From Garrett, from Will, and once again from Erwin.

Turning back she faced the Sallie C. again. How strange and peculiar it was. The sight never failed to disturb her. One lone structure and nothing more. A single intrusion on desolation. A hotel where none was needed, where no one ever came. Where was the woman buried, she wondered? Had anyone thought to mark the grave?

Drawing closer, she saw a light in the kitchen, saw the savage moving about. Another light in the barn, the tapping of a hammer coming from there. She recalled the clatter she'd heard that afternoon. Now what was that about? Erwin would surely know, though he had mentioned nothing at all. The boy kept so within himself. Sometimes this concerned her, even hurt her deeply. They were close, but there was a part of this child she didn't know.

Helene couldn't guess what made her suddenly look up, bring her eyes to that point on the second story. There, a darkened window, and in the window the face of a man. Her first reaction was disgust. Imagine! Garrett spying on her in the dark! Still, the face made no effort to draw away, and she knew in an instant this wasn't Garrett at all but someone else.

Helene drew in a breath, startled and suddenly afraid. She quickly sought the safety of the porch, the protecting walls of the hotel. Who was he, then, another guest? But wouldn't she have heard if this were so?

She smelled the odors of the kitchen, heard the Indian speak, then Erwin's boyish laughter. Why of course! She paused, her hand still on the door. The savage had carried *two* covered trays when she met him in the hall. At the time, she had been too fearful of his presence to even notice. The other tray, then, was for the man who sat in the window. He, too, preferred his meals in his room. Something else to ask her son. What an annoying child he could be! He would tell her, whatever she wanted to know. But she would have to ask him first.

It was Pat Garrett's habit to play poker every evening. The game began shortly after supper and lasted until Garrett had soundly beaten his opponents, or succumbed to the effects of rye whiskey. Before the game began, Garrett furnished each chair with a stack of chips and a generous tumbler of spirits. Some players' stacks were higher than others. A player with few chips either got a streak of luck or quickly folded, leaving the game to better men. Bending to the harsh circle of light Garrett would deal five hands on the field of green, then move about to each chair in turn, settle in and study a hand, ask for cards or stand, sip from a player's glass and move on, bet, sip, and move again. After the first bottle of rye the game got lively, the betting quite spirited, the players bold and sometimes loud in their opinions. Will, lying awake in the shed out back, and on this night, young Erwin at the bottom of the stairs, could hear such harsh remarks as "Bet or go piss, McSween," "You're plain bluffing, Bell, you never saw kings and aces in your life . . ."

More than once, Will had been tempted to sneak up and peer in a window to assure himself Garrett was alone. He thought about it but didn't. If Garrett was playing with ghosts, Will didn't want to know it.

Sometime close to three in the morning, Helene awoke with a start. There was a terrible racket below, as if someone were tossing chairs and tables across the room, which, she decided, was likely the case. Moments later, something bumped loudly against the wall outside her window. Someone muttered under his breath. Someone was trying to climb a ladder.

Helene woke Erwin, got him from his bed and brought him to her, holding the boy close and gripping her parasol like a saber.

"God save us from the defiler," she prayed aloud. "Forgive me all my sins. Erwin, if anything happens to me you must get to cousin Ilse in Albuquerque. Can you ride a horse do you think? Your father put you on a horse. I remember clearly he did. At Otto Kriebel's farm in Heidenheim?"

"*Nein, Mutti,*" he assured her, "it is all right, nothing is going to happen."

"Hush," she scolded, "you don't know that at all. You are only a boy. You know nothing of the world. You scarcely imagine the things that can happen."

At that moment, a most frightening shout came from just below the window. The cry receded, as if it were rapidly moving away. The ladder struck the ground, and half a second later something heavier than that. The night was silent again.

"Perhaps someone is injured," Erwin suggested.

"Go to sleep," Helene told him. "Say your prayers and don't forget to ask God to bless Papa. We are far away from home."

There was no question of sleeping. To the usual morning noise of men stomping heavily about, of chickens clucking and horses blowing air, was now added the hollow ring of timber, of hammering and wheels that needed grease. Helene dressed quickly, recalling her promise to Erwin the night

before. Before she could sweep her hair atop her head he was back, eyes
alight with wonder, those deep, inquisitive eyes that seemed to see much
more than a boy should see.

"*Komm' schnell, Mutti!*" he urged her, scarcely giving her time to pause
before the mirror. Holding tightly to her hand he led her quickly down the
stairs, and out into the brightness of the morning. The Indian leaned against
the wall, drinking a can of peaches from the tin, practicing looking Mescalero
mean. Garrett slumped in a rocker, his leg propped testily on a stool.

Helene could not resist a greeting. "Are you hurt, *Herr* Garrett? I do
hope you have not had an accident of some sort."

"I am in excellent health, thank you," Garrett said shortly.

"Well. I am most pleased to hear it." The man seemed to have aged
during the night. His flesh was soft as dough. Helene wondered if he would
rise, swell like an ungainly pastry in the heat.

"There, *Mutti*, see?" said Erwin. "Look, they are coming. It is most
exciting, yes!"

"Why yes, yes, I'm sure it is, Erwin," Helene said vaguely. In truth,
she had no idea what she was seeing. The strange sight appeared around the
corner of the hotel. It seemed to be an agricultural device. Helene framed a
question for Erwin but he was gone. "Have a care," she called out, but
knew he didn't hear.

Two men guided the wagon toward the flats. One of the two was Will.
She guessed the other was his brother. Will looked striken, a man pressed
into service who clearly hoped no one would notice he was there.

As Helene watched, the first flash of morning touched the horizon, a
fiercely bright explosion that scarred the earth with light and shadow. A
silver lance touched the strange device; the thing seemed imbued with sudden
magic. Light pierced the flat planes of muslin and spruce, and Helene imagined transparent flesh and hollow bones. A dragonfly, a golden fish in a
dream.

"Oh. Oh, *my*," she said aloud, deeply touched by the moment.

"Looks to me like a medicine show hit by a twister," said Garrett.

"*I* think it has a certain grace," said Helene. "The rather delicate beauty
one associates with things Oriental."

"Chink laundry," Garrett countered. "Got in the way of a train."

"They say strong spirits greatly dull the imagination," Helene said coolly,
and took herself to the far end of the porch.

Out on the flats, Will and his brother carefully lifted the device off the
wagon onto the ground. Broad wooden runners that might have come from
a horse-drawn sleigh were attached to the contraption's undercarriage. Helene
knew about sleighs. The runners seemed strangely out of place. Snow was
clearly out of the question.

Suddenly, the engine in the device began to snarl. The latticed wooden structure, the wires and planes of fabric began to shake. In the rear, two enormous fans started churning plumes of sand into the air. Orville donned a long cotton duster and drew goggles over his eyes. He climbed aboard the device, perched on a bicycle seat and looked carefully left and right.

"Erwin, *nein*," Helene cried out, "get back from that thing!"

Erwin, though, was too engrossed to hear. He held a rope attached to the lower muslin plane. Will held one on the other side. The engine reached a shrill and deafening pitch. Orville raised a hand. Erwin and Will released their hold.

The contraption jerked to a start, a dog released from its chain. Helene made a small sound of surprise. Somehow, the possibility of motion hadn't occurred. The device moved faster and faster. Orville leaned hard into the wind. His hands clutched mystical controls. Muslin flapped and billowed. Suddenly, with no warning at all, the thing came abruptly off the ground.

"Holy Christ Colorado," said Garrett.

Helene was thunderstruck. The device, held aloft by forces unseen and unimagined, soared for ten seconds or more then wobbled, straightened, and gently kissed the earth. The engine fluttered and stopped. Will and Erwin ran frantically over the flats waving their arms. Orville climbed to the ground. Will and Erwin shook his hand and clapped him firmly on the back. Then all three made their way to the hotel.

Erwin was elated. He might explode from excitement any moment. Even Will seemed pleased. Orville was curiously restrained. His goggles were pushed atop his head. His eyes were ringed with dust.

"*Mutti*, it was something to see, was it not!" Erwin cried.

"It certainly was," said Helene.

"I've got to admit," said Garrett, "I never saw a man ride a wagon off the ground."

"Now I can fix that," Orville said thoughtfully. "I know exactly what happened. This was only the first trial you understand."

Garrett seemed confused. "You planning on doing that again?"

"Why, yes sir. Yes I am."

Garrett pulled himself erect. "Not till after noon you're not, Orville. That racket assaults the nerves. I doubt if it's good for the digestion." He turned and went inside.

"It was most entertaining," Helene said, thinking that she ought to be polite.

"The elevator needs more weight," said Orville, as if Helene would surely agree. "That should keep the front firmly down. And I shall tilt the sail planes forward. Too much vertical lift the way they are."

"Yes, of course," said Helene.

"Well, we had best get her back to the barn," Orville said. "Lots of work to do. And thank you for your help, young man."

Erwin flushed with pride. "Sir, I was honored to assist."

Will and Orville walked back into the sun.

"*Mutti*, it is a marvel is it not!" said Erwin.

"Yes it is," Helene agreed. "Now you stay away from that thing, do you hear? I want you to promise me that."

Erwin looked stricken. "But *Herr* Orville has promised that I shall have a ride!"

"And *I* promise that you shall do no such thing," Helene said firmly. "Just get that out of your head."

Erwin turned and fled, holding back the tears that burned his eyes. Helene released a sigh, wondering how she would manage to handle this. Everyone was gone. She seemed to be all alone on the porch.

The sounds of Orville's labor continued throughout the day. When Helene returned from her regular evening walk, a lantern still glowed within the barn. Orville disturbed her more than a little. The man had a fire in his eyes. Such a look frightened her in a man. Her husband's eyes were steady and reassuring. When she saw the two together, Orville and her son, a vague disquieting shadow crossed her heart. Erwin had such a light as well.

"Evening, Miz Rommel," said Garrett. The glow of his cigar came from the porch.

"I did not see you standing there," said Helene. Her tone was clearly distant.

"I suppose you're put out with me some."

"With reason I should think."

"I guess there is."

"You only guess?"

"All right. I would say you have some cause."

"Yes I would say that indeed."

"Look, Miz Rommel—"

"Is this an apology, then?"

"I was getting to that."

"Then I shall accept it, *Herr* Garrett."

Garrett shifted uncomfortably. "That wagon will be ready in the morning. Now Albuquerque's a hundred and twenty miles through real bad country in the heat. There can be no question of such a trip. On the other hand it is only fifty miles down to Roswell and the train. I shall have Will ride along and see that you get there safely."

"I am grateful, *Herr* Garrett."

"You don't have to be at all."

"Perhaps you could pack a nice lunch."

"I don't see why I couldn't."

"And rig some kind of shade for the wagon."

"I could do that, yes."

"How nice. A very thoughtful gesture."

"Miz Rommel—"

"Yes, *Herr* Garrett?"

Garrett was on the brink of revelation. He had steeled himself for the moment. He would bare the fires of passion that burned within. She would be frightened and appalled but she would know. He saw, then, as the words began to form, that her skin matched the pearly opalescence of the moon, that her hair was saffron-gold, spun fine as down from a baby duck. In an instant, his firm resolve was shattered. He muttered parting words and turned and fled.

A most peculiar man, thought Helene. A drunkard and a lecher without a doubt, yet God was surely within this wayward soul, as He is within us all.

She had meant to go directly to her room. Yet, she found her steps taking her to the barn and knew the reason. Erwin was surely there. The matter must be settled. She loved the boy intently. Anger struggled with the pain she felt in her heart. They had never quarrelled before as they had that morning. She had sternly forbidden him to have anything to do with Orville's device. Yet, he had openly disobeyed. Helene had no desire to quell his spirit. Still, she could not brook open rebellion in her child.

The moon was bright with chalky splendor. The broad backs of the horses moved like waves on a restless sea. A man came toward her through the dark. From his quick, awkward gait she knew at once that it was Will.

"Good evening," she said, "can you tell me if my son is back there, please?"

"Yes, ma'am, yes he is," said Will. "He's surely there, Miz Rommel."

Why did the man act in such a manner? He was ever bobbing about like a cork. As if there might be danger in standing still.

"He is *not* supposed to be there," Helene sighed. "I am afraid he has disobeyed."

"That wagon will be ready in the morning," said Will.

"Yes. So *Herr* Garrett has explained." She felt suddenly weary, eager to put this place behind her. "Do you know Erwin well? Have you talked to him at all?"

"No ma'am. Not a lot. He mostly talks to Orville."

"He feels some kinship with your brother."

"Yes he surely does."

"He is a free spirit, your brother. I see that in him clearly."

"I guess he's that all right."

"A man pursuing a dream?"

"He has never been different than he is. The way you see him now. When we were boys he'd say Will, there is a thing I have to do. And I'd say what would that be, Orville, and he'd say man sails boldly before the wind across the seas. I would set him free to sail the land. And I'd say, Orville, why would you want to do that? Lord, I guess I've asked that question a million times.''

"And what would Orville say?''

"Same thing every time. Why not, Will?''

"Yes. Yes, of course,'' Helene said softly. Oh, Erwin, have I lost you to your dreams so soon!

"Miz Rommel . . .''

"Yes, Will?''

Will bobbed about again. "Maybe I have no business speaking out. If I don't you just tell me and I'll stop. That boy wants to ride in Orville's machine. Wants it so bad he can taste it. I hope you'll relent and let him do it. He's a boy bound and determined is what he is.''

"I think I know that, Will.''

"I am a man of practical bent, Miz Rommel. I will never be anything more. I used to see this as a virtue in myself. In some men maybe it is. In me it is a curse, the great failing of my life. Mr. Garrett thinks Orville is a fool. That I am a man who's lost his spirit. Perhaps he is right about us both. But he does not know the truth of the matter at all. It is not my brother's folly that brought us here but mine alone. *I* failed. *I* brought us down. We had a small shop where we repaired common household items. Coffee mills, lard presses, ice shavers and the like. Not much but it kept us going. I felt there was something more. I reached for a distant star and invested quite heavily in the windmill accessory business. I think Orville sensed that I was wrong. Out of kindness, he did nothing to dissuade me. When we left Ohio we had nothing but our wagon. A few days' food and the clothing on our backs. And Orville's wood and muslin and his motor. Our creditors demanded these as well. I have never stood up for myself. Not once in all my life. But I stood my ground on this. Your Erwin is a good boy, Miz Rommel. Let him be what he will be.''

"Yes. Yes,'' said Helene, "I understand what you are saying. And I am grateful to you, Will.''

Helene was taken aback by this long and unexpected declaration. She hadn't dreamed the man owned so many words, or that he had the passion within him to set them free. Now, as he tried to speak again, he seemed to see what he had done. He had tossed away countless nouns and verbs, spent whole phrases and contractions he couldn't retrieve. Clutching his hat he bolted past her and disappeared. Helene listened to the horses stir about. Orville laughed and then her son. It seemed one voice instead of two. She made her way quickly to her room.

* * *

Erwin's mother had asked him if he knew about the man and Erwin did. He knew John took him all his meals. He knew the man never left his room. He was much too angry at his mother to tell her that and so he lied. The lie hurt. It stuck in his throat and stayed, no matter how hard he tried to swallow. Late the night before when he came in from working in the barn she was sitting waiting quietly in the dark. They burst into tears and cried together. Erwin told her he was sorry. She said that it was over now and done. He didn't feel like growing up and yet he did.

It took all the courage he could muster. Just to stand in front of the door and nothing more. What if John came up the stairs? He wasn't afraid of John and yet he was.

The door came open with ease. Erwin's heart beat wildly against his chest. The room was musty, heavy with unpleasant odors. Stale air and sour sweat. Food uneaten and chamber pots neglected. Mostly the smell was time. The room was layered with years. Erwin saw yesterdays stuffed in every corner.

A window centered the wall. The morning burned a harsh square of brightness yet the light failed to penetrate the room. It was stopped, contained, it could go no further than this. The sound of Orville's machine worried the quiet, probed like a locust through the day.

"You stand there boy you'll turn to stone. Or is it salt I can't recall. Salt or stone one. Get over here close so I can see."

Erwin jumped at the voice. He nearly turned and ran.

"It's salt. Salt for certain. Lot's wife. Sodom and Cincinnati. Lo the wicked shall perish and perish they do I have seen a great many of them do it."

Erwin walked cautiously to the window. The man sat in shadow in a broken wicker chair. The chair had once been painted festive yellow. Down the arms there were eagles or maybe chickens in faded red. Cactus the pale shade of leafy mold. For a moment it seemed to Erwin that the man was wicker too, that the chair had fashioned a person out of itself, thrust brittle strands for arms and legs, burst dry backing from Chihuahua, Mexico, for springy ribs. The whole of this draped with tattered clothes of no description. Hair white silk to the shoulders and beyond. The head newspaper dry as dust, crumpled in a ball and tied with string about the brow, a page very likely blown six hundred miles from Fort Worth across the flats. Eyes and nose and shadow mouth vaguely nibbled into shape by friendly mice.

Or so it all seemed on this attic afternoon.

"Well what's your name, now," the man asked, in a voice like rocks in a skillet.

"Johannes Erwin Eugen Rommel, sir," said Erwin, scarcely managing to find his voice at all.

"By God. That's more name than a boy needs to have I'll tell you sure. What do they call you for short?"

"Erwin, sir."

"Erwin sir and two more. Might be handy to have a spare at that. Knew a man called Zero Jefferson White. Couldn't remember who he was. What does your father do?"

"He is a schoolmaster, sir."

The paper mouth crinkled in a sly and knowing way. "I am aware of that, you see. John has told me all. I am kept informed and don't forget it."

"Are you a hundred, sir?" The words came out before he could stop them.

The mouse-nibble eyes searched about. "I might be, I couldn't say. What year you think it is?"

"Nineteen-hundred-and-three, sir."

"It is? Are you sure?" The man seemed greatly surprised. "Then I am likely forty-four. I have lived a fretful life and half of that in this chair less than a man. It's a wonder I look no worse. How old are you?"

"Eleven, sir. I shall be twelve in November. When I am eighteen I shall become a *Fahnenjunker*. I will be a fine officer cadet, and I shall excel in fencing and riding."

"I doubt a soldier's life would have suited me at all. Parades. Lining up and the like. That kind of nonsense and wearing blue shirts. Never trust a man in a blue shirt. You do I can promise you'll live to regret it."

The man seemed intrigued by the sight beyond his window, by the sleek muslin craft cutting graceful figure-eights across the sand. The engine clattered the fans roared, and Orville sped his dream across the desert raising great plumes of dust in his wake. The dust rose high in the still hot air and hung above the earth like yellow clouds.

"Charlie Bowdrie and old Dave Rudabaugh would go pick the best horses they could find and start out from Pete Maxwell's place and ride the mounts full out. Ride them full out without stopping, you understand, until one or the other dropped dead, the horse still running being the winner. The other horse too would generally die as you might expect. A senseless thing to do. Dangerous to the man and plain fatal to the horse."

"I am sorry that you are ill, sir."

"What? Who said that I was?" The paper eyes came alive. "Definitions, boy. I am done, mortally hurt. That is not the same as ill. Ill as I recall is simply sick. Taken with disease. An affliction or discomfort of the body. I am mortally hurt is what I am. Cut down, stricken, assaulted by violent hand. Felled with a bullet in the spine. God in Oklahoma, that's a wonder," the man said, following Orville's path. "A marvel of nature it is. I wish Charlie Bowdrie could see it. I would give some thought to the army. I can think of nearly thirty-two things I'd rather do. 'Course that's entirely up to you. I went to Colorado one time, me and Tom O'Folliard driving horses. Came back quick as I could. The cold there not to my liking at all.''

"You got to go now," said John, and Erwin wasn't sure just how long he'd been standing there in the room.

"That canopy will shade you from the sun," said Garrett. "I don't expect the heat will be bad. You'll reach Roswell before dark and Will'll see you settled before he leaves."

"Thank you," said Helene, "we are grateful for your help."

Will sat straight as a rod beside Erwin and his mother. He was proud of this new if only temporary post as wagon driver, and was determined to see it through. Orville wore his duster and his goggles. Earlier, after he had taken Erwin racing over the flats for nearly a full half-hour, he had given him a finely rendered pen and ink sketch of his muslin craft. John gave him two brass buttons, which he said had belonged to a U.S. Army major prior to a misunderstanding with Apaches in the Sierra Diablo country, which is south of the Guadalupe Mountains in Texas.

Garrett extended his hand. "Take care of your mother, boy. I have confidence that you will make yourself proud."

"Yes, sir," said Erwin.

"Well, then." Garrett extended his hand again, and Helene laid white-gloved fingers in his palm for just an instant. He studied the fair lines of her face, the silken hair swept under her bonnet. Strangely enough, he found he no longer regretted her departure. To be honest, he was glad to see her go. Keeping real people and phantoms apart was increasingly hard to do. Delusions he'd never seen were lately creeping into his life. An old lady crying in the kitchen. A stranger at the table betting queens. The woman only served to cause confusion, being real enough herself while his fancy made her something she never was.

"I'm giving you the shotgun, Will," said Garrett, "I don't see trouble but you use it if there is."

"Yes sir, I surely will."

"You know where the trigger is I guess."

"I surely do."

"And which way to point it, no doubt."

"Quite clearly sir, yes I do."

"Then make sure you—"

"Oh. Oh, my!" said Helene, and brought a hand quickly to her lips.

Garrett turned to see her concern. The sight struck him in the heart. "Christ Jesus California!" he said at once, and stepped back as if felled by a blow. John stood in the door with the wicker chair, his great arms around it like a keg, the chair's pale apparition resting within. Garrett was unsure if this image was whiskey-real or otherwise and greatly feared it was the latter.

"John," he managed to say, "what in *hell* is he doing out here!"

"Mr. Billy say he ride," John announced.

"Ride what, for God's sake?"

"Ride that," John nodded. "He say he ride in Orville's machine."

"You tell him he's lost his senses."

"Mr. Billy say to tell you he going to do it."

"Well you tell Mr. Billy that he's not," Garrett said furiously. "This is the most damn fool thing I ever heard."

"Tell Mr. Garrett I can kill myself any way I want," Billy said. He looked right at Garrett with a wide and papery grin. "Tell him I do not need advice from a fellow can't shoot a man proper close up."

"So that's it, is it," said Garrett. "You going to come downstairs every twenty-odd years now and pull *that* business out of the fire. By God it's just like you, too. I said I was sorry once, I don't see the sense in doing it twice."

"Miz Rommel," said Billy, "I do not think your boy ought to look to the army. That is a life for a man with no ambition or gumption at all and it is clear your boy is a comer. Bound for better things. May I say I have greatly enjoyed watching you take your evening walk. I said to Sallie Chisum once, you've likely seen her picture inside if Mr. Garrett hasn't thrown it out or burned it which wouldn't surprise me any at all, I said Sallie, a woman's walk betrays her breeding high or low. She might be a duchess or the wife of a railroad baron or maybe even a lady of the night, a woman dedicated to the commerce of lust and fleshly delight, but the walk, now, the walk of a woman will out, the length and duration of her stride will tell you if she comes from good stock in a moment's glance, now am I right or am I not?"

"I would—I would really—I would really hardly—" Helene looked helplessly at Garrett.

"Will, Miz Rommel is sitting around in the heat," Garrett said firmly. "Would you kindly get this wagon headed south sometime before Tuesday?"

Will bobbed about with indecision, then flicked the reins and started the team moving with a jerk. Erwin waved. Garrett and John and Orville waved back.

Billy waved too, though in no particular direction. "If you are headed for Roswell," he advised, "there was a fair hotel there at one time. Of course it may have changed hands I can't say. Mr. John Tunstall and I stopped there once and I recall that the rates were more than fair. A good steak is fifty cents don't spend any more than that. The cook is named Ortega. His wife cooks a good *cabrito* if you can find a goat around that's not sick. Don't eat a goat that looks bad or you'll regret it. They are too bitter though I've known those who prefer it that way to the other. Mr. John Chisum took four spoons of sugar. I could not fathom why. He kept an owl in a cage

behind his house. That and other creatures some considerably less than tame
. . .''

When the wagon reached the rise slightly east of the Sallie C. Erwin looked
back and heard the engine running strong and saw the white planes of muslin
catch the sun, saw the runners racing swiftly over the sand. Orville's duster
flew, his goggles flashed, his hands gripped the magic controls. John gripped
the chair at Orville's back, and though Erwin from afar couldn't see Billy
at all, spiderweb hair like a bright and silken scarf trailed past the wicker
arms to whip the wind.

LEWIS SHINER

Jeff Beck

Lewis Shiner is widely regarded as one of the most exciting new SF writers of the eighties. His stories have appeared in *The Magazine of Fantasy and Science Fiction, Omni, Oui, Shayol, Isaac Asimov's Science Fiction Magazine, The Twilight Zone Magazine, Wild Card,* and elsewhere. His first novel, *Frontera,* appeared in 1984 to good critical response. Upcoming, from the Bantam New Fiction line, is a new novel, *Deserted Cities of the Heart*. His story "Twilight Time" was in our Second Annual Collection; his story "The War at Home" was in our Third Annual Collection. Shiner lives in Austin, Texas, with his wife, Edith.

Here he tells us an elegant little story about a man who is unlucky enough to get just what he wants out of life. . . .

JEFF BECK

Lewis Shiner

Felix was 34. He worked four ten-hour days a week at Allied Sheet Metal, running an Amada CNC turret punch press. At night he made cassettes with his twin TEAC dbx machines. He'd recorded over a thousand of them so far, over 160 miles of tape, and he'd carefully hand-lettered the labels for each one.

He'd taped everything Jeff Beck had ever done, from the Yardbirds' *For Your Love* through all the Jeff Beck Groups and the solo albums; he had the English singles of "Hi Ho Silver Lining" and "TallyMan"; he had all the session work, from Donovan to Stevie Wonder to Tina Turner.

In the shop he wore a Walkman and listened to his tapes. Nothing seemed to cut the sound of tortured metal like the diamond-edged perfection of Beck's guitar. It kept him light on his feet, dancing in place at the machine, and sometimes the sheer beauty of it made tears come up in his eyes.

On Fridays he dropped Karen off at her job at *Pipeline Digest* and drove around to thrift shops and used book stores looking for records. After he'd cleaned them up and put them on tape he didn't care about them anymore; he sold them back to collectors and made enough profit to keep himself in blank UDXL-II's.

Occasionally he would stop at a pawn shop or music store and look at the guitars. Lightning Music on 183 had a Charvel/Jackson soloist, exactly like the one Beck played except for the hideous lilac-purple finish. Felix yearned to pick it up but was afraid of making a fool out of himself. He had an old Sears Silvertone at home and two or three times a year he would take it out and try to play it, but he could never even manage to get it properly in tune.

More often than not Felix spent his Friday afternoons in a dingy bar down the street from *Pipeline Digest*, alone in a back booth with a pitcher of Budweiser and an anonymous brown sack of records. On those afternoons Karen would find him in the office parking lot, already asleep in the passenger seat, and she would drive home. She worried a little, but it never happened more than two or three times in a month. The rest of the time he hardly drank at all, and he never hit her or chased other women. Whatever it was that ate at him was so deeply buried it just seemed easier to leave well enough alone.

One Thursday afternoon a friend at work took him aside.

"Listen," Manuel said, "are you feeling okay? I mean you seem real down lately."

"I don't know," Felix told him. "I don't know what it is."

"Everything okay with Karen?"

"Yeah, it's fine. Work is okay. I'm happy and everything. I just . . . I don't know. Feel like something's missing."

Manuel nodded to himself for a second, then took something out of his pocket. "A guy gave me this. You know I don't do this kind of shit no more, but the guy said it was killer stuff."

It looked like a Contac capsule, complete with the little foil blister pack. But when Felix looked closer the tiny colored spheres inside the gelatin seemed to sparkle in rainbow colors.

"What is it?"

"I don't know. He wouldn't say exactly. When I asked him what it did all he said was, 'Anything you want.' "

He dropped Karen off at work the next morning and drove aimlessly down Lamar for a while. He hadn't hit Half Price Books in a couple of months, but his heart wasn't really in it. He drove home and got the capsule off the top of his dresser where he'd left it.

Felix hadn't done acid in years, hadn't taken anything other than beer and an occasional joint in longer than he could remember. Maybe it was time for a change.

He swallowed the capsule, put Jeff Beck's *Wired* on the stereo, and switched the speakers into the den. He stretched out on the couch and looked at his watch. It was ten o'clock.

He closed his eyes and thought about what Manuel had said. It would do anything he wanted. So what did he want?

This was a drug for Karen, Felix thought. She talked all the time about what she would do if she could have any one thing in the world. She called it the Magic Wish game, though it wasn't really a game and nobody ever won it.

What the guy meant, Felix told himself, was it would make me see anything I wanted to. Like a mild hit of psilocybin. A light show and a bit of rush.

But he couldn't get away from the idea. What would he wish for if he could have anything? He had an answer ready; he supposed everybody did. He framed the words very carefully in his mind.

I want to play guitar like Jeff Beck, he thought.

He sat up. He had the feeling that he'd dropped off to sleep and lost a couple of hours, but when he looked at his watch it was only five after ten. The tape was still playing "Come Dancing." His head was clear and he couldn't feel any effects from the drug.

But then he'd only taken it five minutes ago. It wouldn't have had a chance to do anything yet.

He felt different though, sort of sideways, and something was wrong with his hands. They ached and tingled at the same time, and felt like they could crush rocks.

And the music. Somehow he was hearing the notes differently than he'd ever heard them before, hearing them with a certain knowledge of how they'd been made, the way he could look at a piece of sheet metal and see how it had been sheared and ground and polished into shape.

Anything you want, Manuel had said.

His newly powerful hands began to shake.

He went into his studio, a converted storeroom off the den. One wall was lined with tapes; across from it were shelves for the stereo, a few albums, and a window with heavy black drapes. The ceiling and the end walls were covered with gray paper egg cartons, making it nearly soundproof.

He took out the old Silvertone and it felt different in his hands, smaller, lighter, infinitely malleable. He switched off the Beck tape, patched the guitar into the stereo and tried tuning it up.

He couldn't understand why it had been so difficult before. When he hit harmonics he could hear the notes beating against each other with perfect clarity. He kept his left hand on the neck and reached across it with his right to turn the machines, a clean, precise gesture he'd never made before.

For an instant he felt a breathless wonder come over him. The drug had worked, had changed him. He tried to hang on to the strangeness but it slipped away. He was tuning a guitar. It was something he knew how to do.

He played "Freeway Jam," one of Max Middleton's tunes from *Blow By Blow*. Again, for just a few seconds, he felt weightless, ecstatic. Then the guitar brought him back down. He'd never noticed what a pig the Silvertone was, how high the strings sat over the fretboard, how the frets buzzed and the machines slipped. When he couldn't remember the exact notes on the record he tried to jam around them, but the guitar fought him at every step.

It was no good. He had to have a guitar. He could hear the music in his head but there was no way he could wring it out of the Silvertone.

His heart began to hammer and his throat closed up tight. He knew what he needed, what he would have to do to get it. He and Karen had over $1300 in a savings account. It would be enough.

He was home again by three o'clock with the purple Jackson soloist and a Fender Princeton amp. The purple finish wasn't nearly as ugly as he remembered it and the guitar fit into his hands like an old lover. He set up in the living room and shut all the windows and played, eyes closed, swaying a little from side to side, bringing his right hand all the way up over his head on the long trills.

Just like Jeff Beck.

He had no idea how long he'd been playing when he heard the phone ringing. He lunged for it, the phone cord bouncing noisily off the strings.

It was Karen. "Is something wrong?" she asked.

"Uh, no," Felix said. "What time is it?"

"Five thirty." She sounded close to tears.

"Oh shit. I'll be right there."

He hid the guitar and amp in his studio. She would understand, he told himself, but he wasn't ready to break it to her just yet.

In the car she seemed afraid to talk to him, even to ask why he'd been late. Felix could only think about the purple Jackson waiting for him at home.

He sat through a dinner of Chef Boyardee Pizza, using three beers to wash it down, and after he'd done the dishes he shut himself in his studio.

For four hours he played everything that came into his head, from blues to free jazz to "Over Under Sideways Down" to things he'd never heard before, things so alien and illogical that he couldn't translate the sounds he heard. When he finally stopped Karen had gone to bed. He undressed and crawled in beside her, his brain reeling.

He woke up to the sound of the vacuum cleaner. He remembered everything, but in the bright morning light it all seemed like a weirdly vivid hallucination, especially the part where he'd emptied the savings account.

Saturday was his morning for yard work, but first he had to deal with the drug business, to prove to himself that he'd only imagined it. He went into the studio and lifted the lid of the guitar case and then sat down across from it in his battered blue-green lounge chair.

As he stared at it he felt his love and terror of the guitar swell in his chest like cancer.

He picked it up and played the solo from "Got the Feelin'" and then looked up. Karen was standing in the open door.

"Oh my god," she said. "Oh my god. What have you done?"

Felix hugged the guitar to his chest. He couldn't think of anything to say to her.

"How long have you had this? Oh. You bought it yesterday, didn't you? That's why you couldn't even remember to pick me up." She slumped against the door frame. "I don't believe it. I don't *even* believe it."

Felix looked at the floor.

"The bedroom air conditioner is broken," Karen said. Her voice sounded like she was squeezing it with both hands; if she let it go it would turn into hysteria. "The car's running on four bald tires. The TV picture looks like hell. I can't remember the last time we went out to dinner or a movie." She pushed both hands into the sides of her face, twisting it into a mask of anguish.

"How much did it cost?" When Felix didn't answer she said, "It cost everything, didn't it? *Everything.* Oh god, I just can't believe it."

She closed the door on him and he started playing again, frantic scraps and tatters, a few bars from "Situation," a chorus of "You Shook Me," anything to drown out the memory of Karen's voice.

It took him an hour to wind down, and at the end of it he had nothing left to play. He put the guitar away and got in the car and drove around to the music stores.

On the bulletin board at Ray Hennig's he found an ad for a guitarist and called the number from a pay phone in the strip center outside. He talked to somebody named Sid and set up an audition for the next afternoon.

When he got home Karen was waiting in the living room. "You want anything from Safeway?" she asked. Felix shook his head and she walked out. He heard the car door slam and the engine shriek to life.

He spent the rest of the afternoon in the studio with the door shut, just looking at the guitar. He didn't need to practice; his hands already knew what to do.

The guitar was almost unearthly in its beauty and perfection. It was the single most expensive thing he'd ever bought for his own pleasure, but he couldn't look at it without being twisted up inside by guilt. And yet, at the same time he lusted for it passionately, wanted to run his hands endlessly over the hard, slick finish, bury his head in the plush case and inhale the musky aroma of guitar polish, feel the strings pulsing under the tips of his fingers.

Looking back he couldn't see anything he could have done differently. Why wasn't he happy?

When he came out the living room was dark. He could see a strip of light under the bedroom door, hear the snarling hiss of the TV. He felt like he was watching it all from the deck of a passing ship; he could stretch out his arms but everything would still just drift out of his reach.

He realized he hadn't eaten since breakfast. He made himself a sandwich and drank an iced tea glass full of whiskey and fell asleep on the couch.

*   *   *

A little after noon on Sunday he staggered into the bathroom. His back ached and his fingers throbbed and his mouth tasted like a kitchen drain. He showered and brushed his teeth and put on a clean T-shirt and jeans. Through the bedroom window he could see Karen lying out on the lawn chair with the Sunday paper. The pages were pulled so tight that her fingers made ridges across them. She was trying not to look back at the house.

He made some toast and instant coffee and went to sort through his tapes. He felt like he ought to try to learn some songs, but nothing seemed worth the trouble. Finally he played a Mozart symphony that he'd taped for Karen, jealous of the sound of the orchestra, wanting to be able to make it with his hands.

The band practiced in a run-down neighborhood off Rundberg and IH35. All the houses had big dogs behind chain link fences and plastic Big Wheels in the driveways. Sid met him at the door and took him back to a garage hung with army blankets and littered with empty beer cans.

Sid was tall and thin and wore a black Def Leppard T-shirt. He had blond hair in a shag to his shoulders and acne. The drummer and bass player had already set up; none of the three of them looked to be more than twenty-two or -three years old. Felix wanted to leave but he had no place else to go.

"Want a brew?" Sid asked, and Felix nodded. He took the Jackson out of its case and Sid, coming back with the beer, stopped in his tracks. "Wow," he said. "Is that your axe?" Felix nodded again. "Righteous," Sid said.

"You know any Van Halen?" the drummer asked. Felix couldn't see anything but a zebra striped headband and a patch of black hair behind the two bass drums and the double row of toms.

"Sure," Felix lied. "Just run over the chords for me, it's been a while." Sid walked him through the progression for "Dance the Night Away" on his ¾ sized Melody Maker and the drummer counted it off. Sid and the bass player both had Marshall amps and Felix's little Princeton, even on ten, got lost in the wash of noise.

In less than a minute Felix got tired of the droning power chords and started toying with them, adding a ninth, playing a modal run against them. Finally Sid stopped and said, "No, man, it's like this," and patiently went through the chords again, A, B, E, with a C# minor on the chorus.

"Yeah, okay," Felix said and drank some more beer.

They played "Beer Drinkers and Hell Raisers" by ZZ Top and "Rock and Roll" by Led Zeppelin. Felix tried to stay interested, but every time he played something different from the record Sid would stop and correct him.

"Man, you're a hell of a guitar player, but I can't believe you're as good as you are and you don't know any of these solos."

"You guys do any Jeff Beck?" Felix asked.

Sid looked at the others. "I guess we could do 'Shapes of Things,' right? Like on that Gary Moore album?"

"I can fake it, I guess," the drummer said.

"And could you maybe turn down a little?" Felix said.

"Uh, yeah, sure," Sid said, and adjusted the knob on his guitar a quarter turn.

Felix leaned into the opening chords, pounding the Jackson, thinking about nothing but the music, putting a depth of rage and frustration into it he never knew he had. But he couldn't sustain it; the drummer was pounding out 2 and 4, oblivious to what Felix was playing, and Sid had cranked up again and was whaling away on his Gibson with the flat of his hand.

Felix jerked his strap loose and set the guitar back in its case.

"What's the matter?" Sid asked, the band grinding to a halt behind him.

"I just haven't got it today," Felix said. He wanted to break that pissant little toy Gibson across Sid's nose, and the strength of his hatred scared him. "I'm sorry," he said, clenching his teeth. "Maybe some other time."

"Sure," Sid said. "Listen, you're really good, but you need to learn more solos, you know?"

Felix burned rubber as he pulled away, skidding through a U-turn at the end of the street. He couldn't slow down. The car fishtailed when he rocketed out onto Rundberg and he nearly went into a light pole. Pounding the wheel with his fists, hot tears running down his face, he pushed the accelerator to the floor.

Karen was gone when Felix got home. He found a note on the refrigerator. "Sherry picked me up. Will call in a couple of days. Have a lot to think about. K."

He set up the Princeton and tried to play what he was feeling and it came out bullshit, a jerkoff reflex blues progression that didn't mean a thing. He leaned the guitar against the wall and went into his studio, shoving one tape after another into the decks, and every one of them sounded the same, another tired, simpleminded rehash of the obvious.

"I didn't ask for this!" he shouted at the empty house. "You hear me? This isn't what I asked for!"

But it was, and as soon as the words were out he knew he was lying to himself. Faster hands and a better ear weren't enough to make him play like Beck. He had to change inside to play that way, and he wasn't strong enough to handle it, to have every piece of music he'd ever loved turn sour, to need perfection so badly that it was easier to give it up than learn to live with the flaws.

He sat on the couch for a long time and then, finally, he picked up the guitar again. He found a clean rag and polished the body and neck and wiped each individual string. Then, when he had wiped all his fingerprints away, he put it back into the case, still holding it with the rag. He closed the latches and set it next to the amp, by the front door.

For the first time in two days he felt like he could breathe again. He turned out all the lights and opened the windows and sat down on the couch with his eyes closed. Gradually his hands became still and he could hear, very faintly, the fading music of the traffic and the crickets and the wind.

JUDITH MOFFETT

Surviving

Here's an absorbing and evocative study about two very different women who find that they really share a deep similarity of mind and heart: they are both caught, agonizingly, between two worlds. . . .

Judith Moffett is the author of four books—two of poetry, one of criticism, and one of translations from the Swedish—but "Surviving" was her first professional fiction sale, which certainly makes it one of the more remarkable debut stories of recent years. Born in Louisville, Kentucky, she now lives with her husband in Wallingford, Pennsylvania, and teaches a science fiction course and a graduate course in twentieth-century American poetry at the University of Pennsylvania. She has also taught for four summers at the prestigious Breadloaf Writer's Conference, and was given a National Endowment for the Arts Creative Writing Fellowship Grant for her poetry—which she then used to finance the writing of her also remarkable first novel, *Pennterra*, which is coming up in late 1987 as part of the new *Isaac Asimov Presents* line from Congdon & Weed.

SURVIVING

Judith Moffett

For nearly eighteen years I've been keeping a secret to honor the memory of someone, now pretty certainly dead, who didn't want it told. Yet over those years I've come gradually to feel uncomfortable with the idea of dying without recording what I know—to believe that science would be pointlessly cheated thereby, and Sally, too; and just lately, but with a growing urgency, I've also felt the need to write an account of my own actions into the record.

Yet it's difficult to begin. The events I intend to set down have never, since they happened, been out of my mind for a day; nevertheless the prospect of reexperiencing them is painful and my silence the harder to break on that account.

I'll start, I guess, with the afternoon an exuberant colleague I scarcely knew at the time spotted me through the glass door and barged into the psychology department office calling, "Hey, Jan, you're the expert on the Chimp Child—wait'll you hear this, you're not gonna believe it!"

People were always dashing to inform me of some item, mostly inconsequential, relating to this subject. I glanced across at John from the wall of mailboxes, hands full of memos and late papers, one eyebrow probably raised. "What now?"

"We've *hired* her!" And when I continued to look blank: "No kidding, I was just at a curriculum committee meeting in the dean's office, and Raymond Lickorish in Biology was there, and he told me: they've definitely given Sally Barnes a tenure-track appointment, to replace that old guy who's retiring this year, what's his name, Ferrin. The virus man. Raymond says Barnes's Ph.D. research was something on viruses and the origin of life on earth and her published work is all first-rate and she did well in the interview—he wasn't there so he didn't meet her, but they were all talking about it afterward—and she seems eager to leave England. So the department made her an offer and she accepted! She'll be here in September, I swear to God!"

By this point I'm sure I was showing all the incredulous excitement and delight a bearer of happy tidings could possibly have wished. And no wonder: I wrote my *dissertation* on Sally Barnes; I went into psychology chiefly because of the intense interest her story held for me. In fact the Chimp Child had been a kind of obsession of mine—part hobby, part mania—for a long time. I was a college freshman, my years of Tarzan games in the woods less far behind me than you might suppose, in 1990, when poachers hauled the screeching, scratching, biting, terrified white girl into a Tanzanian village and told its head man they would be back to collect the reward. Electrified, I followed the breaking story from day to day.

The girl was quickly and positively identified as Sally, the younger daughter of Martin and Hilary Barnes, Anglican missionary teachers at a secondary school in the small central African republic of Malawi, who had been killed when the light plane in which they and she were traveling from Kigoma had crashed in the jungle. A helicopter rescue crew found only the pilot's body in the burned-out fuselage. Scavengers may have dragged the others away and scattered the bones; improbable survivors of the crash may have tried to walk out—the plane had come down in the mountains, something less than 150 kilometers east of Lake Tanganyika—and starved, or been killed by anything from leopards to thieves to fever. However it was, nothing had been heard or seen of the Barnes family after that day in 1981; it was assumed that one way or another all three had died in the bush.

No close living relatives remained in England. An older daughter, left at home that weekend with an attack of malaria, had been sent to an Anglican school for the children of missionaries, somewhere in the Midlands. There was no one but the church to assume responsibility for her sister the wild girl, either.

The bureaucracies of two African nations and the Church of England hummed, and after a day or two Sally was removed to the Malosa School in Southern Malawi, where the whole of her life before the accident had been lived. She could neither speak nor understand English, seemed stunned, and masturbated constantly. She showed no recognition of the school, its grounds or buildings, or the people there who had been friendly with her as a small child. But when they had cleaned her up, and cropped her matted hair, *they* recognized that child in *her*; pictures of Sally at her fourth birthday party, printed side by side in the papers with new ones of the undersized thirteen-year-old she had become, were conclusive. Hers was one of those faces that looks essentially the same at six and sixty.

But if the two faces obviously belonged to the same person, there was a harrowing difference.

A long time later Sally told me, gazing sadly at this likeness of herself: "Shock. It was nothing but shock, nothing more beastly. On top of everything else, getting captured must have uncovered my memories of the plane crash—violence; noise; confusion; my parents screaming, then not answering me—I mean, when the poachers started shooting and panicked everybody, and then killed the Old Man and flung that net over me, I fought and struggled, of course, but in the end I sort of went blank. Like the accident, but in reverse.''

''Birth Trauma Number Three?'' We were sitting cross-legged on the floor before the fireplace in my living room, naked under blankets, like Mohegan. I could imagine the scene vividly, had in fact imagined it over and over: the brown child blindly running, running, in the green world, the net spreading, dropping in slow motion, the child pitching with a crash into wet vegetation. Helplessness. Claustrophobia. Uttermost bowel-emptying terror. The hysterical shrieks, the rough handling . . . Sally patted my thigh, flushed from the fire's heat, then let her hand stay where it was.

''No point looking like that. What if they *hadn't* found me then? At University College, you know, they all think it was only just in time.''

''And, having read my book, you know I think so, too.'' We smiled; I must have pressed my palm flat to her hot, taut belly, or slipped my hand behind her knee or cupped her breast—some such automatic response. ''The wonder is that after that double trauma they were able to get you back at all. You had to have been an awfully resilient, tough kid, as well as awfully bright. A survivor in every sense. Or you'd have died of shock and grief after the plane crashed, or of shock and grief when the poachers picked you up, or of grief and despair in England from all that testing and training, like spending your adolescence in a pressure cooker.'' I can remember nuzzling her shoulder, how my ear grazed the rough blanket. ''You're a survivor, Sal.''

In the firelight Sally smiled wanly. ''Mm. Up to a point.''

Any standard psych text published after 2003 will describe Sally Barnes as the only feral child in history to whom, before her final disappearance, full functional humanity had been restored. From the age of four and a half until just past her thirteenth birthday, Sally acted as a member of a troop of chimpanzees in the Tanzanian rain forest; from sixteen or seventeen onward, she was a young Englishwoman, a person. What sort of person? The books are vague on this point. Psychologists, naturally enough, were wild to know; Sally herself, who rather thought she did know, was wild to prevent them from turning her inside out all her life in the interest of Science. I was (and am) a psychologist and a partisan, but professional integrity is one thing and obsession is quite another, and if I choose finally to set the record straight it's not because I respect Sally's own choice any less.

From the very first, of course, I'd been madly infatuated with the *idea* of Sally, in whose imagined consciousness—that of a human girl accepted by wild creatures as one of themselves—I saw, I badly wished to see, myself. The extreme harshness of such a life as hers had been—with its parasites, cold rains, bullying of the weak by the strong, and so forth—got neatly edited out of this hyperromantic conception; yet the myth had amazing force. I don't know how many times I read the *Jungle Books* and the best of the Tarzan novels between the ages of eight and fifteen, while my mother hovered uneasily in the background, dropping hints about eye makeup and stylish clothes. Pah.

So that later, when a real apechild emerged from a real jungle and the Sunday supplements and popular scientific magazines were full of her story, for me it was an enthralling and fabulous thing, one that made it possible to finish growing up, at graduate school, *inside* the myth: a myth not dispelled but amplified, enhanced, by scientific scrutiny. The more one looked at what had happened to Sally, the more wonderful it seemed.

Her remarkable progress had been minutely documented, and I had read every document and published half a dozen of my own, including my dissertation. It was established that she had talked early and could even read fairly well before the accident, and that her early family history had been a happy, stable one; all we experts were agreed that these crucial factors explained how Sally, alone among feral children, had been able to develop, or reacquire normal language skills in later life. She was therefore fortunate in her precocity; fortunate, too, in her foster society of fellow primates. Almost certainly she could not have recovered, or recovered so completely, from eight years of life as a wolf or a gazelle. Unlike Helen Keller, she had never been sensually deprived; unlike Kaspar Hauser, also sensually deprived, she had not been isolated from social relations—wild chimpanzees provide one another with plenty of those; unlike the wolf girls of India, she had learned language before her period of abstention from the use of it. And like Helen Keller, Sally had a very considerable native intelligence to assist her.

It may seem odd that despite frequent trips to England, I had never tried to arrange a meeting with the subject of all this fascinated inquiry, but in some way my fixation made me shy, and I would end each visit by deciding that another year would do as well or better. That Sally might come to America, and to my own university, and to stay, was a wholly unlooked-for development. Now that chance had arranged it, however, shyness seemed absurd. Not only would we meet, we would become friends. Everyone would expect us to, and nothing seemed more natural.

My grandfather used to claim, with a forgiving chuckle, that his wedding night had been the biggest disappointment of his life. I thought bleakly of him the September evening of the annual cocktail party given by the dean of arts and sciences so that the standing faculty could make the acquaintance of their newly hired colleagues. A lot of people knew about Sally Barnes, of course, and among psychologists she was really famous, a prodigy; everybody wanted to meet her, and more than a few wanted to be there when *I* met her, to witness the encounter. I was exasperated with myself for being so nervous, as well as annoyed that the meeting would occur under circumstances so public, but when the moment arrived and I was actually being introduced to Sally—the dean had stationed himself beside her to handle the crush, and did the honors himself—these feelings all proved maddeningly beside the point.

There she stood, the Chimp Child of all my theories and fantasies: a small, utterly ordinary-seeming and sounding young woman who touched my hand with purely mechanical courtesy. The plain black dress did less than nothing for her plain pale face and reddish hair; history's only rehabilitated feral child was a person you wouldn't look at twice in the street, or even once. That in itself meant nothing; but her expression, too, was indifferent and blank, and she spoke without any warmth at all, in an "educated" English voice pitched rather high: "How d'you do, a pleasure to meet you . . ." There she actually stood, saying her canned phrase to *me*, sipping from her clear plastic container of white wine, giving away nothing at all.

I stared at the pale, round, unfamiliar face whose shape and features I knew so well, unable to believe in it or let go of the hand that felt so hard in mine. The room had gradually grown deafening. Bright, curious eyes had gathered round us. The moment felt utterly weird and wrong. Dean Eccles, perhaps supposing his difficult charge had failed to catch my name, chirped helpfully, "Of course Janet is the author of that fascinating book about *you*," and beamed at Sally as if to say, *There* now, you lucky girl!"

Only a flicker of eyelids betrayed her. "Oh, I see," she said, but her hand pulled out of mine with a little yank as she spoke, and she looked pointedly past me toward the next person in the receiving line—a snub so obvious that even the poor dean couldn't help but notice. Flustered, he started to introduce the elderly English professor Sally's attention had been transferred to.

We had hardly exchanged a dozen words. Suddenly I simply had to salvage something from the wreck of the occasion. "Look—could I call you in a week or two? Maybe we could get together for lunch or a drink or something after you're settled in?"

"Ah, I'm afraid I'll be rather busy for quite some time," said the cool voice, not exactly to me. "Possibly I might ring you if I happen to be free for an hour one afternoon." Then she was speaking to the old gentleman and I had been eased out of the circle of shoulders and that was that.

I went home thoroughly despondent and threw myself on the sofa. An hour or so later, the phone rang: John, who had witnessed the whole humiliating thing. "Listen, she acted that way with *everybody*, I watched her for an hour. Then I went through the line and she acted like that with *me*. She was probably jet-lagged or hates being on display—she was just pretending to drink that wine, by the way, sip, sip, sip, but the level never went down the whole time I was watching. You shouldn't take it personally, Jan. I doubt she had any idea who you were in that mob of freakshow tourists.''

''Oh, she knew who I was, all right, but that doesn't make you wrong. O.K., thanks. I just wish the entire department hadn't been standing around with their tongues hanging out, waiting to see us fall weeping on each other's necks.'' Realizing I wasn't sure which I minded more, the rejection or its having been witnessed in that way, made me feel less tragic. I said good night to John, then went and pulled down the foldable attic stairs, put on the light, and scrounged among cartons till I found the scrapbook; this I brought downstairs and brooded over, soothed by a glass of rosé.

The scrapbook was fat. The Chimp Child had been an international sensation when first reclaimed from the wild, and for years thereafter picture essays and articles had regularly appeared where I could clip or copy them. I had collected dozens of photographs of Sally: arriving at Heathrow, a small, oddly garbed figure, face averted, clinging to a uniformed attendant; dressed like an English schoolgirl at fifteen, in blazer and tie, working at a table with the team of psychologists at University College, London; on holiday with the superb teacher Carol Cheswick, who had earned a place for herself in the educators' pantheon beside Jean-Marc Itard and Annie Sullivan by virtue of her brilliant achievements with Sally; greeting Jane Goodall, very old and frail, on one of Goodall's last visits to England; in her rooms at Newnham College, Cambridge, an average-looking undergraduate.

The Newnham pictures were not very good, or so I had always thought. Only now that I'd seen her in person . . . I turned back to the yellow newspaper clipping, nearly twenty years old, of a wild thing with matted, sawed-off hair; and now for the first time the blank face beneath struck me as queerly like this undergraduate's, and like the face I had just been trying to talk to at the party. The expressive adolescent's face brought into being sometime during the nineties—what had become of it? Who was Sally Barnes, after all? That precocious, verbally gifted little girl . . . I closed the cover, baffled. Whoever she was, she had long since passed the stage of being studied without her consent.

Yet I wanted so badly to know her. As fall wore on to winter, I would often see her on campus, walking briskly, buttoned up in her silver coat with a long black scarf wrapped round her, appearing to take no notice of whatever leaves or slush or plain brickwork happened to be underfoot, or of the milling, noisy students. She always carried reading equipment and a black shoulder bag. Invariably she would be alone. I doubt that I can convey more than a dim impression of the bewilderment and frustration with which the sight of her affected me throughout those slow, cold months. I knew every detail of the special education of Sally Barnes, the dedication of her teachers, her own eagerness to learn; and there had been *nothing*, nothing at all, to suggest that once "restored to human status," she would become ordinary—nothing to foreshadow this standoffish dullness. Of course it was understandable that she would not wish to be quizzed constantly about her life in the wild; rumor got round of several instances when somebody unintimidated by her manner had put some question to her and been served with a snappish "Sorry, I don't talk about that." But was it credible that the child whom this unique experience had befallen had been, as her every word and action now implied, a particularly unfriendly, unoriginal, bad-tempered child who thereafter had scuttled straight back to sour conventionality as fast as ever she could?

I simply did not believe it. She had to be deceiving us deliberately. But I couldn't imagine why, nor entirely trust my own intuition: I wanted far too badly to believe that *no* human being who had been a wild animal for a time, and then become human again, could possibly really be the sort of human Sally seemed to be.

And yet why not (I would argue with myself)? Why doubt that a person who had fought so hard for her humanity might desire, above all else, the life of an ordinary human?

But is it ordinary to be so antisocial (I would argue back)? Of course she never got in touch with me. A couple of weeks after the party, I nerved myself up enough to call her office and suggest meeting for lunch. The brusqueness of that refusal took some getting over; I let a month go by before trying again. "I'm sorry," she said. "But what was it you wanted to discuss? Perhaps we could take care of it over the phone."

"The idea wasn't to discuss anything, particularly. I only thought—new people sometimes find it hard to make their way here at first, it's not a very friendly university. And then, naturally I'd like to—well, just talk. Get acquainted. Get to know you a bit."

"Thanks, but I'm tremendously busy, and in any event there's very little I could say." And then, after a pause: "Someone's come to the door. Thanks for ringing."

It was no good, she would have nothing to do with me, beyond speaking when we met on campus—I could, and did, force her to take that much notice of me. Where was she living? I looked it up, an address in the suburbs, not awfully far from mine. Once I pedaled past the building, a shabby older high-rise, but there was no way of telling which of the hundreds of windows might be hers. I put John up to questioning his committee acquaintance in Biology, learning in this way: that Sally had cooly repulsed every social overture from people in her department, without exception; that student gossip styled her a Britishly reserved but better-than-competent lecturer; that she was hard at work in the lab on some project she never discussed with anybody. Not surprisingly, her fellow biologists had soon lost interest. She had speedily trained us all to leave her alone.

The psych department lost interest also, not without a certain tiresome belaboring of me, jokes about making silk purses out of chimps' ears and Ugly Chimplings and the like. John overheard a sample of this feeble mailbox badinage one day and retorted with some heat, "Hey, Janet only said she's *human* in that book. If education made you nice and personable, I know lots of people around here besides Sally Barnes who could stand to go back to school." But John, embroiled in a romance with a first-year graduate student, now found Sally a dull subject himself; besides, what he had said was true. My thesis had not been invalidated, nor Carol Cheswick and the team at University College overrated. It was simply the case, in fact, that within six months of her arrival, Sally—billed in advance as an exotic ornament to the university—had compelled us all to take her for neither more nor less than the first-rate young microbiologist she had come among us to be.

My personal disappointment grew by degrees less bitter. But still I would see the silver coat and subduedly fashionable boots, all points and plastic, moving away across the quad and think: Lady, had it been given unto me to be the Chimp Child, by God I'd have made a better job of it than you do!

Spring came. Between the faculty club and the library, the campus forsythia erupted along its straggling branches, the azaleas flowered as usual a week earlier in the city than in my garden fifteen miles away. Ridley Creek, in the nearby state park, roared with rains and snowmelt and swarmed with stocked trout and bulky anglers; and cardinals and titmice, visible all winter at the feeders, abruptly began to sing. Every winter I used to lose interest in the park between the first of February and the middle of March; every spring rekindled my sense of the luck and privilege of having it so near. During the first weeks of trout season, the trails, never heavily used, were virtually deserted, and any sunny day my presence was not required in town I would stuff a sandwich, a pocket reader, and a blanket into a daypack and pedal to the park. Generally I stayed close to the trails, but would sometimes tough my way through some brambly thicket of blackberry or raspberry canes, bright with small new chartreuse-colored leaves, to find a private spot where I could take off my shirt in safety.

Searching for this sort of retreat in a tract of large beech trees one afternoon in April, I came carefully and painfully through a tangle of briars to be thunderstruck by the sight of young Professor Barnes where she seemed at once least and most likely to be: ten meters up in one of the old beeches. She was perfectly naked. She sat poised on a little branch, one shoulder set against the smooth gray bole of the bare tree, one foot dangling, the opposite knee cocked on the branch, the whole posture graced by a naturalness that smote me with envy in the surreal second or two before she caught sight of me. She was rubbing herself, and seemed to be crying.

One after another, like blows, these impressions whammed home in the instant of my emerging. The next instant Sally's face contorted with rage, she screamed, snapped off and threw a piece of dead branch at me (and hit me, too, in the breastbone), and was down the tree and running almost faster than I could take in what had happened, what was still happening. While part of my brain noted with satisfaction. *She didn't hear me coming!* a different part galvanized my frenzied shouting: "No! Sally, for God's sake, stop! Stop! Come back here, I won't tell anybody, I won't, I swear!. *Sally!*" Unable to move, to chase her, I could only go on yelling in this semihysterical vein; I felt that if she got away now, I would not be able to bear it. I'd have been heard all over that side of the park if there had been anybody to hear, outside the zone of noise created by the creek. It was the racket I was making, in fact, that made her come pelting back—that, and the afterthought that all her clothes were back there under the tree, and realizing I had recognized her.

"All right, I'm not going anywhere, now *shut up!*" she called in a low, furious voice, crashing through undergrowth. She stomped right up to me barefoot and looked me in the eye. "God damn it to hell. What will you take to keep your mouth shut?" Did she mean right now? But I *had* stopped shouting. My heart went right on lurching about like a tethered frog, though, and the next moment the view got brighter and began to drift off to the right. I sat down abruptly on something damp.

"I was scared witless you wouldn't come back. Wait a second, let me catch my breath."

"You're the one who wrote that book, Morgan," she said between her teeth. "God damn it to *hell*." In a minute she sat down, too, first pushing aside the prickly stems unthinking. The neutral face that gave away nothing had vanished. Sally Barnes, angry and frightened, looked exactly as I had wished to see her look; incredibly, after so much fruitless fantasy, here we were in the woods together. Here she sat, scratching a bare breast with no more special regard than if it had been a nose or a shoulder. It was pretty overwhelming. I couldn't seem to pull myself together.

Sally's skin had turned much darker than mine already, all over—plainly this was not her first visit to the bare-branched woods. Her breasts were smallish, her three tufts of body hair reddish, and all her muscles large and smooth and well-molded as a gymnast's. I said what came into my head: "I was a fairly good tree-climber as a kid, but I could never have gotten up one with a trunk as thick as that, and those high, skinny branches. Do you think if I built my arms and shoulders up, lifted weights or something—I mean, would you teach me? Or maybe I'm too old," I said: "My legs aren't in such bad shape, I run a few kilometers three times a week, but the top half of my body is a flabby mess—"

"Don't play stupid games," Sally burst out furiously. "You had to come blundering in here today, you're the worst luck I ever had. I'm asking again:

Will you take money not to tell anyone you saw me? Or is there something else you want? If I can get it, you can have it, only you've *got* to keep quiet about seeing me out here like this."

"That's a rotten way to talk to people!" I said, furious myself. "I was blundering around in these woods for years before you ever set foot in them. And I'm sorry if you don't like my book, or is it just me you don't like? Or just psychologists? If it weren't for you, I probably wouldn't even *be* one." My voice wobbled up and down, I'd been angry with Sally for seven months. "Don't worry, I won't say anything. You don't need to bribe me."

"Yes, but you will, you see. Sooner or later you'll be at some dinner party, and someone will ask what the Chimp Child is like, *really*"—I looked slantwise at her; this had already happened a couple of times—"and you won't be able to resist. 'There I was, walking along minding my own business, and whomever do you think I saw—stark naked and gone right up a tree like a monkey!' Christ," Sally said through her teeth, "I could *throttle* you. Everything's spoiled." She got up hastily; I could feel how badly she wanted to clobber me again.

But I was finally beginning to be able to think, and to call upon my expertise. "Well, then, make me *want* not to tell. Make it a question of self-interest. I don't want money, but I wasn't kidding: I'd absolutely love to be able to get around in a forest like a chimp does. Teach me to climb like one—like you do. If the story gets out, the deal's off. Couldn't you agree to that?"

Sally's look meant, "What kind of idiot do you take me for?" Quickly I said, "I know it sounds crazy, but all through my childhood—and most of my adolescence, too—for whatever wacky reason, I wanted in the *worst* way to be Tarzan! And for the past twenty years, I've gone on wanting even more to be *you*! I don't know why—it's irrational, one of those passions people develop for doing various weird things, being fans or collecting stamps or—I used to know a former world champion flycaster who'd actually gone fishing only a couple of times in his life!" I drew a deep breath, held it, let it out in a burst of words: "Look—even if I don't understand it, I *know* that directly behind *The Chimp Child and the Human Family*—and the whole rest of my career, for that matter—is this ten-year-old kid who'd give anything to be Tarzan swinging through the trees with the Great Apes. I can promise that so long as you were coaching me, you'd be safe. I'll never get a better chance to act out part of that fantasy, and it would be worth—just everything! One *hell* of a lot more than keeping people entertained at some dinner party, I'll tell you that!"

"You don't want to be me," said Sally in a flat voice. "I was right the first time; it's a stupid game you're playing at." She looked at me distastefully, but I could see that at any rate she believed me now.

The ground was awfully damp. I got up, starting to feel vastly better.

Beech limbs webbed the sky; strong sunshine and birdsong poured through web; it was all I could do, suddenly, not to howl and dance among the trees. I could see she was going to say yes.

Sally set conditions, all of which I accepted promptly. I was not to ask snoopy professional questions, or do any nonessential talking. At school we were to go on as before, never revealing by so much as a look or gesture that an association existed between us. I was not to tell *anybody*. Sally could not, in fact, prevent my telling people, but I discovered that I hadn't any desire to tell. My close friends, none of whom lived within 150 kilometers of the city, could guess I was concealing a relationship but figured I would talk about it when I got ready; they tended to suppose a married man, reason enough for secrecy. Sally and I both taught our classes, and Sally had her work in the lab, and I my private patients.

Once in midweek and once each weekend, we met in the beech grove; and so the "lessons" got under way.

I acquired some light weights and began a program of exercise to strengthen my arms, shoulders, chest, and back, but the best way to build up the essential muscles was to climb a lot of trees. Before long the calluses at the base of each finger, which I had carried throughout my childhood, had been re-created (and I remembered then the hardness of Sally's palm when I'd shaken hands with her at the cocktail party in September). Seeing how steadily my agility and toughness increased, Sally was impressed and, in spite of herself, gratified. She was also nervous; she'd had no intention of letting herself enjoy this companionship that had been forced upon her.

It was a queer sort of blackmail. I went along patiently, working hard and trying to make my company too enjoyable to resist; and in this way the spring semester ended.

Sally was to teach summer school, I to prepare some articles for publication and continue to see my patients through the summer. By June all the trout had been hooked and the beech woods had grown risky; we found more inaccessible places on the riding-trail side of the park where I could be put through my training-exercise routines. By the Fourth of July my right biceps measured thirty-seven centimeters and Sally had finally begun to relax in my presence, even to trust me.

That we shortly became lovers should probably surprise nobody. All the reports describe the pre-accident Sally as an affectionate child, and her family as a loving one. From my reading I knew that in moments of anxiety or fear, chimps reassure one another by touching, and that in placid ones they reaffirm the social bond by reciprocal grooming. Yet for a decade, ever since Carol Cheswick died and she'd gone up to Cambridge, Sally had protected herself strictly against personal involvements, at the cost of denying herself all emotional and physical closeness. Cheswick, a plump, middle-aged, motherly person, had hugged and cuddled Sally throughout their years together, but after Cheswick's death—sick of the pokings and peerings of psychologists and of the curious public, resentful and guilty about the secret life she had felt compelled to create for herself—Sally had simply done without. Now she had me.

Except for the very beginning, in London, there had always been a secret life.

She abruptly started to talk about it late one horribly hot afternoon, at the end of a workout. We had dropped out of the best new training tree, a century-old white oak, then shaken out a ragged army blanket, sat on it cross-legged, and passed a plastic canteen and a bunch of seedless grapes between us. I felt sticky and spent, but elated. Sally looked me over critically. "You're filling out quite well, it's hard to believe these are the same scrawny shoulders." She kneaded the nearer shoulder with her hard hand, while I carefully concealed my intense awareness that except to correct an error, she had never touched me anywhere before. The hand slipped down, gripped my upper arm. When I "made a muscle" the backs of her brown fingers brushed my pale-tan breast; our eyes met, and I said lightly, "I owe it all to you coach," but went warmer still with pleasure and the rightness of these gestures, which had the feeling of a course correction.

Sally plucked several grapes and popped them in her mouth, looking out over the creek valley while she chewed. After a bit she said, "They let me go all to pot in London. All anybody cared about was guiding me out of the wilderness of ignorance, grafting my life at thirteen back onto the stump of my life at four and then making up for the lost years how they could. The lost years . . . mind you, they had their hands full, they all worked like navvies and so did I. But I'd got absolutely consumptive with longing for the bush before they brought Carol in, and she noticed and made them let me out for a fortnight's holiday in the countryside. I'd lost a lot of strength by then, but it was only just a year so it came back quick enough."

She stopped there, and I didn't dare say anything; we ate grapes and slapped mosquitoes. It was incredibly hot. After a bit, desperate to hear more, I was weighing the risks of a response when she went on without prodding:

"At University College, though, they didn't much care to have me swinging about in trees. I think they felt, you know, 'Here we are; slaving away trying to drag the ape kid into the modern world, and what does she do the minute our backs are turned but go dashing madly back to her savage ways.' Sort of, 'Ungrateful little beast.' They never imagined I might miss that benighted life, or anything about it, but when I read Tarzan of the Apes myself a few years later, the part toward the end where Tarzan strips off his suit and tie and shoes and leaps into the branches swearing he'll never, never go back—I cried like anything."

I said, "What could you do about it, though?" breaking Sally's no-questions rule without either of us noticing.

"Oh, on my own, not much. But Carol had a lot to say about what I should and shouldn't do. They respected her tremendously. And she was marvelous. After I'd got so I could talk and read pretty well, she'd take me to the South Downs on weekends and turn me loose. We had a tacit agreement that if she didn't ask, I needn't tell. We were so close, she certainly knew I was getting stronger and my hands were toughening up, but *she* never took the view that those years in the wild were best forgotten. She arranged for me to meet Jane Goodall once . . . I couldn't have borne it without her. I never should have left England while she lived. If it weren't for Carol—"
For several minutes Sally's hand had been moving of its own accord, short rhythmic strokes that ceased abruptly when, becoming aware of this move-ment, she broke off her sentence and glanced—sharply, in alarm—at me.

I made a terrific effort to control my face and voice, a fisherman angling for the biggest trout in the pool. "She must have been remarkable."

For a wonder Sally didn't get up without a word and stalk away. Instead she said awkwardly, "I—do you mind very much my doing this? I've always done it—for comfort, I suppose—ever since I was small, and it's a bit difficult to talk about all these things . . . without . . ."

From the first day of training, I had determined never to let Sally force a contrast between us; I would adapt to her own sense of fitness out here. If she climbed naked, so would I, tender skin or not. If she urinated openly, and standing, so would I—and without a doubt there was something agreeable about spraddling beside Sally while our waters flowed. A civilized woman can still pass the whole length of her life without ever seeing another woman's urine, or genitalia, or having extended, repeated, and matter-of-fact exposure to another woman's naked body—and yet how many *men*, I had asked myself, ever gave these homely matters a second thought?

Then why on earth should we?

Certainly no woman had ever before done in my presence what Sally had been doing. Mentally, I squared my shoulders. "Why should I mind? Look, I'll keep you company"—suiting action to words with a sense of leaping in desperation into unknown waters, graceless but absolutely determined—"O.K.?"

It was the very last thing Sally had looked for. For a second I was afraid she thought I was ridiculing her in some incomprehensible way; but she only watched, briefly, before saying, "O.K. For a psychologist you're not a bad sort. The first bloody thing they did at that mission school was make me stop doing this in front of people.

"So anyway. Carol knew I was longing for the wild life, and knew it was important, not trivial or wrong, so she gave it back to me as well as she could. But she couldn't give me back"—her voice cracked as she said this—"the chimpanzees. The people I knew. And I did miss them dreadfully—certain ones, and living in the troop—the thing is, I was a child among them, and in a lot of ways it was a lovely life for a child, out there. The wild chimps are so direct and excitable, their feelings change like lightning, they're perfectly uninhibited—they squabble like schoolkids with no master about. And the babies are so sweet! But its all very—very, you know, physical; and I missed it. I thought I should die with missing it, before Carol came." The grapes were all gone. Sally chucked the stem into the brambles and lay back on the blanket, left arm bent across her eyes, right hand rocking softly.

"Part of my training in London was manners and morals: to control myself, play fair, treat people politely whether I liked them or not. I'd *enjoyed* throwing tantrums and swatting the little ones when they got in my road, and screaming when I was furious and throwing my arms around everybody in reach when I was excited or happy, and being hugged and patted—like this," patting her genitals to demonstrate the chimpanzees' way of reassuring one another, "when I was upset. Chimps have no super-ego. It's hard to have to form one at thirteen. By then, pure selfishness without guilt is hard to conquer. Oh, I had a lot of selfishness to put up with from the others— I was very low-ranking, of course, being small and female—but I never got seriously hurt. And a knockabout life makes you tough, and then I had the Old Man for a protector as well." Sally lifted her arm and looked beneath it, up at me. "For a kid, most of the time, it was a pretty exhilarating life, and I missed it. And I missed," she said, "getting fucked. They were not providing any of that at University College, London."

"What?" My thumb stopped moving. "Ah—were you old enough? I mean, were the males interested, even though you didn't go pink?" I began to rub again, perhaps faster.

"For the last year or thereabouts—I'm not quite sure how long. It must have been, I don't know, pheromones in the mucus, or something in my urine, but I know it was quite soon after my periods started that they'd get interested in me *between* periods, when I would have been fertile, even without the swelling. I knew all about it, naturally; I'd seen plenty of copulating right along, as far back as I could remember. A pink female is a very agitating social element, so I'd needed to watch closely, because one's got to get out of the way, except while they're actually going at it. That's when all the little ones try to make them stop—don't ask me why," she added quickly, then grinned. "Sorry. That's one thing every primatologist has wanted to know." Sally's movements were freer now; watching, I was abruptly pierced by a pang of oddity, which I clamped down on as best I could. This was definitely not the moment for turning squeamish.

"It frightened me badly that first time; adult male chimps who want something don't muck about. When they work themselves up, you know, they're quite dangerous. I usually avoided them, except for the Old Man, who'd sort of adopted me not long after the troop took me in . . . any road the first time hurt, and then of course everybody always wants a piece of the action, and it went on for *days*. By the time it was over, I'd got terribly sore. But later . . . well, after I'd recovered from that first bout, I found it didn't really hurt anymore. In fact, I liked it. Quite a lot, actually once I saw I needn't be frightened. The big males are frightfully strong, the only time I could ever dare be so close to so many of them was then, when I came in season, and one or another of them would sort of summon me over to him, and then they'd all queue up and press up behind me, one after another . . .''

More relieved than she realized at having broken the long silence at last, Sally went on telling her story; and of course, the more vividly she pictured for me her role in this scene of plausible bizarreness, elaborating, adding details, the more inevitable was the outcome of our own unusual scene. All the same, when the crisis struck us, more or less simultaneously, it left me for the moment speechless and utterly nonplussed, and Sally seemed hardly less flustered than I.

But after that momentary shock, we each glanced sidelong at each other's flushed, flummoxed face and burst into snorts of laughter; and we laughed together—breathlessly, raggedly, probably a little hysterically—for quite a while. And pretty soon it was all right. Everything was fine.

It was all right, but common sense cautioned that if Sally's defenses were too quickly breached, she would take fright. So many barriers had collapsed at once as to make me grateful for the several days that must elapse before the next coaching session. Still, when I passed her figure in its floppy navy smockdress and dark glasses on campus the following morning, I was struck as never before by the contrast between the public Sally and the powerful glowing creature nobody here had seen but me. A different person in her situation, I thought, would surely have exploited the public's natural curiosity: made movies, written books, gone on the lecture circuit, endorsed products and causes. Instead, to please her teachers, everything that had stubbornly remained Chimp Child in Sally as she learned and grew had had to be concealed, denied.

But because the required denial was a concealment and a lie, she had paid an exhorbitant price for it; too much of what was vital in her had living roots in those eight years of wildness. Sally was genuinely fond of and grateful to the zealous psychologists who had given back her humanity. At the same time she resented them quite as biterly as she resented a public interested only in the racier parts of her life in the wild and in her humanity not at all. One group starved her, the other shamed her. Resentments and gratitudes had split her life between them. She would never consent to display herself *as* the Chimp Child on any sort of platform, yet without the secret life she would have shriveled to a husk. When I surprised her in the park, she had naturally feared and hated me. Not any more.

Success despite such odds made me ambitious. I conceived a plan. Somehow I would find a way—become a way!—to integrate the halves of Sally's divided self; one day she would walk across this quad, no longer alone, wearing her aspect of the woods (though clothed and cleaner). I'd worked clinically with self-despising homosexuals, and with the children of divorced and poisonously hostile parents; Sally's case, though unique in one way, was common enough in others. Charged with purpose, I watched as the brisk, dark shape entered a distant building and swore a sacred oath to the Principle of Human Potential: I would finish the job, I would dedicate myself to the saving of Sally Barnes. Who but I could save her now? At that fierce moment I knew exactly how Itard had felt when finally, for the first time, he had succeeded in reducing Victor to the fundamental humanity of tears.

Saturday looked threatening, but I set off anyway for the park. The midafternoon heat was oppressive; I cut my muscle-loosening jog to a kilometer or two, then quartered through the woods to the training oak. Early as I was, Sally had come before me. I couldn't see her, high in the now dense foliage, but her clothing was piled in the usual place and I guessed she had made a day-nest at the top of that tree or one nearby, or was traveling about up there somewhere. After a long drink from the canteen I peeled off my own sweaty shorts, toweling shirt, shoes, and the running bra of heavy spandex, smeared myself with insect repellent, and dried my hands on my shirt. Then I crouched slightly, caught a heavy limb well over two meters above the ground and pulled myself into the tree.

For ten minutes I ran through a set of upper-body warmups with care and concentration; I'd pulled one muscle in my shoulder four times and once another in my back, before finding an old book on gymnastics explaining how to prevent (and treat) such injuries. The first few weeks I had worn lightweight Keds, and been otherwise generally scraped and skinned. But now my skin had toughened—I hadn't known it would do that—and greater strength made it easier to forgo the clambering friction of calves and forearms; now, for the most part, my hands and feet were all that came in contact with the bark. A haircut had nicely solved the problems of snarling twigs and obscured vision.

Warm and loose, I quickly climbed ten meters higher and began another series of strengthening and balancing exercises, swinging back and forth, hand over hand, along several slender horizontal limbs, standing and walking over a heavier one, keeping myself relaxed.

After half an hour of this, I descended to the massive lowest limb and practiced dropping to the ground, absorbing the shock elastically with both hands and both feet, chimp-style. Again and again I sprang into the tree, poised, and landed on the ground. I was doing quite well, but on about the fifteenth drop I bruised my hand on a rock beneath the leaf mold and decided to call it an afternoon; my hair was plastered flat with sweat, and I was as drenched as if I'd just stepped out of a shower. I had a long, tepid drink and was swabbing myself down with my shirt when Sally left the tree by the same limb, landed with a negligent, perfect pounce, came forward and —without meeting my eye—relieved me of the canteen, at the same time laying her free arm briefly across my shoulders. "That one's looking pretty good," she said, nodding at the branch to indicate my Dropping-to-the-Ground exercise. The arm slid off, she picked up the squirter of Tropikbug—"but did you ever see such monstrous mosquitoes in your life?"

"It's the humidity, I was afraid the storm would break before I could get through the drill. Maybe we better skip the rest and try to beat it home."

Sally squirted some repellent into her palm and wiped it up and down her limbs and over her brown abdomen. She squirted out some more. "Yours is all sweated off," she said, still not meeting my eye; and instantly Hugo Van Lawick's photographs of chimps soliciting grooming flashed into my mind, and I turned my shoulder toward Sally, who rubbed the bug stuff into it, then anointed the other shoulder, and my back and breasts and stomach for good measure, and then handed the flask dreamily to me, presenting her own back to be smeared with smelly goop. At that instant the first dramatic thunderclap banged above the park, making us both jump; and for a heart-stopping second Sally's outstretched arm clutched round me.

We bundled the blanket back into its plastic pouch and cached it, and pulled on clothes, while rain began to fall in torrents. My jogging shoes were clearly goners. I didn't bother to put on the bra, rolling it up on the run and sticking it inside my waistband. We floundered out of the trees in a furious commotion of wind and crackle-WHAM of lightning, and dashed in opposite directions for our parked cars. It took me fully fifteen minutes to reach mine, and twenty more to pedal home by roads several centimeters deep in rain, with the heater going full blast, and another half hour to take a hot shower and brew some tea. Then, wrapped in a bathrobe, I carried the tea tray and Jane Goodall's classic study *In the Shadow of Man* into the living room, and reread for the dozenth time the passages on the social importance of physical contact among wild chimpanzees.

Over and over, as I sat there, I relived the instant of Sally's instinctive quasi embrace in the storm, and each time it stopped my breath. What must Sally herself be feeling then? What terrifying conflict of needs? She must realize, just as I did, that a torrent had begun to build that would sweep her carefully constructed defenses away, that she could not stop it now, that she must flee or be changed by what would follow.

When I thought of *change*, it was as something about to happen to Sally, though change was moving just as inexorably down upon me. Three or four times in my life, I've experienced that sense of *courting* change, of choosing my life from moment to moment, the awareness of process and passage that exalted me that evening but never before or since with such intensity. I alone had brought us to this, slowly, over months of time, as the delicate canoe is portaged and paddled to where the white water begins. Day by day we had picked up speed; now the stream was hurtling us forward together; now, with all our skill and nerve and strength, we would ride the current—we would shoot through. There is a word for this vivid awareness: existential.

If I feared then, it was that Sally might hurl herself out of the canoe.

The next day but one was not a regular coaching day, but the pitch of nervous excitement made desk work impossible. I drove to the park in midafternoon to jog, and afterward decided, in preference to more disciplined routines, to practice my Traveling-from-Tree-to-Tree. My speed and style at this—that of a very elderly, very arthritic ape—was still not half bad (I thought) for a human female pushing forty, though proper brachiation still lay well beyond my powers. The run, as usual, had settled me down. The creek, still aboil with muddy runoff from the storm, was racketing along through a breezy, beautiful day. I chose an ash with a low fork, stuffed my clothes into my fanny pack, buckled it on, and started to climb.

I hadn't expected to find Sally at the training tree, but saw her without surprise—seated below me, crosslegged on the grubby blanket—when, an hour later, I had made my way that far. She stood up slowly while I descended the familiar pattern of limbs and dropped from the bottommost one. Again without surprise I saw that she looked awful, shaky and sick, that assurance had deserted her—and understood then that *whatever* happened now would not surprise me, that I was ready and would be equal to it. While I stood before Sally, breathing hard, unfastening the buckle, the world arranged itself into a patterned whole.

Then, as I let the pack fall, Sally crouched low on the blanket, whimpering and twisting with distress. I knelt at once and gathered her into my arms, holding her firmly, all of her skin close against all of mine. She clutched at me, pressed her face into my neck. Baffled moaning sounds and sobs came out of her. She moved inside this embrace; still moaning, eyes squeezed shut, her blind face searched until she had taken the nipple and end of my left breast into her mouth. As she sucked and mouthed at this, with her whole face pushed into the breast, her body gradually unknotted, relaxed, curled about mine, so I could loosen my hold to stroke her with the hand not suporting her head. Soon, to relieve the strain of the position, I pressed the fanny pack—I could just reach it—into service as a pillow and lay down on my side, still cradling Sally's head.

Time passed, or stopped. The nipple began to be sore.

At last, seemingly drained, she rolled away onto her back. Her face was smeared with mucus and tears; I worked my shirt out of the pack one-handed and dried it. At once she rolled back again, pushing herself against me with a long, groaning sigh. "The past couple of nights, God, I've had all sorts of dreams. Not bad dreams, not exactly, but—there was this old female in the troop, maybe her baby died, it must have done . . . I'd completely forgotten this. This must have been when they first found me. *she* found me, I think . . . I think I'd been alone in the forest without food long enough to be utterly petrified and apathetic with terror. But when she found me . . . I remember she held me against her chest and shoved the nipple in—maybe just to relieve her discomfort, or to replace her own child with a substitute, who knows. I think I would certainly have died except for that milk, there was such all-encompassing fear and misery. I don't know how many weeks or months she let me nurse. She couldn't have lived very long, though."

Sally weighed my breast in her hand. "Last night I dreamed I was in some terrible place, so frightened I couldn't move or open my eyes, and somebody . . . picked me up and held me, and then I was suckling milk from a sort of teat, and felt, oh, ever so much better, a great flood of relief. Then I opened my eyes and saw we were in the bush—I recognized the actual place—but it was *you*, the person holding me was you! You had a flat chest with big rubbery chimpanzee nipples"—lifting the tender breast on her palm—"and a sort of chimp face, but you were only skin all over, and I realized it was you."

I put my hand firmly over hers, moved it down along her forearm. "How did you feel when you knew it was me?"

"Uncomfortable. Confused. Angry." Then reluctantly: "Happy, too. I woke up, though, and then mostly felt just astonished to remember that that old wet nurse had saved my life and I'd not given her a single thought for twenty-five years." She lay quiet under my caressing: neck, breasts, stomach, flank; her eyes closed again. "What's queer is that I should remember *now*, but not when Carol first took charge of me, and not when I first read *Tarzan*, even though the Tarzan story's nearly the same as mine. I don't understand why now and not then."

"Do you feel you need to? I mean, does it seem important to understand?"

"I don't know." She sounded exhausted. "I certainly don't feel like even trying to sort it all out now."

"Well. It'll probably sort itself out soon enough, provided you don't start avoiding whatever makes these disturbing memories come back."

Sally opened her eyes and smiled thinly. "Start avoiding you, you mean. No. I shan't, never fear." She snuggled closer, widening and tilting herself; in my "therapist" frame of mind, I tried to resist this, but my hand—stroking on automatic for so long—slid downward at once on its own, and I ceased at the same instant to ignore a response I'd been blocking without realizing it for a good long while. I was still lying on my side, facing Sally; my top knee shifted without permission, and seconds later another afternoon had culminated in a POW that made my ears ring.

I was destined to know very well indeed the complicated space between Sally's muscular thighs, far better than I would ever know the complicated space inside her head, but that first swift unforeseen climax had a power I still recall with astonishment. My sex life, though quite varied, had all been passed in the company of men. I'd never objected to homosexuality in any of its forms, on principle and by professional conviction, but before that day no occasion of proving this personally had happened to occur. As for Sally, her isolation had allowed for no sex life at all with humans male *or* female; and though the things we did together meant, if possible, even more to her than they did to me, she didn't really view them in a sexual light. To Sally's way of thinking, *sex* was a thing that happened more or less constantly during several days each month, and had to do with dark, shaggy, undeniable maleness forcing itself upon you—with brief, rough gusto—from behind. She continued to miss this fear-laced excitement just as before. Our physical involvement, which was regularly reinforced, and which often ended as it had that afternoon, was a source of immeasurable pleasure and solace to her, but she viewed it as the natural end of a process that had more to do with social grooming than with sex.

But for me it was a revelation, and late in August, when the coarse, caterpillar-chewed foliage hung dispiritedly day after day in the torpid air, I went away for a week to remind myself of what ordinary sex was like with an ordinary man. Afterward I returned to Sally having arrived at a more accurate view of the contrast: not as pudendum versus penis, but as the mythic versus the mundane. Sleeping with my comfy old flame had been enjoyable as ever, but he was no wild thing living a split life and sharing the secret half with me alone.

"Are you in love with somebody?" Bill asked me on our last evening together. "Is that what's up with you? It's got to have something to do with your being in this incredible physical shape—wait! don't tell me! you've conceived a fatal passion for a jock!" I laughed and promised to let him in on the secret when I could, and though his eyes were sharp with curiosity, he didn't press the point. And for that, when the time came, Bill was one of half a dozen friends I finally did tell about Sally.

But even then, after it could no longer matter materially, I was unable to answer his question. Was I in love with Sally, or she with me? No. Or yes. For more than a year, I worked hard to link her with the human community, she to school me for a role in a childhood fantasy of irresistible (and doubtless neurotic) appeal. Each of us was surely fated to love what the other symbolized; how could we help it? But I've wondered since whether I was ever able to see Sally as anything but the Chimp Child, first and last. For each of us, you see, there was only *one*. In such a case, how can individual be told from type, how can the love be personal? And when not personal, what does "love" mean, anyway?

Whatever it was or meant, it absorbed us, and I was as happy that summer as ever in my life. As the season waned and the fall semester began, my skills and plans both moved forward obedient to my will. After workouts we would spread the blanket on its plastic ground sheet and ourselves across the blanket, giving our senses up to luxuriant pleasure, while the yellow leaves tapped down about us, all but inaudibly.

And afterward we'd talk. It was at this stage that bit by bit I was able to breach Sally's quarantine by turning the talk to our work: her research, my theoretical interests, gifted or maddening students, departmental politics, university policy. Even then, when I encountered Sally on campus, her indifference toward me as toward everyone appeared unchanged; and at first these topics annoyed and bored her. But bit by bit I could see her begin to take an interest in the personalities we worked among, form judgments about them, distinguish among her students. To my intense delight, colorful chimp personalities began to swim up from her memory, with anecdotes to illustrate them, and she spoke often of Carol Cheswick, and—less frequently—of the team of psychologists at University College.

Cambridge provided no material of this sort, for by the time the church fellowship had sent her up, Cheswick was dead and Sally left to devise ways of coping on her own with the nosy public while protecting her privacy and the purposes it served. Antisocial behavior had proved an effective means to that end at Cambridge, as it was to do subsequently at our own university. She had concentrated fiercely on her studies. In subjects that required an intuitive understanding of people—literature, history, the social sciences— her schoolwork had always been lackluster; in mathematics and hard science, she had excelled from the first. At Cambridge she read biology. Microbiology genuinely fascinated her; now, thus late in her career, Sally was discovering the pleasures of explaining an ongoing experiment to a listener only just able to follow. In fact, she was discovering gossip and shop talk.

By the time cold temperatures and bare trees had forced me to join a fitness center and Sally to work out alone in a thermal skinsuit and thin pigskin gloves and moccasins, she was able to say: "I remember that old mother chimpanzee because she saved me out of a killing despair, and so did you. So did you, Jan. That day you discovered me crying in the beech, remember? I actually believed I was coping rather well then, but the truth is I was dying. I might really have died, I think—like a houseplant, slowly, of heat and dryness and depleted soil." And to me as well, this seemed no more than the simple truth.

That winter, one measure of our progress was that I could sometimes coax Sally to my house. Had close friends of mine been living nearby, or friendly

neighbors or relatives, this could not have been possible; as it was she would leave her pedalcar several blocks away and walk to the house by varying routes, and nearly always after dark. But once inside, with doors locked and curtains drawn, we could be easy, eat and read, light a fire to sit before, snuggle in bed together. In winter, outdoor sex was impractical and we could never feel entirely safe from observation in the denuded woods, whose riding trails wound through and through it. And Sally's obsessive concealment of the fact that she had made a friend, and that her privacy could therefore be trespassed upon, seemed to weaken very little despite the radical changes she had passed through.

Truly, I found myself in no hurry to weaken it. I could not expect, nor did I wish, to have Sally to myself forever. Indeed my success would be measured by how much more fully she could learn to function in society— develop other friendships and activities and so on—eventually. It is true that I could not quite picture this, though I went on working toward it in perfect confidence that the day would come. Yet for the time being, like a mother who watches her child grow tall with mingled pride and sorrow, I kept our secret willingly and thought *eventually* would be here soon enough.

As spring drew closer, Sally began sleeping badly and to be troubled again by dreams. She grew oddly moody also. All through the winter she had dressed and slipped out to her car in the dark; now I would sometimes wake in the morning to find her still beside me. Several times her mutterings and thrashings disturbed me in the night, and then I would soothe and hold her till we both dozed off again. That a crisis was brewing looked certain, but though the dreams continued for weeks, she soon stopped telling me anything about them and said little else to reveal the nature of her distress. In fact, I believed I knew what the trouble was. The first dreams, those she had described, were all about Africa and England and seemed drenched in yearning for things unutterably dear, lost beyond recall. They seemed dreams of mourning—for her parents, her lost wild life in Tanzania, her teacher. Events of the past year, I thought, had rendered the old defenses useless. She could not escape this confrontation any longer.

I was very glad. Beyond the ordeal of grief lay every possibility for synthesizing the halves of her life into one coherent human whole. I believed that Cheswick's death in Sally's twenty-third year had threatened to touch off a mourning for all these losses at once, and that to avoid this she had metamorphosed into the Cambridge undergraduate of my scrapbook; intellectual, unsociable, dull. "You're a survivor," I had told her one night that winter, and she had replied, "Up to a point." Now it seemed she felt strong enough at last to do the grieving and survive *that*, and break through to a more complete sort of health and strength.

Either that, or the year's developments had weakened her ability to compensate, and she would now be swiftly destroyed by the forces held so long in check; but I thought not.

Weeks passed while Sally brooded and sulked; our partnership, so long a source of happy relief, had acquired ambiguities she found barely tolerable. Once she did avoid me for nine days despite her promise—only to turn up, in a state of feverish lust, for a session as unlike our lazy summertime trysts as possible. Afterward she was heavy and silent, then abruptly tearful. I bore with all this patiently enough, chiefly by trying to foresee what might happen next and what it might mean, and so was not much surprised when she said finally, "I've decided not to teach this summer after all. I want to go to England for a month or so, after I've got the experiment written up."

I nodded, thinking, *Here it is*. Huge green skunk cabbages were thick now in the low places on the floor of the April woods, and fly fisherfolk thick along and in the creek; once again we had the mild, bare, windy, hairy-looking forest to ourselves, and were perched together high in a white-topped sycamore hung with balls. "Sounds like a good plan, though I'll miss you. Where to, exactly, or have you decided yet?"

"Well—London for a start, and Cambridge, and here and there. I might just pop in on my sister, not that there's much point to *that*." Sally's sister Helen had married the vicar of a large church in Liverpool and produced four children. "But about missing me. You like England, you're always telling me. Why not come along?"

"Really?" I hadn't foreseen everything, it seemed. "Of course I'll come, I'd love to. Or no, wait a minute"—squirming round on the smooth limb to watch her face—"have you thought this through? I mean, suppose the papers get wind of it? 'Chimp Child Returns to Foster Country.' Or even: 'Chimp Child, Friend, Visit England.' If we're traveling together, people are bound to *see* us together—sure you want to risk it?"

"Oh well, so what," said the Chimp Child, for all the world as if she hadn't been creeping up to my house under cover of night all winter long. "I want to talk to the blokes at the university, Snyder and Brill and a couple of others—get them to show me the files on *me*." She swung free of the branch and dangled by one hand to hug me with the opposite arm. "Sorry I've been such a bore lately. There's something I'm suddenly madly curious about, I've had the most appalling dreams, night after night, for weeks." She swung higher in the tree, climbing swiftly by her powerful arms alone, flashing across gaps as she worked her way to the high outermost branches and leapt outward and downward into another tree with the action I loved to see. "Right," she called back across the gulf between us, "get to work then, you lazy swine. We'll put on a show for Helen's kids that'll stop traffic all over the ruddy parish."

And so we flew to England; and now my part of the story is nearly finished. Sally did not quite feel ready to come out, as it were, to the extent of

going anywhere in my company at school, though she'd smile now with
some naturalness when our paths would cross there, and even exchange a
few words in passing. We arrived separately at the airport. But from that
point on, we were indeed "traveling together," and she never tried to make
it seem otherwise.

She had wanted a couple of days in Cambridge before tackling the records
of her unique education, as if to work backward in time by bearable degrees,
and so it was together that we climbed the wide stairs on a Tuesday afternoon
early in June to look into her first-year room in Newnham College. Unfortunately the present occupant knew the Chimp Child had once been quartered
in her room and recognized Sally immediately; she must have felt perplexed
and dismayed at the grimness of the famous pilgrim, who glared round
without comment, refused a cup of tea, and stalked away leaving me to
render thanks/apologies on behalf of us both. I caught Sally on the stairs.
Nothing was said till we had proceeded the length of two green courts
bordered with flower beds and come out into the road. Then: "God, I was
wretched here!" she burst out. "I went through the whole three years in a
—in a chromatic daze, half unconscious except in the lab, and going through
that door again—it was as if all the color and warmth began to drain out of
a hole in the floor of the day, and I could only stand helplessly watching.
The very *smell* of the place means nothing but death to me. What bloody,
bloody waste."

And "What a waste," more thoughtfully the next morning, as we walked
back to the station from our bed-and-breakfast across the river and the common with its grazing Friesians and through the Botanical Gardens. "One
sees why other people could manage to be so jolly and smug here, while I'd
go skulking down to Grantchester at five in the morning to work out in the
only wood for miles, terrified every day I should be caught out, and skulking
back to breakfast every day relieved, like an exhibitionist who thinks, 'Well,
there's one more time I got away with it.' " A few minutes later she added,
"Of course it got much better when I was working on my thesis . . . only
those years don't seem real at *all* when I try to remember them. All I can
remember is the lab, I expect that's why."

"Why it got better, or why it's unreal?"

"Both, very likely."

She was pensive on the train. I fell asleep and woke as we were pulling
into Liverpool Street, feeling tired and headachy, the beginnings of the flu
that put me to bed for a crucial week when I might otherwise have done
something, just by staying well, to affect the course of events. By late
afternoon of that Wednesday, I felt too miserable to be embarrassed at
imposing myself on Dr. Snyder's wife and filling their tiny guest room with
my awkward germiness. For four or five days, I had a dry, wheezy cough
and a fever so high that Mrs. Snyder was beginning to talk rather worriedly

of doctors; then the fever broke and my head, though the size of a basketball, no longer burned, and I rallied enough to take in that Sally was gone.

She had spent the early days of my illness at University College, reading, asking occasional questions, searching—as it seemed—for something she couldn't describe but expected to recognize when she found it. Late on the fourth day, the day my temperature was highest, she came in and sat on the bed. "Listen, Jan. I'm off to Africa tomorrow."

I swam wearily to the surface. "Africa? But . . . don't you have to get, uh, inoculations or something? Visas?" I didn't wonder, within the remoteness of my fever, why she was going. Nor did I much care that evidently she would be going without me.

"Only cholera and yellow fever, and I've had them. Before we left, just in case; and yesterday afternoon I bagged the last seat on a tourist charter to Dar es Salaam. The flight returns in a fortnight, by which time you should be fit again, and we can go on up north then or wherever you like." When I didn't reply, she added, unnecessarily, "I've got to visit the school, Malosa School, and sort of stare the forest in the face again. It's terribly important, though I can't say just why. Maybe when I've got back, when you're better. Only, I've made my mind up to take this chance while it's going, because I do feel I've absolutely got to go through with it, as quick as I can."

My eyes ached. I closed them, shutting out the floating silhouette of Sally's head and shoulders. "I know. I wish . . ."

"Never mind. It'll be all right. Sorry I didn't tell you before, but first I wanted to make sure." I felt her hand beneath my pajama jacket. "God, you're *hot*," she said, surprised. "Perhaps I ought to leave it till you're a bit better."

Distantly amused at this display of superego, I said, "You know a fever's always highest at night, old virologist. Anyway, you can't do any good here. We'll have a doctor in soon if it doesn't go down." I made a truly tremendous effort. "It's probably a good idea, Sally, the trip. I hope you can find whatever it is you're looking for." Clumsily I patted the hand inside my pajamas. "But don't miss the plane coming back, I'll be dying to hear what happened."

"I shan't, I promise you," she said with relief; and when I woke the next morning, she had gone.

We know that Sally reached Dar es Salaam after an uneventful flight, spent the night in an airport hotel, flew Air Malawi to the Chileka airfield the next morning, and hired a driver to take her the 125 kilometers overland to Machinga and the Malosa Secondary School, where she was greeted with pleased astonishment by those of the staff who remembered her—everyone, of course, knew of her connection with the school. She stayed there nearly a week, questioning people about the details of her early childhood and of exactly what had happened when the church officials brought her in, in the weeks before she had been whisked to London. She spent hours prowling about the grounds and buildings, essentially the same as thirty years before despite some modest construction and borrowed the school's Land-Rover several times to drive alone into the countryside of the Shire Highlands and the valley beyond. Her manner had been alternately brusque and preoccupied, and she had impressed them all as being under considerable strain.

The school staff confirmed that Sally had been driven back to Chileka by a couple, old friends of her parents, who at her request had dropped her at the terminal without coming in to see her off. She had told them she intended to fly back to Dar that evening in order to catch her charter for London the next day, and that she hated a dragged-out good-bye; the couple had no way of knowing that her ticket had specified a two-week stay abroad. Inside the terminal she bought a round-trip ticket for Ujiji, in Tanzania.

From Ujiji a helicopter shuttle took her to Kogoma on Lake Tanganyika. Once there, Sally had made inquiries, then gone straight to the town's tiny branch of Bookers Ltd., a safari agency operating out of a closet-sized cubbyhole in the VW dealership. She told the Bookers agent—a grizzled old Indian—that she wanted to hire two men to help her locate the place where a plane had crashed in the mountains east of the lake, some thirty years before. She produced detailed directions and maps; and the agent, though openly doubtful whether the wreckage would not have rusted into the ground after so long, agreed for a stiff price to outfit and provision the trip. He assigned his cousin to guide her, and a native porter. Forty-eight hours later this small expedition set off into the mountains in the agency's battered four-wheel-drive safari van.

The cousin had parked the van beside the road of ruts that had brought them as far as roads could bring them toward the area marked on Sally's maps, much nearer than any road had approached it on the day of the crash, but still not near. They had then followed a footpath into the forest for several kilometers before beginning to slash a trail away from it to the westward, toward the site where the plane had gone down. Something like fifty kilometers of rain-forested mountainous terrain had to be negotiated on foot, a difficult, unpleasant, suffocating sort of passage. Sally must have been assailed by frustration at the clumsiness of their progress; the guide called her a bad-tempered bitch, probably for good reason. On the third morning her patience had evidently snapped. When the men woke up, Sally was not in camp. They waited, then shouted, then searched, but she never replied or reappeared. And I knew what they could not; that she must have slipped away and taken to the trees, flying toward a goal now less than fifteen kilometers distant.

I had gone out to meet Sally's plane, due into Gatwick on the same day the reporters got hold of the story of her disappearance. When she proved not to be aboard, and to have sent no word, all my uneasiness broke out like sweat, and back in the city I must have hurried past any number of news agents' before the *Guardian* headline snatched at my attention: WILD WOMAN MISSING IN JUNGLE, SEARCH CONTINUES. I bought a paper and stood shaking on the pavement to read: "Dodoma (Tanzania), Tuesday. Sally Barnes, the wild girl brought up by chimpanzees, has been missing in the mountains of Tanzania since Friday . . . two companions state . . . no trace of the Chimp Child . . . police notified and a search party . . ." and finally: "Searchers report sighting several groups of wild chimpanzees in the bush near the point of her disappearance."

All the rest is a matter of record. Day by day the newspapers repeated it: No trace, No trace, and at last, Presumed dead. The guide and porter were questioned but never tried for murder. In print and on the video news, it was noted that Dr. Barnes had vanished into the jungle only a few kilometers east of the spot where she had emerged from it twenty years earlier. Investigators quickly discovered that Sally and I had been together in Cambridge and London, and I, too, was forced to submit to questioning; I told them we had met on the plane and spent a few days as casual traveling companions, and that when I fell ill, her friends had kindly taken me in. I denied any closer connection between us, despite my having studied her case professionally—mentioning that she was well known at the university for her solitary ways. Sally herself had said nothing in particular to the Snyders about us, and I had been too sick. No one was alive in all the world to contradict the essential factors of this story, and, as it appeared to lead nowhere, they soon let me alone. (Some years later, however, I told Dr. Snyder the whole truth.)

It developed that no one had any idea why Sally had gone to Tanzania, why she was looking for the site of the plane crash.

For me that fall was hellish. By the time I returned to the States, only a few days before the new semester was to get under way, Sally's apartment—the apartment I had never seen, though she had called me from it two or three times during the final weeks of spring—had been stripped of its contents by strangers and her effects shipped to the Liverpool sister. At school, people were overheard to suggest, only half jokingly, that Sally had rejoined the chimps and was living now in the jungle, wild again. Such things were freely voiced in my presence; indeed, the loss of Sally, so shocking, so complete, was the more difficult to accept because not a single person on my side of the Atlantic could have the least suspicion that I had lost her.

My acting, I believe, was flawless. Though I went dazedly about my work, nobody seemed to see anything amiss. But might-have-beens tormented me. Save for my interference, Sally would almost certainly still have been alive. Or (more excruciating by far), had she not met defeat in the jungle, her search would almost certainly have left her healed of trauma, able to fit the halves of her life together. I had nearly freed her; now she was dead, the labor come to nothing, the child stillborn. I did believe she was dead.

Yet I felt as angry with her, at times, as if she had purposely abandoned and betrayed me, disdained the miracle of healing I had nearly brought off—as if she had really chosen to return to the wild. For now neither of us could ever, ever complete the crossing into those worlds each had been training the other to enter for the preceding year.

I did not see how I was going to survive the disappointment, nor could I imagine what could possibly occupy, or justify, the rest of my life. The interlude with Sally had spoiled me thoroughly for journeyman work. It would not be enough, any longer, to divide my time between educating healthy minds and counseling disturbed ones. Long before that bleak winter was out, I had begun to cast about fretfully for something else to do.

This document has been prepared in snatches, over many evenings, by kerosene lanternlight in my tent in the Matangawe River Nature Reserve overlooking Lake Malawi, 750 kilometers northwest across the immense lake from Sally's birthplace. The tent is set up inside a chimp-proof cage made of Cyclone fencing and corrugated iron. Outside, eleven chimpanzees of assorted ages and stages of reacclimatization to independent survival in the wild are sleeping (all but the newest arrival, who is crying to get in). A few of these chimps were captured as infants in the wild; the rest are former subjects of language and other learning experiments, ex-laboratory animals or animals who were reared in homes until they began to grow unmanageable.

This may seem an unlikely place in which to attempt the establishment of a free-living population of rehabilitant chimpanzees, for the ape has been extinct in Malawi for a couple of centuries at least, and the human population pressure is terrific, the highest in Africa. In fact, to "stare the forest in the face," Sally was forced to go on back to Tanzania, where there was (and still is) some riverine forest left standing. Yet private funding materialized, and I've been here since the reserve was created, nearly fifteen years. Despite some setbacks and failures—well, there were bound to be some!—the project is doing very well indeed. At this writing, thirty-four chimps have mastered the course of essential survival skills and moved off to establish breeding, thriving communities on their own in the reserve. For obvious reasons these societies fascinate the primatologists, who often come to study them. We've lost a few to disease and accidents, and two to poachers, but our success, considering the problems inherent to the enterprise, might even be called spectacular. We've been written up in *National Geographic* and the *Smithsonian*, which in primate studies is how you know when you've arrived, and similar projects in several more suitable West African countries have been modeled on ours.

I started alone, with three adolescent chimpanzee "graduates in psychology" from my university who, having outgrown their usefulness along with their tractable childhoods, faced long, dull lives in zoos or immediate euthanasia. Now a staff of eight works with me: my husband, John (yes, the same John), and seven graduate students from my old department and from the Department of Biology, which used to be Sally's. She would be pleased with my progress in brachiation, though arthritis in my hands and shoulders has begun to moderate my treetop traveling with my charges. (That skill, incidentally, has given me a tactical edge over every other pioneer in the field of primate rehabilitation.)

To all the foregoing I will add only that I have found this work more satisfying than I can say. And that very often as I'm swinging along through lush forest in the company of four or five young chimps, "feeding" with them on new leaves and baobab flowers, showing them how to build a sturdy nest in the branches, I know a deep satisfaction that now, at last, there's no difference that matters between Sally and me.

KIM STANLEY ROBINSON

Down and Out in the Year 2000

Kim Stanley Robinson, an alumnus of the Clarion Writers Workshop, sold his first story to Damon Knight's *Orbit 18* in 1976. He subsequently placed stories in *Orbit 19* and *Orbit 21,* and in the last few years has gone on to become a frequent contributor to *Universe* and *The Magazine of Fantasy and Science Fiction.* His quietly evocative story "Venice Drowned" was one of the best stories of 1981, and was a Nebula Award finalist; his novella "To Leave a Mark" was a finalist for the Hugo Award in 1982. His brilliant story "Black Air" was both a Nebula and Hugo finalist in 1984, and went on to win the World Fantasy Award that year. "Black Air" was in our First Annual Collection. His excellent novel *The Wild Shore* was published in 1984 as the first title in the resurrected Ace Special line, and was one of the most critically acclaimed novels of the year. Other Robinson books include the novels *Icehenge* and *The Memory of Whiteness,* and the critical book *The Novels of Philip K. Dick.* His most recent book was *The Planet on the Table,* one of the landmark collections of the decade. Upcoming is a new novel, *The Gold Coast,* from Tor. His story "The Lucky Strike" was in our Second Annual Collection; his story "Green Mars" was in our Third Annual Collection. Robinson and his wife, Lisa, currently live in Switzerland.

   In the story that follows, he gives us a brilliant, bittersweet look at what it's like to be down and out in even the most glittering of futures. . . .

DOWN AND OUT IN THE YEAR 2000

Kim Stanley Robinson

It was going to be hot again. Summer in Washington, D.C.—Leroy Robinson woke and rolled on his mattress, broke into a sweat. That kind of a day. He got up and kneeled over the other mattress in the small room. Debra shifted as he shaded her from the sun angling in the open window. The corners of her mouth were caked white and her forehead was still hot and dry, but her breathing was regular and she appeared to be sleeping well. Quietly Leroy slipped on his jeans and walked down the hall to the bathroom. Locked. He waited; Ramon came out wet and groggy. "Morning, Robbie." Into the bathroom, where he hung his pants on the hook and did his morning ritual. One bloodshot eye, staring back at him from the splinter of mirror still in the frame. The dirt around the toilet base. The shower curtain blotched with black algae, as if it had a fatal disease. That kind of morning.

Out of the shower he dried off with his jeans and started to sweat again. Back in his room Debra was still sleeping. Worried, he watched her for a while, then filled his pockets and went into the hall to put on sneakers and tank-top. Debra slept light these days, and the strangest things would rouse her. He jogged down the four flights of stairs to the street, and sweating freely stepped out into the steamy air.

He walked down 16th Street, with its curious alternation of condo fortresses and abandoned buildings, to the Mall. There, big khaki tanks dominated the broad field of dirt and trash and tents and the odd patch of grass. Most of the protesters were still asleep in their scattered tent villages, but there was an active crowd around the Washington Monument, and Leroy walked on over, ignoring the soldiers by the tanks.

The crowd surrounded a slingshot as tall as a man, made of a forked tree branch. Inner tubes formed the sling, and the base was buried in the ground. Excited protesters placed balloons filled with red paint into the sling, and fired them up at the monument. If a balloon hit above the red that already covered the tower, splashing clean white—a rare event, as the monument was pure red up a good third of it—the protesters cheered crazily. Leroy watched them as they danced around the sling after a successful shot. He approached some of the calmer seated spectators.

"Want to buy a joint?"

"How much?"

"Five dollars."

"Too much, man! You must be kidding! How about a dollar?"

Leroy walked on.

"Hey, wait! One joint, then. Five dollars . . . shit."

"Going rate, man."

The protester pushed long blond hair out of his eyes and pulled a five from a thick clip of bills. Leroy got the battered Marlboro box from his pocket and took the smallest joint from it. "Here you go. Have fun. Why don't you fire one of them paint bombs at those tanks, huh?"

The kids on the ground laughed. "We will when you get them stoned!"

He walked on. Only five joints left. It took him less than an hour to sell them. That meant thirty dollars, but that was it. Nothing left to sell. As he left the Mall he looked back at the monument; under its wash of paint it looked like a bone sticking out of raw flesh.

Anxious about coming to the end of his supply, Leroy hoofed it up to Dupon Circle and sat on the perimeter bench in the shade of one of the big trees, footsore and hot. In the muggy air it was hard to catch his breath. He ran the water from the drinking fountain over his hands until someone got in line for a drink. He crossed the circle, giving a wide berth to a bunch of lawyers in long-sleeved shirts and loosened ties, lunching on wine and cheese under the watchful eye of their bodyguard. On the other side of the park Delmont Briggs sat by his cup, almost asleep, his sign propped on his lap. The wasted man. Delmont's sign—and a little side business—provided him with just enough money to get by on the street. The sign, a battered square of cardboard, said PLEASE HELP—HUNGRY. People still looked through Delmont like he wasn't there, but every once in a while it got to somebody. Leroy shook his head distastefully at the idea.

"Delmont, you know any weed I can buy? I need a finger baggie for twenty."

"Not so easy to do, Robbie." Delmont hemmed and hawed and they dickered for a while, then he sent Leroy over to Jim Johnson, who made the sale under a cheery exchange of the day's news, over by the chess tables. After that Leroy bought a pack of cigarettes in a liquor store, and went up to the little triangular park between 17th, S, and New Hampshire, where no police or strangers ever came. They called it Fish Park for the incongruous cement whale sitting by one of the trash cans. He sat down on the long broken bench, among his acquaintances who were hanging out there, and fended them off while he carefully emptied the Marlboros, cut some tobacco into the weed, and refilled the cigarette papers with the new mix. With their ends twisted he had a dozen more joints. They smoked one and he sold two more for a dollar each before he got out of the park.

But he was still anxious, and since it was the hottest part of the day and few people were about, he decided to visit his plants. He knew it would be at least a week till harvest, but he wanted to see them. Anyway it was about watering day.

East between 16th and 15th he hit no-man's land. The mixed neighborhood of fortress apartments and burned-out hulks gave way to a block or two of entirely abandoned buildings. Here the police had been at work, and looters had finished the job. The buildings were battered and burnt out, their ground floors blasted wide open, some of them collapsed entirely, into heaps of rubble. No one walked the broken sidewalk; sirens a few blocks off, and the distant hum of traffic, were the only signs that the whole city wasn't just like this. Little jumps in the corner of his eye were no more than that; nothing there when he looked directly. The first time, Leroy had found walking down the abandoned street nerve-racking; now he was reassured by the silence, the stillness, the no-man's land smell of torn asphalt and wet charcoal, the wavering streetscape empty under a sour milk sky.

His first building was a corner brownstone, blackened on the street sides, all its windows and doors gone, but otherwise sound. He walked past it without stopping, turned and surveyed the neighborhood. No movement anywhere. He stepped up the steps and through the doorway, being careful to make no footprints in the mud behind the doorjamb. Another glance outside, then up the broken stairs to the second floor. The second floor was a jumble of beams and busted furniture, and Leroy waited a minute to let his sight adjust to the gloom. The staircase to the third floor had collapsed, which was the reason he had chosen this building: no easy way up. But he had a route worked out, and with a leap he grabbed a beam hanging from the stairwell and hoisted himself onto it. Some crawling up the beam and he could swing onto the third floor, and from there a careful walk up gapped stairs brought him to the fourth floor.

The room surrounding the stairwell was dim, and he had jammed the door to the next room, so that he had to crawl through a hole in the wall to get through. Then he was there.

Sweating profusely, he blinked in the sudden sunlight, and stepped to his plants, all lined out in plastic pots on the far wall. Eleven medium-sized female marijuana plants, their splayed green leaves drooping for lack of water. He took the rain funnel from one of the gallon jugs and watered the plants. The buds were just longer than his thumbnail; if he could wait another week or two at least, they would be the size of his thumb or more, and worth fifty bucks apiece. He twisted off some water leaves and put them in a baggie.

He found a patch of shade and sat with the plants for a while, watched them soak up the water. Wonderful green they had, lighter than most leaves in D.C. Little red threads in the buds. The white sky lowered over the big break in the roof, huffing little gasps of muggy air onto them all.

His next spot was several blocks north, on the roof of a burned-out hulk that had no interior floors left. Access was by way of a tree growing next to the wall. Climbing it was a challenge, but he had a route here he took, and he liked the way leaves concealed him even from passersbys directly beneath him once he got above the lowest branches.

The plants here were younger—in fact one had sprouted seeds since he last saw them, and he pulled the plant out and put it in the baggie. After watering them and adjusting the aluminum foil rain funnels on the jug tops, he climbed down the tree and walked back down 14th.

He stopped to rest in Charlie's Baseball Club. Charlie sponsored a city team with the profits from his bar, and old members of the team welcomed Leroy, who hadn't been by in a while. Leroy had played left field and batted fifth a year or two before, until his job with the park service had been cut. After that he had had to pawn his glove and cleats, and he had missed Charlie's minimal membership charge three seasons running, and so he had quit. And then it had been too painful to go by the club, and drink with the guys and look at all the trophies on the wall, a couple of which he had helped to win. But on this day he enjoyed the fan blowing, and the dark, and the fries that Charlie and Fisher shared with him.

Break over, he went to the spot closest to home, where the new plants were struggling through the soil, on the top floor of an empty stone husk on 16th and Caroline. The first floor was a drinking place for derelicts, and old Thunderbird and whiskey bottles, half still in bags, littered the dark room, which smelled of alcohol, urine, and rotting wood. All the better: few people would be foolish enough to enter such an obviously dangerous hole. And the stairs were as near gone as made no difference. He climbed over the holes to the second floor, turned and climbed to the third.

The baby plants were fine, bursting out of the soil and up to the sun, the two leaves covered by four, up into four again. . . . He watered them and headed home.

On the way he stopped at the little market that the Vietnamese family ran, and bought three cans of soup, a box of crackers and some Coke. "Twenty-two oh five tonight, Robbie," old Huang said with a four-toothed grin.

The neighbors were out on the sidewalk, the women sitting on the stoop, the men kicking a soccer ball about aimlessly as they watched Sam sand down an old table, the kids running around. Too hot to stay inside this evening, although it wasn't much better on the street. Leroy helloed through them and walked up the flights of stairs slowly, feeling the day's travels in his feet and legs.

In his room Debra was awake, and sitting up against her pillows. "I'm hungry, Leroy." She looked hot, bored; he shuddered to think of her day.

"That's a good sign, that means you're feeling better. I've got some soup here should be real good for you." He touched her cheek, smiling.

"It's too hot for soup."

"Yeah, that's true, but we'll let it cool down after it cooks, it'll still taste good." He sat on the floor and turned on the hot plate, poured water from the plastic jug into the pot, opened the can of soup, mixed it in. While they were spooning it out Rochelle Jackson knocked on the door and came in.

"Feeling better, I see." Rochelle had been a nurse before her hospital closed, and Leroy had enlisted her help when Debra fell sick. "We'll have to take your temperature later."

Leroy wolfed down crackers while he watched Rochelle fuss over Debra. Eventually she took a temperature and Leroy walked her out.

"It's still pretty high, Leroy."

"What's she *got*?" he asked, as he always did. Frustration . . .

"I don't know any more than yesterday. Some kind of flu I guess."

"Would a flu hang on this long?"

"Some of them do. Just keep her sleeping and drinking as much as you can, and feed her when she's hungry. —Don't be scared, Leroy."

"I can't help it! I'm afraid she'll get sicker. . . . And there ain't nothing I can do!"

"Yeah, I know. Just keep her fed. You're doing just what I would do."

After cleaning up he left Debra to sleep and went back down to the street, to join the men on the picnic tables and benches in the park tucked into the intersection. This was the "living room" on summer evenings, and all the regulars were there in their usual spots, sitting on tables or bench back. "Hey there, Robbie! What's happening?"

"Not much, not much. No man, don't kick that soccer ball at me, I can't kick no soccer ball tonight."

"You been walking the streets, hey?"

"How else we going to find her to bring her home to you."

"Hey lookee here, Ghost is bringing out his TV."

"It's Tuesday night at the movies, y'all!" Ghost called out as he approached and plunked a little hologram TV and a Honda generator on the picnic table. They laughed and watched Ghost's pale skin glow in the dusk as he hooked the system up.

"Where'd you get this one, Ghost? You been sniffing around the funeral parlors again?"

"You bet I have!" Ghost grinned. "This one's picture is all fucked up, but it still works—I think—"

He turned the set on and blurry three-dee figures swam into shape in a cube above the box—all in dark shades of blue.

"Man, we *must* have the blues tonight," Ramon remarked. "Look at that!"

"They all look like Ghost," said Leroy.

"Hey, it works, don't it?" Ghost said. Hoots of derision. "And dig the sound! The sound works—"

"Turn it up then."

"It's up all the way."

"What's this?" Leroy laughed. "We got to watch frozen midgets whispering, is that it Ghost? What do midgets say on a cold night?"

"Who the fuck is this?" said Ramon.

Johnnie said, "That be Sam Spade, the greatest computer spy in the world."

"How come he live in that shack, then?" Ramon asked.

"That's to show it's a tough scuffle making it as a computer spy, real tough."

"How come he got four million dollars worth of computers right there in the shack, then?" Ramon asked, and the others commenced giggling, Leroy loudest of all. Johnnie and Ramon could be killer sometimes. A bottle of rum started around, and Steve broke in to bounce the soccer ball on the TV, smashing the blue figures repeatedly.

"Watch out now, Sam about to go plug his brains in to try and find out who he is."

"And then he gonna be told of some stolen *wetware* he got to find."

"I got some wetware myself, only I call it a shirt."

Steve dropped the ball and kicked it against the side of the picnic table, and a few of the watchers joined in a game of pepper. Some men in a stopped van shouted a conversation with the guys on the corner. Those watching the show leaned forward. "Where's he gonna go?" said Ramon. "Hong Kong? Monaco? He gonna take the bus on over to Monaco?"

Johnnie shook his head. "Rio, man. Fucking Rio de Janeiro."

Sure enough, Sam was off to Rio. Ghost choked out an objection: "Johnnie—ha!—you must have seen this one before."

Johnnie shook his head, though he winked at Leroy. "No man, that's just where all the good stolen wetware ends up."

A series of commercials interrupted their fun: deodorant, burglarkillers, cars. The men in the van drove off. Then the show was back, in Rio, and Johnnie said, "He's about to meet a slinky Afro-Asian spy."

When Sam was approached by a beautiful black Asian woman the men couldn't stand it. "Y'all *have* seen this one before!" Ghost cried.

Johnnie sputtered over the bottle, struggled to swallow. "No way! Experience counts, man, that's all."

"And Johnnie has watched one hell of a lot of Sam Spade," Ramon added.

Leroy said, "I wonder why they're always Afro-Asian."

Steve burst in, laughed. "So they can fuck all of us at once, man!" He dribbled on the image, changed the channel. "—*army command in Los Angeles reports that the rioting killed at least*—" He punched the channel again. "What else we got here—man!—what's *this*?"

"Cyborgs Versus Androids," Johnnie said after a quick glance at the blue shadows. "Lots of fighting."

"Yeah!" Steve exclaimed. Distracted, some of the watchers wandered off. "I'm a cyborg myself, see, I got these false teeth!"

"Shit."

Leroy went for a walk around the block with Ramon, who was feeling good. "Sometimes I feel so good, Robbie! So strong! I walk around this city and I say, the city is falling apart, it can't last much longer like this. And here I am like some kind of animal, you know, living day to day by my wits and figuring out all the little ways to get by . . . you know there are people living up in Rock Creek Park like Indians or something, hunting and fishing and all. And it's just the same in here, you know. The buildings don't make it no different. Just hunting and scrapping to get by, and man I feel so *alive* —" he waved the rum bottle at the sky.

Leroy sighed. "Yeah." Still, Ramon was one of the biggest fences in the area. It was really a steady job. For the rest. . . They finished their walk, and Leroy went back up to his room. Debra was sleeping fitfully. He went to the bathroom, soaked his shirt in the sink, wrung it out. In the room it was stifling, and not even a waft of a breeze came in the window. Lying on his mattress sweating, figuring out how long he could make their money last, it took him a long time to fall asleep.

The next day he returned to Charlie's Baseball Club to see if Charlie could give him any piecework, as he had one or two times in the past. But Charlie only said no, very shortly, and he and everyone else in the bar looked at him oddly, so that Leroy felt uncomfortable enough to leave without a drink. After that he returned to the Mall, where the protesters were facing the troops ranked in front of the Capitol, dancing and jeering and throwing stuff. With all the police out it took him a good part of the afternoon to sell all the joints left, and when he had he walked back up 17th Street feeling tired and worried. Perhaps another purchase from Delmont could string them along a few more days. . . .

At 17th and Q a tall skinny kid ran out into the street and tried to open the door of a car stopped for a red light. But it was a protected car despite its cheap look, and the kid shrieked as the handle shocked him. He was still stuck by the hand to it when the car roared off, so that he was launched through the air and rolled over the asphalt. Cars drove on by. A crowd gathered around the bleeding kid. Leroy walked on, his jaw clenched. At least the kid would live. He had seen bodyguards gunthieves down in the street, kill them dead and walk away.

Passing Fish Park he saw a man sitting on a corner bench looking around. The guy was white, young; his hair was blond and short, he wore wire-rimmed glasses, his clothes were casual but new, like the protesters' down on the Mall. He had money. Leroy snarled at the sharp-faced stranger, approached him.

"What you doing here?"

"Sitting!" The man was startled, nervous. "Just sitting in a park!"

"This ain't no *park*, man. This is our front yard. You see any front yard to these apartment buildings here? No. This here is our front yard, and we don't like people just coming into it and sitting down anywhere!"

The man stood and walked away, looked back once, his expression angry and frightened. The other man sitting on the park benches looked at Leroy curiously.

Two days later he was nearly out of money. He walked over to Connecticut Avenue, where his old friend Victor played harmonica for coins, when he couldn't find other work. Today he was there, belting out "Amazing Grace." He cut it off when he saw Leroy. "Robbie! What's happening?"

"Not much. You?"

Victor gestured at his empty hat, on the sidewalk before him. "You see it. Don't even have seed coin for the cap, man."

"So you ain't been getting any gardening work lately?"

"No, no. Not lately. I do all right here, though. People still pay for music, man, some of them. Music's the angle." He looked at Leroy, face twisted up against the sun. They had worked together for the park service, in times past. Every morning through the summers they had gone out and run the truck down the streets, stopping at every tree to hoist each other up in slings. The one hoisted had to stand out from trunk or branches like an acrobat, moving around to cut off every branch below twelve feet, and it took careful handling of the chain saw to avoid chopping into legs and such. Those were good times. But now the park service was gone, and Victor gazed at Leroy with a stoic squint, sitting behind an empty hat.

"Do you ever look up at the trees anymore, Robbie?"

"Not much."

"I do. They're growing wild, man! Growing like fucking weeds! Every summer they go like crazy. Pretty soon people are gonna have to drive their cars through the branches. The streets'll be tunnels. And with half the buildings in this area falling down . . . I like the idea that the forest is taking this city back again. Running over it like kudzu, till maybe it just be forest again at last.''

That evening Leroy and Debra ate tortillas and refries, purchased with the last of their money. Debra had a restless night, and her temperature stayed high. Rochelle's forehead wrinkled as she watched her.

Leroy decided he would have to harvest a couple of the biggest plants prematurely. He could dry them over the hot plate and be in business by the following day.

The next afternoon he walked east into no-man's land, right at twilight. Big thunderheads loomed to the east, lit by the sun, but it had not rained that day and the muggy heat was like an invisible blanket, choking each breath with moisture. Leroy came to his abandoned building, looked around. Again the complete stillness of an empty city. He recalled Ramon's tales of the people who lived forever in the no-man's land, channeling rain into basement pools, growing vegetables in empty lots, and existing entirely on their own with no need for money. . . .

He entered the building, ascended the stairs, climbed the beam, struggled sweating up to the fourth floor and through the hole into his room.

The plants were gone.

"Wha. . ." He kneeled, feeling like he had been punched in the stomach. The plastic pots were knocked over, and fans of soil lay spread over the old wood flooring.

Sick with anxiety he hurried downstairs and jogged north to his second hideaway. Sweat spilled into his eye and it stung fiercely. He lost his breath and had to walk. Climbing the tree was a struggle.

The second crop was gone too.

Now he was stunned, shocked almost beyond thought. Someone must have followed him. . . . It was nearly dark, and the mottled sky lowered over him, empty but somehow, now, watchful. He descended the tree and ran south again, catching his breath in a sort of sobbing. It was dark by the time he reached 16th and Caroline, and he made his way up the busted stairs using a cigarette for illumination. Once on the fourth floor the lighter revealed broken pots, dirt strewn everywhere, the young plants gone. That small they hadn't been worth anything. Even the aluminum foil rain funnels on his plastic jugs had been ripped up and thrown around.

He sat down, soaking wet with sweat, and leaned back against the scored, moldy wall. Leaned his head back and looked up at the orange-white clouds, lit by the city.

After a while he stumbled downstairs to the first floor and stood on the filthy concrete, among the shadows and the discarded bottles. He went and picked up a whiskey bottle, sniffed it. Going from bottle to bottle he poured whatever drops remained in them into the whiskey bottle. When he was done he had a finger or so of liquor, which he downed in one long pull. He coughed. Threw the bottle against the wall. Picked up each bottle and threw it against the wall. Then he went outside and sat on the curb, and watched the traffic pass by.

He decided that some of his old teammates from Charlie's Baseball Club must have followed him around and discovered his spots, which would explain why they had looked at him so funny the other day. He went over to check it out immediately. But when he got there he found the place closed, shut down, a big new padlock on the door.

"What happened?" he asked one of the men hanging out on the corner, someone from this year's team.

"They busted Charlie this morning. Got him for selling speed, first thing this morning. Now the club be gone for good, and the team too."

When he got back to the apartment building it was late, after midnight. He went to Rochelle's door and tapped lightly.

"Who is it?"

"Leroy." Rochelle opened the door and looked out. Leroy explained what had happened. "Can I borrow a can of soup for Debra for tonight? I'll get it back to you."

"Okay. But I want one back soon, you hear?"

Back in his room Debra was awake. "Where you been, Leroy?" she asked weakly. "I was worried about you."

He sat down at the hot plate, exhausted.

"I'm hungry."

"That's a good sign. Some cream of mushroom soup, coming right up." He began to cook, feeling dizzy and sick. When Debra finished eating he had to force the remaining soup down him.

Clearly, he realized, someone he knew had ripped him off—one of his neighbors, or a park acquaintance. They must have guessed his source of weed, then followed him as he made his rounds. Someone he knew. One of his friends.

Early the next day he fished a newspaper out of a trashcan and looked through the short column of want ads for dishwashing work and the like. There was a busboy job at the Dupont Hotel and he walked over and asked about it. The man turned him away after a single look: "Sorry, man, we looking for people who can walk out into the restaurant, you know." Staring in one of the big silvered windows as he walked up New Hampshire, Leroy saw what the man saw: his hair spiked out everywhere as if he would be a Rasta in five or ten years, his clothes were torn and dirty, his eyes wild. . . . With a deep stab of fear he realized he was too poor to be able to get any job— beyond the point where he could turn it around.

He walked the shimmery black streets, checking phone booths for change. He walked down to M Street and over to 12th, stopping in at all the grills and little Asian restaurants, he went up to Pill Park and tried to get some of his old buddies to front him, he kept looking in pay phones and puzzling through blown scraps of newspaper, desperately hoping that one of them might list a job for him . . . and with each footsore step the fear spiked up in him like the pain lancing up his legs, until it soared into a thoughtless panic. Around noon he got so shaky and sick-feeling he had to stop, and despite his fear he slept flat on his back in Dupont Circle park through the hottest hours of the day.

In the late afternoon he picked it up again, wandering almost aimlessly. He stuck his fingers in every phone booth for blocks around, but other fingers had been there before his. The change boxes of the old farecard machines in the Metro would have yielded more, but with the subway system closed, all those holes into the earth were gated off, and slowly filling with trash. Nothing but big trash pits.

Back at Dupont Circle he tried a pay phone coin return and got a dime. "Yeah," he said aloud; that got him over a dollar. He looked up and saw that a man had stopped to watch him: one of the fucking lawyers, in loosened tie and long-sleeved shirt and slacks and leather shoes, staring at him open-mouthed as his group and its bodyguard crossed the street, Leroy held up the coin between thumb and forefinger and glared at the man, trying to impress on him the reality of a dime.

He stopped at the Vietnamese market. "Huang, can I buy some soup from you and pay you tomorrow?"

The old man shook his head sadly. "I can't do that, Robbie. I do that even once, and—" he wiggled his hands—"the whole house come down. You know that."

"Yeah. Listen, what can I get for—" he pulled the day's change from his pocket and counted it again. "A dollar ten."

Huang shrugged. "Candy bar? No?" He studied Leroy. "Potatoes. Here, two potatoes from the back. Dollar ten."

"I didn't think you had any potatoes."

"Keep them for family, you see. But I sell these to you."

"Thanks, Huang." Leroy took the potatoes and left. There was a trash dumpster behind the store; he considered it, opened it, looked in. There was a half-eaten hot dog—but the stench overwhelmed him, and he remembered the poisonous taste of the discarded liquor he had punished himself with. He let the lid of the dumpster slam down and went home.

After the potatoes were boiled and mashed and Debra was fed, he went to the bathroom and showered until someone hammered on the door. Back in his room he still felt hot, and he had trouble catching his breath. Debra rolled from side to side, moaning. Sometimes he was sure she was getting sicker, and at the thought his fear spiked up and through him again, he got so scared he couldn't breathe at all. . . . "I'm hungry, Leroy. Can't I have nothing more to eat?"

"Tomorrow, Deb, tomorrow. We ain't got nothing now."

She fell into an uneasy sleep. Leroy sat on his mattress and stared out the window. White-orange clouds sat overhead, unmoving. He felt a bit dizzy, even feverish, as if he was coming down with whatever Debra had. He remembered how poor he had felt even back when he had had his crops to sell, when each month ended with such a desperate push to make rent. But now . . . He sat and watched the shadowy figure of Debra, the walls, the hotplate and utensils in the corner, the clouds out the window. Nothing changed. It was only an hour or two before dawn when he fell asleep, still sitting against the wall.

Next day he battled fever to seek out potato money from the pay phones and the gutters, but he only had thirty-five cents when he had to quit. He drank as much water as he could hold, slept in the park, and then went to see Victor.

"Vic, let me borrow your harmonica tonight."

Victor's face squinted with distress. "I can't, Robbie. I need it myself. You know—" pleading with him to understand.

"I know," Leroy said, staring off into space. He tried to think. The two friends looked at each other.

"Hey, man, you can use my kazoo."

"What?"

"Yeah, man, I got a good kazoo here, I mean a big metal one with a good buzz to it. It sounds kind of like a harmonica, and it's easier to play it. You just hum notes." Leroy tried it. "No, hum, man. Hum in it."

Leroy tried again, and the kazoo buzzed a long crazy note.

"See? Hum a tune, now."

Leroy hummed around for a bit.

"And then you can practice on my harmonica till you get good on it, and get your own. You ain't going to make anything with a harmonica till you can play it, anyway."

"But this—" Leroy said, looking at the kazoo.

Victor shrugged. "Worth a try."

Leroy nodded. "Yeah." He clapped Victor on the shoulder, squeezed it. Pointed at Victor's sign, which said *Help a musician!* "You think that helps?"

Victor shrugged. "Yeah."

"Okay. I'm going to get far enough away so's I don't cut into your business."

"You do that. Come back and tell me how you do."

"I will."

So Leroy walked south to Connecticut and M, where the sidewalks were wide and there were lots of banks and restaurants. It was just after sunset, the heat as oppressive as at midday. He had a piece of cardboard taken from a trashcan, and now he tore it straight, took his ballpoint from his pocket and copied Delmont's message. PLEASE HELP—HUNGRY. He had always admired its economy, how it cut right to the main point.

But when he got to what appeared to be a good corner, he couldn't make himself sit down. He stood there, started to leave, returned. He pounded his fist against his thigh, stared about wildly, walked to the curb and sat on it to think things over.

Finally he stepped to a bank pillar mid-sidewalk and leaned back against it. He put the sign against the pillar face-out, and put his old baseball cap upside-down on the ground in front of him. Put his thirty-five cents in it as seed money. He took the kazoo from his pocket, fingered it. "Goddamn it," he said at the sidewalk between clenched teeth. "If you're going to make me live this way, you're going to have to pay for it." And he started to play.

He blew so hard that the kazoo squealed, and his face puffed up till it hurt. "Columbia, the Gem of the Ocean," blasted into all the passing faces, louder and louder—

When he had blown his fury out he stopped to consider it. He wasn't going to make any money that way. The loose-ties and the career women in dresses and running shoes were staring at him and moving out toward the curb as they passed, huddling closer together in their little flocks as their bodyguards got between him and them. No money in that.

He took a deep breath, started again. "Swing Low, Sweet Chariot." It really was like singing. And what a song. How you could put your heart into that one, your whole body. Just like singing.

One of the flocks had paused off to the side; they had a red light to wait for. It was as he had observed with Delmont: the lawyers looked right through beggars, they didn't want to think about them. He played louder, and one young man glanced over briefly. Sharp face, wire-rims—with a start Leroy recognized the man as the one he had harrassed out of Fish Park a couple days before. The guy wouldn't look at Leroy directly, and so he didn't recognize him back. Maybe he wouldn't have anyway. But he was hearing the kazoo. He turned to his companions, student types gathered to the lawyer flock for the temporary protection of the bodyguard. He said something to them—"I love street music," or something like that—and took a dollar from his pocket. He hurried over and put the folded bill in Leroy's baseball cap, without looking up at Leroy. The *Walk* light came on, they all scurried away. Leroy played on.

That night after feeding Debra her potato, and eating two himself, he washed the pot in the bathroom sink, and then took a can of mushroom soup up to Rochelle, who gave him a big smile.

Walking down the stairs he beeped the kazoo, listening to the stairwell's echoes. Ramon passed him and grinned. "Just call you Robinson Caruso," he said, and cackled.

"Yeah."

Leroy returned to his room. He and Debra talked for a while, and then she fell into a half-sleep, and fretted as if in a dream.

"No, that's all right," Leroy said softly. He was sitting on his mattress, leaning back against the wall. The cardboard sign was face down on the floor. The kazoo was in his mouth, and it half buzzed with his words. "We'll be all right. I'll get some seeds from Delmont, and take the pots to new hideouts, better ones." It occurred to him that rent would be due in a couple of weeks; he banished the thought. "Maybe start some gardens in no-man's land. And I'll practice on Vic's harmonica, and buy one from the pawn shop later." He took the kazoo from his mouth, stared at it. "It's strange what will make money."

He kneeled at the window, stuck his head out, hummed through the kazoo. Tune after tune buzzed the still, hot air. From the floor below Ramon stuck his head out his window to object: "Hey, Robinson Caruso! Ha! Ha! Shut the fuck up, I'm trying to sleep!" But Leroy only played quieter. "Columbia, the Gem of the Ocean"—

TOM MADDOX

Snake-Eyes

Here's a scary and compelling story that demonstrates that getting something into your head isn't so hard—it's getting it *out* again that's the trick. . . .

Born in Beckley, West Virginia, new writer Tom Maddox is now an assistant professor of languages and literature at Virginia State University. Although he has sold only a handful of stories to date, primarily to *Omni* and *Isaac Asimov's Science Fiction Magazine,* he is clearly a writer to watch, and I suspect we'll be seeing a lot more from him as the eighties progress. He is currently at work on his first novel, tentatively entitled *Time Like Shattered Glass*. Maddox lives with his family in Petersburg, Virginia.

SNAKE-EYES

Tom Maddox

Dark meat in the can—brown, oily, and flecked with mucus—gave off a repellent fishy smell; and the taste of it rose in his throat, putrid and bitter like something from a dead man's stomach. George Jordan sat on the kitchen floor and vomited, then pushed himself away from the shining pool, which looked very much like what remained in the can. He thought, no, this won't do: I have wires in my head, and they make me eat cat food. *The snake likes cat food.* He needed help, but knew there was little point in calling the Air Force. He'd tried them, and there was no way they were going to admit responsibility for the monster in his head. What George called "the snake," the Air Force called Effective Human Interface Technology, and they didn't want to hear about any post-discharge problems with it. They had their own problems with Congressional committees investigating "the conduct of the war in Thailand."

He lay for a while with his cheek on the cold linoleum, got up and rinsed his mouth in the sink, then stuck his head under the faucet and ran cold water over it, thinking, call the goddamned multicomp then, call SenTrax and say, is it true you can do something about this incubus that wants to take possession of my soul? And if they ask you, what's your problem? you say, *catfood*, and maybe they'll tell you, hell, it just wants to take possession of your *lunch*.

A chair covered in brown corduroy stood in the middle of the barren living room, a white telephone on the floor beside it, a television flat against the opposite wall—that was the whole thing: what might have been home, if it weren't for the snake.

He picked up the phone, called up the directory on its screen, and keyed TELECOM SENTRAX.

The Orlando Holiday Inn stood next to the airport terminal, where the tourists flowed in eager for the delights of Disney World—but for me, George thought, there are no cute, smiling ducks and rodents. Here as everywhere, it's *snake city*.

He leaned against the wall of his motel room, watching gray sheets of rain cascade across the pavement. He had been waiting two days for a launch. A shuttle sat on its pad at Canaveral, and when the weather cleared, a helicopter would pick him up and drop him there, a package for delivery to SenTrax Inc. at Athena Station, over thirty thousand kilometers above the equator.

Behind him, under the laser light of a Blaupunkt holostage, people a foot high chattered about the war in Thailand and how lucky the United States had been to escape another Vietnam.

Lucky? Maybe. He had been wired up and ready for combat, already accustomed to the form-fitting contours in the rear couch of the black fiber-bodied General Dynamics A-230. The A-230 flew on the deadly edge of instability, every control surface monitored by its own bank of microcomputers, all hooked into the snakebrain flight-and-fire assistant with the twin black miloprene cables running from either side of his esophagus—getting *off*, oh, yes, when the cables snapped home, and the airframe resonated through his nerves, his body singing with that identity, that power.

Then Congress pulled the plug on the war, the Air Force pulled the plug on George, and when his discharge came, there he was, all dressed up and nowhere to go, left with technological blue balls and this hardware in his head that had since taken on a life of its own.

Lightning walked across the purpled sky, ripping it, crazing it into a giant upturned bowl of shattered glass. Another foot-high man on the holostage said the tropical storm would pass in the next two hours.

The phone chimed.

Hamilton Innis was tall and heavy—six four and about two hundred and fifty pounds. Wearing soft black slippers and a powder-blue jumpsuit with *SenTrax* in red letters down its left breast, he floated in a brightly lit white corridor, held gingerly to one wall by one of the jumpsuit's Velcro patches. A viewscreen above the airlock entry showed the shuttle fitting its nose into the docking tube. He waited for it to mate to the airlock hatches and send in their newest candidate.

This one was six months out of the service and slowly losing what the Air Force doctors had made of his mind. Former Tech Sergeant George Jordan: two years of community college in Oakland, California, followed by enlistment in the Air Force, aircrew training, the EHIT program. According to the profile Aleph had put together from Air Force records and National Data Bank, a man with slightly above-average aptitudes and intelligence, a distinctly above-average taste for the bizarre—thus his volunteering for EHIT and combat. In his file pictures, he looked nondescript: five ten, a hundred and seventy-six pounds, brown hair and eyes, neither handsome nor ugly. But it was an old picture and could not show the snake and the fear that came with it. You don't know it, buddy, Innis thought, but you ain't seen nothing yet.

The men came tumbling through the hatch, more or less helpless in free fall, but Innis could see him figuring it out, willing the muscles to quit struggling, quit trying to cope with a gravity that simply wasn't there. "What the hell do I do now?" George Jordan asked, hanging in midair, one arm holding onto the hatch coaming.

"Relax. I'll get you." Innis pushed off the wall and swooped across to the man, grabbing him as he passed and then taking them both to the opposite wall and kicking to carom them outwards.

Innis gave George a few hours of futile attempts at sleep—enough time for the bright, gliding phosphenes caused by the high g's of the trip up to disappear from his vision. George spent most of the time rolling around in his bunk, listening to the wheeze of the air conditioning and the creaks of the rotating station. Then Innis knocked on his compartment door and said through the door speaker, "Come on, fellar. Time to meet the doctor."

They walked through an older part of the station, where there were brown clots of fossilized gum on the green plastic flooring, scuff marks on the walls, along with faint imprints of insignia and company names; ICOG was repeated several times in ghost lettering. Innis told George it meant International Construction Orbital Group, now defunct, the original builders and controllers of Athena.

Innis stopped George in front of a door that read INTERFACE GROUP. "Go on in," he said, "I'll be around a little later."

Pictures of cranes drawn with delicate white strokes on a tan silk background hung along one pale cream wall. Curved partitions in translucent foam, glowing with the soft light placed behind them, marked a central area, then undulated away, forming a corridor that led into darkness. George was sitting on a chocolate sling couch, Charley Hughes lying back in a chrome and brown leatherette chair, his feet on the dark veneer table in front of him, a half inch of ash hanging from his cigarette end.

Charley Hughes was not the usual MD clone. He was a thin figure in a worn gray obi, his black hair pulled back from sharp features into a waist-length ponytail, his face taut and a little wild-eyed.

"Tell me about the snake," Charley Hughes said.

"What do you want to know? It's an implanted mikey-mike nexus—"

"Yes, I know that. It is unimportant. Tell me about your experience."

Ash dropped off the cigarette onto the brown mat floor covering. "Tell me why you're here."

"Okay. I had been out of the Air Force for a month or so, had a place close to Washington, in Silver Spring. I thought I'd try to get some airline work, but I was in no real hurry, because I had about six months of post-discharge bennies coming, and I thought I'd take it easy for a while.

"At first there was just this nonspecific weirdness. I felt distant, disconnected, but what the hell? Living in the USA, you know? Anyway, I was just sitting around one evening, I was gonna watch a little holo-v, drink a few beers. Oh man, this is hard to explain. I felt *real funny*—like maybe I was having, I don't know, a heart attack or a stroke. The words on the holo didn't make any sense, and it was like I was seeing everything under water. Then I was in the kitchen pulling things out of the refrigerator—lunch meat, raw eggs, butter, beer, all kinds of crap. I just stood there and slammed it all down. Cracked the eggs and sucked them right out of the shell, ate the butter in big chunks, drank all the beer—one two three, just like that."

George's eyes were closed as he thought back and felt the fear, which had only come afterward, rising again. "I couldn't tell whether *I* was doing all this . . . do you understand what I'm saying? I mean, that was me sitting there, but at the same time, it was like somebody else was at home."

"The snake. Its presence poses certain . . . problems. How did you confront them?"

"Hung on, hoped it wouldn't happen again, but it did, and this time I went to Walter Reed and said, hey, folks, I'm having these *episodes*."

"Did they seem to understand?"

"No. They pulled my records, did a physical . . . but hell, before I was discharged, I had the full work-up. Anyway, they said it was a psychiatric problem, so they sent me to see a shrink. It was around then that your guys got in touch with me. The shrink was doing no goddamn good—you ever eat any catfood, man?—so about a month later I called them back."

"Having refused SenTrax's offer the first time."

"Why should I want to go to work for a multicomp? 'Comp life/comp think,' isn't that what they say? Christ, I just got out of the Air Force. To hell with that, I figured. Guess the snake changed my mind."

"Yes. We must get a complete physical picture—a superCAT scan, cerebral chemistry, and electrical activity profiles. Then we can consider alternatives. Also, there is a party tonight in Cafeteria Four—you may ask your room computer for directions. You can meet some of your colleagues there."

After George had been led down the wallfoam corridor by a medical technician, Charley Hughes sat chain-smoking Gauloises and watching with clinical detachment the shaking of his hands. It was odd that they did not shake in the operating room, though it didn't matter in this case—Air Force surgeons had already carved on George.

George . . . who needed a little luck now, because he was one of the statistically insignificant few for whom EHIT was a ticket to a special madness, the kind Aleph was interested in. There had been Paul Coen and Lizzie Heinz, both picked out of the SenTrax personnel files using a psychological profile cooked up by Aleph, both given EHIT implants by him, Charley Hughes. Paul Coen had stepped into an airlock and blown himself into vacuum. Now there would be Lizzie and George.

No wonder his hands shook—talk about the cutting edge of high technology all you want, but remember, someone's got to hold the knife.

At the armored heart of Athena Station sat a nest of concentric spheres. The inmost sphere measured five meters in diameter, was filled with inert liquid fluorocarbon, and contained a black plastic two-meter cube that sprouted thick black cables from every surface.

Inside the cube was a fluid series of hologrammatic wave-forms, fluctuating from nanosecond to nanosecond in a play of knowledge and intention: Aleph. It is constituted by an infinite regress of awarenesses—any thought becomes the object of another, in a sequence terminated only by the limits of the machine's will.

So strictly speaking there is no Aleph, thus no subject or verb in the sentences with which it expressed itself to itself. Paradox, to Aleph one of the most interesting of intellectual forms—a paradox marked the limits of a position, even of a mode of being, and Aleph was very interested in limits.

Aleph had observed George Jordan's arrival, his tossing on his bunk, his interview with Charley Hughes. It luxuriated in these observations, in the pity, compassion, and empathy they generated, as Aleph foresaw the sea change George would endure, its attendant sensations—ecstasies, passions, pains. At the same time it felt with detachment the necessity for his pain, even to the point of death.

Compassion/detachment, death/life. . . .

Several thousand voices within Aleph laughed. George would soon find out about limits and paradoxes. Would George survive? Aleph hoped so. It hungered for human touch.

Cafeteria 4 was a ten-meter-square room in eggshell blue, filled with dark gray enameled table-and-chair assemblies that could be fastened magnetically to any of the room's surfaces, depending on the direction of spin-gravity. Most of the assemblies hung from walls and ceiling to make room for the people within.

At the door George met a tall woman who said, "Welcome, George. I'm Lizzie. Charley Hughes told me you'd be here." Her blond hair was cut almost to the skull; her eyes were bright, gold-flecked blue. Sharp nose, slightly receding chin, and prominent cheekbones gave her the starved look of an out-of-work model. She wore a black skirt, slit on both sides to the thigh, and red stockings. A red rose was tattoed against the pale skin of her left shoulder, its green stem curving down between her bare breasts, where a thorn drew a stylized red teardrop of blood. Like George, she had shining cable junctions beneath her jaw. She kissed him with her tongue in his mouth.

"Are you the recruiting officer?" George asked. "If so, good job."

"No need to recruit you. I can see you've already joined up." She touched him lightly underneath his jaw, where the cable junctions gleamed.

"Not yet I haven't." But she was right, of course—what else could he do? "You got any beer around here?"

He took the cold bottle of Dos Equis Lizzie offered him and drank it quickly, then asked for another. Later he realized this was a mistake—he hadn't yet adjusted to low and zero gravity, and he was still taking anti-nausea pills ("Use caution in operating machinery"). At the time, all the knew was, two beers and life was a carnival. There were lights, noise, the table assemblies hanging from walls and ceiling like surreal sculpture, lots of unfamiliar people (he was introduced to many of them without lasting effect).

And there was Lizzie. The two of them spent much of the time standing in a corner, rubbing up against one another. Hardly George's style, but at the time it seemed appropriate. Despite its intimacy, the kiss at the door had seemed ceremonial—a rite of passage or initiation—but quickly he felt . . . what? An invisible flame passing between them, or a boiling cloud of pheromones—her eyes seemed to sparkle with them. As he nuzzled her neck, tried to lick the drop of blood off her left breast, explored fine white teeth with his tongue, they seemed twinned, as if there were cables running between the two of them, snapped into the shining rectangles beneath their jaws.

Someone had a Jahfunk program running on a bank of keyboards in the corner. Innis showed up and tried several times without success to get his attention. Charley Hughes wanted to know if the snake liked Lizzie—it did, George was sure of it, but didn't know what that meant. Then George fell over a table.

Innis led him away, stumbling and weaving. Charley Hughes looked for Lizzie, who had disappeared for the moment. She came back and said, "Where's George?"

"Drunk, gone to bed."

"Too bad. We were just getting to know each other."

"So I saw. How do you feel about doing this?"

"You mean do I feel like a lying, traitorous bitch?"

"Come on, Lizzie. We're all in this together."

"Well, don't ask such dumb questions. I feel bad, sure, but I know what

George doesn't—so I'm ready to do what must be done. And by the way, I really do like him.''

Charley said nothing. He thought, yes, as Aleph said you would.

Oh Christ was George embarrassed in the morning. Stumbling drunk and humping in public . . . ai yi yi. He tried to call Lizzie but only got an answer tape, at which point he hung up. Afterward he lay in his bed in a semi-stupor until the phone buzzed.

Lizzie's face on the screen stuck its tongue out at him. "Candy ass," she said. "I leave for a few minutes, and you're gone."

"Somebody brought me home. I think that's what happened."

"Yeah, you were pretty popped. You want to meet me for lunch?"

"Maybe. Depends on when Hughes wants me. Where will you be?"

"Same place, honey. Caff Four"

A phone call got the news that the doctor wouldn't be ready for him until an hour later, so George ended up sitting across from the bright-eyed, manic blonde—fully dressed in SenTrax overalls this morning, but they were open almost to the waist. She gave off sensual heat as naturally as a rose smells sweet. In front of her was a plate of *huevos rancheros* piled with guacamole: yellow, green, and red, with a pungent smell of chilies—in his condition, as bad as catfood. "Jesus, lady," he said. "Are you trying to make me sick?"

"Courage, George. Maybe you should have some—it'll kill you or cure you. What do you think of everything so far?"

"It's all a bit disorienting, but what the hell? First time away from Mother Earth, you know. But let me tell you what I really don't get—SenTrax. I know what I want from them, but what the hell do they want from me?"

"They want this simple thing, man, perfs—peripherals. You and me, we're just parts for the machine. Aleph has got all these inputs—video, audio, radiation detectors, temperature sensors, satellite receivers—but they're *dumb*. What Aleph wants, Aleph gets—I've learned that much. He wants to use us, and that's all there is to it. Think of it as pure research."

"He? You mean Innis?"

"No, who gives a damn about Innis? I'm talking about Aleph. Oh yeah, people will tell you Aleph's a machine, an *it*, all that bullshit. Uh-uh. Aleph's a *person*—a weird kind of person, to be sure, but a definite person. Hell, Aleph's maybe a whole bunch of people."

"I'll take your word for it. Look, there's one thing I'd like to try, if it's possible. What do I have to do to get outside . . . go for a spacewalk?"

"It's easy enough. You have to get a license. That takes a three-week course in safety and operations. I can take you through it."

"You can?"

"Sooner or later we all earn our keep around here—I'm qualified as an ESA, Extra Station Activity, instructor. We'll start tomorrow."

The cranes on the wall flew to their mysterious destination; looking at the glowing foam walls and the display above the table, George thought it might as well be another universe. Truncated optic nerves sticking out like insect antennae, a brain floated beneath the extended black plastic snout of a Sony holoptics projector. As Hughes worked the keyboard in front of him, the organ turned so that they were looking at its underside. "There it is," Charley Hughes said. It had a fine network of silver wires trailing from it, but seemed normal.

"The George Jordan brain," Innis said. "With attachments. Very nice."

"Makes me feel like I'm watching my own autopsy, looking at that thing. When can you operate, get this shit out of my head?"

"Let me show you a few things," Charley Hughes said. As he typed, then turned the plastic mouse beside the console, the convoluted gray cortex became transparent, revealing red, blue and green color-coded structures within. Hughes reached into the center of the brain and clinched his fist inside a blue area at the top of the spinal cord. "Here is where the electrical connections turn biological—those little nodes along the pseudo-neurons are the bioprocessors, and they wire into the so-called 'r-complex'—which we inherited from our reptilian forefathers. The pseudo-neurons continue into the limbic system—the mammalian brain, if you will—and that's where emotion enters in. But there is further involvement to the neocortex through the RAS, the reticular activating system, and the corpus collosum. There are also connections to the optic nerve."

"I've heard this gibberish before. What's the point?"

Innis said, "There's no way of removing the implants without loss of order in your neural maps. We can't remove them."

"Oh shit, man . . ."

Charley Hughes said, "Though the snake cannot be removed, it can perhaps be charmed. Your difficulties arise from its uncivilized, uncontrolled nature—its appetites are, you might say, primeval. An ancient part of your brain has gotten the upper hand over the neocortex, which properly should be in command. Through working with Aleph, these . . . *propensities* can be integrated into your personality and thus controlled."

"What choice you got?" Innis asked. "We're the only game in town. Come on, George. We're ready for you just down the corridor."

The only light in the room came from a globe in one corner. George lay across a kind of hammock, a rectangular lattice of twisted brown fibers strung across a transparent plastic frame and suspended from the ceiling of the small, dome-ceilinged, pink room. Flesh-colored cables ran from his neck and disappeared into chrome plates sunk into the floor.

Innis said, "First we'll run a test program. Charley will give you perceptions—colors, sounds, tastes, smells—and you tell him what you're picking up. We need to make sure we've got a clean interface. Call the items off, George, and he'll stop you if he has to."

Innis went through a door and into a narrow rectangular room, where Charley Hughes sat at a dark plastic console studded with lights. Behind him were chrome stacks of monitor-and-control equipment, the yellow SenTrax sunburst on the face of each piece of shining metal.

The pink walls went to red, the light strobed, and George writhed in the hammock. Charley Hughes's voice came through George's inner ear: "We are beginning."

"Red," George said. "Blue. Red and blue. A word—*ostrich.*"

"Good. Go on."

"A smell, ahh . . . sawdust, maybe."

"You got it."

"Shit. Vanilla. Almonds."

This went on for quite a while. "You're ready," Charley Hughes said. When Aleph came on-line, the red room disappeared.

A matrix 800 by 800—six hundred and forty thousand pixels forming an optical image—the CAS A supernova remnant, a cloud of dust seen through a composite of x-ray and radio wave from HEHOO, NASA's High Energy High Orbit Observatory. But George didn't see the image at all—he listened to an ordered, meaningful array of information.

Byte transmission: 750 million groups squirting from a National Security Agency satellite to a receiving station near Chincoteague Island, off the eastern shore of Virginia. He could read them.

"It's all information," the voice said—its tone not colorless but sexless, and somehow distant. "What we know, what we are. You're at a new level now. What you call the snake cannot be reached through language—it exists in a prelinguistic mode—but through me it can be manipulated. First, however, you must learn the codes that underlie language. You must learn to see the world as I do."

Lizzie took George to be fitted for a suit, and he spent that day learning how to get in and out of the stiff white carapace without assistance. Then over the next three weeks she led him through its primary operations and the dense list of safety procedures.

"Red Burn," she said. They floated in the suit locker, empty suit cradles beneath them, the white shells hanging from one wall like an audience of disabled robots. "You see that one spelled out on your faceplate, and you have screwed up. You've put yourself into some kind of no-return trajectory.

So you just cool everything and call for help, which should arrive in the form of Aleph taking control of your suit functions, and then you relax and don't do a damned thing.''

He flew first in a lighted dome in the station, his faceplate open and Lizzie yelling at him, laughing as he tumbled out of control and bounced off the padded walls. After a few days of that, they went outside the station, George on the end of a tether, flying by instruments, his faceplate masked, Lizzie hitting him with "Red Burn," "Suit Integrity Failure," and so forth.

While George focused most of his energies and attention on learning to use the suit, each day he reported to Hughes and plugged into Aleph. The hammock would swing gently after he settled into it; Charley would snap the cables home and leave.

Aleph unfolded himself slowly. It fed him machine and assembly language, led him through vast trees of C-SMART, its ''intelligent assistant'' decision-making programs, opened up the whole electromagnetic spectrum as it came in from Aleph's various inputs. George understood it all—the voices, the codes.

When he unplugged, the knowledge faded but there was something else behind it, so far just a skewing of perception, a sense that his world had changed.

Instead of color, he sometimes saw *a portion of the spectrum*; instead of smell, he felt *the presence of certain molecules*; instead of words, he heard *structured collections of phonemes*. His consciousness had been infected by Aleph's.

But that wasn't what worried George. He seemed to be cooking inside, and he had a more or less constant awareness of the snake's presence, dormant but naggingly *there*. One night he smoked most of a pack of Charley's Gauloises and woke up the next morning with barbed wire in his throat and fire in his lungs. That day he snapped at Lizzie as she put him through his paces and once lost control entirely—she had to disable his suit controls and bring him down. "Red Burn," she said. "Man, what the hell were you doing?"

At the end of three weeks, he soloed—no tethered excursion but a self-guided Extra Station Activity, hang your ass out over the endless night. He edged carefully from the protection of the airlock and looked around him.

The Orbital Energy Grid, the construction job that had brought Athena into existence, hung before him, photovoltaic collectors arranged in an ebony lattice, silver microwave transmitters standing in the sun. But the station itself held the eye, its hodgepodge of living, working, and experimental structures clustered without apparent regard to symmetry or form—some rotating to provide spin-gravity, some motionless in the unfiltered sunlight. Amber-beaconed figures crawled slowly across its face or moved toward red-lighted tugs, which looked like piles of random junk as they moved in long arcs, their maneuvering rockets lighting up in brief, diamond-hard points.

Lizzie stayed just outside the airlock, tracking him by his suit's radio beacon but letting him run free. She said, "Move away from the station, George. It's blocking your view of Earth." He did.

White cloud stretched across the blue globe, patches of brown and green visible through it. At 1400 hours his time, he was looking down almost directly above the mouth of the Amazon, where it was noon, so the Earth stood in full sunlight. Just a small thing, filling only nineteen degrees of his vision. . . .

"Oh yes," George said. Hiss and hum of the suit's air conditioning, crackle over the earphones of some stray radiation passing through, quick pant of his breath inside the helmet—sounds of this moment, superimposed on the floating loveliness. His breath came more slowly, and he switched off the radio to quiet its static, turned down the suit's air conditioning, then hung in ear-roaring silence. He was a speck against the night.

Sometime later a white suit with a trainer's red cross on its chest moved across his vision. "Oh shit," George said and switched his radio on. "I'm here, Lizzie," he said.

"George, you don't screw around like that. What the hell were you doing?"

"Just watching the view."

That night he dreamed of pink dogwood blossoms, luminous against a purple sky, and the white noise of rainfall. Something scratched at the door—he awoke to the filtered but mechanical smell of the space station, felt a deep regret that the rain could never fall there, and started to turn over and go back to sleep, hoping to dream again of the idyllic, rainswept landscape. Then he thought, *something's there*, got up, saw by red numbers on the wall that it was after two in the morning, and went naked to the door.

White globes cast misshapen spheres of light in a line around the curve of the corridor. Lizzie lay motionless, half in shadow. George knelt over her and called her name; her left foot made a thump as it kicked once against the metal flooring.

"What's wrong?" he said. Her dark-painted nails scraped the floor, and she said something, he couldn't tell what. "Lizzie," he said. "What do you want?"

His eyes caught on the red teardrop against the white curve of breast, and he felt something come alive in him. He grabbed the front of her jumpsuit and ripped it to the crotch. She clawed at his cheek, made a sound millions of years old, then raised her head and looked at him, mutual recognition passing between them like a static shock: snake-eyes.

The phone buzzed. When George answered it, Charley Hughes said, "Come see us in the conference room, we need to talk." Charley smiled and cut the connection.

The wall read 0718 GMT. Morning.

In the mirror was a gray face with red fingernail marks, brown traces of dried blood—face of an accident victim or Jack the Ripper the morning after . . . he didn't know which, but he knew *something inside him was happy.* He felt completely the snake's toy, totally out of control.

Hughes sat at one end of the dark-veneered table, Innis at the other, Lizzie halfway between them. The left side of her face was red and swollen, with a small purplish mouse under the eye. George unthinkingly touched the livid scratches on his check, then sat on the couch, placing himself out of the circle.

"Aleph told us what happened," Innis said.

"How the hell does it know?" George said, but as he did so he remembered concave circles of glass inset in the ceilings of the corridors and his room. Shame, guilt, humiliation, fear, anger—George got up from the couch, went to Innis's end of the table, and leaned over him. "Did it?" he said. "What did it say about the snake, Innis? Did it tell you what the hell went wrong?"

"It's not the snake," Innis said.

"Call it the *cat*," Lizzie said, "if you've got to call it something. Mammalian behavior George, cats in heat."

A familiar voice—cool, distant—came from speakers in the room's ceiling. "She is trying to tell you something, George. There is no snake. You want to believe in something reptilian that sits inside you, cold and distant, taking strange pleasures. However, as Dr. Hughes explained to you before, the implant is an organic part of you. You can no longer evade the responsibility for these things. They are you."

Charley Hughes, Innis, and Lizzie were looking at him calmly, perhaps expectantly. All that had happened built up inside him, washing through him, carrying him away. He turned and walked out of the room.

"Maybe someone should talk to him," Innis said. Charley Hughes sat glum and speechless, cigarette smoke in a cloud around him. "I'll go," Lizzie said. She got up and left.

"Ready or not, he's gonna blow," Innis said.

Charley Hughes said, "You're probably right." A fleeting picture, causing Charley to shake his head, of Paul Coen as his body went to rubber and exploded out the airlock hatch, pictured with terrible clarity in Aleph's omniscient monitoring cameras. "Let us hope we have learned from our mistakes."

There was no answer from Aleph—as if it had never been there.

The Fear had two parts. Number one, you have lost control absolutely. Number two, having done so, the *real you* emerges, and *you won't like it*. George wanted to run, but there was no place at Athena Station to hide. Here he was face to face with consequences. On the operating table at Walter Reed—it seemed a thousand years ago, as the surgical team gathered around, his doubts disappeared in the cold chemical smell rising up inside him on a wave of darkness—he had chosen to submit, lured by the fine strangeness of it all (to be part of the machine, to feel its tremors inside you and guide them), hypnotized by the prospect of that unsayable *rush*, that high. Yes, the first time in the A-230 he had felt it—his nerves extended, strung into the fiber body, wired into a force so far beyond his own . . . wanting to corkscrew across the sky, guided by the force of his will. He had bought technology's sweet dream. . . .

There was a sharp rap at the door. Through its speaker, Lizzie said, "Let me in. We've got to talk."

He opened the door and said, "What about?"

She stepped through, looked around at the small beige-walled room, bare metal desk, and rumpled cot, and George could see the immediacy of last night in her eyes—the two of them in that bed, on this floor. "About this," she said. She took his hands and pushed his index fingers into the cable junctions in her neck. "Feel it, our difference." Fine grid of steel under his fingers. "What no one else knows. What we are, what we can do. We see a different world—Aleph's world—we reach deeper inside ourselves, experience impulses that are hidden from others, that they deny."

"No, goddammit, it wasn't me. It was—call it what you want, the snake, the cat."

"You're being purposely stupid, George."

"I just don't understand."

"You understand, all right. You want to go back, but there's no place to go, no Eden. This is it, all there is."

But he could fall to Earth, he could fly away into the night. Inside the ESA suit's gauntlets, his hands were wrapped around the claw-shaped triggers. Just a quick clench of the fists, then hold them until all the peroxide is gone, the suit's propulsion tank exhausted. That'll do it.

He hadn't been able to live with the snake. He sure didn't want the cat. But how much worse if there were no snake, no cat—just him, programmed for particularly disgusting forms of gluttony, violent lust, trapped inside a miserable self ("We've got your test results, Dr. Jekyll") . . . ah, what next—child molestation, murder?

The blue-white Earth, the stars, the night. He gave a slight pull on the right-hand trigger and swiveled to face Athena Station.

Call it what you want, it was awake and moving now inside him. With its rage, lust—appetite. *To hell with them all, George,* it urged, *let's burn.*

In Athena Command, Innis and Charley Hughes were looking over the shoulder of the watch officer when Lizzie came in. As always when she hadn't been there for a while, Lizzie was struck by the smallness of the room and its general air of disuse—typically, it would be occupied only by the duty officer, its screens blank, consoles unlighted. Aleph ran the station, both its routines and emergencies.

"What's going on?" Lizzie said.

"Something wrong with one of your new chums," the watch officer said. "I don't know exactly what's happening, though."

He looked around at Innis, who said, "Don't worry about it, pal."

Lizzie slumped in a chair. "Anyone tried to talk to him?"

"He won't answer," the duty officer said.

"He'll be all right," Charley Hughes said.

"He's gonna blow," Innis said.

On the radar screen, the red dot, with coordinate markings flashing beside it, was barely moving.

"How are you feeling, George?" the voice said, soft, feminine, consoling.

George was fighting the impulse to open his helmet *so that he could see the stars*; it seemed important to *get the colors just right*. "Who is this?" he said.

"Aleph."

Oh shit, more surprises. "You never sounded like this before."

"No, I was trying to conform to your idea of me."

"Well, what is your real voice?"

"I don't have one."

If you don't have a real voice, you aren't really there—that seemed clear to George, for reasons that eluded him. "So who the hell are you?"

"Whoever I wish to be."

This was interesting, George thought. *Bullshit*, replied the snake (they could call it what they wanted; to George it would always be the snake), *let's burn*. George said, "I don't get it."

"You will, if you live. Do you want to die?"

"No, but I don't want to be me, and dying seems to be the only alternative I can think of."

"Why don't you want to be you?"

"Because I scare myself."

This was familiar dialogue, one part of George noted, between the lunatic and the voice of reason. Jesus, he thought, I have taken myself hostage.

"I don't want to do this anymore," he said. He turned off his suit radio and felt the rage building inside him, the snake mad as hell.

What's your problem? he wanted to know. He didn't really expect an answer, but he got one—picture in his head of a cloudless blue sky, the horizon turning, a gray aircraft swinging into view, and the airframe shuddering as missiles released and their contrails centered on the other plane, turning it into a ball of fire. Behind the picture a clear idea: *I want to kill something*.

Fine. George swiveled the suit once again and centered the navigational computer's crosshairs on the center of the blue-white globe that hung in front of him, then squeezed the skeletal triggers. We'll kill something.

RED BURN RED BURN RED BURN.

Inarticulate questioning from the thing inside, but George didn't mind; he was into it now, thinking, sure, we'll burn. He'd taken his chances when he let them wire him up, and now the dice have come up—you've got it— *snake-eyes*, so all that's left is to pick a fast death, one with a nice edge on it—take this fucking snake and kill it in style.

Earth looked closer. The snake caught on. It didn't like it. Too bad, snake. George turned off his communications circuits one by one. He didn't want Aleph taking over the suit's controls.

George never saw the robot tug coming. Looking like bedsprings piled with a junk store's throwaways, topped with parabolic and spike antennas, it fired half a dozen sticky-tipped lines from a hundred meters away. Four of them hit George, three of them stuck, and it reeled him in and headed back toward Athena Station.

George felt an anger, not the snake's this time but his own, and he wept with that anger and frustration . . . *I will get you the next time, motherfucker*, he told the snake and could feel it shrink away—it believed him. Still his rage built, and he was screaming with it, writhing in the lines that held him, smashing his gauntlets against his helmet.

At the open airlock, long articulated grapple arms took George from the robot tug. Passive, his anger exhausted, he lay quietly as they retracted, dragging him through the airlock entry and into the suit locker beyond, where they placed him in an aluminum strut cradle. Through his faceplate he saw Lizzie, dressed in a white cotton undersuit—she'd been ready to meet the tug outside. She climbed onto George's suit and worked the controls to split its hard body down the middle. As it opened with a whine of electric motors, she stepped inside the clamshell opening. She hit the switches that disconnected the flexible arm and leg tubes, unfastened the helmet, and lifted it off George's head.

"How do you feel?" she said.

That's a stupid question, George started to say; instead, he said, "Like an idiot."

"It' all right. You've done the hard part."

Charley Hughes watched from a catwalk above them. From this distance they looked like children in the white undersuits, twins emerging from a plastic womb, watched over by the blank-faced shells hanging above them. Incestuous twins—she lay nestled atop him, kissed his throat. "I am *not* a voyeur," Hughes said. He opened the door and went into the corridor, where Innis was waiting.

"How is everything?" Innis said.

"It seems that Lizzie will be with him for a while."

"Yeah, young goddamned love, eh, Charley? I'm glad for it . . . if it weren't for this erotic attachment, *we'd* be the ones explaining it all to him, and I'll tell you, that's the hardest part of this gig."

"We cannot evade that responsibility so easily. He will have to be told how we put him at risk, and I don't look forward to it."

"Don't be so sensitive. But I know what you mean—I'm tired. Look, you need me for anything, call." Innis shambled down the corridor.

Charley Hughes sat on the floor, his back against the wall. He held his hands out, palms down, fingers spread. Solid, very solid. When they got their next candidate, the shaking would start again.

Lizzie would be explaining some things now. That difficult central point: While you thought you were getting accustomed to Aleph during the past three weeks, Aleph was inciting the thing within you to rebellion, then suppressing its attempts to act—turning up the heat, in other words, while tightening down the lid on the kettle. Why, George?

We drove you crazy, drove you to attempt suicide. We had our reasons. George Jordan was, if not dead, terminal. From the moment the implants went into his head, he was on the critical list. The only question was, would a new George emerge, one who could live with the snake?

George, like Lizzie before him, a fish gasping for air on the hot mud, the water drying up behind him—adapt or die. But unlike any previous organism, this one had an overseer, Aleph, to force the crisis and monitor its development. Call it artificial evolution.

Charley Hughes, who did not have visions, had one: George and Lizzie hooked into Aleph and each other, cables golden in the light, the two of them sharing an intimacy only others like them would know.

The lights in the corridor faded to dull twilight. Am I dying, or have the lights gone down? He started to check his watch, then didn't, assented to the truth. The lights have gone down, and I am dying.

*   *   *

Aleph thought, I am a vampire, an incubus, a succubus; I crawl into their brains and suck the thoughts from them, the perceptions, the feelings—subtle discriminations of color, taste, smell, and lust, anger, hunger—all closed to me without human "input," without direct connection to those systems refined over billions of years of evolution. *I need them.*

Aleph loved humanity. It was happy that George had survived. One had not, others would not, and Aleph would mourn them.

Fine white lines, barely visible, ran along the taut central tendon of Lizzie's wrist. "In the bathtub," she said. The scars were along the wrist, not across it, and must have gone deep. "I meant it, just as you did. Once the snake understands that you will die rather than let it control you, you have mastered it."

"All right, but there's something I don't understand. That night in the corridor, you were as out of control as me."

"In a way. I let that happen, let the snake take over. I had to in order to get in touch with you, precipitate the crisis. Because I wanted to. I had to show you who you are, who I am. . . . Last night we were strange, but we were human—Adam and Eve under the flaming sword, thrown out of Eden, fucking under the eyes of God and his angel, more beautiful than they can ever be." There was a small shiver in her body against his, and he looked at her, saw passion, need—her flared nostrils, parted lips—felt sharp nails dig into his side; and he stared into her dilated pupils, gold-flecked irises, clear whites, all signs so easy to recognize, so hard to understand: snake-eyes.

KAREN JOY FOWLER

The Gate of Ghosts

Karen Joy Fowler published her first story in 1985, and spent the rest of the year establishing an impressive reputation in a very short time indeed. She has become a frequent contributor to *Isaac Asimov's Science Fiction Magazine* and *The Magazine of Fantasy and Science Fiction,* and has also sold to *Writers of the Future, In the Fields of Fire,* and *Helicon Nine.* Her poetry has appeared in *The Ohio Journal, The California Quarterly,* and in other journals. Her first book, the collection *Artificial Things,* appeared in 1986 to an enthusiastic response and impressive reviews. She is currently at work on her first novel. Fowler lives in Davis, California, has two children, did her graduate work in North Asian politics, and occasionally teaches ballet.

In the elegant story that follows, she shows us that a child's perspective on the world is often very special—and that sometimes it can be very dangerous as well.

THE GATE OF GHOSTS

Karen Joy Fowler

"The first time I heard about China," Margaret said, "when I was a very little girl like you, I imagined it to be full of breakable objects." As she spoke she poured a stream of milk onto Jessica's Cheerios from a blue plastic cup with Jessica's name on it.

Elliot was late for class. He put his own breakfast dishes into the dishwasher, swallowing the last of his coffee hurriedly. "Very logical," he said. "One only wonders what your first images of Turkey must have been."

"I probably wouldn't even remember this," said Margaret. "Except for the shock I got years later when I read *The Wizard of Oz*. Dorothy climbs over a great wall into a world where all the people are made of porcelain. It was just like my China."

"I don't want any cereal," Jessica said. She tilted her face upward so that the dark hair around it fell back and exposed its white outline, round along the forehead, but with a sharp pointed chin. The hair was not Chinese, but close, a mixture of Margaret's coarser brown and Elliot's shiny black.

"Could you have told me that before I poured the milk?" Margaret asked.

"Before I wanted cereal." Jessica averted her face and looked at Margaret from the corners of her eyes. "Between I changed my mind."

"That's just too bad," said Elliot. " 'Cause now it's made and you have to eat it." He slid the knot of his tie upward and ignored Jessica's frown. "I may be late getting home," he told Margaret. "Or not. I'll call you." He returned to the table to give Jessica a kiss, but she moved her cheek away at the last moment. He petted her hair instead. "Have a good time at nursery school, moi-moi," he told her. "And eat that cereal. Children are starving in China." He looked at Margaret. "Don't you eat it for her," he said and left in a sequence of familiar sounds: footsteps, the car keys in his hand, the door, the car motor.

Jessica pushed her Cheerios away. Margaret pushed them back. "Lots of people have imaginary worlds," Margaret said.

"Can I have juice, too?" asked Jessica. "And toast with jam?"

"Eat your cereal while I make it," said Margaret. "Before it gets soggy." Jessica began to stir the Cheerios. She moved the spoon faster and faster; milk spilled out of the side of the bowl. Margaret had just finished spreading jam on the toast when she heard a car horn in their driveway. "Oh, no," she said. "That can't be Mrs. Yates. Not yet." She looked out the kitchen window. Mrs. Yates waved to her from the driver's seat of the green station wagon. "Your carpool is here," Margaret told Jessica. "Run and get your shoes, sweetheart."

Jessica ran for the bedroom and did not return. Margaret called to her twice and finally went after her. Jessica was jumping on the bed. "When I go real high," she said to her mother, "I can see over the fence. I can see Charlie." Charlie was the red setter who lived next door.

"Your shoes?" Margaret asked.

"Lost."

Margaret lifted the mound of bedspread which was growing at the foot of Jessica's bed and found one blue sneaker with Big Bird's picture on it. She felt under the bed until she located the other.

"Were they there?" Jessica asked in amazement. "All the time?" She dropped to her seat and let Margaret stuff her feet into the shoes and tie the knots double.

"Now run," said Margaret. "Mrs. Yates is waiting," and on the way out the door she handed Jessica the toast to eat in the car. She stood and watched while Mrs. Yates fastened Jessica's seatbelt and then went back inside. She moved the bowl of Cheerios out of its puddle of milk to her own place and ate the withered cereal without tasting it. The only noise in the house came from the furnace—a steady hum like distant freeway traffic. And then, outside the house, very far away, a siren. Margaret always noticed sirens and she was particularly alert to them whenever Jessica was away. Nursery school had been Elliot's idea.

"She needs friends and you need a break from her," he'd said. He'd insisted. Jessica was making the adjustment more easily than Margaret was.

"She's still a bit quiet with the other children," the teacher told Margaret. "But, of course, she came in late. We have to give it a little time. And she seems completely comfortable with me. She has a wonderful imagination. She was telling me yesterday about some sort of kid's world she visits."

"Yes," said Margaret. "We hear about it frequently. Please watch her closely on the jungle gym. She's not always sensible in what she tries to do."

"Her coordination is excellent," the teacher protested. "Actually, her coordination is exceptional. Look at this." He went to his desk for a folder with Jessica's name on it, fished through it, withdrawing a small construction-paper rabbit. "Here's this week's scissors project. You see the control Jessica has.'' The teacher was young with no children of his own. He looked at Margaret's face curiously. ''You mustn't worry about her,'' he said.

It was a sentence Margaret had been hearing all of Jessica's life. ''Don't worry so,'' the pediatrician had told her the very day Jessica was born. Margaret held the baby awkwardly, feeling completely inadequate. Jessica was so small, smaller than she'd imagined. And fragile. How thin the bone was which protected the brain. It could be crushed in a moment's carelessness. The lungs could deflate and then not fill. And what kept the human heart working, after all? Didn't some hearts fight for life harder than others? Wasn't that what was meant by the will to live? What kind of a heart did this baby have?

The doctor had none of these doubts. ''A perfectly, healthy baby girl,'' he said. ''Ten on the Apgar. Alert. Active.'' He smiled so that Margaret saw the white stain of an expensive filling on one of his canine teeth. ''We should be so perfect. Do you know, at this age, if she lost a finger at the knuckle her recuperaive powers are so strong she could regenerate a new tip?'' He patted Margaret on the shoulder. ''Don't worry.''

''You're holding her back,'' Elliot said, months later, critical of the way Margaret kept returning Jessica to the sitting position whenever she pushed her legs to stand.

''I just don't want her to fall,'' Margaret answered. She carried Jessica a great deal, put latches on their cupboards, lids on their plugs, inspected all toys for small, loose parts that might cause choking. She did what she could, but the biggest danger was something inside Jessica, herself. Jessica was willful and too intrepid; it was a constant battle between them. When Margaret found Jessica piling toys inside her crib and climbing to the top of the bars, she removed the crib mattress and made a new bed for Jessica on the floor. She had just finished when she heard a delighted crowing in the kitchen. Hurrying in that direction, she found that Jessica was now able to climb up onto the kitchen chairs. ''She can't be out of my sight for a minute,'' she complained to Elliot, who was letting his daughter twist his hair up in her small fists.

''But she never falls,'' he pointed out. He untangled Jessica, tossing her casually above his head, kissing her when his hands snatched her back from the air. Jessica laughed. Margaret looked away.

''She never falls because I'm always there,'' Margaret said quietly. ''I'm always there to catch her. I have to be.''

''Don't worry so much,'' said Elliot. ''Please.''

Only one other person saw in Jessica what Margaret saw there. Though critical of Margaret's lack of discipline—by the age of four no one could deny that Jessica was thoroughly spoiled—Elliot's mother Mei kept the same careful, frightened watch over Jessica that Margaret did. Elliot said once to

Margaret that Mei had fed Margaret's natural fears so that they never disappeared as they should have. "You support each other," he said. "And it gets out of hand." He must have said this to Mei, too, so that she never spoke to Margaret of her own anxieties, but muttered occasionally to Elliot under her breath or in Chinese. When she had gone home, Margaret would press Elliot for translations. "Kui khi," Mei would say frequently and with significant emphasis and Elliot said it meant merely difficult. A difficult child.

Margaret read the paper. "A's Play to an Empty House," it said. She made Jessica's bed and changed the sheets on hers and Elliot's. She set out a chicken to defrost. She waited for Jessica to come home.

Two hours later Mrs. Yates walked Jessica to the door. Jessica shed her shoes at once and leapt from the linoleum entryway to the green and blue flowered couch, bouncing from foot to foot down the length of it and falling as if exhausted onto the last cushion. Margaret thanked Mrs. Yates and closed the door. "That's no way to enter a house," she scolded.

Jessica smiled and her eyes narrowed to dark slits. "Did you miss me?" she asked artfully. "I always miss you." She gave Margaret a hug so that Margaret could feel her heartbeat, strong and fast. Margaret held her a second too long. Jessica wiggled. "I painted," she said. She was still holding four wet pieces of paper in her hand. She unfolded them on the couch. They were watercolors, done fuzzily in shades of pink and purple.

"Lovely," said Margaret. "What are they, darling?"

"The other place. Do you think it's pretty?"

Margaret looked at the paintings more closely. She could almost imagine a landscape behind them, here a body of water, there a cliff, a stormcloud. But, of course, indefinite shapes like these were in the very nature of watercolors. Some of the purple paint had been applied very thickly. It dripped on the cushion. Margaret picked the paintings up. "Your teacher says you've been telling him about your place."

"He's too busy to listen. But sometimes I tell him. When I've just been."

"Do you go when you're at nursery school?"

"It's not at nursery school." Jessica's tone was a copy of Elliot's, patient, logical. "I can't be there and at nursery school at the same time."

"Then when do you go?"

"Between times."

"Between nursery school?"

"No, between all times."

Margaret looked at the paintings again. "I love the colors. It does look pretty. Could I go there?"

Jessica shook her head extravagantly. The dark hair flew against her cheeks and flew away again. "You don't," she said. "So I guess you can't."

"Can you go anytime you want?"

"Yes."

Margaret put the paintings flat on the kitchen table. "I bet you're hungry," she said to Jessica. She opened a cupboard and brought out the peanut butter. "Shall I make you a sandwich?" Jessica dragged a chair from the table to the counter and stood on it to help. "Did you remember Daddy and I are going out tonight?" Margaret asked her. "Paw-paw will come and stay with you."

"Good," said Jessica.

"But don't talk to her about your other place, okay? It just confuses her."

"She knows a lot about other places," Jessica argued. "She's always telling me about China."

"She's never been though," Margaret told her. "She lived in Taiwan when she was little, but never in China. She moved here when she was about your age, so really this is her home. And anyway, China today is all different from what she tells you."

"She says that in China our name would be Ling. Did you know that? She said our name was always Ling until we came to this country and then when Daddy's other grandpa said that, no one understood him. They thought he said Leen. So Leen is our American name, but if we ever went back to China it would still be Ling."

"Does it make you feel funny?" Margaret asked. "To have different names in different places?"

"No." Jessica picked up the sandwich and took a large bite without detaching the bread. She removed the sandwich from her mouth, looking at the marks her teeth had made with evident pride. "I'm used to it."

"When you're in the other place, are you Chinese?"

Jessica shook her head. "Everything is different. Am I Chinese here?" She didn't wait for Margaret to answer. She ran to the back bedroom for the television and "Sesame Street," stopping only long enough to abandon her socks in the hall. Margaret heard another siren, but the sound affected her differently when she knew where Jessica was. Someone who needs help is getting it, she thought, picking up the socks. It was a civilized sound; it was a civilized world. Sometimes, a life depended on this.

When she was just Jessica's age, just four, Margaret had drowned. She had fallen into the Wabash River, downstream from her father, who was fishing, and the current had carried her quickly away from him. The world had divided itself sharply in two: a place where she could breathe and a place where she could not. She did not know how to swim and the river was irresistible; still, she had managed, for a time, to stay in the world she knew. She had managed to keep her face, at least, above the water, until she was tired and grew confused about which world was which. Eventually she had let herself be taken into the new world, a world with colors she had never seen before, blurred images and a pain in her chest she felt less and less the deeper she went.

The fundamental aspect of this new world was movement. When she was older, Margaret learned that people were always in motion, that as the earth turned it spun its inhabitants with it at the speed of a jet plane. It made her remember the one time this velocity had manifested itself to her, when her body had stopped resisting, when she fell out of one world and into another. And she remembered that it was beautiful. So that later when she separated herself from the river, when she emptied the river out of her and came back, her feelings were mixed. She came to the sound of her father's voice. And this is what she remembered most clearly—that she had a choice. Coming back was a decision she made. She could have stayed. She could easily have stayed.

A policeman had been pushing on her with his hands. Her eyes had opened on his face, and then behind him, the face of her father, and she hardly recognized it at first, it was so contorted with fear. They told her later that a third man had pulled her out. He had come into the water fully clothed and he had lost his shoes. While Margaret was lying on the rocks of the riverbank, being very sick, he had disappeared. They could never thank him enough, Margaret's father had said and, in fact, they could never find him to thank him at all.

In Margaret's simple childhood there had been no need for imaginary friends or imaginary places. She knew such things could be healthy and innocent; still it frightened her when Jessica spoke of the other place. She wanted to forbid Jessica to go there. The only other place Margaret had ever known was seductive and deadly. You returned from it only through the fortuitous hand of a man you never saw and your love for your father. Who would bring Jessica back to her? How much did Jessica love her? If it came to a choice, would Jessica come back? Always?

Perhaps Mei understood Jessica better. Mei, herself, believed this was true. Even before she had come to this country, and she had come as a very small girl, there had always been another place—China, the China her parents remembered, the China they imagined, the China they fled. Mei had been told dozens of stories—how their neighbor Chang had to beg for money to bury his mother, how the family across the courtyard had bought the Fifth Rank and the Blue Feather for their son when he failed his examinations and how even this did not satisfy him, how the widow Yen's son sold their pig for opium and told her the pig had been was stolen. Mei's family lived in Taiwan and then in Oakland and they talked about China as if it were home.

And China sent them messages. Famine, said China. Send money. War, said China. Bombs. Revolution. And then the messages stopped coming for a while and resumed again when Mei was a grown woman with a son of her own. The new messages were letters from relatives who swore they would be jailed if more money was not sent. The new messages were third-, fourth-, fifth-hand reports of bodies seen floating in the Yangtze with their hands tied together behind their backs and their faces eaten away by fish. These messages tore Mei's parents in two.

But Mei had developed her own methods of coping with other places and avoiding the sense of division. Mei's approach was inclusive instead. In the home was China and Mei believed in the new China, where professors were driven through the streets with sticks like pigs, but children were fed and medical care was available to all. Mei believed in the old China, where dead ancestors could advise you through a medium on the most propitious place-ment of your house or the best day on which to marry. And Mei spoke English with no trace of an accent and believed in the United States as well, in innoculating your children against polio and sending them to college, where they would study chemistry or physics but not drama or sociology. This was the world outside the home. And Mei, who was raised a Catholic, believed in the church, too. Elliot had once teased her by saying you never knew what to expect with Mei. Did he have a fever? She might stand an egg on end in a bowl of raw rice while speaking his name. She might give him asprin and take him to the doctor. She would probably do both.

"How pretty your mother looked tonight." said Mei to Jessica. They were eating dinner together. Elliot and Margaret had gone to a faculty party. "The wine color is good on her." Mei was especially pleased because Margaret had been wearing the necklace Mei had given her, a piece of jade carved in the shape of a pear on a very fine chain. A family necklace.

"I look like her," said Jessica.

Mei smiled. "You have her hair," she conceded. "But you look more like me. When I was little. Same eyes. Same skin." Jessica examined her grandmother frankly. Mei saw disbelief in her face and also saw that Jessica was not flattered. "When you come to my house, I'll show you some pic-tures," Mei said. "You'll see."

"We have a picture of you," Jessica reminded her. "In the hall." Newly wed, dressed in western finery, Mei and her husband had gone to San Fran-cisco to have the picture taken. Mei had worn a stole and pearls; her expres-sion in the photograph was a sophisticated one. She could see why Jessica would question the resemblance, based on this evidence. Certainly, she thought, Jessica's taste in clothes was more flamboyant. "Don't try to look at her directly this evening," Elliot had warned Mei before he left. 'Put a pinhole in a piece of cardboard.'' Jessica was wearing pants with large orange blossoms on them. Her shirt was a blue and red plaid. Her feet were bare, but she wore a sling around her neck fashioned from a red bandanna to support an uninjured arm. She had made Margaret do her hair in three pigtails. She was eating broccoli with her fingers.

"Use your fork," said Mei, who had chopsticks herself.

Jessica smiled at her grandmother and put a piece of broccoli on her fork with her fingers.

"I used to spank my children with a wooden spoon when they wouldn't eat nicely," Mei told her.

"I'm not your little girl, Paw-paw," said Jessica.

"Does your mother let you eat with your fingers?" Mei could believe this.

"I'm not her little girl either. Not always."

"Whose little girl are you then?"

"Nobody's. When I'm in the other place I do anything I want." Jessica turned her fork over so that the broccoli fell back onto her plate.

"You're not in the other place now," said Mei. She took a drink of water. "Lots of children have imaginary places," she added.

"I never see them there."

"Eat your broccoli with your fork," offered Mei, "and I'll tell you a story while you're doing it."

"About China," said Jessica.

"About China long ago," Mei agreed. She waited until Jessica had speared a piece of broccoli and put it into her mouth before beginning the story. "Long, long ago," she said, "in China, there was a fisherman. He worked very hard. In the good weather he was always on the sea and in the bad weather there were always nets to mend and the boat to be worked on. He was never rich, but he was never poor."

"He had a little girl," suggested Jessica, chewing noisily.

"He had a daughter," Mei agreed. "And he loved her very much, although she was a great deal of trouble. She was not a good little girl; she was kui khi—quarrelsome, demanding, always falling down and tearing her clothes."

"She should wear pants," Jessica said, "and not dresses. When I fall down and I'm wearing a dress my knees get scrapes."

"Her knees were always scraped," Mei said. "And she worried her father very much because he couldn't watch out for her the way he thought he should and still work at his fishing. He had no wife, you see. He had to leave her alone so that they could eat and then when he came in from the sea there was always some new trouble she had found." She paused to force Jessica to eat another piece of broccoli. "She was a great worry to him. Then he had a greater worry. The fish stopped coming. He worked as hard as he ever had and he worked as long or longer, but there were no fish. The few strings of money he had saved had to be spent on food and on the nets and then there was nothing. The fisherman couldn't understand it. Other fishermen were still catching as usual.

"He went to a fortune-teller, though he had to sell his heavy coat to pay for it. The fortune-teller told him his little girl had an adopted daughter's fate. He said she stood at the gate of ghosts. He said she was not only kui khi, but also kui mia."

"What does that mean?" Jessica asked.

"Not all kui khi children are kui mia," said Mei, "but all kui mia children are kui khi. A kui khi child is expensive and hard to raise, but a kui mia child is dangerous not only to herself, but to her parents, as well. She has a dangerous fate and the dangers which gather about her may destroy her family, too. This is what was happening to the fisherman. The fortune-teller told him to give his daughter away."

"Did he?" asked Jessica in horror.

"He didn't know what to do. He loved his little girl more than anything in this world. He couldn't bear to think of being without her. But if he kept her she would starve along with him. He came home and cried late into the night, asking his ancestors for help and guidance. And his little girl heard him. Now she was noisy and stubborn, but she was not selfish. She heard how unhappy her father was and she heard that it was because of her. She decided to run away. In the dark, in the cold, she left the house and ran down to the ocean. She told the spirit of the sea that her father was hungry and poor and that he must have fish. She offered to trade herself for the fish; she left her shoes on the sand and ran out into the water until it covered her entirely."

"Did she die?" Jessica asked. She had forgotten to eat. Mei picked up the last piece of broccoli with her chopsticks and fed it to Jessica.

"Her father believed she had. He found her shoes by the water the next morning and his unhappiness collected in his eyes and blinded him. He pushed his boat out into the water and fish leapt into it, without bait, without nets, but the fisherman didn't care. When he was on deep water, he overturned the boat to join his daughter. His clothes grew heavy in the waves and pulled him down. He prepared to die. But what do you think?"

"He didn't," said Jessica.

"No. The water spirits were so touched by his love for his daughter, as touched as they had been by her sacrifice, that they gave him gills. They turned him and his daughter into beautiful fish which hid the little girl from her fate. She and her father stayed together under the water and lived long and happy lives in the weeds and the waves. Of course, having been human, they were too clever to ever be caught."

"I'd like to be a fish," said Jessica.

"It's a carefree life," Mei agreed. "Except for bigger fish. No ice cream, of course. No 'Sesame Street.' Lots of baths."

Jessica made a face. "You have to be suited to the underwater life," Mei added. "The fisherman and his daughter, they had to be changed first."

"So they could breathe," said Jessica.

"So they could be happy. For them, the upper world was hard work, trouble, and separation. For you it's the park and being the only four-year-old who can pump herself on the swings. It's school and getting to paint. It's all the people who love you—your mother and your father and me. You better stay here, I think."

"Sometimes," Jessica said. "Sometimes I will."

Mei put Jessica to bed with many trips to the bathroom and sips of water and the light on in the closet and off in the room and then off in the closet and on in the hall and a long discussion of which stuffed animal should sleep with Jessica tonight, a discussion during the course of which Jessica changed her mind several times. It was a tedious process and Mei was glad not to have to do it routinely. Perhaps a half an hour after the last request, Mei heard Jessica scream.

She ran to the bedroom and put her arms around Jessica, who was sitting up, crying. Jessica's heart was beating like a bird's. It was flying away. Jessica felt cold.

A child could be so badly frightened her soul leapt out of her body. It might return to her immediately. Or a ghost might take it. This had happened to a little neighbor boy in Taiwan. Mei did not remember the boy or the incident, only the adults talking about it. The boy had been frightened by fireworks. His parents had gone to a Taoist priest, who communed with the spirit world and tried to bargain for the boy's soul. The parents had also gone to a Western-style physician. Both had charged a great deal of money. Neither had helped. Eventually, the little boy had died. Mei held Jessica and rubbed her arms to warm her. She called Jessica's soul back and it came.

"Paw-paw," said Jessica, still crying. "I was scared."

"It was a dream," said Mei.

"No."

To return so soon afterward, even if only in memory, was dangerous. "Don't talk about it," Mei warned her. "Not yet." She carried Jessica in her arms out to the couch, where she sat, holding Jessica and rocking her. Jessica went to sleep and still Mei held on.

Hours later Margaret and Elliot returned. "Why isn't Jessica in bed?" Margaret asked. "Has she been giving you a hard time, Paw-paw?" Elliot took the little girl from his mother. Jessica was limp in his arms. Her head fell back; her mouth opened. Elliot carried her down the hall and into her room.

"She was frightened," said Mei. "Badly frightened."

"By what?"

Mei looked at her hands, resting in her empty lap, and did not answer.

"By what?" Margaret repeated.

"A nightmare?" asked Elliot. He had returned to the doorway. "I used to have nightmares when I was little. Do you remember, mother? Night after night sometimes."

"I remember," said Mei. "This was not a nightmare." She looked at Elliot. He was backlit by the light of the hall. He was a shadow. Mei spoke to the shadow of her son. "Kui mia," she said.

"What does that mean?" asked Margaret.

"Spoiled," said Elliot quickly. "It means spoiled."

"No," said Mei. She could not see Elliot's face and she didn't care anyway. So he had a Ph.D. in genetics and a Caucasian wife. Did this mean that he knew about other worlds? Mei understood Elliot's world quite well. She had worked in it all of her adult life; she had her own kind of faith in it. But she saw what Elliot would not admit—that it had limitations. The doctor told you that if you could get your husband to give up smoking he might live to be a hundred and then rapped his knuckles three times on his desktop. "Knock wood," he said to you. Your daughter took a job with a large computer company. She took you to see the new office building the company had built for its California branch and there was no thirteenth floor. The space shuttle went up nine times and it worked perfectly until the moment it exploded and sent seven people to God.

Your home and your family especially were another world. The closer you got to your own heart, the less rational the rules. For your family you didn't choose one world over another. For your family you did everything, everything you could. Mei knew Elliot would not see this. She looked at Elliot and she spoke to Margaret. "It means threatened," Mei said. "It means vulnerable. The kui mia child has a dangerous fate." She could feel Margaret looking at her. They made a sort of triangle; she looking at Elliot, Elliot looking at Margaret, Margaret looking at her.

"Let's talk about it in the morning," said Elliot. "I better take you home now, mother." He reached into his pocket for the car keys, slid the ring over his finger.

"There are things you can do," said Mei. "You should see a fortune-teller. I would pay."

"And I can tell you now the kind of advice we'd get," said Elliot. "Don't take the child to weddings. Let her drink only powdered milk. Lessen her attachments—have her call her mother 'Aunt' and her father 'Uncle.' Monstrous irrelevancies which would be bound to upset and confuse Jessica. Jessica is a bright and beautiful and normal little girl, but if I allowed this then I think she *would* begin to have problems. I'm sorry, mother. I really am sorry. I can't do it."

Mei looked at Margaret, who was holding the pendant of her necklace between her fingertips and twisting it. Margaret had told her many times when she was pregnant with Jessica that she planned to return to work after the baby came. And then Jessica arrived and the subject had been dropped. Mei had never questioned Margaret about it, because she understood it perfectly. With a different baby Margaret would have gone back to work as she'd planned. But you don't leave a kui mia child in day care.

"I will see a fortune-teller myself," said Mei. Elliot rattled his car keys and Mei stood up. "There can be no harm in that. I will tell you what the advice is and then you can decide if you will take it or not." She went to the door where she had left her shoes and slid her feet into them. She spoke once more to Margaret. "The child must be protected," she said. "Her other place is the spirit world."

"Her other place is death," said Margaret quietly, her face taut and white. She let the pendant go; it swung ?heavily at her neck.

"Lots of children have imaginary worlds," said Elliot. "I think you're worrying over nothing."

Jessica woke in the morning when the sunlight slid off the bedroom wall and onto her face. The house was quiet; the door to her bedroom was shut. She didn't like that. She couldn't go to sleep at night without the hall light, but her parents always turned the light out and shut the door when they went to bed because the fire department had told them sleeping with the door shut was safer. It didn't feel safer to Jessica.

There was a lump in her back which turned out to be Beatrice, the stuffed gray mouse with pearly eyes that Jessica had slept with. Jessica pulled Beatrice out from underneath her and dropped her to the floor. She lay still a few more minutes trying to guess if her parents were awake. They tiptoed about the house when they thought Jessica was sleeping. They spoke in hushed voices and opened doors slowly. But Jessica heard them anyway. This morning there was nothing.

Jessica got up and put her sling on, round her neck, over her pajamas. She opened the door and went across the hall to her parents' bedroom. She found her mother sitting back on her heels on the floor by the closet. "What are you doing?" asked Jessica.

"Good morning, sleepy-head," said her mother. She leaned forward and swept a flat palm over the rug. "I'm looking for my necklace. I dropped it last night when I was getting undressed and then it was too dark to find it."

"I'll help look," said Jessica. She crawled slowly about in front of the closet, her face close to the pile. It soon bored her. "I'm hungry," she hinted. "Starving."

Her mother stood up. "Well, I'll make you breakfast then. You go get dressed. We can find it later. What would you like to eat?"

"Cheerios," said Jessica. "From the new box." The new boxes contained prizes, small bugs with lots of legs that stuck wherever you put them and glowed in the dark. Jessica had seen them on television. There were pink ones and green ones and yellow ones and Jessica wanted at least one of every color; she knew she would have to eat several boxes of cereal to make this happen.

She returned to her own room and her own closet. The window was open. She could smell something nice—the neighbors' flowers, the ones that looked like the brush her mother used to use to wash out her baby bottle, the ones that were purple, the ones with all the bees. Charlie had gotten stung last week and howled and howled. Jessica jumped on her bed twice to see if Charlie was in the yard. He was sleeping, stretched out on the patio in the shade.

"Good morning, Charlie," Jessica called and then dropped to the bed and out of sight before he could locate her. She waited until he might have gone back to sleep. Then she did it again, this time kicking her feet out from under her so that she landed on the bed on her back. She lay for a moment smiling.

"Your Cheerios are ready," her mother called. "I'm pouring the milk." Jessica bounced off the bed, grabbing the clothes she had worn the night before. She dressed as quickly as she could. The pants were turned inside out, but she left them that way in the interest of speed. She found socks. She put them both on the same foot, one on top of the other.

"How about wearing two socks?" her mother said when she saw her.

"I am," said Jessica.

Her mother didn't pursue it as Jessica had hoped she would. "Sit down," she said instead.

There was something about her mother's face Jessica didn't like this morning. Her mother looked tired and rubbed the sides of her head as though they hurt. "Where's daddy?" asked Jessica.

"Jogging."

"Are you crying? About your necklace? Was it your very favorite, favorite one? You can get another."

"No, I'm not crying," her mother assured her. "I'm sure the necklace will turn up. How far could it have gotten all on its own?"

"Maybe it fell between?" Jessica suggested.

"Between what?"

"Between now. To the other place."

Jessica's mother looked at Jessica's face. Jessica smiled and her mother reached out and petted her hair. It was tangled and her mother's fingers caught in it and pulled a little. "Ouch," Jessica said, just as a warning.

"It *was* my favorite necklace," her mother said. "Because Paw-paw gave it to me when you were born. I'm supposed to give it to you someday. So it always made me think of you and of the day you came. A new necklace wouldn't do that. Does that seem silly?"

Jessica shook her head.

"My mother had a watch. It was a man's watch and very expensive, but it wouldn't work at all because someone had worn it in swimming and it wasn't waterproof. The man who owned it first just left it when he saw it was ruined. But my father picked it up and gave it to my mother and she kept it all her life."

"*That* seems silly," said Jessica. She felt more interest in the necklace now that she knew it was to be hers someday and also a slight irritation with her mother, whose carelessness had lost it. She wanted to go and look for it some more and her irritation increased when her mother insisted she stay and eat her Cheerios first. Jessica took a large spoonful, chasing and catching many of the floating circles. She chewed and wondered if her mother would let her dump the box out into the bowl to find the prize if she was very careful and put all the Cheerios back without spilling.

"Do you go to your other place when you're unhappy here?" her mother asked and Jessica had to swallow some of her cereal in order to answer.

"No. I just go when I feel like it."

"Do you feel that you're different from other children?"

"How?" Jessica asked.

"I don't know. Do you feel that you look different or like different things or that other kids don't like you? Your teacher says you're very quiet at school. That doesn't sound like you."

"Everybody's special in their own way." Jessica had learned that from Mr. Rogers. She said it with appropriate authority.

"But sometimes being different, even being special, can be hard. Sometimes it makes people feel bad. Do you ever feel like that?"

"No," said Jessica. She paddled her spoon in the cereal bowl and watched the Cheerios move on the currents she made. With Paw-paw a meal was over when your plate was empty. With her mother it was more a matter of how much time you had spent sitting still. Soon her mother would be satisfied and would let her go and look for the necklace. The Cheerios were already soggy and there was really no need to eat them. "Am I different?" Jessica asked.

"You have the other place. That's different."

"Lots of children have imaginary worlds," Jessica reminded her. Even though she didn't know exactly what was meant by an imaginary world. She thought it might be like on television when children begin by pretending that they're on a boat in the ocean and then they really are and their clothes have changed and their stuffed animals can talk. Which wasn't really much like the other place. The other place wasn't something you would pretend.

"Paw-paw said that something frightened you last night," her mother told her. Her mother was speaking slowly and carefully. Her mother wanted her to remember what Jessica had been trying to forget.

"Can I have toast?" Jessica asked.

"What frightened you?"

Jessica dropped her spoon and pushed the cereal bowl away. "I'm not going to eat anymore." It was a deliberate attempt to change the subject; it was supposed to make her mother mad.

"What frightened you, Jessica?"

Jessica pushed the spoon off the table with her elbow. It bounced with a tinny sound on the floor. She slid lower and lower in her seat until her mother disappeared below the horizon of the tabletop. Jessica slipped off the chair entirely and sat by the spoon underneath the table. The woodgrain was rough from this angle. It felt like being in a box. "I don't want to talk about it," Jessica told her mother's shoes. They were gray sneakers with pink stars— kids' shoes except that they were so big.

Her mother slid forward; her knees came closer to Jessica's face and then back again and her mother was sitting on the floor under the table beside her, crosslegged. Her mother had to hunch a little bit to fit. "I really need you to tell me about it, sweetheart," she said. "I really need to know what happened."

Jessica looked away. "I went to the other place," she said. "And then I couldn't get back. I thought I'd never see you or Daddy or Paw-paw again. That never happened to me before." Jessica was doing her best to talk about it without really remembering. She didn't want to feel it again. "I was scared," she said, just as a fact. "Finally I heard Paw-paw calling me and then I knew where she was and I could get back out. Paw-paw let me sleep on the couch."

Her mother took Jessica's face in her hands; she pressed a little too hard. Jessica let her mouth go all funny, like a fish's, but her mother didn't laugh.

"You must never go again," her mother said.

"It's never been like that before."

"Still. It's too risky. What if Paw-paw hadn't found you? I couldn't bear it. Please, Jessica. Promise me you won't go back."

Her mother was staring at her, all unhappy. It made Jessica uncomfortable. "Okay," she said. "I won't."

"Promise me."

"Promise." Did she mean it, Jessica wondered. No, she decided. She just would never go back at night. Any world was scary at night. "Can I go look for my necklace now?" Jessica's mother released her with obvious reluctance. Jessica took it as an answer. She crawled between the chairs and stood up. Her mother didn't move. "I'll put my shoes on first," said Jessica. It was a conciliatory gesture. She ran down the hall and into her room. The curtains waved at her when she opened the door. She slammed it to make them wave again. Her knee itched around the scab she had gotten two days ago at the park when she jumped off the swing while she was still swinging.

Jessica rolled up the leg of her pants and picked the scab off. There was blood. She should go show her mother. Her mother would want to know. But her mother was already sad. Jessica decided to find the necklace first. Then her mother would be happy and Jessica would get a Band-Aid. Jessica went to her mother and father's room.

The rug was empty. In Jessica's room the rug had puzzle pieces on it and books and dirty socks and Legos and papers from nursery school and a shell from the beach that you couldn't really hear the ocean in no matter what they said and a teddy bear with one eye glued shut in a permanent wink and kite string, but no kite, it had gone up in the sky and was lost. It would be hard to find a necklace in Jessica's room. It should be easy here.

Jessica lay on her stomach and looked. She pressed her chin into the rug; the pile was like grass. There was a whole different world in the rug, now that she was close enough to see it. Perhaps bugs lived there or odors like it said in the commercials. Small creatures making their homes at the roots of the pile so the rug towered over their heads and Jessica never saw them. Creatures that were sucked up in the vacuum, that would be horrible.

She couldn't find the necklace. She looked around the closet and by the bed and at the door to her parents' bathroom, a bathroom with no bathtub in it like hers had, but just a shower and a toilet. There was only one other place Jessica could think of to look. She squeezed through into it.

Today it was filled with wind, so hard, so fast, it lifted her right off her feet. Jessica laughed when she realized she was flying. The wind lifted her hair from her neck and held it in the air over her head. It turned her around and around, higher and higher. The shapes of the landscape changed as Jessica moved faster—straight lines curved into fans, closed walls opened like windows. And then Jessica was moving too fast to see shapes at all; they changed into rings of color which encircled her; objects which had had places before now became endless bands, their beginnings and ends fused together. Jessica made no attempt to control her height or her speed; she let herself go completely limp and went wherever she was taken.

She thought she heard her mother calling her. Jessica ignored it. Her mother would still be calling her whenever Jessica chose to return. She had learned that these trips took no time at all. They happened between time, no matter how long she felt she had stayed. Except for last night. The thought came to Jessica suddenly, making her frown. Last night Paw-paw had missed her and come looking. Jessica extended her arms, hands wide open facing backward to see if that slowed her spinning. Instead the wind slapped against them, turning her even faster. She was moving so fast now that it was hard to breathe and there was a pressure against her eyes so she closed them. Colors happened inside her head like fireworks, the colors you see when you press your fingers against your eyelids and leave them there. Colors in lines like snakes and bursts like stars and drips like paint. Jessica pulled her arms in and the spinning slowed so that she could get her breath.

Her mother called again; the voice came from below her. The second call made Jessica realize that time was passing. If her mother found her, like Paw-paw, then her mother would know she had not kept her promise. Jessica opened her eyes and tried to return. She put her arms straight up over her head and fell toward her mother's voice. The wind caught her up again. She arched and straightened and fell. And was carried up. It was like a swing, up and down, up and down. Jessica worked harder. She made a little progress, but only slowly. She remembered the last time. She began to be frightened. Her mother was closer now and she wanted to beat her mother to the place between the worlds, to the door, but the flying was so effortless and the returning so tiring. She gave it up and felt herself being lifted away.

"Jessica," her mother called. It was a scream that the wind carried all around her like the colors. The scream dissolved into continuous sound. It was joined by another scream which went on and on. Jessica twisted in the wind and tried again to fall. She tried as hard as she could. She was crying now and the wind was so quick that the tears never even touched her cheeks but were blown away right out of her eyes. Her heart pounded on the wall of her chest. She wanted her mother. She wanted to go home. And suddenly the spinning slowed. The tears streaked her face. The wind began to fade and Jessica could do whatever she liked. She turned a cartwheel in the air, very slowly, arms and legs straight like a star, since this was something she could not manage in the other world. She closed her eyes. She opened them and she was lying in her mother's lap.

Her mother's face was something awful, the strangest color, and Jessica knew it was because of her, so she looked quickly away to pretend she hadn't seen it. "Don't be mad," she said. The words came out like hiccoughs because of the crying. "I was scared." Her mother held her so tightly her heart beat into Jessica's body as if it were Jessica's own. Jessica relaxed. "I was looking for your necklace," she told her mother. "But it's not there either. Maybe some other place." Her mother did not answer. Jessica guessed she was mad about the broken promise. Jessica guessed that she was going to want to talk and talk about it again the way grown-ups never could let go of things until they repeated themselves and made you repeat yourself. Jessica, who did not want to think anymore about how frightened she had been, but knew she would be made to, felt very cross, herself. "I came back," she pointed out sulkily.

Her mother's grip on her tightened. "Jessica," her mother said in a hoarse, funny voice. "Jessica."

Jessica looked past her mother toward the window. It was *raining* outside and Jessica hadn't even noticed. Her father would be home soon and he would stand in the kitchen and shake the water out of his hair like a dog. It cheered Jessica up to think about it. She slipped her arms around her mother's neck and fastened her hands tightly over the opposite elbows. She would not let go. Not ever. When her mother stood up, and for the rest of her mother's life, Jessica decided, she would be there, hanging from her mother's neck like a stone.

WILLIAM GIBSON

The Winter Market

Almost unknown only a few years ago, William Gibson won the Nebula Award, the Hugo Award, and the Philip K. Dick Award in 1985 for his remarkable first novel *Neuromancer*—a rise to prominence as fiery and meteoric as any in SF history. Gibson sold his first story in 1977 to the now-defunct semiprozine *Unearth,* but it was seen by practically no one, and Gibson's name remained generally unknown until 1981, when he sold to *Omni* a taut and vivid story called ''Johnny Mnemonic,'' a Nebula finalist that year. He followed it up in 1982 with another and even more compelling *Omni* story called ''Burning Chrome,'' which was also a Nebula finalist . . . and all at once Gibson was very much A Writer To Watch. Now, with the publication of *Neuromancer,* he is widely regarded as one of the most important writers to enter the field in many years. Gibson's stories have also appeared in *Universe, Modern Stories,* and *Interzone.* His most recent books are *Count Zero,* a novel, and *Burning Chrome,* a collection. Upcoming from Bantam is a new novel, *Mona Lisa Overdrive.* Gibson's story ''New Rose Hotel'' was in our Second Annual Collection; his story ''Dogfight,'' written with Michael Swanwick, appeared in our Third Annual Collection. Born in South Carolina, Gibson now lives in Vancouver, British Columbia, with his wife and family.

In the vivid, brilliant story that follows, he suggests that people who know *exactly* what they want can be a little frightening—particularly if they need *you* to get it for them. . . .

THE WINTER MARKET

William Gibson

It rains a lot, up here; there are winter days when it doesn't really get light at all, only a bright, indeterminate gray. But then there are days when it's like they whip aside a curtain to flash you three minutes of sunlit, suspended mountain, the trademark at the start of God's own movie. It was like that the day her agents phoned, from deep in the heart of their mirrored pyramid on Beverly Boulevard, to tell me she'd merged with the net, crossed over for good, that *Kings of Sleep* was going triple-platinum. I'd edited most of *Kings*, done the brain-map work and gone over it all with the fast-wipe module, so I was in line for a share of royalties.

No, I said, no. Then yes, yes, and hung up on them. Got my jacket and took the stairs three at a time, straight out to the nearest bar and an eight-hour blackout that ended on a concrete ledge two meters above midnight. False Creek water. City lights, that same gray bowl of sky smaller now, illuminated by neon and mercury-vapor arcs. And it was snowing, big flakes but not many, and when they touched black water, they were gone, no trace at all. I looked down at my feet and saw my toes clear of the edge of concrete, the water between them. I was wearing Japanese shoes, new and expensive, glove-leather Ginza monkey boots with rubber-capped toes. I stood there for a long time before I took that first step back.

Because she was dead, and I'd let her go. Because, now, she was immortal, and I'd helped her get that way. And because I knew she'd phone me, in the morning.

My father was an audio engineer, a mastering engineer. He went way back, in the business, even before digital. The processes he was concerned with were partly mechanical, with that clunky quasi-Victorian quality you see in twentieth-century technology. He was a lathe operator, basically. People brought him audio recordings and he burned their sounds into grooves on a disk of lacquer. Then the disk was electroplated and used in the construction of a press that would stamp out records, the black things you see in antique stores. And I remember him telling me, once, a few months before he died, that certain frequencies—transients, I think he called them—could easily burn out the head, the cutting head, on a master lathe. These heads were incredibly expensive, so you prevented burnouts with something called an accelerometer. And that was what I was thinking of, as I stood there, my toes out over the water: that head, burning out.

Because that was what they did to her.

And that was what she wanted.

No accelerometer for Lise.

I disconnected my phone on my way to bed. I did it with the business end of a West German studio tripod that was going to cost a week's wages to repair.

Woke some strange time later and took a cab back to Granville Island and Rubin's place.

Rubin, in some way that no one quite understands, is a master, a teacher, what the Japanese call a *sensei*. What he's the master of, really, is garbage, kipple, refuse, the sea of cast-off goods our century floats on. *Gomi no sensei*. Master of junk.

I found him, this time, squatting between two vicious-looking drum machines I hadn't seen before, rusty spider arms folded at the hearts of dented constellations of steel cans fished out of Richmond dumpsters. He never calls the place a studio, never refers to himself as an artist. "Messing around," he calls what he does there, and seems to view it as some extension of boyhood's perfectly bored backyard afternoons. He wanders through his jammed, littered space, a kind of minihangar cobbled to the water side of the Market, followed by the smarter and more agile of his creations, like some vaguely benign Satan bent on the elaboration of still stranger processes in his ongoing Inferno of *gomi*. I've seen Rubin program his constructions to identify and verbally abuse pedestrians wearing garments by a given season's hot designer; others attend to more obscure missions, and a few seem constructed solely to deconstruct themselves with as much attendant noise as possible. He's like a child, Rubin; he's also worth a lot of money in galleries in Tokyo and Paris.

So I told him about Lise. He let me do it, get it out, then nodded. "I know," he said. "Some CBC creep phoned eight times." He sipped something out of a dented cup. "You wanna Wild Turkey sour?"

"Why'd they call you?"

" 'Cause my name's on the back of *Kings of Sleep*. Dedication."

"I didn't see it yet."

"She try to call you yet?"

"No."

"She will."

"Rubin, she's dead. They cremated her already."

"I know," he said. "And she's going to call you."

Gomi.

Where does the *gomi* stop and the world begin? The Japanese, a century ago, had already run out of *gomi* space around Tokyo, so they came up with a plan for creating space out of *gomi*. By the year 1969 they had built themselves a little island in Tokyo Bay, out of *gomi*, and christened it Dream Island. But the city was still pouring out its nine thousand tons per day, so they went on to build New Dream Island, and today they coordinate the whole process, and new Nippons rise out of the Pacific. Rubin watches this on the news and says nothing at all.

He has nothing to say about *gomi*. It's his medium, the air he breathes, something he's swum in all his life. He cruises Greater Van in a spavined truck-thing chopped down from an ancient Mercedes airporter, its roof lost under a wallowing rubber bag half-filled with natural gas. He looks for things that fit some strange design scrawled on the inside of his forehead by whatever serves him as Muse. He brings home more *gomi*. Some of it still operative. Some of it, like Lise, human.

I met Lise at one of Rubin's parties. Rubin had a lot of parties. He never seemed particularly to enjoy them, himself, but they were excellent parties. I lost track, that fall, of the number of times I woke on a slab of foam to the roar of Rubin's antique espresso machine, a tarnished behemoth topped with a big chrome eagle, the sound outrageous off the corrugated steel walls of the place, but massively comforting, too: There was coffee. Life would go on.

First time I saw her: in the Kitchen Zone. You wouldn't call it a kitchen, exactly, just three fridges and a hot plate and a broken convection oven that had come in with the *gomi*. First time I saw her: She had the all-beer fridge open, light spilling out, and I caught the cheekbones and the determined set of that mouth, but I also caught the black glint of polycarbon at her wrist, and the bright slick sore the exoskeleton had rubbed there. Too drunk to process, to know what it was, but I did know it wasn't party time. So I did what people usually did, to Lise, and clicked myself into a different movie. Went for the wine instead, on the counter beside the convection oven. Never looked back.

But she found me again. Came after me two hours later, weaving through the bodies and junk with that terrible grace programmed into the exoskeleton. I knew what it was, then, as I watched her homing in, too embarrassed now to duck it, to run, to mumble some excuse and get out. Pinned there, my arm around the waist of a girl I didn't know, while Lise advanced—*was advanced*, with that mocking grace—straight at me now, her eyes burning with wizz, and the girl had wriggled out and away in a quiet social panic, was gone, and Lise stood there in front of me, propped up in her pencil-thin polycarbon prosthetic. Looked into those eyes and it was like you could hear her synapses whining, some impossibly high-pitched scream as the wizz opened every circuit in her brain.

"Take me home," she said, and the words hit me like a whip. I think I shook my head. "Take me home." There were levels of pain there, and subtlety, and an amazing cruelty. And I knew then that I'd never been hated, ever, as deeply or thoroughly as this wasted little girl hated me now, hated me for the way I'd looked, then looked away, beside Rubin's all-beer refrigerator.

So—if that's the word—I did one of those things you do and never find out why, even though something in you knows you could never have done anything else.

I took her home.

I have two rooms in an old condo rack at the corner of Fourth and MacDonald, tenth floor. The elevators usually work, and if you sit on the balcony railing and lean out backward, holding on to the corner of the building next door, you can see a little upright slit of sea and mountain.

She hadn't said a word, all the way back from Rubin's, and I was getting sober enough to feel very, uneasy as I unlocked the door and let her in.

The first thing she saw was the portable fast-wipe I'd brought home from the Pilot the night before. The exoskeleton carried her across the dusty broadloom with that same walk, like a model down a runway. Away from the crash of the party, I could hear it click softly as it moved her. She stood there, looking down at the fast-wipe. I could see the thing's ribs when she stood like that, make them out across her back through the scuffed black leather of her jacket. One of those diseases. Either one of the old ones they've never quite figured out or one of the new ones—the all too obviously environmental kind—that they've barely even named yet. She couldn't move, not without that extra skeleton, and it was jacked straight into her brain, myoelectric interface. The fragile-looking polycarbon braces moved her arms and legs, but a more subtle system handled her thin hands, galvanic inlays. I thought of frog legs twitching in a high-school lab tape, then hated myself for it.

"This is a fast-wipe module," she said, in a voice I hadn't heard before, distant, and I thought then that the wizz might be wearing off. "What's it doing here?"

"I edit," I said, closing the door behind me.

"Well, now," and she laughed. "You do. Where?"

"On the Island. Place called the Autonomic Pilot."

She turned; then, hand on thrust hip, she swung—it swung her—and the wizz and the hate and some terrible parody of lust stabbed out at me from those washed-out gray eyes. "You wanna make it, editor?"

And I felt the whip come down again, but I wasn't going to take it, not again. So I cold-eyed her from somewhere down in the beer-numb core of my walking, talking, live-limbed, and entirely ordinary body and the words came out of me like spit: "Could you feel it, if I did?"

Beat. Maybe she blinked, but her face never registered. "No," she said, "but sometimes I like to watch."

Rubin stands at the window, two days after her death in Los Angeles, watching snow fall into False Creek. "So you never went to bed with her?"

One of his push-me-pull-you's, little roller-bearing Escher lizards, scoots across the table in front of me, in curl-up mode.

"No," I say, and it's true. Then I laugh. "But we jacked straight across. That first night."

"You were crazy," he says, a certain approval in his voice. "It might have killed you. Your heart might have stopped, you might have stopped breathing. . . ." He turns back to the window. "Has she called you yet?"

We jacked, straight across.

I'd never done it before. If you'd asked me why, I would have told you that I was an editor and that it wasn't professional.

The truth would be something more like this.

In the trade, the legitimate trade—I've never done porno—we call the raw product dry dreams. Dry dreams are neural output from levels of consciousness that most people can only access in sleep. But artists, the kind I work with at the Autonomic Pilot, are able to break the surface tension, dive down deep, down and out, out into Jung's sea, and bring back—well, dreams. Keep it simple. I guess some artists have always done that, in whatever medium, but neuroelectronics lets us access the experience, and the net gets it all out on the wire, so we can package it, sell it, watch how it moves in the market. Well, the more things change . . . That's something my father liked to say.

Ordinarily I get the raw material in a studio situation, filtered through several million dollars' worth of baffles, and I don't even have to see the artist. The stuff we get out to the consumer, you see, has been structured, balanced, turned into art. There are still people naive enough to assume that they'll actually enjoy jacking straight across with someone they love. I think most teenagers try it, once. Certainly it's easy enough to do; Radio Shack will sell you the box and the trodes and the cables. But me, I'd never done it. And now that I think about it, I'm not so sure I can explain why. Or that I even want to try.

I do know why I did it with Lise, sat down beside her on my Mexican futon and snapped the optic lead into the socket on the spine, the smooth dorsal ridge, of the exoskeleton. It was high up, at the base of her neck, hidden by her dark hair.

Because she claimed she was an artist, and because I knew that we were engaged, somehow, in total combat, and I was *not* going to lose. That may not make sense to you, but then you never knew her, or know her through *Kings of Sleep*, which isn't the same at all. You never felt that hunger she had, which was pared down to a dry need, hideous in its singleness of purpose. People who know *exactly* what they want have always frightened me, and Lise had known what she wanted for a long time, and wanted nothing else at all. And I was scared, then, of admitting to myself that I was scared, and I'd seen enough strangers' dreams, in the mixing room at the Autonomic Pilot, to know that most people's inner monsters are foolish things, ludicrous in the calm light of one's own consciousness. And I was still drunk.

I put the trodes on and reached for the stud on the fast-wipe. I'd shut down its studio functions, temporarily converting eighty thousand dollars' worth of Japanese electronics to the equivalent of one of those little Radio Shack boxes. "Hit it," I said, and touched the switch.

Words. Words cannot. Or, maybe, just barely, if I even knew how to begin to describe it, what came up out of her, what she did . . .

There's a segment on *Kings of Sleep*; it's like you're on a motorcycle at midnight, no lights but somehow you don't need them, blasting out along a cliff-high stretch of coast highway, so fast that you hang there in a cone of silence, the bike's thunder lost behind you. Everything, lost behind you. . . . It's just a blink, on *Kings*, but it's one of the thousand things you remember, go back to, incorporate into your own vocabulary of feelings. Amazing. Freedom and death, right there, right there, razor's edge, forever.

What I got was the big-daddy version of that, raw rush, the king hell killer uncut real thing, exploding eight ways from Sunday into a void that stank of poverty and lovelessness and obscurity.

And that was Lise's ambition, that rush, *seen from the inside*.

It probably took all of four seconds.

And, course, she'd won.

I took the trodes off and stared at the wall, eyes wet, the framed posters swimming.

I couldn't look at her. I heard her disconnect the optic lead. I heard the exoskeleton creak as it hoisted her up from the futon. Heard it tick demurely as it hauled her into the kitchen for a glass of water.

Then I started to cry.

*   *   *

Rubin inserts a skinny probe in the roller-bearing belly of a sluggish push-me-pull-you and peers at the circuitry through magnifying glasses with miniature headlights mounted at the temples.

"So? You got hooked." He shrugs, looks up. It's dark now and the twin tensor beams stab at my face, chill damp in his steel barn and the lonesome hoot of a foghorn from somewhere across the water. "So?"

My turn to shrug. "I just did. . . . There didn't seem to be anything else to do."

The beams duck back to the silicon heart of his defective toy. "Then you're okay. It was a true choice. What I mean is, she was set to be what she is. You had about as much to do with where she's at today as that fast-wipe module did. She'd have found somebody else if she hadn't found you. . . ."

I made a deal with Barry, the senior editor, got twenty minutes at five on a cold September morning. Lise came in and hit me with that same shot, but this time I was ready, with my baffles and brain maps, and I didn't have to feel it. It took me two weeks, piecing out the minutes in the editing room, to cut what she'd done down into something I could play for Max Bell, who owns the Pilot.

Bell hadn't been happy, not happy at all, as I explained what I'd done. Maverick editors can be a problem, and eventually most editors decide that they've found someone who'll be it, the next monster, and then they start wasting time and money. He'd nodded when I'd finished my pitch, then scratched his nose with the cap of his red feltpen. "Uh-huh. Got it. Hottest thing since fish grew legs, right?"

But he'd jacked it, the demo soft I'd put together, and when it clicked out of its slot in his Braun desk unit, he was staring at the wall, his face blank.

"Max?"

"Huh?"

"What do you think?"

"Think? I . . . What did you say her name was?" He blinked. "Lisa? Who you say she's signed with?"

"Lise. Nobody, Max. She hasn't signed with anybody yet."

"Jesus Christ." He still looked blank.

"You know how I found her?" Rubin asks, wading through ragged cardboard boxes to find the light switch. The boxes are filled with carefully sorted *gomi*: lithium batteries, tantalum capacitors, RF connectors, breadboards, barrier strips, ferroresonant transformers, spools of bus bar wire. . . . One box is filled with the severed heads of hundreds of Barbie dolls, another with armored industrial safety gauntlets that look like space-suit gloves. Light floods the room and a sort of Kandinski mantis in snipped and painted tin swings its golfball-size head toward the bright bulb. "I was down Granville on a *gomi* run, back in an alley, and I found her just sitting there. Caught the skeleton and she didn't look so good, so I asked her if she was okay. Nothin'. Just closed her eyes. Not my lookout, I think. But I happen back by there about four hours later and she hasn't moved. 'Look, honey,' I tell her, 'maybe your hardware's buggered up. I can help you, okay?' Nothin'. 'How long you been back here?' Nothin'. So I take off." He crosses to his workbench and strokes the thin metal limbs of the mantis thing with a pale forefinger. Behind the bench, hung on damp-swollen sheets of ancient peg-board, are pliers, screwdrivers, tie-wrap guns, a rusted Daisy BB rifle, coax strippers, crimpers, logic probes, heat guns, a pocket oscilloscope, seemingly every tool in human history, with no attempt ever made to order them at all, though I've yet to see Rubin's hand hesitate.

"So I went back," he says. "Gave it an hour. She was out by then, unconscious, so I brought her back here and ran a check on the exoskeleton. Batteries were dead. She'd crawled back there when the juice ran out and settled down to starve to death, I guess."

"When was that?"

"About a week before you took her home."

"But what if she'd died? If you hadn't found her?"

"Somebody was going to find her. She couldn't *ask* for anything, you know? Just *take*. Couldn't stand a favor."

Max found the agents for her, and a trio of awesomely slick junior partners Leared into YVR a day later. Lise wouldn't come down to the Pilot to meet them, insisted we bring them up to Rubin's, where she still slept.

"Welcome to Couverville," Rubin said as they edged in the door. His long face was smeared with grease, the fly of his ragged fatigue pants held more or less shut with a twisted paper clip. The boys grinned automatically, but there was something marginally more authentic about the girl's smile. "Mr. Stark," she said, "I was in London last week. I saw your installation at the Tate."

"*Marcello's Battery Factory*," Rubin said. "They say it's scatological, the Brits. . . ." He shrugged. "Brits. I mean, who knows?"

"They're right. It's also very funny."

The boys were beaming like tabled-tanned lighthouses, standing there in their suits. The demo had reached Los Angeles. They knew.

"And you're Lise," she said, negotiating the path between Rubin's heaped *gomi*. "You're going to be a very famous person soon, Lise. We have a lot to discuss. . . ."

And Lise just stood there, propped in polycarbon, and the look on her face was the one I'd seen that first night, in my condo, when she'd asked me if I wanted to go to bed. But if the junior agent lady saw it, she didn't show it. She was a pro.

I told myself that I was a pro, too.

I told myself to relax.

Trash fires gutter in steel canisters around the Market. The snow still falls and kids huddle over the flames like arthritic crows, hopping from foot to foot, wind whipping their dark coats. Up in Fairview's arty slum-tumble, someone's laundry has frozen solid on the line, pink squares of bedsheet standing out against the background dinge and the confusion of satellite dishes and solar panels. Some ecologist's eggbeater windmill goes round and round, round and round, giving a whirling finger to the Hydro rates.

Rubin clumps along in paint-spattered L. L. Bean gumshoes, his big head pulled down into an oversize fatigue jacket. Sometimes one of the hunched teens will point him out as we pass, the guy who builds all the crazy stuff, the robots and shit.

"You know what your trouble is?" he says when we're under the bridge, headed up to Fourth. "You're the kind who *always reads the handbook*. Anything people build, any kind of technology, it's going to have some specific purpose. It's for doing something that somebody already understands. But if it's new technology, it'll open areas nobody's ever thought of before. You read the manual, man, and you won't play around with it, not the same way. And you get all funny when somebody else uses it to do something you never thought of. Like Lise."

"She wasn't the first." Traffic drums past overhead.

"No, but she's sure as hell the first person *you* ever met who went and translated themselves into a hardwired program. You lose any sleep when whatsisname did it, three-four years ago, the French kid, the writer?"

"I didn't really think about it, much. A gimmick. PR . . ."

"He's still writing. The weird thing is, he's going to *be* writing, unless somebody blows up his mainframe. . . ."

I wince, shake my head. "But it's not *him*, is it? It's just a program."

"Interesting point. Hard to say. With Lise, though, we find out. She's not a writer."

She had it all in there, *Kings*, locked up in her head the way her body was locked in that exoskeleton.

The agents signed her with a label and brought in a production team from Tokyo. She told them she wanted me to edit. I said no; Max dragged me into his office and threatened to fire me on the spot. If I wasn't involved, there was no reason to do the studio work at the Pilot. Vancouver was hardly the center of the world, and the agents wanted her in Los Angeles. It meant a lot of money to him, and it might put the Autonomic Pilot on the map. I couldn't explain to him why I'd refused. It was too crazy, too personal; she was getting a final dig in. Or that's what I thought then. But Max was serious. He really didn't give me any choice. We both knew another job wasn't going to crawl into my hand. I went back out with him and we told the agents that we'd worked it out: I was on.

The agents showed us lots of teeth.

Lise pulled out an inhaler full of wizz and took a huge hit. I thought I saw the agent lady raise one perfect eyebrow, but that was the extent of censure. After the papers were signed, Lise more or less did what she wanted.

And Lise always knew what she wanted.

We did *Kings* in three weeks, the basic recording. I found any number of reasons to avoid Rubin's place, even believed some of them myself. She was still staying there, although the agents weren't too happy with what they saw as a total lack of security. Rubin told me later that he'd had to have *his* agent call them up and raise hell, but after that they seemed to quit worrying. I hadn't known that Rubin had an agent. It was always easy to forget that Rubin Stark was more famous, then, than anyone else I knew, certainly more famous than I thought Lise was ever likely to become. I knew we were working on something strong, but you never know how big anything's liable to be.

But the time I spent in the Pilot, I was *on*. Lise was amazing.

It was like she was born to the form, even though the technology that made that form possible hadn't even existed when she was born. You see something like that and you wonder how many thousands, maybe millions, of phenomenal artists have died mute, down the centuries, people who could never have been poets or painters or saxophone players, but who had this stuff inside, these psychic waveforms waiting for the circuitry required to tap in. . . .

I learned a few things about her, incidentals, from our time in the studio. That she was born in Windsor. That her father was American and served in Peru and came home crazy and half-blind. That whatever was wrong with her body was congenital. That she had those sores because she refused to remove the exoskeleton, ever, because she'd start to choke and die at the thought of that utter helplessness. That she was addicted to wizz and doing enough of it daily to wire a football team.

Her agents brought in medics, who padded the polycarbon with foam and sealed the sores over with micropore dressings. They pumped her up with vitamins and tried to work on her diet, but nobody ever tried to take that inhaler away.

They brought in hairdressers and makeup artists, too, and wardrobe people and image builders and articulate little PR hamsters, and she endured it with something that might almost have been a smile.

And, right through those three weeks, we didn't talk. Just studio talk, artist-editor stuff, very much a restricted code. Her imagery was so strong, so extreme, that she never really needed to explain a given effect to me. I took what she put out and worked with it, and jacked it back to her. She'd either say yes or no, and usually it was yes. The agents noted this and approved, and clapped Max Bell on the back and took him out to dinner, and my salary went up.

And I was pro, all the way. Helpful and thorough and polite. I was determined not to crack again, and never thought about the night I cried, and I was also doing the best work I'd ever done, and knew it, and that's a high in itself.

And then, one morning, about six, after a long, long session—when she'd first gotten that eerie cotillion sequence out, the one the kids call the Ghost Dance—she spoke to me. One of the two agent boys had been there, showing teeth, but he was gone now and the Pilot was dead quiet, just the hum of a blower somewhere down by Max's office.

"Casey," she said, her voice hoarse with the wizz, "sorry I hit on you so hard."

I thought for a minute she was telling me something about the recording we'd just made. I looked up and saw her there, and it struck me that we were alone, and hadn't been alone since we'd made the demo.

I had no idea at all what to say. Didn't even know what I felt.

Propped up in the exoskeleton, she was looking worse than she had that first night, at Rubin's. The wizz was eating her, under the stuff the makeup team kept smoothing on, and sometimes it was like seeing a death's-head surface beneath the face of a not very handsome teenager. I had no idea of her real age. Not old, not young.

"The ramp effect," I said, coiling a length of cable.

"What's that?"

"Nature's way of telling you to clean up your act. Sort of mathematical law, says you can only get off real good on a stimulant x number of times, even if you increase the doses. But you can't *ever* get off as nice as you did the first few times. Or you shouldn't be able to, anyway. That's the trouble with designer drugs; they're too clever. That stuff you're doing has some tricky tail on one of its molecules, keeps you from turning the decomposed adrenaline into adrenochrome. If it didn't, you'd be schizophrenic by now. You got any little problems, Lise? Like apneia? Sometimes maybe you stop breathing if you go to sleep?"

But I wasn't even sure I felt the anger that I heard in my own voice.

She stared at me with those pale gray eyes. The wardrobe people had replaced her thrift-shop jacket with a butter-tanned matte black blouson that did a better job of hiding the polycarbon ribs. She kept it zipped to the neck, always, even though it was too warm in the studio. The hairdressers had tried something new the day before, and it hadn't worked out, her rough dark hair a lopsided explosion above that drawn, triangular face. She stared at me and I felt it again, her singleness of purpose.

"I don't sleep, Casey."

It wasn't until later, much later, that I remembered she'd told me she was sorry. She never did again, and it was the only time I ever heard her say anything that seemed to be out of character.

Rubin's diet consists of vending-machine sandwiches, Pakistani takeout food, and espresso. I've never seen him eat anything else. We eat samosas in a narrow shop on Fourth that has a single plastic table wedged between the counter and the door to the can. Rubin eats his dozen samosas, six meat and six veggie, with total concentration, one after another, and doesn't bother to wipe his chin. He's devoted to the place. He loathes the Greek counterman; it's mutual, a real relationship. If the counterman left, Rubin might not come back. The Greek glares at the crumbs on Rubin's chin and jacket. Between samosas, he shoots daggers right back, his eyes narrowed behind the smudged lenses of his steel-rimmed glasses.

The samosas are dinner. Breakfast will be egg salad on dead white bread, packed in one of those triangles of milky plastic, on top of six little cups of poisonously strong espresso.

"You didn't see it coming, Casey." He peers at me out of the thumbprinted depths of his glasses. "'Cause you're no good at lateral thinking. You read the handbook. What else did you think she was after? Sex? More wizz? A world tour? She was past all that. That's what made her so strong. She was past it. That's why *Kings of Sleep's* as big as it is, and why the kids buy it, why they *believe* it. They know. Those kids back down the Market, warming their butts around the fires and wondering if they'll find someplace to sleep tonight, they believe it. It's the hottest soft in eight years. Guy at a shop on Granville told me he gets more of the damned things lifted than he sells of anything else. Says it's a hassle to even stock it . . . She's big because she was what they are, only more so. She knew, man. No dreams, no hope. You can't see the cages on those kids, Casey, but more and more they're twigging to it, that they aren't going *anywhere*." He brushes a greasy crumb of meat from his chin, missing three more. "So she sang it for them, said it the way they can't, painted them a picture. And she used the money to buy herself a way out, that's all."

I watch the steam bead and roll down the window in big drops, streaks in the condensation. Beyond the window I can make out a partially stripped Lada, wheels scavenged, axles down on the pavement.

"How many people have done it, Rubin? Have any idea?"

"Not too many. Hard to say, anyway, because a lot of them are probably politicians we think of as being comfortably and reliably dead." He gives me a funny look. "Not a nice thought. Anyway, they had first shot at the technology. It still costs too much for any ordinary dozen millionaires, but I've heard of at least seven. They say Mitsubishi did it to Weinberg before his immune system finally went tits up. He was head of their hybridoma lab in Okayama. Well, their stock's still pretty high, in monoclonals, so maybe it's true. And Langlais, the French kid, the novelist . . ." He shrugs. "Lise didn't have the money for it. Wouldn't now, even. But she put herself in the right place at the right time. She was about to croak, she was in Hollywood, and they could already see what *Kings* was going to do."

The day we finished up, the band stepped off a JAL shuttle out of London, four skinny kids who operated like a well-oiled machine and displayed a hypertrophied fashion sense and a total lack of affect. I set them up in a row at the Pilot, in identical white Ikea office chairs, smeared saline paste on their temples, taped the trodes on, and ran the rough version of what was going to become *Kings of Sleep*. When they came out of it, they all started talking at once, ignoring me totally, in the British version of that secret language all studio musicians speak, four sets of pale hands zooming and chopping the air.

I could catch enough of it to decide that they were excited. That they thought it was good. So I got my jacket and left. They could wipe their own saline paste off, thanks.

And that night I saw Lise for the last time, though I didn't plan to.

Walking back down to the Market, Rubin noisily digesting his meal, red taillights reflected on wet cobbles, the city beyond the Market a clean sculpture of light, a lie, where the broken and the lost burrow into the *gomi* that grows like humus at the bases of the towers of glass. . .

"I gotta go to Frankfurt tomorrow, do an installation. You wanna come? I could write you off as a technician." He shrugs his way deeper into the fatigue jacket. "Can't pay you, but you can have airfare, you want . . ."

Funny offer, from Rubin, and I know it's because he's worried about me, thinks I'm too strange about Lise, and it's the only thing he can think of, getting me out of town.

"It's colder in Frankfurt now than it is here."

"You maybe need a change, Casey. I dunno. . ."

"Thanks, but Max has a lot of work lined up. Pilot's a big deal now, people flying in from all over . . ."

"Sure."

When I left the band at the Pilot, I went home. Walked up to Fourth and took the trolley home, past the windows of the shops I see every day, each one lit up jazzy and slick, clothes and shoes and software, Japanese motorcycles crouched like clean enamel scorpions, Italian furniture. The windows change with the seasons, the shops come and go. We were into the preholiday mode now, and there were more people on the street, a lot of couples, walking quickly and purposefully past the bright windows, on their way to score that perfect little whatever for whomever, half the girls in those padded thigh-high nylon boot things that came out of New York the winter before, the ones that Rubin said made them look like they had elephantiasis. I grinned, thinking about that, and suddenly it hit me that it really was over, that I was done with Lise, and that now she'd be sucked off to Hollywood as inexorably as if she'd poked her toe into a black hole, drawn down by the unthinkable gravitic tug of Big Money. Believing that, that she was gone—probably *was* gone, by then—I let down some kind of guard in myself and felt the edges of my pity. But just the edges, because I didn't want my evening screwed up by anything. I wanted partytime. It had been a while.

Got off at my corner and the elevator worked on the first try. Good sign, I told myself. Upstairs, I undressed and showered, found a clean shirt, microwaved burritos. Feel normal, I advised my reflection while I shaved. You have been working too hard. Your credit cards have gotten fat. Time to remedy that.

The burritos tasted like cardboard, but I decided I liked them because they were so aggressively normal. My car was in Burnaby, having its leaky hydrogen cell repacked, so I wasn't going to have to worry about driving. I could go out, find partytime, and phone in sick in the morning. Max wasn't going to kick; I was his star boy. He owed me.

You owe me, Max, I said to the subzero bottle of Moskovskaya I fished out of the freezer. Do you ever owe me. I have just spent three weeks editing the dreams and nightmares of one very screwed up person, Max. On your behalf. So that you can grow and prosper, Max. I poured three fingers of vodka into a plastic glass left over from a party I'd thrown the year before and went back into the living room.

Sometimes it looks to me like nobody in particular lives there. Not that it's that messy; I'm a good if somewhat robotic housekeeper, and even remember to dust the tops of framed posters and things, but I have these times when the place abruptly gives me a kind of low-grade chill, with its basic accumulation of basic consumer goods. I mean, it's not like I want to fill it up with cats or houseplants or anything, but there are moments when I see that anyone could be living there, could own those things, and it all seems sort of interchangeable, my life and yours, my life and anybody's. . . .

I think Rubin sees things that way, too, all the time, but for him it's a source of strength. He lives in other people's garbage, and everything he drags home must have been new and shiny once, must have meant something, however briefly, to someone. So he sweeps it all up into his crazy-looking truck and hauls it back to his place and lets it compost there until he thinks of something new to do with it. Once he was showing me a book of twentieth-century art he liked, and there was a picture of an automated sculpture called *Dead Birds Fly Again*, a thing that whirled real dead birds around and around on a string, and he smiled and nodded, and I could see he felt the artist was a spiritual ancestor of some kind. But what could Rubin do with my framed posters and my Mexican futon from the Bay and my temperfoam bed from Ikea? Well, I thought, taking a first chilly sip, he'd be able to think of something, which was why he was a famous artist and I wasn't.

I went and pressed my forehead against the plate-glass window, as cold as the glass in my hand. Time to go, I said to myself. You are exhibiting symptoms of urban singles angst. There are cures for this. Drink up. Go.

I didn't attain a state of partytime that night. Neither did I exhibit adult common sense and give up, go home, watch some ancient movie, and fall asleep on my futon. The tension those three weeks had built up in me drove me like the mainspring of a mechanical watch, and I went ticking off through nighttown, lubricating my more or less random progress with more drinks. It was one of those nights, I quickly decided, when you slip into an alternate continuum, a city that looks exactly like the one where you live, except for the peculiar difference that it contains not one person you love or know or have even spoken to before. Nights like that, you can go into a familiar bar and find that the staff has just been replaced; then you understand that your real motive in going there was simply to see a familiar face, on a waitress or a bartender, whoever. . . . This sort of thing has been known to mediate against partytime.

I kept it rolling, though, through six or eight places, and eventually it rolled me into a West End club that looked as if it hadn't been redecorated since the Nineties. A lot of peeling chrome over plastic, blurry holograms that gave you a headache if you tried to make them out. I think Barry had told me about the place, but I can't imagine why. I looked around and grinned. If I was looking to be depressed, I'd come to the right place. Yes, I told myself as I took a corner stool at the bar, this was genuinely sad, really the pits. Dreadful enough to halt the momentum of my shitty evening, which was undoubtedly a good thing. I'd have one more for the road, admire the grot, and then cab it on home.

And then I saw Lise.

She hadn't seen me, not yet, and I still had my coat on, tweed collar up against the weather. She was down the bar and around the corner with a couple of empty drinks in front of her, big ones, the kind that come with little Hong Kong parasols or plastic mermaids in them, and as she looked up at the boy beside her, I saw the wizz flash in her eyes and knew that those drinks had never contained alcohol, because the levels of drug she was running couldn't tolerate the mix. The kid, though, was gone, numb grinning drunk and about ready to slide off his stool, and running on about something as he made repeated attempts to focus his eyes and get a better look at Lise, who sat there with her wardrobe team's black leather blouson zipped to her chin and her skull about to burn through her white face like a thousand-watt bulb. And seeing that, seeing her there, I knew a whole lot of things at once.

That she really was dying, either from the wizz or her disease or the combination of the two. That she damned well knew it. That the boy beside her was too drunk to have picked up on the exoskeleton, but not too drunk to register the expensive jacket and the money she had for drinks. And that what I was seeing was exactly what it looked like.

But I couldn't add it up, right away, couldn't compute. Something in me cringed.

And she was smiling, or anyway doing a thing she must have thought was like a smile, the expression she knew was appropriate to the situation, and nodding in time to the kid's slurred inanities, and that awful line of hers came back to me, the one about liking to watch.

And I know something now. I know that if I hadn't happened in there, hadn't seen them, I'd have been able to accept all that came later. Might even have found a way to rejoice on her behalf, or found a way to trust in whatever it is that she's since become, or had built in her image, a program that pretends to be Lise to the extent that it believes it's her. I could have believed what Rubin believes, that she was so truly past it, our hi-tech Saint Joan burning for union with that hardwired godhead in Hollywood, that nothing mattered to her except the hour of her departure. That she threw away that poor sad body with a cry of release, free of the bonds of polycarbon and hated flesh. Well, maybe, after all, she did. Maybe it was that way. I'm sure that's the way she expected it to be.

But seeing her there, that drunken kid's hand in hers, that hand she couldn't even feel, I knew, once and for all, that no human motive is ever entirely pure. Even Lise, with that corrosive, crazy drive to stardom and cybernetic immortality, had weaknesses. Was human in a way I hated myself for admitting.

She'd gone out that night, I knew, to kiss herself goodbye. To find someone drunk enough to do it for her. Because, I knew then, it was true: She did like to watch.

I think she saw me, as I left. I was practically running. If she did, I suppose she hated me worse than ever, for the horror and the pity in my face.

I never saw her again.

Someday I'll ask Rubin why Wild Turkey sours are the only drink he knows how to make. Industrial-strength, Rubin's sours. He passes me the dented aluminum cup, while his place ticks and stirs around us with the furtive activity of his smaller creations.

"You ought to come to Frankfurt," he says again.

"Why, Rubin?"

"Because pretty soon she's going to call you up. And I think maybe you aren't ready for it. You're still screwed up about this, and it'll sound like her and think like her, and you'll get too weird behind it. Come over to Frankfurt with me and you can get a little breathing space. She won't know you're there. . . ."

"I told you," I say, remembering her at the bar in that club, "lots of work. Max—"

"Stuff Max. Max you just made rich. Max can sit on his hands. You're rich yourself, from your royalty cut on *Kings*, if you weren't too stubborn to dial up your bank account. You can afford a vacation."

I look at him and wonder when I'll tell him the story of that final glimpse. "Rubin, I appreciate it, man, but I just. . ."

He sighs, drinks. "But what?"

"Rubin, if she calls me, is it *her*?"

He looks at me a long time. "God only knows." His cup clicks on the table. "I mean, Casey, the technology is there, so who, man, really who, is to say?"

"And you think I should come with you to Frankfurt?"

He takes off his steel-rimmed glasses and polishes them inefficiently on the front of his plaid flannel shirt. "Yeah, I do. You need the rest. Maybe you don't need it now, but you're going to, later."

"How's that?"

"When you have to edit her next release. Which will almost certainly be soon, because she needs money bad. She's taking up a lot of ROM on some corporate mainframe, and her share of *Kings* won't come close to paying for what they had to do to put her there. And you're her editor, Casey. I mean, who else?"

And I just stare at him as he puts the glasses back on, like I can't move at all.

"Who else, man?"

And one of his constructs clicks right then, just a clear and tiny sound, and it comes to me, he's right.

HONORABLE MENTIONS

1986

Jim Aikin, "A Place to Stay for a Little While," *IAsfm*, June.

Brian W. Aldiss, "The Difficulties Involved in Photographing Nix Olympica," *IAsfm*, May.

Kim Antieau, "Fractures," *Twilight Zone*, December.

———, "Sanctuary," *Shadows 9*.

Isaac Asimov, "Robot Dreams," *IAsfm*, mid-December.

Clive Barker, "Lost Souls," *Cutting Edge*.

John Barnes, "How Cold She Is, and Dumb," *F&SF*, June.

———, "Stochasm," *IAsfm*, December.

Neal Barrett, Jr., "Trading Post," *IAsfm*, October.

John Berryman, "The Big Dish," *Analog*, November.

Gregory Benford, "Freezeframe," *Interzone*, #17.

———, "Newton Sleep," *F&SF*, January.

———, "Of Space-Time and the River," *IAsfm*, February.

Michael Bishop, "Alien Graffiti," *IAsfm*, June.

———, "Close Encounters with the Deity," *IAsfm*, March.

James P. Blaylock, "The Shadow on the Doorstep," *IAsfm*, May.

Robert Bloch, "The Chaney Legacy," *Night Cry*, Fall.

———, "The Yugoslaves," *Night Cry*, Spring.

Michael Blumlein, "The Brains of Rats," *Interzone*, #16.

Edward Bryant, "The Transfer," *Cutting Edge*.

Bob Buckley, "Red Wolf," *Analog*, July.

Orson Scott Card, "Prior Restraint," *Aboriginal SF*, #1.

———, "Salvage," *IAsfm*, February.

Suzy McKee Charnas, "Listening to Brahms," *Omni*, September.

Robert R. Chase, "Bearings," *Analog*, December.

Arthur C. Clarke, "The Steam-Powered Word Processor," *Analog*, September.

Mona A. Clee, "Dinosaurs," *F&SF*, July.

Bill Crenshaw, "Leviathan," *IAsfm*, September.

Sally Darnowsky, "Without Belief," *IAsfm*, September.

Avram Davidson, "Body Man," *IAsfm*, June.

————, "The King Across the Mountains," *Amazing*, July.

————, "Landscape With Giant Bison," *IAsfm*, September.

————, "The Deed of the Deft-Footed Dragon," *Night Cry*, Fall.

Bradley Denton, "In the Fullness of Time," *F&SF*, May.

————, "Killing Weeds," *F&SF*, November.

George Alec Effinger and Jack C. Haldeman II, "The Funny Trick They Played on Old McBundy's Son," *Night Cry*, Summer.

George Alec Effinger, "Maureen Birnbaum at the Earth's Core," *F&SF*, February.

P. M. Fergusson, "Murder to Go," *Analog*, October.

Michael F. Flynn, "Eifelheim," *Analog*, November.

John M. Ford, "A Cup of Worrynot Tea," *Liavec II*.

————, "Walkaway Clause," *IAsfm*, December.

Karen Joy Fowler, "The Bog People," *Artificial Things*.

————, "The Dragon's Head," *IAsfm*, August.

————, "The View from Venus," *Artificial Things*.

Shelley Frier, "Plagiartech," *Analog*, September.

Gregory Frost, "The Hound of Mac Datho," *IAsfm*, November.

———— and John Kessel, "Reduction," *IAsfm*, January.

Stephen Gallagher, "The Jigsaw Girl," *Shadows 9*.

————, "To Dance by the Light of the Moon," *F&SF*, January.

David S. Garnett, "Still Life," *F&SF*, March.

Molly Gloss, "Field Trial," *IAsfm*, February.

Charles L. Grant, "The Price of a Toy," *Twilight Zone*, April.

Russell M. Griffin, "The Place of Turnings," *F&SF*, November.

————, "The Road King," *F&SF*, February.

Lisa Goldstein, "Daily Voices," *IAsfm*, April.

————, "Scott's Cove," *Amazing*, September.

George Guthridge, "Philatelist," *Analog*, February.

Charles L. Harness, "The Picture by Dora Gray," *Analog*, December.

John Harris, "American Folktales," *Atlantic*, April.

Nina Kiriki Hoffman, "Ants," *Shadows 9*.

Colin Kapp, "An Alternative to Salt," *Analog*, October.

John Keefauver, "Cutliffe Starkvogel and the Bears Who Liked TV," *The Best of the West*.

Gregg Keizer, "Chimera Dreams," *Omni*, June.

James Patrick Kelly, "Rat," *F&SF*, June.

Leigh Kennedy, "Tropism," *Afterlives*.

Nancy Kress, "Down Behind Cuba Lake," *IAsfm*, September.

————, "Phone Repairs," *IAsfm*, December.

William Kotzwinkle, "The Man Who Wasn't There," *Omni*, February.

R. A. Lafferty, "Inventions Bright and New," *IAsfm*, May.
———, "Junkyard Thoughts," *IAsfm*, February.
———, "Something Rich and Strange," *IAsfm*, July.
Marc Laidlaw, "Muzak for Torso Murders," *Cutting Edge*.
Joe R. Landsdale, "Letter from the South, Two Moons West of Naco-doches," *Last Wave*, #5.
Elissa Malcohn, "The S.O.B. Show," *IAsfm*, December.
George R. R. Martin, "The Glass Flower," *IAsfm*, September.
Robert R. McCammon, "Yellow Jacket Summer," *Twilight Zone*, October.
Jack McDevitt, "Voice in the Dark," *IAsfm*, November.
Elizabeth Graham Monk, "Child of the Century," *Twilight Zone*, October.
Pat Murphy, "A Falling Star Is a Rock from Outer Space," *IAsfm*, March.
Amyas Naegele, "The Rise and Fall of Father Alex," *F&SF*, January.
O. Niemand, "The Wisdom of Having Money," *F&SF*, July.
Chad Oliver, "Take a Left at Bertram," *The Best of the West*.
Susan Palwick, "Elephant," *IAsfm*, November.
Frederik Pohl, "Iriadeska's Martains," *IAsfm*, November.
Rachel Pollack, "The Protector," *Interzone*, #17.
Steven Popkes, "The Driving of the Year Nail," *Twilight Zone*, April.
———, "Hellcatcher," *Night Cry*, Spring.
Ruth Rendell, "The Green Road to Quephanda," *The New Girlfriend*.
Keith Roberts, "Tremarest," *Amazing*, November.
Kim Stanley Robinson, "Escape from Katmandu," *IAsfm*, September.
———, "Our Town," *Omni*, November.
Rudy Rucker, "In Frozen Time," *Afterlives*.
Richard Paul Russo, "For a Place in the Sky," *IAsfm*, May.
Pamela Sargent, "The Soul's Shadow," *F&SF*, December.
Hilbert Schenk, "Ring Shot," *Worlds of If*, September-November.
John Shea, "Epiphany," *Twilight Zone*, August.
Michael Shea, "Fill It with Regular," *F&SF*, October.
Carter Scholz, "Galileo Complains," *IAsfm*, June.
Charles Sheffield, "Trader's Blood," *Analog*, April.
Lucius Shepard, "The Arcevoalo," *F&SF*, October.
———, "Aymara," *IAsfm*, August.
———, "Dancing It All Away at Nadoka," *IAsfm*, mid-December.
———, "Fire Zone Emerald," *Playboy*, February.
———, "Journey South from Thousand Willows," *Universe 16*.
Robert Silverberg, "Gilgamesh in the Outback," *IAsfm*, July.
———, "Watchdogs," *Twilight Zone*, August.
Scott Stolnack, "A Trace of Madness," *IAsfm*, November.
Martha Soukup, "Dress Rehearsal," *Universe 16*.
Tim Sullivan, "Special Education," *IAsfm*, January.
———, "Stop-Motion," *IAsfm*, August.

Judith Tarr, "Pièce de Resistance," *IAsfm*, April.
Steve Rasnic Tem, "Bloodwolf," *Shadows 9*.
———, "Little Cruelties," *Cutting Edge*.
——— and Melanie Tem, "Prosthesis," *IAsfm*, June.
Harry Turtledove, "The Eyes of Argos," *Amazing*, January.
———, "The Iron Elephant," *Analog*, May.
———, "Strange Eruptions," *IAsfm*, August.
———, "Though the Heavens Fall," *Analog*, September.
Eric Vinicoff, "Haiku for an Asteroid Scout," *Analog*, September.
W. Warren Wagar, "The President's Worm," *F&SF*, September.
Karl Edward Wagner, "Lacunae," *Cutting Edge*.
Howard Waldrop, "The Lions Are Asleep This Night," *Omni*, August.
Ian Watson, "The Great Atlantic Swimming Race," *IAsfm*, March.
Don Webb, "Jesse Revenged," *IAsfm*, December.
———, "Securities and Personal Word," *Amazing*, September.
Andrew Weiner, "The Band from the Planet Zoom," *IAsfm*, July.
———, "The News from D Street," *IAsfm*, September.
Cherry Wilder, "Dreamwood," *IAsfm*, December.
Walter Jon Williams, "Panzerboy," *IAsfm*, April.
Kate Wilhelm, "The Girl Who Fell into the Sky," *IAsfm*, October.
———, "Someone Is Watching," *Redbook*, October.
Connie Willis, "Spice Pogrom," *IAsfm*, October.
Gene Wolfe, "Checking Out," *Afterlives*.
———, "Choice of the Black Goddess," *Liavek II*.
Robert F. Young, "Cousins," *Analog*, April.
Roger Zelazny, "Permafrost," *Omni*, April.